HERE ARE SOME OF THE MEN AND WOMEN WHO FOUGHT THE BATTLE FOR AMERICAN SOIL. . . .

Robert Collins—He's Roosevelt's man, assigned to spearhead an uprising against the Nazi oppressors. But he hadn't planned on falling for a woman who could cost him his country—and his life.

Dietrich Abetz—The ultimate Gestapo officer and Himmler's man in New York, the head of German security inspires terror in everyone around him. And with good reason—his devotion to duty is matched only by his capacity for cruelty.

Patrick Kelly—America's premier collaborator and the wealthy head of the Pan Semcola Oil Company, his ambition knows no bounds. Yet all his powerful connections can't protect him from the traitor in his own bed.

Turn the page to meet more of the characters in CLASH OF EAGLES. . . .

Sylvie Lamont—As the beautiful mistress of Patrick Kelly, she is part of the Nazi social elite. But her outrage at Nazi brutality wakes something deep within her, something she never knew was there.

Friedrich Radner—The German culture czar, he has bittersweet memories of his days as a struggling musician in New York before the war. He's committed to being a humane leader—in spite of the demands of a vicious regime.

Leila Fox—A Jewish actress who's determined to succeed in the new Nazi-run theater, she takes a Christian name—and acquires a powerful German lover.

Harold Kresky—A union leader and seasoned fighter, he conceives a brilliant plan of industrial sabotage that will prevent the Nazis from building an air force—unless Kresky acts too soon.

Paulie Lazar—A young hood in the making, he thinks he can work both sides of the street. But the twisted loyalties of an occupied city are more dangerous than he's bargained for.

Ludwig Beck—The kommandant of New York, he is viewed by his comrades almost as an exile, being punished for his rumored opposition to Hitler in Europe. His activities, however, are far more subversive than most of them imagine.

CLASH OF EAGLES

Leo Rutman

FAWCETT GOLD MEDAL • NEW YORK

For Bette
and August

Acknowledgment

I wish to express my thanks to Dr. James Shenton of Columbia University for his enthusiastic encouragement, for his recall of time and place, and for torch lights along the invasion route. And to Bob Fenton, who was there for the whole seven year roll and kept calling me Lucky.

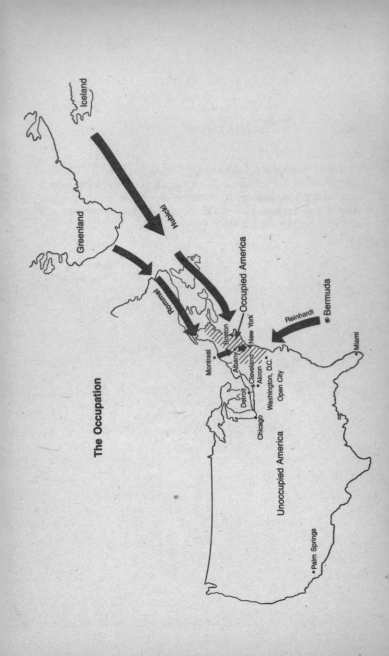

The Occupation

The Uprising

PROLOGUE

LUFTWAFFE DAWN RAIDS AT ESSEX, KENT, AND SUSSEX STOP
STRAFING CIVILIAN AND MILITARY TRAFFIC STOP RAF SUS-
TAINING HEAVY LOSSES STOP LUFTWAFFE BOMBING BRITISH
RAILWAY SYSTEM AT WILL STOP MUCH CHAOS CONFUSION STOP
EXPECT INVASION WITHIN NEXT 24 HOURS

COLLINS

INVASION ON STOP GERMAN PARACHUTE AND GLIDER LAND-
INGS AT FOLKESTONE AND HYTHE STOP GERMAN INVASION
CRAFT SPOTTED NEAR DOVER STOP SANDGATE AND LONDON
ALSO UNDER AIR BLITZ STOP GOING OUT TO THE COUNTRYSIDE
FOR A LOOK

COLLINS

DOVER FALLEN TO GERMANS STOP CHURCHILL ON RADIO TO
NATION STOP IF COUNTERATTACK FAILS GERMANS WILL WIN

1

QUICK STUNNING VICTORY STOP ROOSEVELT MUST ACT STOP BRITISH MORALE DEMANDS IT STOP WAITING IMPATIENTLY FOR YOUR PEARLS OF WISDOM

COLLINS

COPY OF DECODED CABLE SENT TO

MR. ROBERT COLLINS
8 GROSVENOR
LONDON, ENGLAND

DATED: JULY 16, 1940. PLACE OF ORIGIN: THE WHITE HOUSE, WASHINGTON, D.C.

ROOSEVELT SYMPATHETIC BUT CANNOT ACT STOP AFRAID AMERICAN INTERVENTION EXCUSE FOR HITLER ASK STALIN TO PERMIT USE OF RUSSIAN TROOPS STOP HITLER HOLDING TRUMPS STOP ASSESS CHANCES BRITAIN HOLDING OUT WITH-OUT DIRECT MILITARY INTERVENTION BY U.S.

DONOVAN

CABLE TO

MR. WILLIAM J. DONOVAN
THE WHITE HOUSE
WASHINGTON, D.C.

DATED: JULY 17, 1940. PLACE OF ORIGIN: LONDON.

WITHOUT U.S. INTERVENTION BRITS HAVE TWO CHANCES STOP SLIM AND NONE STOP ROMMEL 7TH PANZER DIVISION TANKS MOVING ON CANTERBURY STOP RAF DECIMATED STOP BRITS LAST STAND MAIDSTONE

COLLINS

CABLE TO

MR. WILLIAM J. DONOVAN
THE WHITE HOUSE
WASHINGTON, D.C.

DATED: JULY 19, 1940. PLACE OF ORIGIN: LONDON

BALLGAME OVER STOP CHURCHILL FLED TO BAHAMAS STOP GERMANS WILL PURSUE STOP KING AND QUEEN TO SAIL CAN-ADA STOP GOD COULDN'T SAVE THE KING NEITHER CAN I STOP WANT TO GO TO DUBLIN AND GIVE LADS YOUR PENSION FUND CONTRIBUTION STOP WHERE THE H . . L IS IT STOP ADVISE

COLLINS

MR. ROBERT COLLINS
8 GROSVENOR
LONDON, ENGLAND

DATED: JULY 23, 1940. PLACE OF ORIGIN: WASHINGTON, D.C.

FUNDS IN YOUR NAME CABLED WESTERN UNION GLASGOW STOP
URGENT YOU GO TO BAHAMAS AND KEEP ME INFORMED ON
CHASE STOP COUNTING ON YOU

DONOVAN

CABLE SENT TO

MR. WILLIAM J. DONOVAN
THE WHITE HOUSE
WASHINGTON, D.C.

DATED: JULY 26, 1940. PLACE OF ORIGIN: GLASGOW, SCOTLAND.

CARETAKER GOVERNMENT UNDER OSWALD MOSLEY AS HEAD
STOP CLEMENT ATTLEE STAYING AS LORD PRIVY SEAL STOP
WILL GO TO BAHAMAS AFTER DUBLIN TRIP TO DELIVER YOUR
PRESENT STOP ALL THE LADS EAGER FOR IT STOP TOP O' THE
MORNING

COLLINS

BOOK I

Chapter 1

TOP SECRET

DATE: August 20, 1941
TO: Führer Adolf Hitler
COPIES TO: Field Marshal Wilhelm Keitel, Chief of the
                    Armed Services High Command
                    General Alfred Jodl, Chief of Planning for
                    Army Operations
FROM: General Heinz Guderian
SUBJECT: OPERATION TOUCHDOWN

Germany has vanquished the British nation. Our next victory will be in America.

This plan for the invasion of the United States is offered for your approval, Führer, with the assurance of General Tojo of the Japanese that in accordance with the treaty signed on August 10, 1941, the forces of the Imperial Navigational Air Force shall launch a massive attack on Pearl Harbor on the first Sunday in December. Though the Roosevelt government expects war with Japan, General Tojo believes that the Americans are unprepared for attack as early as December. The Pearl Harbor strike will pave the way for our invasion by concentrating the full attention of the American government and the deployment of air, naval, and ground forces off the Hawaiian Islands and the West Coast of America.

With this in mind we should use the next two months to ship supplies and troops to weather stations in Iceland and Greenland. This subterfuge would allow us to deliver large supplies of bombs, torpedoes, and other high explosives. Though the sending of troops will alarm the Americans, the few thousand men deployed on each island will be perceived as troublesome but hardly the size of an invasion force. Existing airfields have been sufficiently developed in the past six months so the Luftwaffe will be able to provide full air coverage for the invasion.

When the Japanese attack occurs, the full weight of the American armed forces, numbering 3,000 combat planes and 344 capital ships (consisting of 17 battleships, 6 carriers, 208 heavy cruisers and destroyers, and 113 submarines) will be mobilized and deployed to their fullest extent around the Hawaiian Islands. In the past year the American army has been built up to 29 regular and armored divisions. The standing army has grown from 100,000 men to approximately 500,000, but none of them have seen combat. Roosevelt will have to prevent Japanese invasion of the Hawaiian Islands and the West Coast. I recommend 1,000,000 Wehrmacht troops to Operation Touchdown, which will give us at least a five-to-one numerical ratio on the East Coast. This is overwhelming in view of the fact that our troops are combat-experienced.

Immediately after Pearl Harbor, I recommend that we formally declare war on the United States, but, for a period of ten days or so after the declaration of war, no significant ship traffic should be permitted. On the evening of December 19, convoys of ships are to sail from Southampton and Dover for our bases in Greenland and Iceland. Because of Japanese bombing raids over California, American reconnaissance of the Atlantic will be minimal. First ships should arrive in Newfoundland on the evening of December 22. Refueling and loading of additional supplies on our ships are to be finished in six hours. Troops will stay on board the entire time and the convoy will sail again just after 1 a.m. for Quebec, where our agents will have prepared for an unopposed landing on the morning of December 24. The timing of the arrival here is critical because we wish to attain the maximum element of surprise in attacking the Americans on Christmas Day. Our agents will be able to draw support from French Canadians hostile to English rule in Canada. Troops, tanks, and heavy artillery would be unloaded by dawn and push immediately for Montreal. If we achieve the full element of surprise, we can roll up Quebec and Montreal, leaving one division in each city to meet any Canadian counterattack. The only immediate threat would be the Royal Canadian Air Force. Therefore, bases at Toronto, Ottawa, and Ontario would be hit at dawn by Luftwaffe Stukas, accompanied by Messerschmitts flying from Iceland and Greenland. These planes would land and refuel in Newfoundland and in captured Canadian airstrips in Montreal and Quebec. They would then be in ideal position to bomb strategic targets during the invasion of the United States.

Montreal should be secured in no less than half a day once we land in Quebec, and every available effort should be made to cut all wire and telephone service between Montreal and the United States so that confirmation of the invasion will be spasmodic and confused.

A frightened and insecure American populace is essential. General von Runstedt and General von Bock would not pause at Montreal but push across the American border for Saratoga and Albany. The optimum would be to arrive on Christmas Eve or Christmas Day, with American families caught with turkey and goose in their mouths. I recommend that Luftwaffe bombing and strafing be made primarily on military targets and selective cities. Extensive bombing of American cities with their large networks of underground trains would be unproductive. We can induce higher levels of panic by reducing a single city to rubble. Our Stukas should hit these primary targets: the naval base at Norfolk, Virginia; the army bases at Fort Belvoir, Virginia; Fort Hamilton, New York; Fort Devons, Massachusetts; and Mitchell Field in Long Island, New York. Paratroop drops around those bases will give the effect of the bases being attacked and freeze their military personnel there.

I recommend the use of the Seventh Panzer Division under the command of General Rommel to drive to New York City through the Hudson Valley. Rommel is a genius at exploiting the psychology of fear and rolling up vast amounts of territory where the enemy has fled. His creativity in finding the Achilles' heel of the enemy will be our secret weapon. Civilians and reservists faced with tanks will crumble and run. It is recommended that in these early battles, a large city, perhaps Albany or Boston, should be leveled so that there can be no doubt as to our ability to do the same thing to New York. We can isolate New York City in two direct moves that will leave it totally helpless. Capture of the Ashokan Reservoir in the Catskill Mountains area would cut the supply of water to the city. The other objective would be accomplished by General Reinhardt after his troops, deployed from Bermuda, land on the New Jersey coast. A direct, relentless push to Newark and its capture would halt the supply of food coming through the Newark terminal. Once we control both the food and water supply of New York City, surrender is inevitable.

At the same time Rommel pushes for New York City, General Hubicki and the Ninth Panzer will land on the beaches of Maine via Newfoundland and drive for Boston. The northeast of America will be caught in a pincer movement. There should be no let up until Boston and New York have surrendered and we command New York State, Connecticut, Massachusetts, and New Jersey.

I believe our chances for a successful invasion of America are excellent. The Americans will still be stunned by the air strike on Pearl Harbor. They will be amazed and totally unprepared for a land invasion in the winter on their own soil. They have not fought on their territory since the American revolution. They are a nation of freethinkers, industrious and opportunistic. But they are *soft*. They have not fought a war in twenty-three years. Their minds are still on postdepression problems. Faced with a crisis of confidence caused by the invasion of the Atlantic Coast, besieged on the Pacific, they will not have the backbone to persevere. It is expected that the American government will retreat behind its Allegheny and Rocky mountains and its five Great Lakes. They form an impenetrable fortress in winter. Peace terms offered the Americans must convey the specific threat to build Luftwaffe bases and use existing American airfields to reduce their industrial centers to rubble. But we must also show the people that life goes on, that the future under Germany is much the same. Declaring and securing New York as an open city is vital to that success. Otherwise we will have a city of zombies living underground and achieve only a Pyrrhic victory. Should the Japanese succeed in landing on the West Coast, then Roosevelt would have to accede to our terms. But I am not sure that Tojo can accomplish this. Therefore, we must blitz the East Coast and let the Americans think on that. I must admit that I have thought of calling this Operation Christmas Stocking, for, in the name of the Führer, we will be delivering a present the Americans will never forget.

AMERICAN PANORAMA
I

The Daily Mirror, Saturday, December 27, 1941
The Inquiring Reporter
LOCALE:
In and around New York City's five boroughs.
QUESTION:
Where were you on Christmas Day?

Dimos Praxis, Williston, Queens. Bakery driver.

"I was driving my route in Forest Hills, dropping off some last minute deliveries for Christmas. It is my business and I open always on holidays. I make a stop on Ascan Avenue and some kids run out in the street and say 'Nazis coming.' What you talk about, I say? Is no joke. I got relatives back in Greece. What kind of game you think this is to play on Christmas? You should be spanked. Kids yell 'No joke. Nazis coming. Heard on radio.' Then, I say, somebody play big joke on radio. Like the man who fool us about men from Mars. People are crazy, I say. No Nazis in America. Not never. Never. This is the best country in world. Best place, 'cause it free. Free, I yell. Now you know who big fool is? Dimos. Dimos never believe again."

Laney Lee, Washington Heights. Waitress.

"Can I speak frankly? There's this fella, Axel Bagella. He's not Jewish but everybody calls him Bagels. He's been after my pants for a long time and I never gave him a tumble. But after Pearl Harbor, he enlisted and I thought, what the heck, if he could be patriotic so could I. So me and Bagels were alone on Christmas in the parents' house. My parents went to the relatives for turkey. Well, we had the radio on and started foolin' around and then the moment of glory came. Suddenly the door opened and my father came in yelling 'Nazis' and Bagels jumped out the window in his bare ass. And that's the last I ever saw of him."

"Your name, sir?"
"H. Walton Withers. I live in the Park Russell Hotel."
"What do you do, sir?"
"I am a lifelong Republican."
"Where were you on December 25, 1941?"
"Same place I always am on Christmas. At the club. Let me tell you something. This talk of Nazis is a Democratic ploy to keep Roosevelt in office forever. The Great Depression was his trick. All those lines of people. Actors, you hear? Just like the Nazis who come will be actors. Roosevelt has the whole treasury at his disposal. He's spending a fortune bamboozling this country so he can stay president. Do you see any Nazis around? I don't. I'm staying at the club and drinking a martini. People in this country are a bunch of damn fools. They'll believe anything."

"Your name, sir?"
"Smith."
"First or last name?"
"Just Smith. Don't ask me my address."
"Where were you on December 25, 1941?"
"I don't know nothin'. Just forget you ran into me. Don't take my picture. Give me that camera. And my name ain't Smith, it's Jones. I don't know nothin'. Leave me alone. I have to get home.

11

Don't you know there's a curfew on? And don't tell anybody you seen me or I'll get you. You hear?"

Chapter 2

Sunday, December 28, 1941
11:30 A.M.

In the distance you could hear the rolling drums. Next came the sound of the boots. The distant crack of one boot magnified ten thousand times, and then the other, beating down on the streets of Manhattan. Creating an image in the mind long before the actual picture took shape. The sound swelling to a crescendo as they got closer and closer. Assaulting the ear like so many rivets driven in. The pain vibrating into the brain with the truth of its message. They are here. They are coming down Fifth Avenue. We are occupied.

The Wehrmacht started at Ninety-sixth Street, led by Colonel Manfred Klausen, commander of the Twelfth Korps that fought so heroically for the fatherland in the bloody battle of Boston. Followed by Shreiner and his men who had captured Ellenville and Monticello, and then Kleist and his troops who had taken New Haven.

Their boots resounded on the pavement of the city's most illustrious street. Down past the children with wounded eyes, past their parents who gripped them tight, past the horrified matrons and the cluster of doctors and nurses who had come out from Mount Sinai Hospital to see them.

From the crevices and pockets of the city people gathered. Congregating at street corners, next to closed stores, as if too shy to reveal themselves. Huddled in front of the Andrew Carnegie mansion at East Ninety-first Street; shivering in front of the Metropolitan Museum of Art at Eighty-second Street; heads down in mournful pose in front of Temple Emanu-El at Sixty-fifth Street and Fifth Avenue. By twelve o'clock on this bitter, bright day, Fifth Avenue was peopled with the curious, the angry, the hostile, the sad, the troubled, the betrayed citizens of New York. These people for whom a march had once meant cheering crowds, music, confetti, and ecstatic cries were to endure a march of occupation. This city that had acclaimed Lucky Lindy and the Babe, Sergeant York and the Fighting Sixty-ninth, was now to cast eyes upon soldiers in gray whose steel had captured it.

The stunned faces of the crowd were a hundred frozen cameos. The weeping old Polack from Warsaw who had come in 1900 and sent for his family five years later; the aged Negro porter who came out of the small residence off Madison Avenue and stood without a coat as if to punish himself with the cold; the seemingly erect policeman who, off duty, wore his uniform and nipped from a pocket flask, muttering obscenities to himself all the while. The tight little smile on the face of Max Ernst, who was a waiter at Rosoff's and had come on a stinking boat in 1912; the lost stare of Joe Doyle, the butcher who had a store on Broadway; the disbelief of Guido Monti, who had a barbershop near Columbia University where he cut the boys' hair for a quarter; the pathos on the trembling mouth of Sally Fletcher, who solicited trade on Hudson Street every night. The boots came without letup. Amid the heartbreak, the anger, the tears. Each thud driving a nail into the soul of every New Yorker lining the pavement.

By twelve-thirty the Wehrmacht moved past the gilded hotels of Fifth Avenue. Past the Sherry Netherland, the Savoy Plaza, the Plaza, past the Pulitzer Memorial Fountain and the statue of General Sherman, who once marched through the state of Georgia. The city's populace, numb with cold, watched them in almost devout silence now. Their faces etched in tableaux of private yet naked intimacy. There was the garbage sweeper holding a broom that seemed to have become both a weapon and pillar of support for shaking legs; the priest clutching a Bible with knuckles white to the bone; the Chinese woman with lips parted, eyes gaping, who was not aware she had wet herself; the derelict, consumed with a racking cough, who kept hawking up mucous and spitting it on the pavement, aiming for a German boot; the retired professor who stood on Fifth and Forty-eighth, hand in his pocket over the pistol he had bought the previous night; the gray-haired blind peddler who had taken off his glasses at the first sound of the Nazi boots and who now, miraculously cured, stared with all too perfect vision at the reality in front of him. There was, finally, the old soldier decorated in his medals and uniform, propped up by a cane, his white hair blowing in the cold December wind, his mouth moving and yet making no sound. A Negro man turned to a middle-aged woman who had first come here in 1915 from Hungary and said, "The lady in the Battery be shedding a tear right now." The woman was terribly white and didn't understand what woman he was talking about, though twenty-six years earlier she herself had wept when she saw the Statue of Liberty.

Now the Wehrmacht had reached Forty-second Street, where a reviewing stand had been set up on the steps of the public library between the two lions which seemed this day to have averted their eyes. On the swastika-bedecked podium stood the reviewing dignitaries: Heinrich von Stulpnagel, the military governor for New York and New Jersey; General Ludwig Beck, the gross kommandant of Manhattan; Standartenführer Dietrich Abetz, commanding German security forces in New York City; General Erwin Rommel, whose Seventh Panzer Division with its tanks had broken the back of the East Coast defense and laid waste to Albany, Saratoga, and the Hudson Valley; Major Hans Speidel, his adjutant; Otto Klinger, von Ribbentrop's personal representative in New York; and other carefully selected guests. As the troops approached, it was Abetz whose arm shot out first, and the others followed suit. Stiff right arms thrown out in the salute to the troops that had captured the greatest city in the world. Lips formed the words "Heil Hitler," as the commanders of the troops ordered "Eyes right." It was as though the sight of the reviewing stand had evoked a common pride in the soldiers, for now the jackboots smashed down on the pavement. The thumps, a savage exhibition of strength, exploding with each thrust. Splitting the ear with its might, stunning the eye with its symmetry.

It was at that precise moment that the music came. The first one to hear it was a high school student, who listened intently and then nudged a friend. The friend tapped another youth, and now the shoulders of the students standing outside a small store on Thirty-eighth and Fifth seemed to move in rhythmic accompaniment. As the first clear wailing sounds of the clarinet were heard, heads turned. Backing up the clarinet was the sweet beat of a vibraphone, played by an American Negro, Lionel Hampton. More heads turned, eyes roved. Whoever had put on the record had found the proper tuning, and Teddy Wilson could be heard tinkling the piano. The effect was electric and immediate.

Someone in the crowd on Thirty-eighth Street screamed "Benny," as Benny Goodman came sweeping in on a very cool, sweet clarinet. Orders banning music for the day had not been obeyed, and now the Wehrmacht was marching to the beat of Benny Goodman's orchestra playing "Stompin' at the Savoy," circa 1938, at Carnegie Hall. As the music swelled and Benny Goodman blew hot boogie, American fists shot into the air. A jumping new beat. The record had segued into "Avalon," and Teddy Wilson tinkled again. The first German soldier missed a

14

step as a dancing American stumbled against him. For the German was only marching, but the American, a red-haired kid named Higgins, was dancing on the streets of his city. This was still America, its music supplied by Americans. Their names were not Kleist, or von Hoffman, or Strauss. Their names were Hymie Shertzer, George Koenig and Babe Russin, Art Rollini and Harry James, Ziggy Elman, Red Ballard and Jess Stacey, Gene Krupa, Johnny Hodges and Cootie Williams. This was their city and their people. Another Wehrmacht soldier and still another missed a step. It was, after all, hard to goose step to swing. Again came the clarinet, and a chorus of voices screamed "Benny." There was commotion and a flurry as the kids who had discovered it yelled it again and again.

On the platform Standartenführer Abetz was gesturing, and men wearing the black uniform and insignia of the SD came running down the sidewalk shoving people out of their way. The Gestapo followed the noise of the music up the steps of a two-story building and abruptly a sweet clarinet riff by Benny Goodman came to a screeching end. Moments later the perpetrator was led downstairs. He was a young man in a faded brown sweater with overalls. Gripped by both arms, the kid, who had a seemingly endless supply of freckles, grinned broadly and wildly. He was shouting something to the crowd as the SD led him away, careful not to damage him. The Gestapo couldn't understand him, but others who had heard Johnny Lugansky repeated what he had said. Indeed, it was repeated all over the city in the next few weeks. "You'll never stop boogie-woogie." Then he was gone, and the brief moment of bravado and rebellion gone with him. The parade continued as if he had never appeared. The brief respite made the reality all the more painful. This reality became clearly evident as the Wehrmacht continued its noisy assault on Fifth Avenue. The bitter cold winter day had frozen the image of occupation on all the assembled. They stood there moist eyed, grim, linked in betrayal and sorrow. The legend of New York City was forever destroyed. The mourners at this funeral had learned that they had been living a lie. They weren't better off, and they weren't different. They were the same as people in Prague, Warsaw, Oslo, Amsterdam, Brussels, Paris, London. The world wasn't round after all. It was flat and terribly small.

If Fifth Avenue was the soul of New York this first day of occupation, the heart of it was Union Square. The span of three blocks running from Fourteenth Street on the south to Seventeenth Street on the north, from Broadway to University Place. Streets filled with racks holding cheap garments and merchandise of every kind. Marked by double-feature theaters, cafeterias, and luncheonettes. Through its scarred veins and arteries passed the hungry, the hopeless, the hawkers and pitchmen, the rabble-rousers, con men, pickpockets and panhandlers, the beggars on roller skates, the faithless and the union faithful. Seeking portents of the future from sightless clairvoyants, buying hope from brewers of tea leaves. Union Square, home of the country's radical movement, the forum for the mass audience and talk of strike. Walking ground for Wobblies, socialists, anarchists, and Communists. Kresky looked at the swelling crowd in Union Square Park and thought, These are my people, this my school. I studied, learned, and graduated from here. This is where I belong this terrible day.

Kresky relit his cigar and blew into his hands. Union Square Park was jammed. Had been since eleven o'clock that morning as speaker after speaker mounted the soapbox to denounce Roosevelt and the American government for surrendering the city without a fight; denouncing the rich and the cowardly who had fled the city; condemning Lehman for fleeing, praising LaGuardia for being arrested; vilifying any Vichy man who would become the Nazis' mayor. Lighting verbal torches, calling for a man on a white horse.

Union Square Park stood on a small elevation. From beneath it came the insistent roar of the subways. At its north end was a large plaza used for parking automobiles. At the southern tip, a bronze statue of Washington that faced Fourteenth Street. Statues of Lincoln and Lafayette also adorned the park. In the center of the park stood the large liberty pole commemorating the Declaration of Independence. At its base were Jefferson's words that Kresky knew by heart: "How little my countrymen know what precious blessings they are in possession of and which no other people on earth enjoy." As if to verify Jefferson's vision, one could look across the park and see Kleins and Ohrbach's department stores.

It was four o'clock, and the warmth of the sun was gone. The people were cold and tired, the speakers hoarse. The lull had lasted for about twenty minutes; the euphoria of rhetoric was wearing off.

The lines of men parted, and Kresky heard applause and calls of "Gaines, Gaines is coming." Joseph Gaines, Moscow's mouth. The man who had Kresky dumped from the ranks when Kresky stood up and denounced the Soviet-German nonaggression pact. Kresky could remember his words precisely. "Let us be rid of this rotten apple, this Trotskyite bastard who seeks to subvert the people's revolution by starting a war with Hitler. The Union of Soviet Socialist Republics wants no war, no conquest.

It wants only to grow and grow. This rotten agent of the capitalists, Kresky.'' Kresky snorted and forced himself to block out the rest. Now Gaines came through the crowd, a little man in a natty black overcoat and fedora, wearing a blue shirt and striped blue tie. He does well by the party, Kresky thought. He's recently back from Moscow, so we'll get the party line on how the members should react here in America.

Gaines mounted the podium. He was five feet seven and wore platform heels to make himself seem taller. He stood there, a slight smile flickering on his mouth. He had a thin mustache and wore silver-rimmed glasses. He was always the man who appeared after the demonstrations in the street and had a statement for the papers that he would issue among bleeding men. It would look very good in the *Daily Worker* the next day.

Gaines was holding up his hand. ''Comrades, history is upon us. We are the vanguard of the future. Nobody will use us for their purposes. Remember the dream of Lenin, of Marx and Engels, was world revolution. It is coming to pass. First, the rotten order here in America, Roosevelt and the rest of the stinking lackeys of capitalism will fall. Listen to the lies as he speaks tonight. Mark the words of a glib, frightened opportunist whose time is running out. He will call for the country to take up arms, to throw the Reich out of New York. But we will not do his bidding. We will not fight his dirty war for him. We will not bleed for him in the streets. We will not be used to reestablish the old order. We are at peace with Hitler. We are allies.''

There were more cries, protests, men screaming from behind Kresky up to the podium. Menacing men advancing. The roar, the cacophony, the noise building into an elongated shout backed by the roaring crescendo of the BMT underground. Then the subway had passed, and the noise of the crowd seemed a disemboweled thing. As if a bull trumpeting his cry had been castrated. What was happening? Kresky looked behind him and saw the lines of men parting in successive waves. As if anointed by the hand of Moses. The image, black gold. A Nazi officer backed by six Wehrmacht soldiers. The man was small with tight eyes. He looked at Kresky for a long moment, then his eyes slid to the podium.

''Abetz, comrade,'' Gaines roared. He was giving the workers' salute to the Nazi officer. Behind him, from the ranks of the party, a collective fist shot forward. Party solidarity. The officer came to attention and gave the Nazi salute.

''Down with imperialist war,'' a voice shouted from the Communist ranks, which swelled with men saluting, waving, and yelling. Gaines led shouts of ''Heil Hitler.'' The German officer

17

stood stiffly in place; then as Gaines beckoned him forward, he climbed astride the platform.

Abetz was on the platform, and from out of nowhere appeared a bevy of photographers, two wearing Nazi uniforms, the others Communist party hacks. The two leaders embraced, held it for the cameras, then broke and posed in a variety of handshakes for the crowd. Men were cheering, edging around the podium. Kresky felt his shoulders being pounded. A bony fist smashed against his head. An elbow dug his side. At the platform there was triumphant pandemonium as Gaines and the Nazi officer, Abetz, were hoisted on shoulders and carried to their cars. Some men sang "The Internationale."

So that's the strategy, Kresky thought. The party stands back and inherits the country after the Americans and Germans dismember it. But that was no strategy.

Kresky stepped forward. "Tell us, Gaines, what you will say when Hitler comes after Stalin. That's next. What words from the other side of your mouth?"

Gaines's mouth curled up as he spotted Kresky. "Look who is among us. The capitalists' man, the Trotskyite trying to sow discontent. But we are not at war with Hitler. This is Roosevelt's war. He inherited it, let him fight it. We are at peace."

Kresky waved the stub of his cigar. "Tell that to the dead in Finland. Stalin has no policy. He only runs from Hitler. He is Chamberlain's brother."

Now there were voices raised in approval and disapproval. Union Square was coming alive again.

"There is no living with the wolf," Kresky cried. "If Hitler swallows America, then Russia is next."

"Liar," Gaines screamed. "Liar. Hitler does not want to fight Russia. He can never defeat us. We will not fight the wars of capitalism or fascism. We will inherit the earth. We are the future."

"You are bankrupt," Kresky roared. "He comes for Russia next. Will you fight him then, Gaines? No, you'll be back in an office, writing weasel lies. You'll be flying to the Kremlin to eat caviar and vodka and tell workers of the world to bleed for Uncle Joe. You stink, Gaines. You're a whore who sleeps with Nazis."

"Get him," someone yelled from the Communist cadre.

"String him up."

"Capitalist mouthpiece," Gaines shouted back. "The future is ours."

Kresky felt someone tugging his arm and followed, keeping his head down, hearing the bellowing, the broken chorus of men who could not stomach infamy. He fought his way through the throngs of men hoarse from shouting and somehow found himself in the BMT tunnel. He stood alone now in the darkness, listening to roaring men, passion in their voices. He heard the shouting, the stamping feet, the exultation and the sorrow. He felt very cold and very alone.

Chapter 3

December 29, 1941

The first Monday of the occupation of New York gave every promise of being a bright, sunlit, crisp winter day. The city was somber and quiet. Everybody knew that the face of the city would be different this day, and now, in the first hours after dawn, it was as if nobody wanted to go out and verify it. The curfew imposed on the city had been respected for the most part. The last IRT train had left 242nd Street at eleven P.M. and reached South Ferry at midnight. Now, as the sun cut a swath through the morning mist, the city was·quiet, the mood surly. People walked head down to subways, to bus stops, without looking at each other, each carrying with him the anger and grief of knowing their government had made no move to defend the city.

11:15 A.M.

Leila walked across Fifth Avenue and Fifty-third Street on this brilliant, sunlit morning back to the Studio Club, the residence hall where she lived. She had just spent a quarter on tea and a bun. She had exactly two dollars and ten cents left in her purse. The engagement to appear in a children's play for Christmas week had been cancelled because of the invasion. That would have paid her twenty-five dollars. Enough to cover her January rent and still leave her nine dollars. Now what to do? The invasion had played havoc with the whole theatrical season. Every ingenue in the city would be applying for waitress jobs. And yet, she had a premonition something interesting was going to happen. Leila was a very instinctive creature. When these flashes of intuition came, she was seldom wrong. This was such a crazy time. Nazis here. And now this actors' strike. As if work wasn't hard enough to get. These insufferable idealists with their altru-

19

ism. Wasn't there theater going on in Paris and London? It isn't the job of the actor to fight. Let soldiers do that. We starve enough in the best of times. A strike was like laying your head on the block for the guillotine. What do the Nazis care if we strike? There'll be plenty of performers who will cross that picket line. She couldn't repress a smile. She had a mental image of herself walking in patrician style past an angry mob of striking actors and actresses and haughtily exclaiming, "Let them eat their press clippings."

In the middle of the block between Fifth and Sixth avenues was the familiar pink granite structure she lived in. She walked up the steps of the Studio Club and fished inside her purse for the key. She let herself in and saw the gray print rug and then the desk. Mrs. Buxton, the manager, was on the phone. She looked terribly pale and was involved in an intense conversation. She saw Leila and involuntarily covered the mouthpiece with her hand. Leila paid no attention and scanned her box for a sign of mail. Of course, there was none. She walked away and then up the stairs toward her room on the second floor. She put the key in the latch and turned it. There was no click. Funny, she was sure she had locked it last night. Perhaps Fay had forgotten to lock it, although it wasn't like her. She stepped inside, ignoring the jumble of clothes on the floor. She slumped on her bed and lay back. She was tired. She had slept at Richard's last night and had spent half the night warding off his patriotic advances. "But, Leila," he kept saying, "the Nazis are here." Then she would have to explain that that was why she didn't feel like it. Richard would nod sensibly, roll over, and then half an hour later begin again. It had been an exhausting night, but at least there had been no consummation. It suddenly occurred to her that it would have been better if she had let him make love to her. But she detested forced lovemaking.

She desperately needed to rest. A good hot tub would relax her, and then she would nap. She sat up and, for the first time, was struck by the disarray in the room. It was little, a square box with two beds posted evenly next to one another, a bureau in the corner, and a desk pushed against the window that overlooked an alley. A number of the bureau drawers had been pulled out and left that way. On the floor were scattered stockings, a compact, and some blouses, and endless pairs of shoes seemed to have been strewn on their green and orange throw rugs. Leila stood up and walked to the closet and saw immediately Fay's luggage was gone.

But what could have happened? She turned and went to the desk. Fay wouldn't leave without . . .

There was a white envelope with Leila's name written across

it. She picked it up but didn't open it immediately. Rather, she felt a sense of breathless panic come over her. Whatever it said, Fay Brophy was gone, Leila would be alone. No, perhaps it was some kind of emergency, perhaps . . . She forced the thoughts to stop and tore open the envelope. The writing was Fay's elegant style in that green ink she liked to think was so grand.

"Dear Leila, I have a chance to get out tonight and I am taking it. Phil Quinn has a pilot's license and whoopee a plane. So when you read this, hopefully, we will have safely made the flight from the Amityville airport to Columbus, Ohio, without being shot down. And from there, dear Leila, it's on to Holy-wood. Want to come? It doesn't sound like there's going to be much of a season on Broadway. If you want to try it, call Phil's brother, Bill. You remember him, the cute stage manager who kept o-o-o-gling you the year we did stock in Falmouth. Seats cost and I know you're broke, but Bill might be able to loan you some cash. Why don't you come? Please. I'll be lonely for you. Sorry I left in such a hurry but to tell you the truth, I was scared to death in New York. Love,"

Underneath she had written *F* with a large flourish. Angrily, Leila crumpled it into a ball. "No, I am not going out to Holy-wood, I couldn't get a job for almost a year when I was there. Why should I go back this time?" She listened to her outburst and laughed shrilly. "I'd rather take my chances with Nazis," she added. But the moment of gaity had passed and she leaned against the bureau and wondered if she could find another roommate, because now she was faced with a thirty-two-dollar bill for January.

She stood in place, eyes closed. Thinking, she told herself, was no good now. A hot bath would relax her. She turned, went into the bathroom, snapped on the light, and turned on the tap. The warm water on her arm made her immediately feel better.

She opened the medicine cabinet and found the bubble bath. She sprinkled a generous amount in the tub. This would be a real three-bubble affair.

She pulled off her clothes and threw them out in the general direction of the room. Poised, she stood in front of the long, full-length mirror and watched herself. Perfect figure, she thought. Slim, graceful stems, real chorus girl's stuff. Tapered waist, trim buttocks, she gave them a little sashay for emphasis. Nice, full breasts—well, maybe not all that full, but lovely things just the same. Perfect iris of a nipple on each one. She stretched the long, graceful neck and then settled down to inspect her features. I am quite beautiful, she thought, and I don't know why I haven't been discovered. There was the fine nose and the thin lips that could smile, pout, admonish, snap, tremble, all without diminishing her beauty. Yet for all their extreme expressiveness they were not a match for her hazel eyes, which were luminescent with fire and emotion, with palpable tenderness. Looking at herself, she was moved for some reason. There is something special about me, she thought. Why hasn't someone noticed? She closed her eyes and shook the question away.

The Nazis are here, Fay is somewhere in the air over Ohio, and I need thirty-two dollars for the rent. She turned toward the tub and emptied the rest of the bubble bath into it. This was going to be a very special tub. She deserved it.

The door to the black Packard limousine opened, and Corporal Hertz jumped out and opened the door for his passenger. Radner stood in front of the brownstone with the pink stone facade and thought this was almost exactly the way he remembered it except for the sign. He went up the steps and rang the bell. When no one answered immediately, he rang it again, impatiently. He heard footsteps and saw the outline of a woman through the beige curtains that covered the inside of the door. It opened slightly, and a stout, middle-aged woman peered out. She saw his uniform, and her eyes did a little roll.

"Please," he said. "May I come in?"

They stood awkwardly in the vestibule while Radner fished inside his jacket for a cigarette and made a mental note to speak English more precisely. "I wish to see a certain room."

"What?"

"I lived here once. Are the rooms the same? How long have you been here?"

He spoke in an almost imperious manner that intimidated Mrs. Buxton. He was lean and hard, the bone structure of his face making him seem aristocratic. He had a movie actor's perfect nose. His striking blue eyes were filled with keen intelligence and yet mirrored a sadness he could not successfully hide.

The woman screwed up her features, as if by this intense display of concentration to show this impressive conqueror that she was cooperating.

"I've been the manager of the Studio Club since it opened in 1932."

A year after I left, he thought. "Room twenty-one. May I see it?" He spoke in a soft, reassuring voice. "It has a special memory for me. You will accompany me. Please, only for a moment, and then I will leave."

Leila was toweling herself when the knock came.

"Oh, God," she murmured. She put on her robe and went to the door. She looked out, saw Mrs. Buxton's face and the Nazi.

"He . . . he would like to see your room."

"Just a minute," Leila said, and closed the door. She tied her robe. Now she opened the door again and found the officer standing in front of Mrs. Buxton.

The officer spoke softly. "Please, do not be alarmed. Let me explain. This is not official. I once lived here. I just wanted to see the room again. Would you mind?"

He saw the girl staring at him and wished he hadn't come. She was young and pretty and seemed to be looking at him for some kind of sign. It was terribly awkward. "All right," she said, "come in."

"Thank you."

"I'll come, too," Mrs. Buxton announced.

"I shall be leaving momentarily." He saw Mrs. Buxton's red face and horrified eyes. But, of course, I shall defile her, he wanted to say. "You may wait outside if you wish."

"I shall," Mrs. Buxton replied.

He followed the girl into the room and closed the door behind them. They stood there inspecting the room.

"I don't know if this is how you remember it. I—we—my roommate and I have been here nine months."

Radner shifted his weight. "It was different then. There was just one bed and there were three cracks in the wall above the bed. Of course, it has been painted. There was a picture of Long Island."

"We took it down. We wanted something more romantic."

He noted the painting of the Riviera. "Of course."

She watched him as he moved to the window. He raised the shade and stared down the alley. Now he chuckled. "I remember there was a drain pipe that would . . . how do you say it . . . gurgle when there was heavy rain."

He turned and saw she was smiling. "Yes, it still does."

"Is that the right word?"

"Yes," she was still smiling.

"Are you a performer?"

"Yes. How did you know?"

"I assumed that most of the girls here are. Are you an actress?"

"Yes."

"Well, if I didn't think it would kill the old woman out there, I would ask you to scream."

Lame joke, he thought, but he was pleased to see she had laughed.

"I could."

23

Now Radner laughed. "No, please don't. I can see the papers tomorrow: 'German officer tortures woman to death.' "

"Yes, except it would say Nazi officer."

He looked at her curiously then. "Are you working now?"

"No. Actually I lost a job because of you."

"Me?"

"The invasion."

They stood there, neither knowing what to say.

"Anything else you would like to see?"

He looked around. "No, no. I shouldn't have come. Thomas Wolfe was right. You can't go home again."

"Perhaps you will find what you lost in the city," she said.

He scrutinized her carefully with his piercing blue eyes.

She answered his silent question. "Isn't that why we always come back?"

"Yes," Radner said softly. "That is why we come back." He paused. "My name is Radner . . . Friedrich Radner. And you are?"

Leila hesitated. Don't tell him . . . tell him . . coalesced into a contradictory thought, and then she saw only the sensitivity and concern in his tremulous blue eyes, as if it were so terribly important to know who she was.

She spoke the name without knowing why she had done it. "Fay. Fay Brophy."

He took her hand and kissed it. She heard him saying, "A pleasure to have met you, Miss Brophy. If I can be of any assistance . . ." She heard the words as if suspended in a dream. Why did I lie, she asked herself. Because Leila Fox is a Jew? Or because Leila Fox is a loser? Or both. No, you're not a loser. Tell him who you really are. But she was frozen by her lie. Then he opened the door, and Leila saw Mrs. Buxton's frightened, forlorn face. Strange, Leila thought, she seems disappointed I'm all right.

Hertz was waiting for him with an anxious look on his face. "Sir, as you asked, I called Colonel Manheim's office to confirm your dinner engagement. He has been taken to the hospital. The secretary thinks it may have been a heart attack."

Radner seemed stunned. "What hospital?"

"Roosevelt."

"Take me there at once."

The car moved up Fifth Avenue, the bare trees of Central Park looking like so many abandoned widows. Clusters of light leaped before him. He was to have dined with Colonel Manheim tonight along with Gertrude Lawrence at Fouquets. Radner had worked under Manheim in Paris and London. A pudgy man with incredible energy and a bon-vivant appetite for life in Paris. Manheim liked to joke that at fifty-five he had gout in both feet.

Manheim had kept the Paris art and theater scene bubbling. Paris was to be the model for New York. He laughed at the actors' strike in New York. "The plays will go on," Manheim announced to Radner. "They must. Our promotions depend on it." Now Manheim, who was visibly overweight, had suffered a heart attack. Radner felt the serenity of the morning completely desert him. Manheim had promised him a promotion to major within six months.

"Faster," he urged Hertz.

Traffic seemed to melt for the car as it sped past the ornate facades, the stiff doormen, and the fascinated eyes. Along Fifty-ninth Street, which Manheim called the "golden glove." Past the Savoy Plaza, the Plaza, the St. Moritz, the Hampshire House, the New York Athletic Club.

The city flashed before him. What was it about New York? Its pulse and excitement like an unchecked fever. Radner had experienced that feeling as clearly as when he lived in the little walkup on Fiftieth Street not far from the Winter Garden where Fanny Brice starred in a musical. He ate spaghetti for a week so he could see her at Wednesday and Saturday matinees. But it seemed he was always starving himself to go to matinees and to buy a good suit so he could make the rounds of the agents and concert managers who never really understood his music. He was the outsider. The German with operatic credits was trying to write hit musicals, but somehow he wasn't contemporary. He was outside the mainstream. And New York was no place to be an outsider. In no city in the world was one more outside, more unsuccessful than in Manhattan. For no city was as contemporary. Not Paris, not Berlin, not London. And Radner never belonged. The poverty and obscurity always had a hand at his throat.

He remembered the breaking point. The audition for Grierson, the famed manager. It was scheduled for the Carnegie Hall studios, and as Radner walked over on the warm, almost sultry October afternoon, he knew something had to happen for him that day. His nerve had given out. He could not go a day longer without the doors opening for him. He knew he shouldn't put it all on this one audition, but he was thirty-three and had been composing for twelve years. There was no more tomorrow.

Grierson was a balding man with thick eyebrows. He sat on a chair in the middle of the room. His cigar smoke filled the small studio. Radner sat opposite him at the piano and played a piece he had composed back in Berlin five years before. He hadn't dared play it for anyone in this country, but Grierson had a reputation for liking originality. The manager half closed his eyes and pushed the fedora he was wearing farther back on his head. Now he looked down at the floor and sent up puffs of smoke. He was a dreamy-looking man with a crooked mouth. He sounded as if he had a perpetual sore throat. "Wonderful stuff, wonderful. Reminds me a Hindemith piece I heard two years ago. But I can't launch it here. It's not schmaltzy enough. It needs to sound like art but come from Tin Pan Alley. Like Gershwin. Take it back to Europe. Get it played there, then contact me."

Radner felt his heart sink. Grierson was giving him the same message. You're outside the mainstream. Radner's gaze fell on his battered shoes. Grierson's piercing brown eyes also came to rest there. I have holes in my shoes, a broken heart, and a growling stomach, Radner thought to himself, and you tell me to go back.

Grierson seemed to read his mind, for he reached inside his pocket and produced a number of hundred-dollar bills. "There's enough here for boat fare and some clothes. Here, take it. Take it, boy. Give it another shot over there." Eyes averted, Radner let Grierson stuff his pocket with money for the trip back. He knew there would be no more auditions. He needed acceptance more than he needed auditions, and the Third Reich would provide that for him. At a party in Berlin he was introduced to Manheim, who had heard an opera of Radner's performed in Hamburg. Manheim made him his protégé. He had risen quickly after that. He was no longer outside. He belonged. He was never going to be an outsider again like that struggling actress, Fay Brophy.

He recalled her face. She was beautiful and vital like this city. She didn't fear him the way the manager of the club did. Many people would pay him homage. It was his city now. He would manage the arts for Manheim. He would determine who was au courant, who was Broadway, and who played in Carnegie Hall. Grierson was dead, and Radner had risen to heights greater than any manager or impresario. The golden glove was his. Yet, as the city leaped before him in blinding yellow hues, he felt strangely cold and empty. He took out the silver flask that Arletty, the great French actress, had given him. The best. From the best. Courvoisier. Made in France. It always went down smoothly and lifted him, but this time it failed. It burned his throat and tasted strangely bitter.

The city slowly groped through the second day of the Nazi occupation, making its way under the bright December sky through the daily rituals that were the signposts of existence. Children played, garbage trucks made pickups, a million people filed into the subways. On Wall Street the brokerage firms operated feverishly, the wireless popping quotations. War commodities became prime investments. In the streets the cabs wove their circular rites of daredevil passage, fire trucks screamed like Valkyries racing to a fire in Hell's Kitchen, tugboats sailed on the Hudson, tankers carrying oil streamed to the docks. On Delancey Street peddlers hawked their stainless steel, their apples glistening in the sun, displaying their piles of scarfs and woolens, shoes, shirts and socks. Katz's delicatessen had been open since seven o'clock. Its warm smells of franks, knishes, fries, and stuffed cabbage enticed the passing traffic of humanity that spilled into the Lower East Side looking for a bargain. On the surface it was all the same. But something was wrong.

The people saw it when they rode the subway. They looked into each other's eyes and read the same message. Why us? Why didn't they fight for us? What's going to happen? The subway cars pulled in, and the people emerged at their stops. At Bowling Green, Union Square, Essex Street, West Fourth Street; at Penn Station, Columbus Circle, Grand Central Terminal, Whitehall, Franklin, Times Square, Rockefeller Center, 116th and Broadway for Columbia University. And always the eyes asked the other eyes. Have you seen them? Are they here? What do they look like?

And they were there. In their gray uniforms with the swastika on the arm, in their black uniforms with the SS armband. In trucks and cars, in pairs, wearing pistols in holsters, carrying cameras, laughing too loudly, talking in harsh, guttural intonations. In their black leather coats and peaked hats, with their brisk walk and their cries. Calling each other Hans, Gunther, Max, Otto, Werner, Heinz, Dietrich, Hermann, Ernst. They were there when you came out of the IRT at Columbus Circle because the hotels on Central Park South had been confiscated for Nazi officers and visiting dignitaries. They were there when you came out of the subway on West Fourth Street because the Women's House of Detention had become a Gestapo interrogation center. They were there when you left the subway at Centre Street because the city jail had been taken over by the SS for keeping subversives and dangerous dissidents. They were there on Fifth Avenue, the officers strolling together, stopping to buy jewelry at Tiffany's, a wallet in Mark Cross, a fur collar in Bendel's, an expensive shirt and tie in Saks. They stood on the steps of the Forty-second Street library between the lions and posed for photos. They walked along the Battery and took photos of the Statue of Liberty. The Wehrmacht corporals and sergeants stood in a line, nickels in hand, and bought stew at the Automat. They bought coffee at Walgreen, noodles in Chinatown, espresso at the Metropolitan Museum, drank hot chocolate and gestured un-

27

der the Third Avenue El. All over the tight little island known as Manhattan, throughout its twelve and a half miles, its 14,211 acres, they were there on its fixtures, among its facades, on top of the Empire State Building, in front of the Chrysler Building, in the Rainbow Room at Rockefeller Center.

But that wasn't the New York of all the people. The people of a city live in its crooks and alleys, in its shadows and its hidden valleys, in its ghettos and tenements, in its parks and scarred streets. They reside in its groceries, its delis, and its pawnshops. There, they barter for goods, they sell their watches, they trade their rings, they pawn their heirlooms and their jewelry. The people of a city are cave dwellers. The observance of daily rituals goes back to the beginnings of man and his first primitive communities. And always there have been the basic laws of survival. Its most basic tenet is eternal. When you're invaded, you hoard food. And you arm.

AMERICAN PANORAMA
II

NYU PROFESSOR COMMITS SUICIDE IN GREENWICH VILLAGE APARTMENT

by John Luten
World Telegram Staff Reporter

(The following story appeared on Page 3 of the World Telegram *of December 31, 1941.)*

The body of Emil Fuchs, professor of Comparative Literature at New York University, was found in his apartment at 10 Washington Square Mews by New York City police. The police were summoned by Professor John Carston, a colleague who also lives in the building. Professor Carston said that the entire hall of the building reeked of gas and that all attempts to rouse Professor Fuchs or gain entrance to his apartment had failed. Professor Fuchs's body was found on the kitchen floor next to the oven. On the table was a note he had written. A coroner's report estimated that Professor Fuchs had been dead since the previous evening.

Professor Fuchs came to this country in 1931 after having taught at the University of Heidelberg for ten years. He was highly regarded as an expert in European Literature, and had been affiliated with the New York University English Department since 1932. Professor Fuchs had left his native country to escape political persecution by the Nazi party when it came to power. He left no survivors but did address his note to the "great community of Americans whom I regard as my family."

The text of the note is here reprinted:

From the time I first saw the National Socialists in Munich in 1924 I knew they were some dark nightmare that had found shape and form. I never took refuge in the rationale of their being a frenzied, isolated group of outsiders, nor desensitized my fears with bland optimism about the common sense of the good people of the republic. When Hitler was given a comfortable jail cell in which to write *Mein Kampf*, when he was permitted to regroup his party and reappear on the ballot, it was fatal to believe in common sense and decency. I left in 1930, after the national election, because it was plain to anyone of intelligence and intuition that the Nazis would come to power. The drift of certain shrewd businessmen to the Nazis was as clear a message as one might want. The day I sailed from Bremerhaven I remember my exact thought. "I am putting an ocean between me and the dark madness of evil that is surging forth in Germany. I am leaving my homeland, but I will never have to wake in the middle of the night, trembling when I hear a knock at the door. There is an ocean between us, an entire continent. Whatever happens in Europe, they can never come to America." And now, incredibly, they are here. I listen to the radio, and it is all clear and yet unbelievable, as if Kafka were writing the broadcasts. They have come after me. A million of them. Prague, Warsaw, Oslo, Paris, London. Now they have New York. They are here. There is no place to hide from them. An ocean was not enough. Not enough.

(The story and the note were carried in full in the afternoon edition of the World Telegram. *By the second edition, the story had been shifted to page 47 with no mention of the note. The five-star final carried a brief announcement of Professor Fuchs's death on the obituary page. Cause of death was not given.)*

Chapter 4

December 31, 1941
5:00 P.M.

The first occupied New Year's Eve in New York City, Collins thought as he got off the train at Broadway and Eighty-sixth Street. He came up the steps and out into the street. The first thing he noticed was that the Christmas lights strung up over Broadway were not lit. The streets were dark. The festive quality had been snuffed out. People trudged grimly along. For tonight, the curfew had been extended to one o'clock. But what was there to celebrate? The air was raw the way New York is in winter; the chill gripped his bones. He pulled the peak of his fedora down to meet the upturned overcoat collar.

He was carrying the identity card of Robert Jackson, an out-of-work attorney. His cover: a visit to New York for his Cleveland law firm that had left him unable to return when the German invasion occurred. The forgery given him by Bill Donovan was a good job, but if he got picked up there would be no matching registration at Gestapo headquarters. He was using a safe house in the Columbia University area, courtesy of the new OSS intelligence service, which FDR had handed over to Donovan. But he would have to recruit and build his own network of spies and saboteurs.

Collins stood, undecided for the moment on whether to get something to eat or walk awhile. Two days before, while he was waiting his chance to slip into the city, Donovan had provided him with a list of men who would help launch the resistance in New York. "Hitler will try to bomb us into submission," Donovan had said ominously. "We have to cripple the airfields and gut their manpower. You have to get to the unions. Make the Germans hire scabs—then kill a few. See who wants to work for them after that."

Since yesterday afternoon, when Collins arrived, there had been meetings and more meetings. With Michael Donetti, who controlled a large group of longshoremen; with Biff Slade, who ran the Brooklyn Naval Shipyard; with Johnny Dunn, who had taken over the leadership of the anti-Nazi IRA faction. Collins had listened without a word while Dunn told him how Jimmy Handy had been arrested that day. There wasn't a cooler man with a gun or a stick of dynamite, and Collins needed him badly. Arching his bushy eyebrows, Dunn said, "The krauts have a line on us. Liam Fletcher and some of the Nazis in our nest helped them land in Montreal and cut the wires to New York. There's a price on your head, Robbie. Fletcher gave them Jimmy, and he'll do you good if he can."

Collins was out of cigarettes and saw a tobacco store across Broadway. He headed that way as the light turned red. There wasn't the kind of traffic you would expect on New Year's Eve. He dodged between two cabs and made it over to the other side of Broadway. He stopped abruptly as two men in leather coats and hats came out. SS or Gestapo. Each one had two cartons of cigarettes under his arm. The short one took out a pack of Chesterfields and lit one for his companion. They stood there smiling, inhaling on freshly lit Chesterfields. They looked over at him, and Collins turned away. Then he heard a voice call to him and he stiffened. His hand should have been on his gun, but it was locked. He heard the voice again.

"*Schatze. Mein schatz.* I give you a pack of cigarettes."

Sagging against a barber pole, Collins watched them chase after a leggy brunette with long hair. He exhaled and felt the tremor in his right hand. His gun hand. Snap out of it laddie, you're in Nazi New York.

He could hear the voice of Mike Donetti, the union leader of the New York waterfront. "This Abetz is no virgin. He worked under Heydrich in Czechoslovakia. The Gestapo is picking off politicals real fast. They got a pipeline to every rotten informer in New York. The Tombs is full of men already. When you're ready to make your move, me and my guys are with you all the way."

Collins sucked in some air. Roosevelt, I warned you. I trailed Hitler's men to the Bahamas and told you about the buildup, but you wouldn't listen. You got caught with your pants down, and because I owe Bill Donovan I'm supposed to be a savior. Well, I'm not.

He wiped his face and turned toward the tobacco store. He was still out of cigarettes, and he wasn't going to be put off by two Gestapo strong arms. He made his way into the store and found himself facing a mild, prissy-looking man in a gray confectioner's coat. He had a white mustache and wore thick glasses.

"A pack of Chesterfields."

The clerk looked helplessly at him. "No Chesterfields."

"Luckies then."

The clerk shook his head. "No cigarettes."

Collins was hot. "I just saw . . ."

"Please, they took everything I had. Everything," he whined.

Collins looked at the empty racks. You're selling to the black market, he thought.

The little man divined his thoughts. "Here, I have a pack of Philip Morris. Take it. Go ahead. I'm closing up . . . my wife is waiting."

Jesus, Collins thought to himself. This is the city I was born in. The people I knew were fearless.

He saw the pack extended to him and took it. The clerk looked like he was about to cry.

"Easy, mate. You got a bathroom?"

Collins stood in the cramped room and used a paper towel to dry his face. He examined it in the dirty mirror. He was a wiry, compact man, lithe and muscular underneath his clothes. He had the same kind of muscular determination in his face. Strong cheekbones, a mouth that would firm up when angered, and a forehead that took on wrinkle lines when he was troubled and tired, as now. Taken together, they gave him the quality of a restless fuse that could detonate instantly. But there were also ameliorating qualities. The mouth could soften and become sensual, the pale blue eyes could change expression and allow the vulnerability to show, and the rumpled brown hair was the kind that took easily to hands running through it.

"You look like hell, laddie," he murmured to himself. He flipped a Philip Morris into the side of his mouth and, after lighting it, put his hand in his pocket and made his way to the front of the store.

The clerk stood framed under the dull overhead light. Collins flashed the pack of cigarettes. "Thanks for the butts. I wasn't here, mate."

"I never saw you in my life."

Collins went out toward Riverside Drive and saw the bare trees whipped by the driving wind. It had been a long time, and yet it was all so familiar. He had lived on Riverside Drive when he went to Columbia and played right halfback on the 1920 Lions. He saw the large old apartment houses, the lights dimmer because this was no longer a free city. I was born here, but I am a stranger, he thought. He remembered cold winter nights coming off the gridiron at Baker Field, tired, bruised, but warm with the camaraderie and the laughter of his teammates. Living from Saturday to Saturday when they wore the light blue uniforms of the Columbia Lions.

He remembered that last game at Baker Field against Johnny Harvard. He had intercepted a pass and run sixty-eight yards for a touchdown while the crowd screamed fanatically. But the Johnnies drove seventy yards in the freezing cold sunlight and, with less than forty seconds on the clock, Sundstrom, their fullback, dragged Collins on his face across the goal line. Then Sundstrom added the extra point, and Harvard won 14–13. In the dressing room, Collins sat slumped over, the tears foamy on his cheeks. A moon-faced Irishman sat down next to him and whispered, "I'm Bill Donovan from the 1901 team. There'll be another game, lad." Then he gave Collins his card. Six months later when Collins got the word from his dad to come to Dublin, it was Bill Donovan who got him a boat ticket and the money to make his way over.

So he owed Bill Donovan. More than one. Bill Donovan had gotten him out of Spain when the boat Collins was running guns on crashed into the rocks at Malaga and the Fascists captured him. Donovan wanted New York to go up in flames. But Collins was the wrong man, trapped in a terrorist role he had long since outgrown. Now he had a meeting with another name Bill Donovan had given him. Harold Kresky. A red renegade who had broken with the party over the Hitler-Stalin pact. A labor organizer who could give Collins workers who would switch from fitting pipes to fitting dynamite sticks. Kresky was the last meeting, and then the night would be over. At the Gold Rail, a place Collins knew from his student days.

Collins stopped in the freezing night and checked his watch. Seven-thirty, and he hadn't eaten. He was tired, and he ached from the cold. He wanted a steak and a warm bath. Then he heard his dad's voice. "When you get tired and you want to pack it in, push a little harder and you'll win, Bobbie boy." Collins slapped his cold hands together and walked on.

6:00 P.M.

Kresky sat rocklike, despite the rattling motion of the subway car, and looked again at the vile photo in the *Daily Worker* that showed Joe Gaines embracing Standartenführer Abetz at the rally in Union Square. When Hitler and Goebbels saw that picture, how they would chortle. Those two would ply Stalin with incense and myrrh until he lay on his back like a fat sow.

The train pulled into the Twenty-eighth Street Station, and an elderly man in a shabby overcoat got on. He sat down across from Kresky. The subway doors closed, and the train lurched on its way again, the lights in the car momentarily dimming. The lights came back on, and Kresky looked once again at the treacherous photo. Gaines embracing the Gestapo on behalf of the party while workers gave the clenched fist salute and sang

"The Internationale." The song of the revolution, the workers' anthem. The party, which had been the hope of men and women throughout the world, now displayed its shame for all to see. Why, he berated himself, did you not leave the party when Stalin held his trials and executed the last of the Bolsheviks? Because, fool, you had too long believed the workers' revolution would change the world. Revolution would come to America as it did to Russia. You believed through all those burning-hot afternoons and freezing mornings, when you stood with the workers of the city in Union Square Park, that you were in the vanguard of a new dawn.

Communism was the road to the nobility of a socialist order. Time after time it was the party that pointed to the injustices of the capitalist order while America slept on. And always Kresky was in the forefront. He was there that August night in Union Square when Sacco and Vanzetti were executed and the police mounted machine guns on the rooftops across the street. He remembered so well the *Daily Worker* posting signs: SACCO MURDERED, VANZETTI MURDERED. And the cry ripped from one collective throat. *No!* He was there that humid, sultry day in August when the party marched on Union Square Park, crying "No more police brutality." The massed line of police, many on horseback, all swinging billies, came at them in an unending line of blue. Kresky fell, fending off two burly Irish cops, hearing their unadorned enjoyment as they clubbed him to the ground, hearing the screams around him, feeling in the kicks to his head the pain of every man and woman sharing this time with him.

His fingers closed on the paper and crumpled it. He wanted to rend it, tear it to shreds, reduce it to fragments so small they would never be seen. Then the futility of it came to him, and he let the paper slip from his hands and fall to the floor of the subway car.

He looked up and saw the old-timer looking at him and then at the paper. The old man leaned forward and spoke in tired, hoarse accents. "Eugene Debs would roll over in his grave if he saw that."

Kresky instantly recognized the sentiments. "Wobbly?"

"One of the first."

He pulled a bottle from his pocket and uncapped it. Then he extended the bottle to Kresky. "Drink with an old hobo who once rode the rails with Joe Hill?"

The sentiment passed like a lightning sliver through Kresky, and he felt his eyes sting. He smiled and took the bottle. "Happy days."

"Happy New Year."

They sat together, passing the bottle back and forth, as they

34

rode uptown, the old man to whatever shelter he would inhabit this night, Kresky to his meeting with someone from the Father Flynn Charity. There had been a flier in his mailbox that morning. It was a calling card from somebody who wanted action. Well, Kresky had formed his cell—Jake Ragosky, Pincus Sobel, Joe Grant, Nate Pearlstein, Abe Woisky, and Eugene Lepentier, who had spent more years in French jails than any three convicts you could name. These men would not sing "The Internationale" to the Gestapo.

The old hobo stood up and fumbled with his fly. "Only one thing to do about that picture." They both laughed like schoolboys engaging in a malicious prank.

This, Kresky thought, is our answer. Yeah, Happy New Year.

10:00 P.M.

The Gold Rail had been Collins's hangout. Even during the football season, he always managed to hoist a few at the long wooden bar lined with faces he could now no longer remember. The booths were always packed. Now the place was half empty. There was talk, but it was careful conversation, not the carefree kind Collins knew. He spotted an empty seat at the end of the bar and pushed into it. He caught the bartender's eyes. "Gimme something to eat . . . anything . . . and a bottle of Rupert's."

The bartender, a short man with the chest of a basso profundo, was wiping a glass. "I got cheese and bacon and potato soup."

Collins's head hung over the bar. "Gimme a bacon and cheese sandwich and a bowl of potato soup. I don't care in what order."

The soup came in a few minutes. It was thick, but only lukewarm. Collins didn't care. He suddenly realized how hungry he was. He ate it all and the four packages of crackers and washed it down with the beer. Now he noticed the quiet. The place was subdued, even gloomy. Like a pub in Dublin when the Tans dropped in for a drink. He ordered a second beer and checked his watch.

He was halfway through a greasy bacon and cheese sandwich when he heard a man's voice. "You with the Father Flynn Charity?"

Collins turned and saw a stocky, well-built man with a generous mop of brown and gray curls, wearing a black workingman's jacket with a white shirt open at the neck. He had piercing brown eyes beneath a high forehead and nose that had been broken more than once.

"My union got the letter from your parish."

The man was obviously Harold Kresky.

"Want something?" the bartender said.

"We'll grab a booth," Collins told him.

"Okay."

"Give us some ale. The Watney's."

"What's the matter, you don't like good German beer on New Year's Eve?" The smile on the bartender's lips was bitter.

They sat at a table in the back near the kitchen. The light was dim and, Collins thought, we probably look like a pair of conspirators.

"Like I said, I got your letter," Kresky began. "Who's your superior at Father Flynn's?"

"Father Donovan. He speaks highly of you."

"Yes. I know of his work, too," Kresky responded. "I'm glad I come highly recommended."

"I've come here to do work for the subway," Collins said. "Underground. I'll have to go very deep. I'll need surveyors."

Disdaining his glass, Kresky drank from the bottle. "Nobody's around. Let's put some cards on the table. I figure the Germans will want to build a large standing air force here. That's the cannon they'll point at Roosevelt's head."

"The Nazis will have to get workers. We'll get to the unions."

Kresky snorted. "Hell, there's a whole unemployed work force out there. Even with the unions helping us, the Nazis will operate."

"What else have you heard?"

Kresky took another swig and spewed up some angry foam. "There's already a call for scab labor at the Grumman plant. If they can get Grumman and Curtiss-Wright working, the Luftwaffe will be in business. Meanwhile, they'll fly in planes from England and Canada. As long as our air force is tied up on the West Coast, the Germans can stockpile planes here."

"Maybe the scabs could be muscled a little bit."

Kresky slugged some more ale. "Sure, you can lean on them. Everything helps, but that's a drop in the bucket. You need industrial sabotage, and only the labor movement can do that."

Collins loosened his tie. "How many can you deliver?"

"Enough."

"Can you get them into Curtiss-Wright and Grumman?"

"How fast?"

"So fast it's like instant coffee."

"Like yesterday?"

"That's right."

"Who do you have?"

"IRA. Good ones."

The bad ones were Nazi collaborators. Like Liam Fletcher, who had put a price on Collins's head for anyone who clipped him.

"You're IRA, aren't you?"

"Could be."

Kresky downed more beer. "You want hired guns, don't you?"

"Maybe."

"You'll get a lot of innocent people killed?"

Collins's mouth tightened. "If it's the thing to do, I'll do it. Nobody's ever roughed up the Gestapo before. Maybe this is the time."

Kresky leaned forward. "That's dumb. That's hardheaded IRA stuff. You're good at creating martyrs. But you don't win."

Collins was thankful he wasn't being tested on an empty stomach. "We fight and we die. Which is a lot better than signing a nonaggression pact with the Nazis."

Kresky's lips turned up in a sneer, but Collins could see the pain in his eyes. "There are a lot of your lads from the IRA who sold out England to the Germans, all in the name of a free Ireland, so come off your platform, Johnny Irish. Or should I call you by your name, Collins?"

Collins felt like he had been jabbed in the face. His hand balled up into a fist.

Kresky's mouth was only inches away from Collins as he leaned across the booth. "Everybody heard about you and your cousin, Mick Collins, back here in the twenties. You had a revolution going, and then you sold it out. You settled for the south of Ireland when you should have taken it all. That's what got Mick Collins killed."

Collins thought the words he once would have spoken. Keep talking like that, and you'll be swimming in the river.

"What are you doing here, Collins?"

They eyed one another impassively. "Let's just say I owe Bill Donovan one."

Kresky pointed a finger at Collins. "You're a mercenary and you got guts. I'll give you that. But you haven't been around this city for years. You think it's just setting off a few bombs and then back to Dublin. It's a job for you. Only it's not a job. If America falls, it's over for the world. This country is the cradle of freedom and, compared to America, Ireland is a fly in the piss barrel. Can you really understand that?"

Collins leaned back. "I didn't meet you for a political sermon, Kresky. If mercenaries weren't successful, I wouldn't be here. Me and Mick invented the Resistance business. It's not about marching in the street screaming for better wages and shorter hours."

Kresky had a bitter smile across his mouth. "Answer me, what's more important for you, New York or Dublin?"

Collins wanted to grab Kresky by the collar and shake him. "In Dublin, we'd die before we'd let the Tans arrest someone and do nothing about it."

"What the hell does that mean?"

"It means, Kresky, that today I went to see Jimmy Handy, the best dynamite man I knew in Dublin, and I got there five minutes too late. Two Gestapo thugs marched him out of the building while a dozen Americans stood around and did nothing. Now he's rotting in a kraut cell. So sing me no songs about the cradle of freedom."

"That won't happen again."

"Won't it? How did the krauts get here? I warned Washington about an invasion, and no one did anything. They stood by and let themselves be invaded. Like the crowd that stood around this morning. Sure, Ireland is tragedy and privation. We may kill each other, but we don't stand around and let our own be picked up and picked off. We never had anything, but we belong to ourselves. America is soft. It was soft when I left twenty years ago. You're living on the legend of a revolution fought a hundred and fifty years ago. You've been sucking on the cow's tit of capitalism too long. You're a working force, not a fighting one. Give the people jobs, a forty-hour week, and their annual dole to take home to the little lady, and you'll buy them off. They're jelly, Kresky, and they've got a depression mentality to boot. The Germans rolled up the Northeast in a week. When the Germans give them jobs, paychecks, and chicken potpie, there'll be the devil's own time raising them to fight. I don't think the people are up to it. The will isn't there. That's why Hitler came in the first place. He knew that an isolationist people wouldn't scrap, and he was right. So let's not hear any more cock about mercenaries. They're a lot braver than anything I've seen around here."

They sat less than six inches apart, staring at one another with angry, unyielding eyes.

Kresky finished his beer. "When the time comes, they'll be out there, all of them, wanting their freedom back."

Collins drained his glass. "Well, until that day comes, I'm in charge. Your people take orders from me. I'm Washington's man."

"There is no Washington anymore."

"I'm still their man."

"Listen to me, Collins. Roosevelt and Donovan don't know what's happening here. You're their eyes. But to be good, you have to care about what happens here. You have to have a soul, too. It's easy to make a splash, but there's more to it than dynamite and martyrs."

"Meaning what?"

"Meaning I'll work with you, but not for you. Meaning I have my own people. If I need fire power, you supply it. If you need industrial sabotage, we'll supply it. I have to know you're here for the long haul. That's the deal."

Collins let it sift around for a moment. Kresky was going to be hell to work with, but he was courageous, he was a professional, and he knew New York. It wasn't Collins's turf anymore.

"You don't pick the targets, Kresky. I have the final say."

Kresky waited a moment and then nodded. "Okay, but I'll be looking over your shoulder. And I'd better like what I see."

Collins caught the eye of the bartender and help up two fingers. He turned back to Kresky. "All right, we're in business. Now I still need trigger fingers and strong arms. Donovan said you had your head busted more than once. I want the goons who did it."

Kresky rubbed his head as the bartender placed two more bottles on the table and said out of the side of his mouth, "Curfew in a few minutes."

Kresky stared into the bottle, as if he were seeing the faces of the men he had stood side by side with and envisioning once again comrades wearing masks dipped in their own blood. "There was a big strike in Hobokon back in thirty-nine. A few of us went down to show them how to organize at a steel plant. The bosses brought in some local talent from New York. One guy was very good. He used a steel pipe and brass knuckles like he was born with them."

"Name?"

"Lazar. Paulie Lazar."

"Were can I find him?"

"He used to work for an old-time hood named Barney Feldstein. Feldstein was sent up in October. Hughie Gagno inherited his mob. You'll have to make inquiries."

"Who else?"

"You can nose around and see who's left from the Murder Incorporated boys. The Jewish hoods will have an extra bone to pick with the Nazis."

Collins eyed Kresky, who was drawing a water line around the bottle with his finger. "How about the volunteers from Spain?"

"Like the Abraham Lincoln Brigade?"

"Yeah."

Kresky didn't respond.

"Your people," Collins said.

"Something like that. They didn't believe in the pact either."

The lights flashed on and off. Collins heard the bartender call curfew and stood up.

"Friday night. Here, same time."

Kresky looked up at him. In his eyes Collins could still see the doubt and the anger. "I'll be here."

He slipped out of the booth and turned to go. Kresky's voice came to him. "They shall not pass."

Collins whirled. "That was Spain and we didn't beat the fascists there."

"This isn't Spain," Kresky said through tight lips.

"No," Collins said softly. "It isn't. The people there wanted to fight."

Outside, Collins felt the cutting wind again. It slapped at his face and head. He wasn't afraid to die, but did he have the heart for this? Maybe Kresky was right. It wasn't just a matter of dynamite. A gangster named Paulie Lazar was the next stop. How was Collins going to wield men like Kresky, Michael Donetti, and Lazar into a functioning Resistance? How was he going to make them brothers in arms? And Jimmy Handy, whom he desperately needed, was in the Tombs.

Suddenly in his ear there was the ring of Mick Collins's drunken and happy voice reciting the St. Crispin's Day speech of *Henry V*. The words locked in place. Words from a better time, when he still believed in victory. "And Crispin Crispian shall ne'er go by, from this day to the ending of the world, but we in it shall be remembered—we few, we happy few, we band of brothers; for he today that sheds his blood with me shall be my brother, be he ne'er so vile."

Collins disappeared into the darkness.

Chapter 5

December 31, 1941
10:30 P.M.

Paulie Lazar stood behind Hughie Gagno, dragging on a coffin nail, while Hughie worked out the deal with Kreutzer, the owner of the Bavarian Brau House. They were in Kreutzer's office on the second floor. It was a tiny little matchbox, undusted and dirty. Kreutzer was a short, roly-poly man who, despite wearing well-fitted suits, could not hide his bulging stomach and chest. He had a thick mustache and popping brown eyes.

"Hooie, I know I promised you thirty pounds veal, but this is New Year's Eve, and the Reich requisitioned everything."

Hughie was not impressed. "Can it. What do you have?"

Kreutzer looked hurt. "Like I tell you. Twenty pounds veal, thirty pounds ham, and plenty chicken and cornish hen."

Hughie pretended to be unimpressed. It was an old gambit Paulie had seen him use many a time. What a tired bit, he thought. It's getting time for you to retire, Hughie. He watched Hughie run a nervous tongue over his chin. When you saw him doing that and took in the snub nose and flitting brown eyes, you knew he was a punk. Even with the expensive black suit, black overcoat, and gleaming black shoes.

"Kreutzer," Hughie said, pushing forward to lean on the desk. "Just don't be holding out on me, or I'll give you to Lazar."

Kreutzer flashed a panicked look at Paulie. "You know I wouldn't hold out on you, Hooie."

You putz, Paulie thought. Hughie is nothing. He happened to be married to Barney's daughter. That's why he got his operation and not me. When Barney Feldstein wanted a strong-arm job, he sent me, not Hughie. If it wasn't for Hughie marrying Anita, this would be mine.

He turned impatiently away and walked to the window. Outside Yorkville was lit up with swastika banners and pictures of their Führer. People were dancing in the street. Paulie could hear the music from the brau house below as the people of Germantown celebrated. This will go on all night, he told himself.

"Hooie," Kreutzer pleaded. "We have to talk a better deal. Sixty-forty is not fair. I supply the meat. Should be fifty-fifty."

Paulie saw Hughie flush. He didn't like his business coming out that way.

Hughie scowled. "Paulie, leave us alone. We got personal business to straighten out."

"Sure," Paulie said. "If you don't need me for nothin', me and Tommy are gonna eat and relax."

"Just make sure you meet me first thing in the morning with Rocky and another driver. And I mean early, Paulie."

"You got it," Paulie said, playing the part of the trusty second-in-command. He went out the door and then down the stairs, muttering "Kiss off, Gagno."

Paulie speared a piece of wurst and demolished it in three rapacious bites, then washed it down with a swig from his stein. He rocked back in his chair, still holding the stein, and watched the excited activity in the Bavarian Brau House. People were yelling to each other, steins of beer floated through the air like so many balloons, accordian music and singing filed the circular tavern. A large swastika framed in red hung down from the ceiling. The front room of the brau house, the barroom, was packed with noisy Bund members in uniform. Some with black trousers, white shirts, and swastika armbands; others in olive garb, and still others wearing the traditional black of the storm troopers.

Paulie drained his stein and laughed. "Jesus, it's flowing like water."

Tommy Emboli, toothpick flashing in the corner of his mouth, made a gesture with a movement of his head. "What the hell we hangin' around here for?"

Paulie fished a toothpick for himself and placed it in his mouth. "What's a better place to talk? Nobody can hear our business."

Paulie smiled and flashed gold-capped teeth. Only gold for Paulie. "Listen up, *paisano*, and you'll hear good. I got only good things to tell you." Paulie brought out a pack of Luckies from his jacket and stuck one in the corner of his mouth opposite the side that held the toothpick. He lit it and threw away the match, still surveying the room with amused wonder. The effort made the flesh under his throat bulge against the collar of his white shirt and black tie. Everything about Paulie seemed just that way. A little too large. He had a thick shock of brown hair that he combed high, exactly in place. At six feet two, broad of chest and shoulders, he was an imposing figure. His mouth, which he had inherited from his mother, was too soft. To compensate, Paulie had long affected a style of moving his lips in a set of smirks, scowls, sardonic smiles, and sarcastic twists. Now his thin, almost girlish eyebrows arched up, his brown eyes flickered with private satisfaction. "Look around you, Tommy. What do you see?"

Tommy had a face like an olive with matching complexion. All his features seemed round except his lips, which had a way of nervously appearing and disappearing as he talked. "What do you think I see? A bunch of drunken krauts who're drivin' me crazy with their music."

Paulie smirked. He took out the butt and deliberately blew three delicately formed smoke rings with his lady's mouth. "Look around again. Look what they're carrying on the trays next to the beer. You see it, *paisan*?"

A waiter with a plate of schnitzel went by.

Paulie clapped Tommy on the shoulder. "Schnitzel, roast beef, pot roast, lamb. Meat, you get it?"

Tommy looked befuddled.

Paulie sneered. "The restaurants up here ain't gonna have any trouble getting it, and the Nazis ain't, but there'll be lots of rich people who will pay through the nose for it. They're gonna want to stockpile it in their iceboxes. It's the old law of supply and demand. That ain't meat, Tommy, it's long green you're staring at."

It was as if somebody had just painted a miracle, and Tommy was a blind man discovering he had sight. "Yeah, it's gonna be like prohibition." The eyes, fresh with sight, lit up.

Paulie clapped him on the shoulders. "That's how Big Al made his bundle. He blasted Dion O'Bannion and those other mick bastards, and the money rolled in. Do you get it, Tommy? All you need is a little supply store."

Tommy was frowning again. "What supply store?"

"What supply store? Hughie owns the protection business in Germantown."

Tommy was a blind man again. "Yeah, so what? That's Hughie. That ain't us, Paulie. We work for him."

Paulie grabbed a waiter going by, held up the stein on the table, and said, *"Zwei."* He turned to Tommy. "You know, I think Hughie might not be big enough for the job."

Tommy shook his head. "Sour grapes."

"Hughie's a punk," Paulie snarled.

"But it's his territory. Barney gave it to him."

Paulie looked mean. "You don't think I could run it?"

Tommy looked bored. "You're dreamin' again. Hughie is holding it for Barney."

Paulie's eyes were consumed with the fires of jealous rage. "You know what his deal with Kreutzer is?"

"What?"

"Sixty-forty."

Tommy shrugged. "Not bad. After all, Hughie ain't Barney."

Paulie leaned back and drank from his stein. He looked immensely pleased with himself. "I'm not makin' no sixty-forty deals."

Tommy lifted his eyes toward heaven as if to say, give me a break. "You ain't makin' no deals, you're taking orders."

"That's what you think."

"What are you sayin', Paulie?"

"Tomorrow we get on our wheels and start driving out to some of the farmers in New Jersey. The next day to Long Island. We find ourselves some greedy farmers and offer them a very good deal. We'll sell their meat. We transport it for them and sell it for them. Then we split the take."

"Split it?"

"Yeah, split. Eighty-twenty. That's the only deal I make."

Tommy mulled it around. "You're sayin' we run a little action of our own."

"Sure. Who's to be afraid of? Hooie?" Paulie said, imitating Kreutzer.

Tommy sat back. He had known Paulie Lazar all his life. They had gone through grammar school together, quit high school together, been in the slammer together. Paulie was big, free with his hands. Tommy was small, wiry, and fast. Paulie had taken care of Tommy. Paulie had big dreams, but Tommy was never sure he had it in him. He'd busted heads, but he was thirty and still a small-time muscle man. But maybe now . . .

"Check," Paulie called.

The two hoods slipped into dark overcoats and pushed their way through the carousing Bund members. Everybody seemed to have a stein in his hand and a song on his lips. A fat black shirt jostled them.

"Outa my fuckin' way," Paulie snarled.

He's feeling cocky, Tommy thought. When he's that way, then he gets that little edge, and you gotta watch out. He's had about six bottles of that kraut beer. That stuff will grow hair on your ass.

They stood on the corner of Eighty-sixth and Third watching the festive New Year's Eve crowds. Across the street a man on a podium was giving a speech. He was decked out in black trousers, a white shirt with the Nazi armband, and a black cap. He stood under a row of gleaming lights. A squad of German soldiers had pulled in, and now Tommy could see German officers taking the platform. The streets were filled with people. Tommy didn't give a crap about the war, but there was something about these krauts, their beer, their loud songs. It was giving Tommy a terrible headache. Across the street the Yorkville Casino had a huge swastika draped over it. All the pastry shops displayed Nazi banners and portraits of Hitler and other guys Tommy didn't recognize.

"Let's get out of here."

"What's the matter?" Paulie asked. "Don't you like kraut New Year?"

"They gives me the creeps."

They moved through the excited throngs, past the swastika-bedecked delicatessens, dance halls, and beer gardens. Girls ran through the streets, distributing flowers and kissing people. A young blonde suddenly stood in their way. She threw her arms around Paulie and kissed him on the mouth. Paulie leaned into her, giving her the rotating groin treatment. The girl broke away, and Paulie, mouth full of lipstick, turned and winked at Tommy.

44

The girl stood back a little shocked. She was all bursting patriotism.

"Heil Hitler," she said.

Paulie grinned. "Stuff Hitler. Come here, *schatz*." He brought her close with a giant arm and kissed her full on the mouth. In the enthusiasm of the moment, the girl leaped into his arms and flung herself about him. Their impetus tumbled them down some stairs under the awning of a flower shop. They righted themselves, and now Paulie was using his tongue, his hand moving under the broad's ass. She struggled, finally broke free from the laughing Paulie, and ran up the steps.

Paulie continued laughing as he wiped lipstick from his mouth. "We're gonna be kings, Tommy. Like I always told you. Remember?"

The girl was back with a black-shirted Bundist. He was beefy with huge forearms.

"Him," she said.

The Bundist confronted Paulie. "Apologize to the fräulein, you American pig."

Tommy looked around. Normally, this was no problem, but up here it wasn't a good idea. Not tonight.

Paulie rolled his shoulders the way he had seen Muni and Cagney do it. "What did I do?"

"I saw you. You soiled her, you pig."

These people are really full of themselves, Tommy thought.

"These hands," Paulie began, "don't soil."

He's drunk, and he's cocky, and that's when he's mean, Tommy knew. Tommy's hand went to the gun under his coat. Just in case.

Paulie and the Bundist were eye to eye. Paulie's gonna let it drop, Tommy realized. Smart.

"Well, pig?"

"Fräulein," Paulie said, holding his hands out plaintively. He turned to the girl as if to offer his hand, then in the same motion swiveled back and plunged a ripping left into the kraut's gut. The kraut went all white as his lunch started to come up. As he crumpled, Paulie's chopping right landed across his temple. It was over that quick.

"C'mon," Paulie said. They walked up the steps, and now the girl was screaming. "See you, baby," Paulie called back.

They made their way through the ecstatic crowds, the Bundists, the German soldiers, the kissing fräuleins, the happy burgermeisters, celebrating the dawn of the new order. Their fantasy had come true, swastika-covered flags fluttering, pictures of their Führer and swelling music, the marching band in the streets, their voices raised in song.

45

"Vedezana, auf Vedezane." Another fraülein pressed into them. This one was older, more buxom, breasts overflowing her blouse. She was singing and spinning around. *"Ich leibe dich, mein schatz,"* she cried.

Paulie winked. "Dick you, too, baby."

Chapter 6

December 31, 1941
10:45 P.M.

The lights of the city glittered back at Patrick Kelly as he stood on the terrace. He was wearing a tuxedo and held a martini in his hand. Behind him, through the open door, he could hear Roosevelt imploring the American people in occupied America to take heart, to display courage in their darkest hour. How many of the people who could hear the broadcast would dare listen to it? A lot, he admitted to himself. The krauts were not jamming the reception on this one. They're curious, too. And they want to hear the great FDR humbled in defeat. Now Kelly was openly smiling. You son of a bitch, you finally got your due. You will go down in history as the first American president who let foreign invaders on our soil. And if the Nips land on the West Coast, you'll lose it all. The whole ball of wax. You arrogant bastard, you presided over our invasion. Kelly remembered being recalled to Washington from Paris to face dismissal as American ambassador. Kelly had demanded and finally got a meeting with FDR. Five minutes of the great man's time. They hated each other, Kelly and Roosevelt. Kelly had backed Al Smith at the 1932 Chicago convention. He had tried to persuade Lucky Luciano and Frank Costello to back Smith, but the gangster chiefs went for Roosevelt, who took their money and support and then turned Tom Dewey loose as a special prosecutor. Luciano was now serving forty years in Dannemora, courtesy of Dewey. Now you know about FDR, don't you, Lucky?

Roosevelt's voice came to him now. "We must not think of defeat," Roosevelt implored. "The German invader will attempt to make a place for himself amongst the people of the United States. In New York, in Boston, in Philadelphia. The invader

46

will use every insidious trick at his disposal to attach himself to the bond and fiber of these cities. He will use every rationalization to suggest he is your friend, that you can live with him, that things are the same. They are not. You cannot live with the enemy. He must be scourged from our nation.''

Kelly's mouth split open in a broad grin. The arrogant SOB was truly desperate. For the hundredth or the thousandth time, Kelly remembered the meeting with FDR and Secretary of State Cordell Hull in which he had warned them that the Germans were a force to be dealt with, that Hitler had to be recognized and handled. Roosevelt hadn't even bothered to answer. He had turned away in that haughty manner of his, the cigarette holder in the corner of his mouth. Treating Kelly as if he were an inferior. Kelly, who had contributed fifty thousand dollars to Roosevelt's 1936 campaign. That had been his successful bid for the ambassador's chair. That's the way the game was played. It was all a game and, if Kelly weren't a Catholic, he would have gone for the whole thing. But the game had taken a funny turn, and now Kelly suddenly had a chance that nobody could have predicted. A chance to crown himself, to humiliate FDR, and to prepare the way for his son Joe.

Fate had dealt him only one son to go along with six daughters. But that was enough. He had an heir apparent, and he was the man everyone would have to come to. He had spent the years since 1937 in Europe dealing with the Nazi hierarchy. Von Ribbentrop had been his entrée. Kelly knew them all. Goebbels was shrewd and tried to pass himself off as an intellectual. Kelly had praised his plays, his unproduced masterpieces. Goering was cynical and vain. Himmler was a pedant, but tenacious and unforgiving. Heydrich was more dangerous than all of them. His glove covered a mailed fist. Von Ribbentrop was a fox, Bormann fiercely ambitious. Hitler he had met three times and found charismatic but elusive. There was something dark and demonic inside him that he hid in state meetings with quick smiles and false heartiness. Kelly knew only one thing. Hitler meant to swallow the world.

But Hitler had to play ball, and that meant the strings would always be pulled by money. By the Deutsches bank, by Farben, by Krupp. By old world money. Kelly loved that. He was noveau riche, and old money hated him. Well, screw them. He had climbed over the backs of the Rockefellers and Fords and, when things shook down, Kelly was going to start a dynasty of his own. Until Hitler came here, Kelly would have bet heavily against a Catholic becoming president for at least fifty years. But now all bets were off. Kelly had the direct line to the horse's mouth. He was the Nazis' link to business here. They knew and trusted him. They would try to use him, of course, but that was part of the game. He had his price, every man did. He would get it by making himself indispensable. It was all in knowing how to cut the deck.

Kelly moved back inside. Sylvie was on the phone. She was wearing a long black evening dress. She looked now as she had at their first encounter at Regine's in Paris.

First you saw her hair—spun gold—and then the eyes that always reminded Kelly of the good fairy in a nursery story the Swiss governess had read his children. The eyes were a gentle blue. It seemed as if nothing harsh ever resided there. For that alone she invoked in him trust, which was as close as Kelly had ever gotten to loving a woman.

Her nose was almost perfect, but with a slightly crooked cast. The mouth smiled so innocently, imparted the softest kisses when she let herself go. Just now her lips were parted in wonder.

"Mother, of course, I will come to Dede's wedding. What has a travel permit to do with . . . Patrick will get it for me. Yes, I know there's a war on, but I wouldn't miss my little sister's wedding for the world. I made this call, didn't I?" She paused to listen to her mother. Kelly pictured the patrician Mrs. Clarissa Lamont.

"Actually, Patrick placed the call. You mean you haven't been able to get through? The calls are monitored?" She cupped the receiver. "Patrick, is that true?"

He nodded.

"You mean to tell me that Mother and I can't call each other whenever we want?"

"I have a special number. But there is a war on, Sylvie. The Germans will allow very few long-distance calls."

"Hello, Mother, are you there? Patrick will arrange it. Don't worry. Of course, I'll come to Palm Beach. Dede is my baby sister."

Kelly moved out of the bedroom and back into the living room, recently redecorated with new furniture from Abercrombies and Saks. Kelly always insisted on new furniture. Anything old world reminded him of the grinding poverty of shanty life in Boston. The claustrophobic, choking air of the ghetto. The deathlike environment he had fought and clawed his way out of. New was modern, shiny, black, blond wood and gleaming glass. New and modern was America, the generation of men like Kelly who had come to power in the 1920s. Bronfman, Joe Kennedy, Paley, Frank Stanton.

Roosevelt's familiar cadence came to him again. "The German cannot stay unless you aid him. Do not offer him shelter, do not give him succor, for that is to bargain with the devil. You

48

cannot sell him gas for his tanks, oil for his engines, fuel for his planes. Industry cannot be converted for his benefit. The German can only live here if you collaborate. Deny him your company, deny him your sons and daughters for his war machine.''

Kelly poured himself another martini. The great man was desperately trying to hide the fact that he had been gang raped.

The economy must keep rolling in the East. That was the key. Once the people were offered jobs, they would play ball. There was a whole, starving work force out there waiting for Krupp and the others. Kelly would show them how to break the unions. He would . . . Sylvie moved past him, and a bare ankle flashed momentarily. She took a martini and sat down across from him. "Patrick, I must speak to you.''

Kelly's thoughts were far away, but he answered correctly as always. "I'm listening.''

"Please, can you turn the radio off? Meister, if you must listen, please do it in my bedroom.''

The old Jew, who looked like he had aged thirty years since that morning, spoke in a hoarse whisper. "I don't know, but I think there is room for hope. I think Roosevelt will save us.''

Every Yid in America is saying the same thing tonight, Kelly thought. He saw Sylvie looking at him and, picking up his cue, said, "Everything will be all right when Roosevelt runs out of speeches and negotiates.''

"I don't understand," Meister said.

Kelly got up and turned away to signal the dialogue was over. "Meister, please," Sylvie said.

The old man padded out, and Kelly turned to her. "You look beautiful, darling. The krauts are going to give you the blitzkrieg tonight." He saw that the word was lost on her. "I mean the rush. You look like the most beautiful woman in the world. I'd propose if I wasn't married." He held out his arms and enveloped her.

She felt his strong arms and was grateful for that strength. Patrick had a way about him. Always. But, for all his charm, she could never feel him. He was hidden away behind those sparkling eyes, watching everyone, gauging them, making odds with himself on how much nerve each person had. He hated Roosevelt, she knew that.

She slipped away from him. "My dress, you'll muss it.''

She wore a clinging black gown. She was the McCoy, he acknowledged to himself. Hell, he wasn't going to leave her yet.

She saw the admiration and desire in his eyes. When she had first met him she had thought it might enable her to find the passion that had always been there in her yet lay dormant. But somehow with Patrick it had never been more than desire and lust. He could excite her but not make her love him. Sometimes he was wicked and she couldn't resist him, but other times she felt like an acquisition. And somewhere in the last year the headaches had come on. She was on the verge of one now.

Kelly smiled genially. "What is it you need?"

He always knew her mind, and it made her feel like a little girl asking her father for a favor. Patrick was generous, but she wasn't his equal. That was clear to both of them.

Sylvie sipped her martini for courage and then began. "Well, I thought I could meet you at the Stork after I left St. Stephen's." She saw his eyes imperceptibly harden. "I know I've been there but I promised Timmy and some of the children I'd let them hear New Year's tolling. Patrick, it would mean so much. . . ." She stopped. She knew he was indulgent toward her work at St. Stephen's Orphanage. Indulgent, but secretly indifferent.

"I need you on my arm at the Plaza," he said quietly but firmly.

She bit her lip and averted her eyes.

"Abetz and General Beck expect you. But of course, we'll go on to the Stork Club later. Let's take a few of the krauts . . ." he caught himself. "We'll lead the German contingent there."

It was closed, she knew, but she made one last effort. "I'll dash over in a cab and then meet you. . . ."

She saw his green eyes go cold. Stone obelisks from the ice age. He looked at his watch and said, "Have Meister call my driver."

He got up and walked toward the terrace. For a moment she had a desperate image of Timmy waiting for her, his face streaming tears. She had found him in the street eating garbage from an overturned can. She had personally taken him to St. Stephen's. He was her favorite, all the boys knew that . . . he was such a love. She always kept her promise to him. She felt the beginnings of one of her awful headaches.

Chapter 7

Midnight
New Year's Eve

The drunk standing on the corner of Seventh Avenue and Forty-second Street blew his horn. The noise came out in a pathetic blah. Above him the news board of *The New York Times* circled around in darkness. There was no sign reading Happy New Year. Indeed there was only an hour till curfew. In Times Square there were a scattered handful of people. The theaters were sealed, the lights were all dim. The Amsterdam that once housed the tapping shoes of George V. Cohan stood dark and shuttered. As the whole street was. Once it had been a cacophony of sound and noise, ablaze with lights and the swelling laughter of people. This night of occupation it mourned for old George M. Cohan's ghost. And as if to verify the memory, a drunk got down on one knee in the middle of the street and began to sing:

> I'm a Yankee Doodle Dandy
> A Yankee Doodle do or die
> A real live nephew of my Uncle Sam
> Born on the fourth of July

Abruptly he pitched over. No one noticed.

"And can you imagine," Abetz was saying, holding his glass up to be refilled, "there I stood in the midst of a Communist rally, and they were saluting and applauding. Some of the swine sang 'The Internationale.' It was almost touching." The glass had been filled, and now he proposed a toast. "To the Russian pact and to the New Year." From the smile on Standartenführer Dietrich Abetz's face, one could easily discern his thoughts on both subjects. There was a general clinking of glasses in the large suite of the Plaza Hotel where the New Year's dinner party was being held. The suite was to be the quarters of the military governor, General Heinrich von Stulpnagel, until his apartment

51

that was being requisitioned was ready. Abetz stood up and finished his champagne.

Otto Klinger leaned over and whispered to Kelly, "Beware of Abetz. He is shrewd and vicious. He has no friends in the party. He lives only to report to Himmler."

Kelly bit off the tip of his cigar. He waited while Klinger lit it for him and gave a perfunctory nod. This worried little man, his bald head ringed with sweat, was von Ribbentrop's man. Kelly couldn't resist giving a bit of the needle. "I'd say Abetz does have one powerful friend."

Klinger's watery brown eyes looked like they were about to unleash a flood of tears. He quickly changed the subject. "Tell me, what you did think of Roosevelt's speech?"

Kelly let out a stream of smoke in Klinger's direction. "As propaganda it made sense, but his trousers have been stolen. The emperor's clothes."

Klinger looked a bit mystified and then seemed to grasp it. "Yes, of course, the emperor's clothes."

"What else could he say?" Kelly concluded.

"Exactly," Klinger agreed. "But what the Führer wants to know is whether Roosevelt will bomb his own cities."

Kelly sipped from a glass of champagne a waiter had given him. Von Stulpnagel had shipped it from Maxim's in Paris. It was, Kelly acknowledged to himself, of superior vintage. "Roosevelt may be desperate, but he's not stupid."

Klinger's eyes got very big. "Then you think he won't?"

Kelly blew more smoke in his face. "He's already earned an infamous place in American history. He's not going to add to that by bombing his own cities and people."

"Yes, yes of course." Klinger nodded his head vigorously, as if he had been given classified information. He drank some champagne. "I think the Christmas tree is wonderful, *ja*?"

The Christmas tree, still filled with decorations, stood blinking at the window overlooking Central Park South. The tree had been left there in the general confusion and panic after the German invasion. The suite had been occupied by the socialite Doris Darcy, who had flown to Palm Springs. Standing by the tree, enjoying the view of the park just now were von Stulpnagel, General Rommel, Hans Speidel, Rommel's chief of staff, and Radner, the handsome attaché to the cultural minister, Colonel Manheim. Manheim had suffered a serious heart attack two days earlier. It had been the topic of gossip and speculation all evening.

Klinger gestured toward Radner. "He will not have it so easy without Manheim. Radner must administer the arts with Abetz and the Gestapo looking over his shoulder and reporting to

Himmler. Radner is only a captain. He has no power. His only hope is that Manheim recovers. Paris flourished under Manheim."

Kelly watched the handsome captain he had met in Paris. The art and theater world in New York was peopled with Jews. Radner was walking into a mine field. He turned to Klinger. "This is not Paris."

"Ach, Paris," Klinger said with a wave of his hand. "Paris is a whore as old as the world. We did not know what to expect, but we should have. She just rolled over and opened her legs." He gave a laugh that was almost a giggle and then, noticing that Kelly was looking about the room, said, "Where is your lovely companion, Mrs. Lamont?"

Kelly did not smile at the tribute. "I think General Rommel has kidnapped her."

"She is one of the great beauties of the world," Klinger gushed.

"That she is," Kelly said. "Excuse me."

"Of course," Klinger said, almost bowing. Kelly turned and walked away from the fawning little man.

He wanted time to observe the scene before him. He wanted to gauge the men he was pitting himself against.

The large room with its thick rug and black curtain had been the site of the dinner party. A long table had been set in the middle of the room. On one side of the bay windows was the Christmas tree, on the other a large picture of the Führer. Kelly tipped an invisible hand to the Führer. So you're here, and nobody thought you could pull it off. But what do you do now? Roosevelt will draft everybody into his armed services, and you cannot cross the Alleghenies and the Rocky Mountains to go after him. Your blitzkrieg is no good during our winter. So you wait for spring and do what? Bomb the Midwest? Hit Roosevelt's heavy industry? That means you have to build air bases here. You need tremendous production at Grumman and Curtiss-Wright. You'll need a huge labor force. Roosevelt will squeeze the unions. So what you do, Führer, is build a huge scab work force. You don't know that now, but I'm going to offer that pearl of wisdom when Krupp gets here. And I'll organize it for you. And after a while when the union boys get tired of starving, they'll break.

Kelly looked around the room at the German officers in their black dress uniforms with the red stripes running down their pants. The suite was filled with gesturing officers, beautiful women, and Christmas decorations. There were always beautiful women where there were conquerors. A number of them were French, having accompanied officers from Paris who had been sent to New York to speed the transition to German rule. Paris, it seemed, was being used as a role model by the Nazis in many ways.

The doors to the suite had been opened, and music filtered up from the Oak Room downstairs. Waltz music to be sure. The Germans were here, and life would go on. Kelly marked the activity in the room and measured the nature of the men there. Rommel, who had stormed down the Hudson Valley, taking West Point in the process, was the most impressive. A daring leader with the instincts of a riverboat gambler. He loved risk. He would be the key to attacking the American Midwest should Hitler decide to go in. He was a handsome man with a great future. Kelly would take Rommel to the Stork Club later and invite him for dinner next week.

Rommel stood now talking to von Stulpnagel and Abetz. Abetz struck Kelly as being insidious and dangerous. He looked like his boss Himmler, and he was just as vicious. He would want to make an impression on New York City. After his jails became full, he would need more space. Abetz had the mentality of the ultimate Gestapo officer. Kelly would use him by pointing him in certain directions, withholding the big bonus till the end. Let him run into problems and then come to Kelly for the solution. You used Abetz. That's what made you superior to him.

Kelly watched Sylvie in animated conversation with the blond, striking Captain Radner. Yeah, he's a ladies' man all right, Kelly thought. There was something in the blue eyes of the young captain with his aquiline nose and tight mouth that Kelly read as tension. Without Manheim he's got the New Yorker theater scene to administer . . . a strike to break. You've got to get rid of the lefties for that. You have to be ruthless. Was the captain ruthless enough? Kelly wanted to size him up so he could make a mental wager. To get up the Nazi ladder, you had to really play hardball. There was something hard in Radner and also something soft, almost a feminine quality. He had probably been some kind of artist himself once. Goebbels had used his artistic failures to make him hate. What about Radner?

The captain made a gesture, and both he and Sylvie began to laugh. He likes women, maybe a little too much. Wait . . . he needs a woman. That's it. And men who need women that way are weak. He'll get himself in trouble and then be tested in the crucible. Then he will have to choose between his ambition and his need. If Kelly had to bet, it would be on the former. No, wait, it wasn't need, it was some idealistic quality in Radner. That's what disturbed Kelly. He carried the seeds of his destruction within himself. Kelly remembered dining with Radner in Fouquet's in Paris. Radner was witty, intelligent, and cultured.

If he were completely cynical, he'd make it big here in New York. But he's not, and Abetz knows it. There's trouble in paradise, Kelly concluded.

Abetz minced over and slid in next to Kelly. "I have passed on your financial recommendation to von Ribbentrop. It will be on his desk along with your personal note to Krupp. I expect Krupp here in January."

Kelly's face was impassive. "I will be honored to meet with Krupp. And I will deliver some very important business leaders for him to confer with. Especially the oil people you will need."

Abetz looked pleased. "I read your memo with great interest. Particularly your recommendation for taking over the financial holdings of the two Jews, Sarnoff and Baruch." Abetz's English was thick and clumsy, but he was obviously very tickled with Kelly's suggestion. "A detailed memo from you would be most welcome."

"I'll send it over in the morning," Kelly said, letting Abetz know he had anticipated him.

"Excellent. Yes . . . the Führer is most anxious for oil, steel, and munitions. All your good work will be duly recorded."

He started to say more, but then Klinger was there, working the room in his obsequious, frightened manner. "Have you heard the joke about why Stalin will not visit New York?" After a pause, he delivered the punch line. "He fears the party will strike for higher wages." Klinger began to roar, but then froze as he saw Abetz eyeing him coldly and Kelly turning away. The effort caused him to explode into a coughing spasm.

As Kelly walked over and took Sylvie's arm, he noted that Radner had been led off by Rommel.

Radner followed Rommel into von Stulpnagel's bedroom and closed the door. On the bed table a small lamp gave off a colored light. The curtains were drawn, and now Rommel went over and opened them. The lights from surrounding buildings played on the lake in Central Park.

Rommel held a cigar between his fingers and a glass of brandy. He was, as always, commanding physically and intellectually, with his inquisitive brown eyes that missed nothing, the fine but determined mouth, the restless, unorthodox mind that made him dare military maneuvers others never dreamed of.

"Well, Friederich, I saw the film of the surrender of West Point this afternoon, and I must congratulate you. Your movie caught everything. Wonderful close-ups. Geobbels wants it immediately to show in Berlin next week."

Radner leaned forward on the bed. "I am grateful for the

opportunity. But I must say, I found the crushing of the Americans sad."

"Their belief in their invincibility is gone. Defeat causes permanent change. But that was our objective. You lived amongst them, so it is difficult for you to view them as the enemy."

Radner stood up, walked to the window, and put his back against the window pane. "When I lived here, there was a girl. Shall I find another?"

Rommel laughed softly. "You are, Friederich, an incurable romantic. You will find another."

"Even in time of war?"

"Especially in time of war. Come let us join the others. Our glasses are empty." He went out leaving the door open. Radner remained staring at the night, at the glimmering water in Central Park. Someone came into the room. It was Otto Klinger.

Klinger is von Ribbentrop's man, Radner reminded himself. He will seem civilized and friendly. And he is no one's friend. He is just a cipher for von Ribbentrop. He remembered Rommel's words: "The only man I trust less than von Ribbentrop is von Papen."

Klinger drank some champagne. "So Manheim lies in the hospital. What will you do first?"

"Stand in for him. Broadway must reopen quickly. I will be dining with Lawrence Langer of the Theater Guild tomorrow evening to offer him very favorable financial inducements to mount new productions. I shall lunch with Maurice Evans and Judith Anderson to discuss an immediate reopening of their production of *Macbeth*. Once the others see plays open they will follow along."

Klinger nodded his head in agreement. "Remember, the Jews are entrenched here. They are charming, talented, wealthy. You are young, not so experienced as Manheim. They will seek to convert you."

Realizing his little slip, Klinger tried to joke it away. "Ach, too much champagne. I meant to say subvert. You understand, Friedrich."

An ironic smile teased itself across Radner's mouth. "The Jews in New York are a force. The Jews here are used to freedom. If we find a place for their leading artists, bankers, and civil leaders, then there will not be a Jewish problem. Our policy toward the Jews here must be more humane." He saw the look in Klinger's eyes go from one of shock to amusement. *He thinks me terribly naive.*

Abruptly there was noise and the discernible sound of excited voices. Klinger rose from the bed and followed Radner from the room.

"The Führer," Abetz cried out. "The Führer is on the phone. From Berlin."

Just now von Stulpnagel was being given the phone by his valet. The military governor straightened his shoulders. He was aware of everyone watching him. "Hallo. Yes, yes, I can hear you." He listened, nodding his head. "Of course, of course. Just a minute, I will tell them." He turned to the hushed crowd of officers and guests. "The Führer sends his personal greetings and wishes for a Happy New Year. He wishes you every success and knows that you will represent the Reich with honor." He turned back to the phone. "Yes, I have told them. Yes, yes. well, it is cold here, but we are warm inside, and we even have a Christmas tree." There was much laughter and delighted whispers. "Yes, we have a number of Americans here. Mr. Kelly from the Pan Semcola Oil Company, Mr. Wakefield, the investment banker, Mr. Clifford from Empire Steel. Yes, yes, it is very cozy and warm here." There was more laughter. "Yes, of course, Rommel is here. Of course," He beckoned Rommel to the phone.

Rommel, erect and graceful, took the phone, handing his brandy glass to an aide. He said something not quite clear, then listened intently. One could see the hardness around Rommel's jaw, the effort of concentration on his face. His eyes gleamed with intensity. "Yes," he responded to an inquiry, "von Runstedt does not find Boston to his liking. He says the people speak peculiar English." Everyone roared. "Thank you, my Führer . . . *vas*?" Rommel put a finger in one ear to block out the noise. Now he turned to the excited crowd.

"The Führer says he is thinking of coming to Washington to address the world's diplomats."

There was great applause. Rommel held up a hand. "Yes, the connection is sometimes difficult. Will you also come to New York?"

The room was silent. "Well, I hope so. New York is quite a magnificent city and as you know intact." Rommel again turned to the people in the room. "The Führer says he is sending an autographed copy of *The Night Before Christmas* to President Roosevelt." Applause was followed by cries of delighted laughter.

"I hope we are not losing the connection. Yes, of course he is here. Abetz."

Standartenführer Abetz stepped forward and took the phone. "Yes, my Führer. Yes, of course. I take this occasion to wish you a Happy New Year. We will work on making better phone connections. So when you call us again . . . yes, yes. You are too kind." Abetz, unlike Rommel and von Stulpnagel, seemed

57

to regard this as a personal call. He was quite overwhelmed. "My Führer, there is not one of us who would not lay down his life for you. Yes, in fact, in encountering some local Communists today, they cheered your name." A new burst of applause filled the room. "Yes, yes, I can assure you, Führer, we will have every success. Yes, you will have my report within a week on that matter. Yes, I bid you *goodnacht* and if I may . . . I would like to have all of you wish the Führer a Happy New Year." Now Abetz snapped to attention, his right arm thrust out. "Heil, Hitler," he screamed. "Heil, Hitler."

It was as if lightning had cleaved the room. Men snapped to, and the words poured out as a torrential river bursts its banks. "Heil . . . heil . . . heil." Radner watched the scene with a bemused smile. He looked up and saw Rommel vigorously saluting. Radner momentarily raised his hand. He turned and saw Abetz eyeing him. He knew the little vignette would be on Himmler's desk via overseas mail pouch within three days.

He gazed around the room and generals and saw General Beck, elegant, commanding, seated by himself on a sofa under the picture of the Führer. The rumor had it that Ludwig Beck, once commander of the general staff, had opposed some of Hitler's military ventures. His current post as gross kommandant of Manhattan was viewed by most as exile. Beck was tall and patrician. His thick black hair was touched with flecks of gray. His dark eyes seemed permeated with some special sense of the moment. He was just paces away from Abetz. Clearly, protocol demanded Abetz call him to the phone. But now Abetz quickly surveyed the room. His eyes lingered on Beck and passed him by. His tiny eyes brimming with emotion suddenly alighted on Patrick Kelly. Abetz listened to his Führer and then called out, "Herr Kelly, the Führer would like a word with you."

Kelly found himself flushing. He made a purposeful effort to seem pleased yet calm. "Good evening, Herr Hitler. I wish you a Happy New Year."

He heard Hitler's harsh tones moderated by a kind of bubbly good humor. Clearly, he was at his peak this night. There was a barrage of German that Kelly did not understand, punctuated by a strident laugh. Then a translator came on and relayed Hitler's babble. Kelly listened carefully and made a show of laughing to indicate how witty the Führer had been.

Kelly turned to the crowd and watched their hungry, expectant faces. Cupping his hand over the mouthpiece, he smiled and his green eyes were filled with genial hood humor. "The Führer said he is looking forward very much to visiting Mein Amerika." Kelly pronounced the last words with just the right accent, and the room exploded into happy applause. Kelly watched them all watching him and, when he was sure he had everyone's attention, he took his hand from the mouthpiece and continued his conversation with Hitler.

Radner noted the scene. Kelly was an accomplished actor . . . no, performer was more like it. He was a man of vaulting ambition, and Radner knew that, of all the Americans here, he was the most important to the Reich and most likely to play a prominent role in Mein Amerika. I must dine with him, Radner thought.

He felt an arm on his shoulder, and there was General Beck leading him off to the same bedroom in which he had talked with Rommel.

Beck had enjoyed a distinguished career and at one time had been the intellectual leader of the general staff. Now, as he and Radner entered the bedroom with its muted light, he said, "Sit for a moment. I know you are impatient to go out into the city, but spare me a few moments."

Beck gestured to the bed, and Radner sat on it. Beck looked like a leading man. He had known glory and now knew exile. The dark eyes showed a mixture of intelligence and sorrow. He poured two glasses of cognac and handed one to Radner.

The gross kommandant of Manhattan strolled to the window and looked out. For a moment he was still, then he threw down some cognac. "It is fantastic," he began. "We occupy New York. We occupy almost all of Europe. The Mediterranean and North Africa bow before us. South America awaits us. Hitler hopes to do what Napoleon, Alexander, and Charlemagne could not, conquer the western world. The Reich, it seems, will live a thousand years." He finished the cognac and walked back to Radner. "But we are like a mighty giant astride an ever-widening mountain. As it splits asunder, the effort required to keep it from doing so will tear the giant apart."

"Rome ruled for centuries," Radner answered.

"We are not Rome," was Beck's reply. "We are not as secure in our conquests. There is still Russia. As for the Americans, we may not be able to take their country from them even with the help of the Japanese. And if the Americans convince the Russians to fight in the East . . . then we will not talk of Rome anymore."

Radner measured his reply carefully. "Russia is our ally. They recognize Hitler's destiny to write history. Look where he has taken us. But I am not an historian or politician. I think there is a wonderful chance here to show the Americans that we are not the enemy, that by blending their vitality with our tradition, the arts can flourish here. As in Paris." He saw Beck looking at him intently. "You think me impossibly naive?"

Beck shrugged. "There is one similarity about art and politics. They stem from impulses of freedom. Without freedom

59

they are merely involuntary flickers. They must have the freedom of response and gesture." Beck walked to the opposite side of the bed so that he was near Radner but not looking directly at him. "If Hitler became ill, if something happened, an act of God perhaps, do you think we would still sit astride the world?"

Radner was silent for a moment. "Why do you ask?"

"One thinks of many things in a strange country. What do I know of this . . . . this Manhattan?"

"I cannot begin to even contemplate it."

"No, of course not," Beck said. "Well, that is enough of this. The old general will go to his suite at the Sherry Netherland. I have had enough of celebration for one night. Tomorrow morning I ride in Central Park. Imagine that. And then what will I do? Dine in a French restaurant, I suppose. See how homesick I am for Germany. I cannot bear to go to Yorkville. They tell me it is absolute frenzy there. I studied in Spandau, and I am gross kommandant of New York. It is . . ." He broke off, shook hands with Radner, and went out.

A few minutes later Radner took his overcoat from Hertz, von Stulpnagel's valet, and walked down the brown carpeted hallway to the stairs. When he reached the lobby, he went quickly through it, ignoring the laughing camaraderie of the officers and the grasping hands of the bellhops. A doorman found him a cab and, once in it, Radner said to the driver, "Times Square. Take Broadway."

They drove down past the winking lights of the movies and hotels. Past the Roxy and the Strand, the Palace and the Criterion and the Loew's State. At the corner of Forty-third Street, Radner had the driver stop by the Whelans drugstore. He paid the driver, told him to keep the change, and got out. The store had closed earlier as so many had for the holiday. But the neon lights that blinked the name Whelans were still on. Radner pressed his face against the window. He recalled how he used to sit and dream over coffee in there. He smiled. Coffee and . . . that's what they used to call it.

He lit a cigarette and pulled his black cashmere overcoat tight around him, using the collar to break the wind. He looked up at the bright neon signs, one piled high above the other on Forty-eighth Street. Coca-Cola blending into Planters Peanuts, climbing up to Chevrolet and topped by the golden crown of Four Roses, surrounded by two men in neon gold drinking it. Above them, heaven and the gods. It was New Year's Eve, but few people were out. The Americans had nothing to celebrate, even with the curfew extended to one o'clock. A few drunks and pathetic revelers forlornly tooting toy horns passed him by.

First we must turn on all the theater lights again. That will be a signal. It will bring people back. Reopening *Macbeth* will start it. He crossed Broadway and walked up toward Forty-fifth Street.

He walked until he got to the Golden where *Angel Street* had been playing. None of the marquees had been changed. He looked up at the names. Vincent Price, Judith Evelyn, and Leo G. Carroll. Price had fled to California, but the other two were here. With a replacement the show could be remounted quickly. He walked next to the Morosco where *Blithe Spirit* with Clifton Webb, Peggy Wood, and Mildred Natwick had closed. They were all here. Possible. He walked back to the Royale where Ethel Barrymore had been starring in *The Corn is Green*. Radner knew Emlyn Williams from London. A letter had been sent to Barrymore and tomorrow Radner would call her. Laughter, Radner thought. There must be laughter. That is the first healthy sign. Reopen *Arsenic and Old Lace* at the Fulton whether Boris Karloff could be located or not. He had asked Gertrude Lawrence to lunch with him. She was a marvelous performer and *Lady in the Dark* was her vehicle. If he could reopen that along with *Macbeth* things would begin to fall into place. He remembered Klinger saying "Actors are like children." Well, in a way they were. If they saw others performing they would follow. Nobody wishes to starve. That is a subject actors are experts in. The audiences would come around; they had to. Then the theaters would blaze with lights again. He could see the people talking now, laughing, going for a late night supper, marveling at the magic they had just witnessed. He turned as a horn tooted in his ear and felt the drunk press against him. He was short and smelled dreadful.

"How about some Old Granddad for your old granddad?"

Radner reached into his pocket and the drunk mumbled, "Terrible, isn't it? Lousy German bastards. I'm gonna kill me one." He leaned in against Radner. "I hear they make Jews wear yellow stars. Well, I'm Irish. What kind of star do I get? They can't leave me out. I'm a star, too. Don't I look like a star? Well?"

Radner slipped a few bills into the man's hand and pushed him away.

"God bless," the drunk called. "Happy New Year. I want a star Any kind, even a yellow one."

Kelly waited for Sylvie, feeling the singular exaltation within himself. It was all there for him. Hitler had singled him out. He could feel the reins being handed him. Money was the ultimate power, but rarely did one have the opportunity to change history without governing. And now it was coming to him. To Patrick Kelly, to Joe Kelly, and to the sons Joe would have. The dynasty was almost in his hand. God, he was full and he needed Sylvie.

Kelly took the decanter from the cabinet next to the bed and poured two drinks. Sylvie was still in the dressing room changing. Kelly went to the window and looked out. The city was dark. He looked at his watch. Three. How strange the silence on New Year's Eve. He smelled her perfume as she came from behind him.

He handed her a drink. She took it and traced her finger around it. The gesture made him palpitate with desire.

"It seems so eerie," she said.

"What?"

"Seeing the city so dark. It's . . . it's unreal."

"Yes, I know. I was just thinking the same thing."

"New York with a curfew. It's . . . it's just not New York."

He downed the brandy. "The people will adjust. It will take time, but life goes on. This fellow, Radner, the cultural officer, was saying he'd like to change that. Handsome chap."

"He's dashing. Johnny Heartbreak."

There was something cool and provocative in her voice. Kelly realized what he wanted to do and, turning into her, let his body come against hers, smelling the perfume that seemed to filter into his pores and made his head and chest pound.

She didn't utter a sound but continued drinking her brandy until his lips found her throat. Then she uttered a groan.

She wants it tonight even more than I, he thought, as he dropped to his knees and slipped open the sash of her silk robe. He felt her hand move to the back of his neck. Her hand was warm and wet. Like she was inside. She guided his head down, at the same time opening her legs.

It was the gesture they both wanted, and now his tongue ran into her, and he heard her glass drop to the rug. He moved his tongue from side to side, transferring the moistness of it to her.

"Never, never stop," she whispered.

Finally, her knees buckled, and she melted to the floor, reaching for his shirt. Her mouth was on Kelly's chest as she undid the buttons, as he pulled the robe from her. Now his shirt was gone, and she undid his pants as his hungry mouth and tongue found her breast. She held him in her hand all stiff and erect as he lavished his lips on her nipples. She arched her neck way back, and he heard the gutteral noise in her throat. It was the sound of some primal creature, and it inflamed him. He felt himself grow in her hands. She was falling back, and he was on top of her.

She gasped when he went inside her, and he felt himself swell even more. He thrust hard, making her part again and again. Deeper, he thought. So deep I come out the other side of you. For a moment he wondered how his pants had come off, and then he felt her arms around him, her nails talonlike on his back. He got his hands under her buttocks and lifted her up. Break my back, he thought. Now as he wrapped her legs around his, he moved back and forth, in and out, her wetness creating a sucking, slithering noise that inflamed them both. "Come to me," she sang, and Patrick Kelly, his chest heaving, stroked her in successive waves of fury. His chest was sopping, the hair on it matted in thick curlicues. He pinned her arms and saw her eyes widen in their cruel cat's abandon, her lips parted, and she was a lewd, lascivious old lecher of a witch, using incantation to arouse him beyond endurance. Now, now, you bitch, witch of a whore. Her nails tore at him, but he felt no pain as he rode and surged till the fury that was in him broke and he bucked drunkenly inside her, hearing the noise in her throat that meant she was coming also. And, as always, her climax was a sudden thing of terrible ecstasy.

Finished, he lay there like a little boy and listened to her panther's growl spreading to infinity. Always she was more and he less in those moments, and it filled him with awe and fear. He had brought her to this and yet, in leaving him, she took his power. Even this triumphant night when Hitler had selected him first among all Americans to build the new America. Somehow, in this basic, primal thing, he was less, she more. And though he tried to dismiss it as his ego, the knowledge left him with a pounding in his chest. A pounding that resounded as he heard and reheard Sylvie, felt her shaking, heard her cry of triumph. Then finally it stopped, and they were mute as each drifted into places unknown to the other.

AMERICAN PANORAMA
III

AMERICAN NEWSPAPERS AND RADIO STATIONS COME UNDER GESTAPO JURISDICTION

by Art Letieri
Daily Mirror Staff Reporter

Friday, January 2, 1942

Standartenführer Dietrich Abetz, head of German security, announced today that radio stations and newspapers in New

York City will have to obtain special permits from his office in order to be licensed to broadcast or print daily editions. Though the standartenführer indicated this was only a formality, he went on to note in his pronouncements that "The recent death of a Professor Fuchs, a long-time German traitor, was given undue and dramatic attention by a New York paper. This cannot be allowed under new official policy set down by Berlin. Although the American people must be kept informed of matters of importance, newspapers and radio stations must not be allowed to flaunt their power." The standartenführer also made reference to radio station WOR, which carried an appeal by one of its commentators asking the question, Where is Johnny Lugansky? Mr. Lugansky is a New York warehouse clerk who was arrested after interrupting a parade on Fifth Avenue by playing swing music. His words as he was taken away, "You'll never stop boogie-woogie," have been scrawled across buildings, subway cars, and chalked on street corners throughout the city.

Exempted from the new restrictions were the *Daily Bund*, the organ of the American Nazi party, and the *Daily Patrician*, a new publication which will feature writers and editors sympathetic to National Socialism, and the *Daily Mirror*. All other papers, including the *Herald Tribune, Daily News, World Telegram, The Sun, Journal American, New York Post*, and the leftist *P. M.* must halt publication and apply for special permits. *The New York Times* has already closed, but it was announced today that the paper will publish in Los Angeles starting Monday. Among the radio stations, WEAF, WOR, WJZ, and CBS will all have to apply for special permits to broadcast. At the moment, the only stations licensed to broadcast will be WGER, the official station of the National Socialists here in New York operated by the Nazi Bund, and WNYC, which will give traffic, weather reports, and music to New York City listeners.

Standartenführer Abetz went on to say, "We in no way mean to deprive the people of New York of their daily papers and broadcasts, but as an occupying force we must be sensitive to those who seek to disrupt rather than speed the necessary aspects of transition. I can assure all those concerned that prompt and thorough processing of their applications will be expedited. All those who indicate to us that they will print proper news and air careful discussion will have no problem in obtaining the necessary permits."

Standartenführer Abetz also announced that henceforth all communications emanating from New York City would be under control of the Internal Security Division of the Gestapo.

Both Western Union and American Telephone and Telegraph will function under the direction of a German communications officer. Citizens needing to make long distance calls or send telegrams to unoccupied America will have to apply for clearance at the telephone company, 120 Canal Street, which has now become Gestapo Control Center. Individuals attempting to place their own call via the operator will immediately be referred to the Gestapo. In addition, German personnel will man telephones periodically and conduct spot checkups of ongoing telephone calls. Long lines are anticipated at the Canal Street office. A source at the telephone company said that the ruling virtually cuts off all communication between occupied New York and the rest of the country.

The Living History
by Smith Dailey

January 4, 1942

As the grim reality of the occupation took hold and with the prospect of a long occupation by German forces in the Northeast of the United States, eminent and ordinary American citizens trudged to Gestapo headquarters on Manhattan's Centre Street seeking exit visas. Indeed, so great has the overflow become that a special office has been opened up at police headquarters on Fifty-fourth Street to handle the crowds. For those lucky enough to get one of the special green cards, now called "green meanies" in New York City slang, there is a ticket on one of the two daily flights from LaGuardia or Newark airports to the American Midwest, from where those who are affluent enough can continue on to California and those who are not begin life anew in Chicago, Cleveland, or Detroit.

Typically, on one such flight from LaGuardia the passengers included socialite Tommy Manville and his sixth wife, former heavyweight champion Jack Dempsey, stripper Gypsy Rose Lee, District Attorney Thomas Dewey, Giants' baseball owner Horace Stoneham and manager Mel Ott, three members of the Radio City Rockettes, socialite Kay Dennis, band leader Guy Lombardo, and a New York City sanitation worker, Emanuel Pelvis. Asked how he got up the airfare plus the substantial bonus the German Gestapo is asking in American dollars (rumored to be two thousand dollars), Mr. Pelvis smiled and said, "I got lucky at craps."

It has become commonplace at Tenth Avenue and Fifty-fourth Street to see the great, the almost great, the infamous, and the notorious rubbing elbows as they wait on line to meet with Gestapo interviewers to secure a flight to unoccupied America. In recent days restrictions have become severe. Anyone deemed vital to the ongoing propaganda war between America and Germany, or anyone who might help the American war effort, is automatically denied an exit visa. Most recently, baseball star Hank Greenberg, violinist Mischa Elman, playwright Robert E. Sherwood, jazz clarinetist Artie Shaw, and singer Kate Smith were denied visas. On the same day, allowed to fly were restaurateur Vincent Sardi, actor Boris Karloff, reporter Westbrook Pegler, and Aleksandr Kerensky, former head of the provisional Russian government that fell to the Bolsheviks in 1917.

But for ordinary American citizens, grim and tragic scenes were played out as husbands pleaded for wives and children to be allowed to leave New York for freedom. Rumors abound of family fortunes being extricated by Gestapo interrogators. Cash, jewels, and securities worth far more than the two-thousand-dollar fee for green meanies change hands. In addition to exacting a high tribute, particularly from Jewish families, certain restrictions exist. Eldest sons who are teenagers and thus could one day fight in the American army are denied visas even when their mothers, younger brothers, and sisters are allowed to go. No American male between the ages of eighteen and forty-eight who passes a German physical is allowed to leave.

These inevitable family tragedies have also escalated the growing black market for green meanies. The perpetrators generally fall into two categories: those who obtain them and then sell them for five and ten times their normal worth, and those who are in the business of forging them. Each day stories grow of hapless American families sold bogus green cards who are then arrested by Gestapo guards at state borders and have to spend whatever money they have left to buy their freedom. It is clear that the Germans will exploit this situation to their great financial benefit. Still, it seems to come down to the elemental fact that those who have the most money will somehow find a way out. As one airport porter at LaGuardia put it, "Them that got it, gets there."

It was a similar scene in and around Washington, D.C., which has been declared an open city. While embassy lights continued to burn late, American government employees and their families fled their homes in suburban Georgetown and the Virginia and Maryland countryside. During the invasion, as fighting raged in nearby Baltimore, Chesapeake Bay was filled with a brilliant flotilla of red- and blue-flagged boats, packed cabin and deck with the old, the very young, and their mothers. The parting of these families, one captain reported, "is as painful as anything I have ever witnessed." Putting out to sea, these ships made for the Carolinas, Georgia, and Florida. Days later, green and white from seasickness, surviving Americans disembarked in ports like Savannah, Georgia, and Charleston, South Carolina, and kissed the ground.

One old salt remarked, "I haven't seen anything like this since the Klondike during the gold rush." Many boats capsized in the choppy winter waves, and in one tragic accident twenty people drowned. Nor is the voyage the only obstacle to be faced. Officials in the South have made every effort to welcome the boat people, but as the mayor of Charleston put it, "We don't have the economy or the housing for these people. Maybe not the food either." Last weekend President Roosevelt signed an executive order ordering railroads to offer free transportation to any and all American refugees desiring it. Packed trains leave each day from North and South Carolina, Florida, and Georgia, for such destinations as Chicago, Cleveland, Detroit, Denver, Kansas City, and Houston. It is estimated that some ten thousand Americans made their way out of occupied territory in the past week.

Chapter 8

January 5, 1942
3:00 P.M.

Leila felt the pressing bodies of the rush hour commuters as the IRT local lumbered into the Fiftieth Street stop. Someone stepped on her shoe, and she turned angrily and flashed a dirty look at a tall man in a brown tweed coat who paid her no attention. The doors opened, and Leila felt herself being pushed into the car by the surging crowd behind her. She found a seat and settled in as the doors of the subway closed and the train lurched off toward downtown. She wiggled her toe, which still smarted from the clumsiness of the oaf now seated across the aisle from her, nose pressed into the *Daily Patrician*, the fascist paper that had become popular since many of the local tabloids had folded up. Leila noted he was wearing galoshes. That made her even angrier. His feet were dry. She was wearing paper-thin shoes with cardboard wedged into both soles. They had not prevented her feet from becoming wet. Something had better change soon. There wasn't a job to be had in town. The shows were only just reopening. Who knew how long before Broadway would be back on its feet? She had filled in for a sick friend waitressing for three nights, and that had enabled her to pay the January rent. But she had no roommate yet and had to pay the entire twenty-six dollars. Mrs. Buxton had given her a six-dollar reduction because of Fay's sudden departure. "I know things are hard, my dear, but they are hard for all of us. You will just have to find yourself a new roommate." When Leila protested that young aspiring actresses were not coming to an invaded city, Mrs. Buxton had held up her hand. "I'm sure you'll find a way, my dear. I know you're resourceful."

The train rolled into Times Square, and a group of passengers waited impatiently for the doors to open. As they got off five German soldiers got on, and abruptly the whole character of the train ride changed. Leila noticed it immediately. Heads were averted, eyes fixed intently on the floor. Everybody in the car seemed to be either reading a paper or feigning sleep. Look at them, she silently told the passengers. All of you, look at them. You can't stay in the house and pretend they're not here. The gray-uniformed fivesome sat down directly opposite her, room having been graciously offered them by the man who had stepped on Leila's toe. For a moment, Leila didn't look at them, but then characteristically she forced herself to do so. She would not be intimidated. She studied them, noting how young and common they really were. Callow was the word. Two of them with broad foreheads, thick lips, and innocent blue eyes looked as if they came directly from the farm. One was older and bored; he was already closing his eyes. The other two were laughing, pointing and gesturing in between exclamations in German. What an ugly language you speak, Leila thought. Harsh, exploding like oaths from your larynx. One of them noted her gaze and smiled at her enticingly. He was nice looking with blue eyes and a smooth complexion. There is no end to your blue eyes, is there? she thought disgustedly. He pulled at his companion and gestured toward Leila. She looked away and saw an elderly Jew with a beard huddled at the far end of the car. What is he thinking? What emotions do those dark eyes encompass? Will they give out yellow stars? Will you become the wandering Jew? And what about you? she chided herself. Will it be any different for Leila Fox? To be a Jew is to be one of history's homeless. It has happened throughout time, so why not here? Because, she answered herself, America symbolized freedom for all. What made it the hope of the world was the belief that it couldn't happen here. With all its flaws, America is . . . was the last refuge.

"Fräulein, fräulein." She looked over and saw the German soldier calling playfully to her. She looked away. And yet in his cry there was nothing offensive. He was a lonely boy, thousands of miles from home, trying to meet a girl. A pretty one at that, she reminded herself, even if she does have holes in her shoes. She debated letting herself be picked up. It would surely mean a free meal and some wine. You did not sneer at free dinner when you had a dollar and sixty cents in your purse. But, of course, she wouldn't do it. A nice Jewish girl couldn't be seen with a German soldier. What would her mother say? "Leila, you'll send me to an early grave. I'll be the shame of the neighborhood." But her mother was in a nursing home. And Leila had her first man when she was sixteen. You have not been a *shane maidl* for a long time. Besides, what was wrong with going out with a German? Not all of them are monsters. How can I claim to be an artist willing to explore all manner of human experience and then cringe at dating a lonely German soldier?

She glanced around the compartment at the people hidden behind papers and magazines. If you knew what I was thinking, would you stone me from the car? They are here, they have captured New York City. They will walk through Central Park where I would chase a ball my father threw me. They will buy beef potpie in the Automat on Forty-second Street where Grandpa Ezra took me every Sunday. They will attend concerts in Carnegie and Town Hall where I learned to love music. They will buy pretzels from the vendors at Union Square, eat ice cream on the Coney Island boardwalk, stand on the observation tower of the Empire State Building and laugh and joke, applaud for the Rockettes at Radio City. They will walk with their women on Central Park West where my father used to pick me up after dance class. I would run to him, and he would catch me in his arms and then take me to the little cafeteria on Eighty-third Street for tea and cake. Once my father took me to see Babe Ruth play at Yankee Stadium, and Lou Gehrig hit two home runs, and I kept calling him Baby Ruth. Now, Yankee Stadium will become a place for the Germans to hold rallies.

She looked back at the German soldiers. We have yeshivas here. Passover is a joyous time of year. I met my first boyfriend, Howard Popkin, at a Passover seder. Instinct made her swivel back and seek out the old Jew. Their thoughts must have been similar, for now his mouth was quivering and she thought that behind his dark glasses he was weeping. And Leila realized why he cried and for whom. All of us in this great city are dispossessed. In this time of occupation we are all Jews.

For the remainder of the ride she ignored the German soldier's attempts to pick her up, empty though her stomach was. She did not look over anymore, and the soldier respected the distance the aisle placed between them. Getting off at Sheridan Square, she heard his low whisper, more in the nature of an appeal than a conqueror's command. *"Liebschen, Liebschen, kommen sie mit mich."* She got off thinking, Poor boy, how lonely you must be.

She saw Alvin Barker give her a little wave from his booth at the Lion's Head Pub and walked briskly back to him. The place was dark and smelled like scotch. She felt at home. Alvin waggled his finger at the waiter and nodded as Leila sat down. "Hello, lady."

Alvin usually had a smile and a little joke for her. This time it wasn't there. Alvin sometimes covered drama for the Associated Press. He was a soft-spoken southerner with large glasses and small brown eyes. He had an unruly thatch of brown hair he never seemed to comb, and his suits were rumpled.

Leila had known him for five years. They had met on the Cape where Leila and Fay were doing ingenue roles in a stock company. Alvin had taken a sabbatical to try to write the great American novel.

The waiter brought their drinks, and Leila's mouth dropped open. "Doubles? Are we celebrating?"

Alvin's fingers worked nervously around the rim of the glass. Then he grasped it and gulped down the drink. She watched his Adam's apple bobbing greedily and knew it would not be good news.

"Better drink up, Leila."

"I better not," she said. "Not on an empty stomach."

"Suit yourself."

"Go ahead."

As he picked at a splinter on the old wooden table between them, his fingers dipped in and out of the light cast from under a battered shade.

"Fay didn't make it."

"What?"

"Didn't make it. There was a storm . . . plane went down."

Leila felt her throat constrict as if a bone were wedged there. "I don't . . . who told you?"

"Phil Quinn. He and I are drinking partners. He said Bill was a good flier, but they just ran into some rough weather."

Leila tried to think, but nothing came. She couldn't feel, either.

"Drink up," Alvin urged. "Go ahead."

He helped tilt her glass, and she let some of the scotch into her throat. It ran into her, warm and harsh, and made her cough, and then she cried quietly for a few minutes while Alvin held her hand.

They stayed there for an hour and tried to piece it all together. Alvin had a few more doubles and finally, when there seemed no more to say, Alvin announced, "I'm crocked."

"What are you going to do for money, Alvin?"

"Hell, didn't I tell you? I got a job working for the *Daily Patrician*."

"But that's a fascist paper. . . ."

Alvin grinned ferociously. "It's a fascist town." He shrugged. "What the hell, I gotta eat."

"You don't see it as . . . as collaborating?"

"I see it as surviving. Hell, it'll be a great chapter for my book."

"The great American novel."

"Sure enough." Now his face was serious. "Look, sweetheart, being here is worth ten years of life. This is like being in Paris during the heyday of the guillotine. When you're free, you just take life for granted. War is what happens in Spain, Poland, China. Sure, I could try to slip out to Hollywood, but it's like being in New York and reading about Warsaw." He drank some more and then put out his hand. "Lordy, I am drunk, so let me just get it out of my system once. I came here a cub reporter fresh out of Alabama, got a job on the rewrite desk of the *News*. Corrected copy for six months, and then a lead in a gin mill got me to the AP. I been there reporting for sixteen years, protected from the world, and I got nothing to write about. I've seen the roaring twenties and the depression thirties. So it came to me one drunk night—I think clearest when loaded—that I needed some experience. Some irrevocable experience. And this is it."

Now Leila saw it clearly. "Once you do it, you can't go back."

"Hey, that's good, and you're sober." He played with his glass again. "Hell, it gives me a point of view, don't it? I made up my mind when I heard about Fay."

Leila looked uncomprehendingly at him.

"Well, there's no more Fay. Isn't that what death is, after you subtract the tears? No more Fay. And if I don't do something soon, I'll be dead of cirrhosis of the liver. No more Alvin Barker, son of Quentin and Phyliss Barker of Mobile." He shoved a newspaper at her. "There's my first column. It's irrevocable."

Leila stared down at a column written by Alvin with his byline

71

in bold letters. It was an interview with a German officer. She saw the name Radner and then the picture. It leaped out at her. It was the German officer who had come to her room. The article said he would have great authority because his superior was hospitalized. She heard Alvin's words again, but differently . . . "No more Leila, no more Leila." And she remembered what she had called herself when Radner asked for her name. Fay Brophy.

"You okay?" Alvin said. "Need something to eat?"

"No, I'm okay."

"Hell you are. Waiter. Two burgers and french fries. And I need something to sober up. Gimme a beer."

Leila looked at Alvin. "Where is his office? Where did you do the interview?"

"Same place. He lives and works in Colonel Manheim's apartment at the Hotel des Artistes. The great, not so great, the talented, the devious, the schemers and dreamers go in and out of his office all day and night. He's got a lot of power for a young man. He can make careers right now. Hell, I had to wait two hours for this interview. Had to prove I could write to my new editor." He watched her in bewildered amusement. "Honey chile, something is brewing there. What in the world are you thinking?"

Leila felt her wet stocking and, pushing her foot back into her shoe, felt the hole. The cardboard had rotted through. "I was thinking about what you said. That there's no more Fay. She'd only exist if she was brought back to life."

Alvin searched her out with his eyes. "Waiter," he snapped, "bring a beer for the lady also. She needs to sober up, too."

5:30 P.M.

It was late in the afternoon and winter darkness had turned to night. The handsome living room gleamed under its lights, taking on the look of a theatrical set. The large windows facing Central Park reflected light from lamps placed in the four corners of the room. An Oriental rug separated the couch he was sitting on from the coffee table and the chair on which his visitor sat. A liquor cabinet in the wall behind the man displayed rows of whiskey bottles glimmering temptingly and the varied labels of scotch, rye, brandy, and wine.

They sat talking over sherry. Radner, legs crossed, his back against the couch, Leila opposite him on a wicker chair.

"I hope you like the sherry. It is very old and has weathered the years gracefully. What may I do for you?"

He watched her in the warm half glow of the room. She was,

he realized, quite beautiful. There was a fineness to her face he had not noticed at first. Now, framed by the changing light and wearing a white blouse with a black sweater over it, she looked vulnerable and soft. She stirred something in him.

"Well, I . . . I seem to have no identification. My purse was stolen from the restaurant I work in."

"Restaurant?"

"I fill in there. I am an actress . . . out of work for a change."

"I see."

"All my papers were in it. My driver's license, voting registration. I have only this." She handed him Fay's Actor's Equity card she had found in their desk.

He read it and then looked up, tapping the card. "So, and you want me to help you get an identity card?"

She smiled, and he noticed the rich mouth.

He's interested, she knew. Play him along.

"Tell me," he asked. "Why are you here?"

"Excuse me?"

"If you could get out, would you?"

She hesitated. What she said would be important, although she did not know why.

"Well, where could I go? Hollywood? I've been and I couldn't get arrested there. It's a very tough town."

"Strange," he mused. "You would seem to be just the type they would seek. You are pretty in a way they are not used to."

"I'll say."

"Tell me this. If you were a great star and I, acting for the cultural minister, came to you and offered you a vehicle to open the new season, what would you say?"

He watched her intelligent eyes flicker, her fine chin set in repose. "I'm not sure what you mean. Would I accept?"

"Yes, and star in a play personally overseen by a German, the enemy."

She waited, pondering it. He liked that.

"A good play should be performed whether it's sponsored by you or anyone else. Of course I would."

"It is because you don't think of me as a Nazi?"

He waited to see if she would try to evade the answer. If she did, he would beg off on helping her.

"I can't think like a star. I'm not. You work your *cosi fan tutti* off to get into a play, so you can get the next part." She paused. "I guess if you become a star, you want to stay one. Once you're in the play, you're on your own. Doesn't matter about who puts it on. That's not how you judge quality . . . is it?"

He stared at her quite intently. I've spilled the beans, she thought.

"Thank you for being so forthright." He held up her card. "Let me make some inquiries. Identity cards are not in my jurisdiction, but I can see what the official policy is. Now I must do some work. Schilker will show you out."

"Thank you so much." She held out her hand.

He took it and felt her warmth, her racing pulse.

"Oh, look, it's snowing."

He turned to the window. "So it is." Still holding her hand, he led her to see it.

Silhouetted like two lovers against his bay window, they watched the flakes fall.

"You have such a wonderful view."

"Yes. I acquired it quite by chance for Colonel Manheim. Well, not exactly. I read the *New York Times* ads from before the invasion."

She turned toward him. "Really? How clever of you."

He smelled her scent. Fay, he thought. Fay Brophy. A gift.

"What are you smiling about?"

"Just something I remembered. I tell you what. I'll call you tomorrow after lunch and let you know."

"Thank you so much."

He led her to the foyer and called Schilker.

"Do you want my number?"

"Yes, of course."

She gave him a card. "I wrote it out just in case."

He took it, but never took his eyes from her. "You will hear from me."

Outside, Leila walked lightly in the falling snow. Where she had trudged before, now she seemed deft and quick. What was it about this man, the strange feeling she had nursed since returning to her empty room that day? He was terribly attractive, yet vulnerable. There was a wound somewhere. Then the other side of her came into play. Yes, he's nice, and he can have any woman in this town. He probably will before this is all done. Men like him eat up little starlets. And you've started this game calling yourself Fay Brophy. You're not Irish. You were a colleen in *Shadow of a Gunman*. You can play anything. But you're not playing. This is not a game. He's a German, and he works for Nazis. Watch yourself. What do you want? I don't know. I just know Leila Fox couldn't get it. She walked on light, sure feet through the fast-falling snow, past citizens, their heads down, scurrying to their destinations, amidst the twinkling lights and honking traffic in Nazi New York.

AMERICAN PANORAMA
IV

NAZI DAYS

January 12, 1942

From the wires of AP . . . German military governor, General Heinrich von Stulpnagel, today announced new food rationing restrictions. Because of the shortage, meat will be on sale only on Mondays and Thursdays. Coupons will be available at local police headquarters. Bread, also rationed, is to be sold on Tuesdays, Thursdays, and Saturdays. In a statement issued today and announced in the *Daily Patrician*, General von Stulpnagel blamed the Roosevelt government for blocking the flow of meat to New York and starving his own people. "It is the German government who will feed you. Know who your friends are."

January 13, 1942

From the wires of AP . . . German military governor, Heinrich von Stulpnagel, met today with religious leaders from the Knights of Pythias, Knights of Columbus, and the Catholic archdiocese to discuss rumors that the German government would limit religious services and freedom of worship. Afterward General von Stulpnagel issued this statement. "We are clearly in accord with the concept of worship of God. At the same time we expect the church to acknowledge its obligation to respect and obey the state. As long as this precept exists, order will be maintained."

January 14, 1942

From the wires of AP . . . German military governor, Heinrich von Stulpnagel, today met with Jewish civic and religious leaders. He stated that a special office had been set up to process requests by Jewish families to leave German-occupied America. The new exit fee for Jews has been raised to ten thousand dollars. In addition, all applicants must pass a security check. All exiting families must leave a member of the immediate household behind. Asked if Jews would be required to wear the yellow star as a means of identification, a common practice in countries occupied by the Germans in Europe, General von Stulpnagel would only say, "This matter is being given serious consideration by Berlin."

January 16, 1942

From the wires of AP . . . It was announced today by the Gestapo in New York that only vital industries in New York will be eligible for gas-rationing booklets. As of today fuel and its distribution in the New York–New Jersey area will be controlled by the Wehrmacht. Those industries that show vital need for fuel will be taken care of on an individual basis. After that will come taxis and public transportation. Pleasure riding will be the last to be considered.

AMERICAN NIGHTS

(The following broadcast was heard on radio band 99.9 at 9:00 P.M. for two minutes on the night of January 17, 1942, before the Germans were successful in jamming it.)

"Good evening fellow Americans. This is Washington Jefferson of *Revolution 1942* broadcasting to you live from somewhere very close. I and my staff are the Voice of Unoccupied America. Do not confuse us with the Voice of America, which comes to you from Los Angeles every night at six P.M. Yesterday we published our first edition of *Revolution 1942*. All the news that's fit to be repressed, we will print and broadcast to you. We will play American swing, read you American protests, feature the voices of Americans fighting for freedom. Make no mistake about it, we are at war. We must fight, we must strike back. John Donne wrote that no man is an island separate from the main. What each of us does, no matter how small, adds up. It will multiply until there is a united America battling the boot of occupation, and we will throw the fascist invader out. Remember, do not think of Christmas as more than it was . . . a temporary defeat. Remember the words of another great hero of this country, John Paul Jones, when asked if he had had enough. I have not yet begun to . . .

(Static prevented further reception of the broadcast)

76

THE LIVING NEWSPAPER

From the wires of AP . . .

(This is a reprint of a performance given at the Federal Theater on January 18, 1942, up to its interruption by Gestapo and local police.)

HEADLINE: BROOKLYN BUTCHER TARRED AND FEATHERED BY NEIGHBORS

(The stage is dark; slowly lights come up. We see streetlights, a sign reading Bay Parkway. The sounds of cars, traffic noises; now residents of Bay Parkway appear. Angry, they gather in front of a cardboard mock-up of a brownstone.)

WOMAN: Come on down, you hoarder, black marketeer.
MAN: C'mon, you pig.
WOMAN: Where's your German friends?
MAN: C'mon, you yellow dog.
WOMAN: You're taking the food out of my children's mouths.
VOICES: Let's go get him.
    Yeah.
    Bring him down here.
(Neighbors exit stage, lights dim; now the people return, dragging a begging little man, Dominick Pasquale. The other actors fade as the light brightens on Pasquale. He occupies the spotlight while the other actors become accusing voices in the darkness.)

PASQUALE: Please, what you want from me?
MAN'S VOICE: You know what. You're a gouger, a profiteer. You're selling meat to the Nazis.
WOMAN'S VOICE: Your children don't starve. Ours do.
MAN'S VOICE: You feed Nazis.
PASQUALE: Please, you no understand. I have wife and kids in Cincinnati. I got to send them money. My wife can no find work in Cincinnati. Who's gonna take care of them?
VOICE: What about our wives and children?
PASQUALE: Please, I have to take care of my son. He's not well.
VOICES: Yeah, and we know how to take care of Nazi butchers. We'll put the mark on you so everybody will know who you are.

(A bucket is brought out and the screaming Pasquale is stripped of his clothes. Now a neighbor steps out into the light, holding a large tar brush. Another has a bucket with feathers. Pasquale cries out. The neighbors close in on him. Cries, vengeful shouts, Pasquale is heard pleading for mercy. The crowd closes on him. Sudden blackness. The crowd disperses and the lights come up on a naked, tarred, and feathered Dominick Pasquale. He crawls toward the audience.)

PASQUALE: Please, somebody help me. My wife, Clara, Clara . . . (He begins to weep.) Clara, please you come home. I'm in disgrace . . . *desgraciado* . . . *desgraciado*. (Over and over he says the word as he crawls through the gutter.)

Chapter 9

January 28, 1942
3:00 P.M.

The truck had stalled just near the Bowery and Paulie had an uneasy feeling. "Well, c'mon," he barked to Rocky Malfetta, who was driving. "Get out there and find out what the fuck is wrong."

For a moment Rocky just stared at him in that blank way of his. Like he was on his stool waiting for the bell to ring and his brains were on Queer Street. Then he muttered something and got out. Moments later the hood came up. Paulie lit a butt. Fucking Rocky had taken too many punches. Paulie couldn't sit still, so he got out. The sun was bright, but it was a bitch of a cold day, and, though the Bowery looked deserted, Paulie didn't like getting stuck there. He had purposely come this way because the krauts stayed clear of skid row. Gestapo headquarters at Centre Street were not far away and the truck was full of meat. Paulie had taken a zigzag route from Long Island to make sure none of his competitors were on his tail. They had come through Brooklyn, switching streets and parkways and finally entered the city via the Manhattan Bridge. It was a good haul from this farmer Paulie and Tommy had found out in Huntington. And Hughie was none the wiser. But there had been a number of hijackings lately. The beef shortage had become worse than anybody imagined. Roosevelt was starving the krauts out. Nothing was coming out of the Midwest. All that good beef was going to Americans involved in the war effort. What could be gotten from the Long Island, Jersey, and Westchester countryside was being confiscated by the krauts. As Tommy put it, "The krauts are gobbling up all the meat." Paulie smiled at that one.

Rocky was puttering around under the hood.

"Well," Paulie growled. "What is it?"

"Could be the transmission."

"What do you mean, could be? Do you know, or don't you?"

"Well," Rocky said, trying to sound like the wise old owl, "this baby had it before. I know how to coax her. Let me try."

Paulie glanced around, looking for a phone. Nothing. Shit. They were right near the bend off Delancey Street, better known as Thieves' Market. The peddlers would be out hawking their wares. What a place for a black market truck full of beef to stall. Paulie rubbed his forehead. Did he hang around with his thumb up his can, waiting for the old punchie to fix the truck, or call Tommy? Tommy would be down in maybe a half hour tops.

"Let me try it one more time," Rocky called to Paulie. He hopped into the cab of the truck and switched on the ignition. There was a brief sputter and then nothing. Abruptly Paulie saw Rocky banging his head against the windowpane.

"What the hell you doing?"

"Don't be mad, Paulie. Don't be."

Paulie jumped up on the running board. As if by divine instinct he looked at the gas gauge. Paulie exploded. "You fucking cauliflower head. Didn't I give you the money to load up before we went out? You spent it on booze. . . ."

Rocky's lumpy features screwed up into a mask of pathos and shame. "No, Paulie, I got it right here. Right here." And he pulled out the gas ration book and waved it pathetically in the air with red, frozen fingers.

"Gimme that," Paulie said, and snatched it away.

"I'm sorry, Paulie," Rocky whined. "I'm sorry."

"Stuff it," Paulie muttered. Now he had to call Tommy. It was his own fault. He never should have depended on the old punchie to get gas. Paulie gripped Rocky by the front of his coat. "Now listen, marble head, I gotta make a call. It'll take me maybe ten minutes to find a booth and get back. No one gets near the truck. If it's a cop, tell him you're waiting for gas. If he asks you what's in it, say you got stones for the quarry they're building."

"What quarry?"

"Doesn't matter what quarry, banana head. You understand? Just some quarry."

Rocky shook his head solemnly. "Yeah, I understand. What quarry?"

"Jesus," Paulie cried. "Jesus. Okay, okay, the quarry up in White Plains near the Post Road in the Bronx."

Rocky brightened. "The quarry up in White Plains near the Post Road in the Bronx." He repeated it like a young child memorizing the alphabet.

"Anybody else tries to get near it, you tell them to bug off. And if they lay a hand on the truck, or try to see what's inside, you flatten them. Use the lug wrench."

"Flatten them," Rocky intoned. "Use the lug wrench."

"I'll be right back," Paulie said. He jumped off the running board and hurried toward Rivington Street. There was a phone booth right there. Paulie knew the neighborhood like the back of his hand. He used to roll rummies down there when he was in grammar school.

The phone was between the Bowery Mission and the Salvation Army Hotel. A Salvation Army man in uniform was using it. Paulie popped a toothpick in his mouth and paced. "C'mon, c'mon," he implored under his breath. He had a mental image of the beef and chicken piled in heaps on each other, emitting a smell that would bring everyone in the Bowery. He stuck a Juicy Fruit in his mouth to go with the toothpick. In front of the mission was the usual collection of stiffs and flops, lying against the building, already so juiced they were nodding off into oblivion.

Paulie turned toward the Salvation Army Hotel and read the sign: BEEF STEW, OATMEAL, AND COFFEE, 5 CENTS. Only where beef had been written, somebody had crossed it out and penciled in *shit*. The word stew caused Paulie more anxiety. The Salvation Army guy was still gabbing away. In another minute . . . Paulie smelled something horrible and looked down at a particularly moth-eaten old buzzard wearing a brown coat that hung to the ground, open-toed sneakers, and a hat that he must have worn when he galloped up San Juan Hill with Teddy Roosevelt and the Rough Riders.

"Bit of a nipper, hey," the old fleabag began.

Paulie turned away.

"Reminds me of the famous blizzard of . . ."

Paulie found a quarter in his pocket. "Here. Now beat it."

The old bum, who had an uneven patch of white and brown hair, took the coin and put it in his mouth. Satisfied, he raised a finger. "Top of the old morning, sport. Top of the morning." He started to gimp away, but, with that antenna so keenly refined in the jungle, detected something in Paulie's anxious stare at the man with the phone.

"Need that phone, hey?"

Paulie reached for a butt.

"I'll have a word with him," the fleabag announced, and hobbled off. He reached the Salvation Army officer and, after surveying him for a few moments, launched into some kind of dialogue. The man tried to ignore him, but in a few moments he covered the receiver with his hand and began berating the bum. The words grew more heated, and suddenly the man was shaking the bum and the receiver dropped away. Paulie saw his chance. He ran to the phone and, ignoring the two men, hung it up. He dropped in his nickel and dialed Tommy, who picked up on the third ring.

"Yeah?"

"It's me. We're out of gas."

"How?"

"The old pug screwed up. Get down here fast. Load up a jerry can from that truck we hijacked. I mean fast, Tommy, before the whole Bowery smells meat."

"I'm on my way."

Paulie hung up and smelled that awful odor. It was the fleabag who had apparently driven off the Salvation Army. Maybe I should hire him to do my muscle work, Paulie joked to himself. He's riper than a four-day-old carcass. The old fleabag gimped after him.

"Gesture of my appreciation," he wheedled.

"Get lost," Paulie said.

"I don't mean to appear ungrateful . . ."

Now Paulie had the lousy old bastard by the collar. "I said beat it before I throw you in the river."

The old hobo put on his most ingratiating smile. "Quarter will buy you coffee and some oatmeal, but I tell you I hanker for some meat."

The words hung there, and Paulie knew this bearded reptile had overheard his conversation. And like all buzzards smelling meat, he wanted some. Paulie turned to lay the old buzzard out with his fist and saw four other bums looking worse than this one closing in. This one was shrewd. He had given a signal that there was a hide to be cleaned. In a moment Paulie was surrounded. They were like flies on flypaper, dripping malice and voracious. Paulie never hesitated. Out came the rod. "Which one of you croaks wants it first? C'mon. Step right up. Now, you got ten seconds to piss off or one of you is dead meat. Maybe you," Paulie said to the leader. "You like meat so much."

Now the man was tipping his cap. "No offense, governor."

81

"I ain't the governor," Paulie answered. "If I see you within twenty yards of me I'll lay you in the river."

Paulie aimed the gun, and the buzzard backed off, as did his men. "Man's got to eat, you know."

"You got a quarter, go have a feast," Paulie said, and aimed the gun again. "Go on. Eat."

A half hour later Paulie and Rocky were waiting in the truck, and Paulie had smoked half a dozen cigarettes. He still had the uneasy feeling. He couldn't shake it off.

"Here he comes," Rocky yelled, and Paulie felt a surge of relief. Tommy, driving a blue Hudson, pulled up alongside the truck.

Tommy was out of the car and Rocky had his arm. "I didn't mean to do it, Tommy. Tell Paulie . . ."

"Never mind," Paulie snapped. "Get the gas in the tank. Move it."

Tommy uncapped the big jerry can he had taken from the car and now, as Rocky tilted it, Tommy unscrewed the gas cap. Paulie lit another weed and sucked in some air. Not so bad, not so . . . coming from Delancey Street were a group of men. Rough men, peddler types, and right there in front, hobbling to keep up, was the fleabag from in front of the mission.

Paulie knew instantly what had happened. It was the word meat. The old fleabag had gone down to Delancey and sold the information. The men who had come here were street Jews. Hungry, sharp, and greedy. Come on, suckers. This is my meat, not Hughie's. No one takes it from me.

"Tommy," Paulie called. "Come here. I said, come here."

Tommy walked over. "What?"

"You got your heater?"

"Sure."

"Where?"

"In my suit jacket."

"Then unbutton your coat and be ready. We got some hustlers who want to take our haul. I'm going to offer them a few bucks. That's just a stall. Get Rocky to the wheel and when I fire my rod you tell Rocky to move. If they get in the way drive over them. But make sure you're in the truck with him."

"What about the Hudson?"

"Give me the keys."

Tommy handed him the keys and hurried back to Rocky.

There were about ten men coming toward Paulie. Their leader seemed to be a bearded man with a brown jacket and a pointy beard. Yiddle, Paulie thought. That was the name he used for the peddlers down on Delancey Street. The man already had a spiel on his lips.

82

"We can help you perhaps?" the man said.

I'd like to bust your head, Paulie thought. "We're fine," Paulie answered. "We're just going on our way."

The man stopped some ten yards away. He saw Paulie's hand in his pocket and Paulie knew the old hobo had mentioned the gun.

"Your truck is broken?"

"It's fine. Just needed some gas."

"Terrible thing to get stuck on a winter day."

"Yeah," Paulie answered. "Terrible thing." He fingered the keys. "You all set?" he called to Tommy.

"All set," Tommy yelled back.

"Where you from?" the bearded leader asked. It was a stall. He snapped his fingers, and the men behind him fanned out in front of the truck.

"Behind you," Tommy yelled.

Paulie looked and saw that about ten more men had come from his rear. Some were carrying chains. One had an axe. Paulie's gun flashed in the sunlight. "I'm the man from cement city," Paulie snapped back. "Now back off."

The sight of his gun froze everybody, and in that moment Paulie eased back toward the Hudson. Now their leader took a few cautious steps. "We are hungry. We have starving families. Give us some of your load, and we'll let you go."

If he gave them any, he was dead. Paulie flashed a wad. "Gelt. Ten bucks a man. Enough to buy a big dinner for your family. Who wants it?"

Nobody moved.

The leader spoke. "It is a matter of more than one meal. I know who you are. You sell to the rich while we starve. My children live on soup and matzo meal. They haven't had meat in two weeks. But you eat, the rich eat, the Nazis eat. . . ."

Paulie raised the gun. "How you gonna have children with your nuts shot off?" He made a mental promise to gun the old hobo next.

The man lunged forward. "Get them. . . ."

True to his word, Paulie aimed the nickel-plated .38 for the bearded man's groin. . . . The gun snapped and the man went down, his hands folded over his abdomen. Now Paulie turned to plug the old fleabag, but as he aimed a brick smashed against his head, and the shot went wild. Paulie reeled back and heard Tommy screaming, "Go, Rocky, go." Somebody had hold of Paulie's arm, wrestling for control of the gun. Two men had Paulie pinned to the Hudson. One had his wrist and was banging it against the car while the other smashed Paulie's face with his fist.

Spitting into the face of the one wrestling for his gun, Paulie drove an elbow into the man's solar plexus. He fell away groaning. Paulie took three more smashes from the other before working his blackjack loose from his pocket. Now. He whacked the man three times on the side of the head, watching the flesh above his eyebrows spurt red blood. Paulie beat him into the ground with three more successive blows. Now and now and now. He turned and saw the other man crawling for the gun. Paulie brought his foot down hard on the man's hand. Paulie looked down into the face of a young kid. Two whiplash blows with his blackjack laid the kid's head open. Paulie had the gun and looked around. Rocky was driving in a crazy kind of circle. Men he had run over lay in the street while others rode the windshield. He was driving like a drunken Chinaman. Then Paulie saw the flat. Somebody had knifed the front tires. Tommy opened fire through the windshield of the truck and two men flew away.

But the truck was wobbling from side to side, and instead of braking it, Rocky tried to gun it. The truck bucked broncolike, twirled, and then, screeching, pitched forward on its side. And seemingly from nowhere came an endless supply of people. Men, women, young boys, old men. They were on the truck slashing the canvas with knives and sharp sticks.

Paulie ran at them, gun cocked. A foot was stuck out and he fell hard to the ground.

"Get off or I'll blast you."

But no one listened and no one cared.

A kid pulled a chicken out and raised it aloft. *"Essen,"* he screamed in triumph. Calling out to all those in the ghetto to come and partake of this windfall. *"Essen,"* he screamed again.

From a sitting position Paulie shot him through the kneecap and now the kid merely screamed. He dropped the chicken as he fell and two men fought over it.

Chopping with furious energy, frenzied, starving men ripped at the canvas. Now it was open and their furious groping hands fought for the spoils.

Paulie was up and he could see Rocky wobbling over trying to save the truck. A man split his head with an axe handle. Rocky, blood flowing, crumpled. Tommy was there. "C'mon, Paulie. Let's go. Let's go."

Paulie stood there gaping. "The meat . . . the meat."

"Fuck the meat," Tommy cried. "Get in the Hudson. . . ."

There was a coughing, sputtering noise, and they turned to see the Hudson in flames.

"You fucking scumbags," Paulie screamed. He aimed the gun, but there was no one and everyone to kill.

Pitched on its side, the canvas hood ripped away, the truck

84

had become a battlefield for men fighting each other for slabs of beef, for plucked and unplucked chickens. Package upon package of chopped meat was ripped open. Some was thrown into the crowd to people who ate it raw. A little woman with no teeth pushed the meat into her mouth and worked her gums back and forth furiously. A large slab of beef thrown into the air resembled a tipped forward pass that finally landed in the arms of an elderly Jewish man with a cane, who hobbled away with two young boys in pursuit.

Abruptly, cars were pulling up. Men with clubs piled out. Gestapo, backed up by police. They caught the old man, and the men in black coats smashed his shoulders and hands over and over.

"Let's go," Tommy said. That was as much as he could say, for then two plainclothes Gestapo were on them with clubs. A driving hammer of a blow broke Tommy's arm. He fell, his mouth open, emitting a cry of agony. Paulie used his pistol on the man's face and felt the teeth crack. But the second man pounded Paulie to the ground. He was a professional, Paulie thought as he fell to his knees, releasing his gun, clutching the man's legs. Then, as the kraut relaxed, Paulie deftly brought his hand around the man's balls and squeezed. The kraut's cry was music.

A squad of police with swastikas on their armbands materialized as if from nowhere, moving without wasted motion, rounding up and clubbing men, women, and children.

"Run," a woman cried to her little boy, handing him the beef. She went down in a heap from a blow and her son, pursued by a car, tried to make it to Stanton Street. The car was upon him, swerving, and the boy was lifted into the air. He fell heavily and was still, the blood from his head spreading under the ten-pound roast beef he had been trying to escape with.

Now more police cars arrived, bolstered by German troops. The area was quickly surrounded. The people were rounded up. The gutted, empty truck lay on its side, a mess of chicken feathers and chopped meat. The ground was littered with smashed people and pounds of meat, chicken claws, and rooster beaks. An old rabbi was dragged from a doorway, still desperately clutching a plucked chicken. "Mine, mine," he cried out, "for my grandchild, for soup."

Paulie crawled along the ground. A couple more feet, and he could turn the corner. Ugh . . . stabbing pain as a boot stepped on his hand. He looked into the face of a German soldier. "Gelt," Paulie whispered. "Here, I got gelt . . . I got . . ." The soldier looked at him peculiarly, then called someone. A

85

man in a black leather coat came over. Paulie reached for his roll. The man sapped him with his gun.

Paulie sat on a stool smoking a butt and rubbing the big egg on the side of his head. His head throbbed, and his nose smarted from the odor of the piss bowl in the corner. He swore silently. He hadn't been in the slammer in seven years. All because that fleabag of a rummy overheard his phone conversation. The cell was illuminated only by a small overhead bulb, and that so covered by grime that its flickering light was a pathetic thing. Like a dying lightning bug. Bars, Paulie thought. Always the bars on the window and bars on the door, now obscured by shadow. He felt the stub burn his fingers, dropped it, and ground it out with his shoe. He put his head in his hands. He figured he had lost about five grand's worth of meat this afternoon. Be smart, sucker. Learn your lesson. Don't come in through the Bowery no more. He wondered how Tommy was. And old Rocky really got laid out. That blow might be the one to finally loosen all his screws. He was going to have to talk his way out of this one. Good thing he had phony papers.

The old-timer on the cot above him leaned out.

"Got a butt?"

Paulie fished out a Lucky and handed it to him. "How long you been in?"

"Since the Nazis invaded. I got caught jack rollin' an officer."

Paulie tried to smile. "I'll be out on bail as soon as I see somebody."

"Who pulled you in? Cops or Nazis?"

"Nazis."

"Ain't no bail with Nazis."

They sat smoking in silence. Suddenly there was a horrifying scream. It was unlike any utterance of pain Paulie had ever heard.

"Jesus," he exclaimed. "What the hell is that?"

The old con flicked an ash as he spoke. "Gestapo uses Zippo lighters on your nuts. They just toast your balls awhile, and you'll tell them anything they want to know."

The ash fell on Paulie's wrist. "Christ," he yelled out.

They came for Paulie about twenty minutes later and led him down gray halls to a little office on the second floor. Behind a desk was a small man with smaller eyes and a clipped mustache. Paulie was escorted by two black-shirted Gestapo men. "Wait outside," the cheese with the mustache told them. He spoke English with a thick accent. Paulie wanted to laugh but knew that wasn't a good move.

The cheese approached him, gesturing for Paulie to sit down. He picked up Paulie's identity card. "Mister Schmidt. Is that correct?"

Paulie grunted, suppressing a smile. He had picked a German name for just this kind of thing. In case he got picked up they wouldn't be so hard on him. He had his story down pat.

The cheese pushed a cigarette toward him. "Try a German cigarette."

"Thanks," Paulie said. They smelled like shit, but he had to butter this kraut.

The acrid smell of the paper and tobacco filled the room. Christ, Paulie thought, I smelled sweeter diarrhea.

"What do you smoke?" the kraut inquired.

"Luckies." Paulie offered him one. The kraut took it but didn't light it. They weren't buddies yet.

"Schmidt," the kraut said, "your father is from the old country?"

"Hamburg," Paulie said. "He got out in 1920. Too many mouths to feed."

"Where were you born?"

Paulie had been hoping for that one. "Hamburg, but I don't remember nothin'. I was one when we got here."

"So," the kraut said. "Now, tell me what you were doing with the meat in your truck."

Paulie put on his most earnest face. "Well, I'm a driver and I got an offer to deliver some stuff to the South Street Market. They didn't tell me what it was. I had a pretty good idea. But I got a wife and kids to take care of."

The German tapped the Lucky Strike on the desk. "Who approached you to do this?"

Again Paulie was all eagerness to cooperate. "Some little guy called himself Bill, but I could tell that was a phony name."

"Yes?"

"Sure, he was a Jew. Not many Jews named Bill. It's a Jew operation."

Abetz leaned back and put the Lucky Strike in his mouth. This one was a smooth liar. Attacked by a group of *Juden*, he blames the whole operation on Jews. But all reports indicated he knew how to handle a gun. He shot a number of the street Jews who had attacked his truck. He used the gun too well to be anything but a criminal, and a police record check showed two Joe Schmidts, both of whom were in jail.

"What do you do besides drive a truck?"

Now Paulie was a choirboy out of St. Mary's. "Nothin'. Sometimes a little moving . . . you know . . . house moving."

"But the gun we found on you had been fired. From the re-

ports, you knew how to use it. You are a good marksman?''
Abetz used the phrase ''Sind sie ein Scharfschütze?'' It was a
phrase Schmidt would have understood if his father really was
from Hamburg. Abetz watched the man's eyes. Nothing regis-
tered there. No, this one was not German. He had chosen a
German name for just this type of situation. He was a criminal
using a false identity. But he was brutal and had no love of Jews.
This one might be of use. Abetz needed some kind of incident.

Abetz lit the Lucky Strike with a gold lighter given to him by
Himmler for his splendid work in sealing off the Warsaw ghetto.
''I am sympathetic, but the fact is you are guilty of working in
the black market. This is a serious crime. I have taken a personal
interest in it because I agree this is Jew work. For that reason I
have taken it out of the hands of the police. This city is filled
with degenerate Jews . . . more so than any other city in the
world.'' He watched Schmidt for any response. He sat there idly
smoking his cigarette. He reminded Abetz of Landorp, who had
been his killer in Warsaw. Landorp watched the world with un-
caring eyes until given a club, a hose, or a knife with a finely
honed cutting edge.

''What do you think of Jews?'' Abetz asked.

Paulie instinctively spat on the floor.

A little quiver of a smile showed itself on Abetz's face. He
had a feeling about this one.

''Then why do you work for one?''

Paulie shrugged. ''There are so many of them.''

''Just so,'' Abetz said in an excited voice. ''Just so. You are
observant. But we have a little surprise. . . .'' He stopped.
''Vermin must be expunged. Do you not agree?'' He didn't pause
as Paulie nodded. ''It is possible I might be inclined to be le-
nient in this case if we could find those who are running this
ring. The Jewish ones, of course.'' He puffed on his cigarette
waiting for Paulie's response.

Paulie's mind raced like a sure winner at Jamaica racetrack.
This little kraut prick wants a Jew to pin this on. He doesn't
give a rat's ass if the guy has been doing it or not. Fine, but I
ain't got anyone to give him. Paulie stalled.

''Well, if you was to let me go, I could make inquiries. Next
time they hired me I could tip you off. But it's tricky. If they
found out . . .''

''I can assure you,'' Abetz interjected, ''we would not jeop-
ardize a source of information. Especially an accurate source.
So if I should let you go I know you would treat this seriously.
Of course, if you didn't . . .''

Paulie's hand involuntarily moved to his groin. The gesture
was not lost on Abetz.

"But I can see you are a serious man. I will tell you something. This town is ridden with vermin. *Juden* and *schwarz* . . . Poles and Lithuanians . . . it must be controlled. Eventually one is with us or with them. *Verstehen?*"

"Yeah, yeah."

"Good. Now here's what we do. I am going to give you back your gun and identity card and a telephone number where you will call me in three days. You will tell the people you work for that you were released because you are unimportant. That you convinced us of that. Tell them you need money badly and need a driving job right away." Abetz paused. "Schmidt, I want the next convoy. That is why you are going free. If you do well you will stay free."

Paulie smiled broadly.

"Now," Abetz said, "before you go we snap your picture so that if you should suddenly disappear we can circulate your photo and find you. Also we fingerprint you."

Paulie stopped smiling.

"We will take care of you, Schmidt, provided we get what we need. You have how many children?"

"Six," Paulie said.

"Well, that is a lot of mouths. I would make sure that once you have proven yourself the trucks you drive would get through. As men of the world we know that the black market is everywhere. It is a fact of life. Somebody must prosper. It might as well be Germans, *ja*?"

"I appreciate the chance."

"I know you do. And of course, if you should hear any other things—you know, about people who want to resist or engage in opposition—you would report that at once."

"Oh, sure."

"Good. We understand each other. Here." He handed Paulie a card. "Call me in three days. In the afternoon." He pressed an intercom button. "Sergeant Hoppman will take you to be photographed."

Hoppman, a thug with a bull neck, opened the door. "Hoppman, take Schmidt to be photographed. Then arrange for him to have a good meal. Anything he wants. In the morning turn him free."

Hoppman clicked his heels. "*Ja*, Standartenführer."

He led Paulie to the door.

Paulie turned. "You won't be sorry."

Abetz looked at him sharply. "If I'm not, you won't be." He turned back to some papers on his desk.

With Schmidt gone, Abetz leaned back. He had taken a chance, which was a departure from his usual methodical, pre-

89

cise way of operating. But there was something about this one. He had those cold, flat eyes like Landorp. It was a hunch, but Abetz needed to gamble. He had a top secret memo from Himmler asking for campsites within the next two weeks. Once locations had been decided, implementation was to begin. Incidents were needed. Provocation. "Reichstag fires must burn" was the way Himmler had put it. This Schmidt, whoever he was, had the feel of a man who could help Abetz burn things up. Yes. Reichstag fires must burn.

Paulie was released at dawn after breakfasting on ham, sausages, and six eggs. He rode uptown on the IRT, hearing a message in the clickety-clack of its wheels. You got a free pass from the Gestapo if you can give them a patsy. Patsy, patsy, patsy. But who? Get somebody, the message came back, or they'll torch your nuts, your nuts, your nuts. Nuts, nuts, nuts. Patsy, patsy, patsy. Suddenly it came to him. Hughie. He would give Abetz Hughie Gagno. Then the meat operation was Paulie's.

He got off at Times Square and walked toward his apartment on Ninth and Thirty-ninth, ignoring the long lines queuing around the bakery for the daily allotment of bread, ignoring the people in meat lines two blocks long. Ignoring the Nazi patrol cars and the snow starting to fall on the city. It had all fallen into his lap. He had a direct line to the Gestapo, and it was good-bye, Hughie. Paulie laughed out loud. Hughie would never know what hit him. Once the Heinrichs put the torch to Hughie's cubes, you would never hear from Hughie again. He didn't have no balls. Paulie roared at his unintentional joke. No balls.

He decided to stop in at Hogan's, which was on Forty-first and Ninth. That's where Paulie got his mail and messages. Jack Turley was shining up the counter, where there were a few baskets of stale chips and pretzels.

"Hey, Paulie," Jack called out.

"I need my mail. You got any messages for me?"

Jack, who was an earnest looking man with bright red hair, looked a bit embarrassed.

"Did you hear?"

"Hear what?"

Jack rubbed his chin.

"What the fuck is it?"

"Hughie."

"What about him?"

"Croaked. He was trying to run a police blockade with his truck. Truck caught fire. Cops must have hit the gas tank. It went up like a Fourth of July cherry bomb."

"Jesus," Paulie intoned.

"Yeah, it's tough," Jack answered. "I know you was close to Hughie. You want a drink?"

"Yeah," Paulie said, falling against the bar. "Hit me with some rye."

He gulped the shot down. Twelve hours ago it would have been great news. But now with the Gestapo connection, it screwed up everything. Now he had no patsy to give Abetz. Christ, will you give me a break.

Jack dropped his mail on the counter. For a moment Paulie stared dully at it. Then he began to thumb through the pile. There was a flier from the Father Flynn Charity. He was about to brush it away when he saw the handwritten message. "Someone who saw your work in Hoboken recommends you highly. If you want to profit from a situation requiring your special talents, be at the Gold Rail bar this afternoon at 1 P.M." Paulie shook his head. The reference to Hoboken was unmistakable. It was a job. But for who? Who the fuck was Father Flynn and his charity?

Chapter 10

January 19, 1942
12:30 P.M.

The two-page newspaper lay discarded on the subway seat. It had been used by a drunk to blow his nose in. The masthead was a reproduction of Patrick Henry calling out "Give me liberty or give me death." As the train lurched into the Seventy-ninth Street station the paper fell to the floor into a pool of spilled soda. It lay on the subway floor waiting to be read.

REVOLUTION 1942

HITLER MEETS GOD

(Into the spotlight comes a little man with the familiar mustache in full Nazi regalia. He speaks in a soft, reverential tone.)

(Looking up at heaven) The almighty, you who look down upon us, of whom we ask nothing more than to bless us in the future as you have in the past. (The Führer is thoughtful for a moment then looks back up toward God.) But as Aryan to Aryan, I must take this moment to ask you why you blessed the *schwarz* Owens at my Olympics . . . and why you blessed the *schwarz* Louis against my Schmeling? Do you not realize the consequences of your actions? Do you not realize what a bad example you are setting? Can you not see how people will misinterpret . . . (now he is raving) you *stupkopf*. You sit around in your beer hall up there and get so *ungepatchen*, you do not know what you are doing. Last week I sent Goering up in a plane to speak with you and you were not there. Such manners. I send the marshall of all my Luftwaffe and you are out playing with fräuleins. You . . . you . . . *schwein-hund*. Your Führer calls you and you are drunk somewhere playing in the pussy willows. If you do not get yourself together I will replace you with someone I can trust like Bormann. He has great doubts about you. He accuses you of impure blood. You are to report to my doctor on *Wurster-strasse* for a checkup immediately. Bormann says you have been seen with a mulatto in Munich. That would explain about your favoring the *schwarze*s. If it happens again, I send the entire Luftwaffe and we bomb you out. *Verstehen sie . . . dummkopf?* Now that we understand each other, heavenly father, when do I get the rest of Amerika?

The train pulled into Eighty-sixth Street and some German soldiers got on. They were laughing and Paulie noticed how the rest of the compartment moved away from them. How long were these guys going to be here? You never could tell when Roosevelt might pull a Pearl Harbor, and Paulie had to make time count. The train rolled out and Paulie went back to thinking who he could turn over to the Gestapo. It had to be somebody who was running in meat. But who?

He got off the train at 116th Street and walked back to the Gold Rail. Paulie was wary. But he also knew a come-on when he saw one. Back when he was a free-lancing strong arm, a lot of little notes and cards used to show up in his mailbox. He walked along Broadway watching the college kids huddled in little groups, reading the latest Gestapo Achtung. Paulie pulled his overcoat collar up. He passed a bar and a flower shop. There were some guys in dark coats standing around the store owner.

Paulie stopped to watch. They were Gestapo for sure. He looked at the name of the store, Golden's. The guy was an Abey. He was in trouble. Some students had gathered around. Bunch of yo-yos. This ain't the movies. No touchdowns. Only Gestapo with Zippo lighters.

The bar was dark and quiet. Just a few students and some truck drivers. Paulie walked to the bar, said "Gimme a Rupert," and took himself a booth. He went back to thinking about who he could give to Abetz.

"Rupert?"

It was the bartender with Paulie's beer. Another voice suddenly said, "It's on me."

Paulie turned and saw a brown-haired guy who wasn't no priest.

"I'm with the Father Flynn Charity."

Collins paid the bartender and slid in next to Paulie.

"So what do you want?"

"A contribution," Collins answered. "What else?"

"People usually pay me if they want a contribution."

"We are a generous charity if service is given."

"I move furniture, do a little other kinds of moving."

"It might be necessary for you to do extensive removal as well."

"You mean like freshly laid cement?"

"That and other work. We need strong arms."

"What's your company?"

"Family outfit. Run by Uncle."

Paulie popped a cigarette into his mouth. "Uncle, huh? Let me see if I got you. You work for Uncle and you don't like sauerkraut."

"Hate it."

They measured one another. East Side yid, Hell's Kitchen mick. Their ancestory the history of the city.

He's a moron, Collins thought. But he's lethal. He has to be guided or he'll go off.

This guy ain't afraid of me, Paulie thought. Watch out for a trap.

"You got credentials?" Paulie asked

"Sure," Collins said. He reached into the brown suit jacket and pulled out money. A fist full. "Recognize it?"

"Yeah, sure. Good outfit." Paulie was silent. "Who the fuck are you and how did you get my name? And no bullshit or I'm gone. You think I'm an eager beaver. I ain't."

"Easy," Collins said. "If you hadn't asked I would have walked out. Got your name from a union guy named Kresky. Said you busted heads in a strike in Hoboken. Another guy named Donetti dropped your name. He was in Jersey City when you worked there.''

Paulie grunted. He felt a little better. ''How do I know you're who you say you are?''

''Because I want you to put the squeeze on the Heinrichs . . . if you follow me. The pay is good. And Uncle will forgive your sins. You might even become a patriot. I could use some more talent.''

''It'll cost.''

''I want guys who can use a gun, can handle jelly and other high quality fireworks. I want guys who can go bang bang you're dead and ask no questions.''

''I can get them. Who's heading this up?''

''Me.''

''Who the fuck are you?''

''Jack Armstrong, all-American boy. I'll take care of you if Heinrich finds you.''

Paulie thought of Zippo lighters and laughed.

''What's the joke?''

''Nothing,'' Paulie said. ''I just like to smile.''

Collins lit a Chesterfield. ''I need someone to help me free a prisoner Heinrich is holding.''

Now we're getting to it, Paulie thought. ''What are you lookin' for?''

''Someone to drive the car and use the gun if it gets hot. There's a good chance it will.''

Paulie held up five fingers.

''That's a lot.''

''Talent costs.''

''Who's the talent?''

''Me. Gettin' a guy out of the Tombs is no picnic.''

''How do you figure the Tombs.''

'' 'Cause that's where they keep prisoners.''

Collins took the proper respite. ''I'll think about it.''

''Yeah, do that.''

''If it's yes, it'll be soon. Next week or so.''

''You know where to reach me.''

Collins stood up. ''You'll hear from me. Oh, you ever seen Charlie Rosen operate?''

Paulie made a face. ''Charlie is no good for hittin' guys' guts. Charlie will sing real easy if they get him. He's a canary.''

''Thanks for the tip,'' Collins said, and walked out.

''Charlie sings good, smells bad,'' Paulie called out after him.

He watched Collins go out the door. Paulie leaned back in his chair. The job was his and so was the five grand. But he wasn't taking it just for the dough. He was doin' it to find out what the

American side was up to. He was no dummy. This was the chance to play both sides of the fence. Score points with them both, and when he saw who was goin' to sweep the pot, Paulie would lay a big bet for himself. This was givin' him the chance to score. It was a real opportunity, the Heinrichs takin' over New York.

He heard somebody laugh, and it touched a forgotten chord. He looked up and saw some truck drivers. They both had their backs to him. Paulie found himself staring at the huskier one. The one with the brown mackinaw and the bushy blond hair. The guy laughed again and Paulie smiled.

"Hey, Nippo."

The truck driver cocked his head.

"Over here, Nippo."

The driver swiveled and stared around the dim bar. He finally caught sight of Paulie and squinted momentarily, then broke out in a big smile.

"Paulie?"

"No one else."

Nipponomick slid off the stool and, carrying a beer bottle, walked over, hand outstretched. "Paulie, how the hell are you?"

Paulie leaned back. "Okay. Jesus, how long has it been?"

Nippo laughed. "Forty million years B.C."

Paulie stared. Jesus, this guy was exactly the same. Curly blond hair, big honker of a Jewish beak, laughing gray-green eyes, mouth dripping with spit. He and Paulie had been booted out of school about the same time. Paulie because he was a perpetual truant who finally decked a teacher. Nipponomick was a joker. Always cutting up, dropping fish down the girls' dresses. One day he set off a stink bomb. "Hey, didn't you drop a stink bomb in the coatroom one day?"

Drool ran from Nippo's mouth. "Teachers' lunchroom." He smiled and all the years melted away. They were back on the corner of Essex Street pinching butts from the ground.

"What are you drinking?" Paulie asked.

"I'm okay."

Paulie felt a little uncomfortable. "Still a T.P.?"

Nippo grinned, but not like in the old days. "Well, now I'm a little more gentle. I like to suck a little, if you know what I mean."

T.P. had been a reference to Nippo's most outrageous gambit. Tit pulling. He would pedal down the East Side on his broken-down bike and, when he saw a well-stacked girl, he would ride by and grab her tit. The startled girl would scream, and Nippo would honk the horn attached to his bike and then speed off. He especially loved to do it to yeshiva girls.

"That's what finally got me kicked out," Nippo said. "It was Faber's daughter." Faber was the school principal.

Paulie stamped his foot in appreciation. "Now I remember. Fuckin' Nippo." They both laughed, and then it gradually faded away.

"So what you doin' these days?" Nippo asked.

"A little furniture moving, some bouncing."

Nippo nodded. "Still the old strong arm."

"Pays the rent," Paulie said. "Better than pushing a truck."

Nippo didn't say anything for a moment. "Driving a truck pays better than you think."

"What do you drive?"

"A little this . . . a little that."

"Suppose I don't like this? Suppose I want a little of that?"

"You could call me and I would see you got that."

"Could I wear it, drink it, or eat it?"

"You could definitely put it on your table."

Paulie fished out a Lucky. "Smoke?"

Nippo held up a hand. "You don't look like you haven't been eating."

Paulie shrugged. "Lots of bread and spaghetti."

Nippo leaned forward. Paulie could see the red stains on his coat and gray shirt. Son of a bitch, it was a meat stain. "How hungry are you?"

"Maybe three porterhouses or a big tenderloin. I got money," Paulie intoned earnestly. "I can pay."

Nippo slapped him affectionately on the back. "I can't get much . . . maybe three nights' worth."

Paulie gripped his arm. "You could? Really? How much?"

"For you, Paulie, a good price."

"Gee, that's wonderful."

"For old times on Essex Street."

Now they were both abruptly uncomfortable. For it wasn't old times.

"Married, Nippo?"

"Yeah, three kids."

"The old ball and chain." Paulie was angry with himself. He shouldn't have asked. He had been given a gift. Take it, take it.

"How do I get the . . ."

"On a hundred and twentieth near Claremont there's a warehouse. It looks deserted. Be on the corner tomorrow night a little after eight. Watch for me to come out. Then follow me about a block. It'll be in the paper bag under my arm. Bring an old box or something so it won't look like you got food."

Paulie snapped his fingers. "I might be tied up tomorrow. Any other nights?"

96

"I would try to make it tomorrow. This guy in Pennsylvania has good stuff."

"Sure," Paulie said. "You're right. I'm hungry already."

Nippo stood up. "You were always hungry. See you, Paulie. Bring gelt." He laughed.

"See you," Paulie called out.

He watched Nippo go out with his companion and then walked to the bar. Jesus, what luck. There was a whole setup. If he played his cards he could have the meat and a patsy for the Gestapo. He slapped his leg. He'd stepped in it this time. He got some change and went to make a call.

January 20, 1942
8:00 P.M.

The detachment of Gestapo all dressed in civilian clothes huddled in an abandoned building that faced the warehouse that held Nippo's black market operation. It was eight o'clock at night, and the cold was a knife that cut to the bone. It slashed into your sinuses and made them ache for warmth. Across the street, shafts of light would appear and then abruptly disappear as men went in and out of the warehouse.

Paulie cupped the butt he was smoking to give his hand a little warmth. It wasn't the way he thought it would be. Paulie was giving Abetz what he needed, an illegal meat market operation run by a Jew. Why did Paulie have to be there? Why did he have to be there to see Nippo get hauled? You asshole, he berated himself. You didn't figure on that. The Heinrich is sinking the hook into me.

Abetz edged his way over to Paulie. "Will there be more deliveries?"

Paulie shook his head. "Could be, but I don't think so. Trucks coming in at night look too suspicious." He was also remembering Nippo telling him to meet him after eight o'clock. That was probably the last run.

"Then we will take them," Abetz declared.

He called over one of his aides and whispered some final instructions, gesturing with his hand in short, violent strokes. Paulie edged away and back against a wall. He felt a little queasy. Must have been something he ate. He took a piece of Topps gum out of his pocket and, tearing off the wrapper with a sharp fingernail, put it in his mouth. Jesus, poor Nippo. But he was only a driver. They would let him off after a few months in the slammer. What they wanted was the Abey who ran the operation. It had better be an Abey.

Paulie saw the Gestapo men going out. For some reason he

97

thought of his father. Bad Jake Lazar. Why was he thinking of the old man now? Then he remembered. There was one time Jake had bought halvah for him and Nippo. Jake was tight as a rusty screw, but this one day he had some pennies to spare. They had wolfed it down. Later Jake came out with a tennis ball and had a catch with them.

Paulie saw the Gestapo men led by Abetz fan out. They moved briskly toward the warehouse. Some surrounded the rear of it while Abetz and six others positioned themselves in front. Abetz had a pistol in his hand. They were going in armed. That was bad. There were some tough guys in this racket. The word was getting around on what would happen to you if the Gestapo pulled you in. If you're running black market meat, you ain't going to be no cherry. What the hell, Paulie thought. I had to do it to get ahead. I ain't going to be no strong-arm punk the rest of my life.

He saw light as the door opened and a man started out, sighted Abetz, and ducked inside. Now a whistle sounded and the Gestapo rushed in. There were shouts. Moments later came the sound of guns.

"You have done well, Schmidt," Abetz was saying. They were in the tiny office he kept at 230 Centre Street. "I have just what I need, a bunch of filthy Jews running a black market operation. Starving their very own to fatten their wallets. It will look very impressive in the morning newspapers." He clapped Paulie on the shoulders. "You have produced excellent results in a very short time. You have earned a reward. The meat confiscated by my men has been divided up. Some for official proof, another portion in a truck downstairs. Here are the keys and papers for the truck."

Reminding himself to look very grateful, Paulie shuffled forward. "I am glad you gave me the chance to prove myself. And I appreciate what you have done. If there's anything else I can do . . ."

A nasty little smile showed at the corner of Abetz's mouth. "Come, I would like you to see what we do to these *Juden* . . . these lice."

Paulie hesitated. Abetz reassured him. "Don't worry, this one is in no condition to recognize anyone."

He exited his office, and with Paulie following they walked all the way down the dimly lit corridor to an office at the far end of the hall. It read HOMICIDE. Abetz opened the door and gestured Paulie to step inside. The room, which had a desk and filing cabinet, opened into another room that had no window and no furniture but a chair. Lying naked on the floor, his body twitching and covered with cigarette burns, was Nippo.

Paulie remembered once getting hit in a fight right in the solar plexus. He still could recall the exact sensation of the blow and all breath leaving him, knees turning to water, his legs crumpling. He fought to keep his composure and look unconcerned.

"He is stubborn," Abetz admitted. "But I don't think he can hold out much longer. You never can tell. Some of these Jews are quite stubborn, even courageous. This one is typical. He drove his own truck and led the ring. We caught him trying to get out and found this in his coat." He produced a newspaper inside which were wrapped three thick porterhouse steaks.

To cover, Paulie reached for a cigarette.

"Take them," Abetz said. "They will go well on your table. I am sure the frau and your children will find them quite delicious."

He closed the package and put it in Paulie's hand. "I want you to observe our methods."

Abetz lit a cigarette and leaned over near Nipponomick. "Good, you are awake. I must say you are a mess. Now if you will cooperate, you can put your clothes on. Have a cup of tea. There are others involved with you. We want their names. I can assure you that beyond going to a work camp, there will be no other punishment. You are criminals, not subversives." He grabbed Nippo by the hair to prevent his head from falling. "You understand, *ja*?"

Nippo groaned and then urinated on himself.

"Now," Abetz gutturally intoned, "who else is there to be picked up? Who else?"

Paulie felt his gut tighten. Poor fucking Nippo.

Abetz now took the cigarette from his mouth and murmured something to Nippo, who shook his head. Abetz took the lit end of the butt and jabbed it in Nippo's testicles.

Nippo writhed like a man given electric shock. His scream filled the little closet of a room. "Don't know nothing . . . you fuckin' scumbags . . . nothing . . . nothing . . ."

Abetz stood up. "Schroeder," he said, "continue."

Abetz led Paulie out of the room. "He is foolish, isn't he?"

Paulie was all sweaty. "Maybe he don't know nothing."

"Perhaps," Abetz agreed. "We shall find that out also. Well, he is of little consequence, this *juden* scum. We have pictures taken after the arrests. He has served his purpose. And you have done well. I am sure you will enjoy the steak this swine was taking home."

Paulie had turned and was about to leave when he heard Abetz's voice. "Come into my office for a moment, Schmidt."

Abetz led the way down the dingy corridor to his office and

went immediately to his desk. He sat down and made a casual show of going through papers while Paulie fidgeted uneasily. Finally Abetz looked up. *"Ein moment."*

Paulie felt the meat package as he squeezed it. Now he saw blood from the fine red meat trickle onto the floor.

Abetz chose that moment to look up. He saw the dripping meat but said nothing. "Sit down, Schmidt."

Paulie felt the beady eyes upon him as he took a chair.

"You know it is nice that you can bring home steak to your family, but once you have finished your dinner, what then? I mean for a man with certain skills, there is the chance to eat this way every night. You follow me, Schmidt?"

The question was, of course, rhetorical. He tossed some records toward Paulie. "You know, Schmidt, just to be on the safe side, we must always take precautions in my profession. I ran a check. These are two Schmidts, both of whom are in prison at the moment. Neither of them interest me. Do you know why? Because neither of them has ever killed a man. Such a man could be useful. Do you follow me, Schmidt?"

Paulie almost leaped to his feet. "I'm not sure."

Abetz nodded his head. "Have you been in prison, Schmidt?" Abetz paused. "Have you ever killed a man?"

Paulie didn't answer.

"I have high hopes for you, Schmidt. You have done invaluable work. And because I sense you have even greater talents, I will give you a chance to use them. If you do well, there are much greater rewards than steak." He paused for only the briefest instant. "This job is very important. It requires someone who can use a gun. Someone who can use it well. You know how well, I am sure. The person it is to be used on is a traitor. A German. He deserves to die. When he does, there will be quite a commotion. He is well protected, so it needs a professional's touch. His name is Beck. He is the gross kommandant of New York City."

Schmidt obviously didn't recognize the name, but neither did he blanch at Beck's title. Abetz was convinced he had the right man.

"The man who does this job will have my gratitude and my protection. Do you know such a man, Schmidt?"

Paulie shifted in his chair. "I might."

"Yes, I thought you might. Because of the delicate nature of this assignment, the man will be unknown to me or my office if he fails. However, if he succeeds, then, Schmidt, this man would be very well taken care of."

"How well?"

"He need only to ask. I am prepared to be generous. Shall we say five thousand dollars? And perhaps other jobs to come.

100

Is that a good offer, Schmidt? I think it is. Certainly, that louse on the floor, that *jüden* scum, would jump at it.''

Paulie cleared his throat. "It is a very good offer."

"I am pleased to hear you agree. Now in this envelope is a picture of this man and samples of his schedule. The man who does the job is to familiarize himself with it and then burn it. Of course, the choice of place and manner of execution I will leave up to him. That is all, Schmidt. I don't want to hear from you until it is over. And one thing more, Schmidt. Here is an ID card. It belongs to the prisoner you just saw. That is to be dropped on the ground or in some incriminating place near the body. Good evening, Schmidt, my regards to Frau Schmidt and the children. Enjoy your dinner. You earned it.''

Abetz waited until the door closed and then took a cigarette from his silver case. He lit it and luxuriously blew out some smoke. Abetz was sure he had made the right choice. Schmidt was an unpolished diamond. He was violent, and he was ambitious. He would do anything Abetz bid him to. Schmidt would not have a change of heart. Abetz held the power of a fingerprint check over him. One that could go on in any case. By the time Schmidt killed Beck, Abetz had no doubt he would know who Schmidt really was. Abetz was sure he would learn that Schmidt was a hardened criminal. Schmidt was a brute. Such men are useful at the right moment. Abetz had great faith in Schmidt. He would kill Beck, leader of the plotters against Hitler. The killing would be laid to the Jew, Nipponomick, who was being tortured inside. A new Reichstag fire would be lit.

Paulie walked to the BMT stop on Centre Street. He had picked up a contract from the Gestapo. The terms were very clear. Either get this General Beck or Abetz got Paulie's prison record. This was a very big job. As big as Paulie had ever had. He was all churning inside. The blame would be put on Nippo. Poor, fucking Nippo. Lying there in his cell with torched balls. Jesus, why did it have to turn out this way? Who figured Nippo to drive his own truck and run a meat operation? Nippo didn't have the brains for it. What the hell, you took your chances. He suddenly realized he was carrying the steaks Nippo had brought for him. He felt his stomach roll. Christ, he couldn't eat them. He saw a wastebasket and was about to drop the package in it but then stopped. Some Heinrich might find it and give it to Abetz. The little kraut knew everything. Paulie felt his nerve ends chill. If Abetz learned Paulie was a Jew, it was over. He walked on in the bitter cold night, trying to forget the image of Nippo lying naked on the floor having his cubes toasted by Abetz's cigarette.

101

He saw a sewer and crossed the street. Bending down over the grating he started to throw the steaks into the scummy water, but stopped. They would be down the tube just like Nippo was. Once Paulie nailed this Beck guy and dropped the ID card, Nippo would be the Judas goat. But what else could he do? Why was he always alone with big decisions that made his head ache? His head had ached ever since the day that big Jake Lazar rattled it against a radiator when he was ten. Ever since then he couldn't think straight. For some reason he couldn't throw the steaks away.

He lit a cigarette and walked to a building and leaned against it. Always alone. Since he was twelve and Jake had run out on Paulie and his grandmother. From then on he had to take care of himself. Lamebrained Paulie, pitching pennies, rolling kids for quarters, running errands for the cheap hoods who hung out on the street. Hustle, hustle. Christ, life was such a hustle. And all the worse because he was a yid. Christ killer. A descendant of those rabbis with their Abe Lincoln beards, and the Hasidim with their screwy Chinese pigtails. Always you had to prove yourself. That meant having a strong right arm and swaggering around like Paul Muni in *Scarface*. Mashing heads and faces came easy because they all became Jake Lazar to him. Jake Lazar, who used to wail the shit out of Paulie and then split before Paulie ever got his revenge.

He cupped the butt and felt his gut tighten. Nippo, I ain't no canary. But he was. He had to do it to make it. Why couldn't he get away from bein' everybody's strong arm? There had been a whole string of guys, but only old Barney Feldstein cared for him. He would clap Paulie on the head and kiss his forehead. He should have had an old man like Barney. Someone to take care of Paulie. But no, he had Jake. Jake who was mean. Now Paulie was mean. But he still wasn't anybody. Now he had a new boss, Abetz. Why was there always a boss over him? Christ, he couldn't think. He could still smell the steam of the old radiator Jake had mashed his head against. Why? Why? He was my old man. Why didn't I have no one to look out for me? To show me the way? Like a brother. Then I wouldn't have to think. It gives me a headache. If Jake hadn't busted my head that day, things might have been better.

Don't be a chump, he cautioned himself. Stop feeling sorry for yourself. Abetz is giving you a chance, take it. It's you or Nippo. Use Abetz until you don't need him. Collins also. Nobody cares, you got to look out for yourself. You got to get to the point where you give the orders and other people put it on the line for you. That's all there is. Nobody stands up for you in life, not your father or anybody else. So just play ball until you're in charge. Hell, that was it. It had to be. Somebody in heaven had given him Hughie and Nippo so he could make it. That was right, wasn't it? But he wasn't sure. He threw away the butt and, pulling up his collar, headed up the street.

He rode head down on the subway, trying to turn off the sound of the grinding wheels of the train and Nippo's searing lament: "Fucking scumbags . . . I don't know nothin'." Why did Abetz have to take him in the room and let him see Nippo screaming like that? If only he hadn't seen Nippo, he could live with what he had done.

He got off at Times Square and headed toward his apartment. An elderly man shuffled toward him with the help of a cane. He had white hair that stuck out from the sides and no hair on top. His long Jew's nose was red and dripping water at the end. "Please," he said, grasping at Paulie's sleeve. "Some gelt. So I can buy bread for myself and the little one." He pointed at a sad-eyed little boy seeking shelter from the snow under the awning of a vegetable stand with no vegetables to be seen. The boy was painfully thin. He was coughing.

Oh, Christ. "Leave me the fuck alone," Paulie said. "I got things on my mind."

"Just a little change."

Paulie thought of the bakery and the endless line. The old man would freeze to death before he got inside; the kid, too.

He suddenly realized he still had the steaks and pushed them on the old man.

"It's meat, take it."

The old man stared in disbelief as a river of mucus leaked from his nose. Suddenly he grabbed Paulie's hand and kissed it.

"Leave me the fuck alone," Paulie cried, and pulled away. He ran down the street.

AMERICAN PANORAMA
V

AMERICA MARCHES ON

NEWSREEL

VOICE OF ANNOUNCER: "Wartime America responds to the emergency. Los Angeles. Hollywood has taken on the full-time job of fighting the war. On dozens of lots and soundstages, Hollywood is busy recreating the perils of the Nazi and Japanese invasions. On this soundstage on the Warner Brothers lot, Errol Flynn is seen preparing a boat to row away an indigent family left stranded in their cabin by the Nazi invasion."

[IMAGE: ERROL FLYNN AND ROWBOAT FAMILY]

"On a lighter note, Hollywood has also become the capital of the parties and social functions designed to raise money for the war effort. Today, for example, we are attending a charity party for the war effort sponsored by Groucho Marx of the famous Marx Brothers comedy team."

[IMAGE: BEL AIR MANSION WITH GREEN LAWN AND MINGLING GUESTS]

"It seems all of Hollywood is here today. Oh, look, there's Deanna Durbin under the big flowery hat, and helping himself at the punch bowl is comedian Bob Hope. And look, there falling all over the croquet green are those grand cutups the Ritz Brothers."

[IMAGE: GROUCHO MARX WITH A CIGAR]

"And now here's our host Groucho Marx. What do you have to say, Groucho?"

GROUCHO: "Well, as you can see there are a lot of moochers in Hollywood. Yes, we are all here to do our part."

[IMAGE: CHICO MARX]

CHICO: "Did someone say part? I need a good part, bad."

SOUND: HONK, HONK

[IMAGE: HARPO MARX CHASING A CUTIE]

ANNOUNCER: "Well, some things never change."

TITLE: MAN OF THE MONTH

ANNOUNCER: "The man of the month for January is Isaac Pfister."

[IMAGE: TENT TOWN IN MOBILE, ALABAMA]

ANNOUNCER: "Here in this crowded wartime city, its streets bulging with newly arrived workers, with families packed into tents, chicken houses, and flimsy shelters, stands Isaac Pfister, a resident of Albany who escaped the German invasion dressed as, of all things, a Nazi. Isaac Pfister tells it in his own words."

[IMAGE: A THIN, INNOCUOUS LOOKING MIDDLE-AGED MAN IN A WEHRMACHT UNIFORM STANDING IN FRONT OF A TENT]

ISAAC PFISTER: "Well, it was this way. When the Germans came to Albany I was working in my job as a school janitor. I was hiding in the basement and I heard someone upstairs. Well, I went up there and found a Heinie using the toilet. As he was sitting down and in no position to defend himself, I clunked him in the head with a pail. Seeing as there was so many Heinies running around out there, I put on his uniform, gun and all. I went out in the street and they put me on a truck. Next thing I knew I was in New York City. They gives us all this funny money and told us to use it. We was quartered in some armory. Well sir, there wasn't much else to do but spend it. I ate like a king. Went to the best restaurants I could find. The waiters looked at me funny, but what could they say? It was just this crazy looking paper. All of us—I mean all the German soldiers—made funny jokes about it. We lit our cigarettes with it, wiped our—wiped our mouths with it, blew our noses into it. Well, pretty soon I figured I'd better escape, but I figured I needed real American money. By this time they had shipped me to Baltimore. So I got me my rifle, and went into this bank and said this is a stickup. Since I had my uniform on, wasn't nobody going to argue with me. Two women fainted, one of them wet her pants. . . . can I say that? Well, I got the money and stole a car and headed for West Virginia. Didn't nobody want anything to do with me there. Everybody run from me. I would go into a gas station and they just gave me free gas and wouldn't listen to me. Finally, I got to Ohio where I was arrested as a prisoner of war. Wouldn't nobody believe my story. Kept me locked up for a week. Treated me pretty miserable. Finally, some bright boy got the idea to write to the school and sure enough Principal Farley wrote back saying they had found a dead Heinie in the toilet with his pants down and no sign of janitor Pfister. Guess I hit him harder than I thought. Now I'm down here looking for a job. They tell me there's lots of work here in Mobile. I sure miss Albany though. Guess I'll get back there one of these days. Well, I'm real hungry now. They'll be serving down at the local place. Gotta go."

[IMAGE: ISAAC PFISTER WAVES]

ANNOUNCER: "America marches on."

Chapter 11

January 25, 1942
2:30 P.M.

The city had turned ugly. Collins could feel it in his bones just as surely as he felt the biting wind. He moved down Eleventh Avenue past the old battered buildings and the dilapidated junkyards, above the tracks of the New York Central Railroad, from which the endless freight trains poured soot and grime on the inhabitants of Hell's Kitchen. Death Avenue, they called it. It was where he had grown up. Learning how to fight on its streets. Playing in Schermerhorn Park, hanging around the slaughterhouse known as Abattoir Place, scrounging for scraps of meat that he could bring home. Going with his mother to Paddy's market under the Ninth Avenue elevated as she shopped for the family's weekly groceries, trying to squeeze the last bit from the scanty wages earned by his father on a tugboat. His father who finally threw it up and went back to Ireland to fight and die. Until he was ten, Collins attended services at the Bethany Church on Tenth Avenue. Then he began to find excuses and realized how weary his mother was of it all. She knew he was his father's son, Ireland would claim him. He moved past the Eighteenth Precinct station, its sour yellow bricks looking for all the world as if someone's guts had been spewed up on them. There, written in bold red letters, were the words MEIN NEW YORK. Next to it, somebody had scrawled in equally vivid red, MINE NEW YORK.

Up ahead he saw the magistrate's court, more widely known as men's night court. It was a gray stone building whose drabness seemed appropriate for the rummies, petty crooks, and muscle men it sentenced to prison. Collins saw the swastika jutting out from the front of the building. It was Gestapo now. They seemed to be the most flourishing organization in town. As each day the war of nerves escalated, as incident piled upon incident, the Gestapo found new headquarters. He carried the *Daily Mirror* under his arm. It described in vivid language the German officer pushed under the wheels of the Number 4 Lexington Avenue train at Grand Central Station. He lay on the tracks looking up at the frozen faces and stone marble eyes of commuters. There was no last minute rescue attempt, and the driver had made no effort to brake the train. The driver was a Negro named Sam Ward, and he was arrested by the police and turned over to the Gestapo, which was handling the investigation.

More provocation was needed. Enough and they would retaliate. When they do, it will be nasty. Now was the time to tighten the screws. To escalate the level of violence. The Huns have to be gutted. That was the phrase Donovan used last night. He had slipped into the city and met Collins at the safe house on 110th Street.

He had a special mission for Collins. He was to meet with General Beck, the German kommandant of Manhattan. Collins smiled bitterly. The first traitor. Beck, according to Donovan, had always opposed Hitler. He had been exiled to New York. Beck was part of the Black Orchestra, a group of highly placed Germans who opposed Hitler. This meeting would be the first of many between Collins and Beck. Information would be passed, plots hatched.

Donovan wanted Collins to pull off something big, and Collins had sent word that Kresky was setting up things at Curtiss-Wright. Now Donovan wanted a target date. Roosevelt needed results. Collins knew that. Curtiss-Wright had to go up soon, and he would see Kresky tonight. He had decided to give Paulie Lazar a retainer. Lazar was a cannon. But he had to be aimed in exactly the right direction. Sabotage was the name of the game now. Assassinations would come later. The German buildup had to be crippled.

The raw air filled him, and Collins shivered involuntarily. Christ, it was all happening so fast and not fast enough. He knew if he didn't pull off Curtiss-Wright, he would be replaced. There would be a succession of resistance leaders until one of them got it right. So get it right, boyo, get it right.

He cut along Fiftieth Street for the IND subway and the train ride to Long Island City. A limping man pushing a cart gimped toward him. As he came abreast of Collins, he spoke. "I got a couple of dogs left."

Collins eyes flickered. He was hungry. He looked down at the graying, limp franks. "How much?"

"Fifty cents a dog."

"Half a buck?"

The man set his lips like a store manager at Tiffany's who had valuable merchandise. There was no question of lowering the price. "It's meat. That's the name of the game."

Collins fished out fifty cents, and the man took a crumbling roll from a dirty cellophane wrapper and, using a battered spatula, spooned the limp gray dog onto the bun. He held it tight in his hand till he had the fifty cents.

The memory of other hungry days and a juicy frank set Collins's mouth salivating as he bit into the dog.

It was like swallowing a mortuary. "Jesus," Collins cried out. "What the hell is it?"

The vendor, a grimy little man with eyes that darted like flies on a carcass, looked unblinkingly at Collins. "Rat, my friend. And don't ask for your half buck back. There's people in this town would gulp it down lickety-split and reach into their pocket for another half a buck."

"You're selling shit," Collins yelled, and threw the dog to the ground.

"I imagine a rat shits just like you and me," the little man said. He pointed to the ground with something shiny and black. "But we made a sale, and you ain't getting your dough back."

Collins saw he was holding a long black knife with a curling point.

"Cut you open faster than a scythe on a bale of wheat," the ugly gremlin of a man said.

Collins turned and walked toward the subway. Abruptly, he stopped and looked back. The little man was bent over gathering up his little gray dog. Somebody else would eat it, no questions asked.

Collins stopped, looked at his watch and then for a cab. He wanted to get to Long Island City early enough to look around. Dublin, twenty years ago, had taught him about learning the terrain in advance. There were almost no cabs in sight; the ones that were had passengers wearing German uniforms. Prepared to give up, Collins suddenly spotted a red-painted cab, limping and sputtering toward him. It pulled up, choking and spitting gas fumes. Collins stood hesitantly next to it.

The cabbie leaned out. "Well, you want a ride or not?"

"I don't know. Can you get me to Long Island City in this thing?"

"Get in."

Collins checked his watch and decided to take a chance.

The car coughed and choked and finally limped off. Collins noted the driver's hack license. Joe T. Bone.

The hackie, a sharp nosed, balding man, threw his head back. "Don't worry. I'll get you there."

"What's this thing run on?"

Joe T. Bone laughed. "I got a secret formula. Bathtub gin and Kreml."

The car sputtered and veered crazily.

"Hair tonic?" Collins heard himself say.

"Sure. Don't knock it. Hell, a man has got to make a living. These are hard times."

They went over the Fifty-ninth Street Bridge, bouncing and wheezing. Joe T. Bone fished out a cigarette. "A man's got to be creative in these times. You have to adapt. Me, I don't pick up any Nazis. Know why?" He then proceeded to answer his own question. "Damn Fritzis are using scrip, you know, paper money to pay their fares. That's how they're bankruptin' Paris. So a few of the guys and me got together. We couldn't let this go on. They give us scrip and get back real American green. So we figured out a way to stop it. Now they give us scrip, we give them back Monopoly money."

They left the bridge behind and drove on beneath the subway overpass. Suddenly up ahead Collins could see a Nazi soldier waving at them. Behind him was an impatient officer standing beside a vehicle that had obviously broken down.

Collins started to tell Joe T. Bone to keep going, but Bone had already stopped.

"What are you doing?" Collins yelled. But Bone, with a bottle in his hand, had already gone outside. Collins could see him now feverishly pouring something into his tank.

Bone jumped back in and started the ignition.

"What the hell are you . . ."

"Just watch this," Bone called out.

The car bounced, groaned, and now jumped forward. The soldier was right in front of them. Bone veered past him and, as he did, the car gave off an incredible mushroom of smoke that enveloped the soldier. Bone was laughing furiously. They lurched past the officer, who looked at them in an amazed, indignant fashion until he too was swallowed up in a huge ball of smoke.

"That's our secret weapon," Bone called out. "It's the fucking Kreml. Mix it with homemade gin, and you could hide an army in the cloud. Jesus, I'd sell it to Washington if they weren't in Palm Springs."

Joe T. Bone rolled on, his cab emitting enough noxious vapor to fill a blimp.

The meeting was in an old junkyard off Ely Avenue in Long Island City. Collins stood amidst wrecked DeSotos, Fords, Buicks, and Pontiacs as the wind cut through him. Surrounded by broken windshields and caved-in hulks—tilted, tireless, running boards ripped loose, the insides gutted and lifeless. Oh, for a hot rum and the brick-topped streets of Dublin. A black car wheeled into the yard. A LaSalle, and it was new. It stopped and the driver got out and beckoned to Collins. He walked over to the driver, who had a Luger pointed at him.

There was a man in civilian clothes in the backseat. Collins advanced and said to the driver, "We met in Prague, or perhaps Warsaw."

The driver opened the door for him, and Collins stepped in and found himself seated next to Ludwig Beck, gross kommandant of New York City.

"You look like you could use a drink," Beck noted. His English was good. He handed Collins a silver flask. It was expensive. The brandy was even more expensive. Collins felt the warm run of his blood. Like a river freed from the ice during the first thaw of spring. He drank some more and then handed it back to Beck.

Beck, Collins noticed, was an imposing man, a man used to giving orders. He spoke softly, "Admiral Canaris, who heads the Abwehr, has joined us. He will furnish me with their intelligence reports. Whatever Canaris provides concerning Hitler's intentions, I will give to you for transmission to Donovan. Enough other information will flow down to me through our network to anticipate Hitler. As for those who serve me, they must not be jeopardized, so the passing of information will be done only through me. Should you be caught, the only one you can incriminate would be me."

Collins lit a cigarette. "I don't talk out of turn."

Beck accepted a light from Collins. "I'm sure you don't or Donovan wouldn't have chosen you, but the Gestapo can be persuasive. We should meet every two weeks. Abetz has me followed, so we must exercise caution."

"What about him?" Collins nodded in the direction of Beck's driver.

"Schreiner has been with me for nine years. He is a Communist who owes the safety of his family to me. He will drive me anywhere with no questions. He doesn't need to know anything else. He cannot tell about what he does not know."

"And what do you know?"

"Guderian is coming here to meet with Rommel. He planned to the last nuance the invasion of the United States."

"I want to know when he plans to arrive and his schedule."

Beck nodded. "If any major staff officer is assassinated, there will be terrible reprisals. Hundreds of hostages will be shot."

"Will Hitler come to New York?"

Beck stared off into the heaps of wreckage. "He has been to Paris once and to London. He is overjoyed at the success of his conquest of America." It was as though Beck read Collins's mind. "If he comes, there will be only one chance. We will need you then."

Collins filed it and moved on. "Have any agreements been signed with American corporations?"

"Yes. With oil and steel companies. I hope to have a list for you. The Reich's man has been Patrick Kelly, the former French ambassador. He is the conduit for Krupp and American business."

"Jump on the bandwagon," Collins said.

"Yes," Beck agreed. "Germany is in a very strong position now. Those who help will be taken care of in the future. It is the psychology of success."

"Kelly was sacked by Roosevelt. What does he want?"

Beck was thoughtful for a moment. "Power. But with him it is more. I met him at the official New Year's Eve party. He smells like a man who wants a title. He has an incredibly beautiful mistress."

"Who's that?"

"Her name is Lamont. Sylvie Lamont." Beck turned to Collins. "You don't take notes."

"I write in my head."

Beck had the flask in his hand, drank, and then offered it to Collins.

"What else?"

Beck let his cigarette fall to the floor. "Unless they see American victories, many business corporations will flock to Hitler. They will seek to position themselves to profit in the new order. By spring, the Luftwaffe will launch attacks on your Midwest. Guderian is a relentless planner and Rommel is a loaded gun. Each day the Japanese win new battles. War is a psychological chess match. Roosevelt must have a military victory to counter Hitler's seeming invincibility. Each new loss makes Hitler seem inevitable. And having seen your people up close, I do not know if they have the will to resist him. They do not seem up to it. Capitalism has corrupted them. Capitalism makes good workers, not warriors."

Collins listened to his own logic being used on him and felt angry.

"Hitler is frothing at the mouth to get at the Soviets," Beck continued. "Like Napoleon he finds the dream of conquering Russia irresistible."

Collins waved off the proffered flask. "For Hitler to attack Russia, he needs most of the million men he has here."

"If he conquers America, he will conscript an army to occupy it. That will free his combat divisions here. He already is doing it in England."

Collins, as he looked at the well-dressed military gentleman seated beside him, had to concede the chilling logic of it. In Beck's smile he saw irony laced with Teutonic arrogance. "We of the Black Orchestra are your only hope."

Collins flashed a bitter grin. "Mad dogs usually make fatal errors."

"I agree with your estimation," Beck replied. "In my view, Hitler will sacrifice by the millions the finest young blood of the fatherland in Russia. On the other hand, he has Guderian, the best strategist in the world, and he has Rommel, von Runstedt, and a score of generals at his disposal."

Collins now stared Beck in the eye. "General, I am sure you are familiar with the old dictum, kill the body and the head dies."

Beck was not fazed. "How many generals can you kill?"

Back in Dublin, Collins thought, we killed a lot of Brits. We even killed them in London. The trouble was there were always more to take their place.

Collins looked around at the gutted graveyard they were in. It was like a symbol of America. And yet it was inconceivable that, from all the rubble, something would not emerge. "Russia and America—that's a big mouthful even for a wolf like Hitler."

"In this I agree with you," Beck replied. "We fear Hitler's ambition will end with Germany destroyed. Put to the torch by a vengeful world."

Abruptly both men lapsed into silence.

"One other thing I should warn you about," Beck added. "That is Abetz. He acts for Himmler. They are aware of me. They know there are others. We must be very careful. Sometimes I think sending me here was more than a way of getting rid of me. I am thousands of miles from the fatherland. It would not be difficult to arrange some kind of scenario involving my assassination and blame your underground."

It was a scenario Collins knew very well. "Then you had better be careful."

"I am," Beck said. "But I will not live in fear of the assassin's bullet."

Collins could see the old general had no premonition of death. Mick had it. "I have signed my own death warrant," he said. But Mick fought that last ambush the way he lived. Without fear.

Beck glanced at his watch. "I must hurry back now. There is a cocktail party. Abetz would miss me." He offered Collins a last drink.

Collins took a swig and then closed it up. "The next meeting?"

"I ride in Central Park each morning. In two weeks' time on

the riding path near Seventy-second Street, I'll drop an envelope for you." He passed a piece of paper to Collins. "That is how it will be done. Memorize it."

He reached over and opened the door. The gesture was both polite and firm. The meeting was indeed over. Collins stepped out, and Beck's driver returned. Moments later the car left the junkyard. Collins leaned against a rusted heap and, grinding out his butt, played over Beck's words. Capitalism corrupts. It does not make good warriors. Well, the devil is here, Yanks. And if you don't have the stomach for it, he'll swallow you alive. Then he remembered something his father used to say about America. "Bobby, it's a strange place, money does the talking. But the people love freedom, and Jesus, would I love to see the scrap when someone tries to take it away.'

But somebody had already taken part of it away, and Collins didn't see the people out in the street demanding it back. No, and Hitler didn't plan to give it back. In that moment something tugged at Collins's brain. An unfinished portrait of torment and turmoil. Flashing eyes, mouths distorted by screams. Collins glimpsed their faces as his ancestors back in Dublin had. He saw it then lost it and stood alone in this graveyard of automobiles where he had conspired with a traitor.

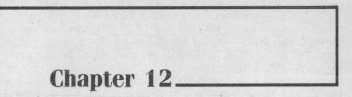

Chapter 12

January 25, 1942
7:00 P.M.

"Don't you see?" Radner was saying, his blue eyes gleaming with excitement at what he was pointing out. "Hamlet, for all his vaunted intellect, is a boy. That's why he is so jealous of his stepfather, Claudius, why he cannot understand his mother's need to remarry so quickly. He is violently jealous of Claudius. He has been recalled from school. What else could he be but nineteen or twenty? Hamlet is a genius but, like any genius who lacks maturity, he does not understand the world. He does not understand a woman's need for a man in her bed. It is written into all the lines of the play. His jesting with Horatio, with the courtiers Rosencrantz and Guildenstern. This is a young man's wit. This is a young man's shock over his mother's early remarriage.''

They sat, separated by a candle, in the Janet of France, a small, intimate French restaurant. Dinner had been oysters on the half shell, pheasant under glass, salad and a bottle of Dom Perignon, followed by a vintage Chateau Lafite-Rothschild. Now, over coffee, brandy, and peach tarts, Radner was elaborating on his vision of the Old Vic's *Hamlet*, which he was mounting in New York. Leila could not help but admire his insights, his ability to articulate ideas and point to how the play delineated those ideas. Looking at him in the flickering light thrown by the candle, backed by the room in warm shadows, orange lines of fire leaping in the fireplace, she felt herself letting go. It was impossible not to be drawn to him. He was so handsome, vital. But it was precisely because he was so attractive, she reminded herself, that he must be resisted. If it is easy, he will hold the whip hand. But within her came a mocking voice. You dine with him, how long before he expects you to sleep with him?

The struggle within her moved her to challenge him. "But in the scene with Yorick, the reference is to a clown he knew more than twenty years ago. Shakespeare did write it, you can't quarrel with that.''

Radner laughed; he was delighted. "Of course, Shakespeare wrote it. Or I should say, he rewrote it for Richard Burbage who was the great actor of his time and of Shakespeare's company. Burbage was too old to play Hamlet as a college youth. Something had to be done to make him seem older. So the grave digger, holding Yorick's skull, says he has been in the earth three and twenty years. It makes Hamlet seem older. There are few great actors who are nineteen or twenty, so that is why we see Hamlet played by older men. Someday, I will mount a production of *Romeo and Juliet* in which the parts are played by thirteen-year-olds. Don't you see how effective their suicides become then?''

He uses "I" more and more, she realized. He is enjoying his sense of power. It is as if he thinks he can make New York over with high culture. He wears his uniform less and less. If Colonel Manheim recovers, it will be a blow to his ego. He is falling in love with his new power.

"Well," he prompted, "what do you think?''

"Yes, then their suicides make sense.''

He studied her. Her beauty was so obvious. She wore a plain black dress with no makeup other than lipstick. Her natural beauty was in direct contrast to the jaded, bejeweled women accepting lights from their fleshy escorts all around them. He

114

reached for her hand and, for a moment, she let it stay there. Only when it remained did she withdraw.

At that moment they were approached by a tall, distinguished-looking officer with black and white hair. Radner stood up. "Please," Ludwig Beck said, "remain seated, Friedrich. Who, may I ask, is the lovely young lady?"

Radner remained standing. "Fay Brophy, may I present General Ludwig Beck, the gross kommandant of New York City."

"Hello."

"Charmed," Beck said, and kissed her hand. "Tell me, have you finished dinner? I thought if you had, you could join me for a drink at my suite. I must confess to being lonely in the evenings here."

Radner looked at Leila and then at their unfinished dessert. "There are still the tarts. . . ."

"Which you dearly love," Beck said, smiling.

Leila found herself laughing. Moreover she found herself fascinated by the tall, commanding figure of General Beck.

"Well," Radner replied, "I am not sure as to how long our discussion will take."

Beck put a hand on his shoulder. "A schnapps in my hotel suite at the Sherry Netherland, and then you will be on your way."

Radner looked at Leila.

"I'd love to," she said.

Beck clicked his heels. "Good. I shall look forward to it. Shall we say in an hour?"

"Our pleasure," Radner said.

"Miss Brophy." Beck took her hand again and then he was leaving, momentarily accompanied by Radner.

Leila's gaze swept around the circular, candlelit room. She noted the German officers and their women huddled in minute tableaux, the businessmen who came and went from New York City without any identity card problem. The expensive women who accompanied them, dressed in black stoles and evening dresses, laughing, gesturing, spooning caviar. This is how the wealthy, the privileged, the collaborators all live. Free from the fear and oppressiveness of occupied New York. They know none of our problems. They have no thought of rent or money. They eat well, sleep on satin sheets, drink real coffee in the morning, they have no problem getting meat. It is a room full of fascists and those who easily accommodate them. What, Leila Fox, daughter of Samuel and Sara Fox of Eastern Parkway, are you doing here?

She became angry at these pangs of conscience. Is it better to starve? To get thrown out of your room because you can't pay

115

the rent? I have the talent, I deserve the chance to make it. Some magical element of fate brought Radner to me. It would be sheer hypocrisy not to take advantage of it. But you are not Fay Brophy, and now the Gestapo is aware of you, the other contradictory voice within her sounded. Then that is the chance I must take. All this means is that I am willing to take risks to get that chance. If I don't have the talent, I won't make it no matter what name I use. Somebody will recognize you, the voice relentlessly accused. How? Leila Fox is anonymous. And Fay Brophy was a singer and bit player. The Germans won't be here forever. I'll say I took her name because I was Jewish. Beware, beware, the voice assailed her, you are glib, you know not what you do. She looked around the room and saw the haves, the rich, the cushy, the influential. She set her jaw resolutely. I am fighting my war, my way.

Radner returned and poured champagne for them, then put a black wallet on the table. "A toast," he said.

"To what?"

"Open it."

She looked at him and then reached out. She had a fleeting intuition as she did. Inside the small black wallet was an identity card in the name of Fay Brophy. Leila felt herself filled with jubilation and guilt at the same time. She started to thank him, but he held up his hand.

"Please, it was a small favor. No more. A toast," he said, smiling generously. "To Shakespeare and to the theater season."

They walked across the newly fallen snow in Central Park toward the East Side, the full moon being a melancholy observer of their nocturnal stroll.

Radner smelled her scent and fought the urge to encircle her waist with his arm, and Leila watched the prints made as their boots sank into the fresh snow. What if he makes a pass here? She felt him brush close to her and tensed.

"I spoke to you of Hamlet," he said, "because I have had an acceptance from John Gielgud to come here and play the part. He arrives tomorrow."

"How marvelous."

"Yes, I saw him play the role in London. His is the definitive portrayal. Eva Le Gallienne is coming to my . . . the office to discuss playing Gertrude."

They walked side by side, the record of their progress being preserved by the snow. Around them the bare trees watched, silent spectators to their minidrama.

She must ask to audition, he knew. But will she offer herself in return? He was intensely drawn to her, but if he slept with her now, it would be ruined. She must not be allowed to believe she could use him.

He stopped and turned in to face her. "You have performed Shakespeare?"

She looked up at him, her face radiant despite the cold. "Yes."

"Would you like to read for Ophelia?"

"I'm not sure," she said.

She's lying, he thought. Any actress would jump at the chance.

Suddenly she laughed. "Of course I want to. How could I not? To appear on Broadway with Gielgud and Eva Le Gallienne is a dream."

She was still smiling, and his hand moved to her waist. He had positioned himself in front of her. He hungered to kiss her.

Leila pointed to the sky. "That's what my mother used to call a midnight sky."

He looked up, and she deftly moved past him.

"Why midnight?"

"Because it is dark and full of omens that we cannot read."

"You are right," he said. "There is hardly a star visible."

He caught up to her and took her arm. "Here, this is yours." He handed her the identity card. He came closer to her. She did not move away. Will you sleep with me for this? he wondered.

Will I lie in his bed for this, she thought.

He spoke softly to her. "Come to my apartment for a nightcap."

She stared at him, her hazel eyes golden and luminous. His head started to dip down, but then she was pushing past him. "I can't. I have to prepare an audition."

He felt a mixture of disappointment and relief. "What audition?"

She whirled and smiled mischievously. "For Ophelia."

He caught up to her. "You can begin tomorrow, but you shall have to earn the part. There will be competition."

She stopped, and now he saw the fire in her. "I shall earn it."

He saw the set of her chin and the fierceness in her. He smiled as he took her arm. "I think we shall come to know each other."

They walked now in silence, the only sound a cracking twig as their boots crunched the snow. A night wind caught the bare trees and shook them. Both of them felt it, shivering with anticipation, their minds pregnant with possibility and anticipation.

She felt his arm again. If I kiss him, all is lost, she thought. It was, she knew, a game within a game. If I sleep with him, then I am a conquest, nothing more.

It cannot be at the price of losing her, he thought. Nor shall

117

I stoop to making her career a condition of what develops. I shall not fulfill her expectation of the conquering womanizer. I shall not allow her to give herself and by doing so remove any possibility of what is between us growing properly. Like all passionate women, and they are the only ones worth having, she must not be allowed to deny her nature or to demean the possibility of love. For that is what we are meant to have.

They walked on in silence, his arm in hers, no words being spoken. Only thoughts and images fused with the hues of their struggle to light their way on the pilgrimage they had begun.

Beck's apartment in the Sherry Netherland was a living room and bedroom that overlooked Central Park. The room was bathed in a subdued light that reminded Radner of a theatrical set. It was managed light. The soft brown bench on which he sat was half in shadow; Beck was in a chair across from him, only the fine features and imperial countenance visible. Behind Radner was the soft light from a table lamp. If I were a member of the audience and yet did not know what play I had come to attend, I should guess a political drama. The room seems to hold dark truths and meanings elusive as a flitting butterfly. Fay had discreetly left them to powder her nose. Beck sipped his cognac; his long legs were stretched out before him. He had unbuttoned his tunic, and his eyes seemed to burn into the rug at his feet. What does he see there? Radner wondered.

"The girl is quite beautiful. You said her name was Brophy. Irish?"

"Yes."

Beck reached for the decanter on the table next to him. "More brandy?"

"Not for the moment."

Beck replaced the decanter. "You know you will bring yourself to the attention of Himmler through Abetz if you use controversial artists."

"Bitte?"

Beck sipped from his glass. "Will you allow Jewish artists to perform?"

"I see nothing wrong with that, but I will use Paris as my guide."

"Perhaps. But this is New York. The Jews dominate the arts."

"I am prepared for that." Radner drank the brandy to hide his anger.

Beck's mouth twisted down, though Radner could not see that. "There are table stakes in a poker game which often carry more weight than is apparent to the eye. Things as they are now in New York are not what they appear. Only after some time will the true weight of these stakes become clear.'' He paused, but clearly not because he expected an answer from Radner. ''Many of us here in New York fear for the future of the Reich. There are hidden fires here. America is not Poland or even England. Simmering fires. I have learned, Friedrich, that those kinds of flames are not easily put out once they erupt.''

''For my part I shall carry a fire extinguisher,'' Radner replied.

Beck chuckled. ''I have heard men in your position say the same thing. They laugh right up to the moment they feel the fire scorch their skin.''

''May I have more brandy?'' Radner asked.

Beck took the decanter and poured brandy into Radner's glass.

''I was young myself once, though it seems centuries ago, and I understand how a young man feels. You are a man of the world, Friedrich, but I also feel you must not let your devotion to the temple of art cloud your judgment. Art is not exempt from politics.''

Leila reentered the room. Beck stood up. ''It is a most marvelous bathroom, is it not?''

''Yes,'' she said. ''The marble is exquisite.''

Beck poured her some brandy, and Leila sat in a soft rose chair, whose color dipped into the room's shadows.

''I was just telling Friedrich that art is not exempt from politics.''

''Art at its best reflects politics,'' Leila observed.

''Yes, yes,'' Beck agreed. ''Nicely phrased. In fact, I think that politics is the theater of life. Yes, I like that phrase also. We have right here in New York a rather unique play with a most interesting cast of characters. Wouldn't you say that, Friedrich?''

Radner moved his fingers around the smooth edge of the brandy snifter. ''Perhaps.''

''And you, Miss Brophy, what is your observation?''

''I don't think I know them so well as to say.''

Beck laughed. ''A fine, political answer. But, of course, you cannot know. Friedrich here does not want to know. I suppose one is permitted that luxury in the world of art. But I, as kommandant, have access to the wireless, to the meetings, to the little schemes and dreams of all the men on the chessboard, so to speak. It is also, I realize, unfair to assess these men as being idle dreamers. After all, we have conquered New York, and where do we go from here? Do we pursue your government, Miss Brophy, or reach some accommodation?''

''I wasn't aware,'' Leila responded, ''that your government wanted peace.''

119

Beck held up his glass in a mock toast. "Nor am I." He smiled bitterly. "Perhaps the Führer will apprise me of his plans."

Leila tasted the brandy on her tongue. What did this strange man want? He spoke in half twists and turns, conjuring up images of political deeds as if he were a chess player assessing many variations on the next move.

Beck pointed out the window. "A lovely place, Central Park. I ride there every morning. It gives a lonely old man great pleasure." He suddenly turned to Leila. "Do you ride?"

"I used to."

He smiled. "Excellent. Friedrich, you must let me usurp some of your time with Miss Brophy. You will be my guest. Soon."

"Of course," Radner murmured.

"I'd like that," Leila said. "But I will be very busy. I plan to audition for a play."

"Yes?"

Hamlet."

Beck turned to Radner.

"John Gielgud has agreed to appear."

"Splendid. I await the opening with great anticipation. You will be my guests at dinner. That is a command, Friedrich."

"It would be an honor."

"Now, I have taken enough of your time. You are young, for you the night holds mystery and the unexpected. For me, it holds only sleep."

He turned and kissed Leila's hand. "You see my back is already quite stiff. I am old."

"On the contrary," Leila said, "I suspect your dreams are full of exciting mysteries."

Beck laughed. "Well, we old men must have our dreams. We shall discuss that sometime." He led them to the door. "Friedrich, you have made an old general feel he is less alone three thousand miles from the fatherland. Many thanks."

They shook hands. Beck turned once more to Leila. "Miss Brophy, a great pleasure. Until we meet again. I will need your number. And you, Friedrich, are you installed in your new apartment?"

"It will be ready next week. At the Hotel des Artistes."

"Good night," Beck said.

They rode the elevator in silence and walked through the lobby where a group of officers were checking in.

They walked on Fifth for some minutes. Leila broke the silence. "He has a strange magnetism. He is like an O'Neill drama. There is a darkness to him that is fascinating, and you want to know what's there although you know it will not be pretty.''

"Yes," Radner said abstractly.

"Who is he?"

"He was formerly Chief of Staff."

"He retired?"

"In a manner of speaking."

Leila's voice had a little more edge than usual. "What happened?"

"He was suspected of opposing the Führer. It could not be proved, but it was known."

"Known?"

"There are ways of knowing these things."

"Do you believe it?"

"Perhaps."

"And now?"

"I don't know."

"What can he do here?"

"Nothing. Hitler is three thousand miles away."

"He seemed to want something from you . . . he seemed to even want it from me. I distinctly felt that. What could he want from you, Friedrich?"

He heard her use his first name for the first time, and it thrilled him. Say it again, he commanded within himself.

"What could it be?" she repeated.

"I don't know."

AMERICAN PANORAMA VI

TIME MARCHES ON

January 25, 1942

Announcer: "Americans across the country respond to the war effort. In San Francisco (Image: Golden Gate Bridge) Yankee star outfielder Joltin' Joe DiMaggio leaves the army induction center at the Presidio. (Image: Joe DiMaggio in army uniform) The Yankee Clipper smiles and waves for the camera."

(Image: New York City at night) Announcer: "In these bootleg films smuggled out of New York City, we can see the Great White Way blacking out at eleven o'clock prior to curfew. Not like the old days. (Image: Lindy's) There's Lindy's, the famous old restaurant now serving its cheesecake and coffee to the German officers and their escorts we see going in. The Stork Club is open and so is Twenty-one, but the most going attraction in wartime, occupied New York is the strip joints. Business is booming says Sally Adams, better known as Fan Tan Sally."

(Image: Tall blonde in white coat) Sally: "I guess we caught on when the Broadway shows had their strike. Germans had to spend their money somewhere. They all come. Officers and privates. Guess they just like to see them feathers come off."

Announcer: "There're new wrinkles also in New York. (Image: Young housewife before microphone) Meet Virginia Schaefer, dubbed German Ginny by American listeners. Each morning and each night she plays songs about home and tells America to give up the war. In this film interview smuggled out of occupied New York, housewife Virginia Schaefer was asked about her nickname."

Ginny: "No, I don't mind being called German Ginny. I'm German and proud of it. I play songs for the boys, tell them to give up the war, Germany wants a truce, they don't want the whole country. Heck, if you can't beat them, join them."

Announcer: "Time Marches On."

Chapter 13

January 26, 1942
6:00 P.M.

Kresky had been up since six o'clock. After he had shaved and dressed, he'd sat waiting at the Port Authority until it was time to board the bus for Paterson, New Jersey. Kresky knew Paterson well. He had participated in a strike led by Big Bill Haywood there back in the teens. It was a workers' town, a leftist town with a long tradition of protest still alive in its ramshackle houses and workers' bars.

Today he was going to Paterson as Ivan Potensky. Kresky fingered the smudged gray-green–bordered identity card Eugene

Lepentier had fashioned for him. Lepentier, an actor with the Yiddish Theater, had a rather piquant background. Raised by criminals in France until he discovered the theater, he was an expert pickpocket and forger. Kresky had put him in charge of forging papers, not only for him but for several others who were to infiltrate Curtiss-Wright. Lepentier had chosen for Kresky the name and identity of a seaman now at rest in a graveyard in Hoboken. Lepentier not only chose actual names for his forged papers, he also researched their backgrounds. "Dead people have a history," he would retort to anyone who questioned his use of the deceased's name. "That makes it legitimate." He loved the word legitimate.

Kresky went over the plan again. Once he got the job at Curtiss-Wright, he would take a room there and go about the business of learning the layout of the plant—its nooks and corners, who of the men hired were soft on espionage, and who needed the work so badly they would inform on fellow Americans. Which of the guards were vigilant, which of them liked their schnapps and beer, which of them could be bribed, and which were placed there by the Gestapo. It had to be done just right, quickly, and with as much knowledge as possible of the running of this plant so vital to the Nazi hopes of bombing America. Curtiss-Wright was the main testing area for engines built on the East Coast. If the engines worked there they were sent to be fitted into Messerschmitts, Heinkels, and Stukas that would bomb and strafe Chicago, Detroit, Cleveland, and other American industrial centers. Collins and Kresky were in complete agreement that the plant was their major target.

Kresky studied the faces of the men on the bus. They were not union. The word had come down from Bill Green and Philip Murray that the AF of L and the CIO would not have one man contributing to the Nazi war effort in America. Their word was backed by fists and steel pipes. But the mailed fist of the union wasn't enough to deter the men on this bus. Men who had lived through the awful years of the Depression. Standing on soup lines, sleeping in flops, watching their families turned out of their houses, having furniture and possessions hauled off. Hunger was a thing you could see etched in a man's face. You could see it there even after he'd had a meal. It was the tight lines around the mouth, the sallow cheeks, the eyes, both hard and pained in the same instant. Years of hunger and deprivation had done that. Sure, there was a war on. Sure, there were foreign troops on American soil. But mouths had to be fed, babies still cried at night for milk, children needed shoes and twenty cents to go to the flickers, your woman craved a new dress every few years, maybe a night out for dinner. What was the point of living in the land of the free and the home of the brave if you couldn't be either? You were free to starve and be homeless. What these men were going to do today was terrible, Kresky thought, but he could understand it. They were helping the enemies of this country perpetuate themselves, and that must not be allowed. Yet he knew that for a lot of them it was simply a job and a means to live. There was loyalty to family that for many of these men came before loyalty to country. It came before loyalty to Washington, which went about its business while these men counted the years in hard lines on their faces and in the eyes of children who knew despair too early.

They got off the bus and trudged along a cobblestone street that led to a school yard where they were to undergo a final papers check. They were led into a tiny bandbox of a gym and told to stand in line by one of the Nazi guards. The place was old and musty. At either end of the gym were baskets without nets. It reminded Kresky of a gym in Queens where he had seen the original Celtics play. You had to score a lay-up—the ceiling was too low to allow for a set shot.

The men stood in line, some smoking, others looking at the floor, some read papers or paperback books. No one talked. They knew who they were. Scabs. The hated name. Men who were willing to do union workers out of a job. The lowest of the low. Even lower, for your boss was the Nazis. But there was the promise of money. That was better than hanging out on a street corner mumbling "Brother, can you spare a dime?" When you starve, you have no brother.

Kresky waited forty-five minutes before he got to the little desk at which was seated a German sergeant and an American in civilian clothes. He had a sharp face with pinched eyes and a tiny mustache. He would be someone with a long record of strike breaking. Perhaps an ex-Pinkerton or railroad dick. He would be looking for troublemakers. Men who might be infiltrating the ranks of the workers to sow dissent. He would have a photo file on hand if he got suspicious. This one was a pro. He would ask certain questions, and if the answers weren't right, you would be detained or asked to leave.

The sergeant read his identity card and thumbed through some lists looking for the name of Ivan Potensky. It was, of course, not there. It was too early for the Nazis to be on to the graveyard gimmick, but eventually they would. He handed the card to the mustached man, who stared at it with a cigarette dangling from the corner of his mouth.

"Potensky, huh. Polack?"

"Yeah," Kresky grunted.

The little man eyed Kresky, trying to make him feel uncomfortable. If the guy was from around the East, Kresky had a good chance to be spotted. But this guy might have been doing his railroad dicking out west. A lot of dicks didn't like to work close to home. Certainly, no one would be expecting Harold Kresky, former Communist and union organizer, to be applying for scab work building Nazi planes. Not the Kresky who opposed the Hitler-Stalin pact.

"So where you worked, Potensky?"

"Mostly sea," Kresky answered.

"Let's see your seaman's card."

Kresky reached into his pocket and produced the dummy seaman's card Eugene Lepentier had made.

The little dick studied it, then looked at his identity card again. "Why do you want this kind of work?"

"Need money."

"What kind of plant work you done?"

"None."

"Know anything about planes?"

"No."

"Where did you hear about hiring?"

"Couple of fellows in a bar."

"What do you think of the Germans?"

Kresky remained impassive. "Don't know much. See some of them around. Never talked to one."

"Do you like them?"

Kresky shrugged. "Don't know. Don't like, don't not like. Don't know anyone."

He held the seaman's card out to Kresky. "This says you're in the maritime union. Why don't they find you work?"

Kresky held out plaintive hands. "No ships sail Iceland, Alaska. All sailors out of work. I gotta eat, pay bills."

"You got a family?"

"No wife. Got mother. She sick. Bills, doctors, hospital."

The little mustached dick now whispered into the sergeant's ear. They conversed for a minute, ignoring Kresky. It was a game to make him uncomfortable. Now the dick looked at him.

"How bad you need the job?"

"Bad."

He shook Kresky's maritime card. "You're in the union, but now you're a scab. What's a scab?"

"A scab is a son of a bitch."

"So, what are you?"

"Me, son of a bitch, too."

The little weasel now stood up and spoke into Kresky's face. His breath was a mixture of whiskey, cigarettes, and halitosis. "You know what you'll find out there at the end of the block?

A narrow street with union people on it. They're protesting. And you know what? You got to walk past them. We'll have guards there, but you're still going to have to walk past them. They'll see your face, they'll spit in it. Maybe somebody will recognize you and call out your name. People will throw rocks, bottles; if it hits you, tough. Maybe they'll see you and get you in town tomorrow or the next night, or the next. We offer no protection. You still want to go?''

Kresky made himself count to ten before answering. "What's pay?"

The man's foul breath was in his face. "Forty bucks a week."

"Not much."

"Next."

He had turned away. It was time for Kresky to humble himself. He put a hand on the little man's shoulder. "Please, mister. I take. Please."

The man waited until Kresky said please a third time, then he returned. "That's better. Okay, Potensky, you got a chance to walk the gauntlet. If you can make it to the bus, you start work this afternoon." He handed the card back to the sergeant, who was busy wolfing down a large cherry danish and coffee. They copied his name down, and Kresky heard the little dick say something about politics.

They came out of the gym and onto the street, Kresky and the fourteen other men who would be the first to walk the gauntlet. It was a gray day with the kind of clinging cold you didn't feel right away. The kind that laid its clammy hand on you and squeezed muscle, nerve, and bone. He tried not to look up the street at the faces on both sides of it. He read his watch: eleven-thirty. Just a five minute walk, and they would be at the buses waiting on the football field. *"Mach schnell,"* a guard barked out. The scabs began to move in single file. Don't look up, he told himself; if somebody recognizes you, you'll be in prison tonight. "You fucking scabs," a raspy voice yelled out. The word cut through Kresky like a knife. Scab, the word he had fought against all his life. The tool of the bosses. Turn men against men. Break the union. Club the strikers and bring in scabs. Let them bleed and starve and see how long they'll hold out with their children starving. "Pussy scabs . . . rotten scab bastards . . . there'll be broken heads tonight . . . we got your names and addresses . . . we'll get your wife and put one in her oven." Kresky desperately wanted to look up at the faces calling out. They were, after all, his people. Men he had fought for, gone to work with, comforted after a beating, gone to union halls to raise money for when they were on hard times. Instead, he hunched up his collar and kept his face down in his walk of shame. Scab shame. "You have to go home at night . . . we got your names . . . we'll be right behind you." Suddenly a man darted out of the pack on the sidewalk and kicked the spindly old man in front of Kresky in the rib cage. He screamed out in pain and then fell. His hands grasped at his ribs, and he tried to crawl. Kresky felt his insides yank down hard. Yet he could do nothing but step over the fallen man. He was on a mission. A bottle shattered somewhere near him. Now a rock was thrown . . . and another . . . and another—the last one hitting the face and smashing the glasses of a little blond man in a brown overcoat and torn brown shoes. Kresky had seen him on the bus, a rabbitlike face with shoes so torn in the front that the socks were visible. Now Kresky passed him, and he gave Kresky a helpless look. If the little man didn't move soon, the crowd would descend on him. He snatched up the broken spectacles and fell back into line.

They kept moving in a slow, steady single file, these fifteen fugitives accepting work from the Nazis. More rocks and bricks pelted down. Bottles smashed, men on both sides of the street shook their fists. The German guards watched it all with no expression. They had their instructions. Let the scabs know that this is what they would have to endure. Just don't let it get out of hand. Now a union man, carrying a hammer, started out of the crowd. Quickly a guard called to another Wehrmacht soldier, and the combat veteran of the American campaign swiftly smashed the union man in the face with the butt of his rifle. He fell, his face a bloody mask. *"Schnell,"* the guards cried out. Kresky took a quick, nervous look ahead. Maybe thirty yards to the buses and then it'll be okay . . . he heard someone come up alongside of him, and then a bull-like fist smashed into the side of his head. He stumbled and saw exploding stars. Don't fall, he told himself, and don't look . . . don't look. His knees buckled, but somehow he stayed on his feet. "You dirty Nazi scab," the attacker chanted at him. His head pounding, he kept walking. He couldn't see clearly yet, but in just a few minutes . . . his feet touched the grass. He shook his head, and there up ahead were the dirty orange buses. The scab buses.

AMERICAN PANORAMA
VII

NAZI DAYS

January 28,1942

VIRGINIA SCHAEFER RADIO SHOW OF
AMERICAN APOCALYPSE CAUSES MASS PANIC
New York City Discovers New Star

by Hubert Kleinsdorf
Daily Patrician Drama Critic

Meet German America's answer to Orson Welles. She's Virginia Schaefer, a housewife who lives in Yorkville in Manhattan. Mrs. Schaefer is the mother of two children and the wife of Bund official Charles Schaefer. She has become known to millions of Americans as German Ginny via her broadcasts over radio station WGER, originating in New York, which shocked America with a script Mrs. Schaefer admits she borrowed from Orson Welles.

Switchboards were lit up from New York to Nevada, from Cleveland to Los Angeles. The Palm Springs White House was deluged with calls, and the American government had to issue an official denial that still did not dispel the rumors that Franklin Roosevelt was dead. The president had to make a special appearance on the radio the next day to prove he was still alive and reiterate that the Japanese had, in fact, not landed on the West Coast. The president called it a hideous trick. Nonsense. Virginia Schaefer is living proof of the ingenuity, talent, creativity, and spark in German-occupied America. She is our newest star. Her mail from Americans across the country is now over two hundred letters in one month. Her historic broadcast began at nine o'clock on January 25 when the excited, emotion-packed voice of a news announcer broke into programmed music to announce Franklin Roosevelt had died. This was followed by remarkably realistic reports of a Japanese invasion on the West Coast. Explosives were heard going off; screams and bombs followed. In Los Angeles, military and police installations were bombarded with calls. With the report of Japanese tanks on the Los Angeles freeway, traffic on the freeway backed up and stalled for ten miles. At least three suicides were reported in Los Angeles. Meanwhile, in San Francisco, air force planes took to the air flying along the Monterey peninsula, desperate for a sight of the Japanese. Air raid sirens sounded throughout the city. People ran to air raid shelters. Hours later, the city, which had come to a stop, was deserted. Cars were packed along the coast road leading out of San Francisco. Not even Orson Welles and his legendary Martians have ever had the effect caused by Ginny Schaefer's incredible broadcast. Telephone lines across the country were tied up for six hours. Scenes similar to the San Francisco evacuation took place in Phoenix, Seattle, Portland, and Sacramento.

Interviewed at her apartment in New York City, Ginny Schaefer had this to say: "I didn't mean to have people kill themselves, but I think Americans need a real scare. This is no game, you know, it's war. Sure, I might try it again. That's the trick of it. It's like the boy who cried wolf. Next time it might be for real."

Chapter 14

January 29, 1942
2:30 P.M.

Leila saw the light on the stage and only the light. The flowers she gripped so fiercely she had no sense or feeling of. She had entered into the dark world of Ophelia's madness and had lived intensely there for three days, shunning all contact with the world and its petty reality, ignoring the notes left under the door, the mail from Fay's parents undoubtedly pleading for some word of their daughter, ignoring the need to earn money, eating the same meals each day. Coffee and a roll in the morning, soup and bread for lunch, stew with whatever they put into it at the Automat at night. Ignoring Radner's calls and saying Ophelia's lines—"How should I your true love know, from another one? By his cockle hat and staff, and his sandal shoon"—over and over into the darkness of her tiny room.

A voice called, "We're ready for you, Miss Brophy."

The voice was like a prod, the words a command. She saw the light on the stage of the Alvin and in it Gielgud, and then next to him a place for her. She walked slowly toward it, the light, white hot, beckoning her. Closer and closer, feeling its presence, blinded by its iridescence. Then she was there, feeling it bathe her, a place in the sun.

A voice spoke to her. "Why, 'tis fair Ophelia."

She scattered some petals and began to speak.

7:15 P.M.

Buffet tables full of caviar, smoked salmon, whitefish, pâté, great hunks of French bread, Virginia and Wesphalian ham to go on it, green noodles with sauce, imported beers, champagne. All of it in gaudy array and seductively displayed in the Hotel des Artistes apartment of Colonel Manheim. It was as if Leila had never eaten in her life. She ate the caviar on delicate crackers, the smoked salmon and whitefish from a gold and green plate, slapped slabs of Virginia ham on French bread smothered in mustard, drank two bottles of beer, and then put leaves of green salad on the green and gold plate.

As she came up for air, she saw the room for the first time. It was not the room that Radner had greeted her in that first time she had come to see him. It seemed to be an adjoining room out of which everything had been cleared. Long tables were joined together to form a square. The floors were bare but exquisitely polished, reflecting the gleaming lights placed at vertical angles in the room. The light above from the chandelier had been dimmed, giving the room an appearance of casual elegance. Uniformed waiters stood next to the iced beer and champagne. There was a bar in the next room. That, Leila saw as she walked toward it, was the room he had greeted her in.

"Champagne?" She turned to the blond, curly haired waiter and said, "Thank you." Now, as he extended the tray, their eyes met. Recognition flickered there and, quickly grasping the glass, she turned away. Who was he? They had been in a play somewhere or taken a class together. She walked away.

She melted into the crowd of people. Some she recognized. Cole Porter was there, and next to him a bearded Monte Woolley. Larry Hart, whom she had once waited on as a hatcheck girl at the Harlequin Club. There was Ponselle, the Met soprano fresh from La Scala, Le Gallienne, Cornelia Otis Skinner, and Nazimova, whom Leila had thrilled to in *The Mother*. How many

130

times had she gone back to see it? Others seemed important. A play agent named Audrey, an investor named Alex, a spectacularly jeweled woman whom men gushed over and called Celeste.

She drifted over to the living room and now there was a flurry in the foyer and cries of "Gielgud, Gielgud" behind her. The great English actor swept in and was surrounded by an entourage of admirers. There were the usual greetings—"Darlings," "You look marvelous"—and then he was moving in her general direction, having spotted someone he knew.

Leila turned, trying to move out of his path, but he kept right for her. How embarrassing, she thought. He'll think I'm trying to get in his . . .

"My dear, I didn't have a chance to tell you how superb you were this afternoon." He stood in front of her, tall with gentle eyes and those wonderful cheekbones. The words dripped from his tongue. "Truly, you were a marvelous Ophelia."

He kissed her hand, and only then did she realize she still hadn't spoken.

"Thank you. It means so much coming from you. I'm just grateful I had the chance to read with you."

He smiled. "We shall read many times together."

What was he saying?

Then he was swept away by a bevy of admirers. Leila turned to watch him, swallowed in love and adoration. She found herself staring into the face of a bearded man with dark bemused eyes.

"It is quite an event, this party, full of little and not-so-little events, hey?"

He spoke English well, but there was no mistaking his French accent. He laughed. "Your pardon, I have not introduced myself. I am Serge Bernard, and I am here at the invitation of Colonel Manheim. And you are . . ."

"Lei—Fay Brophy."

He kissed her hand. *"Enchanté.* Would you like some champagne?" Before she could respond, he had taken her arm and was guiding her to the bar in the living room. It was dark and terribly intimate in the room. He gave her a glass and gestured back to the other room. "It is terribly exciting, but noisy. One must have a respite." He held up his glass. "To your beauty. You are breathtaking."

"Thank you."

He set the glass down on the piano and lit a cigarette he had taken from a gold case. "Yes, this party is formidable. Radner will win over New York. He has a great future in front of him."

"You think so?"

"But of course. He settled this actors' strike of yours. That is only the beginning. New York will accommodate itself to the

131

Nazis as Paris has. Yes, you see I have no trouble saying Nazis. They are a fact of life. One either rises with them or disappears without them. Yes, Radner shall rise. They tell me Manheim will not come out of the hospital alive. A pity. A great patron of the arts, a bon vivant in the truest sense."

He looked at her sharply. "Tell me, what do you think of the philosophy of accommodation?"

"You shouldn't say it too loudly in the streets?"

He laughed. "That is wonderful. But who lives in the streets but those who have disappeared? For we artists, there is the life of the senses, no? Do you know what Cocteau faced when the Nazis came to Paris? His greatest problem was wondering where he would get his opium. Of course, he obtained it. He knows that art and artists outlast wars. We are culture. Above wars and business and all those other cycles of change."

"Don't we have something to do with change?"

"But, of course. That's what makes us unique. Those of us who are superior . . . who have the wits . . . the talent . . . the imagination . . . we are challenged to succeed. And we do. Shall I tell you what made me notice you? Not your beauty, but the way you ate. My God, I think I counted four pâtés, two orders of fish, endless caviar and ham. Such an appetite."

She fought her embarrassment. "That was plain and simple hunger."

"Of course it was. And you will succeed. Your appetite for life will not be dulled by politics. Ah, our host."

Leila turned and saw Radner enter, throwing off his black coat, a scarf worn dashingly about his neck. Now Serge Bernard approached and embraced him.

"So, how is Paris?"

"Corrupt, but flourishing. How is New York?"

"Cold. How are you?"

"Warm and cozy."

Leila turned and walked back to the buffet room where people pressed in against each other, perfume and scent swirling in the air, snatches of conversation in German, French, and English assaulting the ear.

"Paris is marvelous. Never been so gay."

"The season is better than I thought. Barrault directs. Claudel and Giraudoux have new plays. Sartre now writes for the theater."

"Well, I hear Thornton Wilder has a new play."

"It's marvelous. I can't understand half of it. You must show it to Radner, Audrey."

"Between us, *mon ami*, I tell you the Germans create the

black market, drive up prices, and then use the gangsters to sell for them. That way both get rich."

"Don't bore me with politics. Tell me about the parties, the scandals."

"Don't you want to hear about the Jewish problem?"

"Please, there is always a Jewish problem."

"Incredible. No yellow stars here. In Paris we have marked them. We know who they are."

"This de Gaulle of yours is a *schweinhund*."

"He is worse, *mon ami*. A terrible opportunist. Not a drop of royal blood in him. He is hiding somewhere in Morocco."

More conversation, innuendos, hidden meanings, fawning gossip by well-fed, sleek, beautiful people. Now a commotion, heads swiveling, people gaping, little whispers and exclamations.

"Rubirosa and Danielle Darrieux."

"My God, she is stunning."

"Never mind her, darling, look at him. *Ravissant*."

"He could ravish me anytime he wants."

She had to break away; it was all too much. She moved through the room and found her way, finally, into the study, which was dimly lit with a table and couch. She saw a staircase. It was a duplex. Now she climbed the carpeted steps and bumped into a man. It was Gielgud. Her apology faded and froze.

"It's you. How wonderful. We didn't have a chance to finish our conversation."

"Please," Leila said. "I just wanted to say how much this afternoon's audition meant to me. I shall come and see your performance every night."

He laughed, the handsome features crinkling, his eyes alive with mischief. "Indeed, you shall see me every night. And we shall read again and again."

Her eyes flashed. "What do you mean?"

Gielgud laughed. "It is not for me to say such things. But I will tell you that your reading glowed. It pierced my skin. You have gotten beneath the madness, Miss Brophy." He bent over and kissed her on the cheek, then he was gone down the stairs.

Leila hurried into the bathroom and locked the door. What he said could only mean . . . she didn't dare hope. And then in a terrible moment it all flashed over her. Joy and despair. Victory and defeat. Why did you have to tell him you were Fay Brophy? Why not Leila Fox? Because there will be a Jewish problem, there always is. But you will go on as Fay Brophy, and you should be Leila Fox. That was your achievement, and now you've lost it. Why didn't you believe in yourself? Stop it. You have succeeded, and that's all. Nothing will stop you now. Why, you hysterical fool, Gielgud just blessed you.

When she came out, Radner was waiting at the top of the steps for her.

"So, I find you at last." In answer to her silent question, he replied, "Gielgud told me where I could find you. He apologized for telling you the good news, but he thought you knew already."

She felt his arm on her shoulder. "Then it's true? I have the part?"

"You were magnificent." He leaned over the kissed her cheek. "You earned it. You don't have to feel you owe anything . . . to anyone."

She was grateful for that, and now he had her arm and escorted her downstairs. "We shall feast on the magnificent food and drink to your success."

Leila smiled. "I ate half the buffet when I got here."

Radner laughed. "Then we shall drink half the champagne."

There were many eyes on them as they rejoined the guests, mingling in the room where now a huge turkey and a roast beef, pink and succulent, had already been carved. Radner snatched two glasses of champagne from a passing waiter and, holding them aloft, gave one to Leila. "Let us drink to your success and to the play."

"When will it open?"

"Gielgud tells me he can start rehearsing in two days. Is that soon enough for you?" He held out his glass and touched hers, and then she saw his eyes. They were far away and there was pain there.

"My dear fellow, where have you been hiding this ravishing creature?"

It was Serge Bernard, and one could see from the brilliant cast in his eyes that he had taken a lot of champagne.

"I have hardly had any time with her at all," Radner protested.

"Well, you won't have much now either. Gielgud asked for you. We'll excuse you."

Radner turned to Leila. "Wait for me."

"But, of course," Serge chimed in, "she is my prisoner."

They watched Radner, pushing his way toward the den and being stopped by two attractive women and then a man and a buxom brunette with heavy lacquered black hair, piled in thick layers.

"Ponselle's hair is quite marvelous," Serge Bernard remarked. "The coils are like so many snakes. Isn't it fascinating how people dress, seeking to disguise themselves and ending up doing just the opposite?"

Leila took in Serge's fine profile, the aquiline nose, the dark eyes full of curiosity and yet somehow jaded, coming brilliantly alive and then lapsing into hooded somnolence, like a hawk ready to strike. Was she his prey?

"Yes, I am that way," he said.

"Which?"

He laughed. "Whatever you are thinking. I am all things to all people."

"Then no one will know you."

"Exactly. But look around this room. It is full of the famous, those who rub against the famous hoping something will come off, and those who are waiting for the mighty to fall so that they may replace them. It is fascinating. A microcosm of existence. Which class do you fall into?"

Leila hadn't expected such directness. "I'm not sure I can answer that."

"Oh, come. Of course you belong to the last class, Fay. It is the right name?"

"Yes."

"You have made a success. Don't ask me how I know. I make it my business to know. I don't waste time talking to nobodies. You shall be part of this new elite society Radner will build here. It will be like Paris. Wild, dizzying, decadent. And you shall be one of its new stars."

"I think you have had too much champagne. I have only gotten a part in a play."

"You are too modest. You are a tiger who has clawed her way through the street. If you are blessed with talent, what will you do? Hide that talent until the Nazis go away? Nonsense. And if they never go away, will the gifted hide their beauty in a cave? Of course not. That's the lesson Radner is teaching tonight. He is saying to the world of art here that this is the way of the world. Paris is as old as the centuries. Wise and corrupt. We know how to accept the invader. I see sixteen-year-olds in Paris with German soldiers. Do you dare think it will not happen here?"

Suddenly she was angry. "No, I don't think it will happen here. This country hasn't been conquered. Not all of it."

Serge laughed. "Some idealism remains. But you will be disabused of it. It is all a game like *chemin de fer*. How do you say it . . . roulette. You know who Picasso is? I will tell you a story Arno Brecker told me. He is a marvelous sculptor. Brecker received a telephone call. Picasso was very frightened. He had been sending money to the Russians before the Russian-German pact was signed. He feared being labeled an enemy of the state. Brecker had Hitler's favor, and he went to see Heinrich Müller, head of the Gestapo in Paris. Picasso, Brecker said, was a great coward despite his leftist public stance. He would have collapsed had the Gestapo gotten him. The great Picasso . . . profiler of

135

Guernica. Artists can have courage in their art, but not in the real world . . . not with Nazis."

He laughed; his eyes were mirthful and yet cold. She could not stand there and let him nail her in his coffin of cynicism.

"Goya painted it. He would have painted the Germans."

"Are you sure?" Serge laughed. He turned his dark eyes on her, and she saw in them only the desire to bring others down to the void where he resided. "Would you truthfully paint the Germans, or will you act in their play? You don't have to answer. You already have."

"But I worked for it," she cried.

He smiled charmingly. "But, of course you did. You could not hide your talent in a cave until they went away. Why should you? Not for a month or for a century. But it is the same. You work for them as I do, as we all shall. We will do anything, be anybody, to have our chance." There was a challenge in his eye that could not be ignored.

"I don't understand you."

He smiled in macabre fashion. "When we were introduced, you started to say another name . . . it sounded like 'lie.' We often give ourselves away in the most fascinating manner. Like Ponselle's hair. You have told a lie."

She started to protest, but it died in her mouth.

"I don't care who you are. You are making the best of it, that is the human condition. Like the sixteen-year-olds back in Paris. Please, I do not accuse you. You are poised on the threshold. You shall be what you want. Only please do not be fool enough to think you are better. You Americans are not better."

She stared directly into his pain-bright eyes. In them there was the cutting knowledge of whatever path of personal betrayal he had traveled. "Yes, you see it. There. Of course, I am a whore."

He stood perched above her like some giant condor poised to devour her. Leila was frozen, his words had turned her to ice. Suddenly she caught sight of the waiter she had come upon earlier. Now she recalled his name. It was Freddy Manning, and he had done a season of stock with Fay and Leila in Falmouth up on the Cape.

It was more than an hour before Radner could rejoin her. Leila had managed to slip into the den and now stared into the darkness of Central Park. She felt his hand on her waist. "I need to be alone with you. We must talk. Meet me downstairs."

"My coat."

"I'll get it."

Minutes later they were in his car, their destination an East Side address Radner had given the driver. His hand found hers, and she waited for him to speak. But whatever emotion had weighed so heavily upon him earlier was still there. They finished the drive in silence.

They stood in front of an apartment house, and Radner guided her into the lobby. There didn't seem to be any doorman. Leila saw their reflection in the large mirror backed to the wall. They were a striking couple. But he seemed even more agitated now. His eyes were angry, hurt. In the elevator he finally spoke. "This is where I live. But I have been unable to spend time here because taking over for Manheim has become such an exhausting business."

They sat in the sunken living room on the soft velvet couch, drinking brandy. The room was simply but tastefully furnished with modern furniture, a wicker chair, a table stocked with liquor and a large bookcase. Above them were several family portraits.

"It's so different," she said, "from the other place."

Radner smiled forlornly. "Yes, I also got it through *The New York Times*. I went back to the ads just before the invasion and found a couple who wanted to sublease. In exchange for getting them an exit visa, I got the apartment."

"Fortunes of war," Leila said softly. "What's wrong?"

He put the glass down and rubbed his hands together in an agitated fashion. "I am quite undone. It has been so hellish. First visiting Manheim, who is close to death. Then in the theater to have that happen. To witness such incredible talent, to hate that talent."

"Was it me?"

His hand reached back to her. "Before I came to your audition, I was at Carol Marley's office. She played me a recording of *Porgy and Bess*. She wants to stage a Gershwin concert." He looked to Leila for understanding. "To hear Gershwin in his full genius, to write such music . . . is worth your life."

"Gershwin is our greatest composer. There aren't . . ."

He looked at her with a kind of mad fury. "But I have written it, don't you understand? I have. They wouldn't do it." His fist came down on the couch. "Do you think I was born a cultural attaché? Did you think I was some well-groomed bureaucrat and ladies' man, born into the upper class, and that's why they gave me the job? Can't you tell another artist? Do you think I helped you get the audition because I wanted you? I knew you were an artist from the beginning."

A thousand questions whirled in her mind. Who was he? What was his music? Why hadn't it been done? Why didn't she sense the artist in him?

He looked up at her, a little boy with a pain he didn't know how to protect himself from. His eyes said help me, love me.

She felt something palpitate in her. He was no longer the striking, handsome, confident officer. He was a child, struggling so desperately to believe in himself, berating himself, hating himself. For her affirmation was further proof of his defeat. Yet now, in this moment, she realized how desirable he was to her. His vulnerability made her tremble with want.

She brought his hand to her cheek. "But we are together, Friedrich. We are here."

He looked into her eyes and now, as she dropped his hand, it fell on her breast. His mouth came to rest on hers. Theirs was no kiss of tenderness, but something fused by the experience of that day. By the hunger, the expectation, the raw pain. Their lips were hot, their mouths wet with saliva, their hands moving all over one another. He had pulled the dress from her shoulders, and now his fevered lips besieged them. Her fingers were pulling at his tie and shirt, and her hands smoothed their way across his chest. Then she was pulling his shirt loose, and it fell to the rug as he fell on top of her. There was a jumble of pulling and tugging, embraces and caresses. His lips found her breasts, and Leila raised and opened her legs, felt the nylon slide down and then a rush of cool air. She was free to accept him. Sobbing with anguish and desire, he came into her, and she, moaning, took him in. Then she was rocking him, he cupping her buttocks, raising her up so he could be even more a part of her. They held on to one another, kissing fiercely, passionately. He saw her face thrown aside, eyes glazed, mouth straining for a lost note. She saw the fury in his eyes, felt the drive of him surging inside her. She felt him expand, grip her even more tightly, crying out something she didn't understand. Then she knew, for she was crying out the same thing, and they were calling in the same voice. She heard him panting from the effort, fought to catch her breath, then felt his head drenched in moisture on her sweaty, wet chest.

They lay that way until she looked up and saw him over her. Then again inside her. Again. Again. Locked. Clinging. Saturated. Finally they fell into a state of exhaustion. Prisoners of their passion and furtive dreams. They lay that way until dawn when the phone rang.

She heard him talking, her eyes only partly open. She saw the outlines of him standing naked, holding the phone. She listened as he spoke in low, clipped, half sentences. In terse words and grunts. He hung up and came back to her. She waited for him to lie down beside her, but he only sat. "Manheim had a stroke. That was Abetz. I am to be at Gestapo headquarters to breakfast with him."

Leila watched him dress. "Friedrich, the Gershwin concert. Will you do it?"

He was holding his boots and his Wehrmacht uniform over his arm. "Not this season," he said very softly.

AMERICAN PANORAMA VIII

AMERICAN NIGHTS

JOHNNY LUGANSKY COMES HOME

by Art Letieri
Daily Mirror Staff Reporter

January 30, 1942

Last Night, Johnny Lugansky came home after six weeks in Gestapo detention. He walked up the steps of the battered six-story building at 500 West Thirty-ninth Street and then climbed five more flights because the elevator was out of order. At the request of his parents, Kasmir and Ida Lugansky, there were just a few close friends invited over. "Johnny don't want no fuss," said his mother, a stoop-shouldered, white-haired woman who came to this country with her husband in 1912. She fought hard to suppress tears as she kissed her only son repeatedly on the cheek. His father patted his son on the shoulders and periodically whispered to him in Polish.

Neighbors kept popping in, however, to share some coffee and sweets with the Luganskys and their son, who electrified fellow New Yorkers by playing Benny Goodman records during the German victory march on Fifth Avenue. Johnny Lugansky would not talk about his time in Gestapo detention at 60 Centre Street. He has lost some weight but feels his mother's home cooking will fatten him up. About his now almost historic deed, he had this to say: "I just wanted to show everyone that the American spirit is still there. And what's a better way than to play some swing music? I love swing. I got over five hundred records by Benny Goodman, Artie Shaw, the Dorsey brothers, Glen Gray, Charlie Barnet, Glenn Miller. I just thought it was the thing to do."

Pressed for his future plans Johnny shrugged and said, "I

done a lot of thinking and I don't want to go back to my job at the factory." His mother interrupted to protest. Johnny bit his lip. "I know we need the money, but I can't be a shipping clerk all my life. I'd like to do something with music. Sure, on the radio. You see, I learned that day that people really need music. Real American music. Well, they do, Ma. That ain't so terrible to say." Johnny Lugansky remembers the old stage shows. He went to them all. "Sure, I did. Jitterbugging in the aisles at the Paramount to Benny Goodman, Sammy Kaye at the Roxy, Tommy Dorsey at the Strand. Somebody has to play it now that those places are closed. I hear there's nothin' on the radio worth listening to anymore."

He switched on the radio and the brown crystals lit up. A German waltz was heard. Johnny fiddled with the radio and got a news broadcast. Finally, the slippery soft sound of Fred Waring and his Pennsylvanians singing "Moonlight on the Wabash" was heard. Johnny and his father sank onto the worn old couch and listened quietly. Neighbors quietly filed out. Mrs. Lugansky, apparently overcome by the emotion of the entire day, went into the kitchen weeping. The song finished and Kasmir Lugansky told his son his mother made his favorite, sponge cake, but that it didn't come out as well because there was a shortage of eggs this week.

I asked Johnny what he thought of the now famous broadcast by German Ginny that turned America upside down. Did they hear it in prison? Although he spoke calmly one could sense of a great deal of emotion in his voice. "Sure, we heard it. They piped it in for all of us. I tell you it put everything in a tizzy. I shared a cell with this older fellow, and he went all white. He had a heart attack when he heard about Roosevelt. They took him to the hospital. I know it was over in a few minutes but it affected me and a lot of the people around me." Johnny Lugansky was quiet for a second and then said, "That was a nasty trick. I mean, when I did it I was only trying to have some fun. But that, what's her name . . . Ginny, German Ginny, she hurt people."

His father reached over and put his hand on his son's arm. They both stood up. It was time for me to leave.

Chapter 15

The four men sat around an ornate table drinking coffee from cups designed with a single red flower. Like the emblem of the Scarlet Pimpernel, Kelly thought to himself. But it would take more than Leslie Howard portraying the Scarlet Pimpernel to save all the people these krauts want locked up. The cups and the rest of the sterling silver set had been a gift to Alfried Krupp von Bohlen und Halbach, son of Gustav, grandson-in-law of Alfred Krupp. Krupp, the greatest dynasty in Germany. Though Hitler stood astride the world with seven-league boots, Kelly thought to himself, the power brokers, old and new, looked to the Krupp family.

He was thin and sharp featured with black hair, a tight mouth, piercing dark eyes. With the death of his brother, Claus, Alfried was the only remaining son of Gustav von Bohlen. There was a joke going around that both Hitler and Alfried answered only to Krupp.

Next to him sat Abetz, plump, sleek, with those hooded eyes. A cat who knows he shall dine on a bowl of mice shortly with no worry about having to hunt for the food. To his right sat von Kleist, the German ambassador to New York, a man with pinched, sharp features and a crown of shiny white hair. Perfect casting for an ambassador, Kelly thought.

Abetz, ever anxious to please, had called the meeting, which took place in a suite with a dark red rug and blue curtains that had been drawn so only the barest hint of sunlight could be glimpsed. A symbolic gesture in view of what what was going to be decided. Now Krupp drained his coffee.

"We have kept political roundups and detention of able-bodied young men at a reasonable pace," Abetz began, "so that there will be no reason to suspect we will be applying the same methods as Heydrich has in England."

Kelly's lips parted just a trifle.

The methods Abetz referred to were the wholesale roundup of

141

young men between the ages of nineteen and thirty-five immediately after the fall of England, and their shipment to work
camps in Germany and Poland. It had been completely effective,
Kelly had to admit, in robbing the Brits of the manpower to
resist.

Now Abetz looked over at Kelly. "But in deference to Mr.
Kelly's views, we have not initiated such procedures here."

Alfried Krupp turned the steel black curtain eyes on Kelly.
There was clearly the need for an explanation.

Kelly never hesitated. Nobody intimidated Kelly. "It won't
work here. You've got millions of Jews, niggers, slews of other
minorities. You tip them they're on their way out, and you'll
have mass riots on your hands. . . ."

"I don't see . . ." Krupp interrupted.

"And you won't have any kind of work force," Kelly said,
speaking over Krupp's words. He saw Krupp's expression change
immediately. "You need that work force to keep the plants going
here . . . and you'll need some of them to complete the Hackensack camp."

Abetz had produced a map, which he now spread across the
middle of the glossy table. His stubby finger pointed to a large
circle on the map.

"What is this place?" Krupp asked.

"Herr Kelly has found a wonderful location," Abetz said.

Kelly's finger found the circle. "Hackensack, New Jersey.
They're called Meadowlands. Swampy and marshy, but my engineers have already started work there. Prisoners of war are
being used as a work force, and the clearing operation has also
begun. They estimate huts and barbed wire will be up in about
a month to six weeks."

"Excellent," Krupp said, shaking his head affirmatively. "So
my workers will be housed there?"

"Of course," Kelly said, smiling.

"As the camp is expanded," Abetz explained, "we shall be
shipping more and more prisoners there, until the time when we
are ready for a major roundup."

Krupp nodded perfunctorily. "To make Curtiss-Wright and
Grumman functional for the Luftwaffe, I want to double normal
production standard. I shall also need a large work force to make
the Kaiser plant into a tank and munitions factory."

"They are easily found," Abetz said as he refilled Krupp's
coffee cup. "And Herr Kelly has come up with the cleverest
idea for breaking the unions."

"You run advertisements," Kelly broke in, "on the radio and
in the papers. You offer living quarters, food—which is scarce
for the average worker—and a hundred dollars a month provided

they last six months. You pay them in scrip, which they save and are supposed to turn in after six months. After six months you make it a year."

Krupp nodded. "Interesting . . . very clever."

"After you extend it to a year," Kelly continued, "they're hooked. It's like they have an investment in continuing to work. And you do it with the politicals as well."

Now Krupp looked unconvinced.

Kelly turned on the charm and the smile of a thousand parties. "Man lives on hope. If he's got a job, if he's getting paper money, it'll quiet a lot of them down."

Krupp actually smiled. "I have been told you are a man ahead of your time, by my father. He is right."

"And," Abetz interjected, "once the camp is ready and the workers flock to us, we will do what we wish with the politicals."

"Yes," Krupp murmured, "of course."

Now he turned to Kelly. "But the unions will fight you here. You have a certain tradition."

Kelly leaned back. "Key leaders have already been arrested. The Bolshies have to work for us . . . after a while, Joe the factory worker is going to get awfully hungry. His kids will be crying for milk and bread. He'll see the scabs getting his work. How long can a man stand that?"

The Nazis around the table exchanged glances. Kelly's logic was undeniable.

"The scabs will break the unions," Kelly said, pounding a hand on the table for emphasis. "People will be lining up to work and live in the camp. Squeeze them on food rations, and they'll come running after you."

Krupp looked at the map. "Ingenious . . . and they get no money. How many will the camp eventually hold?" He looked at Abetz.

"A quarter of a million," Abetz said, his face glowing.

Von Kleist looked worried. "So many? Won't a large armed force be necessary?"

"There will be soldiers of the Reich," Abetz interrupted him, "and there will also be an auxiliary corps. Herr Kelly also suggested this. Men sympathetic to the Reich who will be paid a higher rate of scrip money, given better rations and quarters."

"They will perform extremely efficiently," Kelly said. "Give a man the right incentives, and he will play ball." Kelly grinned. "That's an American expression."

"There are always troublemakers," Krupp said as he sipped more coffee.

"They shall be screened out and kept away until we are ready to . . . ready to deal with them," Abetz informed him.

Krupp laid down his cup, and now the steel in his eyes was transferred to his tone. "I told the Führer I wanted two million more men."

"You shall have them," Abetz said in a voice that indicated he had long been prepared for the demand.

"Who will you round up first?" Krupp said as he got up and moved to the window, as if by this gesture disassociating himself from the sticky business at hand.

"The *schwarz*," Abetz answered. "They are strong and will make excellent workers. We will exclude most of them from the Hackensack camp. We estimate we can draw from New York, Boston, and Philadelphia over a million, perhaps close to two. For that reason we have doubled the guard allotment around the Harlem, Philadelphia, and Boston ghettos.

"Then there are Slovaks, Chinese, other groups that will give us half a million. When that is finished we shall begin the raids on the Jewish ghettos. Eventually fathers and sons will be separated, brothers and cousins. The sons will be sent to work in Europe while the fathers perform for us here. In this way, each will think that his performance as a worker will bring the son back after a year or two in the fatherland or Poland or England."

"When you go in," Kelly warned, "you have to go in hard. You had an easy time in Europe. The Jew here is a different breed of animal. He's used to his freedom. He fought for it in the ghetto. You have to pick some of them off now, then wait. But you can't wait too long."

Krupp looked back at the men at the table. "It seems that the Jew here does present a more difficult problem. There must be a solution . . . one more final and permanent."

He looked at Abetz and Kelly, who showed no expression.

Now Abetz broke the silence. "Yes . . . there shall be."

Krupp walked back to the table. "New York seems so . . . how do I say it? Normal. The Americans don't seem to be interested in putting up a fight." He looked to Kelly for an answer.

Kelly ran a cigar over his fingertips. "They're still disorganized. Their minds are on the Japs. But they'll be floating people in. Something will happen. Unless I miss my guess, plans are already in the works. They're not going to lay down for you."

Krupp looked now at Abetz. "The Führer wishes air attacks on Cleveland, Detroit, and Chicago to begin no later than February. I want double the workers you have at Curtiss-Wright and at Grumman. I want the most precise security precautions around

144

those plants and the airbases where the Luftwaffe will land. Is that understood?''

Abetz looked confident as he spoke. "That has been taken care of. In addition, we have penetrated certain elements where we are sure the Americans will wish to draw their resistance from. We are prepared.''

Kelly bit the tip off the end of the cigar. "You might consider making a deal with the gun guys.'' He saw them looking at him. "With the gangsters . . . the mob. They'll control your black market. Make a deal with them and you'll not only starve the people out, you'll get muscle.'' He paused. "And you'll get firepower. They specialize in elimination. Get them before Roosevelt makes a deal with them.''

Krupp and Abetz exchanged looks.

Kelly lit his cigar, waiting for his tidbit to have maximum effect. "Get Vito Genovese back. He had to get out to beat a murder rap. He's with Mussolini. Get him back and put him in charge of your civilian muscle squads. The American resistance will show itself. Get Genovese back and keep Luciano in jail. Get Genovese back and put a shotgun in his hand. Whatever he charges, he's worth it.'' Kelly blew out some smoke. "That's the way things are done in this country.''

Krupp looked surprised, Abetz amused, while von Kleist seemed apprehensive.

"They are so powerful?'' Krupp finally asked.

"They are,'' Kelly said genially, "a law unto themselves. They found out in the twenties they could buy almost anyone. They are a potent weapon we must have on our side.''

Nobody said anything. Kelly was giving them their marching orders.

Krupp rubbed his chin, locked into some private vision. Now he caught the eye of von Kleist. "Herbert, you look so worried. You are too civilized for such matters.''

Von Kleist's watery blue eyes seemed tired and lifeless. "Perhaps. It is just that this America troubles me. It is vast. It is not like occupying Denmark, Belgium, or even England. It seems to me, the Americans are a large mass, unmanageable—'' He struggled for the proper word. "—like a herd you see in their western movies. I have an uneasy feeling that they can run wild . . . how do you call it?'' He looked at Kelly.

"You mean stampede.''

"Yes.''

Kelly blew out some smoke. "That's why there are cattle pens. There are ways of handling large herds. You may lose a few strays here and there . . . you may have a stampede, but they are manageable.''

Everyone seemed satisfied except von Kleist, who still looked apprehensive.

"An excellent meeting," Krupp said. "Most productive. Standartenführer, I will want a word with you later, but for now I would like to be alone with Herr Kelly."

Abetz almost jumped out of his chair, while von Kleist rose wearily, though he also seemed greatly relieved at being released from whatever further plans were about to be set in motion.

Krupp waited a few seconds after Abetz and von Kleist had left and then extracted from a briefcase under the table a sealed document. "This is a decree signed by the Führer. All defense, automobile, and arms plants on the East Coast are now to be owned and managed by Krupp."

He sat down opposite Kelly, who smoked his cigar. "Have you spoken with Ford and Kaiser?"

Kelly flicked an ash. "Yes. But they are not going to do anything unless you hit the cities where they have plants. You have to bomb them to make a dent in their attitude."

A small smile showed itself on Alfried Krupp's mouth. "And so we shall."

"Even then," Kelly pointed out, "troops will have to be landed. You must capture Cleveland, Detroit, Akron."

Krupp nodded. "We shall bomb them. Then, in the spring, the Führer has promised me we shall send Rommel into their midst."

Kelly looked up at the smoke curling up toward the ceiling. "When I meet with Cordell Hull and Morgenthau I shall point out that it would be advantageous to deal with you now. But of course they'll sit on their cards."

Krupp nodded. Now he leaned forward. "Tell them nothing more than they expect to hear. But also warn them that it would be a great advantage to them to come to the table. Better to lose the East Coast than the entire country."

Kelly savored that thought and his cigar at the same instant. "A peace treaty would be the end of Roosevelt's presidency."

Krupp spoke quietly, so quietly that Kelly had to inch forward to hear his words. "The Führer has approved a raid using paratroopers on Pittsburgh. If all goes well we shall have the city and its steel mills in a day."

"When?"

"Within the next month. Guderian has worked out a precision strike. It will come on a clear night. We will hit the city with parachute troops and at dawn take the city."

"There is a reserve force there," Kelly warned. "You'll need tanks."

Krupp rubbed his chin pensively. "It is Guderian's belief that

146

the paratroopers can induce enough panic to get control of the city.''

Kelly's green eyes became small and sharp. He was like a panther in a tree prepared to leap upon its quarry. "If you use artillery, you'll risk destroying some of those plants. And I think you'll need them. Pittsburgh is Steel Town, U.S.A. You've got coal miners there. You're not getting a virgin.''

"Guderian's troops have taken half the world. They know how to fight. They are not steel workers and miners, they are soldiers.'' Krupp's contempt for the Americans could not have been more clear. He looked up at Kelly. "Simply tell Hull and Morgenthau that we don't wish to level any more cities. Tell them we want a protectorate in the East. We are prepared to consider some kind of partnership. We would like some reciprocal trade agreement that would enable us to build a partnership with the United States. One that would stand the test of time, allow us to be allies and to form an alliance against common enemies.''

"Like Russia perhaps.''

Krupp nodded affirmatively. "Excellent. You can be more specific when we have Pittsburgh.''

Kelly's eyes gleamed intensely. "Are you sending von Kleist with me?''

Krupp leaned back. "I told the Führer I thought it best if you went. Designating you as our negotiator and ambassador-at-large will make it official and final. For you represent the reality. Germany is here to stay.''

Now they were both silent. The time had come to negotiate the price. Neither was a man who had any patience for the amenities of a negotiation.

"The Führer,'' Krupp began, "may come to Washington. Perhaps you could suggest an appropriate time.''

Kelly set his cigar on the table, the fiery point jutting out like a weapon timed to go off. "He should come and address the diplomats of the world. In the American Senate. I will introduce him myself. You, of course, will be there. That would be followed by my appointment as regent of the Northeast and all other American territory conquered by the Reich. I want the proclamation naming me as regent to be an official ceremony with a swearing-in process. The Führer would be my honored guest along with you and, of course, your father if he is well enough to come. There shall be a ball and a state dinner.''

Kelly stopped and let Krupp envision his dream.

Krupp's eyes came alive. "Yes, it has appeal. It will make everything very official.'' He laughed softly. "Inevitable.'' He let it float in the air, this portrait Kelly had painted for him. "Would you suggest before or after we storm the Midwest?''

From the immediacy of Kelly's response, it was obvious he had given a great deal of thought to it. "As soon as possible. The psychology of a new order must be impressed upon the people. The Reich is here to stay."

Krupp threw his hand out in the air as if he were grasping an invisible scepter and crown. "You shall have it. You shall have it all. When I return to Berlin after my visit here, I shall immediately meet with him. I am sure he will be enthusiastic."

There was a slight tremor in Kelly's voice that belied his calm expression. "He must come."

Krupp waited only a brief moment. "He shall, as will others." He let his picture dangle now before Kelly. "Goering has a passion to come to New York."

Kelly's eyes were bright and luminous, as if some private furnace within him was being vigorously stoked.

"Yes," Krupp said, "it will be a great social event." And noting Kelly's eyes, added, "Even a historic one."

Abruptly, the blinding light of ambition was gone from Kelly's eyes and he turned them on Krupp. "The major American industrialists will all have to come to me then, and they can do it officially. Trade agreements can begin. Reciprocal trade. You have many friends here, Alfried. Many."

Krupp smiled. He was just thirty-five, but he had grown immeasurably sure of himself since Claus had died.

"You have a list for me?" He held out his hand.

Kelly reached into his pocket and produced an envelope.

He handed it to Alfried Krupp. Krupp read it slowly and carefully. It was impressive. Many large American firms would accept reality. Then for a moment his eyes stopped as he thought of Kelly's words. "A peace treaty would be the end of Roosevelt's presidential hopes come the next election." And in Kelly's mind, who better to succeed him than Kelly himself. He will, Alfried Krupp knew in that moment, do anything for us. And a man who will do anything can be used. Yes, thought Alfried Krupp, Patrick Kelly will be the Reich's most humble servant.

AMERICAN PANORAMA
IX

NEW YORKER ARRESTED FOR
IMPERSONATING HITLER

Lugansky Arrested by Gestapo Again
by a Staff Correspondent

Tuesday, February 3, 1942

Johnny Lugansky, New York City's most illustrious patriot, did it again yesterday. Only days after his release from Gestapo detention headquarters, he was arrested at 4:32 P.M., jitterbugging with a couple of vivacious brunettes while dressed as none other than Adolf Hitler. The impersonation caused a sensation around the city. Yet it was only prompt intervention by the Gestapo that saved Lugansky from a militant crowd that had gathered in front of the public library. Mr. Lugansky had set up his record machine somewhere across the street, and as the Benny Goodman band played "One O'Clock Jump" he leaped out in front of the two lions that grace the steps of the library and danced up a storm.

As the crowd, which at first seemed dazed by the impersonation, grew, so did its anger at the reminder of the occupation that the city must endure. Mr. Lugansky's practical joke grew increasingly irritating as he danced on and the crowd went from shouting to throwing stones and bottles to finally closing in to assault the New York Führer. A New York City policeman, who witnessed the incident and called Police-Gestapo headquarters, is credited with alerting the Gestapo, who arrived just as Mr. Lugansky had been grabbed by two burly citizens intent on decorating his face with their fists. Mr. Lugansky was carried away yelling, "You'll never stop boogie-woogie."

Mr. Lugansky's extraordinary impersonation began when a

black-uniformed, black-booted, mustached Adolf Hitler turned up at the German Bund radio station, WGER, on East Eighty-third Street in the Yorkville section of the city. Demanding to see German Ginny, Mr. Lugansky caused an elaborate furor at which it is reported one secretary fainted, and the station manager fractured his elbow. Reportedly, he was so shocked at seeing the "Führer" he vigorously saluted and threw his right elbow into a fire extinguisher. In the scuffle that subsequently developed, the station's news announcer was knocked unconscious by one of his aides. At 10:30 A.M., local police received the first calls reporting that someone dressed as Adolf Hitler was seen fleeing down East Eighty-second Street.

At intervals that followed in the hectic day, Adolf Hitler was reported at Tiffany's buying a brooch; at Mark Cross department store ordering a pair of monogrammed gloves; carrying a sign saying "Eat at Joe's Diner" while patrolling West Thirtieth Street and Sixth Avenue; and drinking beer with local patrons at Delahanty's, a bar on West Fortieth Street where Mr. Lugansky is a regular. Perhaps Mr. Lugansky's most dramatic appearance of the day was at 2:30 P.M. when he surfaced at the top of the Empire State Building and, after giving the Nazi salute, ordered a party of German soldiers to "jump." The soldiers, after getting over their initial shock, attempted to capture Mr. Lugansky, who successfully evaded them by dropping packages of burning film, known as "stink bombs."

The day was put into perspective by Joe Delahanty, the owner of Delahanty's, whom I spoke with. "Johnny told me he had something in mind. It was terrific but maybe a little crazy. I hope he don't get into trouble for it. I'm afraid this time he won't be out so fast. But I think it showed the people of the city a good example."

Chapter 16

February 4, 1942
3:00 A.M.

Sylvie lay in bed wide awake. She had spent the day shopping and had come home to learn that Patrick was staying at the Hotel

Pierre because of important meetings with visiting businessmen and the Germans. He couldn't even spare the time to come home and sleep with her. She hated sleeping alone, and for some reason her pills were not helping. She felt so abandoned.

God, was there no one she could confide in? As a child, growing up in Baltimore, she used to pray a lot. When had that stopped? When had she stopped believing? Perhaps she could pray now. Don't be ridiculous. Try it. She closed her eyes. Our Father who art in heaven . . . oh that's wrong. Just say what's in your heart. I'm so terribly alone. I have been ever since my father, my real father left us. Actually, it was mother who threw him out. He believed in me and that made me better. Since then nobody has and I don't either. There have been men. Men with money and power to take care of me. They've loved me in their way. I suppose Patrick does. But it's not right.

She sat up. Dear God, there must be something better than this life I lead. Once I felt good and clean inside. But then it left me. Why did it go? Tell me. I have something good to give. But to whom? Where is it? She heard the beat of her heart and felt she was perilously close to the answer. She thought of horses and now she was gasping. Why this panic? It must be because I have no escort for the horse show and the dinner-dance. She suddenly had a wonderful idea. She'd call von Stulpnagel. He fancied her, and Patrick would approve. He loved buttering up the Germans.

The last pill she had taken began to act on her. She was drowsy. She was falling back in space to a time when she was younger. She was on a horse riding across the water. They went so fast, skimming like a motorboat. Faster and faster, and then the horse was gone and Sylvie was alone on top of the water being dragged by a rope and crying. Help me, she cried. Help me. But no one heard. And no one came.

3:20 P.M.

Sylvie walked idly on Fifth Avenue. Her headache had subsided to a dull throbbing, thanks to the pills given her by Dr. Jacobsen. She had stopped for a coffee and pastry at La Pâtisserie. The place was full of Germans. What a horrible season it had become. Oh, to be in Palm Springs. The stories coming back were so exciting. If she had only known Patrick was going. She would insist he take her the next time he met Morgenthau. She'd give him a good time in bed, that would do it. Either that or she would just take that little pass Patrick had given her and go to Los Angeles herself.

She walked into Glenda's on Madison and Fifty-eighth and

looked for Mr. Klein. She had been coming to the store for seven years. It had the latest Paris and Milan styles and Mr. Klein had always been extraordinarily kind. The decor was dark, with an Oriental rug and lounge chairs, and espresso was served while you waited. The place was rather empty, and Sylvie could see Mr. Klein was not on the floor. She recognized one of the salesmen, known to her only as George.

Sylvie approached him. He was busy adding some figures. "Good afternoon, George."

He looked up, startled. "Oh, Miss Lamont, how are you?"

"Fine. Is Mr. Klein in?" George seemed rather white now. "I called before and someone said he's not here anymore. I said that's impossible. He's been here for years."

A pained expression had come to George's face. "Actually, he's not been here . . . that is . . . he had to take a vacation. . . ."

"Vacation?"

"A leave. He hasn't been feeling well. Perhaps I could help you."

"Well, I hope someone can. I ordered a special heel put on those rose shoes. You know, the ones from Sans Souci of Milan. Nobody seems to know. Could you help me? Here's the ticket. I must have them for tomorrow night."

George took the slip. "Let me see what I can find out. Please make yourself comfortable."

He went in the back while Sylvie sat down. She found herself drumming her fingers on the hard black leather of the chair. Perhaps a cigarette. She opened her purse and saw the green ticket. Oh, better put that away. She had a zipper compartment and slipped the green pass with the swastika on it inside. She reached for her Pall Malls and then remembered she had given them up. Someone had suggested it might help the headaches. She looked up and saw a man walking toward her. It was Purdy, Mr. Klein's assistant.

"Hello, Miss Lamont, how are you?" It was said with an obvious false heartiness and made Sylvie uneasy.

"George has given me your receipt. I know those shoes you ordered, but we seem to be having some trouble locating them."

A look of horror crossed Sylvie's face. "But I must have them. They're the only things that will match the outfit I shall be wearing."

Purdy, a man who shaved so closely his face seemed all blue, held up a hand. "We will make every effort. But in the meantime I have a new shipment from Paris of shoes by Duvalle."

Sylvie's voice rose an octave. "I ordered shoes from Milan . . . the rose ones. Where is Mr. Klein?"

Purdy, who had a thin, sharp nose and a mortician's lying mouth, drew himself to attention. "Regretfully, Mr. Klein has retired."

"Retired? George just said he was on a leave. Where is he? He knows. Perhaps he took them home to hold for me."

Purdy's face showed no expression. "Mr. Klein is no longer with us."

"I want my shoes."

"We will make every effort. But if I may please show you the Paris collection."

Now Sylvie's headache had returned. Her temples pounded. "Where is Mr. Klein? I insist on speaking with him. Where does he live? Give me his phone."

Purdy looked offended. "I am the manager, Miss Lamont."

"I want Mr. Klein," Sylvie shrieked.

George was suddenly there. "Please, Mr. Purdy, let me." He led Sylvie by the arm toward the front of the store and now he was whispering. "Please, you will get Klein in more trouble."

"Trouble, what are you saying?"

George was whispering. "He was denounced."

It made no sense to Sylvie. "Denounced?"

"He had your shoes the other night. He took them home, in fact. I saw them. He was going to drop them by your building himself the next morning."

"At last. Then where is he? I must have them. I'll call him."

"You can't. You'll get in trouble."

It was the last straw. "Give me his address."

George looked pained. "I beg you. Don't go. It is all too terrible."

"What is his address, or shall I call Mr. Purdy?"

"Purdy," George murmured, "he is the one." He gave her a slip of paper and then took her arm. He looked as if he would cry. "Tell Morris we all . . . are terribly sorry."

Mr. Klein lived at 111 Pierrepont Street in Brooklyn Heights. It was a brick brownstone with neat shutters on the windows. Sylvie got out of the cab and handed the five dollar bill to the cabbie. "Keep the change."

She took the slip of paper George had given her and read the address again. One-eleven. She went up the stairs, thinking to herself that it was such a cozy little house. Exactly what she would expect from Mr. Klein, who was always well groomed in a dark suit and so polite and helpful, not like that awful Purdy.

She went inside the darkened hallway and searched for his name. He was on the second floor, and Sylvie rang the bell. She waited impatiently, tapping her fingers. Why didn't someone answer? It was five o'clock, almost dinner time. Somebody had to be home. She rang a second and a third time. Now a voice came to her. "Who is it?"

"It's Miss Lamont. Sylvie Lamont to see Mr. Klein. About my rose shoes. He'll know."

She heard some voices and then a response. "Please come in." The buzzer rang and Sylvie went inside.

She went up some carpeted steps, the door opened, and she saw Mr. Klein framed in the light.

"Please, Miss Lamont, come in. I have your shoes here." He led her into the kitchen. "How did you find me?"

"George," Sylvie said. "He thought you might know about my shoes. May I sit down?"

"Of course, of course." He pulled out a kitchen chair and Sylvie sat down.

"Can I get you something?"

"Just a glass of water."

He ran the water while Sylvie looked around. She could see someone peering in from what must be the living room.

"There you are."

Sylvie drank the water. She felt her headache returning. She opened her purse and sought her pill vial.

"I'll be right back." He exited in the direction of the living room. Sylvie could hear him talking to a woman. There was another man's voice. They sounded distressed, tense. Surely her visit couldn't have . . . she had evidently come at a bad time.

Now the woman's voice came back to her and Sylvie detected frightened emotion. Perhaps a death in the family. She would leave immediately after she got the shoes.

Mr. Klein returned looking distressed. He was wearing a white shirt that was rumpled. His gray pants badly needed a pressing. He had on old bedroom slippers and now she saw he hadn't shaved in some time.

"I had them here but I can't seem to locate them." He saw the startled expression on Sylvie's face and moved to reassure her. "Oh, they're here, I just have to find them. If you will just be patient I'm sure . . ."

"Of course," Sylvie replied. "I'll wait."

He went back inside. He was so rattled. Sylvie had never seen him this way. Something wasn't right. Everybody at the shop had been so uncomfortable, secretive. And Purdy, he simply was not up to Mr. Klein's standard. She heard more conversation in the back. Mr. Klein was arguing with another man, a younger one. Moments later he came out.

He was a well-built young man with brown flat hair that wouldn't quite sit down as it met his forehead. He had tight brown eyes and he looked bookish. That is, he looked like a scholar. He wore a white shirt, had on a slipover and corduroy pants.

"Good evening. I'm Joel, Mr. Klein's son."

"Good evening."

"Is there anything I can get you? More water?"

"Thank you." She didn't want any more but the son looked even more uncomfortable than his father.

He returned with the water, and after placing it in front of her sat down across from her. He was twisting a rubber band.

It was their discomfort with what should have been perfunctory that forced Sylvie into asking a question that she normally would have avoided. "Have I come at a difficult time?"

The son was taken aback, and his fingers went to a little blemish on his chin. He'd probably cut himself shaving and she felt a swell of caring for his extreme youth.

"No . . . well, it's just that we were in the middle of something. . . ."

"You go to school?"

Now he was more comfortable. "Yes . . . Brooklyn College."

"What are you studying?"

"Law . . . pre-law. I'm just in my freshman year."

Abruptly, there came the sound of Mr. Klein yelling and Sylvie clearly heard the woman sob. This was too much. All for her shoes. Sylvie stood up. Joel's response was to jump up and bar her way back toward the sound of the argument. "I'll get my father," he said.

Sylvie heard the woman crying, more exclamation from Mr. Klein, then the sound of the boy's voice. Something fell to the floor and Mr. Klein came out. Now as he came close she could see he was close to tears.

"I'm terribly sorry, Miss Lamont. I can't seem to find them. We have such a mess back there. I brought them with me and I intended to drop them off at your building. I should have given them to George . . . I'm sorry."

He clearly felt so bad that Sylvie extended her arm to him. "I've come at a bad time. But I'm sure you'll find them. Then bring them to the store and . . ."

He bit his lip.

"You are coming back, aren't you?"

For a moment he was an object petrified in stone. Then he shook his head and began to cry.

Displays of emotion always left Sylvie feeling embarrassed. As if she were an eavesdropper at a funeral. Now she felt the same way but worse, for his crying had become sobbing. The boy appeared. "Papa, Papa." He led his father into the living room and Sylvie followed. Klein collapsed onto the couch, putting his face into his hands. The sobs, Sylvie felt, were like bricks of pain being pulled from Mr. Klein. She should have left, but somehow she couldn't.

Now he stopped and said to his son, "Go to your mother, I'll be all right. Go. It's all right." The boy retreated, throwing a disapproving look at Sylvie. It clearly said, Why don't you leave us?

Mr. Klein had regained his composure. "I promise I will find your shoes, but it may take some time. I will find a way of getting them to you. As soon as we complete the packing . . ."

"Packing?"

His hand went to his mouth to block further slips.

"Please, Mr. Klein, what is going on? Everybody at the shop was so mysterious. Purdy said you had retired. George said something about a leave. I insisted you were the manager."

The look of pain in his eyes was unbearable. "I am not just the manager. I am the owner. It is my shop, and they have taken it from me and given it to Purdy."

"They?"

He wiped the tears. "The Nazis. They are confiscating businesses owned by Jews. They are being turned over to others."

She heard the shock in her voice. "Others?"

His shoulders sagged as if the weight of the world rested on them. "Others like Purdy. He denounced me to the Gestapo. It is a trick, a little game they play. It is just the beginning. They will encourage others like Purdy to do the same. Bring forth the latent anti-Semitism that is always waiting in the bottle to be let out. The Jew is the enemy. The Jew is the money lender, the banker, the one who exploits labor. It has been effective for them in Europe and now . . ."

"But this is America."

His smile was as old as that of the first Jew who felt the sting of the Roman lash. "Yet it has happened. Purdy has taken my store. He will pay himself handsomely and give the rest to the Nazis. Tribute."

"But what did he tell them?"

"It doesn't matter. I am a Jew. That is enough. It will happen to others. Get the Jew out, replace him with an Aryan."

Sylvie couldn't imagine what to say except, "But they gave you something. Something . . ."

He shook his head. "Yes. They gave me a paper saying the German government was confiscating my business and property."

Her headache was going to blow her head open. "But . . . but

156

. . . my shoes . . . the charity ball. Oh, I can't believe this has happened."

Now his arm was around her. "There, there, I will find them. . . ."

She turned on him. "But you're packing. You're going someplace. I must have those shoes . . . it'll ruin my outfit. I can't wear the magenta dress unless I have those rose shoes. It's too late to get a new outfit now."

She was desperate, and Mr. Klein understood. "I know exactly what you are facing and . . ."

"Papa, enough. Get rid of her. We must pack." It was Joel, and he was flushed with anger. He stood in front of a large, framed photograph of an aged man with a white beard and white scarf draped around his shoulders. On his head he wore a black cap. What was it called?

His father stood up. "Joel, go inside."

"No, I won't. How can you think of shoes at a time like this? You comfort this woman, and Mama sits in the bedroom crying for her home. Papa, what is she to us?"

His father gestured helplessly to his son. "But her shoes . . ."

The boy was incredulous. "We have to give up our house, our lives, and you worry about shoes. My God . . ."

Mr. Klein looked helplessly from his son to Sylvie. His wife's sobbing was again clearly audible, and he murmured, "Excuse me," and disappeared into the bedroom.

Sylvie stood facing Joel. "Why don't you go?" he said accusingly.

"You don't understand . . ." she started to say.

"What are your shoes next to our lives?" The saliva flew from his lips. "We have to run. Run before they announce the yellow star. Don't you people understand what is going to happen here? Do you think because you go to your balls and dinners that you can ignore what will happen here? My father has owned that shop for twenty years. It is his life. What are your shoes to that? And he . . . runs and plays the merchant. He is not a merchant anymore . . . he is a displaced Jew."

The boy's wrath had gone completely through her.

Behind the boy was a painted portrait of Roosevelt who, along with the old Jew in the photograph, watched their confrontation with knowing eyes.

Sylvie heard the choked whisper that was her voice. "Where will you go?"

The boy's words were like machine gun bullets. "Wherever we can. He will spend his life's savings getting us out. There are people who will make their fortunes smuggling out displaced Jews. And you know something . . . we will be the lucky ones.

157

For those who cannot escape or who stay behind because they think they will not be touched, they will pay the price for us all. And people like you will wear fancy shoes.''

"Enough." Klein had returned from the bedroom. "Go inside . . . go." The boy left, and they were alone. "He is young and angry . . . you must forgive him. He has not learned the way of the world yet.''

He led Sylvie back into the kitchen. "I will look for your shoes, but everything is such a mess. There is one person who may have the same thing. Here, I wrote it out on a card for you. Her name is Sophie. She has a little place on the East Side. She and I often help each other. She carries the same line . . . go see her. Tell her I sent you.''

"Will she have the rose shoes?''

"It's possible. It's worth going.''

Sylvie took the card. "Where will you go?''

Klein threw up his hands. "Don't ask. I don't know. Someplace in free America.'' He opened his shirt and showed her a money belt. "Everything I have saved is here. It was for the children . . . for their children. Now I must use it to buy our way out. They have raised the price of an exit visa to twentyfive thousand dollars. I don't have that much. But there is enough for the black market trade.''

She waited at the Clark Street station for the northbound IRT. The whole trip had been so incredibly wretched, right up to discovering that she had no more money in her purse. Asking someone for cab fare was out of the question. She had never before in her life taken a subway, and now she stood on the platform with a Negro woman, undoubtedly a maid or cleaning woman. She looked at Sylvie's fur coat.

Some other passengers came by and also appraised her carefully. She felt they didn't like her. Oh, why didn't the train come? Her mouth was dry, but at least her head felt better. She saw the Topps chewing gum machine and opened her bag and searched for a penny. There must be one, she thought. But there wasn't. She sighed and gave it up.

There was a bench and Sylvie went to it. She was tired. It had been such an upsetting afternoon. Tomorrow she would call this Sophie woman. But poor Mr. Klein. Poor, poor fellow. She looked down at the subway platform beneath her and the stone stained and dirty. There was a shiny new penny. If only she could get it. Her mouth was so dry. But she couldn't bend down. She just couldn't. But nobody was watching. One quick scoop and she would have it.

She looked around and now the stocky Negro cleaning woman

caught her eye. She was seated on the opposite end of the bench. There was a little smile on her lips. She had seen the penny and was daring Sylvie to reach for it. Go ahead, her eyes said, but I will see you. Sylvie tried to stare her down and could not. The woman, who had a flat nose, big lips, and a black kerchief, would not avert her eyes. If I could cover it with my foot and drop a kerchief and then somehow . . . suddenly the woman moved over, leaned, and scooped it up. She stood up as the train came rolling in, a triumphant smile in her eyes. Sylvie's headache was worse than ever.

They ate beluga caviar and drank champagne by soft light in the dining room. Sylvie wore a blue silk robe and matching pajamas with the turquoise slippers she had bought in Paris. Patrick was dressed in a black silk robe she had gotten for him at Mark Cross just before the Christmas invasion. He puffed on a cigar and looked very pleased with his trip.

Sylvie slipped down to the thick white llama rug and leaned back against the couch. "What time will you leave?"

Patrick's face was creased by a mocking grin. "You won't stir for many hours after I'm gone."

Sylvie took a cigarette and beckoned Patrick for a light. He knelt down next to her.

"Mother is in Palm Springs," she said. Her lips turned up to a petulant pout.

The smile of the devil was in Patrick's dancing green eyes. God, he was full of himself. "You know I would love to have you come, sweetheart," he said, "but this is top-level business for the Reich."

Whenever he used that awful word "sweetheart" she knew he didn't give a damn at all. This trip to Palm Springs to meet with—what was the secretary of state's name . . . Hall? No, Hull . . . and the other one . . . "Patrick, who is the second man . . . the other one?"

Kelly blew out a mouthful of smoke and grinned. "Morgenthau. Henry Morgenthau . . . secretary of the treasury. Now they'll have to reckon with me."

"What will happen?"

He was silent for a moment . . . far away. "Happen? Oh, nothing. It'll just be a fencing match. A few feelers about a negotiated truce. But it's all bluff."

"Why?"

"Because, my sweet, until the climax of the Jap thrust on the West Coast, it's all a stall. Roosevelt is safe behind the Alleghenies and the Rocky Mountains. Hitler can't do anything about attacking the Midwest until the spring, although"—and now he grinned broadly—"Roosevelt may have a few surprises coming to him from out of the sky."

She saw his faraway look and knew not to pursue the topic. "You look very pleased."

He patted her head. "I am. The American government in exile has to deal with me. That's just the beginning."

"Beginning?"

"You'll see," he said softly. "They'll all see. Hull and his president didn't have five minutes for me three years ago. Now they'll host me, and it will be a long meeting. And they'll write me. It's a different game now."

Suddenly his lips were in her neck. She arched it for him, and his hand came to her breast.

"Wait, Patrick," she whispered.

"Why?"

"I need to talk."

To emphasize this she jumped up and walked to the curtains and pulled the sash. The city to the west beckoned to them. The lights of the West Side, proud harbingers of freedom and reminders of loss.

"I rode on the subway today, Patrick."

He looked at her oddly. "You?"

"I went to see if I could get those shoes I needed for the ball. I had to go to the house of Mr. Klein, the owner. They've taken his shop from him."

Patrick was relighting his cigar. "Who has?"

"The Germans. They've given it to his manager."

Patrick rolled the cigar around in his mouth.

"Mr. Klein said it was because he's a Jew."

Patrick puffed thoughtfully. "There'll be some of that. I'm sure he was given a fair price. People will have to . . ."

"People?" she said, more sharply than she meant to. "That store was his life. And he wasn't given a fair price." How she resented his talking to her as if she were some kind of child.

She saw him looking directly at her, and now she could no longer control her feelings. "The poor man will have to use his life savings to get his family out." She realized she was biting her nails. "How would someone get out of New York illegally?"

Patrick didn't answer right away. "If you can slip into the country up the Hudson Valley or in Connecticut or get to the Pennsylvania border. You need bribe money. He'll make it."

She looked at him inquiringly.

Patrick rolled the cigar around in his mouth. "He has the money. The Jew is very resourceful, I've found. He always has money put away."

His tone when he said "Jew" was clearly contemptuous. She

felt something rise up in her and then realized he was still talking.

"The Jew is going to have to realize that there is a new order and a new way. Others will, too. It sounds hard, darlin', but you'll see, everything will work out. The German occupies countries in Europe, and life goes on. People have a way of thriving on what you give them. It's their nature. So you'll have a little more state control here, but what's so bad about that? Roosevelt let the Bolshies thrive here. If it was up to me, they'd all have been put away a long time ago. Hell, we're still not out of the Depression. People need to work. Do you know Hitler rebuilt Germany completely from the depths of depression? Got the factories open, built an autobahn from one end of Germany to the other. Built a great army. Stabilized the mark." He stopped, and Sylvie saw how much he relished the Germans being here. And she knew in that moment he was somehow wrong. Germany and American didn't stand for the same thing. How could things work out? And there was something in it for Patrick. Something he desperately wanted. Then it was too much, and she had to put it away. It meant something she didn't want to know about.

"But if Mr. Klein is caught?"

He shrugged. "Some kind of state work. Nothing terrible."

"But he's had to give up his life's work. Why can't the Germans let people who want to leave just go? Why keep them?"

She saw his indulgent look. He came toward her. "If I'm successful in Palm Springs, things may ease up. The Germans don't want things to go badly here any more than the Americans do. I'm sorry about your Mr. Klein, but things like that happen in war."

"Yes," she said softly, "war."

Patrick settled in next to her on the floor. "That's why that green card I gave you is so valuable. You can travel anywhere with it."

She stared at him "Anywhere? I could visit Dede in Palm Beach?"

He smiled. "I told you that there are few of them issued. You could have sold it to your Mr. Klein today and he could have gone anywhere."

Sylvie felt her stomach begin to go tight. "His family, too?"

"Of course."

Now he was in close to her and moving to kiss her. "Don't lose it." He found her mouth and pushed her back on the rug. She gave him her lips but she wasn't all there.

"I want you," he whispered.

She gave him a peck and then put her hand on his chest. "I want to do my nails first."

"Sylvie."

"In a few minutes, Patrick. Be patient. You'll be rewarded in time. All those who do good works are . . ."

"I do very good work."

"Don't be vulgar." She got up.

He took her hand. "Hurry . . . I really can't wait."

She gave him a cool stare and then walked off to the bedroom. Twenty minutes later he moved inside her. He was potent and hungry for her, the smell of her scent driving him to bring her to the heights he felt now. It was like some hard thing had formed in her and he, by the force of who he was, by the sheer want of her, could melt it down and reduce her to still another triumph. He lunged and pulverized, bent her to his will, but always this hardness came back at him. Firm, unyielding, ungiving. It was as though her essence had fled. He thrust and thrust at it and she lay, eyes closed, mouth parted, a part of him and yet apart unto herself.

They lay silent, separate. Damn her, he thought. I'm about to grasp the comet by the tail. The heavens beckon, and I can't make her come. I can't make her moan in pleasure. I can't make her wriggle and dance for me. Perhaps it was just time to move to another one. Mistresses were hardly new for him. When one wore out, he sent her some jewelry and faded away. That's how this strange twilight world away from his family was.

One day you slept with a stranger, and desire was a thing of memory. How much of it was him, how much her? It didn't matter. Long ago he had accepted his dual life. There was his family back in Philadelphia—Grace, his wife, was a pleasant, attractive woman who gave him six children and knew how to bury herself in being a dutiful mother and did not ask questions when Kelly returned home to spend weekends. There was that and the women he needed for conquests. That was the way he lived. He'd wait until Palm Springs was over and see how he felt about Sylvie. Something pricked him in that moment. He knew he was rationalizing. There was something about her that got under his skin. It was why he could trust her. He trusted only one other woman besides Sylvie, and that was Grace, mother of his children. What was it? Why, he could have anyone he wanted. He felt the anger and clenched his fists. Tomorrow he would humble Morgenthau and Hull, and he lay here now feeling rejected by a beautiful but simple creature. What did he want from her? What did she have that he could possibly want? She was just class pussy. His father had taught him about class pussy. "The juices in them smell better," his father had said. "Class

162

pussy is better than good Irish whiskey, but not as good as gold. Just never fall in love with it.'' He lay there desperate to say something, but he knew it would make him smaller. He knew what she was. Never, never give in to a woman.

She heard Patrick's soft breathing and stopped feigning sleep. The day had been catastrophic. First Mr. Klein and what he faced. Then there was the Negro cleaning woman with the flat nose and triumphant eyes. Why had the cleaning woman hated her so much? Why was the penny so important? The sleeping pill lay under her pillow but, though Sylvie had three times picked it up, she would not take it. She was close to something. Why did the woman do it? Why were there people who wished to humiliate her? Because they saw something weak in her. Just as Patrick did. He tolerated her so he could take her cruelly as he had just done. They knew she was there to be violated. Because she was a victim? But that couldn't be. She had all the advantages in life. She came from the finest lineage. The Lamont family and Maryland were synonymous. Her mother's house had all those portraits of the entire family. No matter who her mother married, she was always Miss Lamont. Al, her second husband, had always made a fuss about it. That's why they finally broke up. He wouldn't toady to her the way the others did. The way her father, Pierre Ramonde, did.

She remembered how cruel and terribly attractive Al was. He would always go on about how he was going to run off with her. He would take her in a boat around the world. A boat . . . that was it. A speedboat. It was their secret. She had gone to her mother one night and told her of the secret. Her mother had said nothing. There was a hint of something in her eyes, but Sylvie was too young to identify it.

Then the next day with Dede and Sylvie sitting on the porch Al came. Sylvie remembered standing up and saying, "Do you have it?" Al had nodded, and Sylvie had hugged him with all her strength. "I have it with me," he had said. "Give me the key," Sylvie remembered saying. Then Al put his hand in his pocket and took it out. It was a toy boat. She remembered at first thinking it was a joke, but he kept saying, "Here's your boat." Her mother had come out and, looking at her, Sylvie saw the cold aloofness. In that moment she knew it all. Her mother hated Al enough to drive him to this, and Al hated her enough to humiliate Sylvie. She was nothing but a pawn between them. That was the first awful humiliation. That's what made her a victim. Nobody had stood up for her, not even Dede. She had never learned to stand up for herself. That's why she ended up with toy boats. The cleaning woman wasn't born anybody, but she had learned how to fight. A penny is worth fighting for. In that moment she saw what fighting meant. What are we if we don't fight for ourselves? Isn't that what little Timmy wanted so badly? Someone to love him . . . to give him self-worth. She had let herself down, many times, but somehow she couldn't betray little Timmy. The most appealing boy in St. Stephen's. There is something fine and good in me. Somebody listen. I have courage. I do. Somehow I must find it.

Chapter 17

Thursday, February 5, 1942
3:30 P.M.

Well fortified with cash, Sylvie had taken a cab down to Sophie's, which was located on Division Street. Sylvie had never been on the Lower East Side. Just the reference to lower anywhere made her prepare for the worst. The cab driver switched from Park Avenue to Third and then swung left along Grand Street. As the smart buildings and doormen of Park Avenue became the steakhouses and book stores of Third Avenue, then gave way to the ancient architecture of Grand Street, she felt as if she had entered another century. A large apartment house caught her eye. It had a surface of brick carved with little stucco inserts. The driver suddenly swung left, and Sylvie sensed it was not a planned turn.

The driver, a middle-aged man with a least a week's growth of beard, must have read her thoughts. He said, "Nazi car. Can't stand those dirty bastards." She looked and saw the name on his hack license, Jacob Feldstein. Was he, like Morris Klein, planning to leave? No, he wouldn't have the money. But would he leave if he did?

Suddenly, like an impish child unable to keep anything to herself, she spoke the question.

The cab driver considered it only briefly. "Leave? Why should I leave? This is my city. Let the goddamn Nazis leave. We should all get guns and bombs and throw them out."

"Would you fight?"

"Would I?" He snorted. "I'll be in the front lines just as soon as something happens. And let me tell you, lady, the way

164

this town is, something is going to happen." He looked back at her in the rearview mirror and lapsed into silence.

He probably wonders if I'm a spy for the Nazis, she thought. She caught her own thinking pattern. Why does "Nazis" seem like such a better word for them than Germans? She thought of that nasty little man Abetz. Yes, "Nazi" was a good word for him.

The cab moved in a zigzag pattern through the Lower East Side. Now along Allen Street under some elevated tracks. Blue and yellow signs advertised quilts for sale, blankets and bed linens. The street was a cacophony of sound and color, of shops featuring vases and lamps, candlesticks, grandfather clocks, rows and rows of plates in endless designs. Sylvie counted no less than six stores displaying antiques. My God, it's another world here.

"This is Division Street, lady. What number did you say?"

"Three twenty-one."

He had to slow for pedestrians, and Sylvie saw row upon row of women's shops. Dresses, sweaters, shoes, gowns were showcased in beautifully laid out plate glass windows.

"Here you are, lady."

Sylvie got out and saw the sign: SOPHIE'S SHOES.

"Lady!"

She looked back, startled.

The cab driver had a plaintive expression on his face. "Would you like to pay me? Two dollars, lady."

"Of course. I'm sorry."

She was still paying him when a man began tugging at her elbow. "Lady, beautiful lady, do I have a bargain for you. Just come into Freddy's."

He was a young man with gleaming eyes, a bit of a mustache, and a very persistent manner. "It's perfect for you, beautiful lady."

Flustered, Sylvie couldn't remember the fare.

The cab driver shook his hand at the young man. "Get away, schlepper. Go on, she's for Sophie."

The man continued to pursue her, however, straight up to Sophie's door.

"Beautiful lady, come on with me. I have a palace to show you. A palace."

"Please, you're hurting my arm." She pulled free and went inside Sophie's.

It was a small room tastefully decorated with shoes of all styles and colors on stands placed along the walls. On a rack that extended up some eight rows were long-heeled black shoes, smart brown ones, slippers touched with inner layers of fur. Sylvie looked for the rose shoes.

A young woman in a white blouse and brown skirt came over. "Can I help you?"

Sylvie turned to her and was struck by the innocence and sweetness of the girl's face. She was no beauty, but she had the quality indigenous to youth. Full of expectation and even exaltation. Life is good. Something even better will happen tomorrow. Sylvie found herself wondering if she had ever been that way.

The girl reddened. She thinks I'm ignoring her.

"I'm terribly sorry. It's just that you have such an attractive display."

She smiled. "Thank you. Can I show you something?"

"I'd like to talk to Sophie."

"She's in the stockroom. Shall I get her?"

Sylvie thought it might be better to speak to Sophie alone. "If you'll just direct me. . . ."

"Oh, I'll take you, no trouble."

She led Sylvie to the back of the store and into a room that was piled high with boxes and shoes spilling out of them. The walls were a faded yellow, accentuated by the one bulb hanging from the ceiling. The shoes rested on old green shelves. The stale residue of rubber and leather permeated the storeroom. The girl led her to a woman who was on her knees muttering to herself as she checked boxes and threw them away, one after another.

"Sophie, this lady to see you."

Still on her knees, Sophie turned and looked up. She had black hair shot through with gray and large brown eyes not untouched by the wisdom of living. She wore a gray sales jacket over her black sweater.

Sylvie thanked the girl, who left them.

"Yes, how can I help you?"

"Mr. Klein sent me. He said you might have a pair of rose shoes that I desperately need for tonight."

"Oh, you're the lady." Now she was up on her feet. "Morris said you'd be coming in."

"Oh, then he spoke with you."

"Better than that. He found the shoes."

Sylvie couldn't contain her delight. "Then you have them?"

"Certainly. Would I tell such a fine lady as you that he found them and not have them?"

She walked toward a little counter that was awash in bills, invoices, and letters. Sylvie spotted the box with Mr. Klein's label.

"Here you are. There's a note inside for you." Sophie handed a brown envelope to Sylvie. The note was neatly typed on matching brown bond.

Dear Miss Lamont,

Most fortunately I have been able to find your shoes and with great pleasure have delivered them to Sophie. I know they will sparkle on your feet at the ball. I am so glad to have found them for you and ask you to forgive the inconvenience of yesterday. I hope in a better time that you will once again return to Glenda's shoe store.

With best wishes,
Morris Klein.

The signature was scrawled as if made under great duress.

Sylvie turned to Sophie. "I'm so relieved and thankful. And I must also thank you."

Sophie held up a hand. "I didn't do nothing. It was Morris. He brought the shoes here himself. You must be a special customer."

The image of Mr. Klein weeping came back to Sylvie, and for a moment she found herself unable to speak. "You say he brought them himself?"

Sophie nodded.

She wanted to take the box and leave. She didn't want to ask the question but she had to. "When will he leave?"

"Leave?"

"I was at his home yesterday. He told me he was taking his family away."

Sophie shook her head. The expression on her face was a mixture of sorrow and acceptance. "Twenty years he built that business and it is taken away from him."

"He'll start again, of course."

A sliver of a sardonic smile showed itself. "With what? They'll bleed him dry to get out of New York. There's a new business in America. Smuggle Jewish refugees out of the East. Charge them the moon. For everybody knows the Jews have gelt salted away."

"Where will he go?" Sylvie couldn't believe who had asked the question. She saw surprise and suspicion in Sophie's eyes.

The answer was, of course, evasive. "As far away as possible."

"California?"

Rose shrugged. "Perhaps. California is very far."

"It's dangerous, isn't it?"

"Yes, it is dangerous."

"He might not . . ." Sylvie stopped. She remembered something. "You are an old friend, aren't you?"

A certain moistness showed in Sophie's eyes. "Yes."

"Will you see him before he goes?"

"Perhaps, I'm not sure."

Sylvie opened her bag and took out the green pass. "See him and give him this." She handed it to Sophie. "It is a special pass issued by German security. I believe he can get himself and his family away with it and there will be no questions. He will not have to spend his savings."

The extent of Sophie's disbelief was indicated in the way she read the pass to herself in German and English. Then she read it silently a second time. She looked up at Sylvie. "It is a fine thing that you do."

"Will you make sure he gets it?"

"Don't worry. Nobody gets this pass but Morris Klein. Those butchers out there would have to cut off my hands and still I wouldn't let go." She put a hand on Sylvie's shoulder. "He'll get it tonight."

"Good." Sylvie picked up the shoe box and prepared to leave.

Sophie's voice came to her and she turned. "You know, my father said to me that all gentiles aren't bad. He said the best of them were like the word itself. Gentle." She extended her hand. "Go gently, Miss Lamont."

Sylvie reached out and took it.

4:40 P.M.

Late in the afternoon the prisoners were to be driven from the Tombs through the Holland Tunnel to the work camps around Paterson, Hackensack, and East Rutherford. By putting the fix in with a cop named McGinty, Collins had been able to establish that Jimmy Handy would be among those transferred. The plan was a simple one. Paulie Lazar, driving a van, would ram the prisoners' truck as it intersected Canal and Broadway. The Nazis would have only three guards with the truck in addition to the driver. The prisoners were all to be freed, which would create enough of a diversion so that Collins could get Jimmy away on foot. Collins was carrying a duffel bag with an overcoat, a cap, and shoes that Jimmy could slip over the gray uniform issued political prisoners. Lazar, speeding away, would be the diversion. The Heinrichs would be led away from Jimmy and Collins. He had picked Lazar because there could be shooting. This was Lazar's chance to prove himself.

Collins waited in a phone booth at the boarded-up gas station facing Canal Street. His watch showed a quarter of five. The krauts would run into Holland Tunnel traffic. Welcome to New York. Canal Street was a big, open street that intersected a few gas stations and warehouses on the West Side before running past a series of small businesses leading into Chinatown and Centre Street where the Tombs was located. Lazar was set up in an old junkyard behind Collins. The thumbs-up sign meant the Heinrichs were coming.

Collins looked east on Canal Street for the truck. The Heinrichs liked to use New York Police trucks so they wouldn't be obvious. It made it a little easier to disguise themselves. The sun was going down, and Collins blew into his hands and rubbed them. Kresky was going to hit the Curtiss-Wright plant. Dynamite would be needed. Jimmy Handy was the best jelly man in New York. Jimmy had been caught here when the invasion broke out. Collins had to have him for the job.

Paulie sat behind the wheel of the van, hand on the gun in his pocket. What if something goes wrong, and I get hauled in? This job was taking him away from trailing General Beck and coming up with a hit plan. Abetz didn't say when it had to be done, but Paulie knew Abetz was a man of limited patience. Like all the bosses Paulie had worked for, Abetz knew only one box score. The result.

Collins checked his watch. The krauts should be along any minute now. He came out of the booth and looked east on Canal. There, the police truck behind a green Buick. Collins put his thumb up, the signal for Paulie in the van. He could hear the engine of the van start up. Collins went over and crouched behind an empty fuel pump. The gas station, like so many, had gone out of business. He saw Lazar's van pull out and line up at the intersection. Now it started forward as the police truck crossed Canal and Broadway.

Gun in hand, Collins was running as the police truck, struck by the van, swerved into the lane of oncoming eastbound traffic. Lazar had gotten the van right into the rear fender of the police truck and kept pushing it. The truck smashed into the fence of a parking lot and stopped. The rear door opened, and two Nazi guards came out. They found themselves looking directly into Collins's pistol. "Drop the guns. Back inside," he yelled. "Let's go," he called to the prisoners. "You're free." Jimmy Handy was the third one out. "Fancy meeting you," he said. Collins locked the door on the two guards.

Collins clapped Handy on the shoulder. "Let's go."

Paulie came over. "Trouble. There's another truck coming. It's Heinrich. Over there."

It was a truckload of soldiers. Christ on the slopes of Calvary, Collins thought. Always the unexpected.

"Give us some cover," Collins said to Paulie. "Lead them on a goose chase. Then try to lose them."

Jimmy Handy had the overcoat, cap, and shoes on. "How do I look?"

Collins slipped him a revolver. "Beautiful enough for a movie."

He watched Paulie Lazar behind the wheel of the van roar out into traffic. Now Paulie leaned out and fired at the Heinrich truck.

"C'mon," Collins yelled. They sprinted out of the parking lot as the first riddling sound of the Heinrich tommy guns were heard.

Instead of going directly home, Sylvie did an odd thing. Night was falling as she wandered like a nomad along the Lower East Side. She had never seen a world like this. Shops, peddlers, vendors selling bagels and something called knishes surrounded her. On other carts she saw shoelaces, overalls, mittens, sun glasses, blouses, sweaters, galoshes. She was pushed and jostled between peddlers, mothers and children, old men with beards, young men like the one outside Sophie's, trying to sell her this and that. "Fine lady, want to buy a watch?" "Lady, lady, do I have a deal for you." "Hey, lady, I'll show you a good time." "A brooch, lady, a genuine brooch." Men and women pushed, elbowed, jammed, shoved, bargained, begged, argued, abused each other. They're like a colony of ants fighting a hostile army, she thought. She knew Mr. Klein came from these people. Only he was one of those who had gotten out, one who had made it. How cruel that it was taken away from him. His life's work. He had made something of himself. He had the charming brownstone apartment in Brooklyn Heights. She couldn't for the life of her think why she had given away her pass. Not that she needed it. But it just wasn't something she would have thought to do. It wasn't even a thought, it was some kind of reflex instinct. What was happening to her?

She saw a little stand with a sign for tea and coffee and stopped. She was frightfully low on energy. Some tea with sugar would lift her. It was then she noticed she no longer had a headache. That can't be, she thought. I haven't taken my afternoon pill. But it wasn't there. She felt her forehead with her hand as if to reclaim the headache that rightfully belonged there. But is was gone.

"What can I give you, lady?" the bald man said to the welldressed lady with the odd smile. He looked her over. A society type, slumming. He had seen those crazies from uptown before.

Sylvie drank the tea without sugar—the vendor had none—and

170

watched a man trying to sell stockings with a run in them to a fat woman with thick, stumpy legs. "With legs like that, you should be grateful for a pair that will fit." Before she could reply, the little worm of a salesman had them in her hand. "I'm giving them away to you. Fifty cents. No? Forty. A quarter. Twenty cents and that's my last . . ."

Sylvie found herself smiling. She wanted to laugh. She used to laugh a lot, till her father left and her second father came, and then her third. She looked up at the street sign: Orchard Street. There was noise and commotion from the other side of Orchard Street. People were scattering and running. There were shouts, frightened cries.

She could see the soldiers now, and the word forming on people's lips, "Nazis." The scattering became full-scale panic as Sylvie heard cries behind her. There was a group of soldiers coming from the other side. Orchard Street was being closed off. They were trying, it seemed to Sylvie, to effect some kind of search. Men were being grabbed and thrown aside, pushcarts overturned, women and children knocked to the ground. Frantic peddlers fell on their knees to retrieve food and goods tossed brutally aside. Whistles were blowing. She stood, frozen in her tracks, still holding her tea. Why can't I move? She turned one way, then the other, and saw a young boy of high school age struggling with a guard. Somehow the boy wrested away the guard's rifle and started running through the screaming crowd. Someone pushed Sylvie to the ground. The Germans began shooting, and there were more screams. People fell and, hugging the pavement, slithered under carts for cover. Suddenly there was just the boy running in a crazy zigzag away from one end of the street, only to be met by the soldiers at the other end. He went down in a fusillade of fire. It was suddenly quiet. A baby wailed. A woman wept. Sylvie sat up. She was only a few yards from where the boy had fallen; a trail of blood ran from him. Sylvie got up and tried to move to him and felt a hand on her arm. It was the little weasel who, moments ago, had been trying to sell the torn stockings.

"Lady, it's no use."

"Let go."

He looked at her as if she were crazy.

"Did you hear me?" She pulled free and then went over to the boy and bent down at his side. He wasn't even eighteen. He had hair like fuzz over his mouth. She felt for a sign of a pulse. His lifeless hand slipped away.

Obviously, the Germans were looking for someone. Not these people who cried, implored, pleaded, as if each were the culprit. Sylvie saw the fat woman who had been engaged with the stock-

171

ing salesman put a soldier's hand on her breast. The soldier and a comrade became hysterical with laughter and threw her into the roundup.

Now the soldiers reached Sylvie and looked at her with some interest. She was too well dressed for this street. One of the soldiers turned to a comrade, a fat wart of a man, and said "*Spion.*" The other one nodded. He grabbed Sylvie's arm and thrust her into the group being rounded up for questioning.

Collins and Jimmy Handy were wedged against a stand that had spilled over. The kid's dead, Collins thought. It's no different than Dublin. The innocent get it in the neck. This roundup was for them. He wondered if Lazar had gotten away. The Nazi officer heading up the search party was working toward them. Jimmy's pale as a ghost. One look at him, and they'll recognize prison pallor.

Suddenly a little rooster of a peddler slid over. "My blankets." He pointed to an overturned cart. For a second Collins thought, incredible, this guy is trying to sell me his blankets. Then he realized they were meant for cover.

Collins nudged Jimmy. "Slip under those. Hurry, I'll lump them up."

Jimmy dropped down and worked his way under three ugly brown barley blankets. The peddler, a gray-haired runt with a jockey cap, slipped a patchwork quilt over the pile and then another gray one Collins wouldn't have used on a horse. He expertly crumpled them up and stepped in front of them. Collins slid in next to him. There was a chance.

A well-dressed blonde was angrily remonstrating with the fat officer in charge of the search. "Do you know who I am?"

The officer, who wore glasses and had a mustache, inspected her carefully. This one was dressed better. He listened. "No," he said with disdain, "who are you?"

"I am a personal acquaintance of Mr. Abetz." In her rage, Sylvie realized she didn't even know his rank. But the name obviously rang true.

The officer's manner changed immediately. "You know Standartenführer Abetz?"

"I will be dining with him this evening," she lied.

"You can verify this with some identification?"

She remembered the green card. It made her even angrier. "I don't need identification. One phone call to Mr. Abetz will identify me. Will you make it or should I? Tell him you are holding Sylvie Lamont, Patrick Kelly's friend."

Hoisted on his own petard, the officer looked around as if seeking verification.

The names Sylvie Lamont and Patrick Kelly rang in Collins's ear. Beck had mentioned her. And Kelly was America's premier collaborator. In what he knew was either an act of inspiration or insanity, Collins moved to them. "Excuse me, perhaps I can help."

"Who are you?" the flustered captain asked.

Collins had out his identity card. "Robert Jackson. I'm an attorney. I have attended a number of parties given by General Beck, your military kommandant. Miss Lamont has been a frequent guest with Mr. Kelly."

The officer studied his card. You've got your way out, chump, Collins thought, take it.

The captain handed back his card. "That call won't be necessary, Miss Lamont. Give the kindest regards of Captain Schnelker to the standartenführer. My thanks to you, Mr. Jackson." He barked something in German and Sylvie and Collins passed through the ranks of soldiers as if they were descendants of Moses at the Red Sea. Collins fought the urge to look back for Jimmy Handy.

Collins took her arm as she was quite pale and he knew it would also look good. "Are you all right?"

She took a deep breath. "I hope so. That was awful. That young boy is dead."

"I know."

"What was it all about?"

What do you care, you rich bitch? "I'm not sure. The Germans were after somebody." He couldn't go back for Jimmy, and he had to play the hand out with the dame. If he suddenly split, she'd get suspicious and report it. That would be the end of his cover.

They walked along Grand Street in the early evening and Collins had a chance to case her. Rich, spoiled, hangs out with the Nazis and the appeasers. Attractive as hell. Probably like a quick thrill. Couple of drinks and maybe he could bed her down. Christ, he needed it. He hadn't been with a woman in almost three months. He knew his desire was also a thing of the spirit. He felt so alone in America. He needed to be loved, if only for a brief time. He remembered something Mick had said. "The glory of killing has no nourishment."

Collins took her arm. "You look like you could use a brandy. May I?"

She stopped. "Yes, that sounds like a good idea, Mr. . . . ?"

"Jackson."

They stopped at a pub in the Village called the White Knight. It was old, woody, somber, and dank. Collins ordered a double scotch for himself and brandy for the rich bitch.

173

The waiter brought the drinks and Collins asked for some nickels. He went over to the jukebox and read the selections, then came back to their booth. "Can I play you something?" She was quiet a moment. She's a real looker, he acknowledged.

"Pick one for me. I'm afraid I'm not up on the current songs."

He went to the jukebox thinking, lady, I been away for years. He found a selection and punched it.

They sat drinking, making no conversation. Bill Kenny and the Ink Spots came on.

I don't want to set the world on fire,
I just want to start a flame in your heart.

"I was thinking about the boy's parents," she said. "How awful it will be tonight."

"No, it'll be worse the day after tomorrow when the numbness wears off and they realize he's never coming back. That's when it's hell."

She looked at him, wondering for the first time who he really was. "What do you do?"

"I'm a lawyer." Better spin out the rest of the yarn, he thought. She might have Kelly make inquiries. Protect your ass. "I'm a tax lawyer. I'm from Cleveland. I got stuck here during the invasion."

"You can't get out?"

"Well, I'm working on it."

She sipped the brandy and made a face.

What's the matter, honey, not good enough for you?

"I'll speak to Patrick when he comes back from Palm Springs. I mean, if you don't mind. You were very helpful and I'm not ungrateful."

She was so polite. Did she make love that way?

"That's not necessary, Miss Lamont, but I appreciate the offer. I am curious though. What is he doing in Palm Springs?"

"I don't know exactly what it involves, but there are negotiations between the Germans and the American government and he's offered his services."

Collins downed the scotch. Oh, I know who you bed down with. The American Reich. Only you people say Hail Hitler. "Care for another drink?"

She shook her head no.

Collins excused himself as Artie Shaw began the beguine.

He came back and got a whiff of her scent as he slid into the booth. It was good stuff. Class. She was a class lass. She needed time, and he had none. It wasn't his style to fool around.

"Will the war be over soon?" He couldn't quite keep the facetiousness out of his voice.

She didn't seem to notice. "It is for that boy, isn't it?"

She seemed soft and vulnerable. You want it as badly as I do, he realized. Perhaps a little blarney and then a simple direct approach. He put his hand under the table and took hers. "For him and a lot of others."

"It makes everything else seem so . . . so pointless." Suddenly she looked around. "Oh, my god. I've lost them. I can't believe it."

"What? Lost what?"

"The shoes. I came all the way down there and . . ." Now she stopped. "It's not really important. I wasn't meant to wear them."

A kid is dead and Miss Class worries about her shoes. He dropped her hand. He had lost interest. End this. "You look like you should go home."

Tears showed in her eyes. "Yes, I should."

"Park Avenue."

"What?"

"That where you live?"

"How did you know?"

"Just a guess. I'll get you a cab."

She looked at him now in a dazed fashion, and then the eyes came into place. "Yes, please." She stood up.

They came out into the street, and Sylvie looked for a cab. "Good-bye, Mr. Jackson."

"Good-bye." He started to move away and then waited. He wanted to hear the address. You could never tell when the information might come in . . . Jesus, did Jimmy get away?

She got into a cab. "Nine-seventy Park Avenue."

The cab moved away, flickering its light beams into the uptown traffic. Then it was one of the many fireflies of night and was lost to Collins's view.

175

AMERICAN PANORAMA
X

YANKEES TO PLAY IN MIAMI
GIANTS IN OMAHA
NO DODGER MOVE TO L.A.

February 4, 1942

From the wires of AP . . . Baseball Commissioner Kenesaw Mountain Landis announced today that the 1942 baseball season will go on as scheduled despite the German invasion of the Northeast of America. Speaking at a press conference called in Columbus, Ohio by NY Yankee General Manager Ed Barrow, Judge Landis announced that the Yankees have completed arrangements with the city of Miami to play their games at the football stadium of the University of Miami. The Giants will play in Omaha, the Boston Red Sox in Minneapolis, and the Philadelphia Phillies and Athletics are to be located in Columbus, Ohio. But Judge Landis has denied the Brooklyn Dodgers' proposed move to Los Angeles. "We cannot play on the West Coast. We don't have the planes to get there." The commissioner added, "Who would identify with the Los Angeles Dodgers?" Commenting on negotiations with the German government to secure authorization for Yankee shortstop Phil Rizzuto to leave his Queens home, Ed Barrow said, "I am not optimistic. Let's face it. He is behind enemy lines."

GESTAPO ISSUES WARRANT FOR RIZZUTO

February 5, 1942

From the wires of AP . . . Yankee shortstop Phil Rizzuto is being hunted by the Gestapo in New York. After a series of inquiries by the Yankees and several newspapers, the German military governor, General Heinrich von Stulpnagel, has alerted the Gestapo to search for Mr. Rizzuto. Though General von Stulpnagel indicated he was concerned about Mr. Rizzuto's safety, informed sources believe that he is one of several

American sport stars the Germans are demanding a heavy ransom for in order to release them from the occupied East Coast of America. They include Chicago Bears quarterback Sid Luckman, Giants football star Ken Strong, shot putter Al Blozis, and Rizzuto's Yankee teammate, Charlie "King Kong" Keller.

RIZZUTO IN MIAMI

February 6, 1942

From the wires of AP . . . Yankee rookie of the year, shortstop Phil Rizzuto, turned up in Miami today for spring training. Rizzuto, who had been officially listed as missing by the Gestapo in New York, would not comment on how he reached Miami, saying only that he did not want to jeopardize the people who had helped him. He said he was looking forward to the 1942 baseball season but would feel strange playing in Miami all season and not in New York. Asked how he felt about being on the Gestapo's wanted list, Rizzuto said, "After you've faced Bob Feller's fastball and lived, you don't worry about the Gestapo."

RIZZUTO MISSING AGAIN

February 7, 1942

From the wires of AP . . . Yankee star Phil Rizzuto is missing again. He checked out of his St. Petersburg, Florida hotel last night and left no word as to his destination. There is an unverified report that the ball player's father is seriously ill back in Hillside, Queens. Ed Barrow, Yankee general manager, refused to comment on speculation Rizzuto has gone back to occupied New York to be with his sick father. An unidentified teammate had this to say: "If anyone can get past the Nazis twice, it's the Scooter. Hell, he's only five feet four."

Chapter 18

Paulie had figured out how to satisfy both Abetz and Collins. It was tricky, but he had played it over and over in his mind till he felt it was foolproof. With Abetz it was a matter of survival. Paulie wasn't getting his cubes roasted by the Gestapo. At the same time, Collins was the man with Uncle Sam's bread. And he hadn't been back to Paulie with any work since the Canal Street rescue job. There had been a fire at Pier 52. Lots of kraut ships went up. That was the work of professionals. Maybe Collins had used the Scalizi mob. They had good waterfront connections. Paulie should have been part of it. It must have paid good bread. He never should have taken on that job as driver. That lowered him in Collins's eyes right away. He should have plugged some Heinrichs when Collins was rescuing his buddy. That would have impressed Collins. Now Paulie would have to find a way of his own. If he didn't, he would be strictly a chauffeur for Collins, and there was no gelt in that.

He had to clip this guy Beck for Abetz. The brainstorm had come to Paulie that, once he did it, he would then make sure Collins found out it was Paulie who did the icing. Paulie would then tell him the hit was for someone else from Uncle Sam and make sure Collins knew that from now on Paulie's price was top dollar. Collins would try to check it out, but Paulie was sure Uncle had floated more than one guy into New York.

Most of this plan had come to Paulie from a file Abetz had given him. The file was on a guy named Delon who had infiltrated the French Resistance for the Gestapo. Delon had offered his services as a hit man to several suspected underground leaders. To back it up, Delon walked into a café in Lyon and shot three Vichy government officials. Paulie really shook his head over how cool this Delon had acted.

Delon walked into the restaurant where the three Vichy guys ate lunch. He ordered a glass of wine and watched the three targets slopping up clams, salad, and wine. Then, as the waiter brought them coffee, bread, and cheese, Delon walked to the table. He called them this French word *"Messieurs,"* which Paulie guessed meant guys. They looked over, and Delon pulled out a pistol and shot each one between the eyes. Then he shoved the rod back in his pocket and walked away without looking backward. Within three days he was contacted by the Resistance. "We now have an agent placed in the Resistance with access to their movements and to names of specific agents," the file said. All Paulie had to do was wait once he hit Beck. Collins would find out and come to him. That would give Paulie his ace. Once he did the hit, Collins would bring him into the firm and, if Paulie ever got into a tight scrape, he could throw Abetz someone from the Resistance. Not that Paulie figured on being a canary. But this was war, and you had to protect your ass. The way Paulie figured it, if he played it right, he could work for both Abetz and Collins and always be protected. If he got caught doing a job for Collins, he'd whistle for Abetz. And if Abetz had any other hits for him, Paulie would just tell Collins he was in demand for private contracting.

Where to clip Beck had come to him when he passed a newspaper stand. Read the Heinrich paper, dummy. He bought it three days in a row, ignoring the dirty looks of the news dealer. On the third day there was a picture of the kraut officers who rode in Central Park every morning. Paulie had cut the picture out and memorized the three krauts' faces and names. There was Beck, the kommandant of the city; von Stulpnagel, the military governor; and von Kleist, the German ambassador. What Paulie had to do was plug Beck and make it look like he was trying to do all three of them. That would cover Abetz's ass. Then he just had to drop Nippo's identity card and get out. It wasn't going to be that easy, and there would be a lot of heat afterward. Beck was big, but Abetz would help him out once he did the knock.

He had spent the last week getting up at five o'clock in the morning to watch the Heinrichs have their little gallop. They generally rode anytime between seven and a quarter to eight. The three of them would ride together, or sometimes it would just be Beck, who was easy to spot because he was tall and had black hair. The little ambassador had white hair. Von Stulpnagel had red hair and was easy to pick out, but he didn't ride as often. They rode with six soldiers about fifty yards behind them. It was too dangerous to try something then. The time to do it was just before or just after. After meant just as they were coming out of the stables, which Paulie didn't like. Too many people around. But he had noticed that each morning before riding they would have their breakfast at Tavern on the Green. Sometimes they would come out together, and sometimes they would drift out separately. Best of all, their guards would be waiting at the stable. That was the time to do the knock.

He had also changed his plan. He would shoot only at Beck. One was how a professional did it. Then everybody would know his signature. If there was a lot of wild shooting, it wouldn't have the same effect. He remembered something old Barney Feldstein had told him. "Paulie, when you do a big knock, do it so everybody knows it was a first class professional. Don't go in blasting, dropping a lot of people standing around. Nobody will use you after that. You'll be a mad dog with rabies, and you know what happens to them."

9:00 A.M.

Collins was out on the street and suddenly his steps were light and quick. The rain had subsided, and a warm mist was forming over Broadway. It was milder today. A reminder that spring was only six weeks away. He headed downtown, seeing the mud and refuse clogged in piles near the sewers. It was seven o'clock. General Beck would be riding in Central Park this morning, and he would drop a little envelope for Collins. Collins had half an hour to get to Sixty-fifth Street. He decided to walk to Ninety-first Street and take the local there. Now, as he walked along Broadway, past its coffee shops, small clothing stores, past Woolworth, Grant's, Walgreen, Nedick's, he felt more optimistic. It had to do with hackies like Joe T. Bone who fought the Heinrich on the city streets each day with Kreml hair tonic and Monopoly money, and that little runt with the jockey cap who covered over Jimmy Handy and helped him escape. There were dozens more who didn't believe the *Daily Patrician* or the *Daily Bund*. They wanted their city back. Jesus, maybe there's a chance after all. A bit of a wind brought the breeze to him, and he felt he could identify it. It was the quality of hope. He wouldn't be here to see the final acts played out, but he would do his part before leaving. As he walked down Broadway he realized the last thought bothered him.

Collins came out of the subway at Sixty-fifth and Broadway and started in the direction of Central Park West. The people were out on the street now heading for work. Heads down, furtive, some looked up at you and checked you out. Are you Gestapo? the looks said. The rain had stopped, but the mist remained. It was more like fog, reminding Collins of late fall days in London when the air was soup thick. He rehearsed the sequence worked out by Beck in a message left for Collins in Central Park. He knew it by heart. "I like to sprint the horse.

180

My guards know that. You set yourself in the bushes along the riding track approximately half a mile from where we start. You will see us coming. When I raise my riding crop that will be the signal. There is a large elm tree that is set just back off the riding track. When I am parallel with it, I shall pull up and turn around to prepare to sprint back. As I turn the horse I will throw you the envelope.''

Paulie had entered the park at Fifty-ninth Street. That way he could come up behind the parking lot of Tavern on the Green. The rows of benches in the park were deserted. The grass was soggy, heavy from the rain. Christ, they might not ride this morning. But it was perfect if they did. Thick with fog, a little warm, lazy guards. The only problem would be getting out of the parking lot after he hit the target. But there were generally only a few drivers there. The bulk of the officers didn't start arriving until about eight o'clock, long after the riders had left the Tavern on the Green. He would shoot from his pocket with a hankie around the muzzle to deaden the sound. If things went right, he would be moving down the sidewalk path out of the restaurant area before anyone knew what was wrong. Then he would walk deliberately across the street and hail a cab. It would have been perfect if there were a subway across the street. Just be cool, that's all. This is your big chance. If you make it, it's steak and lobster, no more ham and eggs.

He came up along the Heckscher Playground. Empty. In the wading pool a small child's sailboat drifted. He reached the playground leading to the Tavern and looked across the parking area at the restaurant. The first thing he saw was the huge swastika flying from the front of it. Then the guards. Shit. It was all wrong. All wrong.

Collins saw the swastika atop the Tavern on the Green. They've taken it over. Probably as an officers' club. He continued walking along the edge of the park where the large black stones that loomed above him were well saturated from the all night rain. He went into the park at Seventy-second Street and, after passing underneath a small wooden shelter, left the footpath to cut across the grass. His shoes squeaked as they sank into the wet sod. A few minutes later he came upon the riding track, its sand made even darker by the rains. He saw the large elm that fronted a rocky slope. His watch read seven-thirty. Beck would be here within fifteen or twenty minutes. Collins lit a cigarette and waited.

* * *

Paulie had to make a fast decision. With all those Heinrichs around the restaurant, there was no chance of getting near Beck. He thought back to his previous trips to the park. He remembered that sometimes the guards would hang back and the two or three bigwig Heinrichs would race their horses ahead. These bigwigs didn't wear uniforms and weren't armed. All Paulie's experience told him to pack it in and go for it someplace else. But the emotional component within him demanded action. Abetz wouldn't wait much longer. Nobody was going to be expecting Paulie in Central Park on a rainy February morning. Heinrich would be on his horse, and there would be a moment when he could be popped. Paulie put his hand in his pocket and felt the .38. He turned and walked toward Seventy-second Street. He could reach the riding path by using the park entrance there.

Collins hugged the tree and read his watch again. Seven-fifty. It would be any minute. He peered out. They were perhaps half a mile away. Beck was riding with a white-haired man, that would be von Kleist, and a red-haired one, von Stulpnagel. They were cantering easily, and now Beck tossed away a cigarette. He prodded the horse with his crop and, responding immediately, the horse bolted forward. Beck rode well, like a man who had been raised riding horses. He was old enough to have been reared in the tradition of the cavalry. He let his body tilt forward so he was one with the horse and yet he still seemed to maintain a graceful, upright position. He covered the ground between himself and Collins in a matter of minutes. He actually went past it, then reined in the horse and began coming back. Collins recognized what he was doing. He would pick up speed again, and the toss of the envelope would be little more than a moving blur. As Beck came back, something distracted Collins, something in the corner of his right eye. He half turned and saw the figure of a man running toward the riding track. In a million light years and a matter of seconds Collins identified him. It was Paulie Lazar.

Paulie had posted himself atop the slope of black rock that faced down on the riding path. He had sighted the three riders as he lay flat on his chest. If Beck didn't get out in front, he would have a real problem. Then, as if in answer to a prayer he didn't know he had made, one of the horsemen broke away from the others. It was the tall, black-haired Heinrich, Beck. And he was pushing that horse down the track like it was the Derby. Then Paulie saw him rein the horse, slowing down in preparation for coming back. Paulie was up off the rock, running, reaching for his gun as he came down the soggy grass. Coming at an angle, Paulie would be at a point to intercept Beck. It was about thirty yards to the riding track, and Paulie covered them like Pug Manders, the Brooklyn Dodgers fullback. He reached the riding track just as the Heinrich was picking up steam for the race back.

Collins saw the nightmare that had been created out of some surrealist vision. Paulie running full tilt down the slope of grass leading to the black dirt track. As he ran, he pulled a revolver. Beck had just thrown the envelope and now, as he urged the horse forward, saw himself confronted by Paulie, gun in hand. You fool, Collins berated himself, stop him.

Paulie stood squarely in front of Beck. The horse whinnied and, sensing danger, reared up. Paulie looked straight into the brilliant eyes of General Beck and read his lack of fear. Beck now used his crop on the horse, and it plunged forward straight at the assassin. Paulie froze, and Beck lashed out with the riding crop, hitting Paulie across the cheek. Paulie fell to the ground as Beck attempted to gallop away. Still frozen, Paulie took dead aim and shot the horse.

Collins was screaming "No, Paulie, no" as he pounded down toward the scene being played out before him. Beck and his horse had both plunged forward to the ground. His breath tortured gasps, Collins came up behind Paulie. As if guided by some sixth sense, Paulie turned, gun in hand, and aimed at Collins. In that moment Collins saw Paulie had absolutely no recognition of him. He's going to shoot me, Collins realized. He fell sideways, trying to dodge the bullet, but it caught him on the side of his knee. He fell screaming "Mother Mary."

Paulie remembered thinking, What is Collins doing here? Then he heard someone coming at him, whirled and saw the Heinrich. You stupid fuck, you should have run away. Paulie blasted him at point blank range and the Heinrich fell forward, hands grasping at Paulie's knees as he fell. Looking down at him, Paulie put another bullet in him. He was about to shoot again when he felt a pistol lash him in the jaw.

Collins kicked Paulie again and again till the gun was loose. He turned to see Beck crawling pathetically on the ground, the blood seeping from him. The clatter of hooves roused Collins as von Stulpnagel and a detachment of men bore down upon them. "Get up," he yelled at Paulie. "You big, dumb bastard."

Paulie stood next to him now. "What the fuck you doing here, Collins?"

"Me?" Collins raged. "What about you? Who ordered this hit?"

Paulie could see the raging anger in Collins. Collins had tried to save Beck. That meant Collins had bought Beck. That's why Abetz wanted him knocked off. He had to think quick. "I wanted to impress you. You didn't give me no hit jobs and I thought you hired Charlie Rosen."

Collins looked at the lethal killer in front of him and remembered how many times in Ireland he had seen violent men with guns act on their own. It would have to be sorted out later. He saw Beck's envelope and scooped it up.

"C'mon," Collins ordered. "Let's get out of here." He turned to face the Nazis on horseback.

"I'll drop a few," Collins yelled. "Go! You hear me? Get us a car. I'll catch up to you."

Paulie took off.

The soldiers bore down the riding track toward the twitching, crawling body of General Beck just yards in front of Collins. As he aimed Collins thought, no generals. No more goddamn generals. He waited until they were close. No more than thirty yards away.

His shot downed the lead rider. It brought the men on horses to a halt. Now, as they dismounted, Collins aimed at a soldier charging him. Blood spurted from his throat. He fell, looking like a man trying to strangle himself with his own hands.

Limping from the pain, Collins ran toward Seventy-second Street, shots echoing behind him. As he ran, he noted the flow of his blood, but the pain wasn't severe. It certainly hadn't touched a bone. Maybe only a flesh wound, they leaked the most. Collins reached Central Park West first and saw the police car. Where was Lazar?

"Drop it," the cop said, pointing his own .38 at Collins.

Collins dropped the gun. Christ, Lazar had run out on him.

"Kick it toward me."

Collins kicked it away.

"Turn your back and up against the wall. Palms flat."

Collins, spread-eagled against the wall, felt the cop searching him.

"Now, just where did you think you were, buddy, in a shooting gallery?" He went down like a flour sack as Paulie crunched him on the side of the head with his pistol butt.

Collins scooped up his own gun. "Let's go." He turned and saw the squad car. He ran over and looked inside, ignoring the gaping looks of people across the street. No keys in the ignition. "Get his keys," he yelled at Paulie.

Collins was in the car and, moments later, Paulie joined him with the keys. He tossed them to Collins, yelling, "Let's shag ass."

Collins ripped the car into a wide U-turn, sending pedestrians sprawling, causing traffic to swerve.

"Here comes Heinrich," Paulie bellowed, and opened fire.

Now they were hurtling down Central Park West, tires screeching.

"I'll turn on the fucking siren," Paulie said. "That'll clear it out." He found the button as if raised in the profession. Siren screaming, they went past Sixty-sixth Street, narrowly avoiding a truck filled with German soldiers.

"Where are we going?"

"Straight up the creek, Lazar. What the hell did you think you were doing? You big, dumb clown. Every Nazi in town will be after us. And if Beck dies . . ." He came to Columbus Circle, and the thought was swallowed as he ran a light, reached Fifty-seventh Street, and turned west.

"Listen, Lazar, I'm ditching the car under the West Side Highway. Then we split up. You go to an address I'll give you along with the keys. You wait there until I get back. I don't care if it takes a week. If you don't wait, I'm giving your name on a contract to the IRA. You got that? My boys. You wait there. You go nowhere. You're working for me. Cross me this time, and you're dead. You understand?"

He heard Paulie laughing.

"What's so funny?"

"You said I work for you. That means I'm your hit man, not Charlie Rosen."

Collins had wrapped the leg with his hankie and then bound it around with the scarf in his pocket. It had begun to throb, and he knew it would stiffen up as the day progressed. He had to get off the street fast. The Gestapo report would indicate that one of the assassins had shot the other in the leg. He moved down Eleventh Avenue, trying not to limp. His destination was Chelsea and the safe house. There would be a lot of Gestapo-police traffic momentarily, and the leg hurt too much to make the thirty block walk to Chelsea. The best bet was the subway. If he could make the IRT Columbus Circle Station before the dragnet was in place, it would be all right. He ought to be able to make it there in less than ten minutes. As he walked across town on Fifty-ninth Street, he folded up his black raincoat and stuffed it into the first trash can he came to. Then he knelt down next to a sewer grating and set a match to Beck's message. Nothing in it was worth Beck's life. He stood up and looked at his watch. Eight twenty-nine.

General Beck had been shot at exactly seven fifty-eight A.M. The stolen police car had been parked and discarded under the West Side Highway at eight-eighteen A.M. Word of the assassination attempt had been radioed to Gestapo headquarters at Centre Street and to police headquarters at Fifty-fourth Street by eight-eleven. By eight-fifteen, police and Gestapo were in motion, sirens screaming. At exactly eight-twenty, elements of the Gestapo and the New York City police force sealed off the entrance to the Columbus Circle IRT station, the Fifty-seventh Street BMT station and the Fifty-seventh Street IND station. Five minutes later, the exits at Seventy-second and Seventy-ninth streets, leading from the West Side Highway, were blocked off. Two minutes later, the Fiftieth Street IRT, IND, and BMT stations were surrounded by uniformed soldiers. Underground, trains were being held at their nearest stations until searched. General Beck's assassin was described as being a large, bulky man in this thirties, wearing a brown overcoat and dark pants.

The second killer was described as having light brown hair, wearing a black raincoat, having gray or brown pants and being wounded in the leg. He had shot and killed one of General Beck's guards and badly wounded another. At exactly eight-twenty, the ambulance carrying General Beck pulled into Roosevelt Hospital at Ninth Avenue and Fifty-eighth Street. A detachment of Gestapo guards led the way into the emergency room of the hospital, and an oxygen mask was placed over the face of the military kommandant of New York City. The attending doctor, George McGrath, a graduate of NYU Medical College, immediately called up to the operating room to schedule an emergency procedure. He then made a second call to request a priest. He had seen these kinds of gunshot wounds before and was taking no chances. If the kommandant, who was known to be Catholic, was not saved and was also not given the last rites of the Church, there would be scapegoats all over the place. Dr. McGrath did not want to be one of them. Under the circumstances, his insight was prescient, yet incomplete. For without question, if General Beck died, an American doctor would be punished for failing to save him.

Collins reached Fifty-ninth Street at eight thirty-three and saw the situation at the Columbus Circle IRT-IND stop. Jesus, they were fast. If they had this blocked off, then the immediate stops above and below Fifty-ninth Street would also be surrounded. A bus had been halted at the side of the intersection that divided Broadway and Central Park West. The manhunt was on. To walk up or downtown with a limp would be to identify himself. The only logical direction was along Central Park South, with its canopies, doormen, and posh hotels housing the Nazi elite and the well-to-do. His best chance was in the enemy's lair.

At Sixth Avenue, Collins could see the cordon of black vehicles forming at Fifth. He could feel his lips moving slightly as he quietly and steadily cursed Paulie Lazar. Of all the people to shoot, Lazar had picked the pipeline to the conspiracy to assassinate Hitler. It confirmed his lifelong theory about the two kinds of luck. Good was never so good as bad was rotten.

His leg was throbbing terribly, and he needed to be off his feet. He knew he'd never get through the blockade forming at Fifth. Cavendish's inside the St. Moritz beckoned to Collins and he went in. He moved past the counter and past the hostess who called to him "Sir . . . sir," to a table where he sat down. She came up to him, a tall, pinched woman looking terribly flustered.

"Thank you," Collins said, holding out his hand for the menu.

"Sir . . ."

"Yes?"

"Next time, allow me to seat you."

"Of course. It's your job, isn't it?"

She flashed him a thousand-daggers expression and let the menu drop to the table. "The waitress will take your order in a few minutes."

Collins sat among the dolls and teddy bears, and admired the bearing of the soft, the fleshy, the fascists, the collaborators, and above all the German officers, who were sitting like spots of elegant gray at almost half the tables. None of these people looked troubled. They would go on eating their pastries and muffins, and when they heard about the shooting of General Ludwig Beck, they would know that its repercussions were not for them. Hundreds across the city would pay for it. Roosevelt and Bill Donovan would talk of it. And Standartenführer Abetz would do a great deal more than talk. But here in Cavendish's, among teddy bears and dolls, pink papers and tasty food, the world would stay a fairyland. He had picked the perfect hiding place. There was only one problem. Eventually he would have to leave it.

Sylvie had waited by the desk at the St. Moritz while they paged General von Stulpnagel. He had only recently moved there from the Plaza. The general, who had been named a judge at the horse show, had invited her last night to discuss some of the finer points of horse breeding. Sylvie had agreed to meet him at eight forty-five.

The concierge looked very ill at ease. "He does not seem to be here. I shall continue to page him, of course."

"I'll wait inside Cavendish's until you find the general." Sylvie had loved Cavendish's since she was a little girl and her father had taken her there for special treats when they visited New York.

Collins was working his way through a second pot of coffee when he saw General von Stulpnagel come in. The red hair was unmistakable. Collins's hand went involuntarily to his face. Stulpnagel had been one of the riding party who had witnessed the shooting. But he had been half a mile away, and Collins had been wearing a raincoat. Stulpnagel couldn't possibly recognize him.

There were two plainclothes SD people with the general. Be casual. He waved to the waitress whom he would ask to bring a newspaper. As he turned, he saw a woman ordering from his waitress.

"Cinnamon toast and a pot of tea."

"Anything else?"

"Oh, I don't think so. I'll just have the toast and tea. Lots of cinnamon."

Collins lips pursed. Without knowing why, any more than he knew why he went into Cavendish's to begin with, he walked to her table. His leg was killing him.

"Hello, Miss Lamont. May I sit down?"

She glanced up at him with wide, saucer eyes.

"Oh, it's Mister . . . uh."

"Jackson." He sat down without waiting for an invite.

Fancy this, he thought. She looked a little tight.

"Looks like we travel in the same circles," Collins said with a smile.

"Yes, indeed."

His leg ached fiercely now. It was an effort not to rub it. He looked down and saw very clearly the drops of blood on the carpet. The waitress came by, and Collins took her arm. "Have you got a paper I could look at? I'm behind on the news."

She was Irish with freckles and a pug of a nose.

"Certainly, sir. Although the news is very bad this morning."

"Really?"

"Yes. The German commander of the city has been shot. It just came over the radio."

"How terrible." Collins read her eyes and knew she didn't share his stated sentiments. Well, you work here, my colleen, and you're safe.

"Yes," she said. "They're operating on him now. Roosevelt Hospital. Just a few blocks away."

Sylvie seemed genuinely shocked. "How incredible."

"I'll get your paper, sir."

Hurry, he thought, before the bloodhounds see the spots.

It was at that moment that von Stulpnagel approached the table. "Miss Lamont."

Collins's hand went to his jacket, and the Colt in his pocket.

Von Stulpnagel reached them and clicked his heels. "My dear, how are you?" He barely looked at Collins.

If I go, Collins thought, I'm taking you with me, Heinrich.

"You have heard the news?"

Collins took the opportunity. "Yes, the waitress has just told us."

Von Stulpnagel looked at Collins in the manner of a prospective buyer eyeing goldfish for his living room.

"This is Mr. Jackson."

Collins stood up, hoping his leg would support him. The pain came to him, and he bit his lip. He was sweaty and pale. As von Stulpnagel took his hand, the waitress returned.

"Here's your paper, sir."

As she left, von Stulpnagel spoke. "*Ein* moment. Where did you hear of the shooting?"

Her eyes widened momentarily. "German Ginny . . . on the radio."

Von Stulpnagel nodded.

Collins made a mental wager that the waitress had heard it through the grapevine first. She's gritty. In a pinch she'd help him. He sat down, grimacing with relief, and took the paper.

"You must understand my distress," von Stulpnagel said to Sylvie. "I was out riding with General Beck when it happened. He had taken his horse for a gallop, and on his return a gunman came out and shot him. And more incredible, another one appeared, and the first one shot him also."

"Was he killed?"

"No, they both escaped, and General Beck fights for his life now. I will go there as soon as I change. We must have our talk at a future time."

Deliberately setting the paper down on the rug to cover the blood, Collins interrupted. "I saw the cluster of cars as I came in for breakfast. I suppose getting about the city will be difficult today."

"It will be impossible."

Sylvie's hand went to her mouth. "But I must get home. I have to pick up a load of coats to be delivered to St. Stephens. I won't have trouble, will I, General?"

"You will. But I think I can help you. My car is outside. My driver will take you home."

"How kind."

"It is nothing. Now, if you will please excuse me . . . Mr. Jackson."

Collins barely made it up to shake the general's hand.

"A great pleasure."

"I'm sure."

He walked away across the dining room to where one of his adjutants and a Wehrmacht colonel were standing, and Collins sank down into his seat. The waitress came over. "There's a call for you."

Collins almost jumped. "Me?"

"You're Mr. Jackson, aren't you?"

He looked at her and saw she was staring at the rug. She knew. He read her eyes again and saw she would give him help. "Excuse me," he said to Sylvie, and followed the waitress.

She led him into the kitchen area. "You can go out the service entrance."

"Thanks, but what happens once I do that?"

She crouched on her knees. "Roll up your pants. Hurry." She had a towel in her hands. "C'mon or you'll lead them right to you."

He pulled up the pants and she took off the scarf and hankie. "How is it?"

"It needs cleaning and some dressing. I'll swab it clean and tie it. You need to be on your back."

She worked quickly using a wet towel to wash it and then tied what appeared to be a strip from a uniform around his leg. She took no notice of the traffic passing in and out of the kitchen.

"There," she said, and standing up she wiped the sweat from his face with a hankie.

"Thanks."

She was silent a moment, then said, "Kill another one," and kissed him quickly. She gestured toward the kitchen, but Collins shook his head.

"Only if I have to. How long will you be on?"

"Till one."

"If I need you I'll come back."

He moved back toward the dining area and sat down next to Sylvie.

"How's your breakfast?"

"Fine."

"Finish it."

"What?"

"Then we'll go back to your place in the general's car."

"After I finish my breakfast, Mr. Jackson, I shall drive to St. Stephen's Church without you."

"Your breakfast is finished now, Miss Lamont. I have a gun pointed straight at you and if you don't believe me you'll see the blood on the rug at my feet. They want me, and if they get me I'll make sure both you and the kraut general go to the hell all fascists richly deserve."

She stared at him quite white-faced. But strangely enough, though he saw shock he didn't see fear. In these moments, you found out exactly what people were made of.

She set down her spoon and looked at the rug. Then she said to Collins, "Would you really?"

Smiling as if he were making the most droll chitchat, Collins answered, "I'll blow your head off if you don't get me out of here."

Five minutes later they went out, his arm in hers. General von Stulpnagel even opened the door for them. Then he led the way to the car and gave instructions in shrill tones to his driver. He kissed Sylvie's hand, shook Collins's, and they were on their way. Four minutes later they were stopped at a roadblock at Fifth Avenue and cleared without question. Fifteen minutes later they were at Park and Seventy-ninth Street, where a green-coated doorman let them out. Three minutes later, they were inside the apartment shared by Sylvie Lamont and Patrick Kelly.

By four o'clock that afternoon, German troops and the Gestapo, using police files, had surrounded the houses and apartments of known radicals throughout Manhattan. Herded into waiting vans, they were taken across the Triborough Bridge to Randalls Island, and then across Little Hell Gate Bridge to Welfare Island. There they were kept in the Manhattan State Hospital for the Insane, which had been evacuated less than two weeks before.

By that evening similar roundups were in effect in the Bronx and Brooklyn. Prisoners arrested were taken to Rikers Island and put in cells in the city's new model penitentiary. In the past month over a thousand Rikers Island inmates had been sent to work camps in New Jersey, Massachusetts, and Westchester. By midnight over fourteen hundred political prisoners had been swept into the Gestapo's net.

At Roosevelt Hospital, a series of operations on General Ludwig Beck was completed by five o'clock in the afternoon. Bullets and bullet fragments were removed from his chest, lungs, and abdomen. The chief of the team of surgeons, Dr. John Hart, walked out of surgery and was taken to the spacious offices of the Roosevelt Hospital administrator. Dr. Hart, a tall, lean man, sat on the couch, still dressed in operation garb. He puffed on a cigarette, simultaneously rubbing his eyes. He had been in surgery for six and a half hours, nonstop.

The door opened, and Abetz came in. He had been out in the city's streets directing the systematic roundups and the search for the two assassins. He wore a dark leather coat and black leather gloves. He removed his hat as he entered the office and lit a cigarette. He perched on the desk and eyed Dr. Hart coldly. "So, doctor, what is the prognosis for General Beck? And, please, no fancy business when you explain. I do not trust doctors, especially American ones." Abetz produced a flask and drank from it. "What are his chances of survival?"

Hart sucked on his cigarette. "I could say fifty-fifty, perhaps a little less. The odds don't mean that much. In cases where vital organs such as the liver and lungs have been severely damaged, the body will regenerate itself during the healing process. But to get to the point where the healing process can take place, the patient must first pass the critical point where his very existence is threatened. A continued series of crises can break the will. If there are no more hemorrhages, no other setbacks, then a fighter such as the general should have better than an even chance of recovery."

"I see." Abetz extended his flask to the doctor, who took it.

"Thank you." He drank, his Adam's apple bobbing as his throat received the brandy.

"I want hourly reports on General Beck's progress. They are to be delivered here, which will now be my office at the hospital."

"Of course. I'll have one of the nurses . . ."

"No nurses, doctor. You. You will stay at the hospital and be available at all times should any change occur. Remember, you, too, bear a degree of responsibility here. . . . Am I clear?"

"Very."

"Good evening, doctor."

Dr. Hart went out, and Abetz came around the desk and sat down. He had been at Gestapo headquarters at Centre Street when the news came in. Schmidt had done his job. Abetz had picked the right man. But the good news was tempered by the fact that Schmidt had forgotten to drop the identity card of the Jew, Nipponomick. That could be traced to the fact that Schmidt was really a Jew named Paulie Lazar. The fingerprint check had clearly identified him. Perhaps Lazar felt some loyalty to this Jew Nipponomick. No. Lazar was a brute, a criminal with no loyalty to his religion or to anyone else.

Abetz rubbed his forehead vigorously. The card was not there. The police had fine-combed the area. Lazar was too good to forget. It had to be the other man. The one Lazar shot at. If he was an accomplice, Lazar would not have shot at him. Therefore it could only be that the man was someone from the Resistance who was meeting Beck. Yet he did not shoot at Lazar. That could only mean that he knew Lazar or recognized him. The events of the shooting as described to Abetz by both von Stulpnagel and two guards could only lead to one conclusion. Schmidt, alias Paulie Lazar, was working for both the Gestapo and for the American underground. At the right moment, the proper leverage applied to Lazar could yield the most interesting results.

Chapter 19

February 7, 1942
4:00 P.M.

Kresky had arrived at the bus terminal at one o'clock. Handy, Collins's man, was due on the one-thirty bus. He was to be carrying some of the dynamite wrapped in clothes in his laundry bag. The rest of it would be on the truck driven by two more of Collins's men. Collins himself was due at five o'clock. His boys were to supply the firepower for the operation while Kresky and his men were to get the dynamite in and start the fire that would ignite the whole plant. It was to be done during the evening shift when the guards were tired, because it was routine, because they had downed a few schnapps. The fire was to be set in the rear of the plant to allow the workers to get out. The dynamite was to be carried in lunch pails by the men who worked the assembly line. That meant Ragosky, Sturmer, Slote, and Kresky, who would all go over on the nine o'clock bus two hours before their shift began. The Nazis had instituted an eleven to seven shift so that workers coming over from New York could leave before curfew.

It was a daring operation, and it needed a lot of good luck for it all to come off, but even if they were only partially successful, they could do substantial damage to the plant. It would hurt German production and, to those living under Nazi occupation, would send a direct message: *Fight back!*

Handy did not come in on the one-thirty bus, or the two

o'clock, or the three o'clock. Kresky ordered another coffee and decided to wait one more bus before placing a call. He had been living in Paterson for the past two weeks under his scab alias, Ivan Potensky. Two weeks as a scab, dodging and ignoring union men who insulted him. Hoping desperately nobody would recognize him. Paterson was a town he had known in his youth, rows of ramshackle wooden houses on whose porches and stoops could be seen the peopled vestiges of dreams turned into nightmares. Painted on the faces of the people who knew only the ethic of work was the grim disillusionment with those they must work for. Trudging each day over the three small bridges that spanned the Passaic River to an endless night of machines, assembly lines, and the never-ending whirring of airplane engines being tested at the Curtiss-Wright plant. While each day the Nazi trucks rolled over the three bridges bringing more and more engines. Bringing ever closer the day on which Adolf Hitler would have his Stukas and Messerschmitts, his Junkers and Heinkels in the air, ready to bomb the heartland of America.

The four o'clock bus rolled in. Kresky got up and walked rather quickly from the barren spot where he had been sitting to the exit of the old wooden bus depot. He slipped a toothpick in his mouth and eased himself against a pole and watched the passengers discharge. As usual the bus was packed. Workers from nearby Jersey towns and from the city came in and out on a continuing basis. About twenty people had gotten off when Kresky spotted Handy. He was wearing a black seaman's peacoat and dark pants. Kresky's relief was mitigated by the fact that Handy got off the bus without a laundry bag.

Kresky watched Handy walk across the street to Hannigans, the dingy bar and grill they had arranged to meet in. Kresky waited two minutes, then followed the same route to Hannigans. He knew he wasn't going to hear good news. He ordered a beer and then walked to the booth at the end of the bar. It was located next to the partly open door of the men's room, and therefore nobody ever wanted it. The pungent aroma of the urinals assaulted Kresky's nostrils as soon as he sat down. Handy was pouring a beer into his glass.

"Trouble?"

Handy's eyebrows stood up. He talked now as usual from the side of his mouth. He was a handsome young man with brownish blond hair, quick blue eyes. "It's worse than trouble. Somebody nailed General Beck in Central Park today. The Heinrichs are turning the town upside down."

"Is he dead?"

"Who knows? They're treating it like he is."

"What happened?"

"I don't know. The Heinrichs sealed off everything coming out. The Port Authority looks like a police station. All these passengers are from the two o'clock bus and they all work here. I only got here because I sang a sad story to an Irish cop about having twelve kids and a job offer. But I had to stash the dynamite."

"Where?"

"It's back in Collins's apartment."

Kresky fought the urge to slam his fist down. "What about your truck?"

"They're searching everything coming out of the city. It's up to the boys if they want to try it, but it's a hell of a risk."

Handy's fingers drummed on the scarred wooden table. Somebody flushed the toilet in the men's room and the acrid smell came at them. Handy smiled. It was the smile of a man arrested for a crime he hadn't committed. "We're in the right place, next to the shit house."

Kresky waited for the five o'clock bus, the one Collins would be on. The streetlights had come flickering on in their grimy way as the darkness fell all around them. Even as the bus unloaded, Kresky was willing to lay odds Collins wouldn't be on it. Kresky stared for a sign of the Irishman among the rows of workers coming off the bus, cigarettes in their mouths, eyes and cheeks drawn tight like masks. Now the bus was finished, and the doors closed. No Collins. No Jake Ragosky.

The two of them sat in Kresky's little furnished apartment just four blocks away from the factory. It had a bed with an old print cover, a faded chair, a stool, and a kitchen with a hot plate. There was an overhead light and a table light that Kresky had bought. It rented for four dollars a week.

"We can't do it," Handy was saying, "unless we have the jelly. Keough and the boys were due here two hours ago. If they don't make it, all you have is a lot of matches."

Kresky hunched forward. "We have to get the dynamite here. It's either you or me, Handy. One of us will have to go back to New York in the morning."

"I'll go," Handy said. "I know where to look for it."

"What about Collins?"

"I'll need to find him, too."

Kresky stood up and walked to the window. He could see men walking wearily toward the bridges that would lead them to the plant. He spoke to Handy without looking at him.

"They'll be rounding up people now, you know that."

Handy's answer came in a quiet voice. "Doesn't touch me. Once we caught some Tans in an apartment, and they used women as hostages. One of them was my sister. She would have been twenty-five yesterday.''

Handy joined Kresky at the window and asked, ''What if your people can't make it? What if they get picked up?''

Kresky spoke almost in a whisper. ''If I have to do it myself, I'll blow the plant. Just bring back the dynamite. Tomorrow night we blow it.''

''What if you don't have your men in the plant?''

''Just get Collins and the dynamite here.''

Handy was reaching for his coat. ''I'll go now. On the next bus. The Heinrichs won't be watching the buses going back to New York so closely. I have a good chance. Getting back will be the bitch.''

Kresky nodded. ''Get the dynamite through, Handy.''

Handy gave him the thumbs up and then went out. Moments later he was visible from Kresky's window. A little figure with a jaunty walk. A mirthless grin appeared on Kresky's mouth. Handy ressembled Jimmy Cagney walking down the prison corridor with Pat O'Brien in a priest's collar next to him. Our Father who art in heaven wouldn't win this war, but maybe angels with dirty faces could.

Chapter 20

February 7, 1942
5:00 P.M.

They had spent the afternoon in Sylvie's apartment listening to what news they could get from WNYC. It had finally gone off the air at five o'clock and had not returned since. Every few minutes Collins would flick it back and there would be only an ominous silence broken by static. Collins laid five to one they would not be back on the air.

Lazar going haywire couldn't have come at a worse time. Tonight Curtiss-Wright was due to go. Collins was to meet Kresky in Paterson at five o'clock. With his leg getting worse and the city an armed camp, there was no way he would get across the George Washington Bridge. A one-legged gimp would jeopardize the entire operation. Kresky was solid. If it were possible,

Curtiss-Wright would go up tonight. It had to go. Collins needed something to show Donovan. All of Donovan's enemies would be on the phone to the president this afternoon. Did you see what the crazy bastard from the IRA did? He assassinated our best contact in the German camp, General Beck. He's lunatic-wild like all the IRA. He doesn't care about America. He just wants to get the money and go back to Ireland so he can shoot and bomb everyone in sight there.

Three times Collins tried walking across the living room without a limp. It wasn't possible, and as he collapsed onto the light blue satin sofa under the picture window, the wound opened again. At that point the rich bitch offered to call her doctor. Collins looked at her with a sarcastic smile. "Herr doctor, you mean."

"I mean Dr. Jacobsen," she said simply.

"Get me some brandy." Collins sneered. When she came back with a glass, he downed it and said, "You think because you give me the name of a Jewish doctor that I'll fall over and kiss you. There'll be plenty of Jews snuggling in bed with the Heinrichs. Save it. I'm not falling over." He watched her as she walked across the room. Beck was dying, Kresky was waiting for the dynamite, and he sat here admiring a rich dame and wishing he had two good legs. Curtiss-Wright should go up tonight, and Collins knew in his bones it wouldn't.

So he sat in the teakwood apartment on Park Avenue with the mistress of America's foremost collaborator and slugged brandy. It killed the pain, but it made Collins feel ugly and nasty . . . and it made him want her.

Night had fallen, and Collins limped over to the window to look at the park. It was pretty with light from the West Side gleaming in the distance. Suddenly Collins remembered something.

"Do you have any servants?"

"Yes, but he's off till the evening."

"What time will he be back?"

"Eight."

"Call him and tell him not to come."

"I can't. I don't know where he is."

"Leave a note you won't be here with the doorman."

"He lives here."

This was like getting bad dice in a crap game, Collins thought. Nothing but snake eyes came up.

"You had better stay off that leg," she said.

"I'm touched."

She walked over and stood next to him. "That's Central Park," she said, almost wistfully, "where he was shot. Was it you?"

"What do you think?"

"I don't know."

He looked at her eyes, but he could read nothing. She must feel something. He could smell her perfume. It was something French. He limped back for the bottle, drank once more, and realized he was in the bag.

Collins's leg ached like the fires of hell were consuming it. He was alone in a posh Park Avenue apartment with the scent of her, the sight of her, and the more he drank, the more he wanted her. It was a mess. He had been full of hope this morning. Now good men would fill Gestapo cells because Paulie Lazar was a moron.

"How long do you plan to stay here?"

Collins poured more brandy. "Till it's safe to go out."

"Does that mean tonight?"

Collins grinned wickedly. "Looks like it. Where are you going?"

"To lie down. I have a crashing headache."

He watched her go off to the bedroom. Well, at least she was out of sight. That would take his mind off his carnal thoughts.

He tried the tall crystal radio again, and the only voices he heard spoke German. Everything was *Achtung*. His leg ached, his head pounded, his groin throbbed, and WNYC was still enveloped by silence. He felt weak and knew he had to lie down. He stumbled to the couch and pitched forward. Ten seconds later he was asleep.

He awoke in the darkness, wondering where he was. He started to move, felt the pain in his leg, and remembered. His mouth was a batch of cotton. What time was it? Didn't the woman say her servant was coming? He sat up and managed to struggle to an upright position.

Think, Collins, think. But he couldn't. All he could think was, I'm besotted. The trouble was, it wasn't his town anymore. He had left here nineteen years ago to go to Ireland. He had lost touch with the people, with the soul and the heart of the city. He was just a mechanic here to do a good workmanlike job till he could go back to Ireland.

This New York was a symphony of madness. People moving faster than trains, driven by the dream of gold in the streets, fortunes to be made, the rapid-fire breathing of the stock market rattling out quotations like the cold heart of a machine gun. Its tenements housing the poor, the underfed, those who survived on bread and bits and pieces, who rode a lifetime on the subway and street trolleys, all jiggling to a crescendo of noise and music that made introspection impossible. The people of a city that offered them numbing, damp winters, hot, sticky, crawling summers. They didn't love it, and they didn't hate it, they just didn't dream anything else was possible. But Whitman and I, we march to a different drummer, and its beat comes from the old sod, and I don't belong here because I can't get in step, and Beck is dying, and Paulie Lazar is going to go off again and, oh Mother Mary, I am drunk.

Gritting his teeth against the angry throb of his leg, he got up and suddenly thought, What if she wanted to escape. She could have feigned sleep, knowing I would go out soon. Then call that red-headed kraut general of hers. His hand went to the gun in his pocket. He kept it there as he made his way gingerly into the bedroom. There was a soft light on the table. She lay under the covers, her head on the pillow. Half-turned to him and half-buried. She looked like a child. All sweet and innocent. Smelling like Cleopatra herself. In that moment Collins knew he was going to have her. What the hell, it had all been a mess. Nothing worse could happen today. If she screamed rape, he'd muscle her out with one punch. Christ, he needed to be spent and peaceful so he could think. He grinned to himself. If the Heinrichs caught him, he would say, "Well I do regret killing General Beck, but the cunt was velvet."

He was laughing to himself as he peeled down. Yes, lady, I smell like sweat, but I also have a thing of terrible beauty for you. He felt the air on his naked body, all cool and clean. Everything was all cool and clean except for his member, which was liquid fire and erect with the fine blood pulsing through it. He felt like he used to when, naked and excited, he would go swimming in County Cork. The wind tickling his body, the muscles of his buttocks quivering, the sheer fineness of it filling him with an exaltation beyond anything he could ever describe. He came over her and pulled the blanket back. She had on a blue blouse that buttoned up the front. He had the power of magic in him now, and not once did his fingers fumble a button. Being possessed of magical powers, his eyes were cat's lenses, and he could see the bra hiding the molded mountains of flesh. He tugged it gently off and, since he was the thief of the centuries blessed with the fingers of a rogue saint, she felt nothing. Ah, but the panties under the skirt. They would need a tug, and that would need more than magic fingers. It would need a wizard's guile. But he had that also. He lowered himself atop her and, still without touching, brought his lips down on her nipples. Now, as she involuntarily groaned in her sleep, his hands went under her skirt and pulled at the panties. They ripped easily, and Collins let himself come down on her. She stirred again, and yet she slept. Yes, she had taken a draught, a potion so strong that were he less artful, she still would not be aware.

He spat on his hand, then a second time, now moving it down to lubricate the path he would follow. She moaned, saying something that sounded like "Patrick." Collins let his mouth run all over her breast. Yes, he thought, give suck to my mouth. Mother Mary, 'tis good. She groaned, but it was more of a conscious thing now, and Collins told himself, Hurry, for you are not Patrick. He followed the moist trail he had prepared and brought his hand under her buttocks, raising her up. Now. Now. He forced and forced and he was big and she awoke, crying out, and he, by the grace of the Virgin, was in.

Sylvie felt the penetration and, eyes wide, was struck dumb. He was moving in her, and it was not Patrick. She felt the violating power of him, a thing of incredible hardness. It was too late, she knew, to fight him. Too late to deny him, but not too late to shun him. He moved farther in but, without her, his triumph was a thing of smaller and smaller proportion. He surged, and she lay still. Ever still.

Mother, I'm there, he thought, and she has turned into a witch. I have the world in my arms, and yet I am a man without a soul. Mother Mary answered him back: "What does it prosper a man if he gain the world but lose himself in the barter?" He looked down into Sylvie's eyes. Please, he implored silently, give me back something. Take something for yourself. Don't leave me alone and afraid, to come by myself. But she did. And the wind roared in his ears, demanding he come. Be free of this fever that rages in you, and so he did, bucking in her. Spraying forth his seed into soil that was barren and hard, from which nothing of splendor, nor rich, nor good would ever grow.

8:30 P.M.

Paulie had spent the afternoon stewing in the safe house on 110th Street. It was a comfortable three-room apartment with a view of the Columbia campus and the Cathedral of St. John the Divine out the kitchen window. He had gone through a pack of butts looking out that window. There were magazines lying on the living room sofa. He had read *Life* magazine three times and then had fiddled with the radio, trying to get the news, but all he got was stations broadcasting in German. Was he in New York or what? He was increasingly uneasy about this story he had told Collins. If Collins figures out Paulie was doing hits for the Gestapo, Paulie was dead. He tried to comfort himself by reasoning he could always give Collins to Abetz. But then Collins's IRA people would come after Paulie. Christ, he had a headache from thinkin' so much.

He had wanted to go out, but Collins's warning haunted him.

200

They had separated under the West Side Highway, and Paulie had walked to Seventy-second Street and managed to hook a cab up to the apartment. Collins had a bad leg, and it was bleeding. Maybe the Heinrichs picked him up. Too much to think about. He checked his watch. Eight-thirty. Grub time. Maybe he'd pick up some information on the street. He took the elevator down and came out into the biting cold February night. He looked and saw the stars glittering. Maybe things weren't so bad. He walked around the corner to the Gold Rail. College kids' hangout. They would know the scoop around town.

He positioned himself at the bar and ordered a Salisbury steak platter. It came a few minutes later with potatoes and cabbage smothered in gravy. Paulie was extra hungry. He cut into the Salisbury and put a huge chunk into his mouth. Three seconds later he spat it out.

"What is that shit?"

The bartender shrugged. "Horse meat. Wash it down with the beer, it won't taste so bad."

Paulie went back to eating and found the bartender was right. Three bottles of beer later he had finished the horse Salisbury. Now it felt like he had a rock in his stomach. Paulie bought a pack of butts, then moved to the telephone in the back and dialed Tommy's number.

"Hullo."

"Tommy?"

"Paulie?"

"Yeah. What's goin' down?"

"Heinrichs are out everywhere. Midtown looks like a Gestapo convention. I ain't going nowhere tonight. Where are you?"

"Uptown. And I'm stayin' here. Who we got at the warehouse?"

"Legs Corona and Frankie."

"See if you can get down there in the morning. I'll be down in the afternoon."

"You all right, Paulie?"

"Yeah, yeah, see you."

Paulie hung up and went back to the bar, where he scammed four bottles of beer from the bartender then headed back for the apartment. What if Collins came and he wasn't there? Back outside he looked up at the sky. The stars were still there, but it didn't make Paulie feel any better.

Paulie slugged down the four large bottles of Schaeffer and read awhile. Finally he lay on his back with his gun in his right hand and fell asleep. He dreamed of a doubleheader at the Polo Grounds and he was there with Nipponomick. Mel Ott hit home runs, Hubbell pitched a no hitter, and Bill Terry hit a line drive

201

that Paulie caught falling out of the right field stands. Then he was falling wonderfully, softly, like a pillow to the ground and he landed . . . hard . . . very hard. He opened his eyes, head throbbing, knees and elbows smarting, and looked into the face of a snub-nosed automatic held by Jimmy Handy, the snub-nosed Irishman Collins and Paulie had rescued. He was angry as hell.

9:00 P.M.

They faced one another across the bed in the silence.

Collins lit a cigarette and leaned forward, not looking at her. Why didn't I scream? she thought to herself.

"What gets you?" Collins asked. "Besides dressing up and wearing sweet perfume?"

She got up and went to the closet and took out a robe. When she had tied it on, she looked at him. "What if I had screamed?"

Collins flicked an ash on the floor. "I would have made sure you didn't do it very long."

"Why?" she whispered softly.

He saw the moistness at the corner of her eyes. My God, she feels something. He sighed. "Because I was drunk. Because I was mean and because I'm low. I'm fighting a war I'm not right for. I'm doing it for money, and that's always wrong."

"Is it?"

He laughed bitterly. "You should know. What are you doing all this for except for money? For that silk robe you've got on, and the blouse I took off, and this place you live in?"

She ignored what he said and, sitting down across from him, said in a suddenly more accusatory tone, "Why did you do it?"

He stood and ran an impatient hand through his hair. "Because . . ."

"Because." The shock in her voice got to him.

"Yes, because. Because I've made love to a hundred sleeping women and all of them had some welcome for me. Some exchange of love. Not just semen. But love. The act of love. Sure, the oldest cliché in the world. Women sell it, men pay for it, but even then I think there is pleasure and sharing. Whoring isn't the worst thing in the world. What you do is. You look surprised. You wear pretty things he bought you, jewelry, negligees, fur coats. You take trips with him to the Riviera or Timbuktu. You're bought and sold. All your life you've been chattel. How many before this Patrick guy?"

Sylvie opened her mouth to protest, but no words came. He had raped her, now he was crucifying her.

"What do you live for? Have you ever loved a man? I suppose when this guy Patrick goes, there'll be someone else. A winner,

202

of course. Like the general in the hotel today. You got him lined up next.''

She was quiet a long time before speaking. ''No. Not him, or any of them. They're horrible creatures. They'll suck the life out of us all.''

Her words, said with a conviction she had never known she possessed, stunned them both. To her amazement she went on.

''Where I grew up in Maryland there was a man who could knock down a horse with one blow. He was the strongest man I ever saw. He had great tufts of hair on his forearms. He walked up to my horse Ginger at the stable and swung at the poor creature and hit her. I remember Ginger wobbled and tried to keep her feet, but she couldn't and she pitched over on her side with the most terrible moan. It was a cry. A cry from a helpless thing before a brute. That's what the Germans are like.''

She was shaking, and the tears streamed down her cheeks.

He started to leave the room, but her next words caught him up.

''What you did to me, they are doing here.''

He was struck by the correctness of it and searched for a logic with which he could defend himself. He saw in her eyes neither anger nor fear.

The apartment door slammed, and they both jumped. Collins reached for his gun.

''It's Meister,'' she said. ''Our servant.''

She was out the door, closing it behind her.

''Meister, is that you?'' She made her way to the foyer where he stood leaning against the closet door. His hair was disheveled, and his lips moved wordlessly.

''What's the matter?''

Sylvie took him by the arm and, leading him to the dining room, sat him down. She took the whiskey from the cabinet and, bringing it back to him, filled the glass she had with her.

''Go ahead.''

He looked at the glass and drank it down.

''What happened?''

Meister appeared to have aged ten years in one day. ''It is happening the way it happened in Berlin and Vienna. People are being arrested in the night. Next will come the pogroms, the killings.''

He took her hand as if to establish contact and ward off the horror. ''They will blame the Jews. A German general dies and a Jew did it. That is the logic of the world. If there is a sin it was a Jew who committed it. For, after all, are we not Christ killers?''

Putting her arms around him, Sylvie said, "You had someone taken?"

He shook his head. "No, but each day I wait for them to come for my nephew, my niece, my grandson, my granddaughter, my brother, my sister. And waiting is worse than being taken."

"Come," Sylvie said, "let's get you to bed. I have something that will help you sleep. In the morning we'll call your family. I'm sure they're all right."

She led him away and Collins could hear his lament. "Why? Why? Why?"

Collins went back to the living room and reached for the brandy then put it aside. He stood at the window looking out at the West Side. There were no lights. We are, he acknowledged, in purgatory.

He heard her come out of the old man's room and go back into the bedroom. He gave her a minute and then went inside. She was lying on her back, the tears in her eyes shining. Liquid tears that would not fall. He wanted to reach out and reassure her, but how could he?

"I'll be gone in the morning," he said.

"Where will you go?"

"Friends."

"You'll need a doctor."

"I'll find one."

"Get me a drink," she said.

He went out, and she sat up and went to the dressing table. She was a sight. Hair askew, lipstick smudged, the drip of him inside her. But it didn't matter. None of it mattered if it was set right.

He came back with a glass and the whiskey bottle. "Say when."

She let him pour her a stiff one. Then she took it and forced herself to drink it. It burned her, and she felt the rising warmth inside her. I feel, she thought, I feel. Now Sylvie turned to Collins. "It has to be made right," she said to him, "do you understand? We have to make it right. I will not be a victim of today. I will not be my horse, brutalized by . . . by . . ." she stopped and took a step toward him. In her eyes he read, help me.

As he moved toward her, Collins remembered an old woman who had tended to him in Dublin one rainy night. She had whispered, "There are miracles. And they come, Laddie, when the very fires of hell scorch your insides."

Collins brought her to him, and his lips all hungry and burning came down on hers. Soft, soft, he told himself. You've got to earn this one. But it was as if her consuming desire to make this night both a beginning and an ending dictated the tempo of their lovemaking. Her lips pressed into his, and now her tongue worked inside his mouth, and they were pressing into one another. Her robe had fallen open, and Collins took the perfumed breasts into his mouth. Her hands moved to his chest, cool, diamond things that felt like alabaster on him. He was on the bed with her and heard a voice saying, "Glory will come to you, Bobby, glory will come."

He was above her, he knew not how. Big and wanting. He didn't want to be too fast, but he did want so badly to be there. To feel her coil around him. To stop all the madness of the day. The hallucination in Central Park, Beck, Paulie, Sylvie, von Stulpnagel . . .

Then he could not remember anything, for he was rushing toward her, and she took him and lay still feeling him.

Make it right, her eyes said.

He moved. Is this right?

Yes.

And this?

Oh yes. Yes. Yes.

Now they moved together. He forward, she side to side. Him deeper, she wider. Gasping for breath, they fell together. His mouth found hers, and they trembled, quivered, lips parting, tongues thrusting, rocking one another. Rocking and hugging. Over and over. Neither knowing where the boundary between them was. Sweaty and sweet. Wild. Like two children rolling over one another down a hill of clover. Down and mad and frightened and shaking and happy to be doing it together. Oh yes, together. Darling, give it to me, give it to me, oh give it to me.

Feel me.

Yes, I can feel.

Feel me all night.

And they were both feeling and falling, calling out into the darkness that is at the core of fear and at the beginning of light. They came to one another like pilgrims before a shrine long imagined that neither had believed really existed. The curtains had not been completely drawn, and now a sliver of moonlight played on the bed. Collins saw her face as for the first time . . . . pale and pure, devoid of the witch's makeup that hid its natural beauty.

Sylvie saw Collins looking at her as if he had had a revelation and did not know what it meant. She could only see in his eyes that he wanted her in a better way than she had ever known was possible with a man. And as if both were guided by the same marvelous instinct, they thrust forward in unison and wondrously were joined together. I have come, Collins thought, to a time out of war. A moment granted by some divinity to weary, beaten soldiers of fortune. Perhaps a gesture of charity, or perhaps to teach us that there is a better thing than this killing that we do.

Now, as he moved to a deeper place inside her than she knew there was, Sylvie saw the spotted pony she used to ride when she was ten. Across a dappled patch of grass crowned with the gold sun. "Don't let go," her father would call. But she did, she let herself go to this stranger who covered her, coveted her, seemed a part of her. In her ears was a humming, music composed by her body, the notes joyous and deep.

Chapter 21

February 8, 1942
8:00 A.M.

They lay in Sylvie's bed, almost afraid to look at one another. To do so was to acknowledge that, despite their intimacy, they were strangers. They had committed an illicit act. They had loved, and now they were afraid.

Collins looked at his watch. "Eight o'clock. What time will your servant be up?"

Sylvie seemed shocked by the intrusion of reality. "I generally sleep late. He won't come until I call for him."

Collins moved to sit up, and his leg betrayed him.

"You're bleeding. I'm going to call my doctor."

"Okay, but wait. First send your man down to the street for the papers. Tell him to find out what he can. Make sure he's out for an hour. Then make some coffee."

She looked at him oddly.

"You can make coffee?"

She reached for her robe. "Please don't look at me."

He sighed. What else could he expect in the light of morning? He turned away and heard her go into the bathroom. Bracing himself, he lowered himself from the bed, putting his weight on the good leg. He tried to walk, and the wounded leg throbbed like the devil. He needed more than a doctor, he needed morphine. With this gimp, the Gestapo would pick him up the minute he hit the pavement.

Collins went to the window and drew the curtains. The sun was vivid on the buildings across the park. Just another shiny morning. As if yesterday in Central Park didn't happen.

Sylvie came out of the bathroom, her hair combed, her face powdered.

Collins looked at her in amazement. "Why did you . . ."

"What?"

"Never mind."

She took a cigarette from the dressing table and put it in her mouth. A rich bitch once more, Collins thought. But she wasn't the same. She wouldn't forget last night.

He looked around at the rather severe room that had been their love nest. Coffee curtains, a large bed with a canopy, the kind of print rug favored by expensive shops, the Oriental lamp, the white dressing table. It spelled her and this Patrick. Winters in St. Moritz, Paris in the spring, the Côte d'Azur in summer, New York in the fall. How inconvenient to be here now that war had come.

"When will Patrick be back?"

She inhaled some smoke. "I'm not sure. But you have to be out of here."

And burn the bloody sheets, he thought.

"I'll have Meister make some coffee and send him out. Then I'll call Dr. Jacobsen."

"Can he be trusted?"

Sylvie looked at the gun protruding from his jacket. "What choice do you have?"

She went out. If she wanted to turn him in, he was done for and he knew it. He hobbled over to the dressing table and took one of her cigarettes. Pall Mall. He set about trying to establish what he would do. No matter what shape his leg was in, he had to be gone once the doctor bandaged him up. Then up to 110th Street to deal with Paulie Lazar, if he had waited. If Kresky had gotten the Curtiss-Wright plant, there would be a call at one o'clock. That might be the only way to find out. After yesterday, Collins was sure the Germans wouldn't allow news of sabotage to be printed.

They breakfasted on coffee and toast with real butter and marmalade. It was incredibly good, but he missed his rotgut swill. He had always enjoyed the hard mickeys they used to roast on sticks in Hell's Kitchen more than he ever did lyonnaise potatoes. But there was no question the real coffee was making him think better this morning. He put down his cup. "Call General Stulpnagel, ask him about the condition of Beck. And also ask him if there were any other incidents last night. Incidents like sabotage.''

She stood up. "You're still ready to blow my head off, aren't you?''

"If I have to.''

"Even after last night?''

"Last night was last night. This morning is this morning. This afternoon you'll be having tea with toast and marmalade, and I'll be eating frankfurters made out of rats.''

"Rats? Are you trying to shock me?''

"No, I'm trying to warn you. Play along with me, and I'll be gone soon. But cross me, and you'll find out how tough I can be.''

"Yes," she said, lowering her eyes, "you are tough.''

She went out, and Collins poured more coffee. What the hell does she want? Flowers? If Curtiss-Wright doesn't go up, I'll lose this job, and the lads in Ireland won't get their fifty grand. Goddamn it, I'm not an American anymore. I shouldn't have gotten involved.

He spent the next ten minutes smoking Pall Malls and drinking coffee. Then she was back, that perfume of hers filling the room and making Collins want to live inside her again.

"General Stulpnagel says Beck is still critical. There is no new word from the hospital on his condition. He is going there now.''

"Nothing unusual happened last night?''

He stubbed the cigarette out in the coffee cup and saw the angry black ashes swirl around. Like bitter tea leaves in a witch's brew. The blackness became a void, and once again he saw the mad dream of Beck riding at a gallop, turning, flinging the envelope. And then there was Paulie Lazar running down the slope, gun in hand.

Stulpnagel would have told her if Kresky blew up Curtiss-Wright. Damn it, he should have been in Paterson last night, not screwing this rich bitch.

"Nothing else happened?" he said sharply. "You're sure?''

"No, nothing. Just a lot of people have been rounded up and are being detained.''

Collins looked down at the cup full of coffee and ashes and then felt something explode in him. "Goddamn," he yelled, and threw the coffee and saw it splatter on her beautiful beige walls.

Dr. Jacobsen came forty-five minutes later. He was a man in his early fifties who parted his hair directly in the middle and wore a heavy mustache. He was dressed in an expensive black suit, white shirt, and tie. He asked no questions about why he was treating Collins in the bedroom of Patrick Kelly.

He is, Collins thought, a doctor who has earned those expensive black suits by treating the idle rich and keeping his mouth shut.

He cleaned the knee with some peroxide and examined it in a manner that left no doubt in Collins's mind that he had dealt with gunshot wounds before.

"You are fortunate, sir. The bullet appears to have missed the bone. I'll clean it and bandage it; after a few days of rest you'll be up and around. Just stay off it for a few days."

"I can't do that."

Dr. Jacobsen studied Collins for a moment before shrugging and saying, "That's up to you, but I think you'll find it quite painful. It will heal more slowly if you walk around."

Collins produced a sardonic grin. "In my line of work, one can't afford to be idle for a few days."

Dr. Jacobsen knew his way around well enough not to ask what line of work Collins was in.

"I need something for the pain," Collins said. "Something strong enough so I won't feel it for a while. Something like morphine."

Jacobsen looked sharply at Collins. "I don't carry . . ."

"Yes, you do. You're the rich man's doctor. Your patients come to you for all that money can buy, and you service them."

Jacobsen stood up. "I don't like your manner. You may be a friend of Miss Lamont . . ."

He stopped because he saw the gun Collins was pointing at him. "Just give me the shot, and skip the injured-party routine. I'm sure you'll make plenty of money giving those that have it what they ask for."

Jacobsen opened his bag and reached inside. He produced a bottle and a hypodermic needle. The bottle was turned over and into the point of the hypodermic. He came toward Collins. "You'll have to stand up."

Collins got up and felt the doctor use a cotton swab on the back of his arm, then he felt the jab of the needle.

"How soon will I feel the effect?"

"In about twenty minutes, perhaps less, the pain will start to ease." He put the needle back into his bag and then turned to Collins. "You're wrong. I won't be treating rich fascists. I won't run. And I won't be calling the police or Gestapo to tell them who I treated today. I'm not afraid of them or you. This is my city. Here." He extended a bottle and fresh syringe to Collins.

"What's that?"

"For when the pain comes back. And it will." He walked briskly from the room.

Collins stood up and hobbled to his clothes. Sylvie returned.

He could see she was visibly upset. She couldn't get it out and instead said, "Would you please dress inside the bathroom?"

When he came out, she was pacing in the living room. He knew the emotional pattern of it even before she spoke. Here comes the scene. You can't just walk out of my life.

Instead she said, "I'm glad we made it right."

The remark caught him off balance. Get out, he warned himself. "Don't get any ideas," he said. "I'm a hired gun."

"So last night was last night."

"Right." She turned away, and Collins knew he couldn't leave it at that. "When you have something like this, an occupation, people do things they normally wouldn't. You have to get the feeling out. There is no more for us. And if there were, it wouldn't be what last night was." He had given her something if she could see it. She went to the window and looked out at the park. She was still there when Collins grabbed his overcoat and left.

11:20 A.M.

He walked away from Park Avenue toward Lexington. If he could get a taxi, he would be at the apartment in fifteen minutes. He made his way as best he could, walking slowly so the limp would not be too obvious. But it hurt, and he cursed Dr. Jacobsen. Where was the miracle of morphine?

It took him ten minutes, but he finally got a cab at Lexington and Seventy-ninth. Collins gave the address, and the driver called back, "Park is closed off. We'll have to go up to 110th Street and cross to the West Side."

"Sure."

Ten minutes later Collins hobbled into the lobby of his building. He saw two old women huddled together in conversation. They stopped talking as he went by. He rode up alone on the elevator, checking his watch once. It had stopped. He put the key in the lock, drawing his gun at the same instant.

If Lazar was still there, he would be edgy. He went in and saw Lazar and Jimmy Handy.

Jimmy laid it all out. Kresky was in Paterson, waiting for the jelly. Joe Keough and Marty Byrnes couldn't get through. But Paulie knew where to get more jelly. Jimmy and Kresky would plant it. Collins and Paulie would supply the cover. Now all they needed were the wheels to carry them and the jelly to Paterson.

Sylvie would give them that. The part of him that went into her last night wouldn't wash away with soap. Christ, we both want more. No, last night wasn't just last night.

Chapter 22

February 8, 1942
2:00 P.M.

The letter had been delivered by messenger to the manager at the Hotel des Artistes. It had been stamped "personal" and, as the manager explained, he had forgotten it because of the excitement over the shooting of General Beck. Now, in a voice that was terribly eager to please, he asked Radner whether he should bring it up. Minutes later, Corporal Schilker brought it in to Radner.

The atmosphere at the Hotel des Artistes had changed markedly since the news of the shooting had been announced. The easygoing and relaxed camaraderie had abruptly vanished. People spoke to each other in short sentences. Questions were asked and answered abruptly. There were no jokes, no loose gossip about what went on last night. Schilker had looked pale and drawn since he brought Radner the news. Radner could clearly read his thoughts. If General Beck is not safe, then who among us is? At one point Radner had called Schilker in and asked him what he thought the Gestapo's response would be. Schilker drew an imaginary line across his throat.

"You don't think they will use restraint?" Radner probed.

"I was in Warsaw when a similar attempt was made. Hostages were executed."

Radner shook his head. "They don't want to do that here. It is more delicate in America."

Schilker had a sardonic expression on his face. "You think so? The Gestapo has used a velvet glove, but I know them. The velvet glove covers a steel fist. Policy will tighten. They will round up people, and there will be restrictive measures. What if they find the assassin was a Jew?"

Radner had no answer.

"Don't you think," Schilker continued, "it is odd that in

211

America, unlike the other countries we occupy, Jews are not identified by a yellow star?''

"I think New York is special," Radner said. "It would inflame the people. They would not accept it the way Jews in Europe have.''

"Possibly," Schilker answered. "But it has been under consideration. Stulpnagel had no definite answer a month ago. Berlin will give him his answer."

Radner dismissed the argument. "We have no proof it was a Jew.''

"Of course not, sir. I was just giving you an example. Things will tighten. You'll see.''

Radner had eaten a late lunch alone. Since Manheim's heart attack, the work load had doubled. But he had found strength and confidence in his love for Fay. Each day she returned from rehearsal tired but radiant. Filled with excitement, she and Radner would discuss the day's rehearsal over dinner. After she worked on her lines, they would retire early and make love through the night. At their early breakfast, she would study lines; he would go over the agenda for the day. Then, after coffee, they would return to the still warm sheets for more of each other. Sometimes late in the day Radner would drop into rehearsal and watch from the back. It was going to be a brilliant production. Fay's career would be launched.

He had planned to take her to dinner tonight, but with Abetz's hounds out all over town, it would be preferable to eat in the hotel dining room. Now he turned his attention to the letter. It came in a plain white envelope, and over his name was written: "Personal: To Be Opened by Addressee Only." Shaking his head, Radner tore it open and read:

Dear Cultural Minister:

I am a friend even though I cannot identify myself. I have come across some news I am afraid you will find distressing. But I think it is important that you, who are in a position of prominence, should know it. There is an actress whom you have been seen with, Miss Fay Brophy. She is not who she claims to be. She is certainly not Fay Brophy. Her name is Leila Fox. She is Jewish. To pretend to be another is not just dishonest, it is criminal. It is most interesting that a Jew carries out this masquerade. It certainly is deceitful and takes advantage of such an important person as yourself.

Since you have taken such an interest in her personally, I thought you should know. If it were to become known who she is, it would be very embarrassing to you and might damage your career. However, please do not take this as a denunciation. It certainly is not that at all. Take it as more of a warning from one who wishes to protect you from such dishonesty.

How I came to the discovery is not important but it is fortuitous for us both. It will help you avoid a troublesome, delicate situation. In return you can help me. Please do not think I am trying to blackmail you. Rather there is a family situation I need help with. Please do not doubt my information, it is authentic. You have only to ask who is Leila Fox of Miss Brophy and you will have your answer. If you believe me, and want to help, meet me at the information booth on the main level at Grand Central Station at five-thirty today.

Your earnest friend

5:10 P.M.

Leila came out of the New Amsterdam Theater and headed for the subway. She was especially tired. It had been a grueling day. Gielgud was trying new things, and he changed so quickly. She had been trying to find a groove and now was not spontaneous enough to Gielgud. There was no time to talk with Tyrone Guthrie, the director. So much time was spent on Gielgud. Hamlet was, after all, a vehicle. And there was Le Gallienne as Gertrude, Willard Foxcroft as Claudius, Burgess Meredith as Laertes. Hold on, girl, she warned herself. This is your chance and you are going to be brilliant. She would work with Friedrich tonight. He would help her to find those responses. No early sheets tonight.

5:17 P.M.

She looked up and saw the crowds waiting to get into the Seventh Avenue IRT. What was going on? There were guards there. They were still searching for those assassins. How irritating. Just when she needed to get home and take a warm shower. She turned in the direction of uptown and started to walk along Broadway. It would take just five minutes, and then she would catch a local at Fiftieth Street.

But at Fiftieth Street the situation was the same. Less of a crowd but still filing in slowly. Then Leila realized why. They were checking people. Looking at identity cards. Suddenly she felt goose bumps. Stop it, she chided herself. You have an authentic pass issued by the Gestapo in the name of Fay Brophy. But you're not Fay Brophy. She turned and walked away.

Grand Central was filled with Gestapo, Wehrmacht soldiers, and New York City police. Saluting no less than four times, Radner entered the Vanderbilt Avenue side and walked down the ramp. Lines had formed for people waiting to enter the subway. Pushing his way past them, hugging the yellow marble walls, Radner found himself in the huge domed arcade that is the heart of the great station. The usual milling crowds were now packed in tighter because of the lines waiting to board trains.

They're checking them one by one, he thought. The lines went all the way back to the marble steps leading down into the vast room that looked more like a stadium. To make things worse, ticket lines were also backed up as plainclothes Gestapo pulled young men out of the crowds for questioning. Idiots, Radner thought. Beck's assassins are long vanished. It was typical of the Gestapo to plod on this way. Nothing would be accomplished. They were so coarse, clumsy, brutishly persistent.

How could he ever meet someone in the jungle of people? Then he realized it didn't matter. He had no idea as to who his phantom letter writer was. No idea of whether it was a man or a woman. The person would have to find him. Using his shoulder as a means of getting through the people in front of him, Radner called out, "Pardon, your pardon." But the crowd now spilling out in all directions spun him around. Righting himself, Radner grabbed the shoulder of the man in front of him. "Move, this is official business. Move, I tell you." Now he had some room and, using his elbow, calling out as he went, he was able to reach the information booth around which angry New Yorkers besieged a poor middle-aged woman who was in danger of losing her glasses. Sweat glistened from the end of her nose.

"I'm sorry, I have no further information. You must have your identity card to get on a train."

"I'm late, lady."

"Well, so is everybody else," she minced. "Your train will wait. All the trains are running late tonight."

"When will this stop?"

She spotted Radner. "Why don't you ask him?"

They turned to Radner. A little man in a gray raincoat, a blond woman in a brown cloth coat. They were angry. They were all angry. Hostile eyes pointed at him, the invader. Radner stared back at them coldly until they turned around and went back to badgering the woman.

He lit a cigarette and called himself a fool for even coming here. What did he hope to accomplish? Why not speak to Fay first? Give her a chance. But there was something terribly authentic about the note. Instinct told him it wasn't a wild denunciation.

"Sir, sir."

Radner felt a tug on his arm and looked down. There was a young boy in a thin blue coat. His face was freckled, and he had a turned-up nose. His hand was held out. A street urchin asking for money.

"Are you Captain Radner?"

"Yes. Is that for me?"

"From the person you expected." The boy extended the envelope, and Radner took it. He gave the boy a quarter.

"Thank you very much."

He made his way back through the lines of angry, yet frightened people. He went up the steps, saluted three more guards, and found himself on Forty-second Street. He crossed the street and stopped under the awning of a bookstore on Lexington Avenue. Then he ripped open the note.

Dear Cultural Minister:

So glad you came. I must apologize for not coming, but I had to ascertain your interest in this whole business. One can't be too careful. Now that I have had proof of your interest in keeping this matter confidential and of truly wanting to help me out, I feel I can trust you. I will be back in touch with you shortly. The next time I will be there, and we can get down to the substance of what I need and you need. I truly believe we can be of mutual benefit to each other. Till then.

Your earnest friend

5:38 P.M.

Leila ducked into the Automat on Fifty-second Street for a cup of tea. She had suddenly felt frightened. Chilled, sweaty, and scared. She needed a respite for a moment. She was empty. She hadn't eaten anything other than a cheese sandwich for lunch. Silly, she chided herself, you're exhausted and tired. Tea with sugar would pick her up.

The large room with its sand-colored stone floor had tables set in a wide arc under harsh fluorescent lights. Leila hurried through the line and got her change. She waited for the cup to fill with hot water, added the tea bag, and looked for a table.

She found a spot across from a monocled old man who was bent over a paper. Leila looked for the sugar, but there was none.

"Pardon me, sir, the sugar?"

He looked at her grumpily and said, "You get one cube from the cashier. That's it, one cube. There's a shortage, you know."

So it was back on another line; this time a young man in a trench coat joined the line behind her. It took five minutes before Leila finally got a small cube wrapped in yellow paper.

Leila swung off the line and turned right into the young man with the trench coat. The face was familiar. Who . . . it was Freddy Manning. Freddy who had acted with both Fay and Leila.

"Hello, Leila, or should I say Fay? Things are really going well for you, aren't they? I saw your name under the billing at the New Amsterdam. No picture? But I guess you can't have everything. They say, what's in a name? You mean if I changed my name, everything would be hunky-dory?"

She tried to swallow, but she couldn't. Her vocal cords were locked. All she could think to say was, "Please don't call me Leila again."

He took her hand as if to say something nicer, but from the curl of his mouth, Leila knew the worst was yet to come. He just didn't want to be too obvious saying it and draw attention to himself. "Don't worry, you're safe now. There'll be another time when you have to explain about shtupping your Nazi."

Chapter 23

February 8, 1942
6:35 P.M.

Collins had called Sylvie and asked her to meet him at McGlades on West Sixty-fifth Street. There had been a wake and now the drinkers were filing in. The booths were situated under dim overhead lights, and the bar smelled of sweat and stale malt. It was the finest smell in the oldest beer hall in the world. There was no better place in the world to be mourned. Collins bought two ryes and two beer bottles. It was the whiskey courage his grandfather had passed on to him. "When all the world is against you and your soul a vale of tears, drink a boilermaker, then another, and another."

She wore a mink coat over a black suit and a soft mauve blouse. She still had too much makeup on. Collins downed his whiskey and to his surprise saw Sylvie drinking hers. They sat in silence.

She looked beautiful and very vulnerable. And he knew even now amidst the blood and dynamite that he wanted her. He put it away. This was business. His business.

"I'm going to ask you for something. Hear me out and just say yes or no. No ifs or buts or pleas of conscience. You understand?"

She nodded.

"I want you to call your friend, the governor general, and ask him for a car to take you out of the city. You have to visit a sick aunt or dedicate a plaque or host a charity tea or kiss the Führer, I don't care what. Just get me an official car to travel in with papers. I'll be your servant and driver. I want the car in"—he read his watch—"one hour."

She stared into her unfinished whiskey, and Collins waited.

"Why do you need it?"

"I said no questions."

She looked directly at him, and he saw how much she had changed. He couldn't brush her aside any more than he could just assault her in bed.

"For a job," he said.

"Do I have to come?"

Collins drank some beer. "It would help."

"And if I don't?"

"We'll try to use the papers to get through without you."

"If I do come?"

"Then you're an accomplice. But I wouldn't hold it over you. In time of war people help out."

It was the way he said *people*. "My kind aren't your definition of people?"

Collins knew any explanation would sound lame.

"Once I'm an accomplice, I have a choice, don't I?" she asked.

"You mean out or in? Yes, you do. But no one expects in."

"Are you using me?"

"We all use each other, but I'm being honest."

"If I go . . . it's dangerous?"

"Yes . . . and if you go, we'll need you to get us back into the city."

"How many of you?"

"Four."

She let her hand fall free from the glass. She stared into the whiskey. "I've never faced anything like this before. I've always been a terrible coward. When that man I told you about knocked

217

down my horse, I covered my eyes. I've hated myself for that ever since.''

He started to reach for her hand but then stopped. No con. "Then this is your chance to get back at him. That's what's so unexpected about life.''

"What?''

"It does offer us a second chance.''

She had seen his hand and withdrawn hers. Now it trembled in her lap. "Do you want me?''

"That's not part of it.''

"Yes, it is.''

Collins looked at her. "Yes, I want you.''

"As terribly as I want you?''

"Yes. But you still don't have to do it. And I'll understand. You shouldn't unless you want to.''

Her head dropped, and she stared into the whiskey. Finally, she looked up. "Give me a cigarette.''

Collins took one from his pack and lit it for her, then handed it over.

"Now give me a nickel.''

"You won't need it. Ask the bartender for the phone. Just say . . .''

"I know what to say. I've been saying it all my life.''

She put her hand on the table, stood up, and now walked, still wearing her mink coat, to the bar where a phone rested. No one looked at her and the bartender handed her the phone. Watching her, Collins felt his stomach coiling inside him. A combination of tension and want.

She talked for some time. More than ten minutes. Then she was back.

"The car will be in front of the Plaza Hotel in half an hour.''

Collins stood up and felt the pain in his knee. The morphine he had injected himself with was finally wearing off. "I have to make a call.'' Two minutes later he came back. "Let's go.''

Thirty-eight minutes later Meister stopped the car in front of Sylvie's building. Collins waited until Meister went inside and then got in the car.

"Papers,'' he asked.

Sylvie took them from her purse.

He reached for the door. "You can still back out.''

"But you have a better chance with me.''

"Yes,'' he admitted.

She looked down at the papers and then back at him. "My headaches have stopped.''

He reached over and closed her purse, then put the Packard into gear.

Twenty minutes later they were at a warehouse on Twenty-third and Twelfth Avenue where a rather large man and a somewhat smaller one stacked some cartons in the trunk and got in. The small one conversed for some minutes with Collins. A few minutes after eight they began the drive up Twelfth Avenue with Collins at the wheel. Nobody spoke.

At eight-thirty they stopped at the entrance to the George Washington Bridge and were confronted by a uniformed German soldier. Collins rolled down the window and handed out the papers. The Wehrmacht noncom read the papers and the signature at the bottom; then he glanced at the passengers, saluted smartly, and waved for them to pass on. Paulie's finger came off the trigger of the gun in his pocket, and Jimmy Handy slumped back in his seat. Then they were rolling on iron with the Hudson dancing below them and the lights of the city blinking out from the mist and the night that was falling. Collins thought of what was ahead and said a silent prayer. As soon as they were over the bridge, Collins gunned it. Under the cover of night, they sped up Route 4 for Paterson, New Jersey, where Kresky was waiting.

9:00 P.M.

Radner had suggested they spend the night at his pied-à-terre on East Sixty-seventh Street. Schilker had packed a basket full of cold chicken, salad, and bread. Radner selected a bottle of white Bordeaux that would enhance the chicken. They ate on the living room floor sitting opposite one another. He had suggested it, hoping the closeness would allow them to talk about what had to be talked about. But he could see it was not working. She had been tight and cold from the time of her arrival. And he now found himself extremely uncomfortable with their proximity. Neither of them could eat. Radner took refuge in drinking and staring into his glass while Leila looked numbly at her lines.

He knew it was no good faking it. It had to be brought out into the open. He watched her thumbing the pages. She seemed brittle and shaky. What was it? Could she have received the same letter? Was the blackmailer playing them both off against one another?

She looked up and saw him staring at her.

"Aren't you hungry?" Radner asked, giving himself a lead into the discussion.

"Not much."

"The play?"

"Yes."

"What is it?"

"Well, it's just that . . . I can't get it down. Gielgud keeps

219

trying one thing and another. I'm not able to keep up . . . I need to rehearse more."

She was lying, just like she lied about her name. The humiliation, the anger within him was too much to bear. He took a breath and let it out. "Who is Leila Fox?"

Her head, which had dropped down, now snapped forward and he saw the pain and anger on her face. He thought she would cry, but she speared him with hostile eyes. "You know. Since when?"

"This afternoon."

"Who told you?"

"It came in an anonymous note. I think it's a blackmailer. I went to Grand Central to meet the person but no one showed up."

Her head dropped down. He was moved to pity, but there was still the anger at being deceived. "Why? Why didn't you tell me?"

She spoke in low, almost indistinct tones. "I couldn't. I don't even know why I lied. Fay is dead . . . in a plane crash. But I used it even before I knew."

"Why?"

"I'm not sure. Leila Fox wasn't getting anyplace. Bad luck is hard to shake. She left me a note, she was gone, you were there, I'm Jewish. I don't know. I just did it. It was crazy but made a certain sense. How could I trust you?"

"Yes," he responded; "perhaps it made sense then. But all this time when you told me you loved me, how could you allow me to believe . . . that you were not a . . ."

Her eyes bored into him. "A what . . . a Jewess?"

"No. I meant how could you allow me to believe you were Fay Brophy."

Now she looked like a trial lawyer. "That wasn't what you were going to say. Was it?"

She had lashed at him, and now he lashed back.

"Don't you see what a position you have put me in? Someone knows who you are. This person wants to blackmail me. If I don't cooperate there is an anonymous letter to be sent to Abetz."

He could see the lacerated look in her eye. "Yes, I do see very well. You're worried about the compromising position I have put you in."

"Well I am the acting cultural minister."

She threw the script at him, catching him on the side of the face. "You don't care about me. What you care about is your career. Doesn't it occur to you that not only Jews are in trouble around here? Now this general gets shot and there'll be roundups. There's a Polish actor working on the stage crew. He says Europe is full of detention camps. Sooner or later everyone becomes a Jew to your government.''

"That is nonsense," he shouted. "Yes, there are a few places to keep politicals. That's all. There are no camps all over Europe. You are hysterical.''

"And you're in a panic. You may get your knuckles rapped by Abetz, or worse, your career may be hurt for harboring a Jewess.''

"Fay, how could you . . .''

"My name is Leila," she screamed.

"How could you do this to me?''

"Do what—lie, or get you into trouble?''

"Both," he yelled in frustration.

"You hypocrite.''

"Don't you see you've opened me to blackmail?''

"No, I don't see. Ignore the blackmailer.''

"Then Abetz will find out.''

"Let him.''

"Then we're both finished.''

"You could always turn me in.''

"Stop it, Fay.''

"I'm not Fay, I'm Leila. Leila.'' She rushed at him, swinging out, lashing and scratching. She pulled at his hair, and now he could no longer be compassionate. He fought back, finally hitting her across the face.

She fell and lay still, looking at him with revulsion. Then abruptly she jumped up and ran into the foyer.

He stood with his hand outstretched, wanting to go to her and wanting her to get as far away from him as possible. Seconds later the door slammed.

He looked at his watch. Almost ten. She would have to be back soon. Curfew was in one hour. He picked up the wine from the floor and sank down on the couch. He drank some and tried to recall how they'd come to this. It was all a jumbled blur. He drank some more, giving himself to the dull thickness the wine created in him. The more he drank, the less he was able to think. It was all such a mess anyway. Fay . . . Leila . . . which one was she? She must have been mad to think she could get away with it. Eventually someone had to recognize her. You fool, you have handled it badly. She needs understanding. He would straighten it out when she came back. They would both be calmer. But what to do? What to do?

He sat that way, drinking, their fight still vivid in his mind. Only when he stood up to go to the bathroom did he look at his watch. It was ten past twelve. Curfew was more than an hour ago. You silly fool. Where are you? Come back. You have to. We're both in this together.

Chapter 24

February 8, 1942
9:10 P.M.

They reached Paterson shortly after nine and made their way to Geary Street. Collins pulled the car up in front of a vacant lot. Jimmy Handy got out of the back of the car and, after looking around carefully, leaned in and spoke to Collins.

"If Kresky's at work, you want me to leave a note?"

Collins rubbed his forehead. "No. If he's not there, we'll just have to kill time till he gets back. He's our entry to the plant."

He watched Jimmy saunter casually toward Kresky's rooming house. Then he turned toward Sylvie. "You all right?"

"Fine, just a little cold."

"You must be hungry."

"I sure as hell am," Paulie complained from the back.

"You can wait," Collins snarled. He still had a score to settle with that lug after this was all taken care of.

Jimmy came strolling nonchalantly back toward the car. "Kresky's home. Says the Heinrichs have doubled the guard at the plant. They're checking every identity card, lunch bag, and box coming into the plant."

Collins knew he would have to talk to Kresky alone. "C'mon with me," he said to Sylvie. "Jimmy and Lazar will get us some food."

Sylvie stood a few yards away while Collins spoke with Jimmy. "Get soup and bread, load up on the starch. Nobody is eating again until tomorrow. What are you laughing at?"

Jimmy head gestured toward Sylvie. "Her in that mink with this street for a background. That's *Life* magazine stuff."

"One of you in the car at all times when you order the food," Collins said, loud enough for Paulie to hear. Now he spoke softly to Jimmy. "Leave Lazar in the car. You order the food and keep the car keys with you."

"I got you," Jimmy said.

Jimmy got in behind the wheel, and they motored off. Collins took Sylvie by the arm and led her toward Kresky's house. Her heels tapping on the sidewalk started a nagging worry in Collins's mind. Anybody who sees her will remember her. Women in stoles don't just show up in Paterson unless they're hookers. He had an idea.

They sat in Kresky's bare, shabby room, Sylvie on the tattered, boxy little couch.

Collins saw Kresky's piercing look. "She got us here," he said.

"It's better if she doesn't hear," Kresky countered.

"I'll go in the hall," Sylvie offered. She walked out.

Kresky held up a hand. "The less she knows the better. In case she's questioned. Somebody has already squealed."

"What do you mean?"

Kresky's teeth flashed. "They didn't double the guard just because a general was shot in New York. Somebody tipped them that there was going to be a sabotage at the plant."

"Got any ideas?" Collins asked.

"Three or four," Kresky said. "That's how many guys on my team didn't make it last night."

"Whoever it is will have to be hit fast when this job is over."

Kresky bit off a toothpick he had been chewing on. "We agree on that."

Now it was Collins whose mouth tightened angrily. "If there's a canary, he gave them your name."

"I know."

"Then what the hell are we meeting here for?"

"I move every week," Kresky said quietly. "The last address the plant has is on the other side of town. The only person who knows I live here is Handy."

Collins breathed a little easier. "Okay. But after we blow the plant, you'll have to push on. And I plan on blowing that plant tonight no matter how many Heinrichs are on guard."

Kresky's smile was hard as an unpolished diamond. "I was hoping you'd say that."

Collins lit a cigarette. "We can't get in the front door. What are our other options?"

"I've been wondering about that all day," Kresky responded. "I was thinking maybe a fire. I could start it on my break. Once it went up they'd have to call the fire department. You could hijack a truck, and . . ."

"Come in blasting?" Collins interrupted. "I thought of that, but if someone did squeal they'll have your name and they'll pick you up as soon as you get there."

Kresky shook his head. "There's no way to get dynamite into

223

that plant that I can figure. Not by me and not by any of the men who work for me."

Collins stood up. "What else comes into the plant?"

"What do you mean?"

"There has to be deliveries. Food, machines, supplies."

Kresky mulled it over. "No food. Supplies, repair parts come in the mornings. Wednesdays. Engines that have been tested go out on Friday."

"Wrong direction," Collins said. "How do they go out?"

"Same way they come in. Train."

"Train?"

"Yeah. The Erie railroad tracks run right up behind the plant."

Collins rubbed his chin. "When do they bring the engines in?"

"Couple of times a week."

"Day or night?"

"Both."

"How many guards on the train?"

Kresky reflected, "Maybe six."

"How about civilian personnel?"

"The train crew."

"Then the engineer would be an American?"

Kresky had gotten the drift. "You'd need a train."

"And an engineer," Collins added.

"I can drive it," Kresky said.

They ate the barley soup and sandwiches Jimmy and Paulie had brought back. Collins watched each of the others, noting their individual characteristics and beginning to place them in the parts they would play. There was Kresky, solid as a rock drinking his tea. He would be the wheel of the train. Jimmy, eating his sandwich in quick little bites, would supply the diversion along with Paulie. The diversion that would give the speeding train a plausible reason for running through its checkpoints. Jimmy and Lazar would blow the three small bridges spanning the Passaic River. That would send the Germans out on a wild goose chase, make everybody jittery. A train anxious to get to its destination at the Curtiss-Wright plant would not be watched so carefully. But just to make sure, they would need one prisoner. A German officer. Sylvie would get them their prize.

He studied her as she tried to eat soup and made a sour face. Not like the food she got at Cavendish's. A high-class dame. But she had to do it. There was no other way.

He led her into the kitchen. It was a drab little room with a sink and icebox.

"I have a plan, but I'll need you to help carry it off."

Under the dim overhead light, she looked pale.

"You're going to blow something up."

He nodded.

"If I go further, there is no turning back?"

"No."

"What do you want me to do?"

"You're going to have a flat tire near the supply depot and ask to see the officer in charge. You'll be in desperate need of help. You'll smile and show a nice piece of leg. You'll do whatever you have to to get him out to look at the car."

"And then?"

"I take over."

"What will you do to him?"

Collins almost smiled. "Don't worry, I won't hurt him. I need someone to speak German so we can get through the checkpoints."

"What do I do then?"

Collins took her hand. "You'll drive this car to the edge of town. I'll draw you a little map. You'll have the car ready for a quick getaway."

"What will happen to the German officer?"

"Don't worry about him. He'll be dropped off. Worry about some of your new comrades."

He saw what he had hoped for. The look of concern on her face. Is that for me? he wondered.

"It's very dangerous, what you're doing, isn't it?"

"Fair to middling, yes." He was pressed against her, and she was all soft and palpitating. Blarney her, he thought. Don't rely on love. Then he smelled her, and he didn't know if it was blarney or love. He kissed her, and she was willing, her lips moist on his. God, he could take her right here on this scrubby kitchen floor.

He gathered them around him back in the living room while Sylvie waited out in the hall. The less she knew the better.

"All right now, here's the way it's going to be. Get it right because the odds are high enough against us as it is."

Paulie stood up. "I'm a hired gun, Collins. I didn't ask for none of this."

Collins's hand came out of his jacket, and the .38 it held was aimed directly at Paulie. "You're in, Lazar. You did a job for free in New York. Now you're lucky enough to get a chance to redeem yourself. Don't even think about ducking out or I'll have your name on a contract while you're still sprouting wings."

Paulie opened his mouth and mumbled, "I'm in."

"All right," Collins began again, "here's how we do it. Jimmy, you and Lazar plant the jelly under the three bridges. How long should it take them?" he asked Kresky.

Kresky did a quick mental computation. "The bridges are a couple of hundred yards apart. Won't take more than a few minutes to lay the dynamite. He looked at Jimmy. "How will you blow them?"

Jimmy grinned. "Simplest way I know. A few sticks in the right places, a wire, and a match."

"That means you'll have to drive to each bridge after you blow the previous one," Kresky said.

Still smiling, Jimmy said, "Like a Fourth of July relay race. Bam, bam, bam."

Collins looked at his watch. "It's nine-thirty now. Start laying the jelly in an hour. Ten minutes from the time you finish, blow them."

Jimmy nodded. "What if you don't have a train?"

"We'll have one. Stack up the bridges somewhere between ten-thirty and ten forty-five. When the last one goes you take your car—"

"What car?" Paulie cut in.

Collins turned on him and gave him a big smile. "The car you're going to wire and steal, Lazar. Or do I have to call Charlie Rosen for that?"

Paulie rolled his shoulders. "Stash the needle, Collins."

Collins turned back to Jimmy. "When the last bridge goes you burn rubber. Head along the river, you'll pick up the tracks . . . where, Kresky?"

"Off First Street," Kresky answered. "You'll run right into it."

"Okay," Collins said. "Once you're there you follow it to the crossing on Elm Street. Park your car, leave the lights on. When we see you, we'll slow down and pick you up. From there on it's the A Train straight for Curtiss-Wright. We go in the back door."

"Do we pay the toll?" Paulie wanted to know.

"I don't know," Collins said. "If we have to blast then you'll get your chance to prove how good you are. We'll have a prisoner and I hope that will get us in. Once we're in, we use jelly sticks. Torch them and throw them in Heinrich's lap."

Everyone was abruptly quiet as the enormity of it hit them.

"Light them up," Jimmy said.

"And get the hell out fast," Collins echoed.

Paulie looked around the room. "Just the four of us?"

"That's it, Lazar. Those are pretty good odds, aren't they, Jimmy?"

Jimmy smiled. A smile that Collins recognized from suicide days back in Ireland. "Just like Dublin, Bobbie boy." He stood up and clapped Collins on the shoulder.

Collins pulled Jimmy over and said softly, "Let Lazar lay the dynamite while you watch the bridge. If he gives you any trouble, kill him."

"Got you."

Paulie stood in front of Collins. "What do we use to blast our way into the plant?"

"Tommy gun special. Jimmy has them in the car."

Jimmy and Paulie went out the door. Kresky stood at the window and watched them walk down the street. When they were out of sight, he turned back to Collins. "The odds in favor of us making it out of there tonight are not very good."

"I know."

"It's not Lazar I'm worried about, it's the woman," Kresky said. "She's a society dish. She'll get cold feet and blow the whole thing for us."

"I don't think so, but we'll find out."

Now Kresky was face to face with Collins. "What'll you do if she starts screaming 'Help me!' and tips them?"

Collins let out some air. "Kill her."

"I'm glad you said that. 'Cause if you don't, I will. Remember that."

"I'll remember. Now let's go hijack a train."

Kresky had not wasted his time in Paterson. He knew how the city was laid out, including the precise location of key supply and communication facilities. The best place to hijack a train would be at the crossing on Second Street before it came into the main freight yard, which was under Nazi control. The essential ingredient was to have a German officer on board before they rolled into the freight yard. To do that, they would have to lure an officer out of the depot and kidnap him.

They had parked the car at the end of the block, a hundred yards from the depot. Collins gave Sylvie some last instructions. "Remember, we want the officer alone. If he thinks he has a chance to score, he'll come."

"And if he doesn't?"

"Then we'll just have to deal with that," Collins said. He squeezed her hand, and she turned quickly and walked toward the freight yard.

Collins walked over to where Kresky was pressed against an abandoned car. It had been completely stripped. Wheels, running board, fender, hood—the works.

"Think she can pull it off?" Kresky asked.

"We're about to find out."

They watched her move slowly down the street along the deserted patch of warehouses that led to the freight depot. If this had been Germany, this whole street would have been full of soldiers. But this wasn't. It was Paterson, New Jersey, and the Nazis had to improvise. After we pull this off, Collins thought, there will be plenty of soldiers here. If we pull it off. Now Kresky started walking in the opposite direction to handle his part of the hijack.

She moved gracefully. Collins could see the sashay of her body creating a rhythm of its own. He suddenly realized that, if they didn't survive tonight, he would not get to make love to her anymore. That would be an awful disappointment.

Sylvie felt how dry her throat was. How did I get here? she kept asking herself. I got here, she thought, because I was dying, slowly dying, and this man made me live. And now I'll have a chance to see how much life means to me. Still she marveled at it. A man invades you, and your whole life changes. Why? Because he made you feel something.

The yard was fronted by a hastily erected wire fence. The smell of gas came from the trucks that rolled into the yards on a regular basis. She could see three of them up ahead. She crossed over some tracks and saw the guards' shack, the one described by the gruff-looking man who was back there with Collins. She stopped momentarily to brace herself. You must play a part, she repeated to herself. Like you did when you played Pollyanna back at Briarcliff School in Baltimore, Maryland. You were outstanding. Miss Pemberton gushed over you. Miss Pemberton should see me now.

As she approached the shack, she remembered something Miss Pemberton used to teach in social etiquette class. Always smile prettily when introduced to a man. She stopped at the wooden cubicle and was met by a young soldier. Why he's barely out of high school, she thought. Simple trusting eyes and dimples.

"Fräulein, I can be of service to you?"

He stammers. You should be able to convince him. Sylvie smiled and said, "I have car trouble. My driver has not come back. I must see the officer in charge."

Kresky had made his way over to Second Street and now, veering right, walked toward the little hut where the operator of the railroad gate would be holed up. There was nothing on the block but warehouses, and the only building remotely near the hut was a tool company closed up for the night. The wind was cold in his face. He reached into his pocket and, feeling the smooth cold steel of the revolver, pulled out his pipe. He felt cool and steady. Only the slightest tremor in his legs indicated to him that his nerves were vibrating.

Peering in, Kresky saw the outline of a man in a sailor's dickey bird cap reading by lantern light.

"Hi, bud, got a match?"

The man looked up. He had scrunched up features, and he peered at Kresky to see if he knew him. "Yeah, I guess so."

Kresky took two steps into the little hut, which smelled of alcohol and cigarette smoke. The man handed him a box of matches. Kresky lit one up and let the flame go to the tobacco. He inhaled and blew out smoke and the sweet aroma of pipe tobacco filled the shack. "Thanks," Kresky said. "By the way, what time's the next train due by here?"

The man reclined back in his chair and closed his eyes. He knew the timetable by heart. "Ten forty-seven."

"Do you drop the gate for it?"

The man leaned forward and opened his eyes. "Flag them all. You never know who is going to take it in his mind to cross the tracks."

Kresky handed him back the matches. "Passenger train, is it?"

The scrunchy features got scornful. "Not along this track. All we get here is freight."

"Those are pretty big, aren't they?"

"Some are. Well, I think I'll lay my head down and get a few winks."

"Aren't you afraid you'll sleep through?"

The man snorted. "Are you kidding? That whistle is my personal alarm clock." He put his head down and was still. Then, sensing Kresky had not left, he opened his eyes. They got very big when he saw Kresky's gun.

Sylvie had made an elaborate fuss, finally even showing some tears. They were enough to convince the young soldier to call the officer on duty. He talked on the phone for some time. Sylvie heard him whisper, *"Sie ist schön."* The conversation was brief after that. The soldier came over to her and said, "The lieutenant will be here soon. If you wish, sit down." He gestured toward a chair in the shack opposite another soldier.

"Thank you," Sylvie replied. "I'll wait here."

She stood by the shack, noting the activity in the depot. Some of the trucks had been loaded up and were driving toward the hut with their lights flashing.

She felt the young soldier's arm on hers. "Please, fräulein, you move here." He guided her back while three trucks rolled past. Now she could see the depot more clearly. Overlooking the yard there was a high tower from which a searchlight moved in an arc. Along the railroad track itself, a makeshift platform had been built for transfers of equipment. Collins had asked her to look for machine gun emplacements. Her eyes roved past the small and large trucks, then past a small lighted building some men came out of drinking coffee. Light poles had been placed in a semicircle around the yard so that the outer perimeter was well lit while the inner ring was in darkness. A train flashing by would be seen clearly. How could they fire at it? There. In front of a wood building she saw a machine gun mounted on a tripod and surrounded by bags of some kind. There was nobody near it. It occurred to her that, if they could get past this supply depot without a fight, it would be a big step in the right direction.

"Fräulein."

"What?" Sylvie whirled and stared into the face of a young officer. The first thing she saw was that his lips were firmly set, and he had not shaved recently. That could mean he was tired and probably also annoyed. He took her in. Sylvie saw by his eyes that he was impressed.

She smiled coquettishly. "Oh thank you for coming. I have broken down . . . oh, do you speak English?"

"Enough," he said quickly. He was not one you could waste time with.

"My car went dead . . . it just died. I sent my driver for help and he hasn't come back yet. I was getting quite frightened sitting there in the dark. I am expected in New York."

He looked at his watch. "New York? You will miss curfew."

She saw by his eyes that he was nobody's fool. "Yes, that's right. I may have some problems. Could you look at it? Perhaps you have a mechanic. . . ."

He was surveying her carefully, like a horse trader inspecting a potential purchase. He was in his late twenties with a good physique, of medium height, but the strong shoulders made him seem taller. Sylvie guessed he was wondering if there was a chance, and she knew that any flirtation by her now would be false. He had to decide it himself. Apparently he had, for he said, "Show me where it is."

She felt her breath catch. Now the thing had been set in motion.

The officer turned to the guard who had helped Sylvie. "Gorman, *kommen sie*."

The word *no* almost leaped from her mouth. He was so young. "Do we need him?" Sylvie said.

The officer grinned at what he perceived was her anxiousness to be alone with him. "Gorman has a way with cars as some men have a way with women. Come. Show me."

They started down the road, and Sylvie felt his hand under her elbow. The proprietary touch. *He means to have me later.*

Well, there was a surprise in store for him. But the young soldier, what would happen to him?

Paulie held the dynamite in his hands, and the power in the tightly wrapped sticks seemed now to be vested in him. He shouldn't have crabbed before. He needed to do something to cover up for shooting the Heinrich, Beck, in Central Park. If he did this right, he was back in solid with Collins. Collins wouldn't look too closely at Paulie's story. He smelled the wind off the river. It reminded him of that time in Delaware when he and Tommy planted dynamite and got the blowup blamed on the union. Only that had been a spring night. Now it was winter, but his hands didn't feel the cold. This was his kind of work. First the jelly. Later on, the tommy gun. He had practiced with the tommy on targets, but had never had a chance to use it for real. Now he had Heinrich.

"How's it going?" Jimmy called.

Paulie smiled and held up his thumb. He finished wedging the last stick to the upright siding of the bridge. He ran the wire over the siding, then down to where the stick was wedged in and back toward Jimmy. Paulie stretched out the line till they were fifty yards from the bridge. Perfect. He looked at Jimmy. "All you need now is a match."

Jimmy read his watch. Above them the moon sent pale gold shafts onto the Passaic River. "All right," Jimmy said. "Let's go to the last one."

Paulie smiled. "Last to be wrapped, first to blow."

Once more feeling the pain in his knee, Collins hugged the old car and peered at the outline of Sylvie. There were two German soldiers. One had the standard officer's cap. She had done her job. But the officer had brought backup. He was carrying a rifle so he wasn't a mechanic. It was cut out for Collins. He had to kill the soldier and take the officer prisoner. He couldn't use his gun. They were too close. A shot would bring the hounds out of the depot. The officer and his guard would inspect Sylvie's car. He would have to strike quickly, lethally. The guard couldn't be left unconscious, so he could bring help later on.

He needed something sharp. Collins slid around the car he was using for cover till he was almost eye level with the front windshield. He prayed somebody hadn't stripped the wipers. There. He felt one. With a strong wrist snap he tore it off. His fingers touched the edge. It was sharp enough if he drove it home just right.

He heard the crack of boots on gravel. They weren't more

231

than ten yards away. Collins heard Sylvie's voice. "No sign of my driver. I can't imagine where he could be."

"Perhaps he was arrested for missing curfew," the officer said with a laugh.

The feet crunched on a few more paces.

"Give me your flashlight, Gorman."

Collins grimaced. You never want to know the name of someone you have to kill. He came from his mother's womb, like we all did.

"Where is the key?" the officer asked.

"I have it in my purse."

"Give it to me, please. Gorman, lift the hood."

Collins listened for the snap of it. There. Now don't find the keys right away. Empty everything out. Keep him occupied like I rehearsed with you. He crept around and saw Gorman flashing his light into the engine. Now.

He ran the ten yards from the stripped car to Sylvie's Packard, feeling the throbbing pain in his knee. Gorman never heard him until the last second, and then Collins was on him. His arm corralled Gorman's throat, cutting off air and circulation, the vital ingredients of an outcry. In almost the same moment the other hand shot straight forward, plunging the metal portion of the wiper into the German's back. The hemorrhaging would be instant. Collins let him fall like a sack and, pulling his revolver from his waistband, turned. He saw the officer, key in hand, watching in disbelief. Collins advanced toward him, gun pointed. "Don't move . . . don't . . . easy." Collins was directly in front of him then and sapped him with the butt of the gun. The German went down instantly.

"Help me get him in the car," Collins snapped.

Sylvie was staring over at Gorman. "Did you . . . did you . . . ?"

"Yes, now c'mon."

She started to quiver and shake. He slapped her across the face hard. She looked at him in the most shocked fashion.

"It was us or them. If he yelled, we were dead. Now, c'mon."

He dragged the officer to the car and shoved his inert body in the back. He gave Sylvie the key. "Drive." He slid in the back. "I'll tell you where to go. We have no time to waste. This is only the beginning."

Kresky checked his watch. Ten forty-three. Still no Collins.

"When's the next train after the ten forty-seven?"

"Eleven forty-nine," the gate guard answered automatically.

"Too late," Kresky muttered to himself. C'mon Collins. C'mon. He looked out of a little hut and saw the lights of a car. Collins, it better be you.

232

The car pulled in and Kresky saw the woman at the wheel. The back door opened and Collins came out holding a gun on a wobbly German officer.

"Give me the phone," Kresky ordered the gateman. He handed it to Kresky, who tore the cord from its connection.

Holding the Nazi officer by the belt, Collins entered the hut. "Get up," Kresky ordered the gate guard. The officer was shoved into the chair.

"How much time?" Collins asked.

"About three minutes."

Collins turned to the guard. "You know the procedure for slowing down the train after the gate is lowered?"

"Yes."

"Get it ready." Collins nodded to Kresky and they stepped outside.

A gust of cold wind assailed them as they faced one another, guns in hand. "I figure it this way," Collins began. "We'll use them both to make it look kosher. We'll be right behind them, guns in pockets. Heinrich will be standing directly on the track. As soon as it stops we walk right toward them, flash our cannons, and board."

"What about him after?" Kresky said, gesturing toward the gate guard.

"Let him go. He's not going to tip anybody."

"And the woman?"

"I'll take care of that now. Keep an eye on Fritz."

"Hurry up."

Collins gimped over to Sylvie. "You okay?"

"I don't know."

"About the guard . . . I'm sorry you had to see it. Someday you'll understand." He saw the hurt in her eyes. Saw how gentle and fine she really was. He wanted to hold her. To make it better. "Now, you know how to get there."

"Yes. I'll be waiting. Your leg—is it bad?"

It was, but he didn't tell her. "If you get stopped, say you're lost. Your car stalled, you sent the driver for help and then tried the car yourself and it started up. That's all."

She started up the car. "Good luck," he said.

She looked up at him. "Be careful."

She was pulling away and Collins heard the whistle of a train in the distance. He moved back to the hut. Kresky stepped out, gesturing with his gun to the gate guard and the Heinrich officer.

"Get the lantern on the track and then drop the gate." Collins turned toward the officer. "You'll be on the track with me right behind you. Anything goes wrong, you're dead."

* * *

Bill Piel, at the throttle of the ten forty-seven, saw the light from half a mile away. He called to Joe Calloway, who was in the lead car. "Joe, light on the track." Piel eased off on the speed and began smoothly applying the brake.

Collins felt the wind snap in his face. "Easy does it. He's seen us. Everybody nice and still."

Piel felt the train slowing. He prided himself on his brake jobs. No jolt, no commotion. The train, wheels screeching on the track, gently came to a halt.

Piel saw Harry Black, the gate guard whom he had known for twenty years. Next to him was a German officer. God, how Piel had come to dislike the Paterson run. Two men were bringing up the rear.

The German officer was abreast of Piel now. Piel looked to him for some explanation and suddenly the two men behind Harry and the officer had jumped out.

"It's our train," Collins cried out. "We're coming on board." Piel saw the pistols pointed at him and his eyebrows shot directly up.

Collins hoisted himself up into the cab. "Who else is on board?"

The gun was wedged into Piel's stomach. "Joe Calloway."

"Where?"

"Car behind us."

"Call him out. Who else?"

"Couple of loaders."

"Where are they?"

"Maybe with Joe."

Collins wiggled the gun. "Get them out."

But there was no need. The three of them had come out of the lead car to see what was up.

"Cover them," Collins called to Kresky.

"We're taking this train," Collins called out. "You can start walking. No telephones. If you do we'll find you. You're all family men. You don't want trouble."

"You're right," Joe Calloway called back. "We don't want trouble. Let's go."

They crossed to the other side of the track under Collins's watchful eye. "Okay Heinrich, up here."

"Can I go?" whined little Harry the gate guard.

"Go ahead," Kresky said. "The same thing applies to you. Don't call anybody."

"What about me?" Bill Piel wanted to know.

"We'll keep you until the next stop," Collins told him.

Kresky had climbed on board. "Between here and there you give me a crash course. I used to run one of these things."

The officer stared angrily at Collins. "You will not go far."

"Well, if we don't, you're dead, Heinrich."

"Perhaps I am dead anyway. And my name is not Fritz or Heinrich."

He's right, Collins thought, but if he believes it he might try something. "We need you to get through the depot. If you co-operate then you get off once we pass it. What is your name?"

The officer said nothing. He's thinking it over, Collins noted. At least there's a measure of doubt there. Once we head into Curtiss-Wright he'll know he has no chance. String him along now.

"What's your name?" he asked again.

"Müller. Hans Müller."

"All right, Müller, I just need you for a passport, then you get off."

Collins watched Müller's eyes flicker. He's trying to figure whether we're just kidnapping the train. Well, he's got something to chew on.

Nodding to Bill Piel he said, "How far to the crossing at Elm Street?"

"Maybe five, six minutes."

Collins smiled at Kresky. "That's when you graduate. Let's hop it."

The train began to snort and chug now as Piel eased the throttle forward. They were rolling, the train picking up momentum.

We were lucky, Collins thought, we got a freight train. A thought tugged at him. "What are you carrying?"

Piel had just sounded the train whistle. "Paint, turpentine, some chemicals for the plant down here."

"Flammable stuff?"

"Very."

Despite the worsening pain in his knee, Collins felt a little better. Sure, it was a suicide run, but at least he was doing something. Not holed up in a Park Avenue apartment drunk and horny. They were taking it to Heinrich. They broke out over the Passaic River and Collins smelled the breeze coming fresh into him. He looked up at the stars; they were bright, glistening things. Like a night long ago outside of Dublin when they waited to rob a mail train.

The first bridge exploded. He heard it and smiled as the scent of the river came still more sweetly to him. He saw the engineer smiling over at him. He knows who's responsible. He gave Collins the thumbs up sign. Collins saw Kresky nodding. Three minutes later the next one went up, and this time Piel gave two blasts with the whistle.

Crouched alongside the engineer, Lieutenant Hans Müller also heard the first two bridges being blown. This is a small operation, he thought, with a big objective. What do we have in the supply depot that they might want? Nothing. Perhaps they just want to make a name for themselves. But the leader had killed Gorman so quickly and professionally. And we are headed east. Beyond the depot is the Curtiss-Wright plant. If I were a professional, that's where I would be going. Since this is a reckless mission, why shouldn't they aim for the stars? The more Hans Müller thought about it, the more logical it seemed that Curtiss-Wright, not the supply depot, was the target. And the more convinced he was of that, the more certain he became that his life was forfeit. The American was just trying to gain his cooperation to get through the depot. In that moment, Hans Müller realized that the depot stop was his only chance to both stop this mission and save his life.

The third dynamite blast resounded. This time Bill Piel ripped off three large toots. They swung away from the river moving toward Elm Street.

"Slow it a little," Collins said to Piel. "Want to make sure my company has enough time to get there."

Piel nodded. "How many?"

"Two. Why?"

"Well, if you didn't have to worry about driving this thing, there'd be four of you."

Collins looked directly at him. "You know what you're saying?"

"You're going all the way, right? I'll take you."

"We're not making the return trip."

Piel laughed. "I retire next week. My old woman been dead these two years, and all I come home to is an empty apartment and my own socks to darn. Eat hash every night in the diner because there's no meat. I know what I'm doing. You wouldn't deprive me now. This is my country. I want it back."

Collins thought it over. "I wouldn't dream of depriving you. You're signed on. You take your orders from me. If I buy it, then my friend's in charge. When I say, you make lightning down the track. Will this thing go?"

"You just watch."

Two minutes later the train began to slow for the Elm Street pickup. Piel handled it smoothly. Collins could see Jimmy and Paulie Lazar running from a Pontiac. Kresky covered Müller while Collins gave the two men a hoist up.

"Nice car you got there," Collins said to Jimmy.

Jimmy grinned. "Yeah, we had to make a quick sale. Drove like a dream."

Jimmy saw Müller. "Got a guest?"

Collins nodded. "When we get to Curtiss-Wright, finish him."

Jimmy winked.

Paulie was fondling the tommy gun Jimmy had given him.

Collins came over. "Can you handle it?"

"Just tell me when."

"Couple of minutes. You'll know."

Collins thumped Piel on the shoulders. "Let's go. Gentlemen, we have a chauffeur courtesy of the management of the Erie Railroad."

Kresky spat down at the track as they pulled out. "First thing management ever gave me."

The train picked up speed, and now they were racing toward the supply depot, the obstacle they had to pass to get to the Curtiss-Wright plant.

Collins had weighed the chances of speeding through the supply depot without stopping. But it was eight or ten minutes beyond that to Curtiss-Wright. The Germans would phone on ahead, and there would be a reception committee awaiting them. They desperately needed the element of surprise.

"What's going to happen when we get to the depot?" he said softly to Bill Piel.

"I'll slow down," he answered. "They want to know what's going through."

Collins bit his lip. They would need a good cover story.

"Stand up," he ordered Müller.

Müller rose, looking at him. Collins wondered if the German had figured out what the real destination was. They would both be playing a game inside a game.

"You're going to be out in front as we come in. Tell them everything is all right. The train is carrying mechanical equipment."

"You still must stop."

"Just remember the whole time we're stopped that you're out in front. If anything goes wrong, the first to show is the first to go. But once we're through, we'll let you off."

"When will I be let off?"

"When we get about an hour past the depot."

Müller took the news stolidly. No use trying to read him, Collins saw. He's made some kind of decision in his mind. He'll either play ball at the depot or try to signal them. Either way he's a dead man.

"It's up ahead, maybe a mile," Piel called to him.

"Watch him," Collins said to Kresky. He slipped back to where Jimmy and Paulie Lazar stood. "You ready?"

Jimmy showed them the double dynamite sticks tied together

by a short fuse. He blew on his tommy gun. "Remember Belfast?"

"I remember," Collins said. "Three to one against us and we shot our way out. We'll do it again. All right, get down."

He turned back toward Kresky and Müller. Christ, if it was only three to one against us now. He looked up at the night sky and breathed in a lungful of the cold air. Hell, this might be the last time.

"Half a mile," Piel sang out.

Collins jammed Müller up against the wall of the cab. "When we stop, you show yourself. Tell them you're riding along with the equipment for delivery to the aircraft plant. It's special delivery. You understand?"

"I may have to get out."

"Fine. Just remember we can still kill you from here."

Müller said nothing. He seemed ready to play the game. Forget the resigned demeanor, Collins told himself. Inside he's a jumble of nerves. It's sixty to forty he'll try something.

The train had appreciably slowed and Piel said, "Comin' in nice and easy. Here we go."

As the train crawled to a stop, Collins felt his nerve ends screw around him. Mother of miracles, are you there?

Now they breaked and Collins heard a voice call out. *"Vas ist los?"*

He jabbed Müller in the leg with his pistol. "Start talking."

The train stopped and Müller leaned out of the cab. *"Hitzig,"* he barked. They were conversing in German, and Collins realized that with an inflection, a word slipped in, he could warn them. He listened to the harsh, guttural exchange, knowing it might already be too late. If I were him, Collins thought, I would sure as hell try to have a pretext for getting out of the train. In that moment Collins would have to decide whether to kill Müller and make a run for it.

The German said something, and Müller whispered to Collins. "It is my supply sergeant. He has a requisition order I must sign. A release of oil. I was working on it when you kidnapped me. If I do not sign it, he will know something is wrong."

"Go ahead."

Müller walked to the back of the cab and opened the door. Jimmy moved to a spot where he could peer out.

Collins called to Jimmy. "What's happening?"

"They're talking."

"What else do you see?"

"Machine gun, two men on it. Pointed at us."

"How far?"

"Fifteen yards."

"Lazar," Collins whispered. "If they open up, you drop the jelly on them."

Collins crawled around to where Jimmy lay. Inching up alongside of him, he could see Müller signing something. Suddenly he reached out. Collins felt his finger tighten round the trigger. A light flashed. Müller's cigarette's was lit. He was saluting and walking back toward them.

"He did it," Jimmy whispered.

Maybe, Collins thought, maybe.

Müller climbed back on and was waving to the men.

The train started up.

Collins grabbed Müller. "Is it okay?"

Müller eyes were bland. "It is okay. I value my life."

Collins scrambled over to Kresky. "You said the conveyor belt was on the lower level?"

Kresky nodded. "That's where they feed the engines. Knock that out, and it'll hurt them bad."

"I want the whole plant," Collins declared.

"I wanted Santa Claus till I was eight," Kresky answered.

"How is the track laid after the unloading area?"

They had picked up speed again and were running full tilt down the track.

Kresky's forehead screwed up as he tried to remember. "Track winds up an embankment. It curves around the plant, then comes down into a straightaway."

"If we went past the loading area and dropped me off, what would I come to first?"

"Boiler room. Pipes that heat the place."

"So anything we start would spark the whole place."

"You need a big fire."

Collins grinned crookedly. "That's what we'll give them. You'll like this, Kresky. A Russian fire. A Molotov cocktail party."

"Where we going to get them?"

"We'll make them."

Collins grabbed Piel. "Where's the chemicals?"

"Second car back."

"Bottles there?"

"Bottles, cans, you name it."

"Slow down so we can get inside. How long till we reach Curtiss-Wright?"

"Ten minutes."

"Make it twenty." He turned to Kresky. "Watch Müller till we get back. Lazar, Jimmy, let's go."

The train curved round a bend, dipped, and slowed down. The three men jumped off and ran toward the rear of the train.

239

Müller's voice came to Kresky as the train moved again. "You really have no chance."

When Kresky didn't reply he continued. "I knew you were after the plane factory from the beginning. But I kept quiet, do you know why?"

"Because life is sweet," Kresky said.

Müller smiled sarcastically. "Because your leader is a fanatic. We have known an attempt would come sometime. Now they are warned."

Kresky's muscles became taught. "How were they warned?"

"I signed a requisition slip there. It said Americans are coming . . . sabotage. What do you think of your chances now?"

Kresky's pistol came up higher. "Better than yours."

"Don't be a fool. In the game of war you save your life. You are riding into a fort. We will all be killed. For what?"

"What's your offer?"

"Surrender to me now. I will take the others prisoner when they return. You will get special treatment for cooperating."

Piel's voice came to Kresky. "Don't listen to him."

"Another fool," Müller exclaimed. "Well? What do you say?"

"I say," Kresky bit off each word, "thanks for tipping us off to your rotten little trap. It's useful information."

Müller snorted. "There is nothing you can do. You're a dead man."

"What does that make you?"

Müller sank down in a disgusted manner.

"That's tellin' him," Bill Piel said.

Müller had planned it all carefully. First the note back there, then this appeal. And since that didn't work, there was the court of last resort. The pistol his sergeant had slipped him. He felt for it now under his waistband, edged into his pants.

Kresky was wondering if they could shoot through the unloading area and throw dynamite sticks. He put the question to Piel.

"I'd have to slow down for you to have any accuracy. They'd get a good crack at us."

Both men became silent. The way ahead was truly suicidal. The train was moving relentlessly. They could hear the sound of the wheels delivering them to a firing squad.

Piel turned then, as if by looking back he could recall the moment of instant bravado when he volunteered for this mission. He saw Müller raising himself up, gun in hand.

"Watch out."

Müller was a supply officer, not a combat one. If he were experienced, he would have shot Kresky. Instead, he fired at Piel to silence the warning. Piel crumpled and, in that moment, Kresky fired and hit Müller. He fell back and Kresky fired again. Müller slumped to the floor. The train continued rolling.

Kresky looked at Piel dying on the floor. "The train," he choked out. "Brake."

Kresky had the throttle in his hand. They weren't moving that fast. He eased off the speed and now applied the brake. The train lurched and then began to slow perceptibly. It came to a stop just as the house lights went out all over Paterson. It was, Kresky thought, exactly eleven o'clock.

He was examining Müller when Collins came running up.

The lantern light revealed the carnage. "Damn it," Collins swore. "Damn."

Now Jimmy and Paulie joined them.

Kresky pointed to Müller. "He tipped them in that note he signed. He was tryin' to bargain with me. They must have slipped him a gun."

"And they know we're coming for sure," Collins said.

"So what do we do?" Paulie asked.

"We keep coming," Collins said. "They'll be waiting for us, and we'll give them a real hot present. We douse the whole train except for the cab. Soak it full of chemicals and all the other crap. Jimmy, you and Lazar start from the last car. Torch them all. After the lead car catches fire, Lazar, you uncouple it. Got it? When all the cars go up, Kresky, you let out the throttle."

They looked at him as if he were crazy.

"It's our only chance. We have to take it. Five flaming cars in Heinrich's lap. We keep going past the yard until we reach the embankment. They you guys supply the cover while I molotov the boiler room."

"Why don't we just volunteer for the electric chair?" Paulie finally said.

"You can have it right now, if you want," Collins answered. "Well?"

Paulie made no move.

"All right," Collins cried. "Now. Let's go."

Paulie and Jimmy ran back toward the lead car while Collins began stripping Müller of his clothes.

Kresky bent over Piel. "I'll get rid of his body."

"He was a good man," Collins said.

"Good," Kresky said. "He was the best. He's what you didn't think this country has . . . heart. The lumpen proletariat. There's a lot more like him."

Collins never stopped stripping Müller's clothes, but he did look up at Kresky. "Maybe you're right."

Chapter 25

The Germans had laid down temporary tracks so that any train bringing in engines or other parts to be tested would come in right behind the plant itself. They had built a sloped embankment that soared past the gray factory. It continued around the plant until it joined the regular track running to northern New Jersey. They had built up the swell of ground on the embankment by adding dirt and layers of coal. The loading yard was shaped like a crescent. The front of the crescent was taken up by a motor pool in which trucks and vans were parked. The rear and sides of the crescent were occupied by some tool and supply sheds. Each side of the crescent was fortified by a machine gun built into a separate pillbox. Both machine gun nests had clear fields of vision and could rake the yard. Now, as the sound of the train could be heard in the distance, both machine guns were pointed directly at the point where the train would stop. The center of the yard was occupied by twenty German soldiers armed with rifles, automatic guns, and grenades. They were under the command of Captain Helmut Schoendorf, chief of plant security. Schoendorf was a man of thirty-five who had been appointed to his position because of the excellent security he had provided in and around Nazi plants in London. It was reasoned by Berlin that he would do equally well in another conquered nation where English was the mother tongue. A tall, muscular man with a jutting jaw and broad chest, he had been in the security office when Müller's message was called in. It had taken him six minutes to have his squad of men lined up in the yard. Now he turned and waved his hand to both search towers, where riflemen had been placed behind the two sweeping searchlights that lit up the yard. Schoendorf looked behind him at the Curtiss-Wright plant with lights on all three levels. He could hear the hum of engines being tested so that they could be sent out and placed in Focke-Wulfs and Messerschmitts. "Engines that will give the Luftwaffe air superiority over the United States in their

242

own country.'' Those words were from a letter written to him personally by Himmler. They were embedded in Schoendorf's mind.

When this pathetic band of saboteurs came into the yard with Müller presumably as hostage, they would be met by crack security troops. Schoendorf had no question of stopping the four men and their train. He had overwhelming strength and fire superiority even without the troops who had been sent to investigate the three explosions. What concerned Schoendorf was capturing these men so that information could be extracted from them. Information that would lead Schoendorf to others in the American underground movement.

His superiors had thought America would be like England, but Schoendorf did not agree. It would be better. Schoendorf would make his reputation here. America was a country of idiots who had never known invasion or fought a war on their own soil. They were already beaten, but they would take many risks such as these idiots with the train. Fools with illusions were the stuff of rapid promotion. Still they were brave. There was no doubt that this was a suicide mission. These men were prepared to die. But they would not be prepared for Müller's message having gotten through. Schoendorf had only one nagging thought. He fervently hoped Müller had not somehow tipped his hand.

Paulie listened to the chug of the wheels, felt the train pounding on the track, felt the trip-hammer of his heart matching it pulsation for pulsation. Everybody had a tough job, but Paulie's was a bitch. Enough so that he cursed himself heartily for ever having shot Beck to begin with. Paulie would have rather faced the Capone mob, guns blasting, than what they had to do now. The plan was nuts. They would need every break in the world to make it come off. Handy was back there now torching the last car. Handy would slop down some chemicals they found in the big oil drums, then light it. With the flame literally right on his heels, he would run to the next car and repeat the procedure. Right up until he had lit all five cars, and then he would jump into the cab. With all five cars burning full blast, the train would head right for the loading yard. At that point it became Paulie's job to uncouple the cab from the lead car. He would do this by stretching out full length with Handy holding onto his legs. One of the hooks holding the engine to the lead car had already been freed. When the second one was loosened, the flaming train cars would catapult off the track and into the Heinrichs. If he got it free. Otherwise, Paulie would be stretched out trying to uncouple the car and the Heinrichs would machine stitch his body full

243

of swiss cheese holes. He cursed audibly. Underground work. It was nuts. Riding full tilt into the German guns with aces and deuces against you.

He heard Collins's voice. "The first car's lit up. Let it out, Kresky."

Paulie tensed. He had a mental picture of Handy running from car to car, hot flames scorching his ass. Despite himself Paulie laughed.

Schoendorf heard the train getting still closer. His pistol came out of his holster and now he held up his hand for all the men to see. When it came down it meant open fire. Schoendorf had no doubt that the opening volley would destroy the confidence of the men in the train. Especially when the snipers from up above and the two machine gun squads caught the train in a triangular crossfire. He only hoped that they would surrender. They were insane to try this and crazy enough to throw away their lives. Himmler would want information, not just dead bodies. Schoendorf would get his personal commendation when . . . He heard the train again. There, now he could see it. *Mein Gott!* It was on fire.

Paulie saw the flames billowing out of the car in front of him. Here came Handy. He stood poised for one moment, then jumped and Paulie grabbed him. Paulie heard Collins's voice, heard the intense urgency in his words. "Get down, we'll hold you."

Now Paulie was sprawled out on the floor, Collins holding one leg, Handy the other, the train rolling and rocking back and forth. Then he was pushed out to hang in midair between the engine cab and the burning car in front of him. His hands were on the grappling hook, his chest wedged against the steel coupling. Teeth bared, arms straining, he lifted up on the hook. C'mon, you bastard. The flame had consumed the whole car in seconds. He could feel the heat now. Licking tongues reaching out for his hands. Throwing hot splinters at him. And he couldn't get the hook to uncouple.

Behind him Collins was screaming "C'mon, Lazar, c'mon."

Paulie realized he didn't have enough leverage. He had to get under it more. "Lower me," he yelled back. "Lower me."

He felt himself fly forward. He was going under; his heart leaped into his mouth. Then they secured him, and Paulie saw he was only inches from the ground. He could smell the earth. He got his shoulder, that balanced weights for so many years, underneath. He thrust up with it once, twice. Bronco Nagursky cracking the line. He felt the big hook give and, like a man suddenly reprieved from hanging with the noose still about his neck, heaved forth with the last effort of his heart and body.

His head shot forward and he felt funny. What had happened? He no longer felt the weight on his shoulder. He was hanging in midair, and the fire wasn't singeing him. He looked up and saw the flaming train leave the tracks and plunge like molten lava into the yard of the Curtiss-Wright plant.

Schoendorf saw the blazing train speeding into the yard. What were they doing? The train must have caught fire. A stray match or cigarette. They are coming in too fast to stop. They have panicked. They are trying to escape the flame that is devouring their train. You fools, he shouted silently within himself. You have played with fire, and now it will burn you up. And my commendation, what of that? He began to run across the yard, beckoning his men to follow him. But none of them saw him. They were all singularly transfixed by the scorching sight before them.

What were they going to do? Schoendorf asked himself as he ran. It must be that they will speed past us and leap from the train once they pass the plant. He was yelling for his men to come as he ran. Then suddenly the engine car flashed by him without anything in back of it. Schoendorf whirled and saw the flaming cars, disengaged from their anchor, leap out into the air, spitting flames as they crashed and careened into the yard, a tumbling, sizzling ball of fire that exploded into the line of men Schoendorf had placed there.

Schoendorf heard the screams, saw a motorcycle with a soldier on it burst into flame and the man aboard it eaten alive. His men were scattered, running, crying, burning. In that moment he saw what the saboteurs had done and was enraged and full of admiration for them in the same instant. The plan had the simplicity of genius. Throw a match. But he had no time for admiration. He was yelling for the machine guns to fire, for his men to follow the engine speeding up the embankment.

They lost speed on the embankment, and Collins could only vent his frustration. "C'mon, Kresky, move this piece of crap."

It was as if Kresky didn't hear him, so intent was he on piloting this chugging thing.

They were laboring, but steadily rising. Kresky heard voices from down below. German voices.

Bullets whistled past them. Kresky heard the bark of Paulie's tommy gun.

Collins saw the crest of the embankment and knew he could wait no longer. He grabbed Jimmy's arm. "Come with me."

He leaped off and came down hard. The knee crumpled, and

he cried out in pain. Get up. They were running along the embankment. From behind him, Collins could hear Paulie blasting away. He must love this, Collins thought.

They reached the crest of the hill, and Collins saw the lights in the rear of the plant. The boiler room. He pointed. "There."

He ran down the slope, ignoring his wounded knee, feeling wild and liberated, the way it was when he played as a boy and someone freed you, yelling "Ollie, Ollie, Ox and free." His mouth was open, and he heard Jimmy yelling joyously at his heels. There was, as he had known all his life, an ecstasy in being close to death. He stumbled to the ground, felt coal and rough chips scrape his palm. He righted himself, kept running, a figure in a German uniform, sticks of dynamite planted like so many flowers in his belt.

He was still running, on hard ground now, as he approached the boiler room. He saw German soldiers coming out of it and was going too fast to stop. He began to yell. *"Amerikaners, Amerikaners."*

The four soldiers turned toward him and now Collins was upon them. He pointed down the slope. *"Amerikaners, Spions, Spions."* The soldiers turned and, with the instinct of divine guidance, Collins leaped away so that Jimmy's tommy gun could have free access to them.

Collins never looked back. With a leap he was inside the boiler room where he could hear the pipes pumping heat, full of lethal energy. Men were stoking coal into furnaces, and Collins, pistol drawn, was yelling, "Get out. Get out. It's going up." Over and over he yelled it. He pushed men aside, screaming "Get out." He pulled loose a dynamite stick. Now, as if going from slow motion to speed faster than light, men crossed the room in panicked frenzy. They dropped shovels, tools, barrels of coal and dashed for safety. Poised to throw a dynamite stick, Collins saw something from the corner of his eye. He pivoted like an adagio dancer, firing in the same instant. The guard went down in a heap. Outside he heard Jimmy's tommy gun still singing. He had six sticks of dynamite out and lit them one at a time. Like a man at tea with all the time in the world. The way his father had taught him the first time.

"Light them like you would a cigarette, Robbie. If you try to speed, your fingers will trip all over themselves."

He lit four of them and threw them like you would a softball, to the east, west, north, and south of the boiler room. Now he pulled out the two doubled stacks. Four sticks in each. He lit the fuses carefully with his lighter and rolled them into the center of the room.

He ran then, thinking that the fuses would burn down in thirty seconds. They were cut short so that no one could scoop them up and put them out. He leaped over the body of the dead guard and then was back out in the night. He ran a diagonal away from the boiler room, knowing he had less than twenty seconds. The sticks would go off and destroy the furnaces. Then the raging fires would eat through the first floor and blow the conveyor belt and the engines on it. The whole factory would be a furnace in minutes. His knee gave out, and he threw himself headlong on the ground, heard the explosion, and realized what he had missed while he ran. The sound of Jimmy's tommy gun.

There were two single explosions, a multiple one, and then an overlapping crescendo. The last one was like a wave hitting the beach, but amplified twenty times. Hell's fire erupted in the plant, and Collins was up again limping toward the embankment.

Schoendorf had kept after the train. He had seen two men leap from it. One wore a German uniform. Now, as he reached the crest, he saw the engine down the emergency line at the juncture leading out. Then he heard the plant go up. *Gott*, he thought, they have done it. A handful of men.

There was shooting, flashlight beams stabbing in the night. Wild shots being fired. Paulie cackled to himself. Heinrich had panicked. Carrying the tommy gun at his side, Paulie ran for the bottom of the slope where Collins and Handy would be. Suddenly he didn't care about being paid. He was wild with the blood surging inside him. Like the street brawls from when he was a kid. He ran along the track and then in front of him was a Heinrich.

"Hans," Paulie called.

The soldier turned and Paulie spoke. "Welcome to New Jersey." He swung the right fist laden with brass, felt the teeth crack, and the soldier slid down the embankment.

Collins wanted to look for Jimmy and he wanted to run for the train. The nerve ends in his knee were screaming. Have a cup of tea and a stroll he told himself.

He limped along the bottom of the embankment. Along the ridge atop it were Heinrichs. How the hell could he get back to the train? How the hell could he . . . he tripped and went down hard, scraping his face. A body. He saw the black turtleneck sweater. Jimmy. Oh laddie, you must have rolled all the way down here when they got you. He turned him over and saw Jimmy's eyes still open. He closed them and said a Hail Mary. Hail Mary, full of grace, why did you let this man die? You bitch. Always, you take the best of us. Jimmy dead and not even fighting for Ireland. Are we Americans or Irishmen? By the time this is over, there won't be enough of us left to free Ireland.

He kissed Jimmy on the forehead and then scooped up the tommy gun. This was a new war. Heil Mary. He saw the Heinrichs up the hill and he didn't care. He was coming straight at them with Jimmy's tommy. Heil Mary, here I come.

Schoendorf saw the German officer coming up the hill. Stop, you fools, it's Müller . . . Müller. The words died in his mouth as he saw the officer open fire with his tommy gun.

Two men fell. The others began to run down the slope. These were, after all, not combat troops, but young men trained to be security guards. They were not prepared to fight madmen. Schoendorf screamed at them. They were disgracing the Reich. Enough. He would lead by example. He took aim at the American dressed in Müller's uniform and someone called to him. "Heinrich, drop it."

A big man in a suit and open white shirt stood in front of him holding a tommy gun. He pulled the trigger. Nothing happened. It had jammed. Schoendorf reached for his pistol. But this big man was amazingly quick. He hurled himself at Schoendorf. They went down in a heap, rolling and plunging down the embankment. The gravel tore at them. They tumbled to a halt, and Schoendorf shook his head to clear it. Where was he? He looked up and saw the American standing over him. Something glinted on his hand.

Laughing, Paulie said, "Welcome to the Jersey bounce." He smashed down then, full in Schoendorf's face, then sideways, using the brass knuckles like the pro he was, over and over till the face beneath him was blood pudding.

Paulie moved off the limp, bloody German officer and saw all the plant levels burning. Christ, it was going up like a Christmas tree bonfire.

Collins heard and then saw what he had wrought. Then someone was calling out to him. It was Paulie Lazar.

"Let's get out of here," Collins barked, and suddenly was falling as his knee collapsed.

It's over, he thought, and simultaneously he felt Paulie scoop him up. He was slung over Paulie's back as Paulie ran down the black coal embankment.

Christ, he's strong, Collins thought. We're alive and Jimmy's dead.

Kresky couldn't stand it any longer. He hopped off the cab and saw the flames twisting ever higher in the air. Collins had done it. They had all done it. Somebody was running along the track. It was that ox Lazar, and he had a man over his shoulder. Kresky ran toward them yelling, "Lazar, here, over here." He heard Lazar laugh. The crazy son of a bitch is laughing. What the hell is he laughing at?

He reached out for Paulie, who brushed by him. "Let's go, old man."

They ran back to the single cab waiting like a good horse for its trusty driver. Paulie dumped Collins on the cab, hoisted himself and Kresky up.

"Let's go," Paulie yelled.

Shots rang out from behind them. Paulie grabbed a tommy gun and opened up.

Kresky pushed forward on the throttle and the train began to roll. Collins lay on the floor thinking, what the hell is taking so long? Forever. It takes forever.

The train bucked and picked up steam down the track. Collins listened for the wheels, but all he could hear was Paulie's tommy gun singing its relentless song while Paulie screamed at the top of his lungs, "Kiss my ass, Heinrich. Kiss my ass."

Lying flat on his back, his mouth a fountain of blood and broken teeth, Schoendorf knew he had suffered a fiasco. Four men had blown up the Curtiss-Wright plant. The plant he was personally in charge of. He could see the flames spiraling in the air, and with them came the realization that America was an ill-fated assignment. He would never gain a promotion. His career, begun at Spandau, nurtured in Prague, Vienna, and London, had ended in Paterson, New Jersey.

Lieing flat on his back, knee throbbing, Collins looked up at the night sky. The stars were white, clear as crystal above him. All over. They had done it. But how? Jimmy was dead. And a young German soldier who I never saw in my life was in the wrong place at the wrong time. He heard Paulie Lazar yelling his victory paean to the Germans. "Let's take the A Train."

BOOK II

AMERICAN PANORAMA
XI

NAZI DAYS

February 12, 1942

"This is German Ginny and I have a special guest for you tonight. A man who has earned the respect of his fellow New Yorkers. I am speaking of Johnny Lugansky. How are you, Johnny?"

"I'm fine."

"How have the Germans been treating you, Johnny? Tell all the Americans how you are. Has anyone hurt you?"

"No."

"Feeding you good food?"

"Yeah, sure."

"Got any complaints?"

"Well, no. But I would like to go home."

"Well, I think the police would like to send you home. But you did something that wasn't very nice. You made fun of a great leader, Adolf Hitler. Come on now, aren't you sorry about that?"

"Well . . ."

"Aren't you? Come on now."

"I guess."

"The Germans have been good to you, haven't they? Come on, be fair about it."

"Well, I . . . yeah, they been fair."

"Johnny, wouldn't you like to see the war over with?"

"Sure."

"Thanks. Johnny. You've been listening to Johnny Lugansky. Johnny wants what we all want. Peace. Goodnight."

AMERICAN NIGHTS

February 22, 1942

From the wires of AP . . . German radio broadcast out of New York City interrupted by American bootleg band. Program heard over WGER in New York cut off by American claiming to be Johnny Lugansky of New York City, who has been in Gestapo custody. Interruption came at 9:13 P.M. this evening on Washington's Birthday as Virginia Schaefer's show was in progress. Abruptly there was static . . . the German Ginny program stopped and the Benny Goodman band playing "Let's Dance" was heard. . . .

"Hi Ginny, happy Washington's Birthday. This is New York's own Johnny Lugansky making a special guest appearance on your show. Yeah, I know I'm supposed to be a prisoner of the Gestapo, but I escaped. I have underground connections. But since I've been your guest so often lately I dropped in. Remember what George Washington said, Ginny? 'I cannot tell a lie.' So I'll have to tell the folks that wasn't me all these weeks on your show. Shame on you, Ginny. And now for all you good people out there I'm gonna play swing, good American swing. I got Benny Goodman, Jimmie Lunceford, Artie Shaw, Charles Barnet, Count Basie, Duke Ellington. All you people out there listen hard. It's going to be like old times. So you want to lead a band, then do it. You hear me, Ginny? This is my country and you can't have it. You can haul me in and I'll only escape again. You'll never stop boogie-woogie. Now let's have a jam session. Here's T.D. Tommy Dorsey playing Pine Top Smith's 'Boogie Woogie.' C'mon you hep cats, let's dance. It's Johnny Lugansky's Make Believe Ballroom."

The Living History
by Smith Dailey

February 28, 1942

Pittsburgh has fallen. After holding out for a week against the Wehrmacht, the great city of steel has fallen. It will go down forever as the Seven Days of Pittsburgh. Whatever soldiers the government had left behind, together with reservists, and tough coal miners with pickaxes and shotguns fought the Wehrmacht in the streets of the city. The biting winter wind and heavy snowfall made the German advance difficult even under the cover of artillery bombardment that reduced the city to rubble. But it was not until the Germans were able to starve the defense by clogging supply routes that Pittsburgh weakened. Men ate dogs, cats, horses, anything that would give them the necessary sustenance to fight the attacking Panzer corps. On the last day, bloody hand to hand fighting went on all night as American soldiers and civilians fought and died for every inch of ground taken by the Nazis. In the midst of the carnage, with men dying, ripped open by bloody wounds, a singular Associated Press photo haunts my mind. A young woman, without even a coat, dazed and bleeding, holding her dead dog, mouth open, as if trying to give utterance to what is beyond words.

In New York, we wait. There are battles near the California coast, broadcasts from Hollywood stars, from the president, from Winston Churchill. They tell us to have courage, to resist, to give no comfort to the enemy. But we wake up and the enemy is all around us. They eat in our restaurants while we face a critical food shortage. Meat is impossible to get. I want a hamburger swimming in onions, a hot dog smothered in sauerkraut, a Hershey bar.

People walk with eyes averted; suddenly you whirl around expecting to see the Gestapo, and there is only the howling wind mocking you. The city in which I have lived for so long, which always has given me hope and renewal as I walked about it. Breathing its soot and dirt, its damp, muggy air in summer, feeling its biting, damp winters, its frenzy that thrills me, its frenetic tempo and chugging of its traffic. The city with its heartbeat resounding like the improvisations of a jazz quartet, its canyons, its people, characters in a daily drama, a vivid panoply of color, ethnicity, diverse languages, common argot, and uncommon dreams. A nation in itself, a blend of fierce ambition, aspiration, and expectation. We have set the model for freedom, and now a gray, clammy hand has laid itself on our souls. Why does no one come? Who are these faceless men who blew up airplane plants in the night? Show yourself, one of you. Become the man on the white horse. We need to see you, to believe in you. Come forth. We will not believe until we see you. We need a hero . . . a visible one. Johnny Lugansky is not enough.

Chapter 26

March 26, 1942
11:30 A.M.

They hadn't been together since the Paterson explosion, and at first they were both shy and uneasy. As if that night when they had come together was a chapter in a story they had read. Not really about them, but two people like them. But when he came into her, it was as though all the pages melted away. As if they belonged so fiercely to one another that it was not possible ever to be with anyone else. Here in this barren apartment he had brought her to, Sylvie wished she could stay forever and live with him inside her.

Inside her, Collins felt a young girl, tight, frightened, needing gentling; but once sure of him, she let go of herself, trusting him, becoming who she was many years ago. And they speeded up, talking, moaning, more urgent now, rushing toward one another, finding and losing themselves in the same instant, till all was silent, and they held one another.

She knew they should sleep, but she felt something restless in him. Something she had sensed as they came.

She waited a moment before speaking. "Are you afraid you'll fall in love?"

He sat up, and she could feel the tension humming inside him.

He reached for a cigarette from the pocket of his shirt, which lay on the floor of the sparsely furnished apartment. He lit it and looked at her. "Maybe I'm just afraid of what's next."

"I don't believe that," she said. "This isn't new to you, this way of life." She felt now that in some way they had lost one another. That perhaps that their night of love and the next filled with violence were all there was really going to be.

"Why haven't you made any effort to contact me?" she asked.

Collins eyes closed briefly. God, he thought, no matter how it comes out, I'm using her.

He looked at her now. "It was too dangerous. You're the mistress of Patrick Kelly. Heinrich is all around you."

"I would have come. I'm here now," she said, sitting up beside him.

He looked away so that she only saw his hard profile and the tensing of his jaw muscles. "Yes," he said at last, "and probably you shouldn't be. If they catch me, I'll be letting down a lot of men who depend on me."

"And don't *we* mean anything?"

"Probably we do, but I don't see how it can work. I live and work underground. You're not part of that world."

"But I could be," she said.

He remained silent, smoking his cigarette.

"I'll work for you. You know I could do it."

Collins ground the cigarette out on the bare floor. The room had a chair and table lamp. In the farthest corner from the window was the mattress on which they sat.

Collins turned to her. "What I need is special."

"I'm not afraid."

He looked down at her slender body, feeling tender and guilty in the same instant. He had to say what he had known he would say, but it didn't want to come out.

"Kelly," Collins said, more harshly than he had intended.

He saw her eyes go wide. "What about him?"

"I want to know everything that he knows."

"You want me to . . . to spy on him."

"Why not? He's the number one collaborator in America. He knows every move the Heinrichs will make before they do. Hell, he's probably making up most of them."

"You want to use me, that's why you brought me here. You don't care about us."

She started to get up, and he pinned her. "I care. More than I should. How do you think I feel about you sleeping with him? He's a fascist . . . a dirty fascist . . . and he's your lover. He's inside you while I'm out there blowing up bridges."

He let her go, and she jumped up and put on her panties and bra. Only then could she face him.

"You helped me in Paterson."

"That was different."

"No," Collins said, "it's not different. We exist on information. I have to know ahead."

She knew he was right, but what he was asking seemed so monstrous. "You want me to go through his papers, his suits, his desk?"

Collins nodded. "He must bring most of it home."

It was the word home. It cut like a knife in her. "But then I'd be . . . I'd be betraying him."

Collins voice was husky. "He's betraying his country."

Her hand went involuntarily to her mouth. Yes, yes, he was. But she still knew she couldn't do it.

Collins saw it in her eyes. "Goddamn it, how can you sleep with a traitor like that?"

It was right but unfair, he knew immediately. She had to come to that herself, and he was playing the jealous lover.

"I don't . . . we haven't much . . ." she stopped. "I won't spy on him. It's beneath me."

"It's war," he said tersely.

There was a knock on the door, and Collins jumped up. It seemed to her he had his pants on at the same time he flashed the gun. There were two short knocks, then a third lone one. Collins let the gun dangle and slipped into his shirt. He went to the door and opened it.

Kresky came in looking agitated and short of breath. He started to speak, and Collins put a precautionary finger to his mouth, then pointed to the bedroom.

Collins walked back in and pointed to her clothes. "Better get dressed."

They dressed silently, barely looking at one another. Once he glanced over and saw the brown brassiere, the firm breasts. Dammit, you can't sleep with the enemy's mistress and fight a guerilla war.

He waited now till she had on her coat. "I'm sorry. I did want to be with you, but there was no way around it."

Her lips trembled. "I can't do it," and she mouthed his name.

"Say it," he whispered.

"Robert, I can't do it."

He took her hand. "Sylvie, there's a newsstand down on Seventy-second and Broadway. If something happens . . . if you . . . Leave a yellow scarf with Wally the dealer. Make sure you cover it over with a newspaper. You better go."

As he watched her walk out, he saw Kresky in the corner of the living room hidden in shadow. The door closed. Now Kresky approached him.

"What are you doing with her?"

Collins didn't answer right away. "Kelly. I want a pipeline to Kelly."

A tight smile ran across Kresky's mouth. "You'll have to keep screwing her."

Collins grabbed him by the collar and his fist doubled. Then he eased off.

Now Kresky was in his face. "Don't get soft on me, Johnny Irish. If she won't do it after that one night with us, she'll never do it. She's a walking time bomb as it is."

"What do you mean?"

"She could give the whole Paterson job away."

Collins fished out another Chesterfield. "She won't."

"What the hell are you doing, Collins? You have no time for jazzing rich broads."

"Don't worry about me. I'll pull my load."

"I worry about everybody," Kresky said. "This isn't Dublin twenty years ago . . . guys get soft."

Collins grabbed his sleeve. "What are you going on about?"

He saw a strange look come into Kresky's eyes, part pain, part savage and brutal.

Kresky spoke in a whisper so low Collins could barely hear him. "I just found out who fingered some of my men at the Paterson plant." He stopped. "It was Ragosky . . . Jake Ragosky. I've known him since the early days in Union Square."

Collins saw the palpable hurt. War, he thought, brings forth the best and the most treacherous in us. "You're sure?" Collins said.

Kresky nodded. "They were going to send his boy away. Shelly. I've known him all my life. Jake sold us to save Shelly. I checked. Shelly was supposed to go to the Tombs."

"Where did you get it from? Who?"

"Sol Hertzog worked for me. He delivers pastry to the fascist pâtisseries. He saw Jake in a teahouse with Shelly. He went back a week later. This time Jake met a Gestapo agent. He sold himself to save Shelly."

"Judas lives on," Collins said softly.

"He's dead," Kresky said. "Tonight. He's mine."

Collins took a deep breath. "You want to confirm it first?"

Kresky shrugged.

They stood facing one another in the empty apartment, the silence vast and all encompassing.

"When's his next meet?"

"This afternoon," Kresky answered.

3:28 P.M.

They sat in Sol Hertzog's panel truck facing the Limerick Teahouse on East Twenty-third Street near Gramercy Park. It was a good place for a meet, Collins thought. Sedate old Gramercy Park. They had been watching the Limerick for about fifteen minutes. Three-thirty, Hertzog had told them. Christ, Collins thought, what if I had to save my son? But that didn't make up for it either.

He turned to Kresky. "Let me do it."

Kresky didn't answer.

They watched the teahouse. Then Kresky nudged him. A man in a leather coat was going in. "Gestapo," he murmured.

They sat and strained for a sign of Ragosky. It was a routine the Gestapo had Ragosky set up, Collins thought. He drops in a few times a week. He's known there so . . .

"He's coming," Kresky whispered.

Collins looked up the street and saw a compact man in a brown felt hat, wearing a work jacket, carrying a lunch pail under his arm.

Ragosky had a mustache and a rocking walk. He looked like a pleasant man, a worker.

From their vantage point they could see him going inside and sitting in a booth. Abruptly he was joined by the man in the leather coat.

Kresky bit his lip.

"We'll take him tonight," Kresky said.

"Take him when he comes out," Collins responded. "He won't be ready. Informers walk away with their head down."

Abetz stood in the shadows of a loft that overlooked the Limerick Teahouse. Next to him was his adjutant, Leichner. Leichner had just driven through the area wearing civilian clothes. Nothing seemed suspicious, but everything was in place. Abetz had worked a long time on Ragosky. Weeks had gone into setting up the Limerick as a meeting place. Then the bait had been dangled. Ragosky, the Pole, was to meet his son. Abetz smiled. Ragosky was an amateur. A man pressed into service in the Resistance. A more experienced man would have known never to meet the son he had saved in the same place that he met his Gestapo contact.

Abetz smiled again. It was a cold thing. Ragosky, of course, was a small fish. But this Kresky, the man he worked for in the Paterson plant, was high in the Resistance. He wasn't the leader, but he would know the leader. Or perhaps he would know the mysterious man who appeared in Central Park when Schmidt shot Beck. Schmidt alias Paulie Lazar. A *Jüden* thug. But that was for another time. The American Resistance was good, Abetz had to admit to himself. The Paterson job had been superb. The sabotage on the docks was efficient and extremely damaging. Their leader was bold and imaginative. But he wasn't invisible. Kresky knew who he was. Of course there was no guarantee Kresky would come for Ragosky. But Abetz had read their files. They had grown up in the labor movement together. Their families had been close. Kresky would consider Ragosky's betrayal as very personal. Abetz gazed up and down the street. The American Resistance would eventually pick up that Ragosky was an informer. If not today, then another Wednesday. Today was a fishing expedition. Eventually a fish would be hauled in. Ragosky, of course, was a dead man. Abetz smiled. He looked at the bookstore that adjoined the Limerick Teahouse. His two best street men, Meizner and Peisner were there. If a fish came, they would haul him in.

Collins felt edgy and tense. He disliked his idea about verifying for Kresky that Ragosky was an informer. They should just have picked him up and sweated it out of him. Informers are always overripe. A few pokes and they come apart like melon long past its time.

Kresky nudged him, and they saw the Gestapo man stand up. He would go to the bathroom, and Ragosky would come out.

Moments later he appeared. He looked furtively around and then hunched up his shoulders and began to walk away. Kresky started up the van.

"Give him a chance," Collins said. "Let him get around the corner."

As they slipped into traffic, they watched Ragosky move in and out of casual pedestrians, past a bookstore, a Chinese laundry, and an Adams hat shop. Then he was at the corner, and Kresky accelerated.

Neither Collins nor Kresky, intent on watching Ragosky, saw the two men in dark raincoats exit the bookshop.

Ragosky was walking along Lexington as the van slid to a halt and Kresky jumped out, calling "Jake."

Collins watched Ragosky turn and saw the terrible look of fear on his face. Kresky had him by the collar and was pushing him toward the van. Ragosky saw Collins in that instant and cried out, struggling against Kresky. Kresky's doubled fist hit Ragosky in the nose. The bone gave way and blood spurted.

Jesus, Collins thought, not that. You'll draw . . .

"*Achtung,*" came the cry, and Collins saw Ragosky's eyes flicker past Kresky.

In one motion Collins leaped from the van to the street, away from where Kresky and Ragosky were struggling. He peeled back along the van, the gun coming out of his coat. Peering out, he saw the two Gestapo men in dark felt hats, Lugers drawn, pushing their way through people. Collins ducked back until they had passed.

Then he came around the van. The two Heinrichs grabbed Kresky, and Ragosky was crouched on the ground like a felled rabbit. Collins took a deep breath and walked into view, in the manner of a pedestrian who had just crossed the street. Kresky's arms had been swung behind his back by the taller German, while the other used his pistol butt on Kresky.

Coming up directly behind them Collins shouted, *"Achtung!"* The tall one turned first. Collins shot him through the heart. He fell away clutching at the terrible pain, which was the last thing he would ever feel. The other one whirled and tried to use his gun, but he was holding the wrong end. Collins shot him through the head.

Collins grabbed Kresky, who had a river of blood streaming from over his right eye. Kresky broke free as he saw Ragosky run down the street.

"Never mind him," Collins screamed.

But Kresky was berserk, and the only way Collins could stop him was to tackle him.

"Later," he said savagely, with all his weight thrown across the union man's shoulders. "We'll pull him in later."

Kresky stared at him as if he had been separated from his senses.

Abetz and Leichner had seen Meizner and Peisner chasing the van and their black sedan came to a screeching stop as they heard gun shots.

"The van," Leichner called out. He jumped out, and two other black-coated men started to follow him leaving only Abetz in the car.

Abetz took in the scene before him. Two of his best men lay dead on the sidewalk, while in the middle of the street lay the two Americans. Get them, now, Abetz screamed silently within himself.

It all happened very quickly, as if it were a movie run at fast speed. And yet it was all terribly clear. The American was on one knee and, taking precise aim, shot Leichner in the chest. Without wasting a moment, he turned in his crouch and fired directly at the blond-haired, blue-eyed Jaworsky, whom the girls could never resist and whom Abetz thought was the stupidest man he had ever met. Jaworsky, coming out of the back door, never made it. He was thrust backward, his head cracking against the frame.

Just then, from the other side of the car, out came Edelhoffer. He fired twice, both shots missing the American who, with rock-steady deliberation, swiveled toward him. *Gott*, thought Abetz, he has no fear. He is a terrible killer and a great one.

Collins had his gun on the beefy, red-faced German in the long black coat and now he fired twice. The second bullet smashed into the eye and then the brain of Edelhoffer. He was dead instantly. Abetz was alone.

He saw the American walk toward the car, stop in front of the windshield, and aim the gun. Abetz was horrified. He felt the bullet was going to hit him precisely on the ridge of his nose. He was going to die, but he could not move. He saw every feature of the American's face, the hard blue eyes, the dirty brown hair, the tight mouth, the utter fearlessness. He was aiming, and Abetz felt himself gag. He waited for the bullet, but nothing happened. Then he saw the American was laughing. Holding up the gun, Collins smashed the windshield with the barrel, sending splinters of glass into Abetz's face.

Somehow he had gotten Kresky into the van, and somehow they were now speeding crosstown. Collins thought of the pudgy little Heinrich sitting in the car.

"That was Abetz," he finally said.

Kresky, holding a bloodred hankie over his eye, looked at him in glazed fashion. "You should have killed him."

Collins's eyes were bright with emotion. "I was out of ammo. There were guns all over the street. All I had to do was pick one up. . . ."

He made a wrenching turn at Twenty-eighth Street and stopped beneath the Third Avenue El. They both hopped out.

"I'll meet you at the apartment at five o'clock," Collins said.

Kresky spat a mouthful of blood. "I want Ragosky."

Collins licked his dry mouth and spat out death. "That's easy. Just get a few of your boys to pick up his kid. Ragosky will come in."

Kresky looked at Collins as if he were a believer just converted to a new faith.

"See you later," Collins said.

They moved off in opposite directions.

Chapter 27

Sylvie had spent a dreadul afternoon trying to sleep, but except for a brief period when she dozed in a half-conscious twilight world, it had been nothing but fitful tossing. She was too

263

full of anger. He wanted to use her to spy on Patrick. He didn't love her enough just to let them be. Oh, you silly fool, she told herself, there's a war on. Did you think because you helped him once, you could then sit it out as a neutral? That's what he's here for. To make war on the Nazis. It was only later toward evening that she realized she no longer referred to them as Germans. Robert had called Patrick a dirty fascist. That was so vindictive. But Patrick was helping the Nazis. Somehow she could not get herself to call him a collaborator.

It was all so dreadful. In taking her that night, Robert had made here aware of who she really was. How could she give him up? Could she tell him that she hardly ever made love with Patrick anymore? Robert, that's all she knew him as. On the return trip from Paterson he had told her. "It's better that you don't know my name." Were those two nights all they were ever going to have? Well, it was war, as he said. And maybe that's all there was.

And so it had gone all afternoon and into the early evening. Till she had gotten up and run a bath. In the warm water, she was finally able to realize that it was no good. Whatever Patrick did, whoever he was, she could never spy on him. Even if it meant the disappearance of that singular person within her whom Robert had liberated, there was no choice. But she felt something in her chest clutch hard as she thought that.

She dressed simply in a black wool suit and put on just a touch of lipstick. Since that night with Robert, she no longer used powder. She walked into the living room and saw Meister at the bar.

She answered his silent question. "I'll have a martini."

She waited while Meister fixed the drink. "Isn't Patrick coming up for a drink?"

Meister looked at her with big, frightened eyes. "He called to say he'll be a few minutes late."

She took the drink from Meister and walked to the couch. "Did he say where he was?"

"I believe he's in his suite."

Sylvie stared at Meister. "In his suite?"

"I was watering the plants and a Na— . . . German car drove up. Mr. Kelly got out with an officer."

Sylvie felt an uneasy tingle. "When was that?"

"While you were taking your nap."

"But that must be hours."

Meister looked at her apprehensively. "Yes . . . there was a report on the radio before. Five men from the Gestapo were shot. Killed by an American."

Sylvie felt her hand shaking. She remembered how Robert had

made her leave so hurriedly. Did it have something to do with him?

"When?" she stammered.

"This afternoon." Meister's eyes were mournful. "They will take an eye for an eye."

"Did they . . . did they catch him?" She was aware her heart was pounding.

"They didn't say anything about that."

She breathed again and drank a large portion of the martini. Her chest felt ready to explode. Of course. It was war and there was no escaping it. The shootings must be why Patrick is meeting with the German officer.

She did something very impulsive then. She drained her martini. She never did that. She could see the amazed look in Meister's eyes as she handed him her glass for a refill. It took him some time to comprehend what she wanted.

She took her second martini from his hand, and without knowing exactly what she was doing next walked to the door. "I'll be back," she called.

She made her way along the thick-carpeted hallway, then walked down one flight to Patrick's floor. She stood in front of the door for a moment. Patrick had a servant, but not on a regular basis. She put her hand on the doorknob and turned. The door opened, and she moved inside.

There was a light in the living room, and the panel doors leading to it were almost closed. Quickly, quietly, she got next to the door and then, amazed at her boldness, eased it open another inch. The light was filled with hazy smoke from Patrick's cigar and the cigarette of the German officer. It was that horrid little man, Abetz. He was speaking.

"Then it is settled. Central Park as you suggest."

"And no more than twenty-five. That will make the point."

Abetz's tone was strident. "That is not enough to compensate for the death of five of my best agents. A larger lesson . . ."

She could see Patrick hold up his hand. "If you kill a lot of people, you will be premature. Hackensack must be ready. New York is a teeming city. It could all explode. You'll have riots. These are the first executions. It will make the point very well."

Abetz reached for his highball and considered Kelly's logic. Now he drank from it. "Yes, I see your point. All right then, twenty-five in Central Park. Five for each of my men. Excellent."

"Broadcast it," Kelly said. "Allow people to come. Make it a spectacle. Have plenty of soldiers there. Next day, you do some roundups. Somebody will talk."

Abetz stood up and slapped his gloves on the table. "Yes, I believe you are right, Patrick. We will wait."

She could see Patrick smiling. "In America we say, he who laughs last, laughs best."

Patrick got up, and Sylvie flew across the foyer and let herself out. As she pounded up the stairs, she could hear Patrick's calm, rich voice, so clear that it could have been easily heard even across a crowded room, saying, "Make it a spectacle."

Now she was in her apartment. She had to warn Robert. What did he say . . . leave a yellow hankie wrapped in a newspaper with Wally at the newsstand on Seventy-second and Broadway. But it was early evening. He would be closed. It didn't matter. She had to go to Robert.

Moments later, wearing her coat and carrying a yellow scarf, she danced out of the apartment. To Meister she said only, "I must run an errand."

Seventy-second and Broadway was a busy intersection, and Sylvie, alighting from a cab, looked about for the newsstand. She spotted it and, almost without looking, dashed between people to get there. Someone yelled at her, but she never looked back. As she reached the sidewalk, she had her hand in her pocket and grasped the scarf. She stopped abruptly. It was closed.

She saw an old man leaning against the stand and beckoned to him. "Do you know Wally? He runs the newsstand."

The old man was thin and hawk-nosed with a dirty white mustache. "Who?"

"Wally. Wally."

He shrugged. "Sure, everybody knows Wally, but he's not around. He went home. Come back tomorrow."

"Where does he live?"

The man looked at her oddly. "Live? I don't know." He gestured with his hand. "Around."

"Around where?"

The man shrugged. "I don't know. Come back tomorrow. Say, what's so important . . . ?"

As she moved away, she felt the tears come and made no effort to stop them. People stopped and then parted for the well-dressed blonde in the expensive fur coat who was sobbing bitterly and walking in no apparent direction.

She made her way to the other side of the street, still clutching the yellow scarf. He's one of them, she thought, and you let him make love to you. He's one of them . . . he's a dirty fascist. A dirty, dirty fascist.

Radner got out of the car Abetz had sent for him and followed Hoppman, the broken-nosed thug of a driver, into the Centre Street offices. He was seething. Here, on the eve of the opening of *Hamlet*, Abetz had summoned him like some underling to a meeting.

He lit a cigarette to conceal his anger and continued to follow Hoppman up the stairs to Abetz's office on the second floor. The walls were gray and old, the lights in the offices dim. Yes, he thought, it is a perfect jail.

They entered Abetz's offices, and another Gestapo agent in a dark suit jumped up.

"I am here to see the standartenführer," Radner said.

There was just a small table light burning on Abetz's desk. Abetz was positioned so that he was somewhere between the light and the darkness. Radner could see the cigarette holder and the smoke curling up from it. He stood there, waiting for some sign of recognition. Abetz was not reading anything, and yet he seemed content to just stare at Radner. This final humiliation was unbearable.

"I must protest," he began.

Abetz's voice came from the darkness, and now his little vulturous face could be seen. His forehead was bathed in sweat, as was the rim of his mouth over his lower lip.

"Captain Radner, you have heard about the shootings this afternoon?

"Surely, you know *Hamlet* opens . . ."

"Five of my best agents were killed by an American. The man was singularly brave. He just sat there and squeezed off each round. You wouldn't know such a man, would you, Captain?"

"Are you mad?" Radner blurted out. "Is this what you brought me here to discuss?"

Abetz picked up a file. "No, of course you don't know him. But you know somebody who does."

Radner threw down his cigarette. "I insist you . . ."

"Silence," Abetz shouted. "You will be quiet until I am finished."

Radner wanted to strike the little beast that was Abetz, but he did nothing other than shift uncomfortably.

"General Beck knows who he is," Abetz said. "General Ludwig Beck surely knows. He is a traitor to the Reich, which is why he was sent to America far from Berlin. But even here he intrigues, only now with the Americans. He has an organization. It is called The Black Orchestra. Have you heard of it?"

Radner had regained himself. "It is a theatrical title, but I can't say I know of it."

Abetz poured a glass of cognac. "Well you shall. For you are going to join it."

Radner's mouth opened in protest.

"Yes you shall. You will go to see Beck tomorrow and offer your services. And your reason shall be that you are horrified by the hostages you watched being shot in Central Park."

Radner recoiled. "Hostages?"

"Yes, and quite a few. These American swine cannot get away with murdering Gestapo. I want this man. I have reason to believe he heads the Resistance. He is too arrogant just to be a shooter. Beck will lead you to him."

Radner could not believe the little man's presumption. "I must protest . . ." he began again.

Abetz threw a file on the desk. "I would like you to read the statement in there. Go ahead."

Radner picked up the file and opened it. It was the statement of a Mrs. Florence Buxton. He began to read: "As a good citizen it is my duty to inform you that the actress who calls herself Fay Brophy is a Jew. Her name is Leila Fox. I can verify this because both girls lived as roommates at the Studio Rehearsal Club which I manage. I became aware of the deception when I passed the New Amsterdam Theater and saw her picture. She is not Fay Brophy. It is an injustice that such a . . ." The paper slid from Radner's hand and fell to the floor.

As he stopped to pick it up he remembered leaving money in an envelope in a locker at Grand Central Station. Then there had been no word from the mysterious blackmailer. Idiot, he thought. She collected from both of us. And in that moment as he straightened up he knew that Abetz had paid Mrs. Buxton more. Perhaps an identity card so she could leave New York.

"But you are not reading," Abetz purred.

"I don't have to," Radner answered.

"Good," Abetz said, "then we understand each other. Your mistress is a Jewess. It is not against the law . . . yet. There are high-ranking officers in Europe, higher ranking than you, who have *jüden* mistresses. But it is not a good idea. And Leila Fox is in violation of the law. She could be sent to a detention cell for such an offense."

He watched Radner carefully to see which way he would respond. For that would tell Abetz if Radner could be broken.

Radner cleared his throat. "I did not know in the beginning. It was only recently that it came to my attention."

Abetz nodded. "I see. Well, there is something to be said for

268

you then. Of course, she is quite beautiful." Abetz leaned back into the shadows. Yes, he had his man.

Now he came back into the light. "She can remain as Fay Brophy, but there is General Beck."

"But I am not trained in these matters, Beck will not . . ."

Abetz held up his hand. "Oh, but he will. You are a man of the arts, a sophisticated one. An astute man. Beck will be receptive."

Radner began once more to protest. Again Abetz held up his hand. "You will witness the executions tomorrow. Beck will not be there. You will go back to Beck and tell him of your disgust with the brutality. That is all. Then we shall see what happens. The executions are in Central Park at twelve forty-five P.M. Be at the official reviewing stand at noon. That is all for now. Oh, just one thing more. Manheim succumbed this afternoon. You shall be named to his position and, if you do well, I shall recommend your promotion to major. Tomorrow evening after your performance we will meet at the Pocantico Hills party. We will slip off together for a moment and find something to talk about, yes, Captain? Good evening."

Radner turned and then heard Abetz's voice. "You shall make an excellent major, I am sure. And you and Miss Fox . . . excuse me, Miss Brophy, are quite a handsome couple."

Abetz poured more cognac and leaned back in the darkness. The events of this afternoon would have repercussions in Berlin. Five Gestapo agents shot by one American. Just when everything had been going so smoothly. Himmler would not like the reports of this afternoon's massacre. Himmler had personally intervened on Abetz's behalf to get him the post in New York. The Führer and Goebbels had wanted to send Heydrich. But Himmler had argued that Heydrich was needed to complete the evacuation and ransom of England. Besides, Himmler feared and hated Heydrich.

The Paterson strike had been a daring expedition. A speeding train derailed and sent in flames into soldiers waiting in place to trap the saboteurs. A reckless but incredibly audacious maneuver. Like today's shooting. How cool he had been. It must be the same man. Possibly he was a gangster, but Abetz doubted it. He didn't have the look of a thug. No, there was something more heroic in his pose. Who was he then? Where did he come from? Was he an American army officer? That was possible. And yet Abetz's instinct told him that wasn't the answer. America had not fought in a war in years. This man had seen considerable action somewhere. Coolness under fire came only from direct experience. Then where? There were just two leads. When this Lazar who called himself Schmidt shot Beck, another American was in Central Park. Was it the same man? Did Lazar know him?

Lazar had vanished into the city, but Abetz had men searching for him. They had already found his address. It was only a matter of time. Then there was the dead man at the Paterson plant. He was an Irishman, a political prisoner who had been rescued in a daring, daylight raid at Canal Street. James Handy. A dynamite specialist from the Irish Republican Army. He frowned. Most of the Irish Republican Army was pro-German. Elements of it had paved the way for the Reich's invasion of Montreal. Was there some connection here?

He stood up and paced. There were Americans who had fought in Spain, but he vetoed the idea. The man who had killed his agents this afternoon and then walked to Abetz's car and aimed the gun was completely unafraid of death. He wasn't a soldier but a mercenary of some kind. Abetz had gotten a good look at him. Sandy-haired, compact, steel in the eyes. In that moment he seemed almost in love with death. Abetz shook his head. He had wanted to keep things quiet until the time for the big push. Genovese was arriving tomorrow. America was to be the capstone to Abetz's career. He had patterned himself after his leader, Himmler. Colorless, cold, efficient. Not like Heydrich, who was bold, flashy, and always initiating some new reckless exploit. Heydrich made enemies both in and out of the Reich. Men of Heydrich's obvious ambition laid themselves open to assault from within and without.

Abetz looked at his watch. It was early morning in Berlin, and Himmler would be reading the reports. He poured another cognac. He had many files on his desk. He would be up all night reading. The first was that of James Handy, the man killed in the Paterson explosion. Somewhere there was a clue to the American killer of this afternoon. Abetz would find it. This American had taunted him. That meant he was reckless. Reckless men inevitably made a mistake. Abetz wanted the American. Somebody knows him. He would find that person. He began to read.

10:30 P.M.

They had found Shelly Ragosky in the late afternoon. He had been lying on his bed in the one-room apartment he lived in on West 102nd Street. The kid had turned very pale but said nothing. He got dressed quickly and, flanked by Hertzog and Harry Elm, left the rooming house.

The call was made to a neighbor of Ragosky's, giving Jake the time and the place to appear. It was a decoy in case the Gestapo were following, but Ragosky had no tricks left. A car

270

had brought him to Riverside Park, where the small knot of men stood in the bushes above the ferry slip at 125th Street.

Collins and Kresky stood off by themselves, occasionally eyeing Jake and Sheldon Ragosky, who were guarded by three men.

They spoke in tight whispers, as if hiding their words from the biting wind.

"What about the kid?" Collins said.

Kresky's eyes were dark tunnels where the Medusa of death resided. "We can't leave him. He'll tell the Gestapo."

Collins's eyes went back in time. To Dublin . . . to the Black and Tans who murdered father and son. It never stops, he thought. What has the boy done? he thought. Survive. When did that warrant a death sentence?

"He's an accomplice of the Gestapo," Kresky said aloud, answering Collins's question.

Collins nodded. "I'll do it."

They walked toward the circle of men, who parted for their leaders. Now Kresky stood directly in front of Ragosky.

"It's time, Jake."

Father and son turned to one another and embraced. "Papa," the boy cried softly. "Papa."

The older Ragosky kneaded the boy's hair and caressed his neck. "It's all right." He kissed him, and then they were parted.

Ragosky, eyes red, turned to Kresky. "He hasn't done anything."

"I know," Kresky said.

"You mean that?"

Kresky nodded imperceptibly. "C'mon Jake."

He took his elbow and led Ragosky down toward the water.

"C'mon boyo," Collins said, and led Sheldon up toward the network of barren trees above them. Trees without leaves. Trees without life.

Collins spoke softly. "It's the code of war, son. But you can take with you the knowledge that your father did it for you."

The boy wept without sound. "He didn't have to do it. I would have been all right in the work camp. It's not fair . . . it's not. . . ." He began to shake and wobble, and Collins caught him.

"It's all right, son. He loved you too much. And there's no sin in that."

"Then why . . ."

"Because the price was other men's lives. It's a hard life, and we have to go about it the best way we can."

The boy stopped crying. He looked into Collins's eyes. "Then kill me, too. I want to die with him." He said it with absolutely no idea that Collins was going to kill him.

"Damn it to hell," Collins said. Would there never be an end to this torment?

The shot came from down below, and the boy sagged. He would have cried out, but Collins's hand covered his mouth.

"I'm letting you loose, but don't say a word or I'll kill you. Now listen. Here's money. You make for upstate. Here's an identity card that belonged to a friend. He's dead. Name's Jimmy Handy. Put your picture on it. Now go. Find a guerilla band up there and join. That's what your father would want you to do. You have to live for both of you. He was a good man. He just loved you too much.

"Go," he said, kicking the boy hard in the rear. The boy ran, and Collins watched him disappear into the bushes. Then he fired once and walked down the slope and whispered to Harry Elm, who nodded. When he was finished Collins walked on and saw the body of Jake Ragosky being dumped in the Hudson.

"Let's go," Collins said. "Let's go, it's curfew."

They walked into the darkness together. The tall, wiry Irishman and the short little Polack. Slipping into the night that, for all its impenetrable contours, was no match for the dark pain of the two men.

Chapter 28

March 27, 1942
12:00 P.M.

The vans pulled up at eleven forty-five. Fifteen minutes later they began herding out the prisoners. Some had been rounded up the previous night; others came from detention cells. The first one to step out was Boris Tomashevsky, an itinerant Ukranian sign painter who had been caught mugging a drunken German soldier on a cold January night. He was followed by Joe Giniss, an Irish fireman who had decked a Gestapo sergeant named Mundt in a bar. The next person out was Alvin Karp, an accountant and City College graduate who had been dragged from his family's home at 333 Ocean Parkway the previous night. They were followed by Ben Epstein, an out-of-work translator; James Gyp Smithers, a Harlem barfly; Skip Monisi, a member

272

of the Italian Anti-Fascist League; James Li Fong, a Chinese cook at the Red Dragon Restaurant; Lupe Serrabian, a Serbian poet; and Morty Green, a bookmaker out of Brownsville.

They were led in single file down the concrete footpath into Central Park, escorted by German soldiers carrying rifles and tommy guns. Some walked with heads down, others looked back and around as if, amongst the crowd gathered outside the entrance, they would find a savior. Louis Martin, a sometime trumpet player up at the Apollo, moved his head back and forth in quick, furtive movements as if he might escape. He even stopped once until prodded in the back by a German soldier's rifle. It was a raw winter day. Yet many of the prisoners wore no coats. They wouldn't be cold very long.

No spectators were allowed inside the park. But there was a considerable number of people standing out on Central Park West. They had started arriving at eleven o'clock, not long after the Bundist radio station, broadcasting on the wavelength once designated for WOR, had announced the executions. Ropes had been put up, and the ever-increasing crowd pushed back till now they were back as far as Sixty-fifth Street. Even with her fur coat on, Sylvie felt very cold. Meister had insisted on accompanying her. They were wedged between a woman who had been reading from a Bible for the past hour and a tall minister whose cheeks and nose were a bright red from the cold. The wait among the crowd of silent people had seemed interminable. It was as if the crowd had become one body, moving jointly back and forth, shivering in the cold. There were more and more spectators, pushing and fighting to get to the stone wall that formed the outer rim of the park and see what was happening inside.

Sylvie had gone again to the newsstand at Seventy-second Street and left the yellow scarf for Robert. What good would it do now? The whole city knew about the executions. You're being dishonest, she answered herself. It's not the executions you want to talk to him about. You heard Patrick planning all this last night. You must break with him. She couldn't believe she was thinking this. He had taken care of her for years. But she couldn't stay with him. There was something rotten in him. He was infected by these Nazis. Nobody could be good inside and think of killing people this way. And suddenly she knew why he had shown no surprise when the Nazi invasion of England was announced. He knew about it. He knew they were coming to England. And he must have known they were coming to America.

A large military truck pulled in and three soldiers emerged from the rear carrying a machine gun. Moving at a dogtrot they went down the path into the park and then into the grass. About seventy-five yards in they found some green blankets, and there they put down the machine gun and set it up on its tripod.

Directly across the street Sylvie could see the trucks unloading, and the prisoners beginning their march into the park. She saw a sallow-faced little man who looked as harmless as a fly, an oafish man with a gray sport jacket, white shirt open at the neck, and three days growth of stubble on his face. Behind him was a young boy who couldn't be more than eighteen or nineteen. His skin was terribly white. He had on a green mackinaw. There were bloodstains on it. She could see the bandage on the back of his head. As he started to walk he began to fall and was propped up by the man behind him, a large Negro.

Sylvie saw the next man and for a moment he didn't register, and then her hand went to her mouth. There, wearing a sandy-colored overcoat, head down, shuffling along like some beaten slave, was Mr. Klein. Morris Klein. But she had given Sophie a pass for him. He and his family should have escaped. How was it possible? She started to yell something, and her voice caught. But how? He walked slowly, heavily, as if tired or in pain. Oh God, they are going to kill that good man. A man who wouldn't leave without making sure I got my shoes.

She didn't know why then but her hand went out. Please, she thought, look at me. See me. See somebody you know before you die. Please, please, it's so important. For whom? a voice inside her called. For you or for him? But he has to, she responded. He has to. He has to do nothing but die, the voice answered. Mr. Klein walked very slowly, looking down at the street he was crossing. Look, look back, she cried within her. And then, as if he could hear her, he did. He took a last look around at the last people he would ever see, and though he looked directly at where Sylvie stood, he made no sign. Then he turned back and, a moment later, disappeared into the park.

They kept coming. Shamus Jackson, a Negro whose mother had slept with a Jewish peddler; Donny Morton, whose twin brother Dickie was somewhere in that crowd on Seventy-second Street; Walter Liebowitz, who had been arrested in his candy store on Pitkin Avenue; Joe Reilly, a bartender at McSorley's; Hank Majewsky, a unemployed carpenter; Billy Mondello, arrested while visiting a Jewish girl named Roz Faber on Delancey Street the previous evening; Buddy Sondstron, a Swedish porter who had tried to help his neighbors, the Gordons of Ocean Parkway, hide in his house; Lazlo Berman, who had fought in the Spanish Civil War in the Czech Brigade and had been under arrest since the Nazi invasion; Alfredo Garcia Mendes, an exiled officer of the Spanish Republican Army who had been sought by the Franco regime for three years.

They came forward, eyes straight ahead, looking up, looking down, looking at the people across the street watching them. Now the last one was out, a Sephardic Jew named Molinas, a tall man in a black suit, the sleeves of which didn't reach his wrists and whose pants barely touched his ankles. He shambled along in a kind of stupor, looking like he might topple over any second. He had been beaten with a nightstick after attacking his interrogator, and the diagnosis had been a concussion. But because his tormentor was an SD officer named Block who claimed to be a nephew of Himmler, Molinas had been chosen to die. Dressed in his black suit with a white bandage wrapped like a turban around his head, he began to walk in the wrong direction. Away from the executions. He was quickly grabbed by a hefty sergeant named Grabner and escorted back into line. Molinas was the last prisoner into the park. Out of the twenty-five chosen to be executed, eight were Jews. There were three Negroes, two Slavs, three Poles, three Italians, two Spaniards, one Chinese, one Swede, one Greek, and one Serb.

armed guards now took their positions in front of the wooden barrier placed at the entrance to the park at Seventy-second Street. The crowd suddenly surged forward and was met by fixed bayonets. The movement subsided.

Inside the park, Standartenführer Abetz stamped out a cigarette and walked over to Colonel Gierring, who was in charge of the firing squad. The prisoners were being formed in a ragged line looking out at the machine gun. Gierring was telling Abetz that this was not like a European execution where the prisoners dug ditches and were shot into them. This would be messy. Abetz agreed. But it would allow for maximum effect on the spectators. A vital lesson was being taught.

On the wooden reviewing stand borrowed from the nearby precinct stood several German officers. Among them were Governor General von Stulpnagel, and General Hubicki standing in for General Beck, who was at his hotel suite recuperating from his recent attack. Behind them was Colonel Lang of the SS. To the far end stood Radner, his keen blue eyes frozen into relentless anger.

What was he doing here about to watch this savage butchery? All because of Fay and her dishonesty. She had compromised him, endangered his career and made him hostage to Abetz. The price for keeping her was very high. And for what? There had been tension between him and Fay since that night. He ground out his cigarette. Stop calling her Fay . . . she's Leila Fox. He realized that in recent weeks he had stopped calling her by any name. That had caused another row between them. Their sex now consisted of violent, hurtling moments when tension became too much. More often she was exhausted from late evening rehearsals, preoccupied with the big break of her career. The break he had given to Fay Brophy. What had he come back to America for? It had all turned bitter in his mouth. What good could come from all this? He was in bondage to Abetz, and nothing could get him out. Not even breaking with Leila Fox. It didn't work that way. And with all of it, he wasn't through with Leila. He needed to command her again. Damn it to hell. He loved her.

The last prisoner herded into the line was the Negro whose name was Big Al Flash. A guard yelled something that indicated all was in order. Gierring shook Abetz's hand and strolled to the machine gun team, who sat on the ground some twenty yards from the line of prisoners.

Gierring whispered into the ear of the gunner, Alfred Klutz, a veteran of the Polish invasion. Klutz nodded. Gierring summoned Lieutenant Horst Werner, who was in charge of the mop-up, then took his position behind the machine guns. He stepped forward as a bright burst of sun suddenly illuminated the cold March afternoon.

Gierring thrust his chest out as the crowd pressed forward outside the park. Those who could see became hushed and still. Colonel Gierring gave the command to his machine gunner. *"Achtung . . . ziehen . . . schuss."* The machine gun began to chatter as Big Al Flash spat on the ground.

Minutes earlier, Collins had maneuvered his way through the crowd to the point where he stood at the low stone wall of the park. He had done this by the simple expedient of coming up behind people and putting his finger in his overcoat, jabbing it into their backs, saying, "This is a gun. Move." He had come here looking for Sylvie. After being given the yellow scarf by Wally, he knew she would be here. She had to be. Then he saw the hostages standing in a row, white, black, yellow, short, fat, slim, swarthy, some wearing coats, others in suit jackets, one with a bandage on his head looking like a department store dummy. Collins watched the colonel in charge conferring with Abetz. Collins had seen the Tans use innocent people as shields, then shoot men down in the street. And the IRA would retaliate. Death squad for death squad. But, Jesus, twenty-five men in Central Park.

He stood at the stone wall barrier of Central Park looking in at twenty-five men who would be cut down in a few minutes.

Twenty-five men, good, bad, indifferent, hard-working, unemployed, worthy, ignoble, brave, cowardly, but mostly unlucky. United in front of a death machine because he had clipped five Gestapo agents. I didn't mean for it to come to this. I was through with killing.

He looked at the hostages, some staring at the ground, others smoking, one reading from a Bible. Something began to trickle into Collins's mind. Collins, the cynical warrior who had seen it all. Collins, who had been so long away that he no longer felt a part of this city he had grown up in and left eighteen years ago. He remembered the first time he had seen the sparkling green of Central Park, when his dad had locked hands with Collins and led the curly-haired little blond boy across the open spaces. He had played ball on its green and dirt ball fields on soft spring nights and drunk beer with the guys. He had roamed the streets of the city, played stickball in Hell's Kitchen, looked at lassies in Washington Square Park, taken the A Train to the Polo Grounds to watch McGraw's Giants, seen the Babe lose the ball in the right field bleachers, and scrambled with all the other little urchins for that precious piece of horsehide. He had jumped off the piers on the East Side, taken the ferry up to Bear Mountain, had his first girl on a tenement rooftop on Fifth-second Street. The two Gestapo chiefs had broken up, and now the colonel was whispering to the machine gunner. Collins's gaze moved back to the row of men who realized they were facing the machine guns and the last moment of their lives. Collins felt the balloon burst in his chest, and the tears come to his eyes. This wasn't the way it was supposed to be, was it, lads? You come in bawling and screaming from your mother's stomach, and you think it's going to be warm tit and hot milk all the way. You're going to grow up and see the world, have a wife and kids, die an old man in your bed, if you die at all. You know by the time you get to be a man you're not going to have it all, but somehow you could never imagine this. Standing on a raw winter's March day, preparing to have a machine gun slice you into Swiss cheese. The Heinrich colonel was bawling the instructions in German, and now Collins caught sight of the big Negro spitting on the ground. Then the machine gun began to talk, and Collins's fist balled up.

They fell like rag dolls, twitching and swaying in the wind. Some dying gracefully, others falling face down, some with their eyes open, others with them closed. But all of them dying. They went down like a row of toy soldiers, neatly synchronized. It was over very quickly. Some moved or crawled a bit. A squad of soldiers led by a young lieutenant moved among them dispatching them with single shots. Something caught Collins's eye.

A body rising. Like Lazarus from the dead. The tall, gaunt man with the bandage on his head. He was up now and reeling in a drunken fashion right in the direction of the machine guns. Collins fought the urge to pull his own pistol out and begin popping. He saw the machine gunners gesturing now; the colonel was yelling in German and they prepared to fire. Just then from behind the staggering hostage came the lieutenant, pistol in hand. He put it to the head of the tall man and fired twice. The man fell to his knees and then would not go farther. He was dead on his knees, Collins knew. All the lieutenant had to do was push him down. Instead he shot him again. The people around Collins were as still as the death they had just witnessed. The machine gunners congratulated each other. The colonel was over to say a good word. Oh, you bloody bastards.

Collins turned away and began pushing through the silent crowd, but nobody moved. He looked at their faces and heard Mick Collins reciting, "For he today that sheds his blood with me shall be my brother, be he ne'er so vile."

He heard the commotion across the street and, pushing his way to the rear of the pressing throng, saw a woman throw a pot of soup in a guard's face. Then they were brawling and breaking loose. Rushing the barrier where the police and soldiers stood together. Tear gas was exploding, the crowd began to break up, and then Collins caught sight of the old man, Meister, and Sylvie beside him. He began to run in their direction.

Those who could see had begun to scream as the deadly noise of the machine gun ended and the crowds now pushed against each other. Someone cried out, a woman screamed, and the milling throngs began to push against the ropes. A man tried to break through and was met with a rifle butt that split his forehead open. The German soldier who had used the butt swung around as a hand grabbed at his helmet, and then a little stooped lady threw a pot of soup in his face. He fell to the ground writhing in agony as the crowd spilled out and began rushing toward the wooden barricade. An elbow caught Sylvie in the head and someone kicked her ankle; she saw Meister go down and instinctively threw her body on top of him. They fell into the street, hearing the yells, the cries, the incessant firing of the guns inside the park. Now, as the people ran toward the park, a German sergeant mounted the wall and hurled a tear gas bomb at the charging group. It exploded in their midst. Another was lobbed, and another.

The crowd was retreating, gagging, crying. Sylvie saw them falling amongst themselves, kicking each other. There was nothing to do but stay down and hope that . . . a body covered hers, and then she heard a voice she knew. "Don't move and you'll be all right. Just stay down beneath me." She knew his weight and she knew his voice. It was Robert.

Radner watched Abetz conferring with and congratulating the Wehrmacht colonel in charge of the executions. So there it was. Savage, senseless retaliation. Paris had not been like this. Paris had been cultured and refined. It had taken to occupation the way a woman did to a new lover. One adjusts. That is the nature of life. That is how it goes on. He would have to walk a very thin, fine line. He left the platform, this strikingly handsome officer with the Teutonic mouth and forehead. He looked the image of a man who had just come through combat.

Collins had managed to spirit Sylvie and Meister through the angry crowd, and now led her into McGlade's after sending Meister home. The old man had looked ashen.

They sat in the back of the pub, drinking Irish whiskey that was being passed out without charge. The crowd was silent, mournful; almost no one spoke. The air was a blend of malt, whiskey, and something intangible that came from the raw insides of the people who sat there choking on their disgrace.

They sat wordlessly for some minutes. Sylvie sipped her whiskey, but noted that Collins downed three quick ones.

"That was you yesterday, wasn't it?" she said.

His blue eyes were like storm clouds, and then they misted over.

He poured more whiskey and threw it down. "Jesus, I was through with it. I wasn't going to live in the shadow of the gun anymore. Christ, I'll never be done with it." He looked at her, and now his eyes were filled with pain. "It just brings more death. It killed my father and my cousin, Mick, and I was done with it." He looked down at the scarred old table filled with the nicks and cuts and the tears of a hundred lovers who had shed them into the old wood, lamenting on the curse of their lives. "I'll never be free of it," he said.

She reached over and took his hand. "I'm glad you did it." She saw his surprise. "I'm sorry about all those people, but it would have come anyway. If not from what you did, from another place. They are monsters, and they must be driven out."

He was surprised by the conviction in her voice. "I'll do what you asked me to," she said. "I want to. Patrick helped plan this. He told Abetz not to kill too many. They're up to something, and I'll help you find out what." She stopped struggling to control the emotion in her voice. "And I'll never sleep with him again."

279

He reached over and took her hand. "Then you better work fast, because he won't keep you very long."

"I will," she said. She gave him a bold look. One filled with possessive love and with something else. "You don't want me to, do you? Well, do you?"

He felt her squeeze his hand for an answer. "No," he said huskily, "I don't."

Still holding his hand tight, she said, "Tell me your name. It can't just be Robert." She saw his eyes tighten into their warrior squint. "Give me something," she implored.

It was crazy he knew, he was at war. If they tortured it out of her, it would help them. But he couldn't deny her. "Collins," he said. "Robert Collins."

She gave him a radiant smile then. "I love you, Robert Collins. Do you hear me? I love you."

They sat staring at one another, and he felt the knot in his throat and the swelling desire within him and within her.

"Can you take me to that apartment?"

He looked at her a moment, saw what was in her eyes, and drained his whiskey. Still holding her hand, he raised her up. "Let's go."

4:30 P.M.

"So, Schmidt," Abetz said with false jocularity, "we have not seen you for a while. Have you been thriving?"

Paulie shifted uneasily. "I been gettin' by."

"Why haven't you reported to me?" Abetz said with just enough bite to make his point.

Paulie bit his lip. "Well, I felt bad. I felt bad I didn't finish the job just right . . . you know, didn't get my man."

They were in Abetz's office and, though it was late afternoon, it seemed like midnight. It was always midnight in Abetz's domain.

Abetz lit a cigarette that was already inserted in his long cigarette holder. "It was most unfortunate you did not drop the identity card of the Jew you led us to."

Paulie reached inside his collar and pulled it away from his neck. He always felt like Abetz was one step ahead of him. That Abetz was playing with him like you did a kid.

"You should know," Abetz began, his face suffused in spiraling curlicues of smoke, "that I could have brought you in whenever I wished, Mr. Paulie Lazar."

Paulie felt the shiv go into his gut and get twisted very deep. Perspiration broke out on his face and under his arms.

Abetz now leaned back in his chair. "You are a *jüden* criminal, and I can have you put away in a cell for the rest of your life." He let that sink in, then smiled ingratiatingly. "On the other hand, Lazar, you have certain talents that I can make use of. There could still be a place for you within the Reich."

Paulie wanted to reassure Abetz, give him some smooth line, but nothing would come. He just stood there and felt the sweat trickle down his body.

"Tell me Lazar—or let's call you Schmidt. What did happen in Central Park that day?"

Abetz waited behind clouds of smoke as Paulie desperately reached inside himself for the story he had long ago prepared for Abetz. "I woulda done the job like I said only this guy came out of the trees."

Abetz nodded. "Yes, tell me about this guy."

Paulie shifted his weight. Jesus, his back hurt.

"Well, he had a meet with Beck. And he had a rod . . . you know, a piece."

"Did you know him?"

Paulie knew this was the whole ball game. He had to make it believable. "Well I didn't really know him. I mean he was a guy I met with."

Abetz studied him carefully. "How did you meet him?"

"I got a note to come to this bar."

"What bar?"

"The Gold Rail, the same place I met Nippo in."

"You mean Nipponomick. Go on. What was his name?"

"He didn't say. But he was from Uncle. You know, Uncle Sam."

Abetz nodded. "Why did he come to you?"

Paulie felt a little confidence return. "Well, ya know I got a good reputation. I do good work. And this guy wanted to know my price."

"I see. Continue."

"Well, we talked dollars and he asked me about a few other guys."

"Other guys?"

"You know, what guys was around that could do special work. Well, we talked awhile, and he said he would get back to me. But I didn't hear nothin'. So I did know him, but not much."

Abetz smoothed his little mustache over his lips. "What do you suppose he was doing in Central Park?"

Paulie smiled his choirboy smile. "I figured he worked with Beck. Beck is what you call a traitor. He's workin' with the Americans."

"Yes," Abetz said. "He is. But then why did not the man as you call him from Uncle Sam, why didn't he stop you?"

281

Paulie shrugged. "He wasn't quick enough."

"He must have been very angry. After all, you had just shot a man important to the Americans. And what did you tell him about your reason for shooting General Beck?"

Paulie was ready for this question. It was the same story he had given Collins.

"I said I was doin' it to show off my work. And my price was high."

"I see," Abetz said smoothly, as if completely taken in. "What happened then?"

"Well, all hell broke loose, guards comin' after us, so we ran, hijacked that police car, and then we split up."

"Has your good work been appreciated?"

Paulie was ready for this one also. He put on his most crestfallen face. "It put me in the shit house. The guy from Uncle never came back to me. I messed up his guy. But I woulda finished Beck if it wasn't for this guy from Uncle Sam."

Abetz put his cigarette down. "Who is this man?"

"I dunno. . . ."

"Silence . . ." Abetz whispered, and it seemed to Paulie in the sudden stillness that he could hear the sound of his own sweat slipping down his legs. "I want him. Do you understand? He is the head of American resistance, Schmidt, and you are going to help me find him. Your freedom depends on it. There is a second man, one called Kresky. Do you know him?"

Paulie shook his head.

"I want him also. Get me Kresky, and I will find this man from Uncle Sam." He paused. "How have you been living, Lazar?"

"Ain't been easy," Paulie replied to a question he had also been waiting for. "A job here and there."

Abetz stood up. "Well, I may have some steady work for you. It will pay you well and is suited to your, shall we say, talents. But, in exchange for allowing you to work and live well, I want you to make contact with the underground. I want this Resistance leader. The man who finds him for me will be well rewarded and well taken care of. Yes. I would say five thousand American dollars is a good reward. Wouldn't you, Paulie Lazar?"

Paulie almost snapped to attention. "That's a lot of green." He took a careful pause. "I'll do my best, but you know I'm not number one with these guys since I winged Beck. It ain't gonna be easy."

Abetz's fist came down on the desk. "This is war, Lazar. People win and people lose. People live and people die." He stopped. He was the Gestapo standartenführer, totally in control. "We are going to win, Lazar. You will find a way." Abetz stopped and inserted another cigarette. "Tell me, Lazar, do you know Mr. Vito Genovese?"

Paulie's eyes popped, and his Adam's apple seemed to lock. "Sure."

"You have met him?"

"Naw. I seen him around though. He was right next to Charlie Lucky. He scrammed to Italy to beat a murder one rap."

"Wait here, Lazar."

Abetz left the room, and Paulie pondered developments. He should have known Abetz was too smart to believe the Schmidt story. Christ, this guy was good. He had pulled Paulie in just like that. Shit, he wanted Collins and Kresky. Especially, he wanted Collins. Five thousand clams was a lot of clams, but you couldn't spend them if you were stiff as a mackerel. And Collins and Kresky were rough and smart. Collins clipped five Gestapo guys, Jesus Christ. How was he going to handle . . .

Abetz was back. Behind him was a short man with black hair. He was small and compact. His dark eyes were like death.

"Hello, Paulie," the little dago said through tight lips. It was Vito Genovese.

Chapter 29

March 27, 1942
6:00 P.M.

The sign outside the brick-walled building said THE PRINCE-TON CLUB. It was located in the East Thirties near Park Avenue. Inside there was a foyer that led down some steps into a long sitting room overpopulated with black leather-backed easy chairs and wooden tables. There was a thick red carpet that ran wall to wall from the foyer through the sitting room, whose size was enhanced because there was no one there except three men who sat in a corner of the room talking in low, muted tones. Above them was a painting of Woodrow Wilson. All about the room there were portraits of men with distinguished beards and muttonchop whiskers who had contributed to the legacy of Princeton University.

None of the three men sitting in the room beneath the portrait of Woodrow Wilson had ever contributed anything to the history of Princeton University. None of them had ever been to the university. In fact, with the exception of Standartenführer Dietrich Abetz, who spent a year in a school of pharmacy, none of the men had ever attended college.

But they were men who had been schooled in unique ways. Graduates of street wars, beer hall brawls, and the wholesale running of bootleg liquor. If these men were awarded degrees, they would be for expertise in violence, in survival, and in cutting a deal.

Patrick Kelly, dressed in an expensive gray suit with a vest, white shirt, and bow tie was there to arbitrate between the two men who sat on his right and left, Vito Genovese from Naples and Dietrich Abetz from Berlin.

"What you ask," Abetz replied to Genovese's previous statement, "is out of the question. I will give you forty percent of the money you take in and twenty-five percent of jewels. All gold belongs to the Reich."

Genovese sucked on a Camel and squinted at Abetz. "You have soldiers. Why do you need me? Take it all yourself."

Patrick Kelly intervened. "Because the standartenführer knows very well that American Jews are more devious than European ones. Your reputation in this case will carry more weight than even the Wehrmacht's or the Gestapo's. Let's say that your strong arms are more suited to treasure hunts in New York City."

The barest signs of a smile crossed Genovese's lips. "Then we should get more than half. We're gonna have to find it."

"I am sure," Abetz said, "that will not be a problem. But the Reich will not surrender its control over the gold."

There was a long silence as Kelly and Abetz watched Genovese thinking. Kelly made a bet with himself. Two to one Genovese gets a percentage of the gold.

"Then we'll fence it for you," Genovese said.

Abetz looked to Kelly for a translation.

"He means that he'll sell it for you and get you market value."

"Better than market value," Genovese said in his hoarse voice.

"The Reich does not plan to sell the gold it collects."

"You have to sell some of it," Vito Genovese said in the softest of tones. "You just have to."

Kelly turned to Abetz. "I think Vito has a point. All that gold, what will you do with it? About twenty percent should be made liquid, and there's no one better than Vito to make the deal for you."

He watched Abetz considering it. Of course, Genovese would steal him blind. Genovese would fence the twenty percent and give Abetz a low estimate of what he actually got. And, of course, Genovese would not report the correct amounts of gold taken from the Jews. In fact, Genovese would not give fair reports on anything he took in, be it cash, jewels, or gold. Abetz was in way over his head. Hell, Genovese came out of the twenties, when Luciano and Lansky put together the modern syndicate and took it away from the Mustache Petes.

Abetz looked to Kelly. "I would recommend the percentage," Kelly said.

"And fifty-fifty on cash."

"Nein," Abetz replied. "Sixty-forty."

Genovese shrugged, and it was all Kelly could do not to burst out laughing. Genovese was letting Abetz have his victory. He would more than reverse those percentages later on.

"But always I will have some Gestapo agents with you."

"Sure," Genovese said.

"Then," Kelly said, "I think we have a deal. Sixty-forty on the cash and jewels. Vito gets to fence twenty percent of the gold. Well?"

"Agreed," Abetz said.

But Vito Genovese wasn't finished. "I want the black market. All of it. After you get your meat for the month, I take the rest."

Kelly nodded to Abetz.

"And I want the town," Vito Genovese said in tight, coiled tones. "That means Charlie Lucky stays in Dannemora."

Kelly took a cigar from his pocket. "I have briefed the standartenführer on the syndicate bosses. What do you want to do about Albert Anastasia?"

Vito Genovese casually took a Camel and lit it. "Just let the word filter down to Albert, and I'll work a deal with him."

Kelly crossed his legs. "What about Frank Costello? He's the pipeline to Charlie Lucky."

Vito's eyes barely flickered. "Frank's in Hot Springs with his casinos. Why should he come back? Frank likes points, not bullets."

"Perhaps we'll hear from him," Kelly said.

Vito Genovese stroked his chin. "Let me worry about Frank Costello . . . if he gets here."

Abetz felt himself lost in this discussion of New York gangster politics. "Mr. Genovese, remember, you may control your associates, but the Gestapo controls New York. You will be given lists of Jews we have accumulated. You begin tonight. Do you understand?"

Kelly watched Genovese pretend to be impressed. "Sure, sure. We got a deal."

Abetz put his stubby hands on the table. He should be working in a grocery store, Kelly thought. "I am giving you this Paulie Lazar. I believe he is tied into the American Resistance. Use him, but I want him watched. I want this American who shot down five of my agents. He is mine. Is that understood?"

Genovese smiled. "Sure. I'll help you. And any contracts you want done, I'll give you a good price."

"A contract . . ." Kelly began.

Abetz held up a hand. "I know what a contract is. I have not wasted my time in New York. And there will be no price. Let us say, it buys my goodwill, Mr. Genovese."

They heard someone coming, and all three men turned. It was Hoppman, Abetz's orderly. He handed Abetz an official communique.

Abetz read it over twice. Then he looked up at Vito Genovese while the document dangled in his hand like a lifeless bird.

He spoke in the mildest of tones. "Frank Costello has left Hot Springs. He is expected in New York shortly."

Kelly busied himself relighting his cigar, watching Vito Genovese's eyes tighten down. Frank Costello was the prime minister, caretaker of the New York syndicate for Lucky Luciano. The mob was serving notice that they weren't ready to accept Genovese as *capo di capo re* in New York.

Kelly cleared his throat. "It could mean war. Better to settle it now."

Vito Genovese said nothing, but his eyes were like twin stilettos. "Frank likes to talk. He don't like guns. Leave Frank to me."

His words drifted up into smoke. There was going to be an internal war in the mob. Everybody in the room knew it. It would be best if Genovese won. He was Mussolini's boy. He couldn't spell patriotism.

"Gentlemen," Kelly said, "let us continue."

They went back to the business of cutting up New York.

Chapter 30

March 27, 1942
6:20 P.M.

From the window of Beck's suite Radner could see night falling on Central Park. Darkness establishing its reign over the dying powers of light. For him the sky was peopled with the reflections of those that died this winter afternoon, hands outstretched, mouths open in a desperate plea for the life so brutally torn from them.

Radner saw Beck studying him. He knew instinctively that he could not volunteer. Beck would have to make the approach. Beck must feel that Radner was permanently marked by the events of the afternoon.

Beck, pretending to be absorbed in his glass of sherry, watched Radner. "So, I take it you have never witnessed a public execution," he said in the most gentle manner.

Radner shook his head. "I would never have gone, but Abetz insisted there be full representation."

"Once, during an armistice on the Western Front," Beck recalled, "I saw the French execute soldiers who failed to advance under fire. I was, of course, younger and in full agreement with their decision, though I knew even then that the charge was suicidal. We spent almost two years during World War I, separated by less than a thousand yards of barbed wire, annihilating each other. No one would admit it was not possible to advance or to win the war."

He drank from his glass. "Help yourself," he said, gesturing to the decanter on the liquor table.

"Thank you," Radner said as he reached over and refilled his glass.

Beck, wearing a robe and seated in a large chair, looked distinctly pale, even in the dim light of the room. "I think, Friedrich, sherry will not be sufficient. Try the schnapps. A large one."

He waited while Radner poured the brandy into a tall glass. Radner held up the glass. "To your good health."

He drained it and saw Beck eyeing him once again, staring inside him.

"So, Friedrich, what brings you here?"

Radner turned the glass over in his hand. "Well, I felt that I should have visited you earlier, but with Manheim dying and to fill his shoes . . ." He stopped. "No, that is not it at all. I am revolted by what I witnessed this afternoon. It was barbaric."

"We do it in other countries," Beck said quietly. "It is the Gestapo's way of making a point." He paused and then added, "It is an exclamation we make all over the world."

"Then it is a statement the world will hold us accountable for," Radner said.

Beck's handsome features were momentarily lost from the light.

The room they were in was the living room of his suite. Beck sat on a chair of deep, plush velvet. The rest of the room with its handsome chairs and full couch was in darkness. Only the bar next to Radner could be seen in the light, and its bottles gleamed wickedly in the light as if they were the ancient potions and brews of some satanic sect.

Radner looked at Beck. "Can we not expect some retribution for all this?"

Beck did not answer. Instead, with some effort, he rose and, using a walking cane, came to the window. "This America," he said, "with its untamed millions and its history of freedom will rise up against us. As Hitler attempts to spread the flag of the Third Reich across the world, others will revolt. They will find common cause. When that happens, Germany will face the most horrendous retribution."

Now he walked toward Radner. "Hitler means to devour the world. It is not possible. It will mean the end of Germany. There are those of us who wish to save Germany."

He looked directly at Radner, who had not expected so straightforward an approach. Radner stood up and refilled the silver glass with brandy.

"When you spoke to me of Hitler and the destiny of Germany on New Year's Eve, I felt you were asking me something else. I have thought upon it many times these past months."

"Perhaps I was," Beck answered.

"I have been growing increasingly uneasy," Radner continued. "But always I reassured myself that I am a man of culture and art, that it is not my place to be involved in these matters. But it seems to me that I am involved. As I witnessed the executions, I realized that I am a part of it. I am an officer of the Reich and represent the fist of oppression." He drank deeply of

288

his schnapps. "It leaves a bad taste, I am afraid. I do not think I shall forget this afternoon and the faces of the victims I saw."

Beck led him to the window. His finger tapped on the pane. "See how the first stars twinkle, Friedrich. Even in the darkest sky there is a moment of light. Tell me, what do you do tonight after the opening of your play?"

"There will be a reception," Radner said. "In the country at the Rockefeller estate. Will you come to the play?"

Beck shook his head. "I would like to but I must rest. The doctor is very firm on that. But I want you to come here tonight after your reception. Come after one. Do not use your regular driver. When you leave the reception there will be a car for you."

Beck saw the question in Radner's eyes. "There is someone I want you to meet."

They stood facing one another, Beck's meaning being very clear. "Will you come?"

Radner set down his glass. "I will come."

10:00 P.M.

Leila moved in contours of light, in shadows of madness, in bursts of Gielgud's soliloquies.

"Get thee to a nunnery."

And as the intensity of light became Ophelia's madness, she said the words though she remembered none of them. Ophelia, dead by drowning, was carried away and heard Hamlet and her brother, Laertes, come to sword point.

Then it was all crashing light and pounding palms. Gielgud and Burgess Meredith kissing her hand. A bouquet of flowers brought down by two pages. Gielgud kneeling before her, kissing her hand as she touched his shoulder in tribute.

Finally, the curtain lowered and, in the total darkness, Leila felt all alone. For she was Fay Brophy, an imposter.

Leila dabbed at her face with cold cream and heard the knock. The door opened and Radner stepped in. Then she was in his arms, smothered in his black tuxedo and the bouquet of white carnations.

He closed the door. "You were . . . magnificent."

"I'll settle for wonderful. Gielgud was magnificent."

Radner nodded. "He was. But you were more than exceptional." His arms came around her waist. She stiffened.

"Leila," he said. "I know your name. It's done. We are in it together. Let's not waste the good by dwelling on mistakes. I want you with me."

He saw her now both pale and luminescent, her green eyes a

mixture of triumph and sorrow. Poor girl, he thought, that you undertook such a deception.

"We'll make out some way," he said.

For a minute the sadness was overwhelming, and then she smiled. "All right, I'll try again."

He took her in his arms and kissed her. Her lips tasted of flowers, and it seemed he was almost ready to draw the nectar, and then the resistance was there. Why couldn't she trust? Because she is a Jewess, he thought. The door opened, and they were overrun by Gielgud and an entourage of well-wishers.

Later, emerging from the stage door entrance, she noted the absence of star gazers, all those autograph seekers and thrill collectors that she had always imagined were a part of being in a hit on Broadway. Even Gielgud, Katharine Cornell, and Burgess Meredith were not enough to offset the pall of New York under the occupation. Now she heard shrill, emotional words.

Walking ahead of her was Adele Glass, well known in New York theatrical circles as the assistant to Hillary Barnes, the producer. She was on the arm of Klaus Meineke, the German surgeon general in New York. He had been flown from Berlin to treat General Beck.

They were being harangued by a little man with a beard, and suddenly Leila was filled with terrible fear as she recognized he was a rabbi. His hands moved in quick, dramatic gestures, almost as if he were a sorcerer invoking a curse upon his intended victim.

"It is a *shanda*," he screamed. "Disgrace, disgrace you have brought upon the family of Glazer. You sleep with this dog of a Nazi. Well then, know what you bring forth will be impure. You will breed litters of evil. Curse the day you were born, curse the disgrace you have brought upon us all. God has forsaken the Glazers, and He has forsaken you.

He continued to invoke disgrace and tragedy as Adele Glass, a comely woman in a dark coat, threw her hands across her face as if to hide from this shrill apparition, this shaman of her people who poked at her with his fingers and screamed to the heavens to be his witness.

Hillary Barnes and Radner stepped forward, and the little man was pushed away, still invoking punishment and retribution.

Klaus Meineke, handsome and dignified, was trying to comfort Adele as Leila came to them.

"Let me," she whispered.

She held Adele against her chest. "Are you all right?"

"I'm fine . . . fine," Adele answered, and then let out an awful sob.

They drove in the country toward the Rockefellers' Pocantico estate. Adele and Leila sat in back, while in front was Klaus Meineke's driver. Adele had insisted that she be alone with Leila. They had gotten to know one another during rehearsals when Adele had assisted the director, Willard Marshall.

But except for a few brief words as they got in the car, Adele had been silent. Now and then she gave a few quiet sobs. Watching the bare trees, the pale glimmer of a moon above them, Leila felt some strange apprehension grip her. It was something far more than this farcical disguise she had adopted for herself. No, up in the heavens, this strange and disquieting element seemed to hang palpably above her and Adele. The stars, easily visible on this winter night, had lost their sheen. They were like pearls in a jewelry display case that someone had rubbed with polish, but neglected to wipe off. They were smeared and dirty. She felt cold and alone. Then Adele began to talk.

"I don't know how it happened. Hillary had gone riding with General Beck a few times and asked me to deliver a package. Klaus was there and . . . he was the handsomest man I have ever met. And the gentlest. Fay, I'm forty-two. I've known a few men in my time . . . but that's all it's been . . . a few. I'm sure you've heard stories about Hillary and me." She held up her hand. "It's all right. I have to tell someone. Well, they're true. I've been his mistress for many years. He loves me in his way. I used to think he might marry me. He says I'm everything he's wanted in a woman. Intelligence, humor, lovingness."

Leila looked at Adele, who had large green eyes that were just a trifle off center, a quality that was magnified when she wore her glasses. She had a nose that was too large, but her full lips were sensuous and alluring. She had high cheekbones and thick brown hair that, when worn long as she had tonight, gave her a kind of proud, pagan look. Leila could see where many men would want her. Despite her enormous intelligence, she underestimated herself.

Adele mustered a smile. "I was always unsure of myself with men. Give me a script, and I can cut it to shreds or put it back together again." She stopped to light a cigarette. "Klaus asked me to dinner. He was alone in New York. We went out, and it seemed we just talked and talked and talked. Three nights later we were lovers. I know it's all crazy. His wife is dead. He wants to marry me. I told him it's impossible. I'm only free of restrictions because I work under Radner's jurisdiction."

Leila bit her lip. Had she been unfair to Friedrich?

Adele took her hand. "I knew something terrible was coming. My family has disowned me. We have relatives in Austria. My cousin was almost beaten to death by brownshirts."

She began to weep quietly again.

"Who was that man . . ." Leila caught herself. My god, she thought, I'm afraid to say rabbi. What have I become?

"He's the rabbi in my family's temple."

"He took an awful chance," Leila said.

Adele clutched her hand. "I must see them tonight, after the party. Please come with me. Please, say you will."

She saw the terrible look of desperation in Adele's eyes and knew it was no longer possible to be just Fay Brophy. She didn't want to go but she had to. "All right," Leila said.

Adele hugged her and then turned her head away and wept quietly.

They continued their eerie ride through the country underneath a moon and stars smudged with the omens of tragedy.

11:30 P.M.

The first floor of the Rockefeller house had been turned into a huge ballroom. Food abounded on gleaming silver plates, while stacked next to them were countless buckets of chilled champagne. Large overhead chandeliers made the house seem like a stage on which an opera was being played out by a cast of thousands. But they were a special cast. They were those who were "in," in this New York that was being created under the swastika.

They were people who did business with the Reich. People who flourished and took over the businesses of people they betrayed. People who looked forward to prospering for years to come. People for whom the coming of the Reich was an event long cherished and for whom the thought of the Germans leaving was unmentionable. People who saw not an interlude but a long succession of history under the banner of the Reich. Fascist New York for them was a dream become real.

Sylvie watched these creatures and felt her stomach tighten as though someone had a drawstring on her. She saw the pictures of Hitler on the dark paneled walls, the red Nazi banners furled around graceful columns . . . poking out, they seemed like horned stags who had just finished a relentless, bloody charge. Up the stairs were more rooms, more dirty fascists, fat businessmen and beefy Bundists, and their women, breasts overflowing like foam spilling from a beer tap. Dark, haughty women with thin, vulturelike mouths, looking to make a conquest. Trying to ascertain who was official Nazidom, who were active fifth columnists and who were simply collaborators. It was very important to know whom you were bedding down with. Everybody was climbing the ladder. As usual, there was a large crowd around Patrick.

She looked around the room at these supporters and beneficiaries of the Reich and had a sudden loss of breath. She was choking, she couldn't breathe properly. She could smell them. To her, they were people who reeked beneath their colognes and perfumes. Like Al, the man who was once to marry her mother. He always wore lots of cologne. It intrigued her. One day she went into his closet. There was a row of his shirts on hangers. She suddenly put her nose to the armpit of his shirt. She remembered the overpowering, unpleasant aroma, her gagging sensation and revulsion. She knew it was some quality of his insides. Rotten, corrosive. That's what these people made her remember.

She turned and left the room to find Patrick to tell him she was going home. This time she would not plead a headache.

Radner moved about the mansion accepting congratulations from theater people, scores of whom he had never met. The New York Reichers he had christened them. The artists were those who wished to work for him. He was hoping tonight's success would keep the more important ones here. Cole Porter, Jerome Kern, and the Lunts had bought their way out. *Hamlet* must stem the tide.

He saw Abetz eyeing him. He was standing with a thin, wiry Italian who wore a black suit and looked decidedly out of place at the Rockefeller estate. They had been conversing for some minutes, and now Abetz whispered something to him. The Italian nodded to Abetz and then suddenly left. Abetz watched him leave and, turning to Radner, gave him a clear invitation. He walked off into an adjoining room that seemed to lead down some stairs. Moments later Radner followed through the same door.

They were in a cool, dark chamber that adjoined the wine cellar. Even this room had royal velvet chairs. There was an overhead bulb and more light from a large standing lamp in the corner. Radner wanted to laugh. He felt like a conspirator in a long-forgotten sixteenth-century opera.

But as Abetz spoke, Radner was quickly aware of the present and the significance of what he had begun.

"You have been with Beck?"

It was a statement of what Abetz expected. Radner knew he had been totally compromised.

"I will see him this evening. In fact, I must leave in fifteen minutes."

"You were effective then. I thought you would be. Listen to me, Captain Radner. Here is what you will do when you meet with Beck and whoever else is there. I am sure that person will test you. You will not be accepted until Beck has someone second his judgment. Be interested, continue to indicate your disgust with the regime, but do not be inquisitive." Abetz paused. His dark eyes flickered. "At the right moment, and only you can judge when that is, inform them that you have been asked to prepare an itinerary in Washington for the Führer. Be vague about the date."

"What kind of itinerary?"

"A cultural schedule."

"I need time."

"There is no time. This is no game we play at. I believe that this information will win them over, and you will be part of a conspiracy to assassinate the Führer. I wish to catch them in the midst of these preparations. Do you understand, Captain? If you are successful, then I shall be most favorably disposed with regard to Miss Leila Fox."

Radner swallowed hard and affected a casualness he did not for a moment feel. "When you have them, I want a letter of safe conduct for Miss Fox, should she choose to use it."

Abetz nodded. "You shall have it when our arrangement is complete. About Miss Fox. It is not just her life you are responsible for. Now, please, do not let me hold you up from the second act of your little play."

Radner went up the stairs, feeling his neck burning and the anguished hum of his nerves. The game had gotten infinitely more dangerous. His own life and career were on the table. A plot to kill the Führer built on lies he would have to invent. If he were discovered . . . !

He moved through the crowd, still accepting congratulations and handshakes from people who had become blurred images. He had come to New York to thrill its people and save its culture. Instead he was involved in a hideous game with his own life at stake. He searched the room for Leila, finally spotted Hillary Barnes, and learned that Leila had left half an hour ago with Adele Glass and Klaus Meineke.

Chapter 31

March 28, 1942
1:21 A.M.

Riverside Drive was dark and deserted except for the periodic patrols that consisted mostly of auxiliary police assigned by the Gestapo to back them up. This was in contrast to the constant surveillance of all the other heavily populated Jewish areas of the city. The Lower East Side, Brownsville in Brooklyn, and the Grand Concourse in the Bronx were subject to repeated searches and watched closely. Only Harlem faced the equivalent of what *jüden* pockets of New York had experienced since the city fell.

Adele had wanted to go alone with Leila and leave Klaus behind, but he refused. And now Leila was glad. For even with the official car, two women alone would have been in constant danger. She could see it in the leering faces of the auxiliary police who had already found the extra benefits of being near unescorted young women.

"There," Adele said to Meineke, who tapped the driver.

Leila looked out and saw the building lights were on on the fourth floor. In front of the building were several cars, civilian cars. She knew immediately something was askew. So did Adele, who let out a cry and opened the door and ran toward the house.

Meineke yelled to his driver to stop and followed after Leila. There were lights in other apartments, and suddenly there was the scream of a woman.

As they reached the curb in front of the house, they found their way blocked by a thick man with a brutish face. He looked like a horse whose mouth had been disfigured. He's some kind of gangster, Leila realized.

He stood blocking their way, hand inside his vest. He had a gun.

Adele tried to push past him and was thrown to the ground. Meineke began to struggle with the man, calling "Heintzel" to his driver. As they grappled Leila went to Adele and helped her up. Behind them, Leila could hear the struggle and then a gasp.

Looking back she saw Heintzel holding a revolver, which he had obviously used to subdue the gangster.

They all looked at each other, wondering what kind of awful outrage was taking place upstairs. There was another scream, and Leila saw Adele's face register emotional recognition. As if she were reversing the age-old fable that a mother can always identify the cry of her child.

"Mama," Adele Glass screamed, and ran into the lobby.

They had already cleaned out the building next door, and Paulie had been amazed how much gelt, jewelry, and bonds they had come up with. And gold. The old grandmothers had hidden them in boxes buried under old dressers and worthless albums.

In the first apartment the defiance had lasted just as long as it took Paulie to sap a young boy. His head split open and blood spurted like oil. "Kindela," the old grandmother screamed, and minutes later as the boy lay glassy eyed and pale, blood still oozing from his skull, gold magically appeared.

"Open the door," Trigger Coppola yelled. "Let them see. Let them all see." And seeing, the people had forked over gelt and gold. In that moment, Paulie knew that Riverside Drive was going to be very good to them.

They were working in miniature squads of three and four. One man stood at the door with his piece while the others went through each apartment and did any heavy duty roughing up that was necessary. Then they had come to this particular apartment on the fourth floor and Johnny DiMona rang the bell, Paulie had an odd feeling. Something different was about to occur. The feeling was reinforced when nobody answered.

Johnny DiMona looked at Paulie. "Kick it in."

On the third boot the door gave, and Paulie, Johnny DiMona, and Snake Sinacola went barging in. The family was huddled in the living room behind a bearded rabbi. As soon as he saw the rabbi, Paulie's gut tightened. Yunkle, you asshole, what the hell do you think you're doing?

Behind them were the father and mother. He was graying and bald, his skin clammy with sweat, eyes filled with some anguished emotion. The woman was diminutive, hair once brown, now mousey gray, with deep pouches under the eyes, the eyes themselves filled with the apprehension of tragedy passed on through centuries. She wore a brown robe and had her arms around a young woman who Paulie figured was no more than twenty. The girl was pretty. Her hair was in pigtails, but her face was now frozen into a mask of fear. She reminded Paulie of a kid standing in front of one of those amusement park windows that distorted your body and facial expression. She had deep brown eyes, a straight nose, and tiny lips that she now bit into, unaware that they were bleeding. She had thrown on a coat over her pajamas. Her head was buried in the mother's chest.

"Don't touch my Rachel," the woman in the bathrobe screamed.

And now there was Yunkle, this small rabbi with a beard longer than Abe Lincoln's, invoking God's wrath upon them.

"You will be punished. Leave the children of Israel . . ."

The rest was lamentation that made Paulie sick. And because Yunkle epitomized the shame Paulie had always felt at being of the same caste, he felt it his place to act.

That the apartment was furnished with paintings depicting scenes with angels and women trying to protect children from spear-wielding soldiers depressed Paulie. It was like walking into some shul. Fuckin' Yids, he thought.

"All right, Yunkle, out of the way."

He threw the rabbi down and grabbed the man dressed in a black suit and white shirt.

"Get it up. All the gelt you got." Paulie put the rod to the man's head and the two women screamed.

"I don't have . . ." That was as far as he got. Paulie whipped him across the side of the head with his pistol.

"Get it," Paulie commanded. "The jewels, too."

He fell down, blood flowing from his ear.

"Abe," the woman screamed, and relinquished the girl. She bent down over him, cradling the man.

Snake pulled her away. "Get the jewel box," he said, flinging the woman toward the bedroom and then following her.

"No pussy," Johnny DiMona yelled to Snake, who, as everybody well knew, would fuck a goat if it wore a skirt.

The girl bent over the father and tried to comfort him while Yunkle was on his knees praying. Jesus, Paulie thought, would I love to drill him.

There was a scream from the bedroom, and Johnny ran inside. Paulie heard him cursing Snake, and then they were all back with Johnny holding a large box.

Johnny tipped it open and out came jewelry and a stack of papers.

"Bonds," Johnny called out. Now he turned the rod to the bleeding man. "Where's the bankbook?"

The man lay on the floor, blood from his forehead drenching the white shirt. He spoke in a quiet, resigned voice. "Esther, give it to them."

Paulie saw the woman's mouth begin to move, and then the lips just worked helplessly as she was crying.

It was at precisely this moment that Adele and Leila burst into the apartment, followed by Klaus Meineke.

Paulie wheeled about, thinking, Who the fuck are these geeks?

Adele saw her father on the floor and in one motion ran to him, leaving Leila in the doorway. She put her hand to her mouth. It was like some modern-day version of the Rape of the Sabine Women. Adele bent over her father, who leaked blood, while her mother struggled with a gangster with eyes set so far back in his head he looked like some kind of serpent. He was pulling a book from her hand—a bankbook—while on the floor seemingly oblivious to it all was the bearded rabbi who had confronted Adele earlier, praying to a God who Leila knew would not hear.

There was another girl—young . . . pretty . . . terrified. It was the niece, Rachel. Adele had mentioned her during the car ride. There were two other hoodlums with guns standing in the pale light of the apartment.

"Leave them alone," called Klaus Meineke, who was followed by Heintzel, still carrying the revolver. Now Heintzel pointed it in the general direction of two of the gangsters. Instinctively, she knew it was a mistake.

Paulie saw the Heinrich with a gun. He never hesitated. The law of the street outweighed any loyalty to Heinrich. And somehow he knew this was a Heinrich Abetz wouldn't miss. Paulie plugged him through the chest. He went white and then fell, sagging in sections to the floor.

Screams . . . more screams. Adele clutched her father. As Klaus Meineke went to her, Leila saw one of the gangsters, a little man, club him to the ground . . . over and over. And she also saw the serpent-eyed gangster dragging Rachel toward the bedroom.

Then all intellectual capacity to evaluate what she saw vanished. Leila ran into the bedroom. The gangster had already thrown Rachel onto the bed and pulled open the top of her pajamas. Stepping back, he began pulling at his belt. Rachel lay there inert, waiting to be violated. The serpent-eyed thug was grinning wildly at her. "You want it, don't you, baby? I got it for you." He had one hand on Rachel's throat while the other ripped the pajama top off. "Nice baby, nice," he whispered. "Come to Snake."

He lowered himself on top of Rachel, and Leila felt herself blacking out. Tumbling into an abyss. She was unable to give utterance to the scream in her throat.

From far away she heard a voice. It was hard and grainy. Then Snake was standing up. There was another man in the bedroom.

Leila became acutely aware that there were no more cries from the living room.

She heard the voice again. "What the fuck are you doing, Snake?"

"Nothin', Vito."

Vito Genovese pointed to Rachel. "You call that nothin'?"

"A lesson, Vito. They got to learn. . . ."

"Shut up. This is business. You know what business is? My business?"

"Sure."

"Shut up. Business is the hours of collection. Knocking off a piece slows up collection. We just opened for business, and you makin' me look bad."

Leila saw that the man called Vito was small, but there was something lethal about him. He had a gun in his hand.

"Snake," he said, "I'm gonna blow your nuts off." He pointed the gun toward the tall gangster's groin.

The effect of those words was incredible. The gangster called Snake was on his knees. "Please, Vito, don't. I fucked up, but never again. Please, Vito, please."

He kept saying it over and over again while the little man kept the gun firmly pointed there. Then suddenly it was over.

"Get out there, Snake."

Back in the living room Vito Genovese looked around at the collection of bodies and crying women. He turned to Johnny DiMona. "What is this shit?"

Johnny bit his lip. "These guys came in. There was a kraut with a gun. Paulie plugged him . . . Snake went crazy."

Vito Genovese looked around at the dead driver. "Good work, Paulie. Looks like you're the only guy knows how to do the right thing."

"My God," the rabbi wailed. It was a cry that pierced everyone in the room. It was followed by a series of lamentations in Hebrew and curses invoked upon the enemies of Israel.

Vito Genovese looked at Paulie and then at the rabbi. "Shut the fuck up."

There was a split second in which Paulie wondered whether Vito would sap him or clip him. Then the little rabbi started in again and Paulie was thinking, you fucking Abey, it's all you bearded assholes that made me ashamed of bein' Jewish.

Vito Genovese took a step forward and brought the gun butt savagely across the rabbi's temple.

The women began to weep again as Vito Genovese said, "Let's get out of here." In the hall Paulie saw some Gestapo types, and then Genovese was pulling him aside. "Paulie," he said in that soft but deadly voice, "take Snake to the basement. Tell him there's a box to be picked up. Clip him."

They rode down in the elevator, Snake pulling at his collar. "Jesus, that was close."

Paulie offered him a cigarette. "Forget it. Just do your job, and Vito will take care of you."

"Yeah, yeah, sure."

They reached the basement, and Paulie led the way.

"Where is it?" Snake called as he followed Paulie.

"Next to the boiler," Paulie called back. He had the piece in his hand as they reached the boiler and the small lights that burned next to it. Paulie noted that there was a coal bin over in the corner.

As Snake reached him, Paulie said, "Over there by the bin."

He let Snake lead the way and now, as Snake turned, he saw Paulie's heater. Even in the semilight, Paulie could see Snake's eyes go from surprise to complete understanding.

"No, Paulie, I didn't do nothin'."

"Vito gave me the word."

He was trembling, knees shaking. "No, Paulie, Vito and my old man go back . . . Paulie, you can't."

He was completely falling apart, and Paulie felt both contempt and great power.

"No, Paulie, I didn't do nothin'. She was Jew shit. . . ." Then he stopped, realizing who he was talking to.

Paulie smiled coldly. "Vito gave me the word."

He fired twice at point-blank range. Both shots hit Snake in the chest. His hands were still clutching at Paulie as he crumpled. Paulie stood over the body and whispered one more time, "Vito gave the word."

1:55 A.M.

Sylvie got off the elevator at Patrick's floor and walked directly to his apartment. She used her key to get in and went into the study where he kept his papers. Robert had told her to look for papers that were marked "confidential" or "secret." They would be stamped that way across the top. They would be from the Gestapo or from the top echelon in Berlin. In particular, Robert wanted anything about military plans or about Gestapo plans for dealing with politicals. Letters between Patrick and a man named Krupp were also very important.

She switched on the small overhead light and began sorting through the papers on his desk. She felt no fear. She was neither ashamed nor guilty. The executions in Central Park had taken care of that. Patrick was one of them.

She went through the papers on his desk like a woman in a department store, looking at this one, then the next. Then she stopped. Silly fool, this is not Bonwit's or Saks. His briefcase will have whatever he's done today. She scanned the room and saw it resting on the floor next to the bed. Patrick liked to read what was on the agenda for the next day. When he came in this morning in the wee hours, he wouldn't sleep until he'd read these papers.

She picked it up and put it on the bed. She switched on the table lamp. From her purse she took out a pencil and pad. "Copy everything," Robert had said. Everything it would be. She snapped open the briefcase and pulled out its contents. The first document was plans for some kind of camp. It was a complete layout. On top, it read "Hackensack Camp Easter Roundup." It was a detailed drawing. Sections were marked off for politicals, for guards, for Jews. Quickly going on she saw there was a report on when the camp would be ready. On Easter Sunday. Following that was a personal memo from Standartenführer Abetz to Patrick detailing plans for "Ransoming the Jews." She read that document and saw the date. It began a few hours ago. She didn't go any further. She began to write, copying first the diagram for the camp.

She worked for an hour, writing neatly, quickly. She was about to stop, after checking her watch and seeing it was three. He would be home soon. Oh, just one more page, she thought. She was amazed at how bold she had become.

She turned the page over and saw it was on official Wehrmacht stationery. It was from a German general named Heinz Guderian. It gave the official timetable for bombing Detroit and Cleveland. Beginning on March 27. She stopped. But that was last night. She turned the page on her pad and began to write furiously.

2:00 A.M.

Following Beck's orders, Radner had asked for a staff driver. This one was different from the tall man who had driven him out from the city. He had a thick bull neck, and his hair was cut very short. As they swung east through Central Park, it occurred to Radner that the meeting would not be at the Sherry Netherland. Beck was not going to advertise a clandestine meeting. As they exited onto Fifth Avenue, Radner noted the bare trees in Central Park. Everything was barren about this winter in New York. He smiled bitterly. This winter of my discontent.

The car went down Fifth Avenue, cut abruptly over to Madison, then did a series of zigzag turns onto Park, Lexington,

301

Third, and then back to Lexington. Abruptly it turned in off Lexington and pulled up in front of a brownstone town house. His door was thrust open by the driver, and Radner found himself in front of the doorbell. He pressed it and waited. Moments later it was opened by a valet in uniform. Radner found himself wondering, Do servants know of these secret plots? and then ridiculed himself for being such a naive fool as to even pose the question.

The apartment was a duplex, and Radner found himself walking up the stairs. Then the servant was gone. A light gleamed from up ahead, and Radner walked into the bedroom. There was a rocking chair in the corner, and a man seated in it. His face was not visible. He wore a dark civilian suit. Radner was uncertain what was expected of him.

His host gestured with his hand. "Please sit down, Captain. General Beck will be here in a few moments. Until then, the introductions will wait. Please help yourself."

He pointed to a table where a drink had been poured for him. "I presume you like good schnapps."

Radner took the drink and, looking at his mysterious host, raised the glass. "To your good health."

The man said nothing. Radner downed the drink.

"Have another," the man suggested.

Radner went about the business of pouring himself another brandy, grateful for the opportunity to turn away from the man who was obviously here to inspect him. He remembered Abetz's phrase. "You will not be accepted till Beck has someone second his judgment." Abetz was correct. Radner was on trial.

It was perhaps five minutes before he heard the door downstairs being opened. Then there was the sound of footsteps on the stairs and, abruptly, the tall, imposing figure of General Beck was in the room.

He rubbed his hands and quickly took off his leather coat. Even in the dim light, Radner could see how pale he was. The wound had taken a great deal out of him, and he should have been in bed sleeping.

"Gentlemen," Beck began, "your pardon for being late. Captain Radner, the man sitting opposite you must for the time being be known only as Ivo. Because of his strategic placement within the intelligence network of the Reich, I cannot identify him. But let me say, he is an officer of a rank similar to your own, and a distinguished one."

Beck poured himself a brandy and sat down on the bed. "And so gentlemen, to work." He finished the drink and set down the glass. "Captain Radner witnessed the executions this afternoon and came to me and offered his help. Am I correct, Captain Radner?''

Radner cleared his throat. ''I am deeply ashamed of what occurred and can no longer divert myself from the conclusion that the Reich must adopt a different policy in America. I do not think I can hold important artists here as in Paris. Daily they flee to California.''

The man called Ivo leaned forward. He had bushy eyebrows and a bulbous nose.

''Captain Radner, a question. Have you been asked to prepare for a special event?''

Radner felt nerve ends go taut. It was his cue. Better than anything he could have hoped for. He looked properly puzzled. ''Event?''

''Let me put it this way,'' Ivo continued. ''If a dignitary in the highest echelons from Berlin should arrive, would you be approached to prepare some kind of schedule of cultural events for this man to attend?''

The blood pounded in Radner's head. They know. Abetz made sure they would know. They are like puppets on his string. Radner sipped some brandy to calm himself. He must play it just right. Then it came to him. Dress the lie in truth. Malicious truth. Leaning forward he said, ''I have been told by Abetz that the Führer comes to Washington shortly. I am to prepare an itinerary for him.''

''Friedrich,'' Beck said. ''The schedule you draw up would also include receptions, is that correct?''

''Yes.''

''In fact, Friedrich, the schedule will be on your desk at the same time as Abetz receives it.''

''Undoubtedly,'' Radner answered. He knew he needed to anticipate them now. ''What is it you wish of me?''

Ivo spoke from the shadows. ''Can you not guess, Captain? There will be performances, cocktail receptions. Certainly Hitler will address the diplomats of the world in the American Senate.''

Radner saw it all now. Abetz had made sure they knew everything. Give them the bait, and they will take it in their mouths. ''You mean to kill him. Do you wish me to do it?''

''Friedrich,'' Beck responded in the gentlest of voices, ''we wish you to get Captain Ivo close enough to act. Will you do it?''

I am an accomplice in a plot to murder the Führer, Radner thought. This is madness.

As if reading his thoughts, Ivo cut in. ''It seems we are asking a great deal, very quickly, Captain Radner, but the fate of Ger-

303

many hangs in the balance. Von Ribbentrop is in Washington now to make preparations. Even Abetz does not know this. If you could find a way to make contact with von Ribbentrop in Washington, and I were to accompany you . . ." He stopped. "You understand? We need to confirm the Führer's arrival time. Will you risk it?"

He was being put to the test with no preliminaries, and Ivo, sitting in the darkness, was both inquisitor and executioner.

"You are asking me," Radner said, purposefully modulating his voice, "whether I will help you assassinate the Führer. And yet it seems I am suspect. I sense that. Please be candid."

Ivo leaned into the light of the table lamp. "Very well. The actress you live with is a Jew."

Radner reeled back as if he had been struck by a blow. But how could they know?

Beck spoke now. "I have men in intelligence circles. We know Abetz has the report on Leila Fox who poses as Fay Brophy. We worry that perhaps he may attempt to use it against you. Has he approached you?"

Radner heard Beck but watched Ivo. There was a movement of his hand toward his jacket. He had a gun. It would have a silencer on it. Radner felt the sweat forming on his neck.

Radner spoke with conviction. His life depended on his performance. "Abetz has confronted me but asked for nothing. Nor am I prepared to give him anything. I will not give up Leila. It is well known that Reich officers have Jewish mistresses. I told Abetz this."

He watched Ivo and Beck weighing his semitruthful confession. How clever Abetz is. Radner had been sent to Beck by Abetz, who knew Beck had access to Gestapo intelligence. If Radner survived the interrogation, he was Abetz's spy. If he failed . . . he was dead. And if he survived his lie, he was beholden to Abetz for as long as this plot existed. But what if he were to tell Beck and Ivo the truth? Join them. No. For even with Hitler dead, Abetz would remain in power. Radner had been cast as the informer, and there was no changing roles now. Check and mate.

He saw Ivo staring at him. I will have to be very careful with him. I will have to go to Washington with him.

Beck stood up and approached Radner. "Can you travel to Washington tomorrow and see von Ribbentrop? We must know Hitler's exact arrival time."

It was all happening so fast. How he handled it would determine their degree of trust in him. He had to prove himself.

"I will call von Ribbentrop in the morning and suggest a matinee of *Hamlet*. The cast will leave tomorrow evening by

304

train and perform in the afternoon. I will travel to Washington tomorrow to make arrangements, accompanied by Captain Ivo.''

Beck clapped his hands. ''Yes, of course. Brilliant, Friedrich.'' Beck turned to Ivo, who nodded.

Radner stood up and felt how shaky his legs were. He could be dead. Instead he shook Beck's hand.

''Friedrich, Abetz sent the killer after me in Central Park. From now on you live every day on the knife. As we all do.''

''I understand.''

Ivo rose. ''I must speak with you alone, Ludwig.''

Beck put a hand on Radner's shoulder. ''Friedrich, I am so glad you have joined us. Wait downstairs. A driver will come for you.''

He went down the stairs, his head throbbing, hearing the furtive voices of Ivo and Beck. He thought of Ivo and how close a thing it had been. He was between Beck and Abetz, and he had been forced to make his bet. Abetz. He must play the double agent in a drama more real than any he had ever witnessed in a theater. Perhaps Abetz did not know of von Ribbentrop's Washington arrival. Radner would call in the morning and inform him. He bit his lip. See how the dog serves his master. He was in quicksand, and Abetz held the rope. He held the rope, and he had baited the trap.

Radner stood in the sitting room and looked out at the street by shifting the curtain. The black, unfathomable night had descended upon New York. Upstairs, two madmen conspired to assassinate Hitler, and Radner was to provide them access.

5:05 A.M.

Radner let himself into the apartment. He had seen the light under the door, but thought Leila had left it on for him. As he entered the living room, he saw the crown of soft brown hair and the light disappearing into that soft sheen he loved to touch.

He came across the sunken living room and bent over the chair and kissed her forehead. ''You were marvelous. . . .'' That was as far as he got. Her green eyes were full of both fury and some terrible pain. What had he come upon?

She was holding a drink. It looked smoky, the way scotch does in a pool of light. He walked to the cabinet and poured himself a drink. What grim scene had he come upon?

He walked back and sat down on a divan. It put him at her feet. He wanted to stroke her leg but that, he knew, would be wrong. She had been violated in some way.

And he, of course, represented the enemy.

They sat in silence for some minutes. He still had his coat on. Finally he could stand no more.

"Well, tell me about it. Anything is better than this."

She looked down at her drink and then spoke in a voice he didn't know. "They're using gangsters. The Nazis are using gangsters."

He stared at her. What more could there be this night?

"They were at Adele's parents' house . . . they beat them . . . they struck a rabbi. Her niece would have been raped. He tore the top of her pajamas off. And I just watched this gangster. I couldn't move. I was terrified. Another gangster stopped it because it was bad business. He called it business."

"But . . . but," he struggled for the words. "Gangsters you said . . . not Gestapo."

"They know . . . they approve," she said. Her voice was the voice of the Jew who has learned he is always guilty. "There were Gestapo men in the hall. Money . . . it's for money and jewels and gold. It's . . . it's despicable."

She dropped the glass on the rug, and Radner quickly moved to put his arms around her. She was shaking. "Please, let me hold you. Please, let me."

In his arms she was taut, vibrating. He kissed her forehead.

"I have to do something," she said. "I have to."

He said nothing. This was shock. It would have to run its course.

"I can't be Leila anymore."

He said nothing, and then she was pushing him away. "I can't be . . ." and then realizing her mistake, corrected it. "I can't be Fay anymore. I have to be Leila."

"Of course," he said. "Of course."

"I'm so ashamed."

"You're tired," he whispered. "It was awful, and it's been too much. Come to bed. I'll hold you. Nothing more. Come."

She let him lead her there and stood mute until he reached to undress her. Then she punched his hand away. Seeing what she had done, she began to cry. First it was a soft, almost mewing, sound, but then it became a thing that racked her chest and convulsed her body.

Somehow he got her into bed and the cover over her. He managed to pull off his overcoat, then he sank down next to her and enfolded her in his arms.

This night should have been their triumph, and now it was ashes . . . all of it. All of it a bitter joke. He was to betray men who conspired to assassinate the Führer. Leila had hidden herself as Fay Brophy, and now they were both totally compromised. She had hopelessly entangled him in her life. Was anything left of their love? What was he risking his life for? Did she love him anymore?

And she thought, We haven't been right since he found out. I've tangled him all up. Nothing is clean anymore. But it never was, you little fool. Did you think you could get by as Fay Brophy forever? It was all useless after what had happened tonight. Fay, Leila, it made no difference anymore. It was the human race against the Nazis. I must do something. I must leave you, Friedrich. I have loved you, but I must go. I must fight. Tomorrow, I must find somebody. "Poor Adele," she whispered.

"What?" he said.

"Adele, what will she do?" She turned to him. "What will we do?"

In that moment her eyes were big and vulnerable, and he remembered how much he had once loved her. He came over her, and she felt something in her stir. Desire is a two-faced coin, she realized, luring and mocking us at the same time. As he began to move inside her, she remembered the snake-eyed thug ripping Rachel's pajamas, and she closed down. Radner, feeling her leave him, came. He felt her body go cold and dry, and then he sank into defeat next to her, his pants soiled by his semen. She was lost to him, and yet he was responsible for her. They were doomed to play it out.

No, this couldn't go on. He would get her to unoccupied America. But that wouldn't free him of Abetz and Beck. The Führer was coming. Coming to Beck, who waited with dagger and pistol. Tomorrow, Washington. Von Ribbentrop. Was it real? Feeling Leila beside him, hearing her deep breathing, he hated her, hated himself. He closed his eyes but knew he would never sleep well again.

Chapter 32

March 28, 1942
12:30 P.M.

Riding a double-decker bus down Central Park West, Leila noted the headlines in the *Daily Patrician* about the bombing raids on Detroit. At the Automat she had heard a muted conversation between two elderly men in which one of them mentioned that a General Motors plant had been hit along with a Chrysler plant. They were both gray-haired men who smoked cigarettes, cupping the butts in their palm as if even the smoke would make them suspect. "They'll get Cleveland," the taller one said. At intervals in their conversation both men looked furtively about. God, she thought, this is what has happened to us. How could she ever have thought that being Fay Brophy was important?

When she had awakened in the morning, Friedrich was gone, and she was both lonely and grateful. She had drawn a hot bath and sat soaking in the tub. The images of the previous evening assaulted her with their vividness. And yet now she could deal with them. Where last evening she had been all raw emotion, this morning she could distance herself and see the awful images. For whatever reason, she had been permitted to witness what this occupation really meant. She knew now that she must do something to stop it.

But what? She was an actress in a play. How could that possibly be translated into anything, whether she was Fay Brophy or Leila Fox? No, wait. She was both Leila and Fay, that could work for her. There was a Resistance in New York. Plants had been blown up, ships in the docks. Somebody had shot five men in the Gestapo. That was it. She had to contact the Resistance and offer to work for them. She couldn't believe it for a moment. Was she really serious? Of course I am. Didn't I become Fay Brophy on a whim? But was it a whim? You knew from the beginning that being a Jew was dangerous. You tried to hide, but it wasn't possible. Adele is your example. It is not possible to carry on this charade anymore. It had made everything between her and Friedrich impossibly tense. She had compromised him. But he was one of them. It wasn't that he was bad . . . it was just that he was one of them. But she couldn't sort that out now. She just knew she had to do something. But how could she possibly contact the Resistance?

It came to her as she walked on Forty-fifth Street to the New Amsterdam for the afternoon matinee. A matinee that would be filled with German officers and their women, idle collaborators, and other hangers on. Of course. She should have thought of it before. But what if it didn't work? It had to. A gust of wind caught her across the face as she turned into the stage door. She remembered last night and felt the choking sensation again. Always remember it, she told herself. She knew exactly what she was going to do after the matinee. It had to work.

2:00 P.M.

The air was raw and gusty and Collins turned up the collar of his overcoat. He didn't like this meet, he didn't like it at all. Sylvie had left the red scarf for him at the newsstand. In it was a little card that said, "Meet me at the Stanhope, three o'clock." Didn't she know the Stanhope was a garden full of collaborators, fifth columnists, and agents? She must have something important and probably thought what a clever place for a meet. Nobody would suspect. Of course not. Only all of fascist New York would be there. Then there was the meeting tonight with General Beck or whoever he sent at Bruno's Chophouse. It was going to be quite a day for him, hip deep in the fascist vat of New York. He dragged deep on his coffin nail and inhaled. He didn't like it, not any of it. He had the heebie-jeebies. Something bum was going to happen.

2:15 P.M.

Sylvie had chosen the heavy wool black coat she had bought on Carnaby Street in London last year. It had deep pockets. She could keep the papers there with her hands inside them. No, that was no good. It wasn't chic for a woman to walk around that way. Men did that. Men in trenchcoats, spies. Oh, stop this. Don't lose your nerve now. But she was right about the coat. Then how to do it? Of course. A muff. Fashionable, and perfect to keep the notes in. Her hands would always be there. A lady always kept her muff with her. She had chosen the cherry-red dress and the red velvet hat that went with it. That was the right kind of outfit for the Stanhope. By being herself, she would seem less conspicuous. And the Stanhope was the perfect place to meet. Patrick always had lunch there. Anyone who came to the Stanhope was in good standing with the Germans.

2:50 P.M.

Collins checked his watch. He had walked past the Stanhope a couple of times, as if somehow he could ferret out what was going on inside. He didn't like it. There was nothing unusual going on, no official cars, no great activity. Occasionally a couple of Heinrich officers would come out looking very smug. What if I blew your heads off? he thought. Damn it, he didn't like it.

He walked around the block again. What was it? He couldn't shake this odd feeling that something was wrong. Of all places, the bar of the Hotel Stanhope. Why not Gestapo headquarters?

309

Stop it. It's going to be simple. You walk in, run into your old friend, Miss Lamont, have a drink, she slips you the papers, and you're off. He threw down his butt and walked back toward Fifth Avenue.

2:55 P.M.

The cab pulled in, and the doorman at the Stanhope jumped lively and opened the door. A beautiful woman stepped out. She had ash-blond hair and was wearing a black coat over a cherry-red dress, matched by a smart red velvet hat. She had her hands in a mink-lined muff. She walked briskly toward the Stanhope as the obsequious doorman followed in her wake, hoping to beat her to the door.

2:57 P.M.

Collins had just gotten to the corner when he saw the phalanx of official vehicles pulling up in front of the Stanhope. He felt the chill lines run down him, and his hand pulled at the small of his back where he had wedged the revolver. Jesus, Mary, and Joseph, what the hell was this? The black cars stopped. And now out came plainclothes Gestapo and officers, all hovering around the last car where the door was opening now. Then a strongly built, elegant looking man stepped out. He wore a leather coat over his uniform and stood there as if he were Alexander the Great. Jesus, it was Rommel.

3:00 P.M.

Sylvie had gone immediately to the bar, then taken a table and ordered a martini. She lit a cigarette after carefully cradling the muff on her lap. She had timed it so that she would have five minutes alone before being joined by Mr. Jackson, the Cleveland lawyer, who had been so kind to her on the Lower East Side. She looked around the darkened room in a casual manner, noting the officers and ladies in light conversation. There were three businessmen sitting in the corner. The bar, which was next to them, had a large mirror that showed the entire room. Faces were reflected in it. Fascist faces. Cruel, unconcerned faces. What did they know or care about the hostages shot in Central Park? They sit here in plush luxury talking deals or seducing each other. She looked down at the deep black rug that covered the entire room and flicked an ash on it.

310

Instinctively, Collins had felt himself stopping and then re-treating backward. Christ, the place would be full of Gestapo agents and Wehrmacht officers. He couldn't go inside. But it must be important. Sylvie must have gotten something from Kelly's papers.

"You."

Collins fought the impulse to whirl around. Instead he stood still and then did a slow turn. He found himself facing a beefy-looking Bundist wearing the auxiliary police insignia on his olive coat. He had a thick mustache, and under his cap the brown, bushy hair showed flecks of silver. He had a rough face, carved like a hatchet. The eyes were brown and suspicious. Careful boyo, Collins warned himself. This one is stupid.

"You have business here?" The man spoke softly, but Collins knew that was a trick.

"No," Collins said. "Just taking a walk."

"Why did you stop?"

Collins tried to be John Doe fascinated by it all. "Just all those cars. Caught my eye."

The auxiliary policeman watched him carefully, apparently deciding something for himself.

C'mon, Collins silently implored. Let me go. I've had my action for this week.

"Your card," the big plug said.

Collins knew that if he protested it would be worse. The card was a good forgery, but if they ever double-checked . . . He made one try. "Listen, I got a client who's waiting up the street."

"Your card," the man said with more conviction.

Stumblejohn, he chided himself. He felt his gun in the small of his back. No, no chance. Clip this guy and the whole Stanhope will be out after you. He reached into his pocket and extracted the blue and white card from his wallet.

The Heinrich snatched the card and looked at it. He read it over as if it were *De Profundis*. Now he looked up at Collins. "Mr. Jackson, Robert Jackson."

Collins grinned. "Yeah, that's me."

"It says you are from Cleveland."

Collins could see a light bulb going on in the Heinrich's thick head.

"What do you do, Mr. Jackson?"

I kill Gestapo. I should kill you. "I'm a lawyer."

"What kind of law?"

The cowlike brown eyes were implacable. He's doing his bit for the Reich.

Think fast, boyo. "Taxes . . . finance . . . that kind of stuff."

The plug considered the answer. "What do you do in New York?"

Collins tried to approximate a sheepish grin. "I was visiting when the invasion came."

"Visiting who?"

Christ. "Friends."

He watched the Heinrich considering that. "Where do you live?"

"With my friends."

"Where?"

"Eighty-sixth street. Near Broadway."

Heinrich nodded. "Where do you work?"

He was in a bind. If he gave him a phony firm, it could be checked. If he said he was trying to get out, the lump in front of him would figure he's got someone worth hauling in. Still, the second was an infinitely sounder choice.

"I free-lance. Look here, I really have an . . ."

The big plug of beef put the card in his pocket. "Come with me." He pointed to a car parked down the block.

"But look . . ."

The plug put up his hand in the manner of a traffic cop stopping a frantic driver. "You are from Cleveland. The Reich has bombed Cleveland."

He had his arm in Collins's arm and was leading him down the street.

"What's that got to do with anything?"

"You may have information."

"Information, what information?" Collins could hear the anger in his own tone.

The plug said nothing till they reached the car. He opened the door and gestured for Collins to get in. Then he walked around and got in beside him. He looked at Collins as he took out a pad. "Cleveland is a military target. I take you to Gestapo headquarters, perhaps they have some questions for you." Collins started to protest, but the plug had already turned on the ignition, and moments later they were moving down Fifth Avenue away from the Stanhope.

3:10 P.M.

Something made Sylvie look toward the entrance to the Stanhope bar. The door opened momentarily as a patron entered, and she clearly saw a bevy of officers, Wehrmacht officers. She

312

got up carefully, and, putting her hands inside the black muff, walked purposefully across the darkened room. Opening the door, she stepped into the lobby. There was a large group of Wehrmacht officers flanked by Gestapo types. She stepped forward and directly into the path of one of them. He wore a uniform. It was Abetz.

She felt her hands inside the muff clench the sheaf of notes, saw his surprised expression turn to one of recognition. Now he was smiling.

"Ah, the lovely Miss Lamont."

He reached for her hand, and now as she disengaged it from the muff the despicable little man brought his dry lips to it.

He looked up at her. "So you have an afternoon schnapps, hey?"

His attempt at charm was disgusting.

"Yes," Sylvie said. She was aware that her voice sounded shrill. "What is all this fuss?"

An ironic little smile played on Abetz's mouth. "But, can you not see? Rommel has arrived."

She followed the direction of his stubby finger and saw Rommel.

"Has he been away?" Sylvie asked. How bold she had become.

Abtz didn't answer right away. "He has been to Berlin, reporting to the Führer."

"Will he be here long?"

There was a peculiar look in Abetz's eyes. "Perhaps. I do not know. But then you can ask him yourself. He will be at the Bundist rally in Madison Square Garden tonight, and you will meet him at the St. Regis dinner. Has Patrick not told you?"

Sylvie put on her absentminded style. "Of course. I'm just distracted. I have a friend who's been ill. She promised to meet me this afternoon, but I fear she's not coming. I must go."

Abetz took her hand. *"Enchanté,"* he said in clumsy French. "May I also compliment you on your charming dress and bonnet. The color is so striking. How do you call it?"

"Cherry red," Sylvie said, feeling his sweaty palm.

"It is so beautiful," Abetz said. "Until tonight."

"I look forward to it," Sylvie said. She turned and walked back into the bar.

Quickly she scooped up her coat and, draping it over her shoulders, prepared to leave. Robert must not come here.

He would see immediately that . . . Someone tugged at her elbow and she whirled around.

It was the waiter. "Your bill, madam." He was an older man with sad eyes. He looked a bit like Meister.

"Of course," Sylvie said. She reached into her purse and took out a five, gave it to the waiter, then quickly walked out.

She came through the lobby now, disregarding the commotion, and quickly pushed her way out into the street.

From his vantage point, Abetz watched her. A beautiful woman. She dressed so impeccably. A woman of breeding. But who is she? One always feels with her that she is a frightened bird. Something in her is suffocating. But what? In that moment Abetz had an insight. She had a rendezvous. A woman does not dress that way to meet a sick friend. He had a feel for these things. So perhaps she is unfaithful to Kelly. It did not mean a great deal, but perhaps sometime it would. Information, Abetz knew, was the most precious commodity one could have in the game he played. One could never have too much information.

3:25 P.M.

The plug had stopped their car to confer with another auxiliary policeman. The way the plug scraped and bowed indicated this was a superior. The plug kept pointing back at Collins. Finally, they approached Collins, who kept his hand inside his jacket.

"Captain Holtzer says they are too busy at Gestapo headquarters today," the plug announced.

Collins let out a breath.

Captain Holtzer beckoned for Collins to get out of the car. He was smoking a kraut cigarette. He had a lipless mouth and thin eyebrows. He probably worked in a hardware store, Collins thought, before being elevated to his position of prominence in Nazi New York.

"Your card, Mr. Jackson, it is stamped for January 1. How did you get it so quickly?"

Collins saw the trap immediately. "I went to Gestapo headquarters. I knew some kind of identification would be necessary."

"Then," the captain said, "there will be a matching card in Gestapo headquarters."

"Of course," Collins replied.

"I shall forward this information to Gestapo headquarters. You may be called in for questioning."

He handed the now useless card back to Collins. The first thing the Gestapo would do would be to check to see if it had really been issued.

"Can I go?" Collins asked.

The captain gestured with his hand.

Collins had just turned when he heard the captain's question. "What is the name of your law firm. Mr. Jackson?"

Collins turned toward the Bundist functionary. "Smith, Frazier, and Fruchter," he said.

5:18 P.M.

Leila had waited at the desk while the manager called up to General Beck's suite, and now she knocked on the door. His valet opened the door instantly and ushered her into the living room of the suite at the Sherry Netherland. The sea blue curtain had been drawn, and Leila could see the rain beating against the window panes. The suite was lit so that the easy chairs, light blue and soft, were clearly visible. General Beck, however, sat in a rocker in relative darkness.

"Please, Miss Brophy. Be seated. Oster, bring us some sherry. And take off your coat. You'll be warm."

As Oster helped her with her coat and served the sherry, she noted that, without cardboard, even expensive shoes were no help against the rain.

"To your successful opening last night," Beck said, and held up his glass. In the light the sherry danced like sheets of fire.

She drank. Drank more than she intended and felt the alcohol warm her. Beck didn't miss it.

"Oster, give Miss Brophy more sherry."

Oster filled her glass and set the bottle with its crossed-line symmetry down on a coffee table that rested between them.

She looked into the half light and saw only part of his face. The crown of hair was not visible.

They look like swords, she thought, those lines on the bottle. She sipped the sherry, wondering how to begin, where . . . she felt like a strolling player waiting to perform a monologue yet to be written.

"And so," General Beck interjected, "why do I have the honor of so beautiful a companion? Not that I mind. I know you have come to accept my invitation to go riding. Well I am afraid I am not quite up to that yet."

She felt herself go back in time to the moment when she read the final monologue from *Romeo and Juliet* in front of her high school class. She had rehearsed it so often she could no longer remember the words. Then she was in front of the class and there was nothing to do but speak the lines.

"I came," she began, "because after Friedrich and I had that nightcap with you, he told me that you were opposed to Hitler. Well I am also, and I would like to do something about it."

There, it was out. She ducked into the sherry.

315

Beck sat in silent darkness. "Well, I may be opposed, but I don't know that . . ."

"My name isn't Fay Brophy, it's Leila Fox. I am Jewish."

There was the audible sound of the rocker as Beck shifted his weight. He stood up and walked to the window and watched the driving rain. He turned.

"You came on your own or . . ."

"No one sent me."

She watched as he turned away and his fingers tapped on the pane. He was wearing a robe over a tie and shirt. He must still be very weak, she thought.

He was facing her again. Standing directly over her. "You know to oppose Hitler is one thing, but to do something another."

"I want to do something," she said very distinctly.

"What could you do?"

"I was hoping you would tell me."

Beck went back to his chair. "Do you know what could happen to you?"

"Yes."

"Do you really?"

She drank the sherry down and now held the empty glass in front of her as if it were a weapon. "Last night, I watched gangsters club Klaus Meineke. They shot his driver and terrorized a Jewish family. They beat a rabbi. They took money. I won't hide from it anymore."

She stopped. She was out of breath . . . out of words.

She heard Beck's voice. "I know. I have a report on it. Meineke is a friend." He paused. "I know also that you are Leila Fox. I knew it weeks ago. You are a very good actress. It is a talent we can use. Does Friedrich know you are here?"

"No."

"If you are to work for me, then he can't know. Not until I say it is all right. Do you understand?"

"Yes."

"Can you do it?"

"Yes."

"Good. I want to use you as a courier. Tonight."

They sat in the elegant suite of the Sherry Netherland and listened to the rain beating against the window panes. It snapped and pelted ever harder. But it was no match for the beat of her heart.

Outside, the rain came down in hard lines. Inside the beanery, with its faded yellow chrome tabletops and harsh light, the smell of greasy lard and rancid food hung over the men hunched down drinking the cheap coffee substitute the diner served. Collins and Kresky sat in a booth near the back. It was a diner favored by drivers and working men. They would mostly meet there and use the safe house only on rare occasions so as not to draw suspicion.

Kresky stirred his rotgut brew and looked into it. He was clearly edgy and tense. The Ragosky thing is still with him, Collins thought.

Kresky spoke out of the side of his mouth in short, clipped phrases.

"I got the word today. The camp . . . in Hackensack. It's not far from being ready."

Collins dragged on his nail. "For what?"

"I don't know. I could guess."

"You think Heinrich is ready to swoop?"

Kresky nodded.

"How soon will the camp be ready?"

"A month."

Collins put the chipped cup to his lips and tasted the bitter swill on his tongue. "Nazi New York. Give me the Black and Tans anytime."

Kresky tasted some of the poison in his cup. Now he looked back up at Collins. "You let Jake's kid go."

Collins could see the bottled-up anger in Kresky. You hate yourself, don't you? That's what happens when you have to execute friends. He should have known Kresky would hear about Collins's letting Sheldon Ragosky go. They were all Kresky's people at the execution.

"You let him go."

"Yeah, I let him go. There was no point in killing him."

Kresky looked incredulous. "Point! The Gestapo was keeping him under wraps. He'll run back to them."

"No, he won't."

"You're playing a hunch, Collins, and that's not good enough."

Of course he's right. I did it on impulse. Once I wouldn't have.

"Where did the kid go?"

"I told him to head upstate."

"He'll never make it. And once he's caught, they'll stick him, and he'll squeal."

Kresky was right. Collins had taken a hell of a chance. He

317

tried to turn away from it. "He doesn't know who I am. Ragosky had already fingered you. We haven't lost anything."

"That's not the point. You're risking the safety of my men. It's that rich bitch, Collins. She's got you dreaming. Heinrich is shooting hostages in Central Park."

Collins fought the urge to grab Kresky's torn peacoat and pull him over the table. "I popped those five Heinrichs in the street, and I'm running the operation here. I'll pop you, too, if you get out of line."

Kresky showed a bitter smile. "Will ya?"

"Try me."

Kresky stuck a cigar in his mouth and chewed on it. "How about Kelly? Would you pop him?"

"If I have to. Look, we don't need another execution. We need a rising."

"Like in the Dublin post office in 1916?"

"No," Collins said, "we don't need any more martyrs."

Kresky's eyes narrowed. "So let's find ourselves a fortress and do it. Hold it to the last man."

Collins swallowed some coffee. "I'd have to take it to Donovan."

"The hell with Donovan. His constituency is Franklin Roosevelt. Donovan's not on the front lines. He didn't see twenty-five men machine gunned. We pick a spot and do it."

"The odds are a half million to one against."

Kresky's eyes were like storm clouds. "Sure, but you're thinking like Donovan and Roosevelt. Paper generals. They look on the map and see Heinrich's divisions here and Heinrich's battalion there. Heinrich is all around us, but we're on an island. Cut the island off from the mainland, and Heinrich can't get his troops here. Kill off the Governors Island ferry and Heinrich doesn't have more than five thousand troops in New York City."

Collins put down his coffee. Kresky was right. "But there are huge steel bridges that bring the whole world into Manhattan. And tunnels."

"Blow the bridges outside the city . . . the ones that connect to access roads. Blow the Pulaski Skyway, the Hackensack and Passaic bridges.

Something began to perk in Collins. "We still need a rising. It has to be just the right spot. And I'd want a diversion . . . like a parachute drop. Just enough men to spook Heinrich. Make him think there's an invasion."

Kresky was silent. There was something in his eyes. As if Collins didn't understand. He tapped his heart. "You don't need Orson Welles's tricks. You just have to get inside the people."

Collins let his butt go out in the coffee. "I'm not sure what's inside the people except maybe fear. The Wehrmacht is steel."

"So are the steel workers."

"Heinrich marched down Fifth Avenue and no one took a shot at them. I still want a parachute drop."

Kresky's eyes closed down. "Then find Donovan . . . fast."

"I'll have to go into the woods for that."

"Do it. I'll mind the store."

"I need a new identity card. I got hauled in by an auxiliary policeman today. Spot check. It'll go right to Gestapo headquarters."

Kresky frowned. "The Gestapo folded up my printing operation this morning. That's why I sent word."

"How?"

"They're not amateurs, Collins. They have a wire to a lot of finks. Like the Ragosky kid." He rubbed the rough stubble of his beard. "I'm going up to the Heights in a little while to see a guy about a new shop. It'll take a week. What do you want to do?"

Collins saw the edge in Kresky's eyes. "I'm not waiting."

"When will you go?"

"Tomorrow or the next day. But you do nothing until I come back."

Kresky wiped his mouth. "Just make sure you come back."

Kresky lit his cigar and Collins turned to the window. It was raining madly. Like pitchforks in hell.

5:41 P.M.

Collins walked in the rain. It was hard times.

He felt the rain on his back and crawling up into his shoes. A rising. Could it really be pulled off? When Paddy Pearse did it in Dublin in 1916, it was symbolic. Pearse and his men were prepared to be martyrs. From it came the seeds of the IRA resistance to the Brits. But that took years. Donovan wouldn't buy any martyrs. He wanted a winner, and so did Collins. Hell, we outnumber the Heinrichs. They have half a million trained killers. But we have eight million people. How many can you kill before your ammo runs out? The Luftwaffe airfields would have to be burned. You didn't just need the Dublin post office. You needed the whole city to rise. And what if the Japs won the battle off the West Coast? What would that do to the heart of the people in New York? What were the words to the song? "We'll take Manhattan . . . the Bronx and Staten Island, too." You need Brooklyn and Queens. And you'd need every neighborhood in Manhattan. Manhattan was the key. From the piers up to

Washington Heights. It was a huge crap roll. If the Americans won on the West Coast, the city could flash. Like long-stored sticks of dynamite. He still liked the parachute drop. Maybe off the coast of New Jersey. Something had to be done. Hackensack was almost ready. The city was bleeding to death. He couldn't wait for new papers to see Donovan. Something had to be done now before Heinrich crushed the people. That's what he would sell Donovan. In the spring there was the advantage of surprise. In one sense he agreed with Kresky. Fighting a war of attrition wouldn't do it. If they waited for the steamy summer, Heinrich would have nailed everything down. Heydrich had shipped out the working force and the young men in England. Give Abetz time and he'll do the same thing.

He saw the subway stop and checked his watch. There was enough time to make it back to the safe house on Twenty-third Street and use the wireless. Send a message to Donovan. Collins was coming to the Maryland countryside tomorrow. He heard Kresky's defiant words as he ducked down the stairs. "Blow the Pulaski Skyway, the Hackensack and Passaic bridges. Everything will back up like a toilet."

6:24 P.M.

Dyckman Street was Kresky's stop, but he remained seated as the subway car opened. He always rode a stop beyond. The Gestapo had picked off too many guys at subway stops. He would walk back from 207th Street. He gnawed his lip. He hadn't been right since he found out Collins had let Shelly Ragosky go. Collins had gotten soft. The dame had gotten inside him. The way a worm does an apple. He still looked good from the outside, but he had turned. There was more to being a revolutionary than using your gun. You needed to be sharp like a razor. And hungry. A woman takes that edge away. You didn't need tricks. You needed to bring the guts of the city out. There's enough love of freedom inside the people to drown Heinrich. Somebody just has to show them the way. Maybe you'd never get out, but you set an example. Shooting hostages in Central Park was quick. It chilled people. What was needed was a fortress. A place you could hold out in for a few days. If you could do that, the people wouldn't stand by and slink back home. New York was a city in which war was fought every day. A city where workers, pickpockets, criminals, radicals, anarchists, Communists walked side by side. A vat full of ethnics. All claiming their right to freedom each day they walked on the turf of New York. It's our island. Just let somebody show them what kind of fight can be made and they'll come out in force. They will. He felt it to the deepest part of him.

The train pulled into 207th Street, and Kresky came back from his vision. He had to see a man named Williams on St. Nicholas Avenue. Lepentier said Williams did work like an "artiste." Kresky smiled. He never smiled anymore. Not when you had to kill your friends for being informers. He remembered Jake Ragosky's face . . . his eyes. "I never asked for favors . . . not for myself . . . but Shelly." Jake's eyes had gotten wet, and Kresky to stop his own tears had aimed the gun. "No more Jake." He bit his lip. Collins had let the kid go. Damnit. If he could kill Jake, then how could Collins get off with letting the kid go? Not the kid . . . Shelly. Kresky had held Shelly on his knee. Enough.

He stepped out of the train into the raw air and saw the driving rain. He saw the subway repair yard in front of him, saw the layover tracks and the trains waiting to be repaired. It was enormous. He knew it ran for blocks and blocks. And just beyond it, forming a defense in the rear, was the Harlem River. He felt something bubble inside him. Oh God, this was it. It had to be. The Dublin post office. Fifty men could fortify and hold it. He peered out. The yard had a bricked building running all the way along Tenth Avenue. And there was a wire fence. If there was one in the front, at the main entrance . . . He turned and made for the stairs. He went down quickly . . . too quickly. He hit Tenth Avenue and slowed down. Relax, get hold of yourself. Walk around the whole place and then we'll see. We'll see. Maybe, just maybe.

6:30 P.M.

Collins waited on the platform. It was like a spy movie. Since Beck had been shot, little information had been passed to Collins. Names of businesses, collaborators, speculation about a German invasion of the Midwest in the spring. Beck had even been off on the bombing of Detroit. He said not until April. Heinrich had beaten him to it by a few days. He better have something hot for Collins tonight. The trip to Donovan in the Maryland country was justified if he had hard information, not just a wild plan about blowing up New York. And Collins had no good identification. If he went to Washington by train or by car, he would be stopped, papers would have to be shown. It was very dicey. Damn it. He had let Kresky push him.

The light was subdued and the platform crowded with men. Workers. Nobody looked right or left. Collins felt his fist ball up. Be patient, laddie. Be patient. He saw the lights of the train

321

and the people inching forward. For some reason he thought of Sylvie. He felt uneasy. What was it? He would see her tomorrow. He pictured her face. He loved her. She was an innocent. She had been mistress to a lot of Kelly types, but she belonged to Collins. Still, something felt wrong. His hand went into his pocket and felt the gun. Then the train came roaring into the station.

6:35 P.M.

Sylvie had spent the afternoon walking around until the rain began to fall and then wandered into a movie. It was some trivial comedy with nobody she could recognize. Well, there was Don Ameche, whom she couldn't stand. Not meeting Robert had evoked pain in her. She cared. God, when was the last time she cared about anything, much less a man? Even to see him for a few minutes would have been so wonderful. She pictured the rumpled brown hair, the hard-soft eyes, the tight mouth relaxing. She felt something. God, she was wet. Wet for the touch of him, for the feel of him inside her. She felt a smile coming to her mouth. This lithe, quick Irishman who had come for her in the night and liberated her from the awful, numbing void she lived in. God, how she wanted him now. She felt the packet of papers in her muff and her hand closed around it. What was she doing here watching some boring, meaningless movie? There was more information to be copied. Patrick wouldn't be back until eight. Tomorrow she would go to the newsstand and leave word again, and this time the meeting would be in some innocuous place. She got up and made her way past other patrons. She stepped on a man's foot and heard an exclamation. Once she would have stopped and apologized profusely. Now, she never looked back.

7:20 P.M.

Kelly sat in the back of his car and watched the rain pouring down on the city. His mother would always say that a hard rain meant there was a valley of tears somewhere. A hard rain meant bad news. He smiled. She was a decent woman who had too many children and was broken and worn from it. But she gave all the children as much as she could. Kelly, being the fifth, had come along too late to get much. His values had come from his father. Moral values that corresponded to whiskey and women, the only things that mattered to Joseph Kelly. Take as much as you can get, as long as you can handle it. But there had been more to life than that, Patrick Kelly learned. The rest of his formal education came in the streets and then in business. His father had also been right about that. "It's always you against the other guy, one on one. Beat him, Paddy, and you'll own him." And that always became the measure of himself. Beat the man, lay the woman. He kept that law, that code in front of himself as he fought his way to the top. As a young blood, he had been surprised at how deals were really struck. Everybody was bent. Everybody could be bought. Sure, Frank Costello would make a deal. New York under the Reich would be just as lucrative as before. And if he didn't make a deal, Vito Genovese would kill him.

The car turned onto Park Avenue. He was close, very close. The crown of regency was almost in his hand. If Joseph Kelly could only see his son now. I have it. A preinaugural convocation at St. Patrick's, the children all dressed in white. The cardinal there to give him his blessing. He felt a tremor within him and checked his watch. Time for a drink, a shower . . . and Sylvie. He needed to get laid. He leaned back. How many men fifty-six years old had the erections Patrick Kelly did?

The rain cascaded down in angry, slashing lines. Beating against his car as if some angry God of the heavens knew the malevolence that had been hatched down at the Princeton Club.

7:27 P.M.

Leila had raced back to the theater in a cab she had somehow gotten to before an elderly matron. The woman had given her a dirty look as they came together at the corner of Fifth and Sixty-second. But Leila had elbowed past her and into the car. She carried a newspaper with her. Inside it was an envelope that would be passed to someone at Bruno's Chophouse tonight some time after eleven o'clock. It had occurred to Leila that the meeting was not far from the Garden rally, and Beck had nodded. "The Gestapo will be about. Be careful. We are being watched very closely by Abetz. When your play ends, dress quickly and go. He will be seated in the bar. He will be wearing a trenchcoat and hat and will have the end seat. Approach him as if you are expecting him to buy you a drink. He will have a volume of Shakespeare. If the book is not there, it is the wrong man. Then say to him, 'Lucky Strikes are really better than Chesterfields.' He will say, 'Try my brand.' Put the newspaper you are carrying down and make whatever small conversation comes up. Leave separately in a few minutes."

The cab scooted past a policeman and next to him a reservist from the Bundists. She felt a little chill. They came into the theater district, and the cab slowed down in traffic. She sat there

323

waiting and then, feeling the newspaper under her arm, could no longer wait. She told the cab driver to pull over and jumped out. She hurried through the dinner crowds, fifth columnists and fascist sympathizers. That's who went to the theater now. She ran in the rain, feeling somehow free and alive. She was doing something. It was going to be like an entrance to a play tonight. As she ran, she wondered why Beck didn't want to tell Friedrich. She should tell him. She had compromised him enough. She ran under the raindrops and then into the stage door of the New Amsterdam and was waved in by Pops Warner. Inside she saw some of the extras gathered around the bulletin board. She saw the notice and read it. The cast of *Hamlet* had been ordered to Washington, tonight. A matinee was to be given at the Ford Theater. They were to be at Grand Central Station before curfew.

7:29 P.M.

His briefcase wasn't there, but Sylvie felt sure that in his desk there must be other documents. She had rummaged through the drawers and found a great deal of correspondence from business people asking Patrick to use his influence with the Germans for one deal or the other. There were also quite a few files relating to Patrick's business interests. A trucking company that had been hired by the Germans to transport food supplies from New York to Philadelphia and Boston. There was also a letter and a contract confirming that Patrick's whiskey distributing company in Boston would supply the Reich with scotch, bourbon, brandy, and other hard liquors. There must be something else here. She turned and looked about. She had only put on the desk lamp. How furtive it all seemed. The curtains were drawn and much of the room was bathed in darkness. She found herself gazing at the large portrait on the wall. It was hidden from the light, but Sylvie knew it well. It was an original painting of the Harvard rowing team on the river near Boston. Joseph Kelly, Patrick's eldest son, had been a member of the Harvard rowing team. Then she realized . . . Patrick's safe . . . of course. She knew where he kept the combination . . . she heard something at the same time she heard his voice.

"Well, what a nice surprise."

He was standing in the darkness wearing his dark overcoat with velvet lapels. She saw his hat as he twirled it in his hands.

"Patrick, you gave me a scare."

She had to think of something.

"I was out of cash. St. Stephen's needs a donation and I

thought you might have some on hand in the desk. How foolish of me, of course it's in the safe.''

He came into the room and dropped his hat on the desk. "How much do you need?''

"A thousand dollars.'' She knew it had to sound important.

"That's a lot of scallions.''

"Patrick, I would replace it in the morning with a check drawn from my account. Father Mulcahy called before. They are struggling, Patrick. The city is occupied, you know.''

"That's true,'' he conceded. "How about you? Are you occupied?''

He had that roguish twinkle in his eye, and Sylvie knew what it meant. As he reached for her, she froze. His hands were on her waist. "I'm not ungenerous,'' he said, smiling. "But you, Sylvie, are you generous?''

He had pulled her close, and his hand moved from her waist to her breast. She could do nothing. His boldness had mesmerized her.

While he was this way, she knew there was no dealing with him, only submitting. His hand roamed the contours of her body. Down her buttocks, up her thigh. She felt herself stiffen. He was crude. She had such contempt for him.

"Give us a kiss,'' he said, and bent toward her, emitting a strong odor of cigar breath. Then his lips were on her mouth.

It was the taste of his mouth, the repellent mixture of whiskey and cigars, that galvanized her. Made the thought clearly coalesce in her mind. This was for him, all for him. It had always been that way when he wanted something from her. As if he owned her. So many times in the past she had wanted to refuse him but had feared his disapproval. It had been that way with the others she belonged to. They knew better . . . were better. But they weren't . . . he wasn't.

Kelly felt the pounding in his head. He was like a high school kid fighting for his first piece, and it was an immense feeling. He felt her stiffen. Well, he had met that before from her. She wanted it. Women always wanted it. And how he loved to make them feel his domination . . . make them whimper with desire. Over and over his father had reminded him, "A stiff prick, that's the only thing they really want.''

"Take off your clothes,'' he said in a choked voice, and she heard the distinct sound of the zipper of his pants. She knew if she let him, he would give her anything she wanted later. She could continue spying on him. No, the insistent message came back. He is violating you. What he is taking is yours and Robert's. It's degrading. No, she would not permit that. Only she

325

could degrade herself, by giving in. And she wasn't afraid anymore.

His pants had fallen to his ankles. Suddenly she saw how
ridiculous he looked. She saw his inflamed face and was amazed
that she could have let him buy her and use her all these years.
She looked at him now with clear eyes. Finally. She had always
been better than this. And she had been given another chance.

"Patrick, you'll catch a terrible cold. Put your clothes on."

He heard the resonance in her voice along with the mocking
disdain of him. She was not only denying him, she was stronger
than he was. He saw the feeling in her eyes and knew in that
moment her will was greater than his.

He also knew in that moment there was another man. That
was what gave her the courage to deny him. All those headaches,
the excuses. Someone else had been in her pants. She couldn't
deny him except for that.

He slapped her as he spoke. "You little whore."

She stood resolutely in front of him, the same undeniable look
of freedom in her eyes, now tinged with contempt. "Patrick, do
put your pants on."

He heard the door slam, and only then did he stoop to retrieve
the striped gray pants that had fallen in a heap around his ankles.

Chapter 33

March 28, 1942
10:32 P.M.

Leila heard the applause and somehow forced herself to stay
for the curtain calls. Always that damn courtesy with Gielgud,
and then he kissed her hand. She heard bravo, bravo, and spotted the rotund, mustached man who had been there the previous
two nights. He came down the center aisle throwing white carnations. He was bald and waddled like a chorus girl. All kinds
of fascists were in vogue these days. He was standing at the
apron now showering the stage with the carnations. When would
the curtain come down? But there was only more applause, more
bows. She wanted to dash from the stage, but that would draw
attention to her. So she waited while the faggy fascist and the

rest of fascist New York cheered them and cheered themselves. The privileged class in this new society. Filled with the smugness of power and the sure knowledge that they were safe for having chosen the right side. She hated them, and she hated herself for being there. It went on for another ten minutes and then finally, mercifully, the curtain came down.

10:47 P.M.

Collins sat at the bar drinking his scotch and reading his volume of Shakespeare. To his rear, fascists and their clones ate veal and lamb, potatoes smothered in sauce, or dumplings. He was in the lair of the fascists, but this time it made more sense. If you were out this late at night, it was safer among the cozy collaborators. They ate and drank well, went to bed, and knew they would have coffee and eggs in the morning.

He did a careful turn and looked around Bruno's restaurant as if he were expecting someone. The place was dark wood and elaborate glass windows with harsh lights completing the baroque effect. It was not quite pub, not class, not theater. It was a little bit of each. The creatures in the room completed the rococo effect. Fat, fleshy men, filling their mouths with shanks of veal and lots of wine. Thin, hawkish women, preening, whispering, all laughing, acquisitive, calling too loudly, flashing money. Laughing for all the world like it would never end. He saw a group of dandies enter. He could almost smell their cologne from his seat. Leading them was a fat goose carrying white carnations, which he threw on the maître d' and just about anybody else in sight.

He buried himself in the thick volume, though it took minutes before he could read a line. Then he found himself among the pages of *Julius Caesar* and idly thumbed it. He lost himself amidst conspiracy, murder, and now on the plains of Philippi, Brutus confronting Cassius. He read the lines he had always treasured. "There comes a tide in the affairs of men, which taken at the flood, leads on to . . ." He heard someone. It was a woman, and she was addressing him. She had placed a pack of Luckies on the bar and said, "Lucky Strikes are really better than Chesterfields."

He turned then and saw her. She was as beautiful as any young girl he had ever met. She had greenish—no hazel—eyes, and a perfect mouth. To complete the couplet he had to say "Try my brand." But for the moment he could say nothing. They stared raptly at one another. He with his rumpled brown hair, intense eyes, and a cigarette dangling loosely from his mouth. She with full, blackish hair, throbbing eyes, and moist lips. They were

327

riveted by one another, and for the moment there were no codes, just a language old as the world.

He finally managed to push his pack of Chesterfields toward her. "Try my brand. Can I buy you a drink?"

"Sure," she said in a husky voice. "What are you drinking?"

"Scotch. Johnnie Walker."

"Okay."

She saw his eyes devouring her and wanted to stay the object of his attention. But she was also trying to figure out how to give him the envelope. She laid the newspaper on the bar as he signaled the bartender and called, "Two more." She noted the thick volume lying before him and saw it was a Shakespeare collection that was open to *Julius Caesar*. He was drumming his fingers on the bar and Leila saw the tension run through him. It was in his body, his fingers, in his face.

The drinks came, and Collins moved one glass over to the girl. She had put the paper on the table with its headline about the Detroit bombing. He looked at it as if curious, then slid the paper over and began reading the folded-over fascist tabloid. He did this for about thirty seconds, then looked up and around to see if he was being watched. It was a quick, seemingly casual look, but one that encompassed the bar and the dining room. Heinrich wasn't likely to be here tonight, but that didn't make him any less cautious. He glanced at the paper again and brought it a little closer.

She had watched him during the whole time and could not help but admire his performance. This wasn't the first time. He said very casually, "You ready to smoke that thing?"

Leila realized the cigarette was in her mouth unlit, and blushing a little, she nodded.

"I used to smoke Luckies a long time ago," he chimed in as he lit a match and held it for her. "But Chesterfields got more of a kick."

He blew out the match and continuing his banter said, "Here's to it." He clinked her glass and they both drank.

Collins had his hand on the newspaper and switched it with the volume, which he slid in front of Leila. The newspaper had now been transferred to his side of the bar next to his hat.

Intent on the transaction, neither saw the young newsboy, hat pulled over his eyes, who slipped into the bar and, flashing the headline to the maître d', quickly won entrance to Bruno's. He moved wraithlike past the tables, startling the diners by flashing the same headline. There was an immediate effect. Men began handing the boy coins and reaching for the paper. The boy was dressed in a black jacket, too thin for the winter, and knickers torn at the knees. As more and more of the diners purchased the early edition of the *Daily Patrician*, there were excited cries and finally applause. A thick man jumped from his bar stool, went to the boy, grabbed at a paper and, upon reading it, shot a fist into the air.

There was a babble of noise, and both Leila and Collins turned in the direction of the dining room. The word "Cleveland" drifted back to them. Then abruptly the fat, balding man was up on his table scattering glasses, showering white carnations on fellow diners. "We bombed Cleveland," he cried, doing a kind of shimmy on the table. "Cleveland, Cleveland." Like many overweight people, he had a certain kind of fleshy gracefulness to his improvised dance. As he moved, he dispensed white carnations among the approving audience.

"It's him," Leila said.

Not taking his eyes off the man, Collins said angrily, "Who?"

"The one from the theater. He kept throwing flowers on stage."

She hadn't meant to offer all that information, but the sight of the disgusting man with his quivering rolls of jelly, toasting the bombing of Cleveland, was overpowering. Now as he danced and cavorted down the aisles, diners were up on their feet applauding. Congratulating each other. A general cry exploded as the crowd chanted, "Cleveland, Cleveland." And the fat queen, head bobbing to music heard only in his head, played prima ballerina.

Men at the bar were yelling and whistling. "It's disgusting," Leila said.

She saw Collins stand up and take the newspaper. He looked as if he wanted to say something. His eyes were bright with emotion. He nodded in the direction of the washrooms. Leila realized she was supposed to leave now.

Collins pushed his way back in the men's room, which was dimly lit and smelled of cigarettes. He found a stall and shut the cubicle door. Opening the paper, he found an envelope taped to the financial page. It was a letter size, not thick. He tore it open and used the lighter he carried in his pocket. At first the letters typed in capital letters were blurred and indistinct. His eyes craved real light. But now he could make it out

THE BAVARIAN WOLF PAINTING WILL BE ON DISPLAY IN WASHINGTON IN APRIL. DATES ARE NOT CLEAR YET. PERHAPS YOU CAN ATTEND THE EXHIBITION. WE ARE TAKING OUT INSURANCE ON THE PAINTING IN CASE OF DAMAGE EN ROUTE. AN OFFICIAL INVITATION WILL BE SENT TO YOU NEXT WEEK.

He read it again, feeling his nerve ends tighten round him. The Bavarian Wolf was Hitler, and he was coming to Washington in a few weeks. Collins attending the exhibition meant a takeout attempt on the Führer. The insurance meant that some kind of assassination plan had been mounted against him. Probably a bomb on Hitler's plane. Beck's next message would have the official arrival date.

He torched the message and envelope. Little pinprick chills danced up and down his back. Hitler was coming. They would have a shot at him, but only one. He now had a full agenda to discuss with Wild Bill Donovan. Wild enough to okay an insurrection and help Beck nail Hitler? We'll see. He had to get out of town on the first train. Before his phony passport was spotted by the Gestapo and put on a list. He remembered the beefy auxiliary policeman. The unexpected always tripped you up.

Leila saw him coming out. He was surprised, but not angry.

Collins slid in next to the girl. She was a novice, he realized. He nodded toward the tables. "Where's Fatty Arbuckle?"

Leila turned toward him. "Choreographing his dance for the invasion of Los Angeles."

He liked that. It was his kind of quip. "You saw him in the theater. You're an actress." Jesus, he was breaking all the rules. "Name?"

She wanted to say Leila, but played it safe. "Fay."

"What play are you in?"

"*Hamlet*. At the New Amsterdam. What do I call you?"

"Tom."

"Like Tom Paine?"

Her hazel eyes danced, and they both laughed.

"Something like that."

"It's your life, isn't it?"

She was quick. He liked that, but he didn't answer. He had to go. His mind flickered to tomorrow. Going through an ID check would be like walking on eggs. Even on an early train. He stood up and saw the girl looking at her watch. She was late for something.

He broke another rule. "Where are you supposed to be?"

"Grand Central Station." She saw his look. She wanted him to know everything about her. "Washington. We're giving a special performance for von Ribbentrop and the diplomats at the Ford Theater . . . where Lincoln was shot. . . ." She stopped. His eyes were blue jade emeralds.

"When do you leave?"

"Less than an hour." She saw in his eyes he was making some decision. And he needed her for it.

"The men who work backstage, they'll be going, too?"

"I don't know. Perhaps."

"I need to go as far as Baltimore with your company. Can you figure out a way to get me on?"

She saw how important it was, and her answer meant she would be with him. "Yes."

The unexpected had come up on the board again. Only this time he had rolled a seven. The girl was a gift. He had to risk it. The Gestapo wouldn't be able to update their checklist before tomorrow at the earliest. This gave him the jump on them. Coming back, he'd be on thin ice. Hell, worry about that later. Go for it, laddie.

He looked at this beautiful gift of a girl. "If something happens, it's not like carrying a message."

"I know. I'll take a chance."

"Once we're on board, I'll stay out of your way," he said.

She wanted to say "don't." Instead she nodded.

He played it back one more time. There was no way to alert Kresky. He'd figure it out. Collins had already radioed Donovan, so he was expected.

He saw her looking at him with those tremulous eyes. "What's the rest of your name?"

She stood up next to him and felt shaky. "Fay Brophy. Yours?"

"Bob Jackson."

Collins picked up his Shakespeare volume and left a tip for the bartender, who was watching them. Their pickup needed a final flourish. He started to whisper to Fay and then felt her arm loop his. "I'd love to share a cab, Bob. It's curfew soon." He winked at the bartender as they made their way out of Bruno's. Behind them the cry of "Cleveland, Clevcland" began to build again.

AMERICAN PANORAMA XII

TIME MAGAZINE

The West Coast And The War
by a Staff Correspondent

March 29, 1942

Despite the prospective Japanese invasion, Los Angeles has become the exiled heart of the free world, as writers, royalty, distinguished leaders, filmmakers, actors, producers, composers, and journalists have come seeking to help the war effort. Among the personages arriving in the past two weeks have been George Bernard Shaw, Lily Pons, Wendell Willkie, John Steinbeck, and Ernest Hemingway. The members of the Group Theater, led by Harold Clurman, arrived after having been smuggled out of New York. Arthur Hays Sulzberger, publisher of *The New York Times*, announced that he had arranged to share his plant on La Brea Avenue with Henry Luce's *Time* magazine.

Not to be outdone, Hollywood's leading men, flexing their movie muscles, donned olive and khaki garb, signing up for tours of duty in the nation's armed forces. Tyrone Power, John Payne, and Robert Preston all enlisted for duty in the marines, while Jimmy Stewart, Gary Cooper, and Robert Taylor volunteered for air force duty. Other Hollywood heroes who enlisted were Clark Gable, Victor Mature, and George Brent. As one veteran Hollywood producer put it, "Pretty soon we are going to have to go to the army, navy, marines, and air force to get the actors we need for our movies." Other stars lent their efforts to bond and war relief drives. Prominent among those have been Judy Garland, Rosalind Russell, Spencer Tracy, Norma Shearer, Janet Gaynor, and, tragically, Carole Lombard. The gifted comedienne was killed returning from a bond rally in Indianapolis when her plane crashed at dawn in the mountains around Las Vegas. Ironically, Miss Lombard and her party saved the lives of three servicemen who were bumped off the plane so that Miss Lombard's party could have seats. The search for the plane and her body was later joined by her grief-stricken husband, Clark Gable.

Two events illuminated the mood of the West Coast and its people, faced as they are with imminent invasion by the Japanese should Hawaii fall. Last week the Joe Louis–Buddy Baer fight originally scheduled for Jersey City was held in San Francisco's Cow Palace, with all proceeds to go to the Army-Navy War Relief Fund. Outweighed by forty-three pounds, facing an opponent with a ten-inch reach advantage, Louis, who had been floored by Baer in their last fight, KO'd Baer in the first round. Asked by a sportswriter after the fight how he would have fared had there been a Nazi boxer in the ring, the Brown Bomber said simply, "I woulda done it faster."

The social gala of the Hollywood season was the benefit program held at the Hollywood Bowl with all proceeds going to the U.S. war relief effort. Although the president did not attend, the roster of guests and entertainers read like a *Who's Who*. Stars of all shapes and sizes were in attendance. From newlyweds George Brent and Ann Sheridan to Errol Flynn,

Humphrey Bogart, Laurence Olivier and Vivien Leigh, Loretta Young, Vice President Henry Wallace, Mickey Rooney and recent bride Ava Gardner, on and on the firmament sparkled with gems. Among the entertainers were Glenn Miller, Benny Goodman, the Dorsey brothers, Judy Garland, Henry Fonda recreating his film role as Abraham Lincoln and reading the Gettysburg Address, Lauritz Melchior, Lily Pons, and Ezio Pinza of the Metropolitan Opera, Bing Crosby, Bob Hope, Abbott and Costello. The master of ceremonies was George Jessel. But with all those glittering, golden names on the program, the highlight of the evening was supplied by a jazz band, Mickey Messer and his Dixieland Five. Messer and his mates were to follow the duet of Eddie Cantor and Al Jolson, just before the scheduled appearance of Fred Astaire and Ginger Rogers dancing "The Continental."

The bowl was swathed in torchlights and the blinding glare of jewelry and the stars who wore them. They had heard the vice president report that the American fleet was holding its own in fighting off the coast of Hawaii. Abruptly, planes were heard. Moments later, Mr. Jessel came out to report that there were rumors that Japanese planes were spotted over Santa Barbara, headed for Santa Monica and possibly Los Angeles. "Anybody," he said, "who wants to leave should do so now." There was silence, and then an incredible thing happened. Nobody moved. Jessel waited for a moment and then, a smile on his lips, said, "Then let us continue." The crowd broke into spontaneous applause. As the stage was prepared for the Astaire-Rogers dance number, Mickey Messer and his Dixieland Five went on as a filler. After playing "Sweet Georgia Brown" and "Tiger Rag," they launched into a number entitled "Johnny Lugansky's Boogie-Woogie," written by Mr. Messer and dedicated to a young man arrested in New York on the day the Nazis marched down Fifth Avenue. The band had gone two minutes into the lively number when planes were heard overhead. It was precisely at the moment that Negro trumpeter Buck Gray was to deliver a trumpet solo. Mr. Gray walked to the mike and, holding up his hand to point upward at what everybody in the bowl knew was above them, said, "I hear 'em . . . fuck 'em." Then, as the audience rose in spontaneous applause, Buck Gray from Pittsburgh, Pennsylvania, ripped loose a trumpet solo tribute to Johnny Lugansky that nobody in the Hollywood Bowl will ever forget. Of that moment Vice President Wallace said later, "We triumphed in our rites of passage."

March 29, 1942

There is a lull. The occupation continues, we await a rescuer in white armor, and no one comes. People live, love, die, kill, escape, swindle, betray, commit suicide. Occupation is woven into the fabric of our lives. Some of it is indelibly American, some of it is symptomatic of war and the conqueror around us. I cannot make sense of it, only report it.

Item: Yankee shortstop Phil Rizzuto has turned up at the Yankee training base in St. Petersburg, Florida, thus ending a two month search for him by the Yankees and the Gestapo. Said the little Scooter, "I was smuggled out via the underground subway."

Item: Army headquarters in St. Louis announced that the Sixth Armored Division activated at Ft. Knox last week will have two divisions of tanks. They will be commanded by Major General Alvan Gillem, a solid career man, and Major General George S. Patton, who, it appears, has been in and out of trouble with high command all his career. His men often refer to him as Flash Gordon or the Green Hornet. It seems he has served with Pershing as a cavalry officer. We don't need cavalry, we need a savior. Let's hope George S. Patton is not a Flash-in-the-pan Gordon.

Item: Two Wehrmacht soldiers went at it fist to fist in Yorkville the other night. It seems that they had been drinking and exchanged pictures of their American brides. Both men became somewhat incensed as it became apparent they married the same woman. Arrested later in the day, Gretchen Schultz, also known as Gretchen Haas, said she loved them both dearly. She also loved their monthly allotments.

Item: A Roseland dancer named Pearl applied at City Hall for a name change. Her last name, of course, is Harbor.

Item: Hollywood producer Glen Adams has announced a film project dealing with the Nazi invasion of New York. Working title: *Black Christmas*.

Item: Eight-year-old Richie Andrusco was arrested by the Gestapo yesterday. It seems he had been making anonymous telephone calls for the past two months saying a bomb would go off in Gestapo headquarters. No one paid much attention until Monday when a Gestapo car exploded down at Centre Street. The next call was traced. Richie is now being held at Centre Street and questioned for information.

The German planes pound Detroit and Cleveland. The Japanese invasion off the West Coast is imminent. Against the advice of key advisors, President Roosevelt has set up headquarters in Palm Springs. Recognizing that the morale of the country is crucial, the commander in chief has chosen to be as near as safety will allow to the fighting with the Japanese. The American navy and the remainder of the British Gibraltar fleet have surrounded the Hawaiian Islands, prepared to meet the invading Japanese expeditionary fleet sailing from Australia. As American and Japanese ships and planes battled daily off the coast of Hawaii, exiled British Prime Minister Winston Churchill summed it up best. "Free civilization as we know it rides on this battle. If the Japanese conquer the West Coast, America will be bombed into submission by the Japanese-German Axis. America dare not lose. It is the last refuge against barbarianism and a world of total night."

Chapter 34

March 29, 1942
10:25 A.M.

Sylvie walked along West Seventy-second Street. She always had the cab drop her on Amsterdam Avenue and then walked the block to the newsstand on Broadway. She had spent the night at Claudette Frazier's apartment. The Fraziers had been in Palm Springs at the time of the invasion, and just before Christmas Claudette had asked Sylvie to oversee the interior decorator who was to redesign the apartment. A key had been left for Sylvie.

She moved in and out among faceless people. Though she had slept little she had no headache. She had no idea where she was going to live. Going back to Patrick was out of the question. She would collect her belongings that afternoon. But first she had to

335

get the information she was carrying in her muff to Robert. The signal would be a white hankie on top of the metal bar over the stacks of the morning's edition of the *Daily Mirror*. She was never to leave the yellow hankie two days in a row. She could hear his voice now. "If we can't meet for any reason, I'll leave the next signal." She looked down and caught a glimpse of her red skirt. My God, she thought, I am wearing the same outfit. When is the last time I did that? She could have put on one of Claudette's dresses. Once she would have.

She crossed toward Broadway and saw the faded green boxlike stand. Usually there were a number of people around it. Now there was no one. She got to the stand and looked at Jimmy, the news dealer with the weatherbeaten face. He was wearing his shapeless gray coat and a derby hat long past its best days. He shook his head. Sylvie looked at her watch. Ten-thirty. She bit her lip. It meant coming back again. She reached into her purse, extracted three cents, and bought the *Patrician*. The headline reported the bombing of Cleveland just as Patrick's notes had said. She stopped and looked around. She wasn't really hungry, but a cup of tea with lots of sugar would go down well. But to get sugar she would have to go downtown. The Mayflower on Central Park West. Patrick would have business breakfasts there. They catered to fascists and German officers. She would kill some time there and then come back. She stepped off the curb and hailed a cab.

Sylvie finished her second cup of tea and put down the cup. Her watch showed five after eleven. She felt better. She looked around the room and was unable to see another woman there. There was a table full of businessmen smoking furiously. At another table, a group of Wehrmacht officers sat having a very late breakfast. New York must be quite a plum assignment, she thought. Something to write home to the frau about.

There was a rush of air, and she turned. The glass doors had opened, and framed in the doorway was a newsboy. Behind him were three others. She recognized the newsboy. It was little Timmy, pointing out the Wehrmacht officers to a boy with a gun. There were other boys with pistols. St. Stephen's boys. None of St. Stephen's boys saw Sylvie. They were intent on the tables where the German officers sat. They began to fire.

She didn't know when she actually heard the bullets, but some fine tuning in her brain brought the sound to her. She heard cries, saw men diving to the floor, and heard dishes breaking. The boys were firing wildly. Suddenly one boy stopped. His gun had jammed. Sylvie saw a waiter crawling on the floor. Only in that moment did she realize she should get down.

One of the boys kicked a table over and covered for his friends as they ran out. As he exited, a German officer gave chase. Sylvie got up, grabbed her coat and muff, and followed him.

She came out of the Mayflower and saw the officer running after the boys as they dashed up Central Park West. She could see Timmy was to the rear. He couldn't run as fast. Now she was in the street waving wildly for a cab. Where? There. One pulled up, and Sylvie yanked desperately at the handle. Inside she pointed uptown. "There are some boys. Catch up to them."

Without knowing where it came from, she had a five in her hand and thrust it in the driver's face. The car started up, and Sylvie rolled down the window. She saw them start to run through the park at Sixty-sixth Street . . . no, that was close to Tavern on the Green. They came running out seconds later as the Wehrmacht officer ran through traffic after them. He was closing on them.

"Hit him," Sylvie commanded.

The driver looked back at her.

"Do it," Sylvie yelled. "I'll give you a hundred dollars. Do it."

The officer ran parallel to the sidewalk but was still in the street and now, as the cab came abreast of him, Sylvie leaned forward and, coming over the driver's shoulder, turned the wheel. The cab bucked, angled right, and hit the officer flush, sending him flying over the sidewalk. Then they were past him, and Sylvie was still yelling.

The boys turned in at Seventy-second Street, and the cabbie drove on as if possessed by this demonic woman in the back seat.

"Cut them off," Sylvie cried.

The cab passed the boys and did a sharp right. She heard the brakes squeal, and the cab stopped. Sylvie stepped out and looked into the faces of the four boys, one of whom had aimed his pistol. It was Eddie Dalton.

"Get in," she said.

Chapter 35

March 29, 1942
11:57 A.M.

The Penn Limited rolled through the Delaware countryside. From the club car Collins could still smell the bacon and eggs that had been served all morning. Bacon, real bacon, for the troupe traveling to Washington to perform *Hamlet*. Back in New York you ate rat.

Fay had gotten him on the train by bantering with the stage hands and introducing Collins as her cousin. Once on the train he had mingled with the company and spent the night amidst stage props stored in the spare luggage compartment. He looked at his watch. Almost noon. They weren't far from Baltimore. Once they got there, Collins would hop it and make for the rendezvous with Bill Donovan. He sat back on two suitcases and lit a fresh butt. Fay had brought him coffee a little while ago. She had guts. A fresh, beautiful lass. He had been right to trust her.

The butt tasted lousy, and he crushed it out. You're edgy. He wanted this over with so he could get back to New York. To Sylvie. Stop it, man. You have to reach Bill Donovan.

He stood up and looked out the window at the frozen ground and the trees now carrying the first burden of leaves. There were all kinds of guerilla bands roaming the countryside, pro- and anti-Nazi. He shook his head. Stop thinking so much. How could he? There were so many balls in the air.

They had gotten the news from boarding passengers when they reached Delaware this morning. Japanese and American ships had engaged each other off the coast of Los Angeles. This was it. If the Japs won, they would invade. America would be caught in a pincer. Hitler on one side, Hirohito on the other. But if we won . . . he caught the identification—"we". . . . then what would Hitler do? He remembered seeing newsreel films of World War I naval battles. Flickering images of guns flashing on and off. A montage of faces, guns firing, the air heavy with smoke. Fires burning, ships sinking. Each day at sunrise the ships would begin firing. Till day's end. If the Japs lost, they'd lose Hawaii also. Roosevelt would attack, and the Japs would be driven back into the Pacific. Then he'd come for the Bavarian Wolf. Hitler knew it also. Damn. It all rode on the next couple of days.

He heard a knock and out came the gun. The door was opening, and Fay Brophy was there, soft and curvy in a green sweater and matching skirt. Long brown hair.

"I heard the conductors talking. We'll be in Baltimore soon."

The gun was back in his pocket, but his hand was still there. "I'll go to the coach car and slip off. Piece of cake," he said, smiling. "Thanks."

The train jumped, and they were thrown together. He felt the shape of her as his hands moved to halt her slide. He quickly let go. He searched for a quip, but it wasn't there. They stood looking at one another.

"You better go," he said.

Five minutes later, Collins had wedged himself into a seat at the far end of the coach. It had perhaps ten people in it. Most of them were men traveling alone. Businessmen or salesmen. Men with permits from the Reich. A couple sat at the far end. The man, short with white hair and a cheap suit, and an anguished expression on his face. The woman, dowdy and plain. They didn't belong. Where were they going?

A thin, sallow-looking man in a brown shapeless suit entered the car. He had a scarf wrapped about his neck. His overcoat and hat were carried in his hand. He came past the couple. Collins saw the little man stand up and reach for the woman's hand. They left the coach car while the sallow faced man took a seat. Now he took off his scarf.

Collins lit a cigarette and tapped a nervous finger against his mouth. The scarf was a signal. Worn for the benefit of the couple. They had gone back to their compartment. They had come into the coach to wait for the man. They were refugees. The man with the scarf was their contact. But why Baltimore? A boat. Over Chesapeake Bay. That had to be it. Their life savings spent on getting out. Collins felt the train slow down. Baltimore? He checked his watch. Not yet. This was just a small depot. A supply stop perhaps. Cut the crap. It was time to move.

He went down the corridor of first-class compartments as the train made its way into the tiny station. Where was Fay? His nerves were jangling like a fire alarm. Then he saw her amidst some of the cast and crew grouped around an open compartment. There was lots of laughter and the air was thick with smoke. See me, he thought. *See me*.

And like an angel of mercy she turned just then. Christ, she was beautiful.

"Hi, got a cigarette?"

She's good, Collins thought. Like she knew me all her life. He lit a butt for her and leaned close. "Whatever this stop is, I'm getting off. Come with me."

She took his arm and they walked back toward the coach as the train came into the small depot. At the far end he looked out the window and saw police and Gestapo standing in the bright sunlight. It was a roust. A refugee roust.

"I'm going in the bathroom," Collins said. "Give me a tap when they get past this car."

He slipped into the tiny cubicle, and Leila stationed herself against it. What was it about him? Electricity went through her every time he spoke. The train stopped.

They came on board, moving with the swift certainty that told you they had been tipped off. One of them pushed past Leila and then stopped.

"Your identity card?"

He was an American, Leila realized, working for the Gestapo. In a sudden moment of insight, she guessed he had been a conductor who had graduated because he became proficient in spotting refugees.

"Your card."

"In my compartment."

"Get it."

He grabbed Leila by the arm and slung her forward. As she was impelled down the aisle, the man behind her, a tall sallow man with a scarf, exited the train.

Collins heard Fay being led away and came out of the bathroom. He moved quickly to the exit door and slid it open in time to see the man with the scarf running along the edge of the tracks. Suddenly there was a shout and a terrible scream.

They were dragging out the little refugee and his wife. Jesus and Mary. The little man was trying to protect her, but his arm was twisted viciously behind his back by a Gestapo agent.

A policeman was in the car. "Your identity cards," the moon-faced cop said. "Everybody sit down. Sit down."

They were pushed back as the cards were collected. Collins handed his over, praying it wasn't on the wireless yet. He had to get off here. Baltimore would be worse. How? Then suddenly Fay was there.

"Darling, what are you doing here?"

The cop looked at her suspiciously as Fay took his arm.

"Officer, he's with us. Stagehand. We're going to Washington to play *Hamlet*. Under orders from the Gestapo. What are you doing here?"

Collins took his cue. "Couldn't find a bathroom."

"C'mon, silly. I'll show you."

The cop looked at them. "Go ahead. Wait a minute. What's your name?"

"Jackson. Robert Jackson."

The moon-faced cop, face embellished in red by years of whiskey, flipped through the cards. He handed back Collins's card. A moment later, as Leila led him toward the private compartments, Collins whispered in her ear, "I'm getting off."

She stopped. "You can't."

"I have to. Just look dreamy and lean all over me."

Abruptly she was Irene Dunne, looking at him with eyes that melted his insides even though he knew it was fake. "They'll arrest you."

"There'll be a car nearby," Collins said. "There has to be."

But what was in her eyes now wasn't a fake, and he knew he had to tell her. Damn, he was getting soft.

"A guy hopped off. He must be a guide. He's over in those woods nearby. He'll help me get a car. I'll get to my meet and be back in Washington tonight. When's the company going back?"

"Matinee lets out at six. We'll catch the eight o'clock."

"I'll be there," he lied.

"No, you won't."

"Then I'll catch the eleven o'clock sleeper from Baltimore."

"I'll be on that train. It comes from Washington."

"No."

"Yes."

The train started to move.

"I'll wait for you."

She had his arm and squeezed tight.

"Okay, okay."

She was kissing his cheek as the train began to pick up speed. Then he jumped.

Collins ran along the track, watching the train recede from view. The image of the couple being hauled off the train leaped in front of him. Who were they? Just people who could no longer live under the swastika. They would be detained somewhere, or worse.

He saw a patch of woods up ahead and cut away from the tracks. The guide he was looking for would be somewhere in the area. Collins's bet was that the man would lay low until the Gestapo and police pulled out. If he guessed wrong, then he was alone in the Maryland countryside, a long way from Bill Donovan.

He entered the woods and was quickly surrounded by thick

trees. He felt a lot safer here than on that bloody train. He moved farther into the grove of oaks. The denseness of the trees was enough to keep out the sun, and he felt the cold air bite into him. He kept going straight ahead, not really knowing why. It was instinct and luck. The guide might have gone in any number of directions. Hell, these woods were as good a guess as any. The trail he followed between the trees had narrowed out. He passed between the rows of trees, knowing that if the guide was there, he might pop Collins at any time.

Up ahead he saw a clearing, and upon approaching it saw the automobile covered over by leaves. It was nestled in the sun. A kind of bucolic painting. He found the gun and quickly transferred it into his overcoat pocket. Ten yards from the car he stopped. It was the getaway car, no question. Careful, Bobbie boy. Taking a deep breath, he stepped forward.

"I'm alone and I need a ride. I'll pay you well. I had to jump the train also. C'mon, let's talk." He took another cautious step. "I'm alone."

There was no response. No sound. He heard a bird chirp and tensed. His father had gotten it right in the back. Suddenly there was a rustling sound, and Collins turned. He saw the sallow-faced man wearing an overcoat. The scarf was gone. His hands were out of his pockets and Collins relaxed. This one was strictly a guide.

"I have to get to a meeting. I need a car."

The man inched forward. "I don't know you."

"I'll pay you well," Collins answered.

The man chewed his lip. "You don't come well recommended."

"Look, if I was Gestapo, you'd be in custody right now."

He saw the man weighing that.

"I want to borrow your car for a few hours. And some instructions."

"How will I get the car back?"

"You'll go part of the way with me and we'll pick a spot to meet later. Then you'll drive me to Baltimore so I can get the late train."

"How late?"

"The last train."

The man shook his head. "That's too late to be out."

"I'll meet you by eight. Then you drop me off."

The man was silent. He gnawed his lip.

"Look, I could pop you right now and take your car."

"Five hundred dollars. Now."

Collins shook his head. "Three now . . . two when you get me into Baltimore."

The man chewed on it, looking intently at the ground.

"All right, I'll get the map from the car."

Collins waited till the man spread it out on the car and then walked over to him. "Who tipped the Gestapo?"

The man shook his head. "Somebody who knew those people. Somebody who wanted their house, their car. The Germans are confiscating property, and whoever turns you in can claim it. When you do this for a while, you know what's happening. I tried to warn them."

They were bloody shrewd bastards, Collins acknowledged. All you have to do is appeal to people's greed.

Collins looked at the map spread out in the dappled sunshine. "Where are we?"

The man pointed to a spot on the map. "Here."

"You pick a drop-off a couple of miles from here. That's where I'll meet you this evening. No questions." He slapped three hundred-dollar bills on top of the map. "Take it," Collins said. "We got a deal."

The man nervously pocketed the money. "It's my car, mister. It's how I make my living. Bring it back."

"I'll be back," Collins said. "Bet on it."

The man pointed again to the map. "Right here is where you'll drop me off. It's just two miles from here."

Collins studied the map, noting the area where he would have to be to meet Donovan. Now he stepped back and looked up, squinting into the sun. "Let's go."

Chapter 36

March 29, 1942
2:01 P.M.

Sylvie had gotten them across town and paid the driver with the expensive wristwatch Patrick had given her. He was in his early forties, wore glasses, and looked hungry. "I don't want to know your name," Sylvie said. "Thank you."

His pinched face seemed to pucker up, and then he took the watch, mumbling, "Thank you. Where do you want to go?"

She paused. She had to get a car and get them out of the city. They were at Eighty-third and Lexington. Then she had an idea.

She spoke quietly to the four boys. Timmy, whom she held by both arms, Eddie Dalton, Francis Morello, and Eugene Felton. "I have to get you out of the city. We'll talk about what happened later. We're going to a movie. You sit inside until I come for you. Do you understand? Do you, Eddie?"

Eddie was the leader, Sylvie could tell that. He was the oldest, a thin child with pockmarks on his face. Scrawny but tough. Eugene was more dreamy looking, he was a follower. He idolized Eddie. Eugene looked like a priest. Thin, ascetic. Francis was heavy and sloppy. His shirt was never tucked in. He had tiny blue eyes and a button nose. And then there was Timmy, sharp faced with sorrowful eyes. Born too old, born alone. St. Stephen's boys. Her responsibility.

She took them into the Trans Lux at Eighty-fifth Street, bought them candy, then went outside to call Meister. He was to bring the car Patrick leased for her. Quickly, no questions. She knew that they had to get an early start. Be out of the city by dark and well on their way to Long Island, to St. Mary's Parish. If all went well she could have them there by five. Please, please hurry, Meister.

Dan Macklin watched the dish in the red velvet dress and hat pace around the lobby and look out periodically. A society swell taking some orphans out for the day. What does she know about the occupation? She sleeps good, eats good, lays good. Buys the kids some caramels and waits around for her boyfriend to come. What the hell is she doing in a newsreel theater anyway? He watched her look out. She had a nice shape. Hell, Danny boy, give it a try.

He slid over to her and smelled her fragrance. Class.

"Can I help you?"

She whirled and he saw how scared she was.

"I'm the manager. You keep looking out."

"Oh," she said, "it's just that I'm expecting a friend."

"Look, I'll buy you a drink. I'll have the usher call when your friend arrives."

She got flustered. "I couldn't do that. He'll be here any minute. . . ."

He took her arm. "No. In my office. I have a little supply there." He winked.

She looked at him coldly. "Please leave me alone."

It was the way she said it. Not nasty, but asserting her class prerogatives over his. I'm above you, she meant. Bitch. She'd wiggle if he stuck it to her. He was aware his face was red. "Well, you can't go in and out this way."

She looked at him. "I'll be gone soon." As she walked away from him, Dan Macklin felt his nails cut into his palm. He'd remember this one.

The boys sat huddled in the theater watching films of Pittsburgh falling and German soldiers posing for the camera. Then suddenly Sylvie was there. "Let's go, boys."

A minute later they climbed into a blue car, three in back and Timmy on Sylvie's lap.

Meister turned to Sylvie. "I'll drive you."

She started to persuade him not to, but then changed her mind. It would look better. They would be stopped, and she would more suit the role if she had a driver. Moments later the blue Hudson moved away, leaving a trail of smoke in its wake.

Dan Macklin had come out to see who was picking up the rich bitch. A lousy chauffeur. She stiffed him just because her chauffeur was coming. Where was she taking those kids in such a hurry? Orphanage kids? Had to be. For some reason he didn't understand, Dan Macklin memorized the license number and wrote it down on a pad back in his office.

3:30 P.M.

The report had come in to Abetz just after lunch. Some children had broken in and started shooting at guests in the Mayflower Hotel. The city was turning ugly very soon. In a climate where vigilantes roam wild, anything could happen. And, of course, Gestapo retribution would be swift. He arched an eyebrow when he noticed that the only fatality had been the Wehrmacht officer killed by the cab. But, of course, the one casualty was perfect. A young lieutenant . . . overzealous . . . courageous. Curfew would be moved up an hour. New roundups were needed. This was a horrible place, this New York. No citizen was safe here.

He pressed the intercom. "Hoppman, I want a search for the cab that killed Lieutenant Brandt. And I want a report on my desk by this afternoon."

Abetz clicked off and reached for a cigarette. He made a small wager with himself that the cabbie had done it on purpose.

4:29 P.M.

They had come over the Fifty-ninth Street Bridge and found their way onto Route 27 which would take them to Long Beach. Sylvie tried to recall what had happened, and it only came to her in bits and pieces. Like flashes from a movie you remember more for individual scenes than for its whole. She had actually made the driver hit the Nazi officer. She saw him flying over the curb. She pushed it away now as she noticed how slowly Meister was driving. The speedometer was at thirty. "Faster," Sylvie said. She saw his hands on the wheel trembling, the lips compressed and white. The poor man. "It's all right," she said, and patted his shoulder.

The boys were pressed in against each other in the backseat. Sylvie turned to them. "Don't be scared. I'm taking you to St. Mary's and you'll stay there for a while. I'll call Father Mulcahy when we get there. Everything will be all right."

She looked at Eddie, then at Eugene and Francis. They looked very pale, although Eddie was trying to put up a brave front. But the sneer wasn't wearing very well.

"They won't take us," Timmy piped up.

Sylvie turned to him. "Of course they will."

He looked up at her, his brown eyes full of emotion. "The other day Sister Grace wouldn't let some boys come in. She said they didn't have enough food."

"That won't happen," Sylvie answered. "I'll pay for your food if necessary."

"What are you going to say?" Eddie Dalton challenged.

"I'll say what has to be said," she answered firmly.

She stared at Eddie, and finally he looked away. She turned back and saw the traffic in front of them. A few trucks and almost no cars. There was no gas to be had. They were passing through a small town. Valley Stream on the Sunrise Highway. She saw some stores and a bus stop with a lot of people waiting. Bundled in coats, red faces with smoke trailing from their mouths and noses.

"I gotta go," Timmy said. "I gotta go bad."

"I'm hungry," Francis chimed in.

Meister looked over at her. The tremors in him seemed now to extend to his entire face. His jaw seemed to be caving in.

"It hurts," Timmy murmured.

She didn't want to stop. She just wanted to get there. "Meister, get off the road."

The car slowed and pulled around a corner and stopped by a store that was adjoined by an empty lot. Sylvie opened the door and Timmy ran out.

"Anyone else?"

Eugene and Francis scrambled out also, leaving Sylvie and Eddie to face one another. She knew he was the one who had thought up their raid. He was not an easy boy. Always angry. He would never know his mother or father, and someone would

346

always pay for that. He looked at her, and she saw his hand go in his jacket pocket and come out with the gun.

"What do we do wid dese?"

5:45 P.M.

Dan Macklin had hoisted a few at the Brau House, and now he leaned against the wall in the back. Kurt, the bartender, always gave him two for the price of one. The Brau House was an old wood tavern in Bundist territory. It smelled of stale malt and echoed with the laughter of winners. Dan Macklin liked that. He had been a loser all his life. Ever since he grew up in the orphanage and realized no one was coming to take him home.

He could heard the loud laughter coming from the bar. Moments ago he had been part of it. He felt queasy in his gut. He hadn't been able to get the rich babe out of his mind. The talk at the bar had been about the shooting at the hotel. Four kids came in and opened fire. Those four orphan kids! The dame who stiffed him was trying to protect them. He had known it as soon as he heard about the shooting. Little bastards. Who did they think they were? When you're an orphan you take what life gives you. Charity. Only the charity stops when you grow up. The rich dame was saving those kids, but she wouldn't give Dan Macklin the time of day. He wouldn't give those kids the time of day either when they grew up.

There was a phone on the wall. He felt the piece of paper in his pocket. The license number of her car was written on it. He knew it by heart. Hell, why should she get away with it? She had never known what it was to live by the rules. And now she was making them up for those little bastards. He laughed. Bastards was right. Well, he had known nothing but rules all his life.

He swayed unsteadily and felt the nausea come to him again. Two for the price of one did that to you. Hell, it wasn't him. It was the booze. He took the paper out of his pocket and reached for the phone. Life was rough, but you had to take your chances. The rich dame should have been nicer to him. He had been a loser all his life. And she had been a winner. Okay, you bitch, now you find out what it's like to lose.

He fumbled with a nickel and dropped it in. The operator came on.

"Get me Gestapo headquarters. The main one."

There was a pause. "Of course, sir."

Moments later a thickly accented voice announced, "Gestapo."

Dan Macklin began to talk.

St. Mary's was at the end of a block, midway between the boardwalk and some one-family houses. The wind from the ocean was fierce, and it made the boys stagger. Sylvie showed them inside the old white building. It faced a lawn that was badly in need of trimming. The place was unmistakably run down. She herded the boys inside and felt the dampness. No heat. A nun with a pale, blotchy face sat at a table. Behind her, Sylvie could see the office.

She approached the nun, who made every attempt to look pleasant but was clearly put off by the intrusion.

"I'm Sylvie Lamont. I'm on the board at St. Stephen's. I want to make arrangements for these four boys, Sister . . ."

The nun looked at her, and for a second Sylvie saw the anger. "Sister Veronica." She realized she had offended the nun.

"Father Mulcahy is a close friend of mine. Is Father Dunne in?"

Sister Veronica smiled perfunctorily. "No, he is ill. Sister Cecilia is in charge."

Sylvie brightened. "Oh, I believe we've met. At the dinner on New Year's. Could you tell her I'm here?"

Sister Veronica didn't answer right away. She had, Sylvie realized, a lifetime of anger hidden behind the placating smile. As the nun walked down the corridor, Sylvie also realized that once such an insight would have been beyond her.

A minute latter the nun returned and beckoned to Sylvie, who left the boys sitting in the corridor.

She walked toward the office wondering whether Meister had thrown the guns in the ocean without being seen. Why she had kept Eddie's she was still not sure.

The office was cold and poorly lit; its walls were badly chipped and cracked. A large crucifix hung over a large slit in the wall. Sister Veronica led her into a small room that appeared to be Father Dunne's office. It was dark and had a desk and chair. There was a heavy, stale odor. Sister Cecilia, a woman with a tired face and deep circles under her eyes, stood up.

"Miss Lamont." She extended her hand. It was cold as death.

"It's awfully cold here. Is there some other place we could sit?"

Sister Cecilia smiled. "Yes, of course. We are used to it. Come, we'll go to the church."

She led Sylvie outside the offices and down the corridor. Sylvie looked at the boys and saw them staring at the steps leading up to the quarters on the second floor. Well, at least it wasn't a Gestapo cell.

The church had eight rows of pews and a singularly large effigy of the crucified Messiah framed against torn black curtains. If anything, Sylvie thought it was colder here, although the light seemed somewhat better. They sat down together in the last row. Sylvie looked into the gray eyes of the nun, saw the redness, the weary, resigned expression. But she was not an unkind woman. And there was no choice but to tell her the truth.

"There are four St. Stephen's boys who must stay with you." She saw the nun trying to comprehend her urgency.

"I'm afraid they are in trouble."

Sister Cecilia's eyes flickered. "Have they disobeyed . . ."

"No, it's more serious then that. Somehow they got hold of guns and tried to use them. . . ."

Sister Cecilia nodded. "I see. And this trouble, can it be rectified?"

"No. They shot at some German officers. No one was hit, but I fear for them in the city. There will be a search. I think they would be better off here."

Sister Cecilia considered her words. She looked very grave. "Have you spoken with Father Mulcahy?"

"No. But I will tonight as soon as I return to the city."

Sister Cecilia took off her glasses. "As you know, Father Dunne is ill. No decision can be made without his approval."

"Can he be called?"

"He has a severe bronchitis." She rubbed her eyes. The woman was exhausted, Sylvie realized. "It would be better if perhaps you spoke with Father Mulcahy and he called Father Dunne."

"Have you space for them here?"

"We don't have any bed space," Sister Cecilia said quietly. "We have blankets." She seemed overwhelmed by all she had just heard. "Can I offer you some tea?"

Sylvie realized how empty she was. She had eaten nothing since that morning. "Well if it isn't . . ."

Sister Cecilia smiled. "It will be old but hot, and perhaps there are some crackers. Excuse me a moment."

She went out, and Sylvie stood up. It was so terribly cold here. She turned now and saw the statue of Christ and walked toward it. She kept her hands in the muff and felt the pages meant for Robert. It would be all right. It had to be. She had killed a man today. It's true he was a German but he was also a human being. She shivered. She needed Robert. Where was he? I love you. Please come soon.

Abetz read the report that had come in. A tip. New York was becoming Paris. People in times of occupation did the most natural thing. They betrayed each other. It was just natural selection. Survival of the fittest. New York was breaking down. Here was a call from a man who had seen four boys and a woman driven off in a car. Orphans, he called them. How would he know that? Why betray them? Was he an orphan himself? The wretched punish the wretched. The license number was of course easily checked. Was it the same four boys? Perhaps. But that was not as important as something else that jiggled his mind. The woman in red with the red bonnet. One did not forget such a fetching outfit on an attractive woman. He had seen one yesterday on Sylvie Lamont. But women such as Sylvie Lamont did not wear the same outfit two days in a year much less two days in a row. Still it pricked at him. He felt sweat break out. What was it? He wasn't going anywhere until he knew more. All his instinct told him that something was about to break. He pressed the intercom. "Hoppman, come in here."

They sat drinking tea that was tasteless but hot. Sylvie would have given her life for some sugar.

"I'm glad you called Father Dunne," Sylvie said.

"I had to. It is not a matter I can take the responsibility for."

"Will he be here soon?"

Sister Cecilia reached out and patted her hand. "Very soon. Then you and he can go inside and call Father Mulcahy."

"Can the boys eat with you?"

"Of course. Dinner is in an hour. Boiled potatoes I'm afraid. I wish we could do more." She squeezed Sylvie's hand. "Please tell me all about it. I can see you are troubled."

The invitation to talk was irresistible. Sylvie needed to confide in someone. "It must have been all the shooting . . . You know how suggestible children are."

Sister Cecilia's eyes were filled with sympathy and curiosity. "But where could they get guns?"

"I don't know. Eddie probably."

"Eddie?"

"Eddie Dalton. He's the one who must have organized it."

Sister Cecilia nodded. "You said no one was hurt."

Sylvie sipped the bitter tea. Thank goodness it was hot. "They were old guns. No one was hurt at all . . . if it weren't for the officer . . ."

"The officer?"

She didn't like going into all this, but it would be in the paper anyway. It would be dishonest not to tell the sister.

"He chased them. He would have shot them. I couldn't let him do that and . . ."

"And?"

"I'm afraid he was hit by the cab I was in."

"I see." Cecilia drank from her cup. "Was he badly hurt?"

Sylvie shuddered. "I believe so."

"Was he killed?"

"Possibly."

"Then the boys are fugitives." Sister Cecilia appeared deeply concerned. "We must help them."

They both drank at the same moment.

"Is there anything else? Anything else you would like to tell me? You mentioned guns."

Sylvie felt a little uncomfortable.

"My driver has taken care of that."

"Your driver . . . of course. It wouldn't do to have guns found."

She was right. "I have one," Sylvie said.

Sister Cecilia's face was grave. "With you?"

"I shouldn't have it," Sylvie exclaimed.

"Let me have it. Quickly. Father Dunne would be upset having a gun in St. Mary's. You do understand?"

"Of course."

Sister Cecilia stood up and put her hand out. There was something very commanding in her presence. Sylvie had the feeling she too should stand up.

"Quickly, he'll be here soon."

Sylvie handed her the revolver.

Sister Cecilia stared down at the small, dull-looking pistol. "Is it loaded?"

Sylvie's hand went to her mouth. "I don't know . . . possibly. . . ." In that moment she saw the nun step back and she felt a chill line run down her back.

Sister Cecilia pointed the gun at her. There was a look of stern and exacting disapproval on her face. "Don't move. Stay exactly where you are."

"But you can't be . . ."

"Don't move," Sister Cecilia repeated. There was a look of implacable enmity in her eyes now. Sylvie realized the nun would shoot her.

"But Father Dunne . . ."

"He's coming . . . any moment. I have also called the police."

They sat in terrible silence for the next five minutes. No words were possible. It smells, Sylvie thought, as if something has died here. As the door opened, she realized something had.

There was a shuffling noise and Father Dunne, thin, stooped, with hard eyes, came forward. He wore a hat and dark raincoat.

Sister Cecilia edged toward him. "The police will be here momentarily."

"And the boys?"

"Sister Veronica has them."

"You can't do this," Sylvie protested.

Father Dunne had taken the gun from Sister Cecilia.

The priest held up his hand. "This is a police matter. The church does not interfere with the law."

"But they are children."

"Children who had guns," Sister Cecilia said.

"I shall pray for them," Father Dunne said, the gun pointed at Sylvie.

She saw his face, saw Sister Cecilia's eyes, wide open but shut like a wall against her, and knew it was useless. The room whirled around her and she sank onto a bench.

"You don't serve humanity," Sylvie said to them both. They looked back at her as though she were hardly there, and she suddenly remembered the notes inside her muff, which now lay on the floor beside the bench.

Father Dunne looked grave and uncomfortable. "I regret this, Miss Lamont, but I cannot circumvent the law."

"Don't you realize the police will hand these children over to the Gestapo?"

The priest's eyes flickered. "Then it is God's will."

She felt a terrible contempt for him. "Would God want you to hand over those children?" She was trembling with rage now, almost in tears. "You're not a man of God or a servant of the church. You're a servant of the Nazis. Anyone who doesn't resist them is a collaborator."

She hated them both. This is what the occupation has done to us, she thought. They've turned us against each other. If we don't fight them, we turn the hatred against each other. You must fight, even now. She looked down at the floor and realized she had to get the muff.

"I have cigarettes in my muff. May I?"

Father Dunne nodded. Sylvie started to bend down, but Sister Cecilia stooped down quickly and scooped the muff up.

"Stop that. It's mine."

Sylvie reached over, and now they were engaged in a tug of war. "How dare you?" As she said it she felt the nun give a sudden twist. She was remarkably strong. The muff was jerked free and Sylvie gave a cry as the sheaf of notes spilled to the floor.

Sister Cecilia picked up the notes and began to read them.

"Give me those," Sylvie cried.

Sister Cecilia stepped back and kept reading, her eyes unrelentingly devouring each page. Then, looking up at Father Dunne, the nun said tersely, "She's a spy."

Father Dunne blinked. "Let me see." He began to read. He read the first page slowly and then the second. He looked up at Sylvie. They had her. Sylvie could see the dim, blinkered light of triumph in their eyes. She had lived well while they starved out an existence. And for them, the bread of spiritual salvation had been meager fare indeed. Then she knew it was not the occupation. It was this priest and this nun. Not all. These two. These two impostors.

"Burn them," Sylvie said. "Not for my sake. For all of us."

Father Dunne held up the notes as if they were the flesh of the Messiah. "I can't do that," he said. "It would be immoral."

Chapter 37

March 29, 1942
10:57 P.M.

Collins slouched behind a newspaper, his eyes half closed. He had been in and out of the lavatory half a dozen times so he wouldn't draw the attention of a cop or a railroad dick working for Heinrich. Another half hour to curfew. He could have stayed in the washroom the whole time, but that would have been too suspicious. He was less conspicuous sitting out here playing the tired attorney returning to New York from a meeting with a client. Not much of a story, but true. Only, his client was Bill Donovan.

"No parachute drop, Bobbie," Donovan had repeated. Roosevelt had thrown everything into the West Coast in case the Japanese won in Hawaii. Roosevelt wouldn't gamble in New York unless he saw a full-scale uprising, and Donovan wouldn't make a pitch for it unless he had a plan. Collins had to come up with a scenario.

Collins reached inside his jacket and pulled out a butt. He looked around the station. Harsh dirty light showed in the domed ceiling. Rows of benches with no more than a handful of people. Drugstores, coffee stands, hat shops, and jewelers, all shut down and neon lights blinking. This place was a tomb where every little sound was magnified and made your heart congeal. A meet had been set up with Frank Costello in Red Hook. Donovan had made a deal with Lucky Luciano's closest ally. Help the Resistance, help your country. Stop Vito Genovese. Costello would play. The mob wouldn't let Abetz and Genovese take their turf without a fight. More than muscle, they could give Collins the grease he needed to sabotage Heinrich's machine. So he had Costello, but he needed a plan for a rising. No parachute drop. The only tangible thing he had gotten was a carton of Chesterfields. Don't knock it, Bobbie boy, they're worth a lot on the black market. He heard footsteps. Two men . . . dicks. He touched his pocket and felt the revolver. Cold comfort it was.

11:13 P.M.

The train had pulled into Baltimore some ten minutes ago, and Leila had peered anxiously out the window for a sign of him. She had reserved this sleeping compartment with its double berths after slipping away from the rest of the company before they took the eight o'clock out of Union Station. In all the excitement of the performance in front of the diplomats in Washington, nobody would miss her except Friedrich. And oddly, he had seen her for only a minute after the performance and then vanished. He had come down to Washington earlier than the company, saying only that he had to make preparations and meet several dignitaries. It seemed plausible, but the hard line that had now become his mouth and the tight expression around his eyes belied that. She had expected to see him going back with the company at eight o'clock, but he had told her that he would be flying back to New York because of urgent business. It was incredible good fortune. How would she have explained taking the eleven o'clock out of Union Station?

She left her compartment now and walked along the corridor till she found the exit and came down the steps looking for a sign of Robert. She looked both ways and saw only some auxiliary police. Did that mean the Gestapo wasn't concerned with the last train out of Washington? Why not?

The train began to move, and she felt her throat catch. Something had gone wrong. Then she heard something and, turning to her left, saw a figure running for the train. Then he was there, sweeping her along with him up the steps.

They stood in the compartment watching Baltimore recede, watching one another with appreciative eyes, not untouched by wonder. Neither of them seemed eager to speak.

Collins grinned. "Nice layout."

"I was frightened you wouldn't get to see it."

"I'll take the upper berth," he said, still smiling.

"I saved you a sandwich, and tea. It's probably cold by now."

"I'm not hungry. I ate something that passed for mackerel in Baltimore."

"You found that man?"

Collins didn't like to talk about his work. But the concern in her eyes touched him. "He was there. I borrowed his car and returned it to him. He brought me to Baltimore and told me where to eat and kill time."

"He takes a risk each time, doesn't he?"

Collins nodded. "He tried to warn that couple this morning. Somebody turned them in and took their house."

He moved to the window and watched the outlines of the countryside. He had to get away from her eyes. She came and stood next to him. The palpable feeling between them was making it very difficult.

Collins fished out a cigarette. He had distributed as many packs as he could in various pockets of his pants, jacket, and coat. It was not a good idea to carry Chesterfields into New York. They weren't available to the occupied zone. When he got back to the city he would stuff them into some empty packs and . . . the train began to slow.

He looked at his watch. "Damn," he swore.

"What is it?"

"Quick, get into bed."

She stared at him as Collins pulled off his coat. "I haven't got time to look at you or you at me. Do it."

She grabbed the pajamas she had laid out and jumped into the bathroom. Collins peeled down, praying that it wasn't a stop. Less than half a minute later he was up in the upper bunk in his shorts, gun under his pillow. Fay came out of the bathroom.

"Douse the light," he whispered.

She snapped it out, and then they both lay in their berths listening to the sound of the train, feeling it crawl along.

And then the train stopped.

Collins dropped to the floor, holding his gun, and transferred a knife from his pants into his sock. Then he climbed back into the upper berth and they both waited. They could hear the footsteps in the corridor.

He felt the gun cold in his hand. But no colder than the sweat beads on his forehead. "Are you scared?"

"Yes."

"Can you still act?"

"Yes."

"We're lovers. You took the late train so we could be alone. Tell them how much they loved you in Washington. Name some Heinrich biggie that was there. Can you think of one?"

"Von Kleist . . . the German ambassador."

"He personally congratulated you."

The footsteps stopped. He could hear voices. Now they were knocking on someone's compartment.

Leila looked up at Collins. "Maybe it's somebody else."

"Maybe." And maybe they just don't know what compartment I'm in. He didn't like it. There was no way to blast his way out of this one.

He could hear them in the compartment next door, and Collins felt his nerves become barbed wire. The voices were muffled but loud. Then the door slammed, and it was their turn. "Hold on," he said.

The knock came, and then the voice. "Open up. Identity check. Open up."

"Answer them," Collins ordered.

"Just a second," Leila called. She got up, mussing her hair. "What is it . . . I'm sleeping."

"Open up."

Collins's finger tightened on the trigger. Hell, it was no good. He came down and played sleepy as he groped for the card in his jacket. As he fumbled he stashed the gun under Fay's pillow. She opened the door, and the compartment light snapped on. Collins whirled. He found himself facing the sallow-faced guide, who pointed at Collins. "That's him."

Next to him was a tall man in a dark coat with a vivid scar on his cheek. He had on a hat, and he was holding a gun. His voice was unpleasant, sharp and dissonant. "Get dressed. You are my prisoners. I am Jaegner."

Jaegner kept the gun on them as the guide went through the compartment like a wind storm. He came up with Collins's gun and flashed a triumphant grin. Collins looked disheartened. *I wanted you to find it, laddie. Just leave me my knife.*

The guide went through his clothes and his coat, crying out as he found the Chesterfields. Now he bent over and checked Collins's shoes. The socks were discarded next to them. He kicked at them and Collins held his breath. He didn't bend down.

The man called Jaegner snarled at them. "Get dressed. Bring them to the parlor car." He left, and the guide covered them with his revolver.

Fay scooped up her clothing and Collins wondered what was going through her mind.

"Where are you going?" the guide barked.

"To dress . . . in the bathroom."

The guide smirked. "Nice . . . nice. Jaegner will like you." He turned his gun on Collins. "Hurry."

Collins knew he should keep his mouth shut, but he couldn't resist a quip. "How about my five hundred dollars?"

The guide pointed the gun at him. "How about five bullets?"

Collins let the man stare him down.

"The war's over for you, hero. Jaegner's got you. In the morning the Gestapo."

Collins dropped his pants for effect and heard the man laugh. Now he scooped them up along with his socks, palming the knife.

They sat in the parlor car facing the guide. Jaegner had not reappeared. Collins gripped the knife and felt it cold and hard against his wrist. The train was moving toward New York, which meant that they were due to be handed over to the Gestapo after Jaegner sweated them. They wouldn't cable the Gestapo, which gave Collins a chance. This was a vigilante operation. He just had to split them up in some way. And he had a hunch.

Jaegner came in now holding a pot of coffee and some cups. He set them down on the table. The guide sat down in a chair near the window. Jaegner had taken off his coat and jacket. His shirt was white with a shoulder holster prominently displayed. He was tall and lean, like his scar. He came toward them, a smile creasing his lips, hand on hips, pelvis extended toward the girl. He looked her over. Oh yeah, Collins thought, I know you. It's the milk run . . . your milk. Before the odds were one in ten. Now they were four in ten. He was still drawing to an inside straight. Just one card. Do it for me Jaegner. Take the girl first.

He saw Jaegner eyeing Leila, and then he knew it couldn't be any other way. First a piece, then he would stomp on Collins to get information to sell the Gestapo. "Could we have some coffee?" Collins asked in a timid voice.

Jaegner smiled, and the scar leaped across his face. "Sure. You want coffee, honey?"

"Yes," Leila said in a voice that sounded like she was in a department store. She's got the nerve, Collins thought. She'll do it. She has to.

Jaegner sauntered toward the coffee, and Collins spoke rapidly. "He'll take you into a private car. You're gonna have to take it all off for him. Tease him, then peel. When he goes for you use this." He palmed the knife to her. "It's a switchblade.

357

When you press the button on the side, it will open. Can you do it?''

She nodded as Jaegner approached them. "How do you like it honey. Sweet, real sweet, I bet." He leered at Collins.

"Lots of sugar," Leila answered.

"Lots and lots," Jaegner said, and filled her cup.

Collins had the picture now. These slugs were bounty hunters for the Gestapo. They promised to get you out of occupied America for a nice price and then sold you to the Gestapo, with whom they had another arrangement. Collins fell into the category of being a bonus. And Fay was one of the extras that came with the job. Jaegner had collected from a lot of women who thought they were saving their families. Life had never been so good to him. Before the Nazi invasion he had been a railroad dick and beat hobos off the trains. The war had given him his chance. Now he had it all.

Jaegner mixed the sugar for Leila and handed her the cup. "It's real coffee. Go ahead, drink it."

Leila saw him measuring her. She took the cup and felt the tremor in her hand. It was real, and Jaegner knew it.

Jaegner walked over to Collins. He stood over him, his supple body arched back in an expression of supreme power. "I understand you took a visit into the country today. Came back with lots of Chesterfields. We're gonna talk about that. You want to tell me anything?''

Collins debated whether to provoke the man.

"You paid five hundred dollars. That's an important visit. Who did you visit?''

"My Aunt Mary. I missed Christmas dinner."

Jaegner's hand lashed out, catching Collins in the face. Collins felt the hot streak of sadism in the man. This one liked to beat on freight bums and helpless women. Jaegner turned to Leila. "What are you doin' travelin' with a guy like this? Do you know who he saw today?''

Leila shook her head. "I think you've made a mistake. Mr. Jackson is a . . .''

"Can it. You're layin' up with a spy. And you're gonna tell me all you know about it.''

Jaegner took Leila by the arm, and the coffee cup fell and smashed on the floor. Collins saw Jaegner's eyes light up. The slap had been for effect. So Fay would crumble once he got her alone.

"Don't worry," Jaegner said. "I'll bring a drink along for us.''

He whispered something to the sallow-faced guide, then led Leila out of the parlor car. When they were in the corridor, the train swayed momentarily, making Leila stumble. Jaegner's hand was at her waist, and it remained there as if Leila were his possession. She broke free, but felt his hand on her arm. "In here, honey."

He had pushed open the door to her compartment. The lights were still on. "Sit down." He gestured toward the lower berth.

Leila remained standing. "Look, I don't know anything. He's just somebody I met on the train today." Her arms were at her sides, her right fist closed around the knife.

Jaegner lit a cigarette. He blew out some smoke. "Well, you're a fast worker then. Shackin' up with him on the way back. You're hot, aren't you?"

Leila sat down. As she did so, she put her hand behind her and felt for the pillow.

She smiled, a little tart's smile where the corners of your mouth gave you away. "If I like someone."

"Actress, aren't you?"

The way he said it, Leila knew what he thought actresses were. She smiled. "Got a drink?" There, the knife was underneath the pillow.

Jaegner smiled. "Well, I just happen to have a little hootch on me." He pulled out a bottle of cheap brandy and filled their cups. He downed his in one prolonged gulp, his Adam's apple working furiously. He refilled the cup. "C'mon, baby, drink up."

Leila took a sip and gagged. Jaegner smiled. This one liked sweet drinks with lots of bubbles.

"So what do you know about this guy?"

Leila shrugged. "Nothing much. He came out of nowhere. The company was standing around and he drifted over. He bought me lunch and we hit it off. I told him I was going to Washington to do a show. Command performance for the diplomats and the Wehrmacht. He got interested."

"You mean he was nosy."

"That's it. He said he had some business in Baltimore and would be coming back at night."

Jaegner lit a butt off his dying one.

"You just met him."

Leila let the smile play across her face more openly now. "He's a good looking guy. Sometimes you get a yen."

"A what?"

"Like an itch."

"You actresses are real whores, ain't ya?"

"No, we ain't," Leila flared. "I gotta like a guy."

"My pa told me about the theater. All actresses are whores. They love a dick in them. And it's fulla Jews. You know until the war I never seen a Jew. Pa told me they had horns in their head 'cause they made a deal with the devil. That's how they got all that money. Well they don't got horns, but they got money. And you're still a whore." He rode through her protest. "Sure you are, but it's okay. I got a soft spot for whores who look good. Girls like you know what it's about. No fuss, just peel 'em off."

He drank some more. She knew he was capable of ravishing and killing her. In that moment she realized he was the reincarnation of the snake-eyed thug in New York.

"Course it depends on what I feel like. Some of these Jew broads start cryin' and hollerin' when I tear off their clothes. Then I fuck 'em and tell 'em if they scream, I'll kill their husband, and they don't want to give it to me, but they do, and then they love it."

Somehow it was just retribution for courting the enemy. For watching passively when the snake-eyed gangster ripped Rachel's robe away. You can't freeze now. She felt the knife again. Use it. You have to.

"You're in for a treat," Jaegner continued. "Instead of that lawyer, you're gonna have me . . . the best lay around. I don't feel like no coaxin', baby. So peel them off. One way or the other, you're gonna come across."

He stood up, slipped off his shoulder holster with the butt of the gun protruding, and began to unbutton his shirt. He got it off and turned to Leila. "C'mon, let's see what ya got."

He pulled her up, and Leila couldn't breathe.

Collins had to move soon. Jaegner wasn't going to engage in delicate foreplay. Maybe the girl could use the knife and maybe not. But Collins couldn't bet on it. And this guide wasn't close enough for Collins to do anything. He'd been around.

"What's your name?" Collins asked.

The man didn't answer right away. He had a toothpick wedged in the side of his mouth. "Jenkins," he finally said.

"Like the prizefighter."

Jenkins gestured with his gun. "Cut the bullshit."

Collins sipped some coffee and tried again. "How come you get the run of the train like this?"

Jenkins gave a tight smile. "We got the right contacts. Conductors see us, they go the other way."

Good, Collins thought. You're an unofficial posse. So if I get rid of you quietly, no one will miss you.

"But you ain't pullin' any tricks," Jenkins said, reading his mind. "I'm a hunter and I know 'em all."

* * *

"C'mon, baby," Jaegner urged. "You done this plenty of times."

His chest and shoulders were covered with tufts of hair, and she could smell the harsh odor of his body. She felt an overpowering nausea grip her. Leila took a deep breath and pulled the sweater over her head.

Jaegner smiled. "I like a pink bra. C'mon, drop the skirt."

Leila unzipped the brown skirt, and it fell around her feet. She felt her resolve fading.

"Nice," he said. "Let's see what you got." He reached over and tugged the brassiere off. A big smile crossed his face. "You got 'em, don't ya? Perfect shape." He reached over, and his huge hand gripped her breast. Now his other hand covered the other breast. "Great tits." Jaegner stepped back. "Lose the slip."

She pulled the slip down and, stepping out of it, stood fully naked before Jaegner. She felt helpless, already violated. Let him do anything he wants to. No, no, this is how he degrades you. Your life is worth more than your fear. Hate him, hate him.

"Nice baby, nice. We're gonna have a good time. A lotta guys like big broads, but I like the perfect ones. Like you. Small waist, perfect tits. Want to see me?"

He unzipped his pants and pulled them off along with his shorts. He stood grotesquely posturing in front of her. "Like it?" he preened. "Like the sermon says, 'My rod and my staff will comfort thee.'" He came forward, put his arms around her while his mouth found her breasts. He sucked and bit, and Leila felt her stomach heave. Let him, don't fight. Not yet. He chewed on her breasts, and she felt the awful humiliation of it. And in that moment she felt sorry for him. He was slobbering on her. Groaning. His mother had never let him suckle at her breast long enough. Deprived children become Jaegners. Suddenly her anger convulsed her body. Your pity threatens your survival. You have to kill him.

"I have to use the bathroom," Collins said.

"No, you don't," said Jenkins. "You don't get out of my sight. Take a leak on the floor. The train ain't gonna mind."

Jaegner had pushed Leila back on the bed. "C'mon, take me in your mouth."

Her head was spinning. A sudden flash of light illuminated the car. Don't panic.

"I'm hot for you. I can't wait."

He was smiling. "You're a whore, and I love whores." Then he came toward her and felt she wasn't ready.

He slapped her hard across the face. "You're dry, you little tease. Bitch." He slapped her again.

"No, I'm always this way. I just need a little attention. C'mon, honey, take care of me."

He was all over her body with his tongue. She let her arms fall back, and she moaned softly. "More, more." Her hand was under the pillow and found the knife. But she could do nothing and, in that moment, she realized with horror that she could only kill him if he was full on top of her . . . inside her. There was no other way. Let him penetrate. You have to.

Collins knew it would have to be bang bang. There was no more time.

"How about some more coffee?"

He gestured, and Jenkins glanced at the pot. "I'll do it." He came forward, gun carefully aimed, and, lifting the pot, filled Collins's cup. Collins let the cup fall to his waist so that Jenkins had to bend slightly. As quick as the cup was filled, Collins threw the coffee in Jenkins's face. He stumbled back with a howl, and Collins was on him.

"C'mon, honey," Leila whispered. "I'm ready for you now."

She had used spit to lubricate herself. Her arm was thrown back and gripped the knife under the pillow. She felt him pressing forward. Felt the enormous swell of him. She had to let him before she could do it. Let him . . . let him. No, the voice within her resounded, and she locked her legs. He drove forward and she closed. "Bitch," he said, and punched her. Her head exploded as he flailed at her, pulling maniacally at her legs. "Fuck me, fuck me," he demanded. She knew then that others had fought him only to give way under this barrage of abuse and punishment. He hit her again, and all thought left her. He threw himself down on her, and the red hot sensation inside her fused her will to the hand that gripped the knife. She pressed the button and, as the blade snapped open, she drove the knife into his spine. Again. She heard her scream become his. It echoed in her ears.

Blinded, Jenkins still was attempting to use the gun when Collins brought his elbow into his windpipe. As he gurgled and dropped the gun, Collins heard the screams. He pounded Jenkins in the face and, grabbing the gun, smashed the man across the forehead. Jenkins went down like a sack. Collins ran toward the private cars.

* * *

362

Jaegner had fallen away. Now, arching his back like some great animal who had been violated, he reached with twitching, spastic fingers for the deadly thing planted near the base of his spine. There was a gurgle of blood in his mouth. And then, trying to grab this bitch who had so terribly maimed him, he felt something tear inside him. He was falling back on the floor . . . reaching, still reaching.

Collins burst in, and Jaegner instinctively tried to grab him. Collins clubbed him once. It was over.

He wanted to say something, but there was nothing to do but hold her and stroke her hair. She didn't cry, but spasms and tremblings convulsed her body. He held her and whispered what his grandmother crooned to him as a boy. "God forgives his own. There is no sin. No sin, no sin, no sin." They stayed like that, the train rolling toward New York, the sound bursting in their ears. The clack of the wheels repeating the insistent message . . . no sin . . . no sin . . . no sin.

He was thinking it when Leila spoke. "Get rid of him . . . please. . . ."

He moved from the berth, released the lock, and pushed at the window. It came up. Jaegner was a huge beast, and Collins felt the enormous strength that had been in the man as he brought him up and, bracing the body, bent it over and pushed hard. Jaegner fell away into the night. Collins scooped up his clothes and threw them out after him. Earth to ashes to dust.

He bent over Leila. "I have to get rid of the other one. I'll be back. All right? Okay? Then we'll be safe."

The train whistled in the night, speeding like a rifle shot to New York, the sound of it assaulting nerve ends and tissue. She thought, How did it happen? How had she killed a man? Because he was killing you. Killing your spirit. And she knew it was right what she had done. You were given another chance, and you atoned. You're not Fay Brophy, you're Leila Fox again.

Friedrich, Friedrich, I tried, but I can't love you. I have to love myself again. I'm sorry, Friedrich, so sorry.

She heard the compartment door open, and he sat down beside her. "Listen to me," she said. "I'm all right. My real name is Leila Fox. I'm Jewish. Much worse has been done to them. Just hold me."

Chapter 38

March 30, 1942
1:20 A.M.

Abetz came to see Sylvie only moments after they put her in the cell. He asked no questions, but instead spoke generally about the seriousness of the moment. He was polite. He pointed out how upset Kelly would be. He said they would talk again in the morning after she had a night to think about events. Reflection was good in moments such as these. After the night they could sort things out. He had been distressed to learn that Sylvie had not eaten. Incredible that the police in Long Beach questioned her for so long without even offering so much as a cup of tea. He left, and within fifteen minutes a steaming pot of tea, a warm Danish, and rolls were brought in. Fresh milk and sugar were served on the tray. Abetz returned to inquire if she was comfortable, clicked his heels, and left.

Though Sylvie had felt terribly empty, suddenly her hunger disappeared. She was cold. It was so dismal and dank in this cell. There was just a cot with a brown, worn blanket and a pillow with no pillow case. Abetz knew what he was doing. She sat for fifteen minutes drinking tea and eating a roll. The cell was very small. Everything was still and quiet. She poured a second cup and drank that with lots of sugar. What if she had to go to the bathroom? She looked at the bare bed again. Tonight she would be sleeping in an elegant dress bought at Henri of Paris—in a Gestapo cell.

But at least she was alone. She hadn't had a moment alone since she'd been betrayed by Father Dunne and Sister Cecilia. First the police interrogation, then the long ride to New York and Gestapo headquarters. Little Timmy crying, and then the other two boys. Only Eddie Dalton had remained impassive, stolid. What was inside the boy? Fatalism, of course. He had accepted what life had given him ever since he grew to realize his parents had abandoned him. Could she be that fatalistic about what awaited her?

The door swung open and she gave a start. A tall matron faced

364

her. She wore a gray uniform. She carried something over her arm. It was a plain cotton dress.

"You are to undress," the woman said.

Sylvie stood up. "Where?"

"Here. Now."

Sylvie could see the look of mean triumph in the woman's eyes. It reminded her of the Negro woman on the platform who put her foot over the penny. It was class hatred. And nothing made class hatred more evident than war and occupation.

"Begin," the woman ordered.

That was part of it also. Giving orders to someone who never even gave you a glance. She moved closer to Sylvie, who had just begun to undo the button of the velvet top. Sylvie moved back, but the woman stayed on top of her.

"Please give me room."

But the woman didn't budge.

"I said . . . would you please . . ."

The matron smiled for a moment and took half a step back. She folded her arms and waited. Sylvie pulled down the skirt and saw the matron motion toward her shoes. She stepped out of them. Now the woman gestured toward her stockings. Sylvie rolled them down. The matron handed her the dress and a pair of slippers. As Sylvie put them on, she saw the matron reach over and pocket a cheese Danish from the plate next to the tea. She put it into the pocket of her jacket.

Sylvie had completed the transformation. The woman sized her up with those mocking eyes. Once again her lips pressed together in the beginnings of a smile. "Come with me," she said. "You have one visit to the bathroom."

Sylvie dozed rather than slept during the night. She was exhausted more than tired. She would think about all that had happened, then finally close her eyes and slip away. But there were always Sister Cecilia's hating eyes to haunt her, and she would waken and sit up in one motion. Then there was only the silence, the darkness, and the cold. Once, not long before the matron came to waken her, she heard a man scream. A sole, solitary note, awful to the ear. The man never cried out again, but his pain rang in her ears until they came to take her out of the cell.

8:17 A.M.

Radner stood in the somber tomb that was Grand Central Station. His eyes were red and ached fiercely. He had sat with the plotters all night. Men who dreamed of killing Hitler. Beck, who

365

fancied himself the savior of Germany. Ivo, who would carry wine bottles filled with explosives and personally hand them to Hitler. What was he doing with these men? He needed Leila. He missed her. What is a man's life without a woman? There is beauty in art and beauty in a woman. The rest is madness and egotism.

His temple was pounding, and he rubbed a hand across it. She hadn't come home, she must have taken the late train back. The sleeper. He would surprise her. Take her to breakfast . . . then home. He had paid the price for her to Abetz. She was his.

He saw her then, and all thought vanished from him. She was beautiful, but there was something different . . . and then he saw the man. Lean, rumpled brown hair, virile. The thought that they had been together intersected with the line of pain in him. Tears flashed in his eyes. Leila, Leila, I love you.

They brushed against one another, their body language totally explicit. He knew that language. He couldn't breathe, nor could he stop watching them. He embraced the darkness, a furtive being with only one thought. She loves another. I have sacrificed myself for her and she has gone to another.

They were moving toward an exit that led out to Vanderbilt Avenue. He started to turn away, but then something terrible in him resisted that. Some impulse that he knew, as he gave way to it, would destroy him. But it was too late. They moved through the exit door and Radner followed.

9:30 A.M.

The boys' choir filled the church with high soprano notes. They were dressed all in white and faced at a forty-five degree angle the rows of pews and the audience. They also faced the pulpit where the archbishop, dressed in white and red, looked benevolently down upon them. He was a balding man with a pinched face and he wore spectacles that seemed to gleam intensely in the artificial light of the church. Behind him was a large gold cross bearing the crucified Messiah with his head tilted severely to the right, eyes closed. Above him, hanging side by side, were the American and German flags. The red, white, and blue contrasting with the severe black of the swastika.

Kelly looked at the boys' scrubbed faces and innocent eyes. Innocence, he thought. You're either born to it or you'll never have it. In shanty row we were never innocent. We knew every turn in the road was crooked and you had to get around the bend before the other guy. But with all that, nothing had prepared him for Abetz's late-night call. Kelly had listened almost in shock to

Abetz's description of Sylvie as a spy. "We have the notes she stole from you. She knows about the Easter Sunday roundup." He heard that phrase over and over. "She knows about the Easter Sunday roundup. She knows . . . knows . . . knows."

Kelly had wanted to rush down, but Abetz had been firm. "Let me handle it." There was a dead Wehrmacht officer, killed chasing after those little bastards from St. Stephen's. Who was this woman he had been with for four years? She had betrayed him. Made him the fool. The man who was to be regent. "Let me handle it." How would Abetz handle it? Kelly should be there. But there was pomp and circumstance. Grace was here with the children. Darlin' Grace, dressed in black. Born to be wife and brood mother. She had a pretty face even now. She had been beautiful once. A New England debutante. Kelly had married up. She was proper and she knew how to look away and not too closely. Class, like Sylvie was class. He looked over at Joe, his eldest, ruggedly handsome in a black suit with his mother's blue eyes and Kelly's roguish mouth. He would have the ladies as his father had. But for the father, the irony was impossible to ignore. One of the ladies had had him. "She works for the Resistance," Abetz had said. He felt a knot in his chest. He was angry. Very angry.

The artificial light illuminated the stained-glass windows, framing the audience, the Messiah, and the two flags. The choir had finished, and now the archbishop was prepared to begin his homily. But before beginning he turned to the tall, erect Irishman who sat in the first row of pews surrounded by his wife and children. One boy and six girls. He bowed to the man he was speaking about. Just a slight inclination of his head. But it was clear to the layers of people packed in neat symmetry behind the leader of the new society. Patrick Kelly. He was smiling now. And as the archbishop finished his salutory words, there was a burst of applause.

5:00 P.M.

The room Abetz used to interrogate her was bare and dusty. A dull overhead light made it seem infinitely more shabby. On the table in the middle of the room was an ashtray. The room reeked of awful German cigarettes. Abetz smoked them continually. He was no longer civil. Good. That made it easier. We have been going through this all day, Sylvie thought. Abetz asking inane questions, pointed questions, telling her it was all over, stopping, beginning again. The horrid little man looked at her through a cloud of dense smoke trailing from the cigarette clenched firmly in his silver-tipped holder.

"Miss Lamont, let me be perfectly clear. You have no bargaining position. A German officer is dead. The papers you were found with contain information stolen from Mr. Kelly. I want the man you were going to turn them over to. Tell me who he is. . . ."

"I don't know."

Abetz removed the cigarette from his mouth. "But you do. You are a spy. That is an offense punishable by death. Even Patrick Kelly cannot save you."

She saw the horrid little man's eyes tighten. She saw the implicit message there. I can save you. Just tell me Robert Collins's name. Tell me where I can find him. Give him over to me, and you are free.

"I won't tell you anything."

Abetz tapped out his cigarette and put it aside. He leaned forward. "Miss Lamont, you are a beautiful woman with many years ahead of you. I am not interested in your motives or what you do with your life after this. But please be clear. You shall not walk away from this without giving up something. Either the information I require or your life."

She looked into his beady little eyes and saw he meant it. He reminded Sylvie of some ferretlike animal who had for years lived in the woods, surviving on the scraps and leavings of lordly beasts of prey. But now, somehow, after a thousand years of skulking about, he had become a lord himself. And he had not forgotten anything that he had suffered or who had inflicted it upon him.

"I won't tell you anything," Sylvie repeated.

Abetz stood up. "There are ways to make people talk. I assure you, you could not stand up to it. You have lived a privileged life, Miss Lamont. You have not known what it is to bargain. Now you must. I want your contact. Give me his name."

She could see that however low-key the interrogation had been, he had crossed over a line. Something was going to happen.

"Come with me, Miss Lamont."

She followed him down a long corridor and up some steps. They had been joined by a bull-necked assistant in a black uniform. Sylvie could see a sliver of light now and then. They opened a door and emerged into a courtyard. At the far end was a man, wearing a gray sack that passed for a prisoner's uniform. He was small and shriveled. She recognized Meister in the same instant she saw the six-man firing squad.

"Give me the name of the man you report to," Abetz said,

"and where he can be found." He pointed to Meister. "Do so now or this Jew dies."

It was said as if he were purchasing a pair of socks. I'll take the red ones.

She started to protest but then stopped. That would be of no use. She looked in his eyes and saw the cold aloofness, the disdain for human life, the disdain for her. The same disdain she had seen in Patrick's eyes. They thought she was less than them. And all her life she had been. Abetz assumed he would win from the beginning. She would not be able to stand up to watching Meister die. This was what it had all been leading up to. All her life this had happened and she had broken. But she had been given one last chance . . . she wouldn't fail.

"May I speak with him?"

She saw Abetz weighing what that would mean. Then he made his decision. "No. I repeat. Tell me his name. Now."

She saw in that moment what would happen. "You'll shoot him anyway. All right, then shoot me with him."

She took a step toward Meister, and abruptly Abetz's hand was there to restrain her. "Hoppman."

Hoppman held her arms firmly, and Abetz looked at her curiously, then walked to the firing squad and called them to attention. As if to mock her, he spoke the commands in English. "Prepare . . . ready . . . aim . . ." He stopped.

Sylvie remained still.

He barked out, "Fire."

The guns spoke in unison, and the bullets hit with terrible impact the little figure in gray. Meister slumped over, and Abetz turned away and walked unhurriedly toward her. She felt nothing for an instant, and then as the rage welled up in her she bit her tongue. She bit hard until the taste of blood was in her mouth. She tasted it as she turned on Abetz. "I will tell you nothing."

March 31, 1942
2:30 A.M.

Abetz sat at his desk and watched Kelly pace. Kelly was clearly unnerved. His mistress was a spy. This boy who had been a street urchin, who stole first money and then power, was no longer in control. Never, never, Abetz had learned early in life, depend on or trust a woman.

"Her life is in her own hands," Abetz said in a flat, emotionless voice.

Kelly stopped and looked at Abetz, seemingly aghast. "But

you have interrogated her all day. You mean to say . . ." He stopped.

"Patrick, she has stolen information. Do you realize what it would mean if such information had gotten into the hands of the Resistance? Once they know of Easter Sunday . . ." He didn't finish.

Kelly whirled toward him. "I know . . . I know . . . but she is of high social standing and breeding. We don't shoot women over here."

Abetz opened the drawer and pulled out a bottle of schnapps and handed it to Kelly. "She will not die . . . if she cooperates. She will not die because you will convince her she should not. Shall I tell you what I believe happened?"

Kelly was drinking from the bottle without bothering with a glass. Abetz saw some of it run down his neck. The riverboat gambler is shaky. "She met a man. She was bored at being your plaything and someone romanced her. She thinks she is in love. Perhaps she even is. It makes no difference. A woman in love, or even one who thinks she is, will betray the world for that man. But she will not die for that man. There is a difference." Abetz was lying, but perhaps Kelly would believe it. The Lamont woman had found a cause. Still, the hand must be played out.

Kelly sat on his desk. "What if I can't convince her?"

Abetz had the blandest of looks on his face. "But you will."

Kelly wiped his mouth with his hand and, in that moment, Abetz no longer noticed the finely tailored gray suit and the sleek, silver hair. He saw Kelly as he must have looked in his youth. A bright-eyed gutter rat, primitive and voracious. "You're right, she has a price. Everyone does."

Abetz sat motionless, tapping on his cigarette holder with one finger. "I want an exact description of the man. I want to know if he is their leader. Patrick, let me remind you of one thing. We have the might of the Wehrmacht here, but we are outnumbered seven to one. We cannot rush troops here from Germany as we could in England or Denmark. We do not want a spontaneous rising. This man is a match. I must have him."

Abetz turned ever so slightly, and his chair creaked. "I could have Hoppman interrogate her."

Kelly's eyes flashed. "Torture? Are you mad?"

A cold smile appeared on Abetz's mouth. "I want this man, and I will do what I need to do to get him."

Abetz rose, and now the two men stood facing one another, implacable and intransigent. Neither would relinquish power to the other. Finally Abetz made a gesture. "Please, we are both under strain. Speak with her. Get her to cooperate. Patrick, who

370

is this woman? How many like her have you had? Go, see her, resolve it, and she leaves in a chauffeured car in the morning. It is not her I want.''

Kelly was on the verge of saying something but then stopped. He nodded. Abetz leaned over and pressed the intercom. ''Hoppman, show Mr. Kelly to Miss Lamont.''

He followed Abetz's burly assistant, down the stairs and along a corridor. They were in the basement. A row of cells. At the far end, a dim light. Hoppman stopped, unlocked a door, and nodded. Kelly went past him and stepped inside.

She sat on a cot that was covered over by a ragged brown blanket. In the dim light she looked minute, pathetic, wearing a simple white cotton dress and slippers. Sylvie Lamont of the Maryland Lamonts. It would've been easier before. Now they were separated by that last night when she rebuffed him.

He stood there, feeling the knot in his throat. Speak, con man. Conjure up some blarney. ''How are you, darlin'?'' Affectionate words from another time.

She looked up at him, and Kelly saw that there was no connection between them. ''Patrick, about the other night . . .''

His heart leaped. Perhaps this wouldn't be so hard.

''I didn't realize you thought so little of me.'' She shook her head and then said quietly, ''They will shoot me in the morning.''

He made a wave with his hand. ''Stuff and nonsense. The old malarkey to scare you. Look, darlin', it's a game. A game you shouldn't be playing. I've played it all my life. It's traders' poker. You give and you get back.''

She rose from the cot. ''Is that it?''

''That's it. Just tell him what he wants to know.''

''And I leave? Free?''

He nodded.

''When?''

''Soon.''

Sylvie stood up and walked the full three feet to the opposite wall. He watched her. How had this happened? She had made him look like a fool. He was to be regent and this little nympho had her pants on fire for some renegade.

''Who is he? Tell me his name.'' He had meant to ask her, but it came out as a demand.

She turned to him again. ''It's always a command performance with you, isn't it, Patrick?'' She shook her head. ''No name. What about the boys?''

''Damn the boys.'' He grabbed her arm and drew her to him. He looked into her eyes and saw he had no sway with her.

"You're a rotten traitor," she said in the softest of voices. "I've been sleeping with a man who collaborates with Nazi beasts. You've sold your country. I should die for sleeping with you."

"Abetz will shoot you. Torture you and shoot you."

"I won't tell him. And I won't tell you."

"Listen, Sylvie, I'll get the boys off. Meister too."

"Meister is dead."

He stopped. Abetz meant business. Well, it was important. "I'm sorry, darlin'."

"No, you're not."

"Sylvie, for God's sakes. I can't fix this one."

She sat down again. He suddenly felt desperate. How much had she told her lover? *Easter Sunday.* "Sylvie, this man is probably gone now, back to Roosevelt. Why die for him? Why let the boys die?"

She stood up and, to his surprise, took his hand. "I'm not dying for him, Patrick. I'm dying for myself."

He squeezed her hand. "Tell me then, I'll do it for you. It's easier that way. What did you tell him?"

Kelly saw the disgust in her eyes as she answered. "I see now. It's not me, it's you. How foolish I've made you look. A man whose mistress betrays him. Why, you've been disgraced before your Nazi friends. Poor Patrick. I won't tell you anything. Just get me a priest. Father Mulcahy. I'd like to see that there's still a good priest in the world. Tell your friend, Abetz. I'm ready to die. Just so I have confession."

She turned away, and he felt utterly powerless. What could he tell Abetz? He heard her voice. What was she saying? She repeated it. "Good-bye, Patrick."

He followed Hoppman down the corridor. He couldn't let her win. The Nazis would never forget what a fool he had been. They would always remember that they had told him their secrets and that they had been wrong to do so. He could feel his shirt sticking to his back, although it was cold.

Abetz was waiting for him, smoking a cigarette in his office. An unfinished glass of schnapps stood in front of him. He looked up at Kelly and saw the answer in his face. She has the stuff of martyrs, Abetz thought. We will have to use Kelly differently. He is not who we believed him to be.

Kelly looked ashen. He rubbed a palm across his forehead. "I'm going to get her priest, Father Mulcahy. He's head of St. Stephen's. Call him and tell him to expect me."

Abetz nodded and called over the intercom to Hoppman. "Have a car ready for Mr. Kelly. You will personally drive him. And call St. Stephen's Church on Sixty-fourth Street and wake Father Mulcahy. Tell him to expect Patrick Kelly."

Abetz sat alone, savoring the schnapps. A priest and nun betrayed her, and she calls for still another priest. A fool's game. And Kelly hopes he can use the priest to convince her to cooperate. Abetz drained his glass. An idea had come to him. A very good one. His best ideas often came when he couldn't sleep or was up late. He checked his watch. Three o'clock in the morning. A time when sinners repented and Machiavellians thrived. He filled his glass with more schnapps and began to examine his idea.

When the call came to St. Stephen's, Sister Olivia took it. It was from the Gestapo, and she was to inform Father Mulcahy that Patrick Kelly was on his way over. Still drowsy, remembering when there was a night porter to answer the phone, the nun made her way up the stairs to the top level where Father Mulcahy slept. Surprisingly, there was a light under his door. And when she knocked, Father Mulcahy, fully dressed, answered the door. He looked very grave, and yet Sister Olivia, while she was clearly worried, knew that this was not the time to ask him why. His eyes had receded into deep sockets, and in them there was a lacerating pain. He listened to what she had to say and, thanking her, said he would be ready. Moments later, Thomas Mulcahy laid out his coat on the bed, went to a trunk in the corner, and produced a revolver, which he jammed into a side pocket of the coat.

It was not yet four o'clock when the two men sat in Kelly's limousine. Hoppman stood out in front. The entire block was deserted. Father Mulcahy looked at the lights. They seemed drab. It reminded him of the Oscar Wilde story of the Happy Prince, who gave the gold from his body to the poor and, when that was gone, had his friend, the swallow, pluck out his eyes, which were made of sapphires. We are blind, God has gone blind. Otherwise, how to explain Father Dunne's response to Sylvie Lamont's request that he help the four boys from St. Stephen's?

He looked now at Patrick Kelly, a man he had never liked, and said, "Father Dunne called me earlier this evening. I have not slept for worrying about Miss Lamont and the boys. Can you help them?"

The priest smelled the alcohol on Kelly's breath as the tycoon spoke. "I believe you are the man who can be of help here, Father. Unless Sylvie tells the Gestapo who her contact in the underground is, she will be executed."

Father Mulcahy felt as if a fist had bludgeoned his heart. "I?

373

You want me to urge her to give away somebody to the Germans?"

Kelly grabbed the priest's arm. "Damn it, they'll kill her." His voice had a stridency Father Mulcahy had never heard in it before. "I have a check for twenty thousand dollars made out to St. Stephen's church. All you have to do is . . ."

"All I have to do is what?"

"Convince her, Father. Convince her."

"And if she won't be convinced?"

"Then get her to confess."

"And I am supposed to betray what I hear in confession? You know what you are asking me to do?"

"I'm asking you to save her life. And the lives of the four boys. Your boys. A Wehrmacht officer was killed in their escape. The Gestapo will not forgive that."

Father Mulcahy was silent for a minute as he weighed what Patrick Kelly had said. His head was bowed as if he were in private communion. Then he looked up. "And will God forgive me if I break my vows?"

"I don't want any bullshit about vows. Five lives are on the table. I've listened to sanctified crap all my life from you disciples of Jesus. Now, you show me what's more important—your vows, or the lives of four children and Sylvie Lamont."

Thomas Mulcahy put his hands over his eyes. Was it his burden to atone for Father Dunne? Was this the way God was testing him? He felt the gun in his pocket. Why had he taken it? Whatever the reason was, it would be made evident to him shortly.

"Take me to her," he said.

As if by sleight of hand, a folded check suddenly appeared between Patrick Kelly's fingers. He slipped it in Father Mulcahy's pocket.

Sylvie saw Father Mulcahy standing there and wondered why she hadn't heard the door open. The priest was a man in his early fifties who never seemed to have lost faith no matter what the circumstances. But now he had aged. Where his face had been ruddy, it was white and lifeless. The deep pits under his eyes were gray as if he had been a prisoner in a cell far longer than she. The door closed behind him.

He took Sylvie's hand. "I'm so sorry for all this. You shouldn't be here." To see her, who had always been the epitome of style and beauty, in this drab cotton dress and slippers was more than he could bear.

His eyes gave him away, for she said, "Hardly what Mark Cross is showing this season."

"No, my dear."

374

"Have you come to hear my confession?"

The priest hesitated. "They say that you don't have to die. That if you tell them the identity of a man you can save your life and the boys." He produced the check. "This check will feed the children at St. Stephen's for six months. . . ."

He couldn't go on, and tears came to his eyes.

Sylvie took his hand. "Father, what is it?"

"I am to hear your confession," he said without looking at her.

"Father, you wouldn't use confession?"

"The boys . . . Eddie, Eugene, Francis, Timmy. I don't know what will happen to them."

She smiled sadly. "You won't do it. You're not like him."

"You mean Father Dunne." He shook his head. "No, I am not like him." He took out the gun. "I brought this. I thought . . ."

Sylvie came to him. "Father Mulcahy. I will confess to you. Please hear me and give me absolution." She took the check from his hand and tore it in two. "Put the gun away," she said. Then she knelt down.

When she had made her confession, the priest said before giving her absolution, "My daughter, do you have anything else to confess?" and she answered, "Father, there will be a terrible slaughter on Easter Sunday. It must be stopped."

They stood side by side staring at the light coming from under the door. The tall Irishman and the short, innocuous looking man who headed the Gestapo in New York. It seemed they had been standing there for an indescribable amount of time. Kelly was so dry, he couldn't swallow. C'mon, you shit-heel of a priest . . . do your job.

The door opened, and Father Mulcahy came out.

He saw both men staring at him intently. Bitter anger surged through him. The one wants retribution, the other his honor saved. He felt the gun in his pocket. Oh that he could use it. He extracted instead the two halves of the check and handed them to Patrick Kelly.

Kelly looked at it with total disbelief. Money had never failed him.

Thomas Mulcahy looked directly at him. "One priest failed the church tonight. I shall not. I am a priest, not an informer."

Abetz did not bother with the exchange. Instead, he walked into the cell. She sat on her cot, seemingly in deep concentration. Now she saw him. "Miss Lamont, perhaps you think that I will not do this . . . you are mistaken. You live in an occupied city. There are laws. The rich are not above the laws."

"But informers are," she broke in. "That would free me,

wouldn't it?'' She saw Kelly enter behind Abetz. ''I am going to make it very clear for you. It was I who grabbed the wheel and made the cab hit the Wehrmacht officer. Do you understand? I killed him. Not the boys. They're innocent.''

''They shall die,'' Abetz said calmly. ''As will you.''

''I'm ready,'' Sylvie said.

''Leave this to me,'' Kelly said.

Abetz advanced toward Sylvie. ''When I leave here I shall give the order for a firing squad. You die within the hour. This is your last chance. Give me his name.''

She looked at him and shook her head. ''What good would his name do you? Once I do that then you'll want his description, and then you'll want me to meet with him so you can arrest him. That's how you work. You're a vulture who eats human flesh. To give you his name is to die. I will not collaborate as Patrick has done.'' She heard herself saying all the right words. All her life she hadn't been able to say them, but now in the end she could. She knew that she would never be afraid again.

Abetz looked into her and saw indeed she had the stuff of martyrs. Her eyes brimmed full of that feeling. It always filled him with disgust. She wanted to die. Then, so be it. ''As you wish.''

He walked from the room, leaving Kelly alone with her. ''Darlin', don't do this. Don't.''

She came to him and stood before him, tiny in her prison attire. She looked at him for a long moment, and he felt infinitesimally small. ''I'm sorry that I didn't live this way always, Patrick. That's the only thing I'm sorry about.''

At quarter of six, an officer came for her. ''May I have a priest with me?''

He seemed embarrassed. ''Spies do not get priests.''

She nodded.

''Come,'' he said.

He led her along the same corridor and up some stairs. There was a door, and when he opened it she discovered herself facing the small courtyard where Meister had been executed. Now it was dawn. Father Mulcahy had given her his cross, and she clenched it hard. She was aware that breathing was difficult, but still the cold air felt good. She wanted to think of many things . . . of Maryland . . . of Maxim's in Paris where she had met Patrick . . . of Dede . . . her mother . . . her father. But she couldn't picture any of them. Then she realized they didn't matter. Only Robert did. In that instant she saw his face over her the first time they made love. In that instant she saw him and

376

she knew how much she loved him. "I love you," she murmured.

She was led to the wall, and now she saw the six soldiers. She closed her eyes, praying softly. The lieutenant was pulling something down across her forehead. She put her hand there.

"A blindfold," he said apologetically. His eyes were sad and yet hard. He has seen many men die in battle, she thought.

"No, please."

Abetz came out into the couryard, and the lieutenant bowed to Sylvie and left. She saw him say something to Abetz. Where was Patrick? she wondered. Odd, it was so cold, and yet she felt nothing. The lieutenant barked an order, and she closed her eyes. See him. See Robert one more time. There was another command . . . and then another. "I love you Robert . . . thank you."

There was a final command, and now the sound of rifles resounding in the little courtyard, and the slim figure in the cotton dress and slippers crumpled and fell down. The lieutenant walked to her, calmly, deliberately, and inspected her. He got up and nodded to Abetz, who turned around and walked inside.

From the window above the courtyard, Kelly watched. When the shot came he clenched his fists. He watched the lieutenant inspect the body and then report to Abetz. Now Abctz was gone, and Patrick Kelly made himself a promise. He meant to think it; a week later he was sure it was a thought. But in actuality, it was spoken. They were words he had used before, but never had he meant them more than now. "You little kraut bastard. I'll break you for this. I really will."

BOOK III

Chapter 39

March 31, 1942
6:00 A.M.

The sequence of events that led to the race took place late in March. Because of the large Jewish population on the Grand Concourse, Standartenführer Abetz had requested soldiers from the Wehrmacht battalion at the Kingsbridge Armory to help beef up the auxiliary police who ringed the concourse. Foot patrols tramped through the streets of the Bronx and inspected the apartment buildings the Jews lived in. Jewish storekeepers who still maintained their businesses, especially those in food, found their supplies confiscated by the police. Candy-store owners learned that their chocolates and ice cream, pretzels and candies, were so much fodder to be consumed by the invader. On a given day, the auxiliary police might loot a dry-cleaning store of its clothes, or smash up a tailor shop to amuse themselves. Random destruction would keep the Jewish population fearful and cowed, and allow the superior manhood of the occupiers to be displayed. It was this absolute belief in Aryan manhood that brought about the incident that led to the race.

Many young Jewish girls attending school came home every day in the late afternoon, or early evening if they went to college. When coming in contact with a patrol they often heard whistles and seductive cries, and it was not long before Jewish girls learned to travel in groups. For students coming home from school together it was easier, but for the Jewish woman who worked downtown in the garment center or a business office it was harder.

The incident involved Rachel Gittlesman, a student at Gompers High School in the Bronx who stayed late after school one day, looking for a prescription for her grandmother. She missed the trip home with her friends and didn't get back to the concourse until after dark. Walking home she saw she was being followed by a group of Wehrmacht soldiers in a military car. They followed her closely, but there was none of the usual jeering or taunts. This was all the more frightening, and eventually

381

she began to run. As she ran along the edge of Van Cortlandt Park, the car suddenly cut her off.

A Wehrmacht corporal named Victor Radl, and a Wehrmacht private, Joseph Schnell, surrounded the girl and dragged her into the car. Lights from the windows of the brown brick buildings facing the park came on as she began to scream. People across the street saw the Wehrmacht soldiers and the struggling girl, but no one dared to confront the soldiers. Instead they watched as Rachel Gittlesman was driven off crying out for help. An hour later Rachel Gittlesman was found lying in the park by Nathan Bernard, an out-of-work shoemaker who had spent the day at his sister's house. Ignoring her warning, he had gone for a walk and heard the girl's cries. She lay under her coat shivering and shaking, too traumatized to move. Nathan Bernard went to her and saw she had been beaten around the face. He saw the torn stockings and panties lying a few feet away. What had happened was all too obvious. He cradled the sobbing girl, whispering in her ear, *"Kindela . . . Kindela . . . mein shane Kindela."*

The Gittlesman ''incident'' aroused the Jewish community on the Grand Concourse. And if the elders in the community counseled caution, the sons were not so inclined. The fathers after all had landed with their fathers on Ellis Island. They were not born here, and their displacement, their foreign accents, their servility was a part of their European heritage. But their children had been born free of pogroms, and the feeling of being American pervaded their experience. They would never be servile.

The first retaliation took place three days later when three Wehrmacht soldiers were attacked by a group of youths wielding baseball bats. Lance Corporal Schlicter suffered a fractured skull, while privates Schultz and Runsacker suffered fractured ribs and a broken arm.

Two nights later, Sergeant Werner Dietzel was seriously wounded in a knifing incident by a lone youth who then outran an auxiliary patrol car, racing along the edge of the Concourse and disappearing amidst a maze of crooked streets and tenement shadows.

The next day, a Wehrmacht corporal named Gretzel, alone in his vehicle, was knocked unconscious, and moments later his car sped down upper Broadway and crashed into a parked bus. Gretzel suffered a broken pelvis, broken cheekbones, and a spectacular array of internal injuries.

The final reprisal over the Gittlesman incident triggered the race. On the evening of March 25, a heavy but not unattractive Jewish woman named Sarah Tucker lingered on Morris Avenue, not far from the Concourse. It was an area regularly patrolled by Corporal Victor Radl. His partner, Private Schnell, had been transferred to a Wehrmacht headquarters on Governors Island. Corporal Radl had been kept in the Bronx because no one really thought the two men had been seen, much less identified.

At eight o'clock on this bitter cold March evening, an hour when Jewish women were never out, Corporal Radl saw the buxom Sarah Tucker standing alone, and he took more than a passing interest. Especially when Sarah smiled at him as he drove up. Moments later they were conversing, and minutes after that he watched her go into her building, having written "6C" on a piece of paper. Victor Radl was not a stupid man, but when it came to women he let the lower part of his anatomy do the thinking. After pulling his car half a block away, which he deemed sufficient to disguise the fact that he was going to 1413 Tremont Avenue, he went into the lobby and pressed 6C. He was buzzed in and, noting the lobby was empty, went to the elevator. He pressed the button three times, muttering impatiently to himself. After kicking at the elevator door, the eager corporal went to the stairs and headed up them. It was a small enough price to pay for the plump Jewish woman upstairs. He knew her type. She wanted to be ravished by the conqueror. Well, she would get that and more. Radl didn't really know if there was an Aryan superman, but he was convinced that if there was, he was its personification. He got to the fifth floor landing in a series of leaps and bounds and looked happily up at the last floor. As he did he was met by a pot of boiling water thrown directly in his face.

The screams of Corporal Radl as he fled back down the stairs will always be remembered by every inhabitant of 1413 Tremont Avenue. Yet not one came out to investigate. They listened in silence as Radl, scalded, screaming in pain, lurched down the stairs and out of the building. He staggered some two blocks, rending the night with his howls before being spotted by a Bundist police car, which took him to nearby Royal Hospital.

What happened to Radl did not alleviate the trauma Rachel Gittlesman would always carry with her. Nor her family's disgrace. But it did seem to close the book on the Gittlesman incident. The Gestapo was not inclined to pursue the matter, nor was Wehrmacht headquarters. But Radl's comrades were. Two nights later Joseph Kessleman's appetizing store was burned to the ground. The next morning a flier was posted in apartment buildings along the Concourse. The pig that maimed Corporal Radl had been challenged to a fight by one Hans Lichter, a Wehrmacht sergeant. Until this *jüden* pig produced himself, a *jüden* store would burn each night. This logic, employed by the men of the Wehrmacht stationed at the Kingsbridge Armory, was worthy of the Gestapo. The Jewish community had obviously uncovered the identity of the Wehrmacht rapist. They would also know who threw the scalding water on Victor Radl. That night, Eilers, a Jewish department store on Tremont Avenue that had served the community for twenty-five years, went up in flames. Eilers was a community institution. The community was being squeezed. Something had to be done.

In truth, the community had not uncovered the identity of Corporal Radl. That had been done by a lone individual. His name was Ben Marks, a wiry one hundred thirty-five pounder who was eighteen years old. He had uncovered Radl by posing as an Irishman who bestowed six cartons of cigarettes and a case of wine on a garrulous auxiliary policeman named Conklin. Conklin had joined the Bund in 1938, broke and out of work. He was a stew bum. Calling himself Jack Foley, Ben Marks had prevailed upon Conklin to tell him who the rapist was, so he could give the soldier some free booze.

It was Ben Marks who knocked the Wehrmacht soldier unconscious and sent him careening down Broadway. And it was Ben Marks who planted a knife in the side of Sergeant Werner Dietzel.

There are no secrets in a ghetto, and though the grand concourse did not qualify as a ghetto, its inhabitants were only once removed from ghetto life, and so identifying Ben Marks through Sarah Tucker was easily done. In fact, Ben Marks was waiting for a delegation of men who came to see him at the Grand Alliance Club in the Bronx on Post Road where he slept. The club was abandoned now, but Ben had a key and stayed there nights.

The men were led by Louis Marks, Ben's uncle. He listened while the group of men stood in the empty gym where Ben Marks slept on a wrestling mat. His nephew had been on the street by himself for the last two years. He was a slight, wiry boy who had never emotionally recovered from the death of his father and mother in a three-month period when he was ten years old. He had lived with Louis Marks for six years, missing school frequently and fighting in the streets. He was given to long, silent, brooding periods. What kept him from being a street ganef was his activities at the Grand Alliance. The thin, curly-haired boy was a sprinter. For a hundred yards the nail-hard boy gave off the kind of sparks one sees in a blacksmith's forge. For a hundred yards he glowed like a furnace.

"I'll fight him," Ben Marks said in that flat, unemotional tone of his. He had a pale white face, a broken nose, and sad brown eyes. "I boxed on the Alliance team."

"Ben," Louis said, "the Nazi is a bullock. One punch and he'll cave your face in."

Ben Marks grinned. He feared no one, his uncle knew. "He's gotta catch me first."

"Don't worry, he will," Louis Marks said. He had an idea. "Why don't you race the Nazi?"

The group of ten men gathered in the cold, bare gym gaped at the thick, burly butcher who cut meat at the Hunts Point Market, all of which went to the Nazis. Louis Marks had deep blue eyes and a mashed nose, the product of too many street fights back on the Lower East Side. He had the reddish-purple veins of a man who had quaffed more than his share of cups. Like his nephew he was fearless, but he was not without *sekel* . . . a Yiddish word used to connote wisdom.

"The Nazis want revenge," Abe Lipsky said. "Not a race."

"They want blood," Solomon Jaffee agreed.

Louis Marks wiped a gob of snot from his nose with the sleeve of his filthy overcoat. It was a brown plaid and had been bought from a dealer on Orchard Street in 1934 for three dollars. He had seen more blood in his life than even the Nazis dreamed of. Since he was a youth, he had spent his life in the abattoir slicing beef. While Nazi soldiers were nestled between the soft teats of their women, he had watched the pools of blood flowing across the floor. Blood. What was blood? There was blood and there was blood.

"I will give the pigs their blood," he said softly. "Benjamin, you be prepared to race."

The boy looked around at the delegation, and the men looked at the boy. They didn't want to sacrifice him, but neither did they want any more fires. Clearly, it was better to sacrifice one than to have the whole community suffer.

"Let me speak with the Nazis," Louis Marks said.

That afternoon the deal was struck. It was made by Louis Marks with Sergeant Gunther Trachtenberg, who was the unofficial leader of the Wehrmacht vigilantes. That the fight was cancelled and a race substituted came about for two reasons. The first was because Louis Marks still offered the Wehrmacht blood. The second was because the Wehrmacht had a sprinter who worked out daily in Van Cortlandt Park. His name was Harry Ernst, and he was world class. Harry Ernst had been on German Olympic teams in 1936 and would have raced against the incomparable Jesse Owens had he not sustained a serious pull of the thigh while practicing for the four hundred meter relay. When Louis Marks proposed the race he already knew about Harry Ernst. And he also knew that the pride of the Germans in their superiority would cause them to accept the challenge.

The blood that would be spilled was easy to provide. As a

385

boy in Russia, Louis Marks had idolized a Jewish youth named David Bornstein. He was swifter than the wind. He could outrun a horse for forty yards. But he was a hero to Louis Marks not because he could outrun a mare, but because he went to his death on behalf of the Jews in the village of Tishenev. He raced to free his sister who had been taken captive by some drunken Cossacks. Bornstein had run a gauntlet . . . a gauntlet of knives. David Bornstein had undertaken to run eighty yards through the Cossacks with a knife thrust in his direction every two seconds. He had done so with incredible skill and the coordination and vibrancy of his youth. Dodged and snaked his way while running full tilt, as first one Cossack and then another thrust straight out with a gleaming piece of steel. And he had finished the race untouched, arms thrown out, a smile of triumph on his face, chest thrown forward. It was a variation of this race that Louis Marks proposed to Gunther Trachtenberg. And by three o'clock that afternoon the race had been agreed to as well as the terms.

It was to be held the next morning just after dawn in Van Cortlandt Park. It would be witnessed by the soldiers who formed the gauntlet, by Louis Marks, and Gunther Trachtenberg. It was to be acknowledged by no one. Not to the Jewish community, and not to Wehrmacht or Gestapo officers. This was a matter of pride. German versus Jew. It was to be a contest of skill and speed, and so that there would be no doubt as to the better man, two races were to be held. The first would allow the two runners to dash a hundred meters, as marked off by Louis Marks and Gunther Trachtenberg, unimpaired. A contest that would determine which man was faster. That would be followed by the running of the gauntlet, to determine which man had the courage and heart that went with his speed.

Louis Marks had no illusions about what he was committing his nephew to. Instead of Cossacks, the gauntlet was composed of Wehrmacht veterans, men who had fought in Denmark, England, Poland, and America. At two second intervals they would spring from attention and thrust out a bayonet point. Each runner faced a sharp-edged knife that would come from either side of the gauntlet. Bayonet thrusts were to be alternated from right to left. Louis Marks realized that it would take a miracle for his nephew not to be seriously hurt. He only hoped that he would not be killed, for he feared that some zealous soldier would thrust out his bayonet before or after the two seconds stipulated.

What Louis Marks didn't know was the caliber of soldier Gunther Trachtenberg was. He wanted no easy victories. He was a man who kissed a dying Polish soldier in Warsaw on the cheeks before executing him. Then the Pole would die as a soldier who had fought gloriously in battle. Trachtenberg knew Harry Ernst well. He had fought at his side in Denmark, England, and America. He knew what a competitor and soldier he was. Ernst wanted to win for the Wehrmacht soldiers in the Bronx, and his pride was such that he would not accept a cheap victory. Accordingly, Gunther Trachtenberg personally picked the twelve men who formed the gauntlet and personally instructed each of them. No man was to lunge with his bayonet until he heard Trachtenberg's command, *"Stoss,"* which would be given every two seconds. Harry Ernst was a great runner. Gunther Trachtenberg never doubted Ernst would win. The Jew would have a fair chance, but Trachtenberg knew what the outcome would be. The only thing he didn't know about was Ben Marks.

He didn't know that until the German invasion, Ben Marks had won a series of outdoor races for the Grand Alliance. He didn't know that Ben Marks ran wind sprints every morning. He didn't know that Ben Marks feared nothing and no one, that when engaged in athletics he was beset by such a furious rush of adrenaline that he saw nothing, knew nothing, felt nothing. He only was driven by a component that mixed a fanatic desire to win with a manic fear of losing. And finally he didn't know that Ben Marks had been offered a track scholarship at NYU by Emil von Ellinghaus, the coach, on the condition that he get his high school diploma. And what Gunther Trachtenberg should have realized was that Harry Ernst had not run seriously for over a year. But even if he had, he would not have believed anyone could stand up to Harry Ernst running a gauntlet of death, especially not a slight Jewish high school youth who knew nothing of war.

Ben Marks listened to his uncle explain the details of both races. He listened attentively and then asked that it all be repeated. Then he nodded, ate a boiled potato and a plate of peas, and went to bed. They were to be up at five o'clock in the morning. The races would take place just after sunrise, which was at seven-fifteen A.M. Both runners would report to the park at six o'clock and would be allowed to warm up in any manner and for as long as they wished. Louis Marks watched the boy eat his food with no expression on his face. He could die tomorrow, and all he did was methodically cut his potato and spoon his peas. What was in this boy? Louis Marks had known him all his life and knew him not at all. This was a boy who had knifed a Wehrmacht soldier, poured boiling water on another, and set an unconscious Nazi speeding along Broadway. A meshuga. But it was more than that. He was without fear. As David Bornstein had been. What could Louis Marks say to him? He was saving the community just as he had jeopardized it.

Louis Marks went to sleep without saying a word to Ben. He

thought he wouldn't sleep at all, but after a time he drifted off. Or perhaps it was that his thought and dream processes became one. He only knew that with total recall he saw the village of Tishenev, saw the great David Bornstein running the gauntlet of Cossack knives, throwing himself across the piece of rope that marked the finish line, exultant, eyes and mouth open in joyous exclamation of himself. And then he saw the smile twist into the mask of agony and death as David Bornstein ran into a saber held by the Cossack captain who had suddenly become a one man welcoming committee at the finish line. Louis Marks heard again the cheers of the Cossacks, saw himself running to David Bornstein, who was already dead from the sword that pierced his heart. It was a bright spring morning with the air redolent of the grassy meadows around them and the smell of flowers. And Louis Marks cried out as he had then. The cry of yesterday became the cry of this night, and he awoke. He rubbed his eyes. There would never be another David Bornstein. His nephew was courageous, but David Bornstein was incandescent. Another like him would never come. He was not a religious man, but he said a silent prayer for Ben Marks. He went to the boy and found him awake and dressed in his track suit and shoes. Spikes lay next to his bed and a warm-up suit. Who knew how long the boy had been up.

"I'll make us breakfast," he said.

"Just tea," Ben Marks said.

Louis Marks started to protest, but the boy had turned away and was rummaging in a bag. Now he held out white sugar cubes.

"Where . . ." Louis Marks began, and stopped. If the boy could knife a Wehrmacht corporal he could steal sugar cubes.

They drank the tea in silence, dipping the sugar in the tea as their grandfathers and fathers had done. Neither talked. What did the boy feel? Louis Marks wondered. Nothing. Good. He will take a knife in the side and fall. Better than a bayonet in his heart. He comforted himself with the thought that the bayonets would never be aimed higher than the waist. Let the Germans have their blood; the community would be saved more fires. He didn't concern himself with the first race. Ben Marks would lose. The boy was fast. But after all, he had maimed three Wehrmacht comrades. He wouldn't be so stupid as to try and win the race. For then they would surely butcher him during the gauntlet. He was so sure of this that he didn't bother to speak to the boy of it. He finished his tea and sugar and heard a knock at the door. He walked through the apartment and opened the door. He saw Gunther Trachtenberg and another soldier with a rifle. No chances were being taken. Louis Marks nodded and walked back to the living room and tapped Ben Marks on his shoulder. The boy stood up, picked up his warm-up suit, and palmed some sugar cubes from the floor. Then he followed his uncle out.

The two Jews walked together in back of Sergeant Gunther Trachtenberg and in front of the Wehrmacht private carrying a rifle. The grand concourse was dark and quiet. It was a mournful silence. As if the small apartment houses were populated with ghost people who remembered life in another time. When children played in the streets below, and the smell of latkes cooking drifted through open windows. A time when the journey from the hellish ghettos of the East Side and Williamsburg had been put behind them. When they assimilated and became Americans, mingled with the other thousands who rode the subways, watched their sons and daughters go to City College, saw them studying to become professionals, pointed with pride to Hank Greenberg, a son of the Bronx who had made it in baseball, rejoiced with other Americans in the triumph of Joe Louis. Democracy worked here. But that was a long time ago, and now the two Jews walked amidst the mournful silence.

7:00 A.M.

The sky was russet-orange in the east. The two runners had been warming up in Van Cortlandt Park for the past forty-five minutes. Phantoms who disappeared into the darkness, legs churning, smoke trailing from their mouths. Neither of them looked at the other. The thin Jewish boy, pale, eyes almost dilated as he searched for the emotion that he used to stoke fires within himself. The German, stocky and powerful, with thick muscular legs. He was a man running against a boy. Harry Ernst had been seventeen when he was chosen for the German Olympic team. Now at age twenty two he had run the hundred meters in 11.2 seconds. That was only four tenths of a second off his best time. He had not run competitively for a year, but he always kept himself in condition. And he was without nerves. Ernst had a face that looked like it had been chiseled by a sculptor. There was nothing spare, no touch of extra flesh. The cheekbones were set like rocks in his face, the jaw jutted out, the line of the mouth was severe, almost harsh. The hazel eyes were hooded, the forehead large, almost massive, the line of hair above it thick and close cropped on the side. It was a visage that had frightened many competitors. He looked out across the darkness and saw brick-topped stadiums, the cinders flying, teeth gritted, chest thrown forward, extended, extended, the noise of the crowd vibrating in him like a kettle drum.

The finish line had been improvised. It was a strip of white

389

sheet held on either side by two Wehrmacht soldiers. It was to be dropped when the chest of the winning runner made contact with it. Now as the first blaze of sun threw a crescent of light on the grass and dirt of Van Cortlandt Park, Gunther Trachtenberg gave a nod with his head. Louis Marks went to his nephew and whispered. The boy nodded, and peeled off his sweat suit. He was painfully thin. He had long, ungainly legs. Louis Marks looked over at the German. Stripped down to his track shorts and shirt, he was a machine. Louis Marks didn't know about Harry Ernst's Olympic record, but he did know the German was experienced. Much more than his nephew. Good. He will win, and that will give the Germans back their pride. Only his nephew shouldn't be badly hurt during the gauntlet race. Yet as he made these silent observations he was bothered. He knew he was keeping from himself something he felt.

The starting line had been marked by a long furrow dug into the ground. The runners were to balance themselves over it. That meant that each had to push off hard and make a long first stride to avoid stepping into the hole. That had been Harry Ernst's idea. The two contestants came together now. Like fighters facing one another for the opening instructions. The lean, sad-faced Jew, dressed in a uniform of white with blue trim, and the stocky German corporal, dressed in black with lines of gold running down the side. He stared directly at the Jewish boy in a hard, unrelenting way. Just enough to intimidate the boy. But the boy didn't seem to see him. He is afraid, the German thought. He dares not look.

They dug in now, testing the ground, practicing the start, shaking wrists and arms as if to loosen their skeletal structure. Then it was finished, and each took his stance. The German was crouched low as if he were a coiled piston ready to be released. The Jewish boy took a more traditional stance, higher, his body tensed, knees pushed forward. The German stared at the ground in front of him; the boy had his eyes riveted on the white sheet a hundred meters away.

Gunther Trachtenberg stepped abreast of them. He held a pistol in his hand. A Luger. It was not conventional, but then this was not a conventional sporting event. It was real, like the gun. He looked at each runner and saw their singular, fused intensity. Religious men in a monastic retreat were no more concentrated. He counted five to himself as he brought the gun up and over his head. He pulled the trigger.

The German seemed to fly forward, whereas the boy took two long, loping steps. Harry Ernst had won many races using that explosive start. In a sprint race there is no time. Winning times differ from losing by fifths of seconds. Steps, half steps, and inches separate winner from loser. Pushing forward, Harry Ernst had a step and a half yard on Ben Marks before they had gone more than twelve meters. Harry Ernst was confident in himself. That kind of lead for him was insurmountable. Getting off to that kind of start took the heart from the man who trailed you. Once you were in front, the adrenaline was released in you. Nothing could stop you. Nothing.

Watching the two runners, Louis Marks felt a peculiar angst in his chest. But all was well. The German was in front. He ran like a well-oiled car, all muscle, all body, throttle out. His nephew, on the other hand, was more of a delicate whippet. He had long strides and seemed ungainly. He trailed the German until sixty meters, but now something was happening. He was closer. For all his sweat and strain, the stocky German didn't cover as much ground. Ben Marks's long legs had closed the space between them. Louis Marks began to jiggle. His mouth was dry and then at eighty meters as Ben Marks pulled even, he knew what it was. It was David Bornstein running against the Cossacks again. Like Bornstein, his nephew ran for the Jews.

Beat the Nazi bastard, he screamed within himself. Beat him.

At sixty meters, Harry Ernst felt the boy close on him. Like all runners engaged in singular duels, a kind of telepathic intuition ruled Harry Ernst's body and mind. One does not see, but one can feel if one is pulling ahead. Just as one can sense someone pulling closer, one can feel a will that has not been broken by your explosive start. So Harry Ernst knew the Jew boy was almost even, and he knew that the boy still had will. He could not let the boy pull even. He reached back for some extra ounce of fire within himself and lunged forward.

But he could not shake Ben Marks, who ate up the ground with long strides, eyes never wavering from the white sheet only seconds away from him. He thought of nothing. He sensed the German, but he never deviated from one thought. Get to the white sheet. Thus Ben Marks ran against himself, while Harry Ernst ran against the knowledge that he had only a bare lead, and at eighty meters had no lead. Now eyes popping, chest straining, neck curiously tilted, he reached for a final effort. But the effect of all this simply was that he had broken rhythm, while the tall Jewish boy never deviated from his.

At ninety meters, Ben Marks pulled one, two steps in front, and Harry Ernst knew he had lost. Three steps, four steps, and as they finished, Ben Marks hit the strip of white a yard in front of Harry Ernst.

Louis Marks punched himself in the side. It was a blow that could have felled another man. But he said nothing. His nephew had won, won. It was only as he suddenly heard Gunther Trachtenberg giving the commands for the gauntlet to form that Louis Marks realized his nephew might die.

The twelve men who formed the gauntlet were all combat veterans. For this race the length had been extended to one hundred yards. Because of the preciseness of the bayonet thrusts, the longer distance was preferable. What Louis Marks had proposed was in complete opposition to the way a sprint is run. A sprint is a contest in which sinew and fiber are thrown into running forward as fast as possible. Now it meant that brakes would have to be applied every two seconds. But slowing meant you risked losing, for this was a race run against a stopwatch. The winner was the runner who finished the race in faster time.

Gunther Trachtenberg walked between the men forming the gauntlet and spoke quietly, but what he said reverberated like cannon shot. This was a contest of honor between brave men. That meant that each soldier on the gauntlet would immediately respond to the command *"Stoss,"* and thrust forward. It did not matter who the runner was. If any soldier deviated in any manner then he would run a gauntlet after the race. The honor of the Wehrmacht was at stake. He looked at the men and then turned on his heel and walked off.

The winter sun was a cold, unloving thing framing the two rows of soldiers on the cold, hard ground of the vast, empty park. Beyond were sloping hills and rocks where lovers would picnic and, on weekends in summer, softball games abounded. But now it could have been the Caucasus of Russia. The two runners stood at the starting line. Gunther Trachtenberg, smoke streaming from his mouth, stood between them and pointed to Harry Ernst. His man would go first. He had no doubt that though the Jew had outrun Corporal Ernst in the race, in this contest of nerve in which a man could be severely wounded or even die, Ernst's combat experience would easily make him the winner. Blood would be spilled, honor reclaimed. It was unthinkable to this fleshy-faced combat veteran with a thick mustache that there were any finer or braver soldiers in the world than could be found in the Wehrmacht.

Harry Ernst took his place and dug in. His jaw was set, and there was a red flush on his face. He would atone for losing. No pain could prevent him from winning this race. He waited, but this time his eyes did not find the ground. Instead he saw the gauntlet. The Luger exploded.

He bolted forward, but not with his accustomed explosiveness. It was more tentative as he came forward, heard the cry *"Stoss,"* and a bayonet was extended forward from the right. He turned sideways, ran left, found the middle. *"Stoss."* Now from the left. *"Stoss."* From the right. He side stepped, drove forward, *"Stoss."* He veered right, left, right. *"Stoss,"* *"Stoss."* Muscles constricted, veins at his temples throbbing and prominently exposed, Harry Ernst evaded five, then seven bayonet thrusts. But then at fifty yards one scraped him. He stumbled, dodged another, and then lunging forward went left instead of right and took a bayonet in the calf.

He screamed, blood spurted, and he stumbled. But he never stopped, somehow finding the rhythm again. Right, left, right. *"Stoss,"* *"Stoss."* He was at seventy-five yards and still going. *"Stoss."* Another stride, the bloody calf suddenly gave and Ernst lurched, stumbled. *"Stoss."* A bayonet found his side. *"Stoss."* Again the bayonet found him. And now he no longer knew which side was right or left. *"Stoss."* Another hit. Now as he crossed the finish line still standing, he held up his hands in agonizing triumph and pitched forward on his face.

No one uttered a sound. Louis Marks was in awe of what he had just seen. The Wehrmacht had butchered one of their own. What would they do to his nephew? He saw a blanket being laid over Harry Ernst by Gunther Trachtenberg, who left him a canteen full of schnapps. Trachtenberg checked his watch again. Twenty-four seconds. It was the Jew's turn now.

The boy took his stance, and Louis Marks felt all the blood rush from his body. God in heaven, he prayed, give me David Bornstein one more time. The gun sounded.

He ran lower than usual. *"Stoss."* He swerved left. *"Stoss."* He went right. He seemed to flow like some antelope or gazelle. Was he Bornstein? As he passed invisibly through one thrust and another parry, Louis Marks knew what it was. The boy knew no fear. He only knew winning and hated losing. Yes. He was Bornstein. At sixty yards it happened. Ben Marks's spiked shoe found the divot, and he lurched. *"Stoss."* He was going to be stabbed, but somehow he did a cakewalk along the ground, the blade missing his head by three inches. He righted himself and magically went left, never forgetting where the next blade would come from. *"Stoss."* Right, left, right. Twenty yards to go, and he was untouched.

The boy stumbled. It was not from a divot or loss of balance. He had been kicked by Private Oskar Krauss who was far down the line of Wehrmacht soldiers. Ben Marks pitched straight forward headed for the next bayonet thrust, the blade gleaming deathlike.

The blade ripped his track shirt and cut his navel as he pulled back. He drove for the finish line as Corporal Max Kemper brought his blade in a curving line upward, like death wielding a scythe. Abruptly, Ben Marks took off. He shot straight up in the air above the bayonet, then, landing, threw himself across the finish line.

Gunther Trachtenberg clicked the stopwatch. Nineteen seconds. He said nothing to the boy who had come loping past him to his uncle, who longed to embrace him but feared to move. Only after Gunther Trachtenberg stalked past him and moved down the line of the gauntlet did Louis Marks show any emotion. The tears streaked his face. "Bornstein, David Bornstein," he said to his uncomprehending nephew. They stood in the cold looking at one another while behind them remained the gauntlet Ben Marks had just run. At the far end Gunther Trachtenberg stood in front of Private Oskar Krauss, and in a voice devoid of emotion told him he was to run the gauntlet. Was that understood?

"Jawohl, Feldwebel."

The men watched while the private stripped off his equipment. He was not permitted to take off his Wehrmacht uniform. Exactly three minutes later, Oskar Krauss stood at the starting line and kneeled down. Behind him Gunther Trachtenberg aimed the Luger. Then he pulled the trigger and Krauss began to run.

Two seconds later, Trachtenberg cried, *"Stoss."*

Chapter 40

March 31, 1942
1:00 P.M.

The 207th Street IRT subway yard faced Ninth Avenue and had the Harlem River at its back. The river, that's what Kresky liked best. Their rear was protected. Kresky and his men had taken the repair station an hour ago. They had marched in, guns drawn, at the lunch break. Forty men, including Kresky. He had given the subway maintenance men two choices. Go now, or stay and fight with us. If you fight, be prepared to die. We're not turning this place over to Heinrich while one man is still alive. He expected three or four would stay. Thirteen men had volunteered. They were given rifles and told to wait in the repair shed. They were in, there was no turning back. Including Kresky, there were fifty-three to take on the Wehrmacht.

Kresky looked across the yard where the subway cars rested on layover tracks. Trains that had to be repaired were stacked next to those that no longer functioned. Gray ghosts that would afford Kresky's men protection. The American flag had been raised quickly and quietly on a makeshift pole set up in front of the repair shed. Just now a fresh breeze caught it, and the flag billowed out. It was a mild afternoon, yet Kresky shivered. It was a long gamble. Sacrificing his life and the lives of the others in the hope that the city would rise. This train yard and the flag must become a symbol.

Once Jake Ragosky would have been here with them. In the night, as in many nights since Kresky executed him, Jake had been in Kresky's dream. Kresky saw himself with the gun pointed at Jake, and then Jake repeated Kresky's words, "It's gotta be, it's gotta be." Kresky came awake then, fists clenched, sweat bathing his throat and neck. He didn't sleep the rest of the night. He never slept much anymore. He knew what had to be done. Take the yard. Collins was off in the countryside asking Bill Donovan for permission. You don't ask, you do it. The people would come. They had to.

He looked out again at the yard. They could hold it for a long time. Not forever, but long enough to make the people see their sacrifice. They could not be ignored. The repair yard ran from 207th to 215th Street. It was bigger than Yankee Stadium. On the Ninth Avenue side the elevated line ran over it and then curved back to upper Broadway. The two side entrances on Broadway were heavily barricaded by overturned subway cars. In the red brick building next to the entrances, Kresky's men were posted at the windows with machine guns. They would be shooting down at the Wehrmacht from cross angles. If the Wehrmacht took a right on 215th Street and came down Ninth Avenue, they would face the front gate of the yard, which also had subway cars blockading it. Making it even more difficult for Heinrich was the chain link fence that ringed the entire yard. It served as a barbed wire enclosure that Heinrich would have to scale. A lot of krauts would die hanging on those wires. Barbed wire and subway cars. Let's see how the Wehrmacht pulls a blitzkrieg here.

Kresky turned to the Harlem River, which now flowed under a soft mist. The river insured that Heinrich had to come to Kresky. Across it ran the University Heights Bridge. The bridge connected Manhattan and the Bronx at 207th Street. The road across the bridge passed over the New York Central railroad tracks.

Beyond the tracks was underbrush and then University Heights, a network of apartment houses that overlooked the river.

The people in those houses would have a direct view of the yard and the fighting. If Heinrich tried to float boats on the river, they would be sitting ducks. It was more than a hundred yards from the underbrush to the rear of the yard. Lots of them would die. Heinrich wouldn't use boats. That would be admitting the Wehrmacht couldn't storm the gates against a handful of working men. No, they would have to come via the front and side entrances, and they would have their hands full. The only spot where Kresky was vulnerable was the subway tracks that ran in and out of the yard. A series of four that sloped away and underground to connections farther down the line. The IND and IRT hauled their cars here for repairs. Heinrich could run trains into the yard. But to do that he would need subway union men, who had friends and brothers in the yard. Heinrich would need his own engineers, and in anticipation Kresky had already scrambled the tracks by having men take switching stations at the same time he took the yard. It would take Heinrich a while to unscramble the mess. In the beginning Heinrich would have to come via the front door.

Kresky saw Paulie Lazar being led toward him along the tracks by two men. The big gangster wore a new brown topcoat and a snappy fedora. Even from here, Kresky could see the bulge of the gun in its holster. Lazar swaggered as he walked. He was a big man now. Executioner for Vito Genovese. It ate into Kresky's gut. The infant labor unions had in their struggles also given birth to the gangsters. The unions needed strong arms to keep a solid front. The unions and the rising young punks had grown up together. Twins. The good child and the bad.

He watched Lazar pick his way between subway cars, looking around suspiciously. He wonders what this is. He can't wait to pass the word on. You'll get your chance. I need you. There are a thousand like you, but you're in place. You're all the same. Lazar was a typical strong arm. He had gone as far as he ever would. But he was important to what Kresky had set in motion. Abetz must get the first word of what was happening here and set in motion the repressive roundups and other tactics that would inflame the people of New York. Abetz was smart, but he was reactive. He would move. There would be a response.

Lazar stopped just a few feet from Kresky. "I got your message. What's up?"

As he spoke, Kresky watched Lazar's hands. "You're riding shotgun for Vito Genovese."

Paulie shrugged. "Could be."

"You hit Bruno's the other night." He saw Paulie's expression change. "You made it look like we did it. But you did it for Heinrich." Kresky pulled out his pistol. "You can't play both

396

sides of the street, Lazar. You're with them or with us." Lazar's little eyes bored into the gun. Oh, how he respected a gun.

"I don't know Vito's plans. He's runnin' things. We hit a bunch of Heinrich businessmen."

"Sure you did. Dressed like workers. Genovese was with Mussolini. Now he's back. Who do you think he works for?"

He saw Lazar's surprised expression. Good act. "Well?"

Paulie shifted uneasily. "Well what?"

"When's the next job?"

He saw Lazar struggling with himself. "I can't eat no cheese."

Kresky pointed the gun. "How about eating bullets?"

Lazar stalled. "What is all this? Custer's last stand? You got guys all over the yard."

"We're taking over."

"Why?"

Kresky jabbed Paulie in the chest with the revolver. "When is the next job?"

Lazar bit his lip. "Tonight . . . spray job when the fights break at the Garden."

"The Golden Gloves?"

"Yeah, we only clip civilians."

Kresky felt the nasty anger surging in him. "What's it all for? What's Abetz setting up?"

"I don't know . . . ya gotta believe me."

Probably the truth, Kresky thought. He inched up. "I want you to take out Vito's hit squad. If you do it, you go to Collins. If you don't, you're with them. If you're with them, you're against us and we'll get you."

Lazar was really rocked. "But then I'm against Vito."

"That's right, Lazar. No more playing both ends. It's war. And only one side can win. You got till tonight to decide. Now get out of here."

When Lazar was a few feet away, Kresky called to him. "If you see Collins, tell him Paddy Pearse is with us."

He watched Lazar making his way back toward the entrance, dwarfed by two grayish subway cars. Everything was gray in New York. The weather, the uniforms, the slime of the collaborators. Lazar was at the gate now, and the men were letting him through. Kresky made a mental bet with himself. Lazar would hop into the next phone booth and call Vito Genovese. Genovese would call Abetz. That was exactly what Kresky wanted. Lazar would have the nickel in his hand right now.

Vito's office was located in the back of the bar down on Grand Street. In the old days it had been the headquarters of Salvatore Maranzano, the last of the big time Greasers before Luciano wiped him out. Now it belonged to Vito Genovese. The room was like a beat-up card deck. A dingy green rug, a dim overhead light, a desk in the corner. Paulie sat on a stuffed couch that had long since popped its stuffing. He had stopped for three boiler-makers before reporting in.

Vito came in and strode directly over to Paulie. He clapped his back. "I just spoke with Abetz. You done good."

Paulie tried to smile. "They got everybody?"

Vito didn't answer right away. "The place is surrounded. Oh, they'll put up a fight, but what's that?" It should have made Paulie feel better, but it didn't. He had a headache. When his head ached, it meant big trouble.

"Got a little bonus for you, Paulie." Vito pulled out a huge roll. Dressed in a dark black suit with a white shirt open at the neck, he looked like just another neighborhood Shylock until you looked into the dark eyes. Christ, it was always midnight there.

Vito stuffed some bills into Paulie's shirt pocket. Then some more, and he didn't put the roll away. He smiled and Paulie felt a shiver. Something was coming.

Vito ground out his cigarette on the floor and walked over to the corner. He came back with a scotch bottle and, taking a long swig, handed it to Paulie. It was Johnnie Walker Red. Smooth.

"Paulie, I got a little job for you. Tonight." Vito held up his hand anticipating Paulie's protest. "Forget the Madison Square Garden shit. That's a quick hit and run. I need you for something more important."

Paulie gaped as Vito slid his arm around his shoulder.

"Listen Paulie, you know Vinnie the Chin?"

Paulie felt like his eyeballs were coming out of his head. "Vinnie Agramonte, sure, I know him."

Vito smiled. "Good. Listen to me Paulie. Tonight, Vinnie's gonna clip Frank Costello."

Christ, Paulie's fuckin' head was pounding.

"Chin's gonna be on the door, you know what I mean. In uniform. Frank is using Dandy Phil Kastel's apartment at 275 Central Park West. He's doin' business. Tonight we close his shop. Chin hits Frank—" Vito took another swig. "—you hit Chin." He stuffed five more century notes on Paulie. "I give you a dime's worth, Paulie. When you clip Chin, another dime more. Are you the man?"

"I'm the man," Paulie said. He felt like he was croaking.

"Good, now listen up. Frank is goin' to a party. He'll be in at midnight, around curfew time. When Chin hits him, you'll be parked across the street. Don't worry about nothin'. Nobody will disturb you there. Chin comes across the street because you're drivin' the getaway car. Drive through Central Park . . . stop . . . clip him. Use a silencer. Dump him in the river. Come straight here when you're finished. You'll be sleeping like a baby with another dime in your pocket tonight. Do this for me, Paulie, and you'll be my number one gun. I give you the job tonight, not Trigger Mike. You know what that means."

Vito stood up. "Remember, straight back here."

Paulie swallowed hard. "Why we clippin' Chin?"

Vito Genovese looked at Paulie with those ice-pick eyes. "While I been in Italy, he been with my Anna." Vito Genovese walked from the room.

5:30 P.M.

Paulie walked under the shadow of the Third Avenue El as rockets went off in his head. It stank. Vito clipping Frank Costello was like killing the president. It was even bigger. It meant bein' king of New York. Vito wasn't letting anybody who killed Frank Costello live. Paulie was the driver, which made him an accessory. There would be a contract out on Paulie tomorrow morning if Paulie was still alive.

The wind cut into his sinuses, and he scowled. He remembered a story Uncle Barney told him about Vito Genovese. Vito fell in love with Anna, and a few weeks later her husband took a long fly off a rooftop after being strangled. Paulie stopped and leaned against the wall of a brick building. Yeah, he had heard the stories about Anna. She'd fuck a goat if it had pants on. Even Vinnie Agramonte. But that wasn't why Vito was doin' it. You hit Frank Costello, you don't leave two triggers around to talk about it. When Paulie came to the office tonight, Vito would put out his lamps. Paulie was a dead man.

He lurched into a beanery and sagged down in a corner booth. People were huddled around a radio up by the counter. What the fuck was it? The waitress came over. "You got any coffee?"

"We got some kind of shit," she said biting off the words. "I wouldn't recommend it."

Paulie pulled out the bottle of rye he had taken from Vito's joint. "Bring it anyway."

"Okay."

"What's goin' on?"

Her saucer eyes flashed out at Paulie. "Didn't you hear? Up

on 207th Street, the Gestapo has got this subway yard surrounded, but these guys won't come out."

Paulie stood up. His gut was on overload. "Where's the john?"

He had been drinking for over an hour. The bottle was gone. But the more he drank, the clearer Paulie became. He had walked out of the yard after seeing Kresky. Word would get back to Collins. Kresky told him to stop the Madison Square Garden spraying. If he did that Collins would take him in. And if he saved Frank Costello, Frank would take him in.

Vito Genovese was the cheapest fuck who ever lived. When he started shoving those bills on Paulie, it stunk like a toilet. After Paulie hit Chin, Vito would hit Paulie and take back his thousand clams. It also meant Abetz didn't need Paulie anymore.

Paulie slugged more whiskey. Fucking Heinrich had ditched him. Used him to find Kresky. Made him into an informer. Made him squeal on Nippo. You little kraut bastard. Who the fuck do you think you are? This ain't your town. You think you can come in here and fuck me over. You and that ginzo Genovese. Big man, Vito, when he had a shotgun in his hand. Paulie drank more booze. Jesus, he was clear as a bell. And smart. You was wrong, Kresky. By standing on the fence I can save my ass. All I have to do is clip the right people. First hit the execution squad, then clip Vinnie the Chin before he hits Costello. He reached inside his jacket and touched the gun for reassurance. Then find Collins. Find him fast, because Vito would put out a contract on Paulie. Well, go ahead, ginzo. After I take out your best triggers, who's gonna do it for you? Something struck him as being wrong with this logic, but another drink replaced logic with conviction. Fuck Heinrich. Paulie was an American. And now he knew exactly what to do. He picked up the empty bottle and threw it directly through the window of the beanery. Three people dived to the floor at the sound. The waitress turned and looked goggle-eyed at Paulie.

Paulie Lazar stood in place and eyed the remaining patrons. "Anybody don't like it?" There was no response. Moving from the table, Paulie swept the coffee cup away and sent it flying across the room. Then, throwing back his shoulders, he staggered forward and was gone into the night.

6:00 P.M.

Night had fallen. The bright lights set up by the police illuminated the chain link fence. Abetz stood by a police car, smoking a cigarette. The repair yard had been surrounded by two-thirty. An initial burst of fire had driven off police. Abetz had arrived on the scene at four o'clock. Within an hour, Wehrmacht troops from Governors Island had arrived. Now some three hundred soldiers ringed the repair yard. Behind them were police and police vehicles. But no order had been given by Abetz.

He stood by himself, chain-smoking, drinking coffee laced with brandy. It was clear what Kresky was doing. He wanted an incident. An incident that would inflame people. That must not happen. Yet neither could Kresky be allowed to sit in the station for any length of time. It was provocative. It would flout the Reich's authority. That would give the scum of New York ideas.

Kresky was looking to create martyrs. It was part bluff and part suicidal. He must not be allowed to create an incendiary incident before next Sunday . . . Easter Sunday.

Kresky's plan was clear, but Abetz picked up the bullhorn and stepped forward. It was a chess match, and this was the first move. An exchange of pawns.

The diminutive standartenführer spoke for the first time. "Kresky, this is Abetz. You are surrounded. Give up now or face annihilation. You and all your men are outlaws. Surrender and you will be treated well. Oppose me and all of you will be killed."

The Gestapo leader stopped and stepped back as if he were a vaudeville performer turning over the spotlight to another act.

Soldiers and police waited. Rifles ready, waiting for a command, waiting for a reply.

It came a minute later. Loud and clear. Through a large bullhorn stolen from the fire department.

"Abetz, this is Kresky. Fuck you."

Chapter 41

March 31, 1942
9:13 P.M.

Madison Square Garden was smoky and noisy, but it wasn't like the old days. No, not by a long shot, Jack Bixwell told himself. To be precise, he was Black Jack Bixwell. Black as the proverbial ace. The only black man in New York who would have the nerve to slip into Madison Square Garden to watch the Golden Gloves tournament. There was standing room in the back, and he had bought himself a ticket for two bits from Wally Brown, whom he knew from the days when Black Jack had been a swift lightweight contender. He had gotten a few looks and heard *"schvarz"* a few times, but that didn't bother Jack Bixwell. For he had come to see Fritzi Machen fight. Machen was going to make it to the finals. He would face Sugar Ray Smith. Jack Bixwell managed Sugar Ray Smith.

Machen was fighting a German kid from Ridgewood in the semifinals. Gerry Nagel. Nagel was big and strong. He was a lefty who could send you bye-bye, give you a kiss to dreamland real fast. He had a left hook that was lethal. Nobody had gotten past four rounds with him. He was good, but Jack Bixwell knew Machen would eat him alive. Machen didn't knock you out. But nobody knocked Machen down. Fritzi Machen was a bull. He pounded your body till you pissed blood, and Machen knew something that only Jack Bixwell knew . . . a secret they shared together. Nagel telegraphed the hook. When he was going to use it, he dropped his right hand, leaving a one-way path to his jaw. Black Jack Bixwell made a little bet with himself that Machen would knock Gerry Nagel out.

Just now he turned to a beefy young man in a soldier's uniform. "Hey, my man, want to play pick the round?"

The soldier looked at him. *"Vas?"*

Black Jack Bixwell laughed and slipped into the noisy throng at the Garden. He had to find himself a sucker. That would be at the front. Madison Square Garden was a series of levels. There was ringside, there was the middle, and there was the balcony. And so Black Jack Bixwell, moving on twinkle toes like he was Bojangles Bill Robinson coming down a set of gleaming stairs on the Apollo stage, began a descent to ringside. Where the money was. Where the action was.

10:13 P.M.

Paulie stood in the hallway of an old tenement building on Second Avenue, watching the garage across the street. He felt the gun in his overcoat pocket. He was sharp now and edgy. He was always edgy before he killed. Edgy was like being hungry, only it was more so. Edgy meant you saw everything very clear. Edgy was like eating raw meat. But he couldn't show it to Scalizi, to Trigger Mike, to Tony Palmieri. One little thing off and they would smell it.

He had done everything just right. First, Jack Hurley had fried him up two pounds of fresh chopped meat and made a pot of coffee. Paulie filled his gut and fed his nervous system. He had it all planned out. They would be leaving in five minutes. Vito wouldn't be there. Vito had to have an alibi for when Frank Costello came home tonight. The cocksucker was probably having dinner with Costello.

The hit squad would be sitting around the old garage, smoking, cracking wise, waiting on orders from the Gestapo for the hit at the Garden. They were just a little edgy, so Paulie had to be very good and very quick. They were all professionals. But Paulie was better because they didn't know he was coming. So he had a half step. He hunched up his shoulders, felt the gun in his pocket, and then stepped out into the street.

10:30 P.M.

Nagel was big and burly, with a mop of black hair. Machen was flat-nosed, with a body like a tank. The jaw was steel and the Garden was pandemonium. Black Jack Bixwell slid in next to Dinty Callaghan. Dinty was king of the books. He kept his parlors open by paying off the police and the krauts. He doubled his vig, and his customers paid it or else. Dinty had a face that must have been given out at Kleins on a bad bargain day. Nothing matched. Small lips, a nose that was all over his face, north and south, and crossed eyes.

"Dinty, my man."

Dinty looked at him. "Nigger, you live dangerously."

Black Jack smiled. "I'll call the round for three dollars."

Dinty smiled contemptuously. "Kiss my ass, Jack."

"A dollar."

Now Dinty smiled. "Jack, I could bet a dime."

"I'll take it."

Dinty spat on the floor. "Take your hustle somewhere else." Jack stood up to go, and Dinty reached over. "Twenty bucks. You call it when the bell sounds."

Black Jack Bixwell did a little dance. "My man."

Dinty Callaghan spat on Jack Bixwell's shoes. "I ain't your man."

10:47 P.M.

Paulie saw someone in front of the garage.

"Hey Tony," Paulie called out.

He had caught a break. He approached Tony.

Tony had come out for a smoke, and now he flipped his hand back and forth. "Feel like rain?"

"Nah."

Tony was the driver. He had to be careful if it rained.

"I thought ya wasn't comin'."

"I'm comin'. I wouldn't miss it." Paulie gripped the gun in his pocket.

"Vito sent you after all." Tony had a face like a choirboy. Never trust a choirboy, Uncle Barney had told him.

"Sure, Vito sent me." Now get his attention. "Give me a butt."

"Sure." Tony reached in his pocket and took his eyes off Paulie, who leaned in and brought Tony to him with his free hand. The gun was already out, and while in this lovers' embrace, Paulie shot Tony Palmieri silently through the heart.

10:49 P.M.

They had felt their way through the first round. Nagel in red trunks cocking the left, Machen, lantern-jawed, hair slicked down, in black trunks, clinching, bobbing and weaving. Whacking Nagel to the belly. Machen was going to club the kid to bits, piece by piece. Punish him. Mutilate him, and then knock him out. Three times, Black Jack had seen Nagel drop the right hand. Machen had seen it, too. Machen always wanted the edge. This round was the time to get it. It was early in the fight. Nagel wouldn't expect it . . . and then suddenly Black Jack knew what would happen. Machen would knock the kid out now. Break his confidence. The kid had never been defeated in his life. He couldn't stand up to being a loser.

Dinty Callaghan turned to Jack Bixwell. "What do you say, nig?" Callaghan loved Nagel. He wanted to take him into the pros.

Jack Bixwell flashed a hundred he had just printed yesterday. "This round."

Dinty Callaghan took out his roll. "Twenty bucks . . . this round. You called it, nig."

The bell sounded. They were in the center of the ring, and then Machen pounded Nagel into the ropes. Nagel came off the ropes looking to throw the left. He cocked it . . . and dropped the right. Fritzi Machen stepped in and threw a six-inch right that tore Nagel's jaw off. He fell like a steer crushed by the slaughterhouse hammer. He was never getting up.

Dinty Callaghan was up with everybody else as Wehrmacht caps sailed high in the Garden. "You fuckin' little nigger. He'll do the same thing to your boy."

10:52 P.M.

Paulie was in the garage. Pete Scalizi saw him first. "Paulie, you see Tony?"

Paulie smiled. "Yeah, he's outside havin' a smoke."

Trigger Mike was the more dangerous. He was checking his piece. Paulie walked over to him. "Nice rod, Trigger. Beauty. Let me see."

Trigger looked up at Paulie from his chair. He loved his guns. He handed it to Paulie. Pete was stretching, his back to Paulie. Now.

With his left hand Paulie took Trigger's gun as his right hand crossed over and flashed his own gun. It was just a quick pop, but it blew Trigger Mike's head off.

Pete Scalizi knew what the pop was. He turned, but his hands were empty. Paulie had the edge. He popped Pete from ten feet away. Right through the chest. Pete went down, clutching his chest.

Two quick steps, and Paulie stood over him. Pete was trying to get his gun from the holster. "Forget it," Paulie said. He put two more slugs into Pete's heart.

11:07 P.M.

The floodlights from the street were reflected on the men's faces. They were quiet. In position, in empty subway cars. Some slept while others kept watch. Kresky stood by a subway car, watching the Heinrich light. How many of them realized what they were giving up? How many really realized? They would never go home to families, see their children, watch a sunset, bite into a roll with lots of butter smeared across it. It was a very long gamble. Who said the people would respond? In his heart, Kresky felt the time had come. But that was intermingled with hope, and hope is illogical. These men had said they would rather die than live under the Nazi jackboot. The few always had to lead the many. We will give a good account of ourselves. They shall not pass except over our bodies. At this moment American and Japanese ships were engaging each other. If the Americans win, anything is possible. If the Japanese win . . . Kresky shook his head.

We will give a good account of ourselves. He had a few surprises for Heinrich. A machine gun set up inside a subway car. Grenades and Molotov cocktails. Like a good general, he would save something for each Wehrmacht charge.

Kresky looked at the large cranes used to lift the subway cars. Caught in the light, they resembled dinosaurs. Next to them were the deserted subway cars. Empty like New York, a city without its heart. It needed a transfusion. Our blood, he thought, will be that transfusion.

11:37 P.M.

Abetz sat at his desk. The room was completely dark. He never sat in a room without light, nor slept in one, but in this rare instance he had surrendered himself to the darkness. This situation had been thrust upon him by the American. With just six days to Easter Sunday and the roundups Abetz and Kelly had been planning for months, what was needed was a quiescent city and populace. Everything as usual. But this American, this daring renegade, had anticipated him. This elusive and cool killer who crouched on one knee had killed five of Abetz's agents. He was somewhere now directing what Kresky was doing. And he would do something else to light the fire. Abetz had to find him. He and I are linked now, Abetz thought. He remembered the American standing in front of his car window aiming a pistol at him. He would never forget it.

What would be the man's next move? He didn't have access to Sylvie Lamont's information. She took that to the confessional with her, Abetz was sure. The priest . . . Father Mulcahy. He would have the information. He would get word to this American. Follow the priest, and from the shadows will come the American.

April 1, 1942
12:03 A.M.

Paulie had been sitting in the car for half an hour and no sign of the Chin. The doorman was a stooped old fart, opening car doors with one hand, taking tips in the other. Costello would be back any minute now. Vito had said Chin would be wearing the uniform. That meant he had to be on the door. It couldn't have been called off. When you plan a hit on a boss, nothing changes it unless he gets you first. Think dummy. Uniform . . . uniform. Jesus, why didn't he think of it before? He hurtled out of the car.

Walking quickly across the street, he noted the limo pulling up in front of the building. Christ, don't let it be Costello. The doorman was bowing and scraping, and Paulie saw it was a couple of white-haired geezers. He moved under the awning and inside, onto the crazy-patterned carpet that ran the length of the lobby. There were elevators on both sides. Paulie chose the east wing, and walking past a potted palm, stood near the door. It was in use.

He positioned himself to the side with his hand in his pocket. C'mon. He heard it coming down.

The door opened. No one came out. Then the elevator man appeared.

He was a giant of a man. Six feet four, broad shouldered, the cap not quite covering the wavy hair. It was Chin Agramonte.

The gun came from Paulie's pocket as he called softly, "Chin."

The giant in the red uniform turned, and Paulie saw the little marble eyes and the face below them, which seemed to be all jaw.

Chin's eyes showed recognition and bewilderment. Paulie had the edge. He raised the gun and popped Chin three times in the chest. Chin's eyes went wide with hurt and surprise as he discovered he was dying and defecating on himself simultaneously.

Paulie never stopped to watch Chin finish his fall. He walked hurriedly past the elderly couple who had now entered the lobby, then past the startled doorman, and strode briskly to his car across the street. The next morning the *Daily Mirror* would report that the doorman said the killer seemed nerveless and unruffled. He was like a postman who had made his delivery and was going home.

12:42 A.M.

Collins had slept like a dead man. All the long weeks and months, and then the trip to Washington had caught up with him. He had gotten home at eight-thirty in the morning and gone immediately to bed. His dreams had been full of bleeding images. The bodies flying from the train, the slashing wind in his face. Then the girl telling him, "I'm Jewish. . . . my name is Leila Fox. And I don't ever want you to leave me or me leave you." Then Sylvie was there. "I love you, Robert." He awakened periodically, hand outstretched. For which one? He should get up. He had things to do, but he had to sleep. He was so tired. Three months' worth of tired.

Finally, at midnight, he stirred and came awake. He was hungry. He stumbled out of bed and into the kitchen. He boiled some water and found the old tin of teabags. Used ones. He had learned that if you put four in a cup, you could brew up a respectable cup of tea. There was a loaf of bread wrapped tightly. He took four pieces and slipped them inside the oven, then lit it with a match. Tea and warm bread. All the comforts of home in Nazi New York.

He sat at the old table, drinking the tea. Eating the bread was like sampling warm earth. But it sufficeth . . . it sufficeth. The dreams came back at him again, assaulting him with their cutting images. He opened the volume of Shakespeare and began to thumb through it. For some reason he stopped when he got to *Richard II*.

The second Richard; weak, indecisive. His finger stopped at John of Gaunt's dying speech. This royal throne of kings, this sceptered isle, this other Eden, demi-paradise, this fortress built by Nature for herself. Against infection and the hand of war, this happy breed of men, this little world, this precious stone set in the silver sea. He read the speech again . . . precious stone set in the silver sea . . . a moat defensive to a house . . . this sceptered isle . . . this England . . . England gone . . . but Manhattan is an island. A moat flows around it. Kresky was right. Cut the island loose from its anchor, and you can take it. Cut Manhattan loose, and you don't need parachute drops. Cut Manhattan loose and Heinrich is . . . there was a knock at the door.

He moved from dreams to reality quickly enough. He had the revolver out and stood aside from the door. He opened the peep and saw a big man with small features. Familiar and yet strange.

There was another knock. "It's me. Paulie. Paulie Lazar."

2:13 A.M.

They sat around a large wood table in the living room of Klaus Meineke's apartment. Radner was at the far end. The plotters, he thought contemptuously. From left to right, General Ludwig Beck, Colonel Klaus Meineke, Ivo, bearded and noble, the only dangerous one. To his left, Herzog, who represented Canaris of the Abwehr. He would be a plum for Abetz. Von Stauffenberg, Ehrlich, Suederstrom of the Wehrmacht. He knew their names like lines in a play. Wicki, Hauptman, Holsheimer, Gudenberg. Good men . . . fools. You have no chance. We wait for the knock at the door, and then I am a knave forever. All of it gone. Leila . . . culture . . . everything. There was only the party and survival. Fools. Do you really think you can kill Hitler?

Beck held up his hand. "Gentlemen, I offer you a toast. We know what must be done. Hitler comes on the thirteenth. If his plane lands, then Ivo and Friedrich will be waiting for him at the opera with two bottles of champagne. To Ivo."

Glasses were raised. The champagne bottles were set to go off. Ivo would present them to the Führer on behalf of the Wehrmacht officers who had served in America. At the buffet reception before the opera. A spontaneous gesture not on the program.

It was Radner's job to get Ivo into the reception. Then Ivo would bow before the Führer and present the package. The bomb was timed to go off within two minutes. Ivo would keep the Führer talking and would die with his Führer. There would be screams, panic, chaos. Radner would go to the phone and call New York. He would give the message, "The present has arrived." If it failed, he would say, "The party is off."

Fools. The present will never arrive. We are all waiting for a knock, and then I will be in hell.

"To Ivo," Beck called again.

"To Ivo," resounded in the room. The Black Orchestra raised their glasses on high. They all drank except for Radner. He put the glass to his lips but he tasted nothing. He held the glass at his lips and he waited. Thirteen men. Perfect, thought Radner, for I am the Judas. We are seated in a circle around our messiah. Our mad messiah waiting for the knock.

"Gentlemen," Beck began. . . .

The knock came.

Beck looked up, startled. Radner saw Ivo start and reach for his pistol. Beck held up his hand. "Klaus, will you see . . ."

The knock came again. This time loud, insistent. Beck stood up. He knew who it was. They all knew. Ivo produced his gun, but Beck's hand was there to restrain him. "Let me see who it is."

He got up, and suddenly he looked very old.

The knock came again.

General Ludwig Beck went to the door and spoke. "Who is it?"

2:18 A.M.

Collins had listened to all of Lazar's babble and, when it was finished, said only, "You've killed half of New York—that won't help Kresky."

The big gangster, a cigarette dangling from his mouth, said quietly, "Nothin's gonna help Kresky." He saw the distress on Collins's face. "Oh yeah, he said to tell ya, Paddy Pearse was with him. Who the fuck is that?"

Collins rubbed his eyes. "Patrick Pearse took the Dublin post office in 1916. That was the first rising in modern Ireland. That was the key."

Paulie nodded. "What happened to him?"

"The Tans shot him."

Lazar didn't say anything, but Collins knew what he was thinking.

"Dumb fuck, huh?"

Paulie shrugged. "If I go into a situation, I want a chance to clip a guy and get out."

Collins nodded. "Sometimes you have to give yourself up. That takes real courage."

Paulie produced a bottle. He opened it, took a huge slug, and handed it to Collins. "So what do we do?"

Collins took the bottle. He downed a prodigious gulp. "You've done enough for one night, Lazar. Hit the couch, I need to think. And leave the bottle."

He sat now in the dim light of the kitchen, inhaling a butt, the bottle in front of him. Kresky had taken the revolution into his own hands. He wasn't coming out alive. But would anything come of it? Paddy Pearse's uprising took years to bear fruit. Killing hostages in Central Park hadn't done anything. Kresky was gambling that the scars would break open now and bleed. He was forcing Collins's hand but the city needed more than martyrs, it needed more than provocation, it needed dynamite. It needed bridges blowing, armories exploding, train tracks gutted, it needed a million people out in the streets. New York needed to be set on fire. It needed not one incident but ten. All stage-managed . . . and even then it needed the people to respond. He had told Donovan they would. But he didn't know.

He drank some whiskey. Cut the island loose. Cut Manhattan free. But that would take organization. It needed Collins to make a plan. How could he plan when he had two women on his mind? Where was Sylvie? How many days had it been? Tomorrow he would go to the newsstand. They would meet, and she would see Leila Fox in his eyes. He couldn't fool Sylvie. Jesus, what the hell was he about? He was here to lead the Resistance and he was worrying about women. Stumblejohn, what are you doing? Kresky was right . . . you've gone soft. You're the alcoholic who thinks he can handle it. You're hooked. You need a woman, which means Dublin is history. You're a man out of your time. You can still shoot fast, but it takes more than that. You have to want it bad, and the fires have gone out. That's why Kresky took the yard.

He got up, found the map of New York and the East Coast in the pantry, and spread it out on the table, using cracked cups to pin the corners down. Next to it he set down pad and pencil. He downed a gulp of whiskey. Then another. Well, he could at least plan it on paper. He was still a paper revolutionary. He had to know how to do it first. And then if the Japanese were defeated off the California coast . . . he caught himself. Mick would have told him never mind that. If you see it clearly enough, you go after it.

He sat down and began making check spots on the map, little

crosses, here, there. Then me made a notation on his pad. He wrote, he smoked, he drank, with John of Gaunt's words in his head . . . this sceptered isle, demi-paradise, this precious stone set in the silver sea, a moat defensive to a house. He smiled as the song came to him. "We'll take Manhattan, the Bronx and Staten Island, too. . . ." He wrote and he kept writing . . . and drank. He wrote and drank until the first rays of dawn showed silver in the pale morning.

5:12 A.M.

Kresky sat shivering in the morning cold, using the subway car behind him as support. The light had been turned off, but the Wehrmacht and police still faced them. Less than a hundred yards away. Would they come today? Would Abetz turn them loose? Was it Abetz's responsibility? Come on, Kresky begged. They had to. They can't let us sit around here. Yes, they can. They don't have to do anything. Then make them do it. Make Abetz do it. Maybe it's not his responsibility. Take it away from Abetz. How? He rubbed his eyes and shook his head. He looked around at the repair yard full of old cars, cranes, and tracks. Most of the men were asleep. Soon it would be time to wake them. Not just the men but the city. They just needed a little luck. He began to walk toward the shed where Bill Leary was sleeping. Leary was the best shot Kresky had. There would only be one shot given him. Leary had to make it.

5:27 A.M.

Collins drained the bottle and set down the pencil. Bravo, he had taken New York. It would take a week to set in motion. He stood up. He was burnt out, tired, and he hungered to make love. That's what happens when you let women in. Which one did he want? He stumbled into the living room past the couch where Lazar slept. Collins stopped. Lazar came awake.

"What's up, Jack Armstrong?"

"You want to kill the other half of New York?"

Lazar lifted his head. "Sure. What do you got in mind?"

"Just stay close," Collins said. "Stay close."

Lazar cackled. "Like flypaper."

"Wake me in an hour," Collins said.

"Where we goin'?"

"To demi-paradise, to a precious stone set in the silver sea."

"Jesus," Lazar murmured, "you better get some sleep."

A tray of breakfast was on Abetz's desk. Rolls, butter, marmalade and jam, a large pot of coffee. "Sit down, Captain." Abetz gestured to Radner. It wasn't a request, and Radner complied.

"Help yourself," Abetz said, gesturing toward the spread. "I love grapes in the morning."

Now Radner saw the bowl of fruit. God, he was tired. Abetz poured coffee. "Sugar?"

"Two, please."

"Cream?"

But Radner had already taken up the cup and drank the strong, dark brew.

Abetz eyed him as a cat would a mouse he might pounce upon at any given moment. "Yes, I know it goes against your grain but think of it this way. These men were traitors and you have done the Reich an invaluable service."

"What will happen to them?"

Abetz held out the bowl. "Grape?" He set it down. "These men are guilty of treason. They will be tried. Some shall be offered choices."

"Choices?"

Abetz made a face. "Some of these men will not wish to come to trial. It depends on the facts. You are tired now. I will have you see a stenographer this afternoon."

"I am free to go?"

Abetz smiled. "Of course," he purred. "None of these men shall know."

"But their wives, their families."

"All have been arrested or put under house arrest. Did you wish to stay in jail?"

"I thought you would make it appear as if I . . ."

"As if you what?"

Radner shut his eyes. You fool. You are Judas.

He felt Abetz's hand on his knee. Abetz had come around the desk. "Captain, you are a hero, not a traitor, don't you see? Not unless you believe in the cause of these men. You have your Jewess and I shall recommend you for a promotion to major. To Himmler personally. The Black Orchestra is no more."

Abetz's lips parted in a sardonic smile. "I should tell you now, Captain, that we have been seeking to catch the Black Orchestra 'in flagrante delicto' for many years. But we needed the right moment. Cut off from the Reich and Berlin, there were no informers who could warn them of the trap."

Radner fought the anger by biting his lip. "You refer to me? The informer . . ."

Abetz's eyes gleamed with triumph. "I refer to the information that the Führer was to come to Washington which you gave to them. Can you guess the rest of it?"

Radner saw it now. "He never meant to come."

"Precisely." Abetz's eyes now twinkled in triumph. "Did you think we would risk the Führer here in this country of *Jüden* and *Schwarz*, these vermin?" He paused. "But it had to be convincing. Authentic. And who would make it more authentic than the cultural minister of the city? Yes . . . yes. And you will, of course, understand why I could not let you know the Führer's real intentions. You played your part superbly."

Radner hid his shame in the gesture of rubbing his eyes. Enough . . . he needed sleep. "What will happen to Beck? I assume deportation and then a trial. . . ."

Abetz looked amused. "Hardly."

"I don't understand."

Abetz went around to his side of the desk and nibbled on a roll. "Trial would be a disgrace for the former chief of the General Staff. He made the choice himself."

"I'm not sure I . . ."

"Captain, you cannot be so naive. He planed to kill the Führer. He faced death by firing squad. He asked for a pistol as soon as he arrived here. Naturally one does not refuse an offer made by a man of his record, a man of honor." The last word was articulated in tones dripping with sarcasm. "Of course, we gave him a pistol."

Radner saw the amusement in Abetz's eyes. "And?"

Abetz tapped his fingers on the desk. "The poor man somehow missed himself. Inflicted a scalp wound without much damage. Can you imagine? This man saw himself taking over the Wehrmacht in America."

"What happened?" Radner cried.

"We gave him a second chance, of course. Extraordinary. This time he wounded himself in the head, but I swear to you he would have survived. I then had Hoppman finish what the general was so clumsily trying to do."

The image of Beck dead, his head bloody, leaped before Radner. He dropped the coffee cup and rushed into Abetz's private bathroom, head thrown forward, as the bile of his stomach poured up into his throat and out his mouth.

Abetz was drinking coffee and smoking when he returned. "Captain, you are tired, and you need sleep. Hoppman will call you later in the day. Now I suggest you get some sleep."

He watched Radner, ashen of face, leave. The young captain

had learned what life is about. He had done his job well. Though he thinks he hates himself for betraying the Black Orchestra, what he despises in himself is the realization that he is not of noble character. He must come to terms with his ambition. Abetz dismissed Radner from his thoughts and began to review his schedule. He would make an early visit to the subway yard to make sure it was under control. There was a meeting with Kelly at the Waldorf to check final details for Easter Sunday. But the two most crucial and pressing matters were checking on Father Mulcahy and the recapturing of the subway repair shop. They were linked together. If Kresky could be taken alive . . . there were ways of making him talk about his leader. In that respect the interrogation of General Beck had failed. Beck had used couriers, or so he claimed. Perhaps, Abetz thought, I should not have given up so quickly. But this priest had been alone with Sylvie Lamont. What passed from her to him? Abetz had a feeling. He picked up the phone. He wanted the current whereabouts of Father Mulcahy.

6:20 A.M.

The taste of his insides was still in his mouth as Radner entered the apartment. He sensed Leila's presence before he saw her. She was lying on the living room couch, shoes off, feet tucked under the pale green dress she wore. She was beautiful. She was in love with another man. How had it all happened? She had something to tell him, but of course he would have to speak first.

"Where have you been staying?"

"With Adele."

"I see."

He saw her suitcases then. Well, he had been expecting that. She looked at him, and then it began. "I can't stay with you anymore. I'm leaving the play."

"Where will you go?"

"That's not important."

"You have no identity."

She stood up. "But I do. I am Leila Fox."

He came forward and took her hand. How could she do this? He was through with her. She had been with another man. "Stay with me. I love you terribly. It will be different. . . ."

She stopped him by kissing his cheek. "Friedrich, something has changed for me . . . someone . . . Friedrich, our situation was never possible . . . we were never . . ."

Now he gently stilled her by putting his hand to her mouth. They both knew.

414

"Over is over," he murmured.

"Friedrich, you're a good man. I got you into this. By leaving, I can help you get out."

He smiled bitterly and saw her look of confusion. He could see she wanted to reach out to him. But it was pity, not love. His anger seared him.

She picked up her coat.

Panic seized him. "What will you do?"

"Work to free my country." She stopped. "I wasn't going to say that, but you see what has happened."

"You leave me with nothing," he blurted out.

She came to him. "Each of us has ourselves. That's all one ever has. Good-bye, Friedrich. I hope there's a better time."

She held out her arms to embrace him, and then suddenly he was pushing her away. "Get out. I know why you are leaving. Do you think I am a fool." He stopped. He saw the hurt in her eyes, and then her pity. It wasn't what he meant to say. I am better than this, you know that.

She picked up her suitcases. "Good-bye, Friedrich."

He watched her walk out, closing the door behind her. He heard it shut and collapsed on the couch.

Leila, come back, on any terms, come back. I did it for you. Now what shall I do?

11:13 A.M.

Collins bought the newspaper and felt his nerve ends curl around him like a string. A yellow cloth was there. A different kind. Not Sylvie's. She used hankies. The newsstand dealer gave him his change and nodded at him. Carrying the paper under his arm he walked toward Amsterdam Avenue and ducked into a walkup. He pushed his way into the vestibule and then slid under the staircase.

The message was carefully printed. He read it over twice.

MR. JACKSON, I HAVE A VITAL MESSAGE FOR YOU. PLEASE COME TO ST. PETER'S CHURCH DURING THE LUNCH HOUR AND TAKE CONFESSION. IDENTIFY YOURSELF AS VALIANT.

It was signed Father Mulcahy. He bit his lip. Shit, whatever it was, it was no good. It could be anything. A trap, bad news, important news. What had happened? He would have to find out. But he wasn't going unarmed. He lit a match and burned the message, grinding the ashes under his foot. Then he left the building with the last phrase playing over: Identify yourself as "Valiant."

St. Peter's Church was located on East Eighty-ninth Street. There was a garden with a black wrought iron fence around it. Collins had stood for a long time on the corner of East Ninetieth Street. He had crossed over a few times, watching the cars. It was a brightly sunlit day and there was the tang of spring in the air. When he was a kid it meant the baseball season was coming. Now, as he looked at the sun reflected on car windows, it meant search out the Gestapo. He checked his watch. Time to go? He was uneasy. Hell with it. Time to go.

It was dark and musty inside the church, and he kept his head down as he walked past the pews toward the confession box situated to the left of the altar. He saw unlit candles and a red velvet curtain. He tried the door. The confession box was empty. He went in.

He knelt down and suddenly felt trapped and claustrophobic. Get out, a voice within him warned. He heard nervous fingers drumming on wood as he spoke. "I have come to confess . . . I am Valiant."

The voice that responded was tense with emotion. "My son, I am glad you've come. I am Father Mulcahy of St. Stephen's Church. Miss Lamont asked me to pass this information to you." There was a pause. "On Easter Sunday the Nazis will round up a large group of young men. Not just politicals. It will start before dawn and will continue all day. They will be taken to the camp at Hackensack. Evacuation will begin the next day."

"Evacuation?"

"Ships will arrive at Montauk during the week."

Collins was stunned. Heinrich was really moving. The priest's voice snapped him back.

"Can you do anything?"

"I don't know. What else?"

"Only that Hackensack is ready. And that she . . . she loves you."

"Where is she?"

"She was arrested by the Germans. She was betrayed. The price of freedom was information. She wouldn't give it."

"What are you saying . . . what price?"

"Abetz had her shot."

He heard his voice, but it belonged to someone else. "Shot! No . . . not Sylvie."

"The price was you. Somehow Abetz knew about you and her. She refused."

Tears blinded him. That's why the replacement. Oh Jesus.

"My son. I see two men. They're Gestapo. I will go out and

416

distract them. While I do this you go past the red curtains. There is a door that will bring you out into the garden. Do you hear? Let me go first.''

Collins's head was bursting. He heard the priest move out of the box and felt for his gun. Collins counted to three and then exited.

Father Mulcahy walked down the aisle. "Yes, can I help you?" The two Germans in trenchcoats said nothing, then unmistakably they saw Collins.

"Stop."

Collins went out through the door and blinked as the sunlight reflected off the grass. He saw the fence.

"Halt."

He turned and saw the gun leveled at him. It was a thin, pale man with a bulldog mouth. Gestapo. End of the line.

"Drop your gun. Carefully." As he said it, he pushed his own gun into Collins's chest.

Paulie stood near a red Buick watching the church. He had tailed Collins all morning. It had been easy. Collins was off his feed. First the newsstand. Now here. What the fuck was he doing in a . . . he saw Collins coming along the black iron fence. Two men had him by the arm. Fuckin' Heinrich. They were heading for a car. Another Heinrich came leading a priest by the arm. They were taking them in.

The adrenaline pumped furiously through Paulie. Do something. He looked over and saw a man getting into the red Buick. Paulie ran around the car.

"Gimme the fuckin' keys."

The salesman in brown tweed and mustache saw a thick brute with teeth bared. Then he was separated from his keys and thrown to the ground. He did not cry out. Paulie was in the car. He switched on the ignition, turned the wheels at a right angle, and came out. He ripped the car into second, then third, and gunned it straight at Heinrich.

Collins heard the screeching tires and some instinct born and refined twenty years ago in Dublin made him move. He dug his elbow into the Gestapo agent, heard him groan, and then leaped sideways.

The red Buick slammed head on into the two agents, backed up, and came forward again. The third agent dropped the priest's arm and stood transfixed. He reached for his gun as Paulie Lazar rammed the Buick straight into and over him.

"Get in," Paulie screamed. "Get in."

He saw Collins grabbing the priest. They were inside in a second, and Paulie, snarling in triumph, roared, "We go, we

417

go.'' Tearing down Second Avenue, Paulie slammed Collins in the ribs. ''You were the easiest tail I ever had.''

1:13 P.M.

Abetz was not smiling. Early in the morning he got the call from Genovese. The assassin hired to execute Frank Costello had himself been executed last night. And there had also been the elimination of Genovese's hit squad. It could only be Lazar. That meant Lazar had gone over to the Americans. Abetz's coup of the night before, the news of which had been wired to Berlin, was dissolving already, a thing of the past. After all, the Black Orchestra was a bunch of amateurs, idealistic fools. And Frank Costello had come back to work for the Americans. The phone rang.

Abetz listened as the police sergeant informed him that three of his agents had been run down by a car while escorting a priest and an unidentified man into custody. Two of them were dead, the third severely injured. The driver of the car and the two prisoners had escaped in a red car. The police had the license plate number. . . . Abetz swore and hung up.

They had the American, the Resistance leader, and let him get away. Abetz had anticipated him, but not Lazar. The red car had been driven by that brute. Who else? Abetz was furious. Lazar was a runaway truck, and his leader a reckless phantom . . . a cat with nine or more lives. Abetz had underestimated the damage Lazar caused. The game was almost over, and Abetz had gotten careless. You couldn't do that with the American. He didn't know the game was over. And he had Lazar. They were loaded guns.

2:00 P.M.

Nothing seemed different in the city other than the warmth of the day. Traffic flowed, pedestrians dodged traffic, people spilled out of the subways. Yet something was different. You could see it in the way the people walked. They no longer seemed furtive strangers in their own city. Now they looked quickly right or left. Almost as if they wanted to make eye contact. The battle was on in Los Angeles. If their country won . . . if something good happened . . . if . . . if . . . if. The sun was warm, the day bright and clear. Spring was in the air. A harbinger. An omen. Jogging the memory with memories of other times . . . baseball openers . . . the smell of beer and franks . . . the ball rocketing off the bat of Joe DiMaggio or Pistol Pete Reiser . . . the crowd surging to its feet . . . finding with one voice the

418

joy of being alive. Freedom . . . freedom . . . the humanity of common joy and common cause . . . freedom . . . never forgotten.

2:33 P.M.

Kresky looked across the river and saw the crowds up on University Heights. There must be three or four hundred there, he thought to himself. The people are out on a fine spring day. They want to see a show. Now if Heinrich would just cooperate. He walked across the yard, slipped behind a small red building, and relieved himself. He came around now and ducked into the repair shed.

He saw Bill Leary, sitting on the steps of a subway car, smoking a butt. His rifle rested next to him.

He approached Leary, who ground out his cigarette. "It's the waiting," he said. "Why don't we start it?" Leary was a man with a ham hock of a face. He always looked angry. If you put that ham hock up in a butcher shop, no one would buy it.

"We will," Kresky answered, "but when I give the word. I want it to count."

Leary got up and walked over to a stepladder he had propped against the wall. He climbed it and looked up. Now he pointed directly at the elevated subway line. "Why don't they put men up on the line. Then they could look down on us."

Kresky came across the shed and stopped next to Leary. "When they do it means more than a military tactic. It means they have to disrupt service. It means acknowledging the rising. They don't want to do that yet."

"Why haven't they called for us to come out since last night?"

Kresky took a long time before answering. "They haven't decided on a strategy, which means they either aren't sure or there's a difference of opinion. What we're waiting for is the krauts to take the elevated and we pick somebody off. An officer of high rank. They can't ignore that."

He could see Leary's fingers working back and forth. "Just be ready," Kresky said. He walked away whispering to himself, "And don't miss."

2:47 P M

They had dumped the car on Riverside Drive and entered the park on Seventy-ninth Street. Collins stood against the rail watching the river. The boat basin, once full of pleasure boats, had been stripped by Heinrich. Father Mulcahy stood next to

419

Paulie, both of them watching Collins. Now the priest approached him and put his arm on Collins's.

"She died the way she wanted to. At peace with herself and loving you. I never knew her to be that way."

Collins swung around angrily. "I got her into this."

"No, you showed her the way to becoming herself. She wouldn't want you to be guilty. She could have made up some lie, told Abetz a half truth. Enough to get her out."

"Why didn't she? Why?"

"Because that wasn't her way. She was a long time coming to this. Don't take it away from her."

Damn it, the priest was right.

"Give her something back."

"What?"

"Give her the city. Take it."

Collins looked back out at the water. Damn it, it was all so quick. He remembered what his dad had told him in Dublin twenty years ago. "Lad, when you become a revolutionary, there is no time to mourn."

From behind them Paulie Lazar called out. "Hey, Jack Armstrong, let's go. We're sitting ducks here."

Collins took a key from his pocket. "There's a safe house on One hundred tenth Street. . . ."

Mulcahy shook his head. "I'm going to my parish." He overrode Collins's protest. "I belong there."

"You'll be arrested."

"Not if other things happen."

"I can't let you. . . ."

The priest laid a gentle hand on Collins's shoulder. "You haven't understood her death yet. You can't stop me. I couldn't stop her. Do you understand? In this time, we do what we must."

Collins put the key back in his pocket. "Then I'll see you soon."

They clasped hands, then Collins broke free and walked to Paulie Lazar. "Let's go."

Paulie gestured to the priest. "They'll make him talk."

"He won't talk."

"Where the fuck are we going?"

"Uptown. I want to see Kresky."

"Sure, we just walk in and say we're delivering roast beef. Hey, Abetz almost got you before. He's gonna be up there."

"I know," Collins said.

"Christ, you're asking for it."

Collins turned to the big gangster. "I'm taking the city. You want to go along with me or wait for Vito Genovese to find you?"

420

Paulie watched Collins walk away.
"Christ, wait up."

Chapter 42

The juice on the *New York Times* marquee on Forty-second Street had been turned on for the first time in three months, and a large crowd had gathered in Times Square. Round and round in dancing white letters came the same news . . . the bad news. TEN AMERICAN BATTLESHIPS SUNK . . . 150 AIRPLANES SHOT DOWN . . . JAPANESE VICTORY SEEN BY EVENING. Over and over the same lines, and still the crowds seemed to grow larger.

Radner stood at the edge of the throngs dressed in a blue suit with matching shirt and tie. Is it history, or is it Abetz's truth, he wondered. He watched the faces of the people. Men in suits, some carrying topcoats over their arms . . . girls and women in long dresses, carrying raincoats. He found himself watching a slim blond girl in a white blouse and gray skirt that didn't hide the slender legs. She had blue eyes, and there was a sheen to her face that months of occupation had not taken away. There was wonderment in her eyes. She keeps reading the same news, but she doesn't leave. She is riveted. They don't believe. They don't want to believe. He saw the same look in the faces of others. A young worker in a brown leather jacket; an elderly man with a cane, white hair askew in the wind; a fat matron in a green wool suit too warm for the day; a pointy-faced young boy no more than fifteen, school books under his arms, his studies the farthest thing from his mind. Why do you watch? What do you expect? It is hopeless. The Reich is here forever. Isn't that why I gave Beck over to Abetz? I have sided with the conquerors.

He turned back and looked at the young girl. Her beauty touched him. She was innocent, longing to be free. If I went to her and started a conversation, she would not turn me away. Because I wear a blue suit and I speak English well. But if I told her who I was, if I wore my uniform, she would reject me. Like Leila. The pain was back, and he turned and lurched away.

The crowd didn't notice the handsome, blond young man dressed in a blue suit, with a sea blue shirt and tie. They continued to stare at the *Times* board flashing the same news . . . TEN AMERICAN BATTLESHIPS SUNK . . . 150 AIRPLANES SHOT DOWN . . . JAPANESE VICTORY SEEN BY EVENING.

He drifted uptown, the sun shimmering in his eyes, forming a kind of cocoon around him, dulling the events of the previous night. He hadn't slept, and his eyes ached fiercely. He slipped on sunglasses as he walked up Seventh Avenue in the direction of Central Park. Nothing was real. In the warmth of the sun he could wish it all away. Pretend he was not an informer. That there was no Leila. No Abetz. He stopped now as black dots danced in front of his eyes. He had a terrible headache. He was all tight and coiled. He needed a woman.

He reached Central Park South and headed west toward Columbus Circle. From his pocket, he pulled out the flask Rommel had given him as a Christmas present and took a large gulp of brandy, then another. It made his blood run and chased the headache from the corners of his temples.

He was almost at Columbus Circle when he heard the music. American jazz. "Honeysuckle Rose." Played by a three-man ensemble. A boy with flaming red hair playing sax, a slim Negro on trumpet, and a blond, curly-haired youth on drums. A crowd had gathered around, and a fair collection of pennies, nickels, and dimes lay in the music case on the ground. The trio had set up in front of the entrance to Central Park. They have courage, he thought. Central Park South is for friends of the Reich.

They played fiercely, driving the music in unison and then in solos. The Negro was slim of build, wearing only a polo shirt, work pants, and sneakers. He caught the lead tossed to him, and now body and head arched back, blew hard-driving rhythms into a solo of fierce intensity. The crowd was clapping as he drove for home and the red-haired player stepped up and joined him. Heads bobbing, bodies bent over, they sprinted home, the drums announcing the glory of their playing. Applause, whistles, cheers followed. A larger crowd was forming. It is spring, Radner thought. Their spring, in their city. In that moment he saw the auxiliary policeman make his way through the crowd and order the makeshift trio to disperse. It was like watching a silent movie. He couldn't hear what was being said, but the body language was all too clear. The auxiliary policeman pointed first at the case with its load of coins and then waved his nightstick. The red-haired saxophonist had his hands spread in a gesture that clearly said, why? But Radner noticed the taut biceps, the intensity fused into those arms.

The policeman gestured with his thumb as the Negro trumpet

player closed around him. The drummer played a soft, muted rat-a-tat, ominous in its soft beat. More heated words, and now the policeman walked to the case and kicked at it, sending coins flying in the air. Then the saxophonist lunged at the policeman, and his right arm snapped up twice. Somebody screamed. The policeman stepped back as if taking a curtain call. His arms were spread wide and the knife protruded from his belly. He staggered and fell back, trying desperately to reach the whistle around his neck. There were screams as the crowd broke into groups of fleeing people. Radner saw the three youths running into the park while the policeman writhed in death agony on the ground.

They were all gone in a matter of seconds. The policeman lay still now, an occasional twitch of his legs being the only movement. Radner stood there drinking from the flask. A man dies on this beautiful spring day, a day pregnant with life. On a day when lovers should be lying on the grass, an impromptu musical set becomes murder. Then in a moment of insight as clear as the piercing sunlight above him he saw it. He realized what he had sensed before as the news flashed in Times Square and the crowds stood transfixed by it. The Americans didn't care about the news; the sign itself was a reminder of the past. A past they could never forget. A past that must be their present again. The Americans wanted their city back.

4:03 P.M.

Kresky could barely breathe. He peered out the window and saw the krauts taking their position on the 207th Street station, which was above the yard. He turned and whispered to Sol Yuretsky. "Get men to the windows. Nobody shoots until I give the word."

He looked out again. The steel helmets of the Wehrmacht soldiers gleamed in the sun. He saw the young officer positioning them. The Heinrichs were doing the smart thing. They have us surrounded from above. They're not planning to attack. Not yet. But you've made a mistake. You've shut off service on the number 1 line. The word's going to get around. Americans have taken over the subway repair shop, and Heinrich is worried. He has to do something.

4:27 P.M.

From University Heights, the crowd could see the soldiers lining the tracks. They could see the row of soldiers and armored cars poised on Ninth Avenue and 215th Street. A gray armada of steel and men. Inside the yard were the subway cars and the Americans. Americans like them. But unlike them they were taking the law into their own hands. They were barely visible. Occasionally one would run from a subway car and disappear into the large repair shed or into one of the brick buildings. They had been there since yesterday, and the Germans hadn't done anything. But they all knew that couldn't last. Not much longer. Beneath the crowd the sun leaped and pirouetted on the Harlem River. It was perhaps a hundred yards from across the Bronx side of the river to the iron-gated fence ringing the repair yard. A barge could float across in a matter of minutes.

You could see the tension in their faces. In the eyes of Joe Reilly, who had worked for the subway line for forty years before retiring last summer, his green eyes freighted with concern and sorrow. In the trembling lips of Mary Reilly, his wife. You could see it in the faces of Abe Wohlman, Marty Gershon, Claire Minsky, Denny Butler, Ike Razzotti, and Tully Barrett, who was on leave from the post office because of fallen arches. They stared across the river at the repair yard. There were Americans there, and something was going to happen.

4:37 P.M.

The young Wehrmacht captain walked along the tracks checking the position of his men. His name was Kurt Waldheim. He had only recently been posted to America. He was tall, with a long nose and shrewd eyes. He regarded what the Americans were doing as a futile gesture, but he longed for them to fight. He hadn't seen action since the fall of England, and he missed it. The fatherland promised him a thousand years of glory. He was writing history. For Kurt Waldheim, history was combat.

Satisfied, he walked back along the track toward the station itself where General von Steuben was waiting. Von Steuben had also only recently arrived in New York. Waldheim knew how anxious his general was to take the subway yard. Only the interference of Abetz and the Gestapo had prevented it. The general had deferred to Abetz only because of his recent arrival. General von Steuben was waiting for him on the platform, using binoculars to view the repair yard. Waldheim hoisted himself up and saluted.

Von Steuben waited while Waldheim lit his cigarette for him. "Tell me, Kurt, how difficult is it?"

"My General, the Wehrmacht could take this yard in less than an hour. What are they? Fifty men or so with rifles. Once we pin them down with overlapping fire they are trapped. Some grenades and a few men will be lost climbing the wire. Once we are in the yard, it is finished."

General von Steuben nodded and took off his cap. He had a thick mane of white hair, and blue eyes. Even though the day was warm, he wore a leather jacket. It was unbuttoned, and on his uniform were combat ribbons and a medal awarded him by the Führer. His boots gleamed brilliantly. He looked every inch a Wehrmacht general.

4:38 P.M.

Kresky had been using glasses to watch the young German officer. He had climbed back onto the platform and now talked with his commanding officer. Bill Leary was crouched next to him. "I don't want him," Kresky whispered. "The one strutting like a Thanksgiving turkey, that's our man."

Leary peered out. "He's still under the overhang. I can't get a good shot."

"C'mon, c'mon," Kresky whispered. "Just a little more."

They both watched, silently nudging their target forward.

"Just the goose," Kresky said, "not the gander."

Then suddenly the goose was there. His uniform rich with decoration, wearing a leather coat, his white hair blowing in the wind.

"Now," Kresky whispered.

General Fritz von Steuben was pointing toward the crowds up on the Heights. It was quite an audience, he was saying. He pointed with a gloved finger. He always wore gloves, even in the hottest weather.

His finger swept the river and came back toward the yard. In that moment there was the crack of a rifle and then its echo as General von Steuben's eyes got very big and a hole appeared in his forehead. He fell forward and pitched off the platform onto the tracks.

Captain Waldheim jumped onto the tracks, knowing his general was dead. He lifted the general's head and saw the empty eyes of General Fritz von Steuben, eyes already robbed of life. Then he was running down the track, pistol in hand, screaming at his men to open fire.

4:41 P.M.

There had been a single rifle shot and then a long silence. For the crowd jammed up on the Heights, the tension was almost unbearable. What had happened? Who had fired? Why? What was going to happen? And then it came. A flurry of rifle fire from the subway station. The soldiers had opened fire. Now came the answering fire from the red brick buildings that ran along Broadway. A soldier toppled over the rail and fell down to Broadway. And as if from one collective throat, a cry ripped loose from the crowd. The Americans were firing on the Wehrmacht. The battle had begun.

5:18 P.M.

Abetz and Kelly sat over sherry in the Princeton Club. Their business was concluded. The train was back on the track. Kelly lifted his glass, and the sherry danced like a lake turned gold. "You'll come to St. Patrick's for the cardinal?"

Abez smiled. It was his business smile. "But of course. Everything is upon us."

"And the Führer?"

"Is on schedule," Abetz replied. "A week from Sunday. I have a meeting with Radner this evening. He will make all the arrangements."

"Have him call me tonight," Kelly said.

Now a curious silence came upon them. They were two poker players with all their cards on the table, and yet both withheld a card. Or seemingly did. The facade of cooperation was being observed. But it was just that. Nothing had been the same since Sylvie. As always when they met, the Princeton Club was deserted. The only witnesses to their meeting were the distinguished but dead gentlemen whose portraits graced the walls.

Kelly leaned over and poured more sherry for them. Abetz watched him, wondering what was responsible for the smug, satisfied expression on Kelly's face. He has come to his senses. Or perhaps he has a secret agenda. There was the sound of someone rushing toward them. It was Hoppman.

"Standartenführer, I have word from headquarters. Fighting has broken out at the subway station. General von Steuben has been killed."

Abetz bolted out of his chair. "The fool. How?"

"He was inspecting the troops along the subway tracks and the Americans shot him."

Abetz swore and stalked from the room. Moments later he picked up the phone in the foyer and dialed impatiently. "This is Abetz. Let me speak with Hetzler." He drummed his fingers on the polished black mahogany table. "Hetzler, listen carefully. I want all subway service on the trains running uptown stopped immediately. Buses also, is that clear? I am leaving now for the subway yard. I shall call you when I arrive there." Abetz

426

slammed down the phone and called out, "Hoppman." Then he was gone with nary a word to Kelly.

Kelly sat in the large room drinking his sherry. The silence was almost eerie. The little kraut had given himself away. He was so contemptuous of Kelly he did not even say good-bye. Well, that would all be taken care of soon. Very soon. Kelly got up and downed his drink. In a few long strides he crossed the room, went down through the foyer and out into the street.

He walked east, noting the mild air, the smell of spring. He was himself again. Every man made a fool of himself over a woman at least once. That was another thing his father had taught him. It was just that Kelly had made his later in life. Well, no matter, mistakes get rectified. Hardball is hardball. Payback is payback. He reached Park Avenue and saw the blue Cadillac waiting. He crossed the street. Yes, it was a fine evening. The scent of spring was always exhilarating.

He crossed the street and opened the door to the waiting car. Slipping inside the back, he saw Vito Genovese. "Hello, Vito. Let's take a ride."

"Go, Frankie," Genovese urged his driver. The car slid into traffic.

Kelly bit off the top of his cigar. "Vito, I have a job for you."

For a moment Vito Genovese's brooding eyes showed a sliver of interest. "Frankie, drive to the river."

"Toward the river," Kelly remarked. "I like that. It's a fine evening, Vito. Spring is finally here."

5:53 P.M.

Lazar came up the subway steps as Collins finished his phone call.

"The subways are out."

"What?"

"Nothing's running up or downtown."

They were standing on the corner of Ninety-first and Broadway next to a beanery. Collins snapped his fingers. "Something's happened up there. Heinrich's moving in."

"We'll never get there," Paulie said. He seemed relieved.

Collins flipped a butt into his mouth. "They'll cut the IND too."

Imitating his leader, Paulie palmed a Lucky Strike into the corner of his mouth. "Hold the light."

Brutus and Cassius, Collins thought, but without a Caesar to assassinate. "Let's go."

"Where?"

427

"To the safe house. I have a messenger coming to carry a message to Garcia. You'll meet her. She's a looker."

Paulie's eyes rolled. "A broad? You're using a broad?"

"I'm using both of you. I'm going up to the yard. It can't fall."

Paulie was still in a state of shock.

Collins laughed. "Wait till you see her."

6:01 P.M.

Radner had picked up the actress at Café des Artistes. She had been lamenting over a director who had given *her* part to his girlfriend. She was tall, dark, and bosomy. She made sure an inch or two of cleavage showed as she bent toward you. She was Armenian, and her life was a tragedy she was forever writing.

It had taken Radner less than five minutes to complete the pickup. Her name was Katerina, and now they sat in his living room. She talked incessantly. He heard nothing. He kept looking at the bedroom, expecting Leila to come out. He could almost see her standing there saying, "Poor Friedrich, is this what you must make do with?"

"If I had only gotten the part. To be so vindictive. He owed me that part. Men are so petty."

He felt the wrenching pain in his chest. He could smell her scent in the apartment. Leila, come back. What we had . . . it isn't gone. But it is, fool. His head beat with thunder and throbbed horribly. He was drawn tight as a bowstring and still this creature next to him babbled her tragedy.

"I have this need to give . . . to . . . to . . . love the audience. From my mouth to love them with poetry . . . with beauty . . . with art."

It was the last word that did it. All the other garbage he could have discounted. But the phrase art from her mouth. She wanted art, did she?

His left hand moved down and inside the brown blouse, tugging the bra loose and cupping her breast. Her eyes widened with surprised pleasure and her mouth came open. He tore down his zipper, and now his right hand moved to the nape of her neck and he pushed her large, voluptuous, nonstop mouth down.

He closed his eyes, waiting for the tension and pain to fly loose from him. To stop thought, memory. But there was no release. He was erect, but he couldn't feel. This despite the fact that she hurtled herself down on him in the performance of her life. He was numb. Like some unyielding brute. He wanted

428

Leila, and this was wrong. "Leila," he cried. He was up, grabbing at the girl. "Get out, get out."

He opened the door, thrust her out, and slammed the door. He heard her cry from the hall, "My bag, my bag." He stood there while she banged and kicked the door. Finally she stopped, and he fell back on the couch. If he could only give himself to sleep. But there was still something to be done to complete his debasement. He was a protagonist in a Greek drama who must destroy himself and, in doing so, destroy those around him. He had known what he would do ever since he stood in the shadows of Grand Central Station and saw the two of them. That was why he followed the American. And now it must be finished for all of them. There could be no half measure. He must be a German, a servant of the Reich. All that was left was winning and losing. You do what you must because you are a conqueror. Abetz had taught him that.

He picked up the phone. He would call the police first. Then the Gestapo. He heard the operator and asked for the police station nearest 110th Street. In a few moments she came back on telling him it was the Twenty-fourth precinct. Moments later he heard a gruff voice announcing the precinct. Radner spoke. "At 535 West 110th Street, there is an American Resistance leader." He did not recognize his own voice. "I do not know the apartment but he is young and handsome. I shall call the Gestapo to inform them I have been in touch with you."

He hung up and put his hand to his head. There, it was done. God, how base. No, it was survival. The only way he could justify what he had done. His hand dropped to the phone. Do it. Finish. No, don't call the Gestapo . . . yes. Do it. Then sleep.

He picked up the phone again.

6:13 P.M.

The first Wehrmacht assault had come less than an hour ago after rifle fire had been exchanged by both sides. Gunner Anderson, who had fought at the Ebro, had seam-stitched a row of soldiers with the machine gun set up in the first subway car. He had impaled six golden warriors as they attempted to scale the eight-foot fence. Heinrich had come to skirmish, Kresky had come to kill. The first Wehrmacht charge was broken in less then ten minutes. Soldiers lay strewn across the street, dead, wounded, twitching, calling for comrades to help them.

The acrid smell of smoke still lingered in the air. Kresky peered around a subway car and then scrambled inside. He had

429

three men with tommy guns lying on the floor, Hank Filipowski, Moe Diamond, and Billy Grimes.

Kresky kneeled down next to them. "They're going to come again soon. I figure before it gets dark. They know we got the machine gun now, but they don't know about you. When Gunner opens up, you come and form a Π. Just spray the gate. You understand?"

Nobody said anything.

"They'll set up their machine gun. Billy, you go for it. Hank, Moe, you riddle the gate, and we'll back you up."

"They could use tear gas," Hank offered. He was a thin, gaunt-faced man with a receding hair line. His eyes were like Kresky's. Dark anthracite coal with no give in them.

"Why don't we wear the masks?" Billy Grimes said. He was five feet seven with bushy hair and eyebrows thick as a shaggy dog. "It'll give them something to think about."

Kresky clapped him on the shoulder. "Maybe it'll save us some tear gas later." The men nodded. Nobody believed it.

Kresky walked to the window and watched the sun-flecked lines on the Harlem River. He saw the crowds up on the Heights watching the siege. C'mon, c'mon. We need you. There isn't much time.

6:17 P.M.

There were no subways or buses, and Leila had been unable to find a cab. She had walked across the park after receiving his call. She walked up Central Park West until she saw what she had been looking for . . . a man getting into his car. She darted across the street, lifting her skirt to make sure the distinguished gray-haired man saw a lovely stem, and said, "I have a terrible emergency, could you help me out?" Scarlett O'Hara would have been proud.

Now she stood in front of the building on West 110th Street. There was a green awning. She hadn't seen Collins since Grand Central Station, but she knew he would call. She felt her heart palpitate. Like someone was in there with a hammer. And she could feel the dampness between her thighs. The sensuous revolutionary. She took a deep breath and walked inside the building.

6:20 P.M.

Abetz stood on the University Heights Bridge, where a squad of soldiers and a machine gun had been set up. He spoke in muted tones to Colonel Messmer. "I suggest you get more troops here. There are thousands up on those Heights."

Messmer was a tall man with a crew cut and a face like a hatchet. He had fought in Poland, England, and America. Now he looked up at the Bronx just across the Harlem River and nodded. "They are cattle with a herd mentality. But one must be careful not to start them running."

"Machine guns," Abetz said, "will suffice."

"Machine guns," Messmer replied, "are a myth. Eventually they run out of ammunition."

"Then have more ready."

Messmer lit a cigarette. "They will also run out of ammunition. We must take the men in the yard quickly, before they achieve martyrdom."

Abetz kicked at a rusty can. "That idiot Waldheim did exactly what Kresky wanted him to. He led a charge into a machine gun."

Messmer was momentarily silent. "He learned a lesson."

"Yes, a lesson. But dead men have no use for lessons. Both he and his general are dead idiots."

They walked away from the bridge, talking softly.

"Will you attack before dark?"

Messmer stopped and looked up at the setting sun. "At twilight. There is a tendency to relax them. Men take on strange shapes. It is just before the night comes when one is most apt to feel fear."

Abetz nodded his approval. "The yard must be taken quickly."

"It will."

"Tanks are a last resort," Abetz cautioned. "It would upset the balance of what will happen this weekend. We want a rebellion crushed, not a slaughter."

Messmer scrubbed out his cigarette. "My men are combat veterans. These men in the yard have never been under machine gun fire and grenades. Tanks will not be necessary."

"They will not give up," Abetz cautioned.

"They will die," Messmer said.

6:25 P.M.

Collins had been right. The broad was a piece. But what the hell was Collins saying to her? Paulie edged closer to the bedroom.

Collins sat on the bed next to Leila, holding the folded-up pages. "This is no picnic going to Red Hook. No subways mean no cabs. Heinrich won't turn the subways on again until the yard is taken.''

"But then, how can you . . . ?''

He put a hand on her lips and felt her soft mouth.

"I don't know how the hell you'll get to the barge.''

"I'll get there,'' she said grimly.

"Tell whoever is there that you want to see Uncle Frank. The mad mick sent you. Give them the pages. Tell them the city has to know about the subway yard. Somebody has to run off the news on a printing press.''

"I wish I could go with you,'' she said.

Paulie peered into the room. Fuckin' Collins was off his nut. He had heard enough. Paulie knew what to do.

"There's one other thing,'' Collins was saying. "There was a woman . . . I loved her.''

"I don't care. . . .''

"They killed her. By firing squad. If you get caught . . .''

"I know. And I won't get caught.''

He saw the courage in her eyes.

"Come back,'' she whispered.

Paulie stood in the kitchen dragging on a nail. Collins was giving his plan to the broad to take to Frank Costello. Collins was crazy. You don't send a broad to Red Hook. Paulie Lazar would find Frank Costello. He looked down at the courtyard and saw some dicks. He could spot a dick at forty miles. And there were cops. Something was up.

Paulie broke the clinch in the bedroom. "Coppers.''

Collins jumped up. "Where?''

They stood at the kitchen window, the girl behind them. Collins bit his lip. Coincidence? No, hell no. Abetz had been on his tail all day. Collins had been pushing his luck since he came to New York. Now it had run out.

6:28 P.M.

Two police cars were lined up in front of 535 West 110th Street, and a squad of men stood listening to their final instructions. Detectives meanwhile had staked out the back courtyard. There was a big fish inside.

6:29 P.M.

Collins faced the girl and Paulie Lazar. "I need a diversion. I'll go down to the basement. . . .''

Paulie cut him off. "They'll put a couple of guys there. Go to

432

the second floor. Wait till you hear something. Then walk out. But don't move until you hear it.''

Collins looked over at Leila.

Paulie was ready for that one. "She'll be on the third floor. They won't be looking for a broad coming out alone.''

Collins wiped his mouth. "That's it then. All right, see you soon.'' He stopped and looked back at Paulie. "Lazar, bring Michael Donetti and twenty men and whatever you can carry, shotguns, tommies. . . .''

"Get out of here,'' Paulie whispered through clenched teeth.

Collins started to move toward Leila. "Go on,'' she said.

They were alone now, and the girl was putting the plans into her bag. Paulie drew his piece. "Give me them.''

She saw the anger in his eyes. "Give me the plans and no bullshit.'' He ripped them from her hand and, now pointing the gun, put into motion what he knew had to be done. "You'll never get to Red Hook and no barge. Five guys will rip your dress off.''

"It's my dress.''

"Yeah, it's also your ass. Mine and Collins's too. Listen up and skip the chippy remarks. You go to a bar on South Street near the piers. It's called Diggers. Ask for Mike Donetti, tell them you were sent by the Irishmen. Tell Donetti Collins is up at the University Heights near the subway yard. He wants to go in. He needs twenty men, guns, and ammo. I'm givin' ya the best part. Find Donetti and you save Collins's life . . . maybe. I'll get the plans to Red Hook. Now get out of here.''

She stared at him in disbelief as he threw open the door. "Go on, this ain't no fashion show.''

She went down the stairs, and Paulie grinned.

He opened his pants and wedged the sheets of papers into his Jockey shorts. Good thing he had put them on instead of boxer shorts. His grin became wider. Collins's rebellion was resting on Paulie's balls.

Zippered up, he put his gun in his jacket pocket and knocked on the door across the hall, 14B. He knocked a second and third time before it opened. An elderly man, bald, with glasses and a white shirt, peered out. Paulie thrust his way in. "I want to see the view.''

6:31 P.M.

The police fanned out. A dick stood in front of them holding a bullhorn.

Paulie looked down at the coppers. You assholes. You want

433

Collins, huh? The window looked out at 110th Street. A crowd was beginning to gather.

The old man wedged in next to him. "Somebody must be in trouble."

Paulie looked down at the old geezer. Old fart must be eighty. The whole apartment reeked of mothballs. Paulie winked. "Just wanted to see what was up."

The geezer had warts on his forehead and no hair. "I've never seen you in the building. Do you live here?"

"Sure," Paulie answered. He reached over and raised the window.

"What are you doing?"

"Just getting in some fresh air."

The detective's voice now blared through to them. He was announcing that the building was surrounded. Paulie hadn't known what he was going to do when he knocked at the door.

"I'm cold," the geezer said. "Close the window."

Paulie turned to the whining old man. He was old and dead, like everything in the apartment. It smelled like a funeral parlor. Jesus, it was awful.

"Do you know I can't pee?" the geezer whined. "Not all day."

Something flickered in Paulie and then he was reaching for the geezer, sweeping him up in his arms. "You've peed enough, you old fuck." Paulie pivoted in one motion, raised the old man in his arms, and sent him hurtling down toward Broadway.

Collins, wedged against the rear of the second floor, heard a scream. It was like someone falling off a precipice. He went down the stairs.

6:32 P.M.

The body of the man had landed on the sidewalk directly in front of three policemen. The man was dead, his face a bloody pulp. A ring of uniformed police formed around him. Had the use of the bullhorn panicked the man they were looking for? Detective Danny Patrick shook his head. He hated anonymous tips.

A crowd had gathered, and the police were occupied in keeping them back. The detectives were bent over the body, huddled in conversation. No one paid attention to the lithe man in a black turtleneck and green jacket who walked out of the building. Nor did anyone stop the attractive, leggy girl who followed him out about two minutes later. They had a dead man, sunny-side up, on the sidewalk.

Carrying a bundle of the old geezer's shirts, Paulie stepped into the elevator and pressed "Basement." This was the riskiest part. He would have to play the surprised bozo coming down to rinse his shirts. He would leave them there, give his name and apartment, and drift out. Bluff. Bluff it all the way.

The elevator door opened, and he stepped out. It was dark. One light was on. He walked toward it.

"Hold it," a voice called.

Dick, Paulie told himself. He turned and saw a squinty-eyed fuck holding a revolver.

"Where you goin'?"

Paulie was Mickey Rooney. "Wash my shirts. That's okay, ain't it?"

The dick came toward him. He had eyes like a bulldog. Shit, Paulie thought. This one ain't no cherry.

"Drop the shirts," the dick called out to him. "Then put up your hands. You ain't no washerwoman."

Shit. He was fucked. He dropped the shirts. "Gimme your ID card," the dick said.

Paulie carefully extracted the extra one he kept in his pocket. The one with his picture that identified him as Alan Nipponomick.

6:47 P.M.

The crowd on University Heights numbered more than a thousand now. The sun had dipped out of sight, but they could see the Nazis in motion on the other side of the river. Something was about to happen. Soldiers were positioning themselves, while in the yard nobody was moving. A terrible silence had come over the crowd. Gone were the hushed bits of conversation, the muted asides, the shoving and maneuvering for better position. Something was going to happen. Like in a prizefight when one fighter had been hurt. The stalk was over. Then there was the sound of a machine gun and an answering volley echoing over and over like a spasmodic death rattle. Puffs of smoke flew in the air as the Americans responded. The Wehrmacht was rushing the main gate again.

6:48 P.M.

Kresky saw them coming and, in the same moment that Gunner Anderson opened up again, he shouted to his three tommy guns. "Now . . . go."

From out of the subway car came three men wearing gas masks and carrying tommies. They positioned themselves to the left and right of the car concealing Gunner Anderson. In lines of concerted fire they shot a continuous stream of bullets at the charging Wehrmacht soldiers.

"Keep them off the fence," Kresky shouted.

Faced with a barrage of machine guns and rifle fire, the Wehrmacht pitched over in front of the fence. Five, six, eight.

The people of the Heights could see the Germans trying to scale the eight foot fence and the deadly fire cutting them down. Abruptly, there was a terrible explosion and screams. The Germans were throwing grenades.

Kresky saw Bill Grimes blown sideways and never took his eyes off the gun. He scooped it up, propped it on one knee, and ripped loose a volley of bullets. "Hold your grenades," he screamed. "Hold them for the next time."

Chapter 43

April 1, 1942
7:13 P.M.

The sky was a mix of orange and purple when the submarine rose to the surface. It came out of the depths of the Atlantic like some angry shark hungry enough for food to show itself. A red light blinked from its conning tower. It moved relentlessly toward the shoreline into the warm circle of gold given off by the Montauk lighthouse.

Guderian and Rommel walked along the beachfront, exact replicas of one another in leather coats and peaked hats. Both held cigarettes in gloved hands. Montauk, on the Eastern tip of Long Island, was fifteen degrees cooler than New York City.

Rommel kicked at the sand. "You cannot keep this news from spreading. The Americans will broadcast it. All of New York will know in twenty-four hours."

Heinz Guderian stopped and looked at the ocean. "They will know in time, although I am sure Abetz will keep them confused for a few days."

"And the Führer?"

A rueful smile showed itself on Guderian's sharp face. "I think he is grateful in some ways. Now Barbarossa can go forward."

A circle of smoke seemed to shoot from Rommel's mouth. "So we invade Russia . . . but what of America?"

"We are to retrench on the East Coast. Control the ports of Long Island and New Jersey. Consolidate and build barricades on the main highways, fortify the bridges. We can hold New York for an indefinite period. The East Coast can be held in the same way."

Rommel stopped and picked up a shell. "How much time is there?"

Guderian stubbed out his cigarette. "The target date for Barbarossa is May. Roosevelt may have retaken Hawaii by then, but it will take a major effort by his land troops. The Americans cannot begin thinking about the East Coast for three months. By that time we will have Russia."

Rommel cast his cigarette in the direction of the ocean. "There will be a major invasion by Roosevelt."

Guderian pushed up his collar. "The Führer's orders are simple. If New York and the East Coast cannot be held, set a torch to it. Deport its young men, and leave nothing standing."

Rommel's face showed no expression. "And then?"

Guderian turned to Rommel. "They will still be reeling when we return . . . after Russia."

Rommel watched a wave hit upon the shoreline, throwing up angry spray. He looked out toward the ocean and its dark, unyielding surface. "One cannot always return, Heinz, even when one wants to."

7:37 P.M.

The subways to upper Manhattan had stopped, but the power of the word flowed from the Bronx to Manhattan via some kind of magical conduit. From witnesses at University Heights to storekeepers, to passing workers, to newsstand and grocery dealers, to schoolboys and truck drivers, itinerant workers and out-of-work salesmen. From cops to sanitation men and firemen, to men of hope and despair, and those of truculent demeanor. A bunch of Americans were holding the subway repair shop at 207th Street and Broadway. They were fighting the mighty Wehrmacht bullet for bullet.

From University Heights, the crowd could see the angry flashes of light as the Americans and the Wehrmacht blazed away at each other. The third Wehrmacht assault had begun only minutes earlier, and the crowd had let out a triumphant cry as the first American grenades landed and exploded amidst the charging soldiers. Piercing screams carried across the Harlem River.

Abetz stood in the Department of Sanitation shed on Ninth Avenue and 215th Street watching the Wehrmacht dying on the eight foot fence. He was fascinated. The triumphs of the Reich on the battlefield had always lived in his mind. England, Poland, Czechoslovakia, Holland, Belgium, France. An unending chain of blitzkrieg victories. And now the vaunted Wehrmacht couldn't take a subway yard. He saw the Wehrmacht charging the wire and the spitting lines of fire lashing out at them. Men dying on the fences, being chopped down at the fences. And beyond fascination and wonder, he felt anger and humiliation. The American had planned this. The reckless American who had a bullet meant for Abetz in his pistol. He wasn't in the yard, he had sent Kresky to do his bidding. But the planning was bold and cunning. A new weapon unleashed with every charge, machine guns, grenades. Of course they couldn't hold out. But they were forcing the Wehrmacht's hand. With the subway car wedged against the entrance to the yard, the side barricaded by brick buildings, the river to its rear, only tanks could breach the yard. Messmer, standing only a few feet away, would have to call the Kingsbridge Armory for them. One didn't need to be a graduate of the military academy at Spandau to realize the Americans had selected a perfect location to hold.

The Wehrmacht was being cut down as they tried to scale the gate. It was useless. He saw six men grappling with the wire— wait, it was a phalanx, and behind them a large figure who threw something . . a grenade. It disappeared into the night and then landed in the subway car where the Americans had set up their machine gun. There was a terrific explosion.

Gunner Anderson and his machine gun went up in the explosion, and Kresky ran toward the subway car. Glass fragments from the car flew like a nest of hornets released from captivity.

The German snipers up on the railroad track poured a volley of fire down on the yard. He ran amidst bullets and screams till he reached the gutted car. It was on fire, a large, devouring flame, and he couldn't get inside. For a moment he looked toward the Heights. C'mon, where are you? We don't have much time left. Collins, where the hell are you? C'mon Irish. There are only a few cards left in the deck. The subway car burned brightly, but it would go out.

8:03 P.M.

Traffic was clogged up and down Broadway and Riverside Drive, forcing Collins to walk on Amsterdam Avenue. If his guess was right, Heinrich would be too occupied with the yard to close access to the Bronx. The Harlem River Bridge was only a little more than a mile downriver from the repair yard. All he had to do was get to the bridge, and if it hadn't been secured he could make it into the Bronx. He figured the odds four to one in his favor.

He reached the bridge at 8:27 P.M. A crowd had gathered and now stood looking upriver at the University Heights Bridge covered over by night. Collins pushed his way through and now found himself jammed against a small Negro boy who stared raptly upriver. The boy's lips moved. What was he thinking?

He turned to Collins, who said quietly, "Don't worry son, we're going to win."

The boy's eyes lit up. Collins nodded, and the boy nodded back. He just needed some hope. That's what all the people here needed. Well then, get going, boyo, and give them some.

He plunged back into the crowd and eight minutes later crossed into the Bronx.

9:13 P.M.

Black Jack Bixwell stirred his watery scotch and jabbed a finger at Joe the Coon. "Big Joe, my Sugar baby gonna take out Fritzi Machen. It's sure."

Joe the Coon had a face and features as large as his bankroll. A bulbous W. C. Fields nose, chopped-liver lips, and eyes hand dipped in dollar signs. They were seated in a booth in the back of Tiny's, a Harlem after-hours joint. Only it wasn't after hours yet. The place was harsh lights and the babes were working the bar. Lotta kraut officers and off-duty police came in to get laid.

Joe the Coon, who wore a brown suit, spats, and derby hat, threw down his bourbon. "I seen Fritzi Machen fight. He one tough bitch."

"Sugar take him. Sugar smooth as silk."

"Sugar outweighed by twelve pounds."

Black Jack smiled. "Don't mean nothin'. Sugar dance for a

439

few rounds . . . then pop . . . pop . . . pop." Jack Bixwell pantomimed a series of exploding left hooks.

Joe the Coon yawned. "How much you want?"

Jack Bixwell never hesitated when talking money with bankers. "Twenty large," he announced.

"Sheet," Joe the Coon guffawed. But Jack Bixwell never took his eye off him.

Joe the Coon picked up his glass and turned it up toward the light. "Who you wan' lay it off with?"

"Dinty Callaghan. He like Machen."

"Callaghan, huh. He seen Sugar fight. Maybe he don't take your money."

"He take it. It's a score, man. I be there when Machen take out Gerry Nagel. Callaghan go for it."

Joe the Coon hunched forward. "Dinty smell it out."

"No he don't. 'Cause it ain't too much. It's just the right figure. He make the odds. He cut it so we don't get more than six to five. If we bettin' fifty, he don't take it. My end is . . ."

Joe the Coon grabbed him by the collar. "Your end is shit. Your end is what I give you. I take it all except five dollars."

Five dollars was five thousand more than Jack Bixwell had. "Ten," he cried.

"Five, and if I lose, you ass be in many pieces."

It was done. He had the gravy train to the . . . there was a woman's scream and everybody was up.

The white man came off the bar, hands spastically trying to retrieve the knife in his gut. He was wobbling like a fighter just blitzed by a Joe Louis left-right combination. He was a dead man, Jack Bixwell knew.

There was pandemonium, screams, and suddenly some cops. What the fuck were they doin'? . . . Oh shit, they were here for their payoff. "Let's go Joe." Black Jack had barely gotten the words out when the walking dead man, shiv in his gut, waved the gun. Oh Christ, he was a dick. He turned, staggered, and then the gun was pointed. He fired three times as he lurched, and the last shot hit Joe the Coon right between the eyes. He fell over, dead meat, and Black Jack Bixwell watched a fortune bleed to death on the floor of Tiny's.

9:39 P.M.

They had taken Paulie to the Seventh Regiment Armory on Park between Sixty-seventh and Sixty-eighth streets. It was a huge brick fortress with three crowning turrets overlooking the city and a neat parapet between them. The Gestapo used it as one of their headquarters, and they kept prisoners in it. Special prisoners, the dick had said. He was in a huge room with a lot of beds. There must have been close to a hundred guys sleeping in this room. Paulie had been brought up there by a soldier while the dicks went to make some calls. They weren't through with him. Maybe they wouldn't get to him till morning. Better find out what was happening.

He tapped a guy, under his blanket but obviously awake. "What's the score here?"

The guy looked up and now put his hands under his head. It was all dark, and Paulie couldn't make out his features. "I dunno. Depends what game you're playin'."

"What are you in for?"

"Heist. You?"

"Building roundup," Paulie lied.

"If you stay here, you're okay," the voice said. "Gestapo took over the Tombs and Rikers Island, so there's a jail shortage. Up here, the basement and fourth floor is police shit. Side rooms downstairs is for Gestapo security."

Paulie felt his bladder revolt. "Gestapo security?"

The man's voice came to him again, but without a face. It was creepy. "Gestapo security keeps a place here 'cause they protect high Wehrmacht officers. Long as you're up here you're okay. If you go to one of the Gestapo side rooms, your soul may belong to God, but your ass belongs to the Gestapo."

Paulie wanted out. "Who's the top trustee here?"

"Only one trustee here, only man can help is the mayor of New York."

"The mayor of New York?"

"The mayor," the voice echoed. "John Law uses him to get coffee . . . and so does the krauts."

"Where is he?"

"He's around."

"Around where?"

"Just around."

"How will I know him?"

"You'll know him."

The guy had turned over, signifying the conversation was over. Paulie yanked him up and held him by the collar. "How will I know him?"

"He's crazy as a fuckin' bedbug. Sometimes he's here. Sometimes he's not."

"What do you mean crazy?"

"He rides his motorcycle up and down the first floor."

Paulie let the guy loose. "A motorcycle on the first floor? They wouldn't let no one . . ."

"He don't got no motorcycle. He just rides it."

441

Paulie lay in the dark and waited. He had Collins's plans for New York wedged into his nuts, he didn't know if he was stayin' here or goin' down to the side rooms, and the only fuckin' help he might get was from some asshole who called himself the mayor of New York and rode a make-believe motorcycle through the armory. Jesus, fuckin' Christ.

10:13 P.M.

The air was redolent with the smell of oil mixed with the odor of clams nesting in the murky depths around Red Hook. It was a smell that could accurately be characterized as evil, old as the centuries. A barge floated in the water, and inside the cabin dim light flashed from two kerosene lamps. Cheap shades hid the interior of the cabin. The barge rocked in the water, back and forth, as if it somehow captured the impatience of the boat's inhabitants.

There were three inside the cabin. Two of them were seated. The other man paced. His name was Socks Lanza, and he ran the New York waterfront. Lanza had deepset eyes, jet black hair, wore a peacoat and crewneck sweater. He was unshaven. The expression in those eyes was as dark as his hair. He chain-smoked and looked over at the two seated men, whom he plainly deferred to. At other moments he stared at the entrance to the cabin as if expecting someone long overdue.

Seated next to Socks Lanza was a large bear of a man in a long black overcoat with a fedora worn so low it covered his menacing eyes. The eyes were in contrast to the large nose. Eyes filled with a litany of vendetta and assassination. His name was Albert Anastasia, and just now he peered out into the darkness.

Directly to his left, occupying an ancient rocking chair, was the man known to the underworld as the Prime Minister. As befitting a man with that designation, he was nattily dressed in a gray pin-striped suit, blue tie and white shirt. His pointed black shoes were expensive and glossy. He parted his dark hair in the middle and had gray eyes that seemingly mirrored his genius for survival. Survival was his life. Knowing how was inbred in him. A cunning passed from generation to generation of peasants in Calabria where he was born. He dragged on his cigarette and made a gesture to Albert Anastasia. "I don't think Collins is coming. From what Donovan told me, he's reckless."

"Could be he's up at the subway yard," Anastasia said.

"Could be, or maybe he got picked up."

Costello sat back in his chair, and it creaked eerily. They were alone in the bare cabin, which had only a large table and two chairs. On the wall, running its entire length, was a fisherman's net of knotted twine. They were men used to such places where they spawned deceit and deception. Frank Costello ground out his cigarette. "The deal I made with Bill Donovan gives us a free hand. All he wants are results. So how do we send a message?"

"I know a way," Socks Lanza growled. "Torch the piers, East and West Side. Nobody can miss that message."

Frank Costello lit another cigarette. "What else?"

"The krauts have been given a free ride," Albert Anastasia said very ominously.

Frank Costello turned to the lord high executioner for the mob and waited.

Anastasia took a gun from his pocket and laid it on the table. "The Resistance has done a lot with dynamite, but nobody has ever hit the krauts where they live."

The suggestion of a smile showed itself on Costello's face. "Where do they live?"

"In Gestapo headquarters on Centre Street."

Frank Costello wasn't smiling now. "How do you get inside?"

Albert Anastasia clutched the pistol by its barrel, almost pointing it at Costello. "We stop out in front and walk in with machine guns."

"How many men?"

Albert Anastasia never hesitated. "Six or seven men with choppers could do a lot of damage. And they'll never forget it. That's a message worth a million."

Frank Costello let it sit there for a minute. "There are hundreds of krauts in there . . . Gestapo."

Albert Anastasia pulled a big cigar from his overcoat and put it in his mouth. "You know what Big Al Capone said to me once? If you was on the third floor of a building, and you heard machine guns on the first floor and people screaming, would you run downstairs and be a hero? Or would you save your ass? Big Al was a genius when it came to hits."

They sat there considering it, as Albert Anastasia, the man who handed out the contracts for Murder Incorporated, lit his cigar. Then he spoke softly words he had said many times. "*Farlo Fiori*. Kill Heinrich. Kill them all."

Outside, the fetid air of Red Hook seemed to grow even heavier by weight of stealth and plot. The old barge rocked and creaked in the water while inside, over kerosene lamps, murder and revolution coalesced and became one.

Collins stood wedged between an old man and a young boy beneath the tenements of University Heights. Below him the tracks of the New York Central lay desolate and unused. Beyond that was the Harlem River, glittering softly under a bright moon. And there was the subway yard, bathed in the artificial light of police and Wehrmacht cars. The river came up to a point where there was a fence. Easy enough to swim that.

He nudged the boy. "When was the last attack?"

He didn't answer at first. Now he turned to Collins. He was snub-nosed and he shivered a little. He was seeing death up close for the first time.

"Couple of hours. Not since it got real dark. Will they come again tonight?"

Collins rubbed his mouth. "I don't know, laddie. If they hold it all night that would be . . ." he didn't finish. That would be significant. Heinrich knows that.

"How many attacks have there been?" Collins asked.

"Three," the old man said. His voice was almost as high pitched as the boys. "Terrible it is."

Collins looked down at the river again. Had Lazar found Donetti? He checked his watch. How much time should he give it? He had been too young for Paddy Pearse's last stand in Dublin. He had missed Mick on that last fateful day. He wasn't missing this one.

11:00 P.M.

Paulie lay on the cot and heard the footsteps. The thud of heavy boots. He closed his eyes and stiffened. Moments later he felt the rifle in his ribs. Then again. Shit. He opened his eyes and saw a big-nosed kraut. "Up. Up."

"Okay. Okay." He got up slowly, stalling around before asking the fateful question. "Where we goin'?"

The answer came back like a rifle bullet. "Side room."

Paulie felt his stomach roll. He stumbled forward as the kraut jabbed him with the rifle. The side room. Salad days were over. He helped Collins lam it, and now it was Zippo lighters and toasted balls.

11:13 P.M.

Kelly had dined at home alone. He never dined alone, even in a restaurant. Eating dinner was high ritual stuff. Since he was a lad he had known that. The day was over, time for its adventures, confessions, heartbreaks to be shared. Even if there was nothing but bits of bacon and some stale boiled potatoes. In the sharing there was camaraderie, love, friendship. Funny he should use that word. Friendship. All his life he had been a lonely man. Aware always of that fact despite the wealth of people in his life. There were constant business meetings, official functions, a wife and seven children, travel, and of course, the women. The gay, radiant, vivacious women he made love to, wined and dined, met in secret rendezvous, or by chance, as with Sylvie in Paris. At Maxim's.

Sylvie. Just her name was pain.

He had put out a contract on Abetz. Closed the deal with Vito Genovese tonight. Ten thousand down. To be done after Kelly was sworn in as regent. Ten days from now. I'm getting him for you, Sylvie. The little kraut bastard didn't have to kill you. Jesus Mary, not you. You were the stuff of lightness and dreams. Beautiful, full of vanity. Mine. No one kills my woman.

He poured whiskey from the decanter and threw it down. Sylvie. Where are you? Looking down. Just to hear you complain about a headache. I wouldn't care. I'd rub your temples, like my ma did with me. Strong hands they were.

He smelled her now. What was it? Not love. But something was all knotted up inside him. If he could only cry, but he had stopped crying fifty years ago. He had lost the habit. So he could only ache and throw whiskey down his gut and smell her. Christ, to be rid of the stinking guilt. Church guilt. I won't have it. I'm Patrick Kelly, regent of America. You hear that, Pa? Regent of America. No woman is worth that. Not even Sylvie. But her name brought the image of her. He guzzled the whiskey and threw the glass across the room, where it smashed and ran down the wall leaving a stain. A stain that would not come off.

The phone rang. A second time, then a third, a fourth. It would not stop ringing.

11:20 P.M.

Leila decided to walk along West Forty-third Street. The lights were still on along Broadway. The ultimate farce was being played out. Shows were still open, concerts were being given. How could she have lived in this world? But she hadn't lived. She had only hidden. At South Street it had been much colder. But the air crackled with something. It was a mixture of hope and anger. Men grouped at Diggers bar, grim at the mouth, talking in quiet tones, the words clipped. What was happening at the subway yard? What about the West Coast? No one knew Michael Donetti, of course. Leave a message. That was all she could do. Meet Collins at 207th Street. Bring men and weapons. She couldn't linger there. No one believed her anyway. It was a trap. Why had she let that big ox take the plans away from her? You should have dared him to shoot you. But he would have. She remembered him now. He was one of the gangsters at Adele's parents' house that night. He was with the Nazis . . . what was he doing working for Collins? She saw Rosoff's up ahead as she passed Town Hall. Who was running it for the fascists now . . . she heard jazz music. It was Benny Goodman playing and it was coming from Town Hall. But Town Hall was dark. Someone had gotten inside, put on a record, and amplified it. Benny Goodman was playing in Times Square.

The music resounded eerily in the night as someone came out of the restaurant. A figure in white, a busboy or a cook. He dipped in and out of the shadows, dancing in elongated joy with an invisible partner. Leila watched in fascination. The people hadn't forgotten. They still wanted to jitterbug. We're going to win, she thought. Somehow, someway. Now "Down South Camp Meet" blared forth and the tall ghost did a split and hip-hopped back into Rossoff's. The street was empty again. But it wasn't. American phantoms still danced. She hurried toward Fifth Avenue. She had to reach Alvin Barker. She would stay at his place tonight, and then in the morning she would somehow get to the subway yard. That's where Collins would be. That's where she should be.

11:38 P.M.

The people on University Heights hadn't moved. They stood on the rooftops of the tenements on Hampden Street and Cedar Street. They stood on the roofs of three-family brick houses. They crowded Landing Road, a crush of human bodies, all watching the subway repair yard across the Harlem River. There was a bright moon out, and it framed the American flag, which still fluttered in the breeze from the top of the repair shed.

The Nazis had raised both sections of the University Heights Bridge. Smart, Collins thought. They have made us all specta-tors. But they have betrayed their fear. Why raise a bridge unless you fear intervention? Jostling, pushing, wedged against each other, somehow we are one. We feel together, we think together, and we will overrun you together. The crowd swayed in unison now, an irregular line of bodies looking down at the river and the subway yard. Above them on the rooftops another wedge of Americans stood silently, whispering, smoking, watching the drama across the river. The subway yard had been dark for a long time. Collins couldn't read what Heinrich was up to. If

Kresky was still there in the morning . . . the lights outside the yard had been turned up.

It was as if the spotlight had been turned up in Radio City Music Hall. Then came the fanfare, only instead of a drum roll it was the rumbling sound of tanks. Two big steel-turreted Volkers now wheeled into place. Guns protruding, they stopped in place, directly in front of the entrance to the yard. Their big guns were pointed straight at the subway car that had been used to block off the main gate. And in that moment the crowd, which had become one body, with one brain and one voice, moaned audibly. It was a low, strangled cry of anguish, coming from somewhere inside the womb of this mass of humanity. As if they had been involved in labor and now the fetus had been prematurely taken from them. Something that was theirs was about to be aborted. And in that moment, Collins knew he had to give them hope. He couldn't let it die for these people. He couldn't wait for Donetti.

11:40 P.M.

Kresky saw the big Volkers rumble into place. He had lost twelve men; another sixteen were wounded. That left twenty-five men with rifles to fight tanks. He looked over at the men in his car. Olafson. Joe Donelly, Skeeter Larsen, Ike Razzotti, Bill Hicks, and Ollie Manson from 125th Street and Seventh Avenue. Manson was a merchant seaman, Olafson a steel worker, Donelly had cut lumber before coming East, Larsen and Razzotti were train workers, Billy Hicks had worked construction on some of the city's biggest skyscrapers. They had wives, families. They had vowed to fight to the last bullet. But there were tanks out there now, and it was almost over. He looked at their tired, blackened, sweaty faces. The air in the car was stagnant, stale with the smell of gunpowder, sweat, blood, fear, and death. They crouched at the windows looking out at the big tanks. He saw their faces, saw the expression on them. Hell, it wasn't over. Nobody had come. But somebody would. We're not leaving until they do. He called over to Billy Hicks. "Get the Molotov cocktails. The krauts want to play rough."

11:43 P.M.

From the Department of Sanitation garage that had been set up as Wehrmacht headquarters, Abetz could see the tanks facing the main gate of the yard. What was Kresky thinking? He had lost his machine gun, and there couldn't be much ammunition left. But that didn't mean he would surrender. He dropped his

447

cigarette and walked over to Messmer. "How much time will you give them?"

Messmer looked at his watch. "I shall give them thirty minutes."

"Let me make a suggestion," Abetz said. "The Americans want martyrs. It is a drama being played in front of thousands of people. If we blow them up now, we give them the story they want."

Messmer rubbed his chin. "Yes, I see what you mean. Go on."

"Let the tanks stay in place till morning."

"Do nothing?"

Abetz smiled. "But we shall be doing something. I shall take troops and Gestapo security up onto University Heights in the morning. I shall spend the night making preparations. At seven o'clock you will give them a chance to surrender. The wait until morning will unnerve them. As you go in, I shall drive the people off the Heights. They will have no time to clutch martyrs to their bosoms. Crowds are like indulgent children. They must not be spoiled."

Messmer rubbed his chin again. "Standartenführer, this morning I read your memorandum about the Easter Sunday roundup. It seems to me you risk rousing the populace by such tactics."

"Or cowing them," Abetz interjected.

Messmer paced back and forth. "It is a tricky business. As a military man I say crush them now and be over with it."

Abetz inserted a new cigarette. "Because of the urgency of Sunday, I must request that you make no attack until I speak with the governor general."

A thin trickle of sweat appeared over Messmer's lips. "As you wish. But I remind you that General von Steuben is dead. The longer we delay in crushing them . . ."

Abetz put his hand on the Wehrmacht colonel's shoulder. "No one is more appreciative than I of the importance of moving decisively. I shall go immediately to see General von Stulpnagel. I shall phone within the hour."

Messmer clicked his heels. "As you wish. I just want it officially stated that I recommend action now."

"It shall be reported," Abetz answered.

Messmer watched the little Gestapo chief walk out of the garage. He did not like the Gestapo, their tactics or their type. They were ignorant of military psychology. These rebels had to be crushed now. Just to survive the night was a moral victory. He looked out at the tanks and the gates of the yard. There was

448

nothing to wait for. Waiting invited the unknown. He reached for his flask of schnapps. He didn't like any of it.

11:57 P.M.

As soon as he saw the cots lined up in the side room, Paulie let out a lot of pent up air. They were all taken, which meant he wasn't so special after all. And he had the whole night to dream something up. Jesus, it was creepy. It was like some room in a big mansion in the movies with all these pictures of dead big shots. All the furniture had been taken out. There were just the cots and sleeping men. Meat for the Gestapo. First thing he had to do was get rid of the plans he had stuffed in his Jockey shorts. If the Gestapo found them, his balls would be served for breakfast. He tapped the guy next to him. C'mon, no one sleeps that good here. Paulie nudged him again, right in the ribs.

"Where's the crapper?"

The guy turned over. Even in the dark Paulie could see the guy was a cupcake. His marbles were rolling around in his head. "How do I get to the crapper?" Paulie asked.

"Napoleon will take you."

"Who?"

"Beware of Bonaparte. Beware of Robespierre."

What the fuck was this?

Paulie got up. Jesus, he wanted out. "The guard. Go into the guard in the hall," a voice called to him.

Paulie feigned a large stomachache, and the soldier on duty smiled. Many men in the sideroom developed stomach problems the night before morning interrogation.

He was led down into the basement and then along a dark corridor. In the dim light Paulie noticed the weapons room. It was heavily locked, but he could see the racks of rifles as he passed. Heinrich's cookie basket.

The lavatory was fitted with a couple of overhead lights and Paulie made a motion to his stomach. The Heinrich smiled again.

Big joke.

Fuck you, Paulie swore as he slid into the booth and locked the door. He dropped his pants and retrieved Collins's pages. All he had to do was tear them up. Flush like a man with the runs, and he was in business. He looked down at the writing. It said Phase One. Flush it, flush it. Instead Paulie Lazar began to read.

Collins had worked his way down to the crowd surging on Landing Road. The big Heinrich tanks were still sitting there. What were they waiting for? What? Damn it, he should be there. Kresky had made the move . . . the right move. Just like it was Kresky who had realized the intrinsic factor about retaking New York. Heinrich's might was concentrated outside the city. In New Jersey, in New Rochelle, in New Haven. Cut off access to the city, and all he had here was thirty or thirty-five thousand men against a city of eight million. Heinrich was outnumbered. This crowd could take Heinrich and the subway yard. They just didn't know it yet. Someone had to send them the message.

Phase One: Set fire to the marshlands near Hackensack. It would take up the Paterson Plank Road with it. Timed to go up as the dynamite under the Pulaski Skyway went off. The huge suspension bridge that ran from Jersey City to New York would crumble. Blow the Passaic and Hackensack bridges. Everything on Route 46 and Route 1 all tied up. Heinrich can't get anywhere. A hundred fifty thousand men, tanks, munitions, all tied up. They'll never get to the Holland or Lincoln tunnels until after we control the city. Kresky was right. It'll all back up like a toilet.

12:04 A.M.

Phase Two, Paulie read. Burn the landing at South Ferry. That leaves twenty-five thousand men on Governors Island with no way of getting out. Torch the landing at 125th Street and at Dyckman Street. Trap the Germans in New Jersey. Paulie dug his finger into his forehead.

Phase Three: Heinrich will have to come through the Hudson Tubes. Torch the BMT and IND lines at Thirty-third Street. Gasoline and fire will make it a hellhole. If Heinrich makes it out of the tunnel, he runs into a concentration of fire. This is where we wait for Heinrich.

Paulie began to sweat. Shit, if all this happened . . . Jesus, Collins was a smart fuck. His eyes skipped quickly down the page. There was more . . . lots more. Phase Four: An attack must be launched on the German outpost controlling Brooklyn Heights . . . Jesus, he was getting dizzy.

Phase Five: Control of the bridges. Men and armed patrols can take control of the access bridges to New York. Heinrich only has a few patrols there. We must take them all . . . the Triborough . . . the Fifty-ninth Street . . . the George Washington . . . the Brooklyn Bridge. . . . Oh Jesus, he was sweating bullets now. This was big stuff. All these different phases. Stuff about the Luftwaffe airfield and the East River going up. It was meant for Frank Costello. Frank Costello could put an army in the street. Paulie couldn't tear this up. It was important shit. But he couldn't be caught with it either. What was he going to do? He felt his stomach roll. Oh Christ, now he really had diarrhea.

It was the worst moment of his life. He could save his ass but lose the war. The man who brought this to Frank Costello could make any kind of deal he wanted later on. Protection from Vito Genovese . . . from Vito . . . from . . . He heard a strange sound. It was like a motorcycle racing through the men's room. Or to be more precise . . . a man imitating a motorcycle racing through the john.

12:05 A.M.

It was after curfew, but Harlem was simmering. The word had gone out. Joe the Coon, Harlem's biggest policy banker, had been shot dead in Tiny's earlier in the evening. He was the man. The man who bankrolled everybody. He was like Dutch Schultz. But Dutch Schultz didn't get gunned down by no cops. Joe the Coon was dead. And somebody was going to pay.

12:06 A.M.

The police van stopped in front of the Seventh Regiment Armory. Three prisoners were let out. One of them was a Negro. This was the fourth stop of the evening for Black Jack Bixwell. He had been taken to three police stations and questioned. He was a witness to the death of Joe the Coon. A policeman had taken a knife in the gut. This man had seen it all. He knew the truth, and it wasn't clear yet whether the truth would be of any use. How it was used had to be determined. This could only be settled by Gestapo security. Headquarters for Gestapo security was the Seventh Regiment Armory. Handcuffed, the little bow-legged Negro was led inside. He was delivered to the night officer and taken down the hall to one of the side rooms.

12:07 A.M.

Paulie Lazar came out of the toilet compartment and saw a man making a right turn, face and lips contorted as he droned like a motorcycle. He couldn't believe it. The mayor of New York was his old punchie pal, Rocky Malfetta.

12:08 A.M.

Black Jack Bixwell was fingerprinted for a fourth time and then led down the corridor to a supply room where he was given a blanket and pillow. He was then led down the hall to a large room and shoved inside. It was stacked with cots and sleeping men. There were large portraits hung on the wall. Pairs of eyes that followed him as he groped his way through the semidark. He found an empty cot and laid down the pillow and blanket. Damn, he was on the verge of a score, and a wild bullet had cost him. Shit, he was the smartest fucker in the world, but he had no luck. What the hell was he going to do now? The fight was tomorrow night. The Sugar boy needed him. His Sugar boy. He heard a voice. It was the man in the cot next to him. What was he saying?

"Napoleon, at last you have come."

12:09 A.M.

Paulie stepped out cautiously. The guard was not there. He reached out and grabbed the mayor of New York. "Hey, Rocky, it's me."

Rocky Malfetta did a U-turn and stopped. "What did you say?"

"Rocky, it's me . . . Paulie."

The punchie's face slowly creased into a large smile. "Paulie . . . Paulie. What happened to him?"

Paulie looked into Rocky's eyes and saw a big vacancy sign. Shit, his marbles were completely scrambled that day on the Bowery. But he was Paulie's only hope.

He grabbed the punchie by the collar. "Rocky, it's me, your buddy. Paulie Lazar. Remember?"

Rocky's eyes struggled as he groped to recall. Something was there. Tears formed. "Paulie . . . Paulie . . . they hit me and hit me."

"I know, I know. Me too. Listen, I gotta get out of here. It's important. Understand?"

Rocky's eyes went big. "Nobody gets out of here . . . just his honor . . . the mayor."

"Yeah, yeah, I know. You gotta take a message for me. It's very important. Papers, Rocky . . . to Frank Costello." He shook him. *"Capisce?"*

Rocky nodded his head. "Costello, I like him. I seen all his pitchures . . . Abbott and Costello."

Oh Jesus.

He was back on his motorcycle as the guard came in.

"Finished? Ah . . . your honor . . . *Vas ist los?*"

Rocky Malfetta stopped his ride and pointed at Paulie. "He wants to see Abbott and Costello."

If Paulie had his rod, the punchie would have been dead on the spot.

Rocky Malfetta revved up his motorcycle again. "Say hello to Paulie for me."

"The side room," Paulie called. "I'm in the side room."

He walked back down and through the basement. He had fucked up. He still had Collins's plan, in the morning there was the Gestapo, and Rocky Malfetta was the only trusty in the joint. This was no fuckin' prison. It was Bellevue.

12:18 A.M.

It was a swim of a hundred yards at best, Collins guessed. The ground below was framed like a picture in front of him. A lot of trees and underbrush leading down to a stone abutment. Beyond lay the New York Central tracks. Beyond that another abutment, and more underbrush, and then a small wooden slip. Nothing in his way, no Heinrich on the tracks. The crowd was very still. Watching the tanks. Waiting. Up on the tenement roofs, the people also waited. It was time to go.

He shouldered his way through the crowd and suddenly broke through. The crowd watched the man who had come from its midst as he disappeared into the underbrush and trees. Moments later he leaped over the stone abutment and ran along the New York Central railroad tracks. Then he was gone again into more trees and bushes. Another thirty seconds went by, and then a woman said, "There he is." The lone American stood by the edge of the water on top of a small ferry slip. He turned to the crowd and threw up his fist. Then, taking a breath, he entered the water at 12:20 A.M. swimming in a strong Australian crawl across the Harlem River.

On the rooftops a thousand and one fingers pointed to his progress. They watched him, a slim, almost minute figure, barely visible under the moonlight. Head bobbing above the water. Swimming for all of them.

12:20 A.M.

Scatman Robbins stood in the shadows of a pawnshop awning on Seventh Avenue. It adjoined Small's Paradise. It was past curfew, but curfew didn't mean shit in Harlem. Not with all the kraut officers who liked to wench black women. The show would be breakin' at Small's in a few minutes. And some fine women would be coming out on the arms of krauts. Krauts who smelled worse than Limburger cheese. They would be beddin' down with fine black stuff. Only tonight some kraut was goin' to sleep early. He fingered the knife in his pocket. Blood for blood. Joe the Coon was dead, killed by some fuck policeman. Well, shit man, the score was going to be even. Scatman Robbins, who once owned a stable of Harlem's finest women, would see to that. Those women had left him for Nazis. Scatman heard applause inside and stepped out from under the awning into the fading light of Harlem. A jewel-encrusted bracelet with several stones missing. He gripped the knife and took a drink from a bottle he was carrying. He leaned against the wall and waited. Somebody would be coming . . . soon.

12:27 A.M.

Collins was only a few yards from the slip and the fence that backed the subway yard. Now he had reached it. And the crowd on University Heights, on its rooftops, along Cedar Street, Hampden Street, and Landing Road, packed as far back as Sedgwick Avenue, cried out. Fists shot in the air and applause echoed over the water. The American had made it. He had made it.

12:28 A.M.

A corporal came running into the garage that was Colonel Messmer's headquarters. He was quite breathless, and Messmer came to his feet.

The corporal saluted. "Sir, an American swam to the yard."

"Vas?"

"Across the river."

"Why didn't someone shoot him?"

"Sir, we need to be on the bridge for that. It is up now."

Messmer slammed down his cigarette. "There will be others. Lower it. I want twenty men on the bridge. Good shooters. If others follow, or if he comes back to rally the crowd . . . kill him. Shoot to kill."

12:28 A.M.

The last few yards Collins got a burst of energy. The water was cold and his arms were heavy as logs. But he was there. "American," he called out. "Get Kresky, I'm Collins." He was swinging his leg over the wire fence as phantoms came out of the subway cars to greet him. Phantoms with strong arms . . . Americans . . . comrades. They led him soaking wet and exhausted to Kresky.

Collins sat on a subway seat smoking a cigarette, watching the men in position at broken windows. Somebody had draped a raincoat over his shoulders. Kresky saw him eyeing the men.

"They're the best."

Collins nodded imperceptibly. "How many you have left?"

"Twenty-five."

"How many you start with?"

"Fifty-three."

Collins raised an eyebrow. "You think Heinrich will wait till morning?"

Kresky rubbed the stubble of beard on his face. "It looks that way. He's got the tanks staring us right in the face, letting us think about it. In the morning he can provide a show for the people."

Collins walked to the window and looked out at the two Volkers, large turret guns pointed straight at the car blocking the gate. Giant creatures of night. He came back to Kresky. "You were right . . . Manhattan is an island. I took some of your ideas, added a few wrinkles, and passed them on to Frank Costello."

Kresky's eyes quivered with emotion. "The government's answer to Vito Genovese. Did you talk to Costello?"

Collins shook his head.

"I sent a messenger."

"The dame?"

"The dame is dead." He saw Kresky's eyes flicker. "I sent a different dame," Collins said, smiling ruefully. "And I sent Lazar to get Donetti and some of his boys up here. No sign so far . . ."

"Lazar?" Kresky spat out the name. "Lazar is Abetz's man. He works for Genovese."

"Not anymore. He wiped out four of Genovese's top guns."

"Did you see him do it? Jesus, Collins, what's happened to you? A half hour after I had Lazar here, the Gestapo showed up."

Collins took a deep breath. "The Gestapo pulled me in. Lazar ran three of them down with a car. Abetz doesn't give up three of his agents just to make Lazar look good."

Kresky shook his head. "Then he's running amuck, killing everyone in sight. Don't count on Donetti being here. Or Lazar."

Collins stood up and squinted out at the tank. "I don't count on anything." He took out his pistol. It was wet. "You got a gun for me?"

Kresky pointed around. "Lots of guns, lots of men." He paused. "You gotta go back, Irish."

"What are you talking about?"

"Irish history. I'm Paddy Pearse, you're Mick Collins. You gotta go back and lead the people over the bridge. The people will be numb after we fall. You gotta take the yard back. If that doesn't bring the people out . . ."

"Damn it, I don't want to go back. My place is here."

"No, it's not. There are martyrs and there are heroes. And it's not by design. It just comes up on the board that way."

"I could have been here first."

Kresky was quiet for a moment before responding. "No, you couldn't. You've been struggling with yourself. I've been hard on you, but I understand. Sarah, my old woman, she's gone. You don't care as much when that happens. When a dame gets under your skin, it's hard not to give a damn. Hell, you play the cards you were dealt. This is my hand. Next shuffle is yours. This can't be for nothing."

Kresky took out his pipe. "The dame . . . what happened?"

"Firing squad . . . Abetz's order. She got me Kelly's plans. There's a massive roundup scheduled for Sunday. The Hackensack camp is ready."

Kresky showed a clenched fist. "Easter Sunday. Sons of bitches. Well, keep stirring the pot, Irish. Make it scalding hot. Get the crowds in the streets. This is your chance."

Kresky's last sentence hung heavy now. The words of a man who faced his last tomorrow.

"Collins, the hell with what's happening in California. This is New York. We can't wait for Frank Roosevelt and his Rough Riders."

"You sound like me talking to Bill Donovan."

A glimmer of a smile showed itself around Kresky's mouth. "I am you. And I'll be with you when you take the yard back. We'll all be with you."

Collins looked over at the men. The lumpen proletariat. Made in Kresky's image. Faces black as boiler plates, eyes red rimmed but undefeated. Leaning on rifles, smoking, looking out at the tanks that would come for them. "Goddamn it, this is my place."

Kresky cracked a smile. "Irish, you got the chance to make history, the first Irish folk hero to live, and . . ." His voice trailed away. They were all beat. And they all knew what they had to do.

Kresky looked over at him. "You gotta go back, Irish."

Collins shook his head. "I know. But not yet. Not yet."

12:46 A.M.

Curfew had been put into effect. The city was dark. In select spots around the city, in restaurants and hotel grills, collaborators, officials of the Reich, and Wehrmacht officers dined and drank. The news from California was good. Very good. The Americans were falling. The Japanese would land in California. They would meet the Reich and divide America. The Reich would live a thousand years as the Führer predicted. There would be a storm trooper in every city in America. Nobody knew anything about a subway yard at 207th Street. And if they did, nobody cared. It would be handled.

1:02 A.M.

Paulie saw the nigger come back to his bed. He had been out trying to con a guard. What did the little jig think he was going to do? Soft shuffle his way out of the Seventh Regiment Armory? Shit, what the hell was he doing thinking about the nigger? He had his own problems. All he had going for him was Rocky Malfetta, the mayor of New York, who thought Frank Costello was Abbott's partner. He rolled over. He wasn't going to sleep. Not tonight.

Someone called over to him. "What you in for?"

It was the nigger. "None of your fuckin' business." That should have been it. But now Paulie was sitting up. "What about you?" he said in a whisper.

They looked one another over. They were both too streetwise to believe there was a way out, but they were just desperate enough to throw bread crumbs on the water. Maybe some gull would come down and nibble.

Jack Bixwell began. "I was standing upside Joe the Coon when he got shot."

Paulie's eyes came open. "Joe the Coon was iced?"

Jack Bixwell's alarm clock went off. This white muscle-head knew who Joe the Coon was. He was a rackets boy, no doubt about that.

"How?" Paulie demanded.

"Some bitch knifed a dick. He come out with his gun, he already on his way to his maker. He started shooting . . . Joe the Coon got it right through the head."

Paulie pursed his lips. "Harlem ain't gonna like that."

Jack Bixwell smoothed his mustache. "Oh, somebody take a knife in the guts tonight. More than that. Some shit is goin' to come down."

"Why didn't the cops hold you?"

457

"They done took me to three precincts. All full up. They arrested a lot of people. I told them I didn't see nothin'. I don't know why I'm here."

You'll know when they toast your nuts, Paulie thought.

"Ain't no Gestapo business," Jack Bixwell said, trying to reassure himself. "What about you?"

Paulie shrugged. "I helped some guy slip a dick raid."

"Just boolshit them."

Yeah, sure.

Jack Bixwell eyed Paulie. This white meat rack was scared. Meat rack wanted out bad. Jack Bixwell probed to see just how bad. "I make it four to one . . . no, make it six to one."

Paulie heard the odds. "You make what?"

"That's the odds on gettin' out of this piss hole tonight."

It was the way he pronounced *tonight* that caught Paulie. The little nigger had to get out fast. "They'll let you go in a day or two."

"Too late," Jack Bixwell lamented.

"Too late for what?"

"Sugar . . . Brown Sugar."

"What?"

"Too late for the fight. My boy, Sugar Smith, fighting in the Golden Gloves tomorrow night. Fightin' Fritzi Machen for the middleweight championship."

Paulie Lazar heard a bell. "I seen Sugar Smith fight. Last year in the Gloves. The kid was smooth. He beat . . . another . . ."

"He beat Tommy Bell. Tommy Bell turned pro . . . knock out ten men. My Sugar outpoint him."

Yeah, now Paulie remembered. The kid was smooth. He had also seen Fritzi Machen fight one night this winter. Amateur boxin' was all that was left since Heinrich come to town. Machen was a bull. He was older. "I make it seven to five," Paulie said. "Machen."

Black Jack Bixwell's eyes lit up. "They'll make it Machen, three to one. There's money to be made."

There was something here all right, Paulie knew that. "Where's the fight?"

"The Garden."

It was something Jack Bixwell saw in Paulie's eyes. Something that made him think Paulie could get up enough money, or perhaps it was just plain illogical hope. "Joe the Coon was gonna bankroll me. You know who he be. Now you look like a man who has some acquaintance with a bankroll. I got Dinty Callaghan primed." Why was he sellin' bullshit to a muscle head?

Paulie listened to the little jig tryin' to sell him a song. The kid had a chance against Machen, but that was not what had

458

caught Paulie's attention. Joe the Coon was dead. Harlem was like a car leaking gas. One match and it would go up. And the fight could be it. Phase Seven of Collins's plan.

Jack Bixwell had concluded his appeal. "I gots to get out. My boy needs me."

Paulie studied the little hustler in the darkness. "You really think he can beat Machen?"

Jack Bixwell shot a left hand and then another. "He can double up on a left hook. He be greatness one day."

Paulie stared at Jack Bixwell and now sank back. "One day," he said softly. Now both men were silent. They were both in the Seventh Regiment Armory, in a Gestapo side room, and it was one night too many. I gotta find the punchie, Paulie thought. I gotta find him.

1:33 A.M.

The city was pitch. Ostensibly sleeping. But it was full of restless, elusive spirits. People gathered around radios, listening for some sign. Had America won? Were the Americans coming? But the night was inky black.

Chapter 44

April 2, 1942
1:47 A.M.

Abetz was ushered into von Stulpnagel's suite at the Waldorf, and the confident smile on his face disappeared when he saw Guderian and Rommel.

Guderian was pacing while Rommel leaned casually but elegantly against the mantel. Von Stulpnagel sat on the plush blue couch. The whole suite was done in blue. The curtains, also blue, were drawn tight. The room was filled with the aroma of smoke.

Running a nervous hand through his red hair, von Stulpnagel rose. "Abetz, the Americans have won in California. We have confirmation from the Japanese War Office in Hawaii."

Abetz's face showed no expression. "So, what must we do?"

Guderian advanced toward him. "We will form a cul-de-sac around the East Coast. Secure all parts along the coast of New Jersey, Long Island, and Massachusetts. Once that is done, we can hold it with half a million troops. The other half a million are needed for Russia. The Führer has given orders that if the Americans threaten New York, it is to be put to the torch. I will dictate a complete memo and have it on your desk at dawn."

Abetz spoke quietly but firmly. "As you know, Easter Sunday is the date for the roundup of young men in New York."

Guderian finished his drink. "The Führer is absolutely firm that we accomplish in New York what Heydrich did in England. Sixty percent of their working force between the ages of eighteen and thirty are in work camps under Reich control."

Abetz's expression was resolute and determined. "It shall be done."

"Abetz," Rommel called from the corner of the room. "Can you keep the news from the people until Sunday? If you cannot, you will have trouble."

Abetz turned to the Reich's daring general, the Führer's current darling. "We shall begin special broadcasts in the morning on the spectacular Japanese victory. The *Patrician* will carry a major story. There will be a parade, a gala musical festivity celebrating it."

"The *Daily Mirror*," von Stulpnagel pointed out.

"The *Daily Mirror* shall not publish anymore. They are in violation of our agreement." Abetz turned back to Rommel and Guderian. "The roundup of young men, Jews, subversives, and radicals will take place on Good Friday. Is that satisfactory?"

Guderian nodded. "I commend you on your zeal. I am sure the Führer will be pleased."

Rommel walked toward Abetz. "I understand you have some flare-up with the Americans."

"A trifle. Some Resistance people have taken a subway repair yard in upper Manhattan. General von Stulpnagel, I have come here to ask that you telephone Colonel Messmer to wait until morning to subdue them. I wish the crowds on the Bronx Heights to see it, and I wish to have my men there. We begin the roundups immediately under the pretext of ending the rising."

Rommel's eyes showed concern. "It should be crushed immediately."

Abetz saw von Stulpnagel's distress.

"This is a matter of internal politics, General, though, of course, I defer to your great war record. But this is New York. I have been here for some months."

Rommel held up a hand in acknowledgment. "Of course."

"General von Steuben is dead," Guderian said.

"I can assure you, they will all be dealt with," Abetz responded.

Von Stulpnagel sighed. "The morning you say."

"At dawn," Abetz replied.

"Very well then," von Stulpnagel said after seeing Rommel's nod.

"And now, gentlemen, if you excuse me, I must be off to my headquarters." Abetz clicked his heels. "Heil Hitler."

The three generals stood in silence in the room. The American victory in California had changed a great deal.

"Can he do it?" Guderian questioned.

"Abetz is very efficient," von Stulpnagel assured him. "Rumors will fly of course, but people will not know for sure. I do believe Abetz has a point. Crushing the rebellion and its spectators will be an ingenious way to begin the roundup."

Rommel came back to the table and poured more sherry. "Perhaps. But rumor can be a dangerous animal. Men will believe it and act on it. Hope thrives on rumor precisely because it is so illogical."

"But a subway yard," von Stulpnagel protested. "Why not a military objective? Something like the Brooklyn Naval Shipyard?"

Rommel drained his glass. "My dear von Stulpnagel. The subway is a symbol. Precisely because it is, I would have crushed this rebellion right away. Each minute it exists is more dangerous."

"Dangerous, a few men in a subway yard. A lucky shot . . ."

"My dear fellow," Rommel said, putting down his glass. "It is because it comes from the heart not the head that is indicative. The Americans don't know where to start, and someone pops up. You see? They dream of reclaiming their city."

"But then why didn't you tell Abetz . . ."

"Come now, von Stulpnagel. It is after all, a handful of men in a subway yard. Not enough to disrupt policy. Abetz is an efficient officer."

"Gentlemen," Guderian said. "I must go. The Americans may dream but the Wehrmacht is reality." He held up his glass. "Their dreams will go up in flames."

1:45 A.M.

Paulie lay on his back holding Collins's sheaf of papers. A shaft of light showed in the room. Moments later he heard a whisper. He looked down and saw Rocky Malfetta crawling on the floor.

"Paulie, it's me. What do you got for Costello?"

461

Paulie couldn't believe it. He had the Collins revolution for Costello. He sat up. "I got something for him, but I don't know where he is. Christ."

He felt Rocky Malfetta's hand on his shoulder. "That's okay, Paulie. I used to run the numbers count to Costello for Tommy Eboli."

Paulie stared at the little geek.

"Just give it to me, Paulie. I know where Costello counts his money."

2:00 A.M.

Abetz was back in his office with a mental list of phone calls he had to make. Once his first phone call would have been to Kelly. But events and priorities had changed. Instead he dialed another number and waited. He heard Vito Genovese's rough voice come on.

"This is Abetz. I wish to see you in my office tomorrow morning at seven. There is an emergency in California. Our movie has been cancelled."

2:45 A.M.

The expensive West Side penthouse apartment was furnished in the style Frank Costello had been accustomed to since the 1920s when he made his mark as a bootlegger. The living room where he sat alone with Albert Anastasia had pictures of Joe Louis and Alfred Smith on the wall. Two large standing lights in opposite corners illuminated the room but not the faces of the two men who planned what would happen without ever being seen. A lifetime habit of contracts, conspiracy, and murder. As you rose in stature, you receded even further into the darkness.

Frank Costello spoke now in that scratchy, hard delivery. Like many Italian children, he had been operated on in untimely fashion when his tonsils were removed. "Albert, they have to be very good boys for the Gestapo. The best."

Albert Anastasia sat as impassively as a pope holding an audience. "I got Pretty Levine, Nick Abruzzi, Carmelo Gigante, Abe Hirsh, the Gallardo brothers, and Bugsy Goldstein."

Costello smiled. "Bugsy Goldstein. Is he as crazy as Bugsy Siegel?"

Anastasia turned to him. "I thought no one was nutsy as Bugsy Siegel until I met Bugsy Goldstein."

The man lapsed into silence. They were waiting for somebody. Someone who would make a difference. A deal had to be cut. There was always a deal, a maneuver that put you one step ahead of everyone. Like the time Lucky Luciano took Joe the Boss Masseria to lunch in Brooklyn, went to the bathroom, and Albert Anastasia, Bugsy Siegel, Vito Genovese, and Joe Adonis appeared and rubbed out Joe the Boss. You always had to have the edge.

"What do you think of the subway yard?"

Albert Anastasia shrugged. "I don't like the odds."

There was a soft knock, and a voice called to them. "He's here."

Both men rose as a short man entered the room. He wore a dark suit and a white shirt without a tie.

Frank Costello stepped forward and extended his hand. "Hello, Vito."

They shook hands and then sat down, their faces hidden from each other. Vito Genovese spoke first. "How was Hot Springs, Frank?"

"Hot."

Albert Anastasia spoke. "Vito, I'm callin' for a table on you."

There was a dramatic silence. A table meant a vote on whether a boss should be hit.

"I wanna hear your reason, Albert."

"Vincent the Chin was hit in Frank's building the other night. I think he was there to hit Frank. Who sent him, Vito?"

Vito Genovese showed no emotion as he spoke. "The Gestapo. They musta got a tip."

"Yeah Vito, and you're top man with the Gestapo."

Genovese turned toward Frank Costello. "Frank, listen."

"You went against the outfit," Albert Anastasia interrupted. "You're the krauts' number one. In this our life, certain things are not forgiven. I'm callin' for a table."

Vito Genovese edged forward. "What do you say, Frank? You want a table on me?"

Frank Costello crossed his legs. "What was Vincent the Chin doin' in my buildin' dressed as a doorman?"

"Frank, business is business. But I changed my mind and stopped Vinnie Agramonte. It's all business, Frank. Let's do a deal."

There was no immediate answer. The air was thick with tension. Vito Genovese's hand drifted toward his pocket. Now he came up with a cigarette. "Like I said, no one from the outfit was around, so I made the best deal I could. But Abetz double-crossed me. You can't trust him."

"I was around," Albert Anastasia said ominously. "I didn't hear from you, Don Vitone."

Vito Genovese got white with anger. His hand quivered.

Frank Costello unfolded his legs. "No hard feelin's, Vito. Not

463

on my part, but the rest of the outfit didn't hear from you on how many points you got from Abetz." He put out his cigarette. "What do you got in mind for Abetz?"

Genovese rubbed his mustache. "I owe the outfit, so I'll take the risk." He paused. "I'll snuff Abetz for ya." He let that sink in. "That's a major league hit. I do it myself."

"From in front or in back?" Albert Anastasia said.

"Fuck you, Albert. I do it and no table."

Frank Costello let it sit there. "All right Vito, it's your contract. Hit him and there's no table."

"How you gonna do it?"

Vito Genovese didn't answer right away. His eyes were dark and melancholy. "He's never alone. It's gonna be harder than Maranzano or Joe the Boss. I gotta take a big chance."

Albert Anastasia looked at Frank Costello, who was watching Genovese carefully. Now Costello spoke in that soft, gravelly manner known only to intimates. "That's the only thing that will square it, Vito. You got forty-eight hours."

"That ain't much time."

"That's what you got."

The deal had been made. Cigars and cigarettes were lit. Smoke swirled in the air. Finally Frank Costello broke the silence.

"What do you hear about California, Vito?"

"Nothin'. I haven't heard a peep. It's the whole ballgame, ain't it?"

There was a rap on the door, and a voice emanating from a primordial creature resounded. Frank Costello excused himself. Two minutes later he returned. "We gotta find a new counting house. There's a little punchie dink out there. He used to run numbers and do drops here. Now he calls himself the mayor of New York."

He held out a sheath of papers to Albert Anastasia.

"What's that?"

"They're from Collins . . . Donovan's man."

The three gangsters looked at each other. A street fly who was a numbers messenger had come right to Frank Costello's door with the goods.

Albert Anastasia stood up. "Who sent him?"

Frank Costello smiled. "A guy in the slammer. Paulie Lazar. Who the fuck is Paulie Lazar?"

Albert Anastasia didn't register any sign of recognition, but Vito Genovese stood up. There was a strange look on his face. "I know Paulie Lazar."

3:45 A.M.

The men sat quietly in the subway car, some dozing, others smoking. Occasionally a whisper was heard. But mostly they were quiet. It was not a time for talk. Collins watched them and then Kresky. This hard-wrought man, carved out of steel and cement. A man in the corner began to whistle. After a while Collins recognized the tune. "The St. Louis Blues." Collins thought of the words. "I hate to see that evening sun go down." He checked his watch. Soon it would be rising. For the last time.

Up on the heights, the crowd was still there. Along Cedar and Hampden streets, on Landing Road. And on the rooftops. Nothing had changed. They shivered and smoked. No one talked much. Occasionally someone pointed out the bridge, which had been lowered and was now occupied by twenty Wehrmacht soldiers, focused on the river. But it was all still and quiet. So were the two giant steel bugs with long guns protruding frontward that waited at the yard's gates.

4:18 A.M.

The Wehrmacht major was drunk, and he weaved back and forth along Park Avenue, which was all dark. He stopped to drink from his bottle and then clasped it to his breast. Goot bottle, goot friend. Now he tripped and fell laughing into a row of flowers planted on one of the islands in the middle of the street. He crawled around laughing and pulled up a fistful of white flowers. He heard a noise. A car. It stopped, and the driver leaned out.

The major presented the flowers as though to a young lady, laughing loudly. Then he saw the gun in the driver's hand. It roared three times at point-blank range. He fell over backward, the flowers falling directly on his chest. The car sped away.

4:20 A.M.

Abetz sat alone, reports of the day on his desk. Harlem was touchy. Their policy gangster had been shot. There was the subway yard. The Americans had retaken California. Kelly had been decidedly sour upon learning the news. Wait till he heard the Führer wasn't coming to Kelly's coronation. Well, Kelly had served his purpose. He would continue to do so. Tomorrow would be busy. He had a lot of work for Vito Genovese. The city must be kept in turmoil, shootings, rumors, fear. That would distract the people. As would the headlines in the morning. The *Daily Mirror* had already been closed down.

His hands moved restlessly through the paper on his desk. Reports, endless reports. He had to be on top of it all. Here was one. From the police. There had been a man thrown from a building on 110th Street. An old man. He came out the window shortly after the police had received a phone call saying a leader of the Resistance lived there. Abetz stared at the sheet. A suspect had been arrested trying to sneak out of the basement and been taken to the Seventh Regiment Armory on Park Avenue and Fifty-sixth Street. His name was Alan Nipponomick. Abetz felt tiny chills run up his back. Nipponomick had been dead for a month. This could only be Paulie Lazar with Nipponomick's papers. And he was in a cell in the Seventh Regiment Armory. He stood up. Abetz pressed the intercom. "Hoppman, my car. Immediately."

4:34 A.M.

Paulie lay back and watched the ceiling. The punchie was gone. No word. Nothin'. What was happening? . . . A line of light showed in the room, and turning he saw two soldiers come in. Instinctively he knew it was for him. They came straight across the room, turned right, and made their way to his bed. One of them shook him roughly. Paulie pretending to sleep, and took another dig.

"What?"

"Kommen sie."

"You got the wrong guy. . . ." He took a sharp nudge with a rifle. He felt his nuts tingle.

4:37 A.M.

The two dicks waited. They had on black topcoats and black hats. They had a warrant for the transfer of the prisoner, Nipponomick. Gross, the Wehrmacht orderly, was tired. His office was a clutter of shelves and papers. Prisoners came and went in the middle of the night . . . the jails were full. He knew he should call Gestapo headquarters, but he was tired. Gross had spent the day with a cute blonde. He was worn out. There were footsteps, and he saw the big oaf flanked by two Wehrmacht soldiers. Gross turned to the detectives. "This is your man."

4:39 A.M.

Handcuffed, Paulie was led out into the street. The sky was gray. Night was surrendering to morning. He felt the ever present hand on his arm. Dicks always had their hands on you. But what the fuck was going on? He was led along Park Avenue to a big, shiny sedan. Something perked in him, like coffee in the morning. It wasn't no dick's car. His stomach rolled over. Vito. He was lunch meat. The car door swung open, and Paulie was shoved in back. He looked up and saw the man's face as if in a dream.

"Hello, Paulie."

It was Frank Costello.

4:45 A.M.

Gross looked up. The two detectives were back. There was another prisoner they wanted. A *schwarz* named Bixwell. Wearily he picked up the phone and called down the hall. He asked for the prisoner, Bixwell. Gross, a crew-headed young man, put down the phone. He wished Lieutenant Munchen was here. He turned to collect the warrant for Bixwell and saw one of the detectives fixing something on his pistol. Gross's eyes got very big. It was a silencer. It was his very last thought. Bugsy Goldstein shot him right between the eyes. As Gross crumpled, Nick Abruzzi caught him and dragged him to the closet.

4:47 A.M.

The two men in black topcoats and hats led the handcuffed prisoner down and across Park Avenue where a big, shiny sedan was parked. The door opened and Jack Bixwell was pushed inside. The two men slid in the front. Seconds later, the powerful Buick came to life and the car headed uptown, and then, taking a left on Sixty-fifth Street, headed across Central Park.

4:50 A.M.

The black military car carrying the head of the Gestapo in New York City pulled up in front of the Seventh Regiment Armory. A bullnecked subordinate opened the door and Standartenführer Dietrich Abetz stepped outside and then hurried up the steps of the armory. He headed immediately for the quarters of the night officer. He walked briskly, impatiently down the corridor. He turned into the office expecting to see the night orderly. But no one was there. Abetz tapped his gloves impatiently. He didn't like it. He stepped out into the hall and called to one of the soldiers on duty.

The morning smiled sweetly and the dew glistened on the grass. Ben Marks had stripped down to his track uniform and now stood shaking arms and legs. Snapping them as if they were spaghetti. The whole trick was to be loose. For ultimately, you ran not against an opponent but yourself. He had been running since he was a very small boy. Every spring there were races. Perhaps not this year, but he had to stay in touch. He loved the ritual of it. The hum of his nerves telling him it was time to begin, the tingling in his body, the pretense that there were other runners. He took his stance and lowered himself into a sprinter's crouch. Body poised, legs dug in, eyes relentlessly focused on the ground. The gun in his head went off, and he gave himself to the challenge. Now, legs pumping, eyes intent on the lane he had created for himself, he ran. Seeing the grass, driving, head locked, eyes focused, testing himself. Now, give it all you've got. He strained forward. There was the wind rushing to him and a noise, some echo he picked up, and then the bullet aimed at his head stilled his senses and thought. He pitched forward on his face, eyes closed. He lay still now, face wet from the dew in the grass, the race unfinished.

From behind a tree in Van Cortlandt Park, the Wehrmacht soldier stepped out. His name was Oskar Krauss. He too had run the gauntlet, and now the score was even. He looked around. It was safe, clear. Nobody had seen him. But it was not a time for lingering. He began to trot and then broke into a run.

Hoppman spotted blood leaking from the closet and, opening the door, found the body of Corporal Kurt Gross. He ran from the office yelling for the standartenführer, who was angrily questioning two Wehrmacht soldiers about the release of the prisoner, Nipponomick.

The first flash of sun jumped on the Harlem River. Collins and Kresky watched it in silence. It was time.

Kresky's eyes found the bridge. "If you go now the sun will give them trouble."

Collins nodded. "Go after the tanks now. If you get lucky you might take them out."

Kresky smiled. "Now you're a warrior again, Irish."

They were in the repair shed, and Kresky pointed to a row of bottles filled with flammable gas. "Cocktails will be served in exactly three minutes."

Collins looked at the four messengers of death. Working men in overalls and grimy shirts. Men who would attack the tanks with Molotov cocktails.

"Let me take one out," Collins said.

Kresky leaned against a large yellow lift. "Listen, Irish, you gotta get back there to take this yard again. We'll hit the tanks, you hit the river. You got a better chance that way."

They stood facing one another now. Mick and Polack. Nothing and everything to say.

"It's my city again."

Kresky put a hand on Collins's shoulder. "Then take it. Irish . . . about Shelly Ragosky . . . you were right. Thanks."

They walked toward the door that opened out onto the yard.

5:11 A.M.

The entry in the night book showed a prisoner had signed out to bring back food. How was such a thing allowed? The night duty officer had left and a corporal who had been murdered let a prisoner sign in and out. And there was no name. Just a title. Abetz slammed his fist on the desk. "Bring me this mayor of New York."

5:12 A.M.

On the rooftops of Cedar Street above University Heights, the sun reflected on a pair of binoculars held by Irv Polkin. He had picked up something in the yard. A man had run to the back fence. And around the large shed some men were carrying out bottles. Bottles? Irv Polkin moved his focus now to the tanks. There were only a few soldiers nearby. The rest of the Wehrmacht were apparently sleeping. He swept his binoculars toward the University Heights Bridge. The soldiers there were not sleeping. They were pointing.

5:13 A.M.

"Go," Kresky said. "Go. Go."

Four men began scaling the fence. Behind them were Kresky and six men with rifles. As they climbed over, Kresky heard a German soldier yell.

Irv Polkin watched in fascination. The Americans were attacking. Men against tanks. With what? Then he saw something flare. The bottles were lit, and the men who had climbed the fence ran toward the tanks. Some German soldiers appeared, but not in time to stop one of the men from climbing on the turret of the tank. He pulled open the turret door and dropped the flaming bottle, then jumped. Another man rolled a flaming bottle at the tank and then fell, hit by rifle fire. Seconds later the tank went up.

5:14 A.M.

Collins heard the explosion and went up the wire fence. He was over and running on the planks of the little slip. In one motion he threw himself into the water.

5:16 A.M.

Irv Polkin saw the soldiers on the bridge begin shooting. There was a man in the water. The crowd, still focused on the burning tank, hadn't seen him yet.

5:17 A.M.

They hadn't gotten the second tank. Two Wehrmacht soldiers had cut down Ollie Johnson and Johnny Nolan. The tank wheeled into position.
"Get down," Kresky screamed.

5:13 A.M.

Colonel Messmer had heard the explosion, and from his vantage point in the garage saw the first tank go up. The Americans were attacking. *"Achtung,"* he screamed. *"Achtung."* . . . Sergeant Polner followed as Wehrmacht soldiers poured from the garage and from the waiting trucks on Broadway. Messmer felt the coolness of air, and the early morning sun blurred his vision. We will slaughter the American *schweinhunds*.

5:19 A.M.

Collins came up and heard the first ping as a bullet hit the water. Another. Ping . . . ping . . . ping. He swam strongly, gathering up breath, and then dived.

5:20 A.M.

The first three blasts from the tank had blown the subway car open, and now the Wehrmacht was pouring in. Kresky stood in

the middle of the yard waiting. "C'mon Heinrich . . . c'mon."
From behind subway cars the Americans came out to meet them.

5:21 A.M.

Irv Polkin could see the fighting going on in the yard. The
Germans kept coming, and now as Americans fell, others closed
in hand to hand fighting. The tank had wheeled into the yard.
The Germans had broken through.

5:22 A.M.

Collins came up and heard yelling from the crowd. For him
or for the fighting in the yard? Ping . . . another bullet rippled
in the water. He kept swimming. He was only twenty yards
away. Go.

5:23 A.M.

The tank gun was aimed at the subway repair shed. There was
a tremendous explosion, and the front wall of the shed disappeared.

Behind the tank, across the yard, Americans fought the Wehrmacht with guns and clubs. On the layover tracks an American
named Jimmy Jones used a rifle butt on a soldier named Gorman. Seconds later Jones took two bullets in the back and fell
on top of the dead soldier.

There were more and more soldiers, adept with bayonets.
Thrust . . . stab. *"Stoss."*

Kresky had taken a bullet in the shoulder. Now leaning against
a subway car, he emptied his rifle. He saw a soldier go down
and begin crawling toward him. There were screams . . . from
dying men. He got to the Heinrich and reached for his grenade
belt. He took a kick in the side and grunted. Looking up, he
saw the Heinrich. He had blue eyes and a face like a hammer.
He lunged with his bayonet. Kresky rolled but still took it in the
shoulder. He cried out. The Heinrich was coming back. A shot.
The soldier keeled over. Get the grenade. He crawled feeling
the pain in his arm. A foot thudded on his hand. He looked up
and saw a Heinrich officer with a pistol. He was smiling. Kresky
raised himself up. "Fuck you . . . Heinrich."

He took a kick in the teeth. Spitting up blood. He said it
again.

Lieutenant Schindel raised the pistol.

Collins, Kresky thought, Collins.

Schindel shot him through the head.

471

5:23 A.M.

Irv Polkin swept the yard with his glasses. There seemed to be only gray uniforms. Wehrmacht. Nobody was left. The Americans were all dead. Polkin bit his lip.

Up on the Heights the crowd was still.

5:24 A.M.

The American flag was being lowered. Irv Polkin saw it. He looked down at the water. A man was coming out. He disappeared into the underbrush.

5:25 A.M.

Collins looked across the river. They were dead, he knew that. He stood up and, unable to contain himself, said, "You sons of bitches, I'll be back."

Chapter 45

April 2, 1942
5:27 A.M.

The sun graced the sweet grass in Van Cortlandt Park. Louis Marks smelled the morning air as he dogtrotted toward where he knew his nephew would be sprinting. He should have caught sight of him already. He felt the bag he was carrying bang his knee. In it was flanken he had taken for himself before the Nazi supply officer arrived. It was meat Louis Marks had stripped with the cleaver he carried in his bag.

He scanned the seemingly endless expanse of ground and saw his nephew lying in the grass. He must have finished and was taking a breather. "Benny," he called. "Benny . . . I got some flanken . . . we eat good tonight." He reached the boy and knelt down, and saw the thin line of blood trickling on the grass, making it turn brown. And somehow before he even turned the boy over . . . he knew. His eyes were closed, yet his body was lukewarm. He brought the boy to his chest and began to sob

472

quietly. They had done it . . . they. He rocked his nephew and cried . . . and the more he cried, the more the feeling came into his chest, till the quiet crying became sobbing . . . till the sobbing became something terrible and corrosive inside him. They had killed him as they had killed David Bornstein. He stood up, brandishing his meat cleaver.

From the distance you could hear the cry. It sounded like someone screaming, "Benny . . . Benny."

5:30 A.M.

Abetz found himself standing on the drill floor of the armory. Cages with iron bars covered most of the floor. The cages contained prisoners. In front of Abetz was a little bit of a man with many teeth missing, wearing gray prisoner's garb. This was the so-called mayor of New York. Behind Abetz stood a flustered lieutenant named Munchen.

"I repeat. Where did you go to in the middle of the night?"

Rocky Malfetta grinned. "To the movies. I seen Abbott and Costello."

Abetz gestured toward a Wehrmacht guard. "You told Private Metz you had brought the detectives with you. What detectives?"

Rocky Malfetta grinned. "I'm the mayor of New York. They work for me."

"The mayor of New York is named LaGuardia, and he is my prisoner."

"I imposed him," Rocky Malfetta said.

"Where is the prisoner Nipponomick?"

Rocky Malfetta screwed up his forehead. "Nyack. That's upstate."

"*Schweinhund.*" Abetz lashed the infuriating little man in the face. He turned on Lieutenant Munchen. "You shall face a court-martial for this. I have lost an important prisoner. Your orderly is dead, prisoners come and go as if this were a hotel. This *schwarz* who was freed, does no one know anything about him?"

The guard looked away. Lieutenant Munchen bit his lip. Abetz said to no one in particular, "Nipponomick is an American named Paulie Lazar. I want him."

Rocky Malfetta suddenly brightened. "You know Paulie?"

Abetz stared. "You know Lazar?"

"Sure. I took him to the movies to see Costello."

Costello. Of course. Vito Genovese's assassination attempt on Costello had failed because of Lazar. And now Lazar was free . . . because of Costello. Abetz turned to Lieutenant Munchen. "The prisoner is coming with me. Call Lieutenant Gearhard and

473

tell him to report immediately and question anyone who spoke with Nipponomick or this *schwarz*, Bixwell. I want a complete report on my desk in two hours' time. Is that understood?''

Acknowledging neither the reply nor the salute from Lieutenant Munchen, Dietrich Abetz pointed to Rocky Malfetta. ''Hoppman, bring the prisoner.''

5:42 A.M.

Slowly the city came to life on April 2, 1942. It promised another bright spring day. Along Broadway and Sixth Avenue, copies of the *Daily Patrician* were dropped off at newsstands. Dealers cut open the string and stared at the headline. JAPANESE WIN GREAT NAVAL VICTORY. The subhead read, ''California Facing Invasion.''

From Times Square to Wall Street . . . from Herald Square to Columbus Circle, the papers were placed on wooden newsstands. Dealers squinted down at the headlines, read them and, sober eyed, looked up at the sky. Jimmy Key at Broadway and Fiftieth Street had run his stand for over twenty years. Since the days of Jimmy Walker as mayor. He puffed on a cigarette that dangled from the corner of his mouth. The *Daily Mirror* was late. Why? He took a nickel from his pocket and gimped over to a nearby phone.

5:50 A.M.

Passengers were coming out of the BMT station at Times Square grumbling. There were no trains running. A haberdashery salesman named Ansel Levin checked his watch as he walked across Sixth Avenue. He managed an Adams hat shop on lower Broadway. He had never been late in thirty years. He stopped and looked up and down Sixth Avenue. There didn't seem to be any buses either.

6:13 A.M.

Abetz congratulated Colonel Messmer on the results of the morning's battle. ''I regret I was not there, but duty of the utmost seriousness prevented it.'' He stopped. ''To the last man? Excellent. Then the crowd has had a lesson in the Reich's military efficiency.'' He smiled at Vito Genovese, who sat across from him. ''I do not wish any attempt to be made to disperse the crowds until I arrive. Arrangements must be made. However, I will need your troops. Those rounded up will be taken

474

away. I shall be there within the hour. And once again my congratulations."

Abetz hung up. "Well, their moment of glory is finished. Now we will begin the business of teaching some lessons." He leaned forward. "California is kaput. Our radio and press announcements will be stepped up. That will not be enough. Distractions are needed. Your kind of distractions."

Vito Genovese smiled. "In Chicago there used to be what was called flying squads. Al Capone liked to use them. Gimme some of your men and some Wehrmacht uniforms for my boys and we'll fly through a few places. Some people will get killed . . . maybe a lot. But they'll get the message. They won't be coming out."

Abetz smiled, "Excellent. Fear for one's life is wonderful motivation for staying in the house. Yes, it should be official. By all means you should wear uniforms."

Vito Genovese stood up. "I'll need papers."

Abetz now stood up. "Hoppman will give you requisition forms. Where will you begin?"

Vito Genovese looked blandly at Abetz. "Somewhere nearby."

He turned to go and heard Abetz's voice. "You know Paulie Lazar is with Frank Costello?"

Vito Genovese raised an eyebrow. "Is he? That'll have to be taken care of."

6:39 A.M.

They were in the living room of Meyer Lansky's apartment on West End Avenue. It was a room that featured a large Persian rug and soft easy chairs. The shades were drawn so that the light was a sometime thing. The chairs were occupied by three men sitting like imperious rulers. From left to right they were Frank Costello, Albert Anastasia, and a burly gangster with a thick mop of hair and small eyes. Paulie Lazar.

In the middle of the room, Black Jack Bixwell bobbed and weaved, hooking and jabbing against an imaginary opponent. "Sugar here, Sugar there. Machen never touch him."

Frank Costello, who was holding a coffee cup, smiled. But if you looked closely you saw the smile was not in his eyes.

"Paulie tells me Fritzi Machen is a lot more experienced."

"Sure he be, but Sugar is greatness."

Frank Costello nodded. "Tonight, huh?"

"Eight o'clock."

"You gonna have some fans there?"

Jack Bixwell stopped his shuffle. "Mr. Costello, you know Harlem be boarded up tighter than a dead virgin."

Frank Costello set down his coffee cup. "Jack, why don't you get yourself a cup of coffee?"

Jack Bixwell went out, and Paulie felt rockets going off in his head. He was alone with Frank Costello and Albert A. Jesus, Vito Genovese couldn't touch him.

Albert Anastasia turned to Frank Costello. "Paulie's idea about hitting the jig ain't bad, but what if the kraut knocks him out fast?"

Frank Costello spoke from swirls of smoke. "Who says we have to wait very long?"

Anastasia picked it up right away. "You mean kill him in the first round?" He smiled. "I love it."

Paulie's brain was swimming. This was how it was done. It was the cream . . . with nuts and cherries on it. He saw himself in Madison Square Garden popping the nigger kid. "Let me do the hit, Frank," he blurted out.

"Paulie,"—it was Albert Anastasia—"you done good. Get yourself some coffee."

"Sure." Paulie shot from the chair as if catapulted.

Albert Anastasia put a cigar in his mouth. "If you want a riot, Frank, you still need to get the jigs to the Garden. And we can't put in the fix with the krauts."

Frank Costello, dressed in banker's gray pinstripes with a blue shirt and tie, nodded. "We don't need the jigs to come. It'll be on the radio. When Sugar Smith gets clipped, Harlem will go up. But, just in case, we buy some insurance."

"What kind of insurance?"

Frank Costello smiled. He had already measured that angle. "We own every precinct captain in New York. Get the three closest to Harlem to come down this afternoon. Tell them we got a brown bag for them. Now we just need a hit man. A good one." He looked at Anastasia. "How about Lazar?"

The lord high executioner of murder was hidden in swirls of smoke. "Lazar clipped Vinnie the Chin. He saved your life. And he's hungry."

Frank Costello raised his eyes just a fraction. "Vito said he sent Lazar there to clip Vinnie the Chin. That means Vito owns Lazar. We can't trust him if there's a war with Vito."

"Well, you know, Frank, whoever does the job could get trampled in the crush. Lazar just might not make it out of the Garden."

"Could be," Frank Costello agreed, "but if he knew that, he wouldn't go in."

"I'll take care that Paulie don't know."

Frank Costello stood up. "I have to make a few calls. And make sure there are two guys on the front door. No more surprise visits." Frank Costello went into the bedroom and, moments later, could be heard talking in a muted tone on the telephone. Albert Anastasia sat there smoking his cigar, enveloped in clouds of smoke.

6:43 A.M.

Abetz read the reports and frowned. The subway workers were out, as were the bus drivers. The Americans had gone on strike. There was another report that a German had been shot dead on Park Avenue. He pressed the intercom. "Hoppman. Check on the interrogation of this mayor of New York. And send Radner in."

Radner heard the rap of Hoppman's knuckles on the desk and went into Abetz's office. "Help yourself," Abetz said, gesturing to the coffee pot on his desk.

Abetz went back to scanning a report. There had been a number of incidents in Harlem last night. A Wehrmacht officer had been stabbed to death outside Small's Paradise. The city was very restive. While Genovese's flying squads would be effective, it might not be productive to attack the crowd on University Heights. The subway yard had been retaken. Inertia and despair would set in. His strategy of last night seemed risky. Let the crowd disperse by itself . . . with just a little encouragement.

"Captain," Abetz began . . . he stopped. "You look extremely tired. Are you well?"

Radner rubbed his forehead. "I have been up walking."

"All night?"

"Yes, if you must know."

Abetz was momentarily thoughtful. "And what have you seen?"

"I . . . it is not important."

"Go on, Captain. Continue."

"I have seen that the Americans want their city back."

It was a childish remark, and Abetz should have dismissed it. But Abetz was tired and edgy. Everything was not smooth.

"Captain, they may want it, but they shall not have it back. Not ever. The Reich will be here for a thousand years . . . and if we are not, it will be because there is no city. Do you understand?"

He saw Radner looking at him with dull and red-rimmed eyes. Abetz had reached for his coffee when the reply came.

"We shall not contain them."

The words cut like salt. "Captain, were it not for the service you performed for me, I would have you thrown in a cell for that remark.''

Radner stood up. "Do what you wish."

Now Abetz looked more closely at Radner. He was on the edge, a pathetic idealist who had come to realize he and his ideals were of no value. He could be used for another few days and then discarded. "Captain, I think you are tired. We will discuss your attitude at another time. What I am most concerned with is that the city and its cultural events proceed smoothly in the next few days. What do we have today? It is matinee day, is it not? Sit down, Captain. Have some coffee."

Radner remained standing.

"I said sit down, Captain."

Radner finally took his seat. He is finished, Abetz concluded. "Well?"

"There are several matinees, a cocktail gathering at the Hotel Carlyle this afternoon at five. And there is the jazz concert at the Cotton Club."

Abetz nodded. "That is on Forty-seventh Street?"

"Yes."

"Captain, it is very important that things run as usual."

"As usual?"

"Guests, important dignitaries, officials of the Reich will be at these functions. I rely on you to make sure everything possible is done to ensure their . . . comfort."

"You mean protection."

"Yes, their protection. I want no incidents."

"I am not a policeman."

It was the way Radner said it. "Captain . . . your insolence . . ."

"I am not an agent of the Gestapo."

A sudden insight came to Abetz. "Has your Jewess left you?"

An amused smile came to Abetz's face and then disappeared as Radner lunged across the desk, grabbing him by the collar. Radner's hand dropped away as the realization of just what he had done came to him.

Abetz rose. "Go home, Captain. You are relieved of all further duties. Go on, you are useless to me."

Radner, pale of face and shaky, moved toward the door. Now he turned. "Standartenführer, I wish to say . . ."

Abetz never looked up. "Get out."

7:09 A.M.

Leila came from the shower wearing a robe Alvin Barker had put out for her. A towel was draped around her head. Alvin had a quaint one-bedroom apartment on Christopher Street. She saw the blanket on the couch where he had slept. He was framed in the little alcove that fronted the nook that served as a kitchen. There was a curious expression on his face.

"What is it?"

He didn't answer right away. "The subway yard fell . . . it just came over the radio."

Her eyes flared. "But the Nazis control the radio."

Alvin couldn't look directly at her. "I know . . . but I wouldn't hold out much hope. Look, maybe your friend wasn't in the yard. . . ."

"I do hold out hope." The towel came off her head. "I'm going up there."

"How? All the subways are out."

"I'll go there. And I'll find him."

He watched her moving determinedly through the apartment, gathering up her clothes. She moved toward the bedroom and turned. "You're coming, aren't you?"

Alvin Barker's wrinkled, weathered face broke into a grin. "Are you kidding? It's history."

7:13 A.M.

Collins's plan lay on the coffee table in front of Frank Costello. He picked it up and read a section. "That's a lot of bridges to go up. Blow the Hackensack and Passaic bridges, the Pulaski Skyway, and then torch the Hackensack Meadowlands. We need to fix a lot of people. And there's no time." He turned to Albert Anastasia. "Tell Longie and Joe it's got to be done." He was referring to the New Jersey mob bosses, Longie Zwillman and Joe Adonis.

Albert Anastasia stood up. "Let me talk to Tony." He moved into the bedroom to call his brother.

Costello looked over at Socks Lanza. "What time will the harbor go up?"

"Five. The piers around South Street and the Battery and up the East River. No harbor traffic after that. But lemme tell you something, Frank, if you could blow everything tonight— Paterson, Passaic, all of it—Heinrich can still come in through the PATH tubes. And they're loaded down with troops In Newark and Jersey City."

Frank Costello leaned back. "Maybe the Virgin Mary will throw us a miracle."

"She ain't on the payroll, Frank."

Albert Anastasia returned. "Tony will pass the word to Longie and Joe, but we got bad news. The subway yard went under. If Donovan's boy was there, he went with it.''

Socks Lanza snorted. "Hell, it's only a subway yard.''

"It's a little more than that,'' Frank Costello said.

He used his cigarette to light another. "We could try to take the yard back. Trains come out of that yard. That means trains go into it.''

Albert Anastasia snapped his fingers. "There's got to be a switching station.''

Frank Costello glanced over at Socks Lanza. "Socksie, can you handle it?''

"You know the subways are out.''

"What do you mean, out?''

"There's a strike. Nobody's showed up. Nothin' is runnin'. So all we gotta do is take a train. The tracks are clear.''

Frank Costello showed a thin smile. "How about if we take the A Train?''

7:33 A.M.

Radner came out of the elevator and saw someone waiting in front of his apartment. It was the Armenian girl. When he reached her, he could see the dark lines under her eyes. Her face looked ravaged. *She has no one, no pride, she is nothing. We are the same.*

The girl's mouth moved. "My bag . . . it's inside your apartment.''

"Of course. Just a minute.''

He fitted the key and opened the door, then turned to her. They were very close, and he could smell the cheap scent she used. He couldn't think anymore. He needed to obliterate his pain with sensation.

"Would you like a drink?''

She nodded. He felt her hand. "Give me another chance . . . I'll do better.''

8:33 A.M.

It was a large apartment, and Paulie was getting restive seated in the bedroom with the nigger who kept up a running stream of chatter about the fight. He was throwing a profusion of left hooks and jabs, planning the fight as he went. "Sugar gonna stab, jab, and move. Stick and move, circle left, circle right. Machen gonna try to lead, but Sugar . . .''

"Shut the fuck up.'' Paulie wanted action.

480

"Hey, Jack." It was Frank Costello. "Come in here. There's somebody I want you to meet."

Jack Bixwell smiled pearly whites at Paulie. "Hey, man, they gonna fade me."

Paulie watched him go. "I'll fade you," he muttered.

In the guest bedroom sat a man in a snappy blue suit. He was king of the books in New York. Dinty Callaghan stood up as Frank Costello came in. Behind him was the little nigger, Jack Bixwell.

Frank Costello held court. "This fight tonight, Jack tells me his boy can win. What do you make the fight?"

Dinty Callaghan looked into space and saw numbers. "Eleven to five, Machen. Sugar is good, but he's a kid, an amateur. If Machen turned pro I'd rate him maybe tenth in the world."

Frank Costello listened. He knew if Dinty Callaghan said tenth in the world, Machen was very good.

"My boy had over a hundred fights in the amateurs," Jack Bixwell chimed in.

"How many rounds has he fought?" Dinty Callaghan challenged. "Lot of six-round bouts. This is eight, and Machen will destroy his body."

"Will the jig last?" Costello said as if Jack Bixwell wasn't there.

Callaghan shrugged. "If he runs, it could go all night."

"Jack, leave us alone a few minutes." Frank Costello didn't look to see Jack Bixwell go. "Talk it up. Take a lot of action on Machen. Take all the action Harlem will give you. Send your boys up Seventh Avenue and hustle jig money."

Dinty Callaghan listened as the prime minister talked. He never once said a word, but he knew. They were gonna kill the jig.

"Whatever you want, Frank."

"Good. Stay here for a minute."

He went out, and Jack Bixwell was back. "Dinty, I want five large on my boy. You gonna fade me?"

Dinty Callaghan smiled and put his arm around Jack Bixwell's shoulder. He towered over the little Negro. He could have crushed him the way a boa does a suckling pig. "Sure, Jack, I'll fade you. I'll fade you all the way."

9:03 A.M.

Collins looked out the window from an apartment located at 2254 Cedar Street. He was wearing a ratty robe supplied by his benefactor, Moe Axler, and drinking a cup of tea. After swimming the river back, he had been welcomed by the crowd and acclaimed its hero. Men thumped his back while women kissed and hugged him. Good revolutionary that he was, he immediately saw the practical value. He had ventured into Heinrich's lair and come back. Others would follow him back. The crowd hadn't broken up. Heinrich would have to disperse them. And if that didn't happen then Collins had a chance to rally them. But he couldn't wait too long.

He suddenly stopped drinking the tea. There, in front of the house in peacoat and cap, was the man he had been waiting for. Part of the milling crowd on Cedar Street. He raised the window, thrust his head out, and called to Michael Donetti.

9:13 A.M.

Lieutenant Max Schindel snapped to attention and said, "Heil Hitler."

Abetz returned the salute. "Sit down, Lieutenant. Have some coffee. It is always hot. Would you care for some breakfast?"

Schindel sat down and removed his cap, revealing flaxen hair to go with his blue eyes. "No, thank you. I come with an urgent message from Colonel Messmer. The crowd remains on University Heights, and he is awaiting word from General von Stulpnagel and yourself as to what action should be taken."

"I have just been on the phone with General von Stulpnagel, and he agrees with me that it will not be necessary for the moment to do anything. In a few hours they will be gone. Were there any prisoners?"

"None. We have collected the bodies and Colonel Messmer suggests two platoons remain there after it is cleared."

No prisoners. Abetz hid his disappointment.

"Are two platoons enough?"

Schindel smirked. "More than enough. They will not be coming back."

Abetz's eyes sparkled. "I am sorry I missed the final attack."

"The Americans came to us. They actually destroyed one tank with Molotov cocktails before we broke through. We killed them down to the last man. I myself shot their leader."

Abetz's eyes widened. "So . . . you killed Kresky. Excellent . . . yes, quite so." Abetz inserted a cigarette into his silver-tipped holder. "Anything else to report?"

Schindel was about to speak when he had a thought. "Before we put a patrol on the bridge, one American from the crowd swam the Harlem River."

Abetz stood up.

"When the fighting broke out, he swam back. Our patrols shot at him, but he appears to have made it back. Brave fellow. I

482

shall include that in my report. I wanted to speak to you about arrangements for the funeral of General von Steuben. He must be shipped back to the fatherland.''

Abetz wasn't listening. His eyes had glazed over. There was no doubt in his mind. It was the American . . . this reckless hero with the eighteen lives of two cats. That meant he was up among the crowd on University Heights. He wouldn't let the crowd disperse. Something was going to happen. But this time Abetz would call the tune.

He looked at the lieutenant. "Talk with Hoppman, and he will make the necessary arrangements for General von Steuben." Abetz stood up. "And now, Schindel, again my congratulations. You must excuse me." Abetz abruptly left the room.

9:40 A.M.

Abetz strode quickly down the basement corridor toward the interrogation room. Now it was imperative that the Heights be left intact. The American was up there and Abetz was going to take him.

On the floor of the dimly lit room lay the mayor of New York. He was naked and semiconscious. They had used the hose and electric wires. Above him were Radatz and Glomb, sleeves rolled up. Both men were sweating profusely.

"Well?" Abetz demanded.

Radatz shook his head. "He doesn't know anything. He is crazy."

"He knows something. He knows where Lazar is and where Costello is. You know, don't you? Don't you?" Radatz turned Rocky Malfetta toward him and Abetz saw the broken face, the blood running from his mouth, where all his remaining teeth had been knocked out. "You know, don't you?"

Rocky Malfetta tried to say something. His mouth formed some kind of word, and Abetz leaned over him. The prisoner had one hand around Abetz's neck . . . while the other grabbed Abetz's testicles.

The mayor of New York squeezed with maniacal force and roared in triumph. Abetz also roared.

It took both Radatz and Glomb to pry the prisoner's hands loose. Abetz lay on the floor for over three minutes while his two aides stomped and beat the prisoner into unconsciousness. Abetz was up now, standing over the scrawny piece of useless flesh on the floor. "Kill him."

Abetz turned and walked from the room in a much slower fashion than he had come in. His testicles ached fiercely, and for a moment he re-experienced the grip of Rocky Malfetta. He

483

was halfway down the corridor when he heard the echo of the shot.

10:00 A.M.

Collins and Donetti sat facing one another across the kitchen table. In the living room there were some ten men, Donetti's men.

Donetti was grinning. "Yeah, somebody left a message for me last night, but who pays attention to that?" He winked. "I know a lot of broads. Hell, I was coming up here anyway. I saw your morning swim."

"I want the yard back," Collins said. Donetti rubbed his stubble of beard. He hadn't shaved in almost a week. "Heinrich ain't going to leave it empty for a while."

"Then we'll take it back."

Donetti grinned again. "I got twenty to thirty guys up here. That won't be enough, but we'll go with you."

Collins pointed toward the window and the crowds. "We have a few thousand people out there."

Donetti took out a revolver and put it on the table. "When?"

"After lunch," Collins said. "When Heinrich gets lazy and some of the troops leave."

Mike Donetti picked up the pistol and produced a pint of whiskey. "I'll drink to that."

10:46 A.M.

The girl lay on the bed, eyes dull and satiated. Radner stood in the bathroom weeping. He looked up and saw the large buttocks jutting out. This was what he had been reduced to.

He walked across the room and, moving to the bureau, opened it. The Luger was there. He picked it up. He hadn't fired since Berlin 1938, but killing a man at three feet hardly called for shooting practice. He walked toward the closet and took out a suit. He should shower. The smell and taste of the girl were all over him. No, he wouldn't shower. Let her stay on him, the smell of her in his nostrils, right up to the minute he killed Abetz. Her odor would be a constant reminder of what he had come to be.

11:17 A.M.

The group of German engineers had started an early lunch break. Meatloaf sandwiches, cole slaw, and beer. Strauss, the sergeant, had managed that. It was a beautiful spring morning.

They lay in the dappled sunshine, laughing, making jokes about women, talking of Düsseldorf, talking of what they would tell their families about America . . . Hitler's Amerika. They lay back on the grass . . . Schnellbacher . . . Kruger . . . Werner . . . Gluck. It was Gluck who saw the shadow on the grass . . . then noted the figure standing up, blocking the sun. He sat up and saw the American . . . there were others. But this one held a meat cleaver and looked like a savage. The man lunged. *"Nein . . ."* Gluck cried out.

11:00 A.M.

A little bald man with frantic eyes hurried up to Jimmy Key's newsstand at Broadway and Fiftieth Street. There was this look on his face. He could hardly contain himself. "These papers are full of shit. I just picked up Roosevelt on my radio. We won."

Jimmy Key struggled to understand. "What?"

"We won. It's over in California . . . the Japs got their ass kicked."

Jimmy Key, standing behind his papers, rocked on his heels. He watched goggle eyed as the bald man swept up all the copies of the *Patrician* and began throwing them away. People were stopping to watch. Jimmy Keys came out from behind his stand. "We won. The Americans won. Spread the word, spread the word."

11:35 A.M.

They were on Riverside and 145th Street. Alvin Barker beckoned to Leila. "Break time, lady."

"I don't need a break."

"Well I do. Lady, we walked over five miles. C'mon."

She joined him, and they sat on a bench looking out toward New Jersey. The morning was fair and mild. The Hudson sparkled. Alvin Barker laughed. "It doesn't seem like anything could be amiss today." He saw she wasn't listening at all. "What if he's not there?"

She turned to him, and he saw the fierceness in her eyes . . . and the love. "He'll be there."

An ironic smile graced Alvin's lips. No casting director in the world could deny her this part. He pulled out a bottle of hootch. "A bit of spiritual restorative."

He had just put the bottle to his lips when there was an awful sound that brought them both off the bench. Coming toward them, belching smoke, was a cracked, beat-up yellow cab. The smoke was pitch black. It stopped.

485

The driver leaned his head out. "Want a lift?"

Leila pounced on him. "Absolutely." She got in. "I want to go to 207th Street." She waited for an argument.

"I'll get you there," the driver said.

Leila stared at him, but only for a second. She called to Alvin. "Well, get in."

Now they were moving up Riverside Drive. The driver cocked his head toward them. "It'll be roundabout, but I'll get you there. My name's Joe T. Bone. What's yours?"

11:54 A.M.

Abetz looked at his reflection in the mirror in his private office. The one he kept upstairs for emergencies. He was dressed impeccably in a dark blue suit, white shirt, and black tie. He approved. He hadn't been in civilian clothes since 1939 when he visited Munich on the only leave he had ever taken. He carefully placed his credentials inside his jacket pocket. Then he took the Luger and placed it inside the shoulder holster. He was ready. Only one more touch remained. He took the black bowler hat and placed it on his head. Now he picked up the phone. "This is Abetz, get me Hoppman." He drummed his fingers impatiently on the desk. "Hoppman, is my car ready? Excellent."

He put the phone down and, stepping forward, surveyed himself in the mirror one more time. Satisfied, he switched out the light. It was time to keep his rendezvous with the American. A rendezvous both had known would come since that moment when they faced one another in the street. Undoubtedly Lazar would also be there. Yes, of course. Abetz turned, opened the door, and walked down the hall. He exited through a door and went down the back stairwell to the street where a car was waiting for him.

12:03 P.M.

The cab pulled up in front of Gestapo headquarters at 230 Centre Street, and a handsome young German officer stepped out. He had no battlefield clusters or medals on his uniform, but he did wear a holster that encased a pistol. He walked slowly up the steps toward the entrance.

12:04 P.M.

The black sedan pulled away from Gestapo headquarters. Seated in the rear of the large car was a short man in a black bowler hat with a trim mustache. Anyone catching a glimpse would have deemed him unimportant and innocuous. Because of his severe dress, he might have been suspected of being a mortician.

12:05 P.M.

Two gray Packards pulled up in front of Gestapo headquarters. Seven German soldiers stepped out. If someone had been looking closely, he might have wondered what German soldiers were doing in civilian cars.

12:06 P.M.

Radner took the stairs up to the second floor. Abetz's office was at the rear, where it was darkest. He loosened the button on the holster. Except for a headache, he felt nothing, only a desire to be finished with it.

12:06 P.M.

At the same instant the seven German soldiers came up the steps. They all had on thick coats, and the tommy guns underneath the coats could not be entirely concealed. There was a glass booth inside the building. An orderly was inside it. Next to him, on both sides, were uniformed guards.

12:07 P.M.

Hoppman looked up. There was a flash of disgust in his eyes, Radner observed. His master's dog.
"I would like a word with the standartenführer."
Hoppman was working on a report. He ignored Radner.
"Would you kindly inform him . . ."
Hoppman continued to write. Now he looked up. "The standartenführer is not in."
"When do you expect him?"
Hoppman continued writing. Finally he stopped. "I have no idea."
"I'll wait."
Hoppman put down his pen. "I wouldn't."

12:08 P.M.

The seven soldiers entered the lobby. They had waited momentarily while checking the lobby. It was clear. Now they stepped inside. Their caps were pulled down so that their faces were not easily seen. They were Americans, and their names were Joey and Albert Gallardo, Nick Abruzzi, Carmelo Gigante, Abe Hirsh, and Bugsy Goldstein. The seventh was a handsome youth known as Pretty Levine. He walked to the orderly who waited for him to identify himself. Pretty Levine showed him a pistol equipped with a silencer. He shot Corporal Huntzecker through the eye.

As he did so, Bugsy Goldstein produced a shotgun and turned it on the two guards. There was an explosive double blast that sent both Germans flying five feet backward. An instant later all the men had brought their machine guns out from under their coats. Four charged down the first floor. Two remained in the lobby, while Bugsy Goldstein took the stairs to the second floor.

12:09 P.M.

Pretty Levine kicked open the door to the Gestapo switchboard located at the rear of the first floor. There were six men and a woman with earphones. The broad was an eyeful. Long blond hair, big tits. What a wild fuck she'd be. She screamed. Pretty hit her with the first volley. Mouth open, eyes bulging . . . he kept shooting. He had no conscious feeling. He kept shooting. He was a toy soldier all wound up. The key had been thrown away.

12:09 P.M.

Hoppman stopped writing as he heard the distinct echo of a large gun. Pulling out his pistol, he shouldered his way past Radner. Then came the unmistakable sound of machine guns chattering away. Drawing his own pistol, Radner followed Hoppman.

12:09 P.M.

They moved swiftly and efficiently through offices on the first floor. Blast Gallardo took the first one and took out three high ranking Gestapo officers. Next door Joey Gallardo sprayed fifty bullets into Obscarführer Kintzel and his aides Bucholz and Gitter.

12:09 P.M.

The six officers sitting around the table were busily planning the Easter Sunday roundup. It was an important meeting . . . Abetz would want . . . there was the sound of machine guns.

Outside the room. The men looked at each other. Captain Lipzig stood up and reached for his pistol. Abruptly, the door flew open to reveal Nick Abruzzi. The meeting was adjourned.

12:10 P.M.

Office doors in the building were opened. Clearly there was shooting down on the first floor. It sounded like war. The doors closed, office lights went out, all interrogations stopped.

In the lobby a group of guards coming from the basement came face to face with Carmelo Gigante, who was six feet seven inches tall. He stood in the middle of the lobby and ripped everything in sight. Directly at his back was Abe Hirsh. They moved like revolving doors. Rotating at a continuous three-hundred-sixty-degree flow. Releasing an arc of machine gun bullets. They killed the three guards and six other men in less than a minute.

12:11 P.M.

The stairwells of Gestapo headquarters were empty. Not one elevator at 230 Centre Street was in use.

12:11 P.M.

There was a shotgun blast on the second floor, glass shattered. A soldier stepped out. Hoppman blinked. Who was this soldier? An impostor. Hoppman took dead aim at the American.

Radner was directly behind Hoppman and saw Abetz's orderly raise his gun. Obviously, the soldier he was aiming at was about to be killed. Then Radner wasn't thinking anymore. He raised the pistol he had brought with him to kill Abetz and shot Hoppman through the back of the head.

Hoppman toppled over. Radner looked up at the American dressed in Wehrmacht uniform. He almost laughed. It was such an obvious camouflage. The man was holding a shotgun, which he now pointed at Radner.

Bugsy Goldstein smiled engagingly at Radner. For some reason, the kraut had killed another kraut who lay on the floor.

Radner dropped the pistol. He wanted to say, No, we don't belong here. It is your city.

All these thoughts raced through his mind and invoked an impulse. He extended his hand toward Bugsy Goldstein. Radner started to say *Leila*. His lips moved, and the word almost came out. But then he took a shotgun blast in the chest, which jolted him back some six feet. He lay still, eyes locked in a vacant stare, the word, the name, unfinished. Bugsy Goldstein stepped past this kraut who had wanted to tell him something.

12:12 P.M.

Lieutenant Schindel had been on the phone when the raid began. He knew immediately that a massacre was taking place. He heard a shotgun blast, screams from the office next door. Schindel went under the desk. He had no compunction about hiding. Victory belonged to the survivor. There would be another battle. These were trained killers. No one else would invade Gestapo headquarters. He lay huddled there as the door to his office was kicked open. Somebody stepped in. Schindel could hear the man's breathing. He stopped his own. The killer came closer. He felt as if he would burst. Then he heard the door slam. He was safe. Safe.

12:13 P.M.

They were all in the lobby now except for Bugsy Goldstein. "Where's Bugsy?" Blast Gallardo demanded. He had a voice like a meat grinder.

12:14 P.M.

Schindel came out from under the desk and, raising himself up, reached for the phone. Frantically, he flashed for the operator. There was no response.

He dropped down again and crawled along the floor. The door was partly ajar. On his knees he peered out. It was clear. He got up and came out into the hallway. He walked slowly, passing an office. The windows were shattered. He didn't bother to look inside as he went past it. Then came a soft whisper. "Heinrich."

Schindel turned and saw Bugsy Goldstein.

12:16 P.M.

Eight minutes after the raid began, the seven soldiers ran from the building. Inside 230 Centre Street there were over thirty dead. The two gray Packards came to life as their respective drivers saw the men. They came running toward the cars. Doors opened . . . doors slammed. The cars took off, heading east.

12:17 P.M.

Next to the main switchboard in Gestapo headquarters was what appeared to be a closet. In actuality it was the Gestapo wireless office. The door was always sealed. From this tiny office messages were received from Berlin and from key sections in the city. It had been set up with help from Western Union. Each Wehrmacht garrison had one. It was almost constantly in use as messages came in all day. Just now there was the frenetic sound of Morse code as more messages poured in. But the operator on duty, Corporal Goetz, lay on the floor huddled in fear. He had been there since the shooting began.

It was quiet now, and he came up. Next door he could hear the constant shrill buzz from the switchboard. He came outside cautiously and saw the door to the switchboard office ajar. He looked inside and saw the carnage. They were all lying in a heap on the floor. Blood ran along the floor. He almost gagged. *Mein Gott*, the Gestapo communication center was out. All the boards were flashing. Goetz stepped over a body and picked up a jack and inserted it. Picking up a headphone he said very softly, "Gestapo headquarters."

12:23 P.M.

The A Train rolled out of the Jay Street Station in Brooklyn. The first three cars were packed with men whose hard eyes said they had seen life in the streets from the time they were kids. Tough guys . . . wise guys . . . from the East Side . . . from Williamsburg . . . Brownsville . . . Hell's Kitchen . . . men in black sweaters who worked the waterfront. They were called Chink . . . Slit . . . Butch . . . Bad Jim . . . Itz . . . Shimmy . . . Snake . . . Paulie . . . Dippy . . . Crusher . . . Duke . . . Blue Eyes Magoon. They were led by Tough Tony Anastasia, Albert A.'s brother. If Tony was going, it was important. Somehow they would have the edge. Tony was tough, but he wasn't stupid. Heinrich had fucked up. When the subway workers went out, no one had turned off the power.

Blue Eyes Magoon turned to Tough Tony, who had features suggestive of the early simians who roamed the lava pits of man's beginnings. "What's the edge, Tony?"

Tough Tony Anastasia, still maintaining the cigar in his mouth and the shotgun on his knee, belched.

A few men talked, but most of them just smoked and squinted at the stations as they shot by them.

Blue Eyes tried again. "We gotta have some edge, Tony. Or it's blood on the moon. Ours."

Tony Anastasia hawked some mucus on the floor and ground it around. "Could be."

The train streaked through the stations of Manhattan. Past station after station. Heinrich didn't know it, but the A Train was coming.

12:33 P.M.

The surging crowd that had poured down Broadway stopped at 242nd Street beneath the subway and the elevated yard. They were led by a man carrying the body of his nephew. Vivid bloodstains marked his white shirt. Tied to his waist was a bloody meat cleaver. As the crowd marched, it had been joined by boys, young men, storekeepers, and the group of twenty who had fought with Louis Marks in Van Cortlandt Park. Men with clubs and axes now carried the rifles of the German engineers.

Stopping in the middle of Broadway, as the crowd formed a circle around him, the tears wet on his cheeks and salty in his mouth, Louis Marks called to the throng. "He was my brother's son . . . my blood. No more pogroms. I die before one more fucking Nazi breathes. Burn it, burn it all. Burn Nazi New York."

A boy yelled, "Burn Nazi New York." Others picked it up until the crowd coalesced into a common visage with one cry from one mouth. "Burn Nazi New York."

The crowd roared it again and again. The Americans wanted their city back.

1:27 P.M.

Colonel Messmer paced the garage that was his headquarters and smoked. He was waiting for a call from Schindel, whom he had sent down to see Abetz. The Gestapo was supposed to clear the crowds off the Heights. There was supposed to be confirmation from von Stulpnagel. He threw down his cigarette. Enough. He would call himself.

As Messmer left the garage and stepped into the bright sunshine, he suddenly saw Sergeant Krantz running toward him. What was happening now?

Krantz almost ran into him. "Americans. They are armed and coming from Broadway. To us."

Messmer slapped the side of his leg. "So the *schwein* haven't learned yet." He turned to the yard. "Leave a platoon there." He gazed across the river. "And have the bridge drawn up. Assemble the rest of the men immediately."

"Yes, sir."

"Krantz, how many Americans?"

"A hundred . . . perhaps more."

Messmer smiled. "Good. We need a little practice."

1:33 P.M.

Collins could see something was happening in the yard. He stood on Landing Road next to Mike Donetti, who was scanning the yard with a pair of glasses.

Donetti grimaced. "Take a look."

Most of the Germans were leaving.

"The bridge," Donetti exclaimed.

Collins quickly shifted the glasses. The soldiers were off the bridge. It was going up.

Donetti spat on the ground. "We swim the river and the fucking krauts could hold the yard with ten men. Just pick us off."

It was that simple. Heinrich had the yard, and Heinrich had raised the bridge. The river would be their burial ground.

Donetti looked nasty. "Jesus, I want a crack at them."

Collins looked equally nasty. "We need a distraction."

At that moment the first shots were heard from beyond Tenth Avenue. Then, more shots.

Collins exploded. "They're under attack. Probably on Broadway. Let's go. Get everybody in the water."

"What?"

"Get everybody you can. Heinrich can't cover everybody."

"They won't come. They're here for the show."

Collins turned to the crowd . . . to the young boys . . . the men . . . the eager faces. "Let's take the yard," he cried.

He ran then. Ran toward the bushes that led to the New York Central tracks.

At first they just stared and listened to Donetti exhorting them on. But then a boy ran down the slope, and another, and another man. Donetti's men followed. "Let's go," Mike Donetti screamed. More men came, and more.

Collins hopped the railroad tracks and ran toward the edge of the water. It was bluff, all bluff, and he would need a few hundred people in the water to do it. You'll get them all killed and come up out of the water with your ammo wet. But he didn't care. Now was the time to take the yard.

He could hear the cries and yells. Well, you have done it now boyo. He ran toward the small slip, thinking Mick wouldn't have done this.

Coming across the wood piling, he looked at the yard and just had time to say "Hail Mary, full of grace," before he hit the water again.

493

Behind him came longshoremen, workers, schoolteachers, vagrants. One after the other diving into the Harlem River and swimming for the yard guarded by twenty Germans with rifles, grenades, and a machine gun.

Halfway across Collins heard the unmistakable sound of a train. But it wasn't from behind him on the New York Central tracks. It was in front . . . and then he saw it. A subway train was sweeping into the yard. He treaded water, staring in disbelief. The train was slowing, and there were shots. Men jumping off. They were Americans. Christ, it was happening. He began to swim again. Long, swift strokes. He had to get to the yard.

Chapter 46

April 2, 1942
1:35 P.M.

They sat in Kelly's living room, the gangster and the soon-to-be-crowned American regent. They drank scotch, and now Kelly handed Vito Genovese a thick envelope. Genovese put it in his jacket pocket.

"Anytime after the middle of the month," Kelly said.

"Whoever they put in his place, I get a better percentage."

Kelly smiled. "More scotch?"

There was the sound of the apartment buzzer, and Kelly stood up. "That'll be Abetz."

He went to the door and opened it. Well, well, Abetz in civilian clothes.

Abetz followed Kelly into the living room. "Gentlemen, good day." He turned to Vito Genovese. "I trust your men are out there doing a good job."

Vito smiled. "Oh, they're out there. Definitely doin' a job."

"Good. If you would wait for me outside, I need a word alone with Patrick."

Genovese finished his drink. He nodded to Kelly. "I'll see you with good news."

"Fine, Vito. Fine."

They were alone now, and Kelly could not resist a jibe. "Why the civilian clothes?"

"In the call of duty," was all Abetz would say. He came forward. "I have disappointing news for you. The Führer does not come." He saw Kelly's mouth drop and hid his satisfaction. "Affairs of state."

Kelly fought to keep his composure. "This is my official swearing in."

"The Führer will personally call you," Abetz assured him. "Goering comes in his place."

Kelly poured himself another drink. He was wearing a blue three-piece suit. "I will invite him myself for the Fourth of July."

They stood measuring one another. It was not the same, each knew. But they were still allies. Much like Hitler and Mussolini.

"A drink?"

Abetz held up a gloved hand. "I have business. Urgent business. I will call you tonight. We shall begin roundups on Good Friday."

Kelly's face showed no surprise. "Why the change?"

"The people are restless. That must be dealt with. Until tonight."

Kelly watched from his window as Abetz entered his car. It was a black Hudson. Curiously unofficial. And in civilian clothes, going somewhere with Vito Genovese. What could Abetz have in mind? He felt a gnawing sensation in his stomach. Hitler wasn't coming. Abetz had known last night when he called. Kelly had lost Abetz's confidence. Well, it was better to know now. The money he had given Genovese was just in time. A new standartenführer was needed in New York. One that paid homage to Kelly. He watched the black Hudson slip away.

Inside the car Vito Genovese noted the two dicks in the front. "Where we goin'?"

Abetz leaned back. "We are going to University Heights. You will find a way to get us there. There is an American I have long sought. He will be there, and I shall arrest him."

"Why the dicks?"

Abetz smiled. "The American would spot my agents immediately. He leads a charmed life. One needs to be very good to take him. I want him. Preferably alive, but if he resists . . ."

"Got ya."

"If we do our work well, he shall face a firing squad tomorrow." Abetz closed his eyes and recalled the American standing in front of of the car, gun pointed at him.

"How will we spot him?"

"Rely on me," Abetz said quietly. "I know him well."

1:39 P.M.

Collins led the Americans swimming toward the yard. Up ahead he could see the fighting in the yard. Heinrich was being overrun. The sound of rifle and machine gun fire echoed in the air. He reached the slip and scrambled up.

1:40 P.M.

From the slopes of University Heights the crowd was crying out its triumph. More people ran down the embankment, scaled it, and ran across the New York Central tracks. Moments later they were plunging into the Harlem River.

1:49 P.M.

The yard belonged to the Americans again. Collins, Tony Anastasia, and Donetti were gathered in a tight knot near the repair shed.

The cigar had never come out of Tony Anastasia's mouth. "Frank Costello sends you regards. He said you might be here."

From Broadway the echo of a machine gun could be heard.

"We gotta do something about that," Mike Donetti interjected.

"No," Collins said. "We fortify the yard. Bring the train around so that the entrance is closed off, and I want snipers up on the subway platform. Mike, take twenty men and start clogging up the roads."

"What do you mean?"

"When Heinrich finds out that we have the yard, he'll call out the troops at the Kingsbridge Armory. I want the streets blocked off so that their tanks can't move through it. Move it."

Donetti turned, calling to his men.

Tony Anastasia rubbed his beard. "There'll be a ton of blood on Broadway. We got another trainload coming."

Collins reached for a cigarette and came out with a sopping wet pack. Tough Tony produced a cigar. "Try one."

Taking it, Collins pointed in the direction of uptown. "We have nothing to celebrate. Heinrich has half a battalion left at the Kingsbridge Armory."

"How many is that?"

"Five hundred men."

Tony Anastasia smiled. "Some of them is cooks."

"How many more you got coming in the next trainload?"

"Maybe a hundred."

Collins looked around. "We gotta get all these kids out of

here." He turned back to Anastasia. "That train you came in on will have to sit on the tracks so Heinrich can't get in the way you did."

Tony Anastasia struck a match and held it for Collins. "Heinrich is gonna have his hands full. We hit Gestapo headquarters at lunch. And we got a few more surprises for him."

Collins inhaled on the cigar and came up coughing and gagging. "Jesus Christ, what the hell kind of tobacco is this?"

"It's like TNT, ain't it?"

Collins saw a dozen men led by Blue Eyes Magoon climb the subway tracks carrying sticks of dynamite. He turned back in the direction of the University Heights Bridge. The bridge was the key to holding the yard. It needed to be lowered, and Americans put on it. Whoever controlled the bridge would hold the yard.

1:49 P.M.

The Germans had spread themselves across 215th Street and Broadway. Machine gunners flanked the east and west sides of the street, while behind them stood a hundred fifty soldiers. Seven platoons, which Messmer had spread out so that they overlapped the side streets. He had posted snipers in several stores. It would be like the Polish cavalry charging the Wehrmacht artillery outside of Warsaw. Messmer had been there. It had been a slaughter.

1:50 P.M.

The crowd led by Louis Marks came straight down Broadway. Up ahead he could see the Germans. He took the pistol from his belt and began running. The others followed.

1:54 P.M.

Messmer stood behind a fruit stand watching the Americans come. He bit into an apple and walked over to Heinz Worst, his nearest machine gunner. "When I lower my stick." Worst eyed the swagger stick and nodded. Messmer stood behind him now, munching the apple . . . waiting. As were his men. He smiled. It was a fine day.

1:55 P.M.

The Americans crowded down Broadway, running at the Germans. They were a mob. Packed three deep, crying out their fury.

1:56 P.M.

Messmer stood there watching the Americans. He dropped his apple and raised his swagger stick. *Kommen*, he thought. Worst stared at him. Messmer's swagger stick came down. The machine guns began their inane chatter.

1:57 P.M.

Louis Marks was the first man hit. He fell to his knees and then came up shooting as another machine-gun volley cut him down along with five other Americans. But still they came.

2:00 P.M.

Messmer watched with grim satisfaction. The Americans were being mowed down. Then, to his left, he heard cheers and screams. They were coming from Ninth and Tenth avenues. He saw Sergeant Kreissler go down. The Americans were shooting from the apartment houses. He screamed to his men, *"Achtung, achtung."*

2:04 P.M.

The Americans on the subway tracks reached 225th Street. Blue Eyes Magoon pointed down. Duke De Stefano followed the arc of Blue Eyes's hand toward the machine gun at the far corner. He nodded and ran up the tracks.

Duke had a six-pack in each hand. He saw the kraut officer yelling at his men, holding a swagger stick. He lowered one six-pack as he scraped a match across the track and lit the bouquet of dynamite. Happy birthday, Heinrich. Duke stepped forward and threw the six-pack. It gleamed red gold in the sunlight. In a second, Duke had the other orchid lit and threw it toward the other machine-gun nest.

An explosion cleaved its way from Colonel Messmer to the machine gunner and his feeder on the east corner of 227th Street. It blew them all to pieces. Ten seconds later the machine-gun nest on the west side of Broadway went up in clumps of blood and flesh.

Blue Eyes Magoon was screaming "Hit 'em," and dynamite rained on Broadway. The Wehrmacht disintegrated, their staunch line crumbling.

Men came from apartment houses and tenements, from stores and shops. Carrying planks with nails embedded in them. Carrying clubs, chains, hammers. One engine, fueled by the anger and humiliation of the last four months.

At 2:06 P.M. the Wehrmacht was overrun.

2:13 P.M.

The audience in the mid-Manhattan version of the Cotton Club chattered away. Loud, caught up in throaty laughter and provocative whispers. They were here to be entertained. This was not the real Cotton Club, the one that had started out in Harlem. It was the tourist version. But who wanted to go to a pit like Harlem when you could import *schwarz* here? The *schwarz* would play jazz and dance for them in their white tuxes. Long-stemmed beauties would cavort and primp for them. The *schwarz* were good entertainers. Good maids and cooks, too. And good in bed. Natural rhythm.

The lights dimmed and the audience, composed of Wehrmacht officers, Reich officials, businessmen, and their perfumed escorts, barely took notice. The curtain was going up and the audience hum dropped a few decibels. On stage was the Jimmy Moon Band. A complete ensemble dressed in white tails, white shoes, white shirts, black ties. Sparkling teeth showed as the band, led by tall, elegant Jimmy Moon stood up and bowed. The audience broke into applause.

From the wings on either side of the stage came six men. They wore top hats and heavy overcoats. They were obviously Chicago-gangster types. What a marvelous parody. The audience applauded as the man in the middle stepped forward. But he didn't smile, and the applause stopped.

Something was wrong. He spoke and his voice sounded like someone drowning in cement. "Get out."

Whispers . . . hushed silence.

From under his topcoat came a tommy gun. The five men behind came forward. They all had tommy guns. A woman screamed.

2:17 P.M.

Leila and Alvin Barker picked their way down along the large crowd now lining Sedgwick Avenue. It had been all on foot since Joe T. Bone's cab gave a final cough and belched forth the most horrible smelling cloud of fumes. After a silent moment of mourning for Bessie, they had come on foot through the East Bronx and finally reached Sedgwick Avenue. The crowd was excited. Children could be seen holding miniature American flags.

Leila clutched Alvin's hand. "Something is happening, c'mon." The crowd was thick and packed three deep.

"Move it," Joe T. Bone sang out. "Comin' through, comin' through."

2:20 P.M.

The four men picked their way eastward along Burnside Avenue. Their car had been left some miles back. It had become impossible to use a car. The Americans were out on the street. They have hope, Abetz decided. That must be crushed. But why was the crowd out? The yard had been retaken by the Wehrmacht.

Beside Abetz, Vito Genovese growled. "Let's try those bushes."

They were crunched in next to a small museum that was backed by trees and underbrush. It led down, and Abetz saw boys disappearing down into the enclosure.

"C'mon," Vito Genovese said, and Abetz and the two plainclothes detectives followed him. As they picked their way down, Abetz felt the branches scrape his face. Below was another street, and as they reached it, he saw the milling crowd.

They worked their way through the crowd via a magic lane that seemed to open for Vito Genovese. They stopped at the corner of Cedar Street. They had a clear view of the Harlem River and the subway repair shop. At that moment the American flag was being raised.

2:21 P.M.

Joe T. Bone saw it and took Leila's arm. "Look."

Something caught in Leila's chest. "He's there," she whispered, "I know he's there."

2:23 P.M.

The men in the yard silently watched the red, white, and blue flag blowing softly in the breeze on the makeshift pole Kresky and his men had erected when the yard was first taken. Collins looked over and saw the bridge was down. Tony Anastasia came over to him.

"We should put people on the bridge."

Collins nodded.

"Look," a hood named Ratso called out.

Following the line of his finger they saw what he had picked up. A mile downriver was the Harlem Bridge, and in the fierce sunlight they could see the outline of men. They were holding an American flag.

2:24 P.M.

Abetz stood among cheering Americans, and his gaze went back to the subway yard. He felt sure the American had done this. Abetz had come for him, and the American was back in the yard. But they would not be able to hold it. Troops would come from the Kingsbridge Armory. The American would need the crowd. He would come back. Then Abetz would have him.

He turned to Vito Genovese. "I will need a phone to be in touch with my office."

Vito Genovese killed the butt he had been smoking. "There's an apartment house full of phones. Why don't we requisition one for you?"

He whispered to the two detectives, Hanrahan and Quigley, two hard-drinking old pros who had made their accommodation with the Reich. They followed him as Vito Genovese pushed his way into 2254 Cedar Street.

2:27 P.M.

Broadway and 227th Street was littered with the quick and the dead. Wehrmacht soldiers and American street fighters lay across each other. Store fronts were overturned. Fruit and vegetables rolled through the gutters like so many rubber balls.

More Americans were pouring from the buildings. They were cascading along Broadway. The mob continued to march down Broadway. Americans who wanted their city back.

2:33 P.M.

The call came in to the Kingsbridge Armory from Corporal Joseph Müller, who had survived the street fighting on Broadway. Colonel Messmer was dead.

The call was taken by Lieutenant Klaus Eberhardt. He then relayed the news to the battalion commander, Lieutenant Colonel Manfried Richter. Within five minutes the remaining four hundred troops were being mobilized and orders had been given for the tank squadron to prepare for combat.

2:35 P.M.

Fires were being lit on Broadway. Cars burned and trucks were overturned. From 215th Street down to 207th Street, Ninth and Tenth avenues, St. Nicholas Avenue, Broadway, and adjoining streets were filled to overflowing. Gas was being siphoned off and spilled across the gutters.

Mike Donetti watched with grim satisfaction. C'mon, Heinrich, he implored. We're waiting for you. He lit a match. He lit another.

2:47 P.M.

A group of Wehrmacht officers stood inside the PATH station at Journal Square in Newark. They were joking and bantering. They were on holiday. The underground train would take them from here to an afternoon in New York, then dinner and some night spots. They were young, newly arrived. They would buy postcards in New York and send them back to families in Berlin, Frankfurt, Munich, Hamburg. This was their first trip. They were assigned to division headquarters here as supply officers. Meat was the commodity they dealt in. They were important cogs in the Reich machine.

Lieutenant Hans Ziegler heard the train first and pointed. He could see the lights. Now closer. It was coming awfully fast. The train whistled past them, and as it did a brandy bottle clattered on the platform.

The train was gone, and the young officers laughed. These crazy Americans. They couldn't even stop a train properly. The officers clapped each other on the back. New York. What a wonderful assignment.

2:48 P.M.

The train sped on down the tracks. It should have been cruising at twenty miles an hour. The next stop was only minutes away . . . Exchange Place . . . the last stop before Manhattan. But the driver, Joe Herlihy, had let the throttle out. He was doing sixty. He was tired of it all, tired of Nazis telling him what to do, tired of stale meatloaf once a week, tired of laughing German officers taking his train to New York. He had started drinking at eleven o'clock that morning, and now as he roared through the tunnel he felt fine . . . just fine. He laughed. Up ahead were the lights of Exchange Place. Time to stop. There wouldn't be krauts at Exchange Place. Stop on a dime and show people how good he was. There. The station loomed, and he eased off and hit the breaks.

The train came bursting into the station, brakes screeching. It leaped past the platform, bucked, skidded, jumped into the darkness ahead, and Joe Herlihy screamed. The train dipped and left the track. One, two, three cars did an unscheduled left. There was a terrible sound . . . an awful crashing that echoed up and down the line. Glass shattered as Joe Herlihy was thrown from his engineer's booth onto the tracks, while next to him, smoking and simmering, engine still on, was his train. It was curved in an S around the tracks, wrapped around itself like a snake.

The young officers back at Journal Square waited for the next train. They had no idea there was no getting to or from New York via the PATH tubes. These crazy Americans.

2:49 P.M.

Vito Genovese stood in the apartment of one Joe Walker. He was drinking some of Joe Walker's finest whiskey and smoking a cigarette. The two dicks had been on the phone for some minutes talking to their precincts. Joe Walker was a diminutive man with the purple red veins of a man who has loved whiskey all his life.

"Just because you're cops, don't mean . . ."

Vito Genovese dropped the butt on the rug and let it burn. "Beat it."

Joe Walker heard the words and then saw Vito Genovese's eyes. He left.

Hanrahan came back now. He eyed the whiskey as he spoke. "Gestapo headquarters was hit."

Vito Genovese looked surprised. "Who did it?"

Grady Hanrahan reached for the scotch. "Professionals in Wehrmacht suits."

"That's real sad."

Pete Quigley came in. "The Cotton Club was hit awhile ago. It was a fuckin' massacre."

Vito Genovese shook his head. "Someone's puttin' on the heat. Why don't you boys go downtown and look into it?"

Both dicks looked at Genovese and then at one another.

Vito Genovese took out a roll and peeled off five one-hundred-dollar bills. He shoved them into Grady Hanrahan's suit pocket. He repeated the gesture with Pete Quigley. "You guys work for me now. Got it? C'mon, I'll walk you to the car."

Grady Hanrahan and Pete Quigley exchanged glances. Events were happening. Americans were rebelling. Power was shifting. It didn't matter. They had seen power shifts before. They were always taken care of. Vito Genovese knew how New York was oiled.

"Leave the booze," Vito Genovese suggested. "You don't want to come in bagged."

They were in the elevator, and Hanrahan turned to the gangster. "How will you get back if we take the car?"

Vito Genovese smiled. "We won't need it. The krauts will take the yard back and then we'll kick some ass up here. Put everything straight."

They all smiled. The elevator stopped and opened to the basement. Vito Genovese gestured. "There's a back way out to Sedgwick."

He stepped out behind the two detectives. As he spoke he drew his gun. "Straight ahead, past the coal bin."

It was Grady Hanrahan who turned to say, "How did you know?"

He saw the gun with its silencer. There was a whooshing sound and Hanrahan went straight back. Pete Quigley knew that sound. His hand was in his jacket as he whirled. *Phtt.*

He crumpled at Vito Genovese's feet. In one motion the gangster bent down and took back his money. He performed the same ritual over Grady Hanrahan's body. He put the gun back in his jacket and calmly reinserted the money into his clip. Then he walked to the elevator and pressed the button.

3:02 P.M.

In the muted light of his bedroom Frank Costello talked to Captain Daniel Ahearn of the Twenty-eighth Precinct located at 2271 Eighth Avenue and Captain Patrick Moriarty of the Twenty-fifth Precinct located at 120 East 119th Street.

"I want the jigs turned loose when the fight ends."

"Christ, Frank," Ahearn protested. "Harlem is crackling . . . my men will get cremated."

Frank Costello opened a suitcase. Inside were two paper bags. "Spread around what you need to . . . the rest is yours. There's twenty large in there. It's easy. Pull your men off at eight o'clock. Let the auxiliary police take the fall."

There was silence in the room.

Ahearn looked at the bag. "What's gonna happen, Frank? We gotta know that."

Dinty Callaghan saw the two chiefs staring at Frank Costello. Frank was the master. He waited. The doorbell rang.

"Get it, Dinty."

Dinty Callaghan made his way to the front door. He opened it, and there stood a hulking Wehrmacht soldier.

He stepped inside and followed Dinty Callaghan into the bedroom.

Captains Ahearn and Moriarty turned and momentarily recoiled. Frank Costello lit a cigarette with a platinum-gold lighter. "You guys know Paulie Lazar, don't you?"

Paulie's face lit up in an engaging smile. "Hey, guys. Like my new suit?"

3:15 P.M.

A fishing boat moved up the Hudson toward the Dyckman Street Landing. As it stopped, one of the fishermen threw a package of fish to the German guards on the slip. There were only six of them. It was strictly a supply depot, seldom used by the Germans.

The soldiers waved back. It was their weekly payoff for not inspecting the boats that belonged to Mr. Lanza. They were still waving when four men with machine guns came out of the cabin and stitched them all up and down with a fusillade of bullets.

Five minutes later the Dyckman Street Landing went up under forty sticks of dynamite. The Upper West Side was no longer accessible by boat from New Jersey.

3:37 P.M.

The sun was warm on Collins's back and neck as he looked out over the yard. There were some sixty men in the yard and another seventy in the red brick building overlooking Tenth Avenue. Another twenty, led by Blue Eyes Magoon, were up on the tracks above 207th Street. And a trainload was on its way. But Heinrich was coming with five or six hundred men. Collins looked across the river at the crowds up on the Heights. We need a riot.

Mike Donetti trotted over. "That's it . . . the bridge is locked in . . . the controls are kaput. That fucker ain't comin' up."

He offered Collins a cigarette, but it was too wet to smoke. Collins took it anyway. He looked out at the river and saw the sun kissing the water. There was no other place in the world he would rather be. "Then let's just wait for Heinrich."

"Yeah," Mike Donetti said. "I got somethin' for him."

They waited.

3:40 P.M.

Leila could see the men in the yard moving about. She kept looking for Collins, but there were too many heads to see over, too much confusion and jumping. The Nazis would be back. Soon. And the crowd knew it. There was an endless supply of Nazis.

Alvin Barker lit another cigarette. It seemed he was never without one in his mouth now. "I'd give anything to be down there."

For some reason she was angry, and he saw it in her eyes. "Don't you understand?" he said. She took his hand and squeezed very hard.

3:47 P.M.

The calls had been made over an hour ago, but it had taken a long time to go through the chain of command. Calls were placed to General von Stulpnagel and to Governor's Island. It had taken a great many calls before an order was given. General von Stulpnagel was very reluctant to act without the advice of Standartenführer Abetz, but he was not reachable. Now the governor general took a call from General Hoffman at the Kingsbridge Armory. Yes, the Americans were to be driven from the yard. Crush them, use tanks. At 3:30 P.M. General Hoffman called in Lieutenant Colonel Manfried Richter.

Twenty minutes later the first tanks rumbled out of the Kingsbridge Armory at Jerome Avenue and Kingsbridge Road. From the air they looked like so many beetles packed in single file. They were flanked on either side by Wehrmacht troops, veterans who had fought in England, at West Point, in the Hudson Valley. Their boots thumped on the streets of the Bronx.

4:52 P.M.

The sun was starting to drop now, and Collins felt a shiver. Where were they, goddamn it? He dragged on a butt and stared across the river. It was the wait. Nobody liked it. Bring on the tanks.

Tony Anastasia slid over to him. "Our train is late."

Collins looked over at Mike Donetti and his men, and then at the assortment of scurvy, streetwise punks Anastasia had brought with him. He started to laugh.

"What's so funny?" the squat little gangster wanted to know.

Collins took the cigarette from his mouth. "There's enough guys with you who have done time to send us up the river for a thousand years."

Tony Anastasia spat. "Nobody is sending me up the river."

4:47 P.M.

A breath of wind tossed Leila's hair, and she felt a chill. He was down there . . . and she would give anything in the world to be with him. If he died . . . no, he wouldn't. The river was so beautiful. Sunlight still shimmered on the water. It was the end of a beautiful day . . . that's all . . . a beautiful spring day.

She couldn't stand it any longer. "Why don't they come?"

"They will," Alvin Barker murmured.

5:06 P.M.

Abetz checked his watch. Just after five. The American has played his last card. I would have had you, but for your resourcefulness. You have had a great run here in New York. But now you will be slaughtered. You won't be coming back, after all. Well, you will die the way you lived . . . recklessly. Yet he felt a twinge of disappointment. They had a rendezvous, and Abetz had been deprived of it. And after all, these rendezvous were why Abetz had chosen the Gestapo. Breaking a man was the ultimate power and pleasure. To see his eyes go wide with fear, pain, and the knowledge that he had lost. That's what Abetz lived for. In the end the American would have cringed. He bit his lip. There was a sound, and Vito Genovese's voice came to him. "Another train . . . they got more men."

Abetz's mouth curled up. What did it matter? The game was up. The Wehrmacht was coming. The crowd cheered, and Abetz felt his nerve ends tingle.

5:10 P.M.

The men in the yard were up as the first man jumped from the train. His name was Phil the Stick Kovalick. He was the strong-arm for Meyer Lansky. He had a face like a mashed potato. He spotted Tony Anastasia.

"We got lost. We ended up in the Bronx. The map was screwed up."

"You can't read anyway. C'mon, get the guys over here."

Collins grabbed Anastasia's arm. "Put twenty men on the bridge. Twenty men with tommies."

Tony Anastasia took off and began barking orders as Collins looked out across the water at the people. Well, c'mon, it's your city. Take it.

507

The Wehrmacht's tanks were stalled. Streets and corners were littered with overturned cars and trucks, with furniture, iceboxes, with every conceivable kind of obstacle. Captain Heinrich Dorfman stood atop the lead tank on Broadway and 225th Street. Spreading out his map, he tried to analyze the contours of this damned city. To get around this improvised roadblock would mean somehow coming through Inwood Hill Park. That meant making a whole circle and coming up Broadway below 207th Street. If he did that, Wehrmacht troops would attack the yard alone. No doubt they would subdue the Americans, but then his force would not receive the credit it deserved. It was Captain Dorfman's tanks that had blown open the yard this morning. But now the Americans had retaken the yard. He looked back. There was a line of his tanks stretching across West Kingsbridge and Kingsbridge Road. He made his decision as he saw Lieutenant Eberhardt running toward him. Dorfman jumped down to meet him.

Eberhardt saluted. "Colonel Richter wishes to know what will be the disposition of your tanks."

Dorfman smiled. "But of course we shall accompany you."

"But the roads are blocked."

"We shall push the blockade out of the way."

"Colonel Richter thought Inwood Hill Park . . ."

"Tell Colonel Richter to go forward, and we shall be right behind you."

Captain Dorfman cut off further conversation with a salute. Eberhardt saluted, backed off, and began running back to his commander. Captain Heinrich Dorfman mounted his tank and, discarding the map, signaled the tank behind him to move. Then he gave the order to his own driver. *"Mach schnell . . . schnell."*

The tanks began to creep forward.

5:33 P.M.

Up and down 215th Street and Broadway gangs of street urchins moved with the reckless fluidity and daring of youth. Gas siphoned off during the afternoon was oozing along the gutters and pavement of Tenth and Ninth avenues. Inside a gutted furniture store Henry "Deak" Manners, a tall youth with wild curls and a harelip, smoked a cigarette and watched as three of his gang ran frantically toward him. Gimpy Lamonica as always beat the others. He began babbling incoherently and received a slap in the face from Deak.

"Slow the fuck down. Who's coming?"

"Soldiers." Gimpy proclaimed. "Nazis."

"Where's the fuckin' tanks?"

"Just soldiers, Deak. Nazis."

In his fantasy, Deak Manners had seen tanks coming and streets of fire. Now he stepped out into the streets where the dead bodies of American civilians and Nazi soldiers lay. Up above in the tenements and on the rooftops were Americans with guns and bricks and Molotov cocktails. Deak Manners walked up the street and produced a wooden matchbox. He struck one against a water hydrant and watched it flare. When he tossed it, lines of fire came crackling to life along 215th Street and Broadway. There were cheers from rooftops and apartment buildings. Deak Manners spread his arms to the sky as if he were some all-powerful sorcerer who had conjured up a vision of hell for his apprentices.

Hands still extended, he turned to them. "Spread the word. Light it all up. Go . . . go."

The youngsters ran, and minutes after Amsterdam Avenue went up. Then Tenth Avenue, Ninth Avenue, St. Nicholas Avenue. Streets of fire.

5:37 P.M.

The Wehrmacht humped it down Broadway in and around blazing asphalt. From street windows and rooftops came rifle shots. Bottles and chairs rained from the buildings.

At 220th Street and Broadway, Colonel Manfried Richter saw the streaking flames and heard the accompanying gunfire. It was an uprising, no question about it. It must be crushed now. He leaped from the car and, resisting Eberhardt's attempts to stop him, ran up the street urging his men forward.

5:42 P.M.

In the subway repair yard at Coney Island, on the edge of Brooklyn, an American flag had been hoisted atop a light pole. They were close to the ocean, and a cutting wind had come up. The faces of the thirty men were rapt with concentration and excitement as the pole jockey, a sanitation worker named Buddy Masters, finished the job. Now the wind caught the stars and stripes and blew them full out. Beneath their flag some Americans cheered. Others cried.

6:23 P.M.

Through the clouds of smoke Blue Eyes Magoon saw the first soldiers. Heinrich was coming. He ran to the subway rail and pumped his fist at Collins. Collins watched the sun dance on the river one time and then looked at Tony Anastasia. "It's time to lock and load." The little two-ton truck snapped the cylinder of his pistol and shoved it in his belt. "It's time to unload."

6:24 P.M.

The Americans waited in the red brick buildings with their shattered windows. From the top of the Broadway line, more snipers were suspended over Broadway. And in the yard where four hours ago American and German soldiers had fought hand to hand, the rest of the Americans were ready. They crouched behind overturned subway cars and inside those that had recently streamed into the yard. Up on the bridge was a group of forty men led by Michael Donetti. Longshoremen, gangsters, laborers, machinists, poolroom sharks, vagrants. Men named Malone, O'Gara, Maffetore, Smithers, Carruthers, Jones, and Schuster. At that moment none of them cared about making history. They were Americans, and New York was their city. The Americans waited.

6:25 P.M.

Blue Eyes Magoon started it. He stood up and, dangling over the railing, screamed, "Heinrich." Then he opened up with his tommy.

The battle for the subway yard at 207th Street and Broadway began again.

6:32 P.M.

The crowds on the Heights watched in silence, the wind from the river whipping their faces. The sun was falling, and the flashes of rifle fire illuminated the darkening sky. Night was coming to the city. Death was coming from that night. There were explosions. Exchanges of grenades and dynamite. And always the sound of tommy guns and rifles.

Leila could see the puffs of smoke and the bursts of fire. It was hypnotic and it was awful. Nothing she had ever read about in history books could equal this. Not Alexander the Great, not Caesar, not Napoleon. It was primitive, brutal, and awesome. Americans outnumbered two to one, fighting with German soldiers for a subway yard. They are fighting and dying for all of us, she thought.

6:39 P.M.

The Heinrichs came up from Tenth Avenue, heading for the bridge. They had been stalled on Broadway by the rifle fire, but now the troops behind them had caught up. They were combat troops.

Collins ran down the subway car, calling for men to follow him. He came out of the car, felt the cool night air, and ran for the fence. Behind him came others. Reaching the fence, he let loose a burst from his tommy. Two Heinrichs fell.

6:59 P.M.

Donetti was the last one still standing. He had only a pistol. Beside him four men were still on their chests firing. They were all hit. Bob Swenson had just taken a bayonet in the chest, right in front of Donetti. Then Donetti was out of bullets, and he knew nothing, only his rage. "You fuckin' scumbags," he screamed and, leaping forward, pounded Heinrich's face with his pistol. Smashing it, smashing it, till the bones broke. A bayonet pierced his back and skewered his lungs. He screamed. There was another Heinrich, and another. The Wehrmacht had overrun the bridge.

7:02 P.M.

Heinrich had the bridge, and now Collins felt a bullet whistle past him. Heinrich was up on the subway tracks. Jesus, they were in a crossfire. "Get back, get back," he yelled. He ran for the cover of a subway car and then felt the bullet in his leg and went tumbling.

7:09 P.M.

The report had come into Wermacht intelligence at Governors Island at 6:25 P.M. The South Street Ferry slip had gone up in flames. There was a raging fire. It meant the thirty thousand troops on the Island could not land in Manhattan. Earlier in the day, ferry slips at Dyckman Landing and 125th Street had gone up. To intelligence officer Lieutenant Karl Diestl, it was obvious. The American Resistance was trying to cut New York off. As the reports came, he shook his head in admiration. It was a gallant effort but doomed to failure. Even with the PATH tubes blocked, there were still the Lincoln and Holland tunnels. There was the George Washington Bridge. We have thirty thousand more troops in Newark and Jersey City. Forty thousand in New Haven. Fifteen thousand in New Rochelle and Westchester. He smiled again. He was still smiling when he heard the roar, and an awful premonition came to him. He ran from the map room out onto the grass and down the slope toward the water.

The East River was ablaze. A burning line of tugs and oil freighters. Boats end to end. A flotilla of them . . . an armada. The Americans had done this. It was formidable. They are blocking access by water. Was this a rebellion or an invasion? He stood transfixed. It was like some god had unleashed this spectacle as a demonstration of his power. The flames. Diestl shook his head. The Americans were everywhere. They couldn't blow the George Washington Bridge or the two great tunnels. But the access roads . . . Lieutenant Diestl turned and sprinted back toward the headquarters building.

7:20 P.M.

The Wehrmacht was on the bridge and on the subway tracks, pouring bullets into the yard.

"It's finished," Vito Genovese sang in Abetz's ear.

Abetz made no acknowledgment. It was the most savage spectacle he had ever seen, and he had watched in fascination.

"No one lives," Vito Genovese said.

Precisely, Abetz thought. The American had no more tricks, no more lives to live. He felt immense disappointment. No, it was more than that. This reckless gamble of the American had failed. Their destinies were no longer intertwined. That moment when the American had smashed the glass of his car was their first and last encounter. He was dying the way he lived . . . a hero.

"We better get back," Genovese reminded him. "My boys need me. Friday is only thirty-six hours away." He checked. "Good Friday. It's late."

Abetz looked around. Yes, it was time to go. He turned and followed Genovese, who was shoving and talking to people and once again a line opened for them.

7:42 P.M.

The thin Negro youth lay on the table in the fighters' dressing room. There was a row of lockers and then the table. Each fighter got it for ten minutes to have his hands taped. Jack Bixwell rubbed the liniment into his boy's shoulders. "You is my

512

Sugar. You gonna skip, dance, and you gonna jab . . . jab . . . jab Machen all night. Dance and jab. Don't you be thinkin' about no knockout. Stick and move.''

He said it as if it were a curse. Now he gentled his tone and whispered into Sugar Ray Smith's ear. "Stick and move, all night long, baby.''

7:59 P.M.

They were pinned into the two subway cars. Heinrich just kept coming. Heinrich was very professional. Heinrich had guts. Favoring the bad leg, Collins fired out the window. The gun clicked. No ammo. Brass knuckles time. In the yard he could see men running, trying to cover for fallen buddies.

Tony Anastasia crawled over to him. "We're dead meat.'' Then he winked. "But we ain't gonna taste so good when they get in.''

He handed Collins a pint. "Finish it.''

Someone screamed and fell over. Bullets poured into the subway car. Collins drained the pint and threw it away. He felt the warmth of the whiskey and spat out the words. "The bridge.''

"What about it?''

"There's ten thousand people up there. Maybe more. The bridge is down.''

Tony Anastasia chewed on his cigar. "They ain't come yet. You wanna try?''

Collins shook his head. "Pick a good swimmer with good legs.''

"You done it already. My money's on you.''

"I left Kresky to die the last time. Not again,'' Collins exclaimed.

"You fuckin' crazy Irishman. We ain't here to lose or to die. I wanna win, and Heinrich's gonna be here in about forty-five minutes.''

Another scream punctuated Anastasia's logic.

The argument was over. Collins began to crawl along the floor. He felt Tony Anastasia's hand on his leg and cried out. "I'd go wit ya, but I can't swim.''

Collins turned. "I'll see you . . . maybe.''

"Don't stop for no Danish.''

The bullets creased the night air as he ran low across the yard. The leg ached fiercely. It was a flesh wound, but they hurt the worst. Bullets pinged around him. He remembered old Mollie Dunleavy, who used to serve the lads stew in Dublin and brush the hair from Collins's eyes. "You lead a charmed life, Robbie, and you're gonna live to be ninety.'' Right now he'd settle for forty-two. He saw the fence up ahead. Go for it laddie. He gripped the fence and started up, feeling the pain in his leg. One step, then another. He had the right leg poised to hit the top of the fence when he took the round in his shoulder. He went down, landing heavily. He lay on the ground smiling to himself between the waves of pain. Well, you finally made it, laddie. You gave it the old college try . . . you'll get to be a martyr's martyr after all and join Mick Collins in heaven or hell. Wherever, he'll have a pint in hand waiting for you.

8:30 P.M.

It had taken an hour to work their way through the crowd back down Sedgwick Avenue and finally over to Burnside Avenue where the car was parked. Abetz had found himself talking more than usual. The sight of the battle had uprooted him from the cool private cell he lived in. War in its most elemental form was something he had never witnessed. He looked at his watch. *Gott*, it was late . . . and he was hungry.

As they reached the car, he turned to Vito Genovese. "You must dine with me."

"Sure," the gangster said as he unlocked the car.

Abetz slid in, and then Genovese was pushing him toward the wheel. Something dug painfully into his head . . . again and again. He was being pistol-whipped. "Please, no more." He fell senseless against the wheel. He felt his hands being looped together and then something put around them. Handcuffs. Now he was shoved over as Genovese turned on the ignition. Abetz was aware his glasses had fallen off.

"Have you gone mad? What are you . . ."

"Shut up."

Again the pistol lashed him.

Abetz sagged over the wheel. Genovese was a brute. Too strong. Wait . . . he will tell you.

"Uncle Sam is supposed to take New York," Genovese croaked in his ear. "I still gotta do business. You understand . . . don't ya? It's all business."

Abetz groped to put it together but couldn't.

"Kelly," Genovese said. "Kelly put out a contract."

"Kelly?"

"That's the way the game is played. You got to be lucky. Like my buddy Luciano. He used to be lucky. Now he's up the river."

Abetz tried to call for help and took another savage blow. "Please." He felt Genovese's hand in his suit pocket removing his handkerchief.

He heard the door slam and tried to move, but he was locked

to the wheel. What was this? Why did Genovese leave the car on? He smelled it. Gas. The windows were closed. Carbon monoxide . . . no, it wasn't possible. He was standartenführer. He smelled it more strongly now. How horrible . . . he was being gassed to death.

Outside the car Vito Genovese quickly stuffed two hankies into the exhaust pipe. Then he stood quietly and smoked a cigarette. If anybody came by, he was just looking after a friend who was taking a nap. A long nap. Up above, the sky was full of stars. In the distance was the sound of gunfire. Vito Genovese smoked a couple of cigarettes. Poor Abetz. He had a heart attack. There wasn't gonna be no fuckin' autopsy with all the hell breakin' loose in this city. Kelly would be happy, and so would Frank C. and Albert A. He waited another five minutes and then looked inside. Abetz was very still. The gangster slid in and quickly removed the cuffs. Glancing down at Abetz, he gave him a little salute off the forehead. Moments later the car door slammed, and Vito Genovese belonged to the shadows.

8:45 P.M.

The nigger kid came down the aisle first. Behind came a little nigger carrying a towel. Seated in the Wehrmacht section, which was about thirty rows back from ringside, Paulie pulled on his collar. This fuckin' uniform was choking him. He had spent over thirty minutes in the john to avoid talking to anyone. He remembered Albert Anastasia's orders. "Paulie, you don't talk to no one. That's a dead giveaway. Only your piece does the talkin' for ya."

Paulie could feel the coiled emotion amongst the krauts. They wanted Machen to leave the nigger for dead. He tapped his piece, which was shouldered under his jacket. He would be.

He heard Albert Anastasia's instructions. "Let it go a few rounds, Paulie. Give the krauts and the jigs a run for their money. A minute into round three you slip down to ringside and pop the jig. Clip him a few times . . . we need lots of blood. When you hit him everybody will go crazy. You drop the gun and put up your hands. We got three cops down at ringside, and they'll take you into custody. The krauts won't touch you, and there won't be no jigs there. They'll hustle you out of the Garden and drive you to a garage where I'll be waiting with a big envelope for you. Do this right, Paulie, and I'll take care of you."

Paulie's hand moved to his chest where the pistol rested in a shoulder holster. The third round. Albert was right. Everybody would be screaming for the kill. The kill, he liked that. If it looked like there would be a knockout in the first two rounds he would have to move faster. But that wasn't likely. Sugar Smith was a slick article. He could have been a champion. He heard the krauts next to him yelling at Sugar Smith. They weren't offering to buy him a beer. The whole kraut section was up. Paulie stood up with them.

Sugar Smith reached the ring and ducked under the top strand. He stood there now in a cheap blue robe, towel around his neck. Jack Bixwell whispered in his ear. "Dance, baby, dance." Sugar shuffled in place. He was tall, with sleepy brown eyes. He saw everything, but showed you nothing of his response. He was cool, lithe, and cocoa brown. He had a handsome nose and thin lips. He could have been a choirboy. He moved in circles, jabbing, weaving, all under the watchful eyes of Jack Bixwell.

Fritzi Machen came down the aisle, the Wehrmacht erupted, and Paulie again jumped up. Cries of "Fritzi, Fritzi" resounded in his ear.

He came up under the ropes in his black and gold robe. He stood there now with his trainer and some kraut officer. The kraut was gesturing and posing. For two cents I'd fill a contract on you, Paulie thought.

Machen was a bull. Thick through the shoulders and chest even under the robe. Thick like an ox through the neck. His brown wavy hair was cut short, and he was beetle browed. His nose was flat, broken half a dozen times. He had gray, shrewd eyes, and he used them now to survey his opponent. The Negro was shuffling in his corner, working up a sweat, seemingly oblivious to Machen. But Fritzi Machen knew there would come a time when the boy would look over. So he waited. He moved to the resin box and elaborately put one foot and then another inside. All the while his eyes never left Sugar Ray Smith.

And now as if on cue, the Negro stopped his routine and looked over to Fritzi Machen. They measured one another . . . boy and man. Fritzi Machen smiled. His eyes never left Sugar Smith. Finally, it was the Negro with those sleepy eyes who looked away.

Jack Bixwell led his fighter over to the resin box. He watched him dip his feet inside and work them around. He rubbed the boy's neck. At ringside another man watched Sugar Smith. Dinty Callaghan, king of the bookies, had seen the Smith kid fight half a dozen times. He was smooth. He could be great one day, but Machen was a pro who knew all the tricks. Machen was not a great puncher, but he would wear you down. He would hit off the clincher, hit low, use the laces of his glove if allowed. It was Machen's fight . . . the nigger would have to take it from him. Callaghan made the fight three to two. Of course, it was all a game. There wouldn't be much of a fight. Sometime during the fight a gun would come out. The nigger was a dead man.

Harry Balogh was making the introduction. "In this corner wearing the white trunks . . ."

8:56 P.M.

It was mild in Harlem, windows were open, radios blaring. "Weighing one hundred forty-nine pounds . . . Sugar Ray Smith."

On 125th Street and Seventh Avenue they listened. In bars and joints, in cracked, peeling apartments, on fire escapes. They heard the babble of voices from the Garden. This was their boy, Sugar. His name was Smith like theirs, and he was fighting the German, Machen. But everybody knew it wasn't really Machen. It was Schmeling . . . Max Schmeling. Hitler's man. The man Joe Louis had left for dead in the first round. The only man to beat the Brown Bomber. Everybody in Harlem knew what this was about. This was Joe Louis and Max Schmeling, one more time.

8:57 P.M.

"And in this corner, wearing black trunks, weighing one hundred fifty two-pounds, Sergeant Fritzi Machen."

The Wehrmacht exploded from their seats, and once more Paulie joined them. The kraut next to him smoking a cigarette that smelled like shit offered Paulie one. The kraut was smiling. Paulie smiled back and took the cigarette.

9:00 P.M.

Alvin Barker dropped Leila's hand. Bright fire burned in the yard as Molotov cocktails exploded. There had been no dynamite charges for an hour. The Americans were out of dynamite. There was heavy fighting around the gate. The Germans were always on the verge of climbing over when American bullets would rake it. The firing was less frequent now. A German had climbed the fence. Another. He reached for Leila's hand. But she was gone.

9:02 P.M.

They stood at center ring, listening but not hearing the referee . . . with eyes only for one another. Machen, the gray eyes probing. Ray Smith . . . sleepy eyed . . . no sign of emotion. They

517

touched gloves now and went back to their corners. Jack Bixwell rubbed some Vaseline over Sugar's eyebrows. "Stick him . . . jab and move. Don't let him get inside."

The bell rang and under hot lights, with the Garden tense and expectant, they shuffled out.

They boxed at long range. Measuring one another. A feint, a shoulder dip, heads bobbing. Machen looking to get inside where he could do damage. The Sugar kid slipped and Machen came inside, but the kid tied him up. Smiling, always smiling, Machen came forward. Now, Jack Bixwell thought . . . stick him. And as if their brains were in perfect sync, Sugar Smith's left flashed. One, two, three times in Machen's face. He blinked. The punches were like bullets. Sugar Smith moved left now, circled right, and threw the jab again . . . pop, pop, pop.

At ringside, Dinty Callaghan permitted himself a little smile. Oh, this Sugar kid was sweet. Sweet as brown sugar.

Sugar worked at long range. He danced and he moved. A jab . . . a hook . . . and as Machen lunged forward . . . he slipped away. Machen lunged again, and the kid countered with a right cross. It landed on Fritzi Machen's mouth. Blood flowed. Still Machen came forward, but the kid was too fast . . . too smooth. God, he was quick. The bell rang.

In Machen's corner, his trainer Kampfelman could be seen pointing to the body and giving an imaginary blow.

They came out for round two. Sugar danced, but he didn't run. He was elusive. He feinted with a shoulder, dodged here, ducked there. And now a left off a left, and a right. Oh, he was quick.

But Machen shook the blows off and relentlessly pressed forward. Cut off the ring, get inside. There, a clinch, and he pounded at the Negro's ribs. Two, three, four times before the kid could tie him up. The referee broke them, and they fought at long range again. Smith pumped three left jabs . . . a hook . . . but an uppercut missed, and Machen got inside again. He dug a left to the belly, and a right. And now he brought his head up and used it on the kid's face.

The Wehrmacht was up cheering. The only one who didn't cheer was Paulie. He knew he should have put on an act but he couldn't do it. He had grown up going to the Garden. He had seen Barney Ross fight . . . there was a Yid with balls. This fuckin' kraut was a brawler, but he had no real skill. The Smith kid was great. C'mon Smith, move, stick. And the kid was doing it again, evading Machen, and now came the retaliation for the butt, two left hooks that Machen never saw. It was a good fight. Too bad Paulie had to clip the kid in the next round. What a time and place for a hit.

The round was over and Paulie prepared to make his way through the solid phalanx of olive-colored uniforms. In that moment he saw the heavy, blond kraut next to him still smiling. Then Paulie felt the kraut's hand on his dick.

His brain was bursting, the blood in him pumped white hot. At any other time, with any other man, Paulie would have mashed him to a pulp. But if he did he blew the biggest hit of his life. A personal contract for Albert Anastasia. "Do this right, Paulie, and I'll take care of you." He would be set forever and under Frank Costello's protection. Vito couldn't touch him. He couldn't fuck this up. He had to hit the jig. Don't make no trouble. The kraut's hand was still on his dick. He smiled. Paulie smiled back. The fat fruit raised his eyebrows and took Paulie's hand. Now he whispered in Paulie's ear. *"Komen sie."* Paulie had something for this guy.

They came out for round three, and the Sugar kid flicked a left, then two more. He was scoring and moving. Dinty Callaghan marveled at it. The kid was a genius. It was ballet. Kids like this come once in two generations. They didn't move by brainpower, but by reflex and instinct. The instinct of the street that teaches them to avoid danger. Dance, oh you genius, dance.

Jack Bixwell smiled. This was his Sugar. A hook off a jab and a right cross. Put your left out and spear his face. He remembered seeing Ray Smith for the first time four years ago in a ratty gym on 135th Street. He was like honey even then. Slide and stick . . . slip, fake, and pump four lefts. Bleed, you kraut bastard.

They had gone down the stairwell, and the fruit led Paulie into the bathroom. The stalls were empty. Paulie could hear the cheering and the din. He should have clipped the nigger kid, and instead he was in the crapper with a kraut fruit.

9:17 P.M.

They came out for round four, and Dinty Callaghan bit off a new cigar. Machen had to do something to change the tempo. He had to rattle the kid, who was in a rhythm known only to him and God. Dinty watched Machen boring in as the kid endlessly circled, firing off flurries of punches. But Machen was relentless. Closing all the time . . . closing. There he was inside, and there was the hand holding the Smith kid around the neck and the low left. The crowd was up, everybody saw it. The referee was between them warning Machen. But Dinty Callaghan had no eyes for Machen, only the kid. They were at long range again, and the kid stabbed and moved. But they were lighter blows. Machen kept coming. He was inside, pounding, and the kid lashed out. They traded blows inside, and Machen scored, and again . . . and again. Dinty Callaghan chewed on his cigar. Machen had done it. He was setting the tempo now. It was the docks of Hamburg, not the music and dance of Harlem.

The fat fruit of a kraut lay face forward in the toilet bowl as Paulie made his way back up the ramp. The krauts had spilled into the aisles. Jesus, he had to get down to ringside.

9:19 P.M.

Leila had fought and inched her way down to Landing Road. Up ahead was the bridge. It was filled with German soldiers. She looked back to the yard where more and more Germans were climbing the wires. She wasn't crying, and she wasn't breathing. Rather it was a combination of both . . . a series of gasps. She was being overwhelmed by panic. We must help them, she thought. We must. In some imperceptible fashion the crowd had edged its way closer to the bridge. The way one inches closer to a three-card monte dealer or a quack salesman selling magic elixir. The instinct to save was there . . . but the Germans were also there . . . and they had a machine gun.

9:24 P.M.

Paulie had made it to ringside sliding in behind a reporter, who turned to protest and then shut up as he felt a thirty-two caliber revolver jabbed into his ribs. Paulie followed the action. The kid had lost his cool and was trading too often . . . not fighting with smarts. And the kraut came in low, really low, and worked over the nigger kid. Pounding heavy body blows to the kidney and ribs. The kid fired back, but Fritzi was hunting him. The bell clanged and Paulie bit his lip. He would have to do it at the beginning of the sixth round . . . no, midway . . . when the crowd was into the fight.

Jack Bixwell used the towel and spoke in quick street accents. "You got to slow him . . . stay away . . . tire him . . . he leanin' all over you." The bell rang. "And don't let him play the possum," Jack Bixwell called out.

They came out under the hot lights for the sixth round. Dinty Callaghan had the fight three rounds to two for Harlem. There, the kid stabbed and ducked and moved. Left . . . right . . . and now suddenly a right uppercut, a good punch that rocked Machen. The kid was in fast . . . punches flew in swift combina-

520

tions . . . Machen was back on the ropes . . . the kid threw a long left . . . Machen reeled. Dinty Callaghan watched the action carefully. Machen had been hurt awfully fast . . . too fast . . . but that's how it happened in a fight. The kid came to Machen.

The crowd was up howling. Paulie was one with them, hand on his revolver. The Sugar kid was on him . . . finish him . . . then I'll clip ya.

Jack Bixwell watched in fascination . . . was this real? Sugar was on him . . . and Machen dipped his shoulder. "Possum," Bixwell screamed. "Possum."

But it was too late . . . Sugar had taken the bait. Machen dug a left to his ribs and then surged in. His cunning trap had been perceived by the pro-German crowd, which roared its approval and sent adrenaline pumping through him. He bored in, bludgeoning Sugar Smith with heavy, thudding blows. Machen knew the effect of a steady assault on a young fighter. He would panic and then try to flail back. So he hammered, pounded, and again Sugar Smith took the bait in his mouth. A right . . . a left . . . four shots to the kidneys, and then Sugar took a right cross to the mouth and went down.

The crowd was bedlam . . . pandemonium . . . eighteen thousand fanatics. The kid sat on the canvas trying to put it back together. Paulie had his gun out . . . now . . . clip him. But he couldn't do it. "Get up," he screamed. "Get up."

The kid was up and on his bicycle as Machen pursued. Gesturing all the while . . . come to me . . . fight. The kid ran . . . the bell rang.

9:28 P.M.

Harlem was silent . . . quiet . . . you heard no sound except the radio and Ted Heusing's voice. "Playing at being hurt, Machen floored Smith with a series of ramlike body blows." Nobody spoke . . . not in the bars, the brothels, the tenements. It was clear . . . Hitler's man was winning.

9:28 P.M.

Jack Bixwell washed his boy's face and rat-a-tatted in his ear. Over and over the same word could be heard. "Possum . . . possum." No one really watched except Dinty Callaghan. He knew the fight would end in the seventh round. He made it four to one. Whoever was out there with a piece would end the kid or Machen would.

521

The bell sounded, and they came to the center ring. Machen the pursuer, Sugar Smith moving back . . . back.

At ringside nobody noticed the Wehrmacht soldier edging in right behind the timekeeper.

The kid stood flat-footed along the ropes. Dinty Callaghan saw it . . . so did Machen. Sugar Smith was out of gas and scared. Machen came forward, looking to unload a big one. The *schwarz* was afraid. Sugar Smith was afraid. Which is what made him so dangerous at the moment as he shifted weight and came off his toes with a left hook that snapped Machen's head back. Then Sugar Smith dipped and threw the right.

Fritzi Machen's eyes rolled and his knees buckled. Dinty Callaghan was halfway out of his seat.

In Sugar Smith's corner, Jack Bixwell whispered to himself, "A thousand punches."

Sugar threw them all. For in this moment he was a street kid with a stick in his hand who had found a sucker with a thousand dollar bill in his wallet. If he could stick him hard enough, he took all the money. You don't miss, and you don't stop. So he stuck him with a left and a jab. He doubled up the jab, and then came the combinations and rights. A thousand punches. Blows thrown from angles the Sugar kid didn't even know he knew. It was street survival. You never had ten dollars in your life and the man had a thousand. Win and live. Lose and die. "A thousand punches." Till Fritzi Machen's face was raw. With the hands of a swift pickpocket Sugar Smith stole back the fight.

The Wehrmacht was up imploring Fritzi Machen to possum out. But he wasn't a possum . . . he was hurt. He was almost in dreamland. Still the Wehrmacht screamed for their hero. Except for one lone Wehrmacht soldier at ringside who yelled, "Kill the fuckin' kraut." In the bedlam no one heard Paulie Lazar's cry.

And now it was Fritzi Machen who screamed as Sugar Ray Smith tore his head off with a left that combined all the sinew and strength of his magnificent, supple body. Machen bounced into the ropes and, coming off, took ten punches without responding.

He's out on his feet, Dinty Callaghan acknowledged as he stood up. But the referee wouldn't stop it. Fritzi Machen had never been off his feet. Machen, on wobbly legs, reached for the ropes as the kid moved in for the kill.

In that moment, Fritzi Machen did the instinctive thing: he brought up his knee into Sugar Smith's groin. Less than ten feet away Paulie saw the low blow and jumped up on the ring apron.

Screaming "You kraut fuck," he too did the instinctive thing. He pulled his thirty-two and drilled Fritzi Machen. Still on fire, he pivoted and plugged Max Kampfelman, the kraut's trainer, right between the eyes.

And at that moment, Dinty Callaghan, grasping what had happened, made the move that earned him a pension for life from the mob. He grabbed the microphone from Ted Heusing and yelled into it, "Sugar Smith has been shot . . . Sugar Smith is dead."

In Madison Square Garden there was a mini-riot. Paulie looked to find Sugar Smith to somehow do the hit, and he couldn't see him. A hundred krauts were in the ring, and they were coming at Paulie. He turned and saw the two cops then . . . and another. They had their pistols drawn. It was a double cross. Paulie started shooting. The three cops fired back.

9:31 P.M.

At the moment that Dinty Callaghan uttered the immortal words "Sugar Smith has been shot," a shotgun exploded in the Gargantua Bar on Seventh Avenue and the body of Ace Slade flew out the door. Within thirty seconds Harlem flew out into the streets as the radio blared details of murder at Madison Square Garden. They ran carrying guns, clubs, and wicked knives that looked like wheat-cutting scythes. They ran in the direction of the auxiliary police who patrolled Harlem, Morningside Heights, and Riverside Drive. They ran looking for Nazi bastards. Ten, fifty, a hundred, multiplying like red ants on a dead carcass. A bomb exploded in the streets . . . a car was torched. Fire streaked in the night. Harlem went up.

9:37 P.M.

Collins had managed to crawl to the ferry slip, which was less than forty yards from the bridge. If he only had some grenades. He had fallen straight over the fence after taking the bullet in the shoulder. It was still there, but unlike his leg which throbbed constantly, his arm was numb. He had watched helplessly as Heinrich surrounded the yard. Anastasia and the last of the men he had brought with him were in the brick buildings that ran along Tenth Avenue. Heinrich would have to fight his way in there. Some twenty men had covered the retreat into the buildings as the rest of the men made for cover. Heinrich swarmed toward the yard, met by Americans with tommies and pistols. They came straight at the Americans with steel bayonets, legs thrown high in the air in a maneuver that somehow brought them

523

closer and offered less of a target. The Americans went down in ones and twos, till suddenly there were none left. And Collins, watching, knew it made Dublin nights seem chivalrous adventure.

He turned to the bridge. The people had to come down off the Heights. But Heinrich had a machine gun there. He could see the outline of the crowd. There were thousands. Some of you will have to die, but we're all dying down here. An awful frustration seeped through him. There were tons of dynamite up on University Heights. Where was the man with the match?

At 9:40 the first tank appeared on Broadway and 207th Street. Of the original group of five tanks that had set out, it was the only one that had made it. Now as it rumbled toward Tenth Avenue, someone could be seen riding on top of it. The tank was marked with a red cluster, which had been put there to denote the fact that it was Captain Heinrich Dorfman's tank. The lead tank. Many times in Denmark, England, Poland, and Belgium, when the tank rode into heavy street fighting, Heinrich Dorfman rode on the top, pistol in hand, surveying the action from the open turret, oblivious to death. And now someone else rode on top of the tank. But it wasn't Heinrich Dorfman, it was an American kid. A punk.

Deak Manners would have rejected this characterization. This tank operation was his now. They had gotten all the tanks but this one. One had hit a truck doused with gasoline at 219th Street and St. Nicholas Avenue and had gone up like Chinese New Year. Another had sloshed through oil-slick streets and, as it negotiated a turn onto Tenth Avenue and 223rd Street, a gimping kid flashed from behind an overturned car and threw a Molotov cocktail directly underneath it. There was a bright red flare and a loud bang, and three seconds later, as the flames crept up into the tank, another bang so much louder that two blocks away there were people whose ears would be ringing from it for another hour.

A third tank skidded off its tracks at 222nd Street and Broadway. Resembling some maddened creature from a dark ancestral past, it skidded, tilted, and finally crashed into a storefront on Broadway. There it was overrun by street hawks. Twenty and thirty condors, clambering on its frame and turret, torches in hand, as if making some mythic sacrifice to the great god of war.

The fourth tank hit a hydrant head-on at 219th Street and stalled as it swirled in water and oil. Several sputtering attempts to restart it had failed, and moments later the crew came out into the chaos and fighting of the Upper West Side.

Deak Manners saw that the fifth tank was headed toward Inwood Hill Park. He knew where it would have to come out of the park, and he cut away to head it off.

Dorfman had realized his blunder within minutes after ordering his tanks to navigate Broadway. The Americans were devouring them . . . a million Lilliputians hog-tying Gulliver. Dorfman thumped the driver on the shoulder. His name was Reinhold Ziegler. Speed was essential. If Dorfman could make it through the park and get to the subway yard, he would be in time to participate in taking it.

Coughing, rumbling, the tank came out of Inwood Hill Park. Dorfman checked his watch: 9:13 P.M. Gunfire echoed in the distance. They were still fighting.

It took Dorfman's tank some nineteen minutes to find its way to Dyckman Street and turn left on Broadway. In that time period it picked up Deak Manners.

9:41 P.M.

The Americans had taken cover in the building. Leila could hear the cries of dying men. The crowd could hear it also and now edged down until the first line of them was only some forty yards from the bridge. Yard by yard, inch by inch, the crowd had moved closer as the fighting intensified and the Germans stormed the brick buildings. The Americans in the building were in a crossfire, caught between the Germans on the subway tracks and the soldiers in the yard.

A low moan sounded from the crowd, and people pushed forward. It was voluntary, it was involuntary. The mob was bursting at the seams. The Wehrmacht soldiers on the bridge knew it. Leila knew it. They all knew it. It was not a direct order but some kind of kinetic feeling between the crowd and the soldiers on the bridge. It was so strong that before the order could be given, the machine gun on the bridge opened up.

9:42 P.M.

Collins had reached the edge of the planks of wood that made up the slip when the Heinrich machine gun began to fire. He heard the dying cries. Now you have to choose. If his arm wasn't so bad he could climb to the bridge from the water. He tried to move it, and now the numbness didn't protect him. The pain ripped through him . . . no good . . . no damn good.

9:43 P.M.

The first burst from the machine gun had laced the crowd, killing more than twenty. They had fallen back. In these seconds they lived a lifetime. There was terror, panic, and there was rage. They regrouped and came forward again.

9:44 P.M.

The tank had moved toward Tenth Avenue and the yard when the machine gun blast vibrated. Slowly the tank came to a halt as Captain Heinrich Dorfman prepared to come up for a look.

Deak Manners's fingers were raw from gripping the tank. But he didn't care about that or his personal safety. Not since a kraut sniper had killed Gimpy Lamonica back on 215th Street. Gimpy was fifteen and had been following Deak Manners since he was eleven. Like Bugsy Siegel had followed Meyer Lansky. Some kraut was going to pay. The tank stopped. Heinrich Dorfman came up to take a look.

Deak crouched down as the turret came open. Then he saw the Heinrich . . . he was looking ahead at the bridge. Deak knew that the kraut was trying to decide where to go.

9:45 P.M.

Dorfman saw the bridge and then turned to the yard. The Wehrmacht was inside.

Collins heard the tank start up and saw it moving directly toward the bridge. A tank gun firing into a crowd could kill people by twenties and thirties. It would be a massacre. He raised himself up and saw the officer half out of the turret. Then he saw the kid moving up behind him. He was carrying a tommy gun.

9:46 P.M.

Deak Manners lunged forward with the butt of the tommy and caught Dorfman. As he crumbled, Deak clubbed him again. Now he yanked savagely at the inert body of Captain Heinrich Dorfman. Seconds later he was discarded. The tank still moved forward.

Dorfman hit the ground like a sack, his skull fractured. That his tank would be pivotal to the fall of the University Heights Bridge was something he would never know. Deak Manners yanked two grenades from his jacket. The tank was almost at the bridge now, and Deak was laughing. He could smell the river. This was home. He used his teeth to pull the pin. Then he dropped the grenades and jumped.

9:47 P.M.

Collins saw the kid jump after dropping off his pineapples. The tank was on the bridge, coming up behind the platoon of soldiers. One of them was running toward it, hands outstretched in a gesture of welcome. Collins counted to three. The tank blew.

The tank blew just as it approached the platoon. It blew and sent shrapnel flying. It blew and killed six soldiers. It blew and made an incredible noise. It blew and gave Deak Manners the cover he needed to pitch two more grenades at the Heinrich platoon.

9:48 P.M.

It had all happened so fast. First the tank exploded, then the grenades . . . and then the crowd heard the rattle of Deak Manners's tommy. There was shooting on the bridge . . . the Nazis were dying. Somebody screamed, "Take it," and the crowd, like a herd of frenzied cattle too long pent up, stampeded.

They swept across the University Heights Bridge now . . . immigrants . . . mockies . . . kikes . . . niggers . . . micks . . . wops . . . men and boys . . . women . . . chattel for the Reich. It was like Times Square at New Year's Eve. There was no stopping. The crowd pounded past the bodies . . . past the wreckage of the tank . . . trampling the wounded and dying on the bridge, surging toward the subway yard, where the Wehrmacht was trying to incinerate the brick buildings they couldn't take.

9:50 P.M.

Leila was swept along in the mad charge. There was only so much room on the bridge. They pushed and jostled, shoved and elbowed. As if no one was aware that there were Nazis over on the other side. Soldiers with guns.

At first as the crowd poured over the bridge, the German snipers up on the tracks had fired at will. But, as a thousand became two thousand became three, the firing stopped. And as the Bronx streamed into Manhattan, the Wehrmacht troops on the IRT overhang fled. Leading the retreat was Corporal Joseph Schlichter, who had marched on Fifth Avenue on December 28, 1941.

9:54 P.M.

A strange thing happened in the subway yard. The Germans had stopped firing. Not all at once, but as if by some uncommunicated cue. As if they were actors in a film. Torches were dropped. Lieutenant Fritz Werblin stared in disbelief as thousands of Americans ran across the University Heights Bridge. A dense, screaming, raging mob. He took a step backward. Then another.

The soldiers gaped at the crowd, which was now across the bridge. They looked at each other.

There was a rifle shot, and Lieutenant Werblin took another step backward and fell over. His pistol clattered on the ground.

The first Wermacht soldier to run was a private named Joseph Vechter. But he was not the last.

9:55 P.M.

Inside the building the Americans lay huddled together. Why was there no more shooting? Tony Anastasia chewed on the stub of his cigar.

"They're running," someone screamed.

No one could understand, and yet everyone understood. They were free. They were alive.

10:20 P.M.

Collins had watched it all from the slip. We have taken back our streets as we will take back our city. We, he thought. I'm one of you again. You hear that Kresky? You were right. In the end that's what it comes down to. We all belong here.

10:37 P.M.

A group of boys who had swum the Harlem River found Collins. He had seen the boys scrambling out of the water and called, "Here, lads . . . here."

10:40 P.M.

You couldn't move in the yard for all the people who had gone out to light up Broadway. Leila had searched relentlessly for a sign of him. She refused to look at the bodies. He was here . . . alive . . . somewhere. It was all so impossible. It was like some great party at which there was an unending rush of guests. But it wasn't guests . . . it was the American people. The Bronx and

Manhattan had joined. Kids kept swimming the river. She saw a bunch of ragamuffins picking their way along the little wood pier, helping a wounded man. . . . suddenly she ran for the fence.

"Easy lads," Collins was saying. None of them saw the girl climbing the fence. She came from in back of them, her heart pumping madly. Then Collins saw her.

The boys stopped. They knew this was special.

Jesus, you're beautiful, he thought. I didn't deserve Sylvie, and I don't deserve you. He thought more but only said, "Hello, lady."

She ran to him, and he said to the boys, "Let me go, lads." But they held him till she got there.

April 3, 1942
12:03 A.M.

Kelly had dined alone. He didn't like dining alone, but there didn't seem to be any place to go. There was a lot of shooting around town. Gestapo headquarters had been hit. That was hardball. It wasn't going to be so easy after all. But on Friday, we will show them.

He sat watching Park Avenue in darkness, drinking brandy. It was time to take the steel fist out of the velvet glove. . . . The doorbell rang. He whirled. Why was he so jumpy? His man was gone and Kelly went to the door. There was a lieutenant from the SS. Kelly bade him enter.

The lieutenant clicked his heels. "Lieutenant Bader, Herr Kelly. I have come with some news I am sure the standartenführer would wish you to know about."

Kelly took out a cigar. He had played the market too long to anticipate what news would be. But it didn't smell good.

"We have just received the news. The New Jersey Meadowlands have gone up in flames."

"But surely . . ."

"It is quite out of control."

The cigar slipped from Kelly's hands. "The camp . . . you can save it? . . ."

Lieutenant Bader was silent. Now he shook his head. "I'm afraid it is quite out of control. It was set in the marshes by professionals, and there is a strong wind tonight."

Kelly felt staggered. "Surely they can be saved," he repeated.

"I'm afraid not. And there is more. We have a report that the Pulaski Skyway has been blown up. Along with the Passaic and Hackensack bridges."

"Never mind the bridges," Kelly said with a touch of his old vigor. "My camp. I built it."

"Herr Kelly . . . you have not grasped it. The Wehrmacht is cut off. Without those bridges, routes Three and Forty-six are completely backed up. The PATH tubes are closed . . . the South Street piers have been destroyed. Harlem is rioting. I have been sent to get you. You are not safe here."

"And Abetz . . ."

"No one knows where he is. Something may have happened."

Vito, he thought.

"Herr Kelly . . . please get your coat. We are in a terrible emergency."

He stood there stricken and white. "I'll get my coat," Kelly said.

He was back in a moment. The door was open. He could see the SS guards. He was cold and put on his coat. "This is temporary. Just rabble. You'll handle them. Goering is coming for my confirmation as regent. In Washington, next Sunday."

Lieutenant Bader held the door for him. "Yes, Goering is coming."

12:37 A.M.

The city ran riot. All its children and its people. They were surging from Harlem to the Bronx, from Coney Island to Washington Heights. Growing from its streets like leaves unfolding in the spring. Carrying torches and pistols, barricading city streets. It was their city, and no one would ever take it from them again. Behind these barricades were the lights. Torches lighting up the city.

The people in the Bronx streamed along Burnside Avenue past the car where the little man slept on. He seemed innocuous as an undertaker, face resting on the wheel. No one looked in on him or noticed. If they had they wouldn't have paid attention. He was just a little man taking a nap.

In the subway yard the crowd remained, fortifying it. Guards were posted. People cascaded from the subway stop. Americans were everywhere.

Torches burned brightly in the night. Their searing flames devouring the midnight sky. Torches held proudly by the people of New York. The Americans had taken their city back.

About the Author

Leo Rutman's novels often focus on New York, its drama and street legends. His previously published books include FIVE GOOD BOYS, a novel about the golden age of college basketball, and SPEAR OF DESTINY, a thriller set on the eve of World War II. Among his published and produced plays are *They Got Jack, Jesus Is A Junkie,* and *Where Is Che Guevara?* He has also been the recipient of playwriting awards from Yale, Brandeis, and Columbia Universities. He is currently at work on a new novel. The author lives in New York City with his wife Bette and son Kristofer.